Dear Reader

I hope you enjoy the story I have put on paper. Many of the incidents actually happened in my own life or to my forebears. My great-grandmother Rhoda Jane Shaw was really buried alive during the tornado as told, and the other tales of Callie's great-grandparents or grandparents are those of my own ancestors. The wonderful writer and herbalist, Adelma Grenier Simmons truly inspired not only me, but thousands of people during her lifetime.

The fictional town of Heartland is loosely based on any small town in central Indiana. However, The Limberlost Historical site is a well-known feature of Geneva, Indiana and the Quilters' Hall of Fame in Marion, Indiana is well-worth a visit. The characters and events are purely the result of my fertile imagination.

All of the recipes are original, with flavor combinations and ideas sparked by the scents of the herbs as I weeded and harvested, or found myself with an overabundance of ingredients. They were tested and revamped with my patient family, friends, and staff as official tasters and reviewers.

The garden information is based on my thirty years of experience gardening with herbs, flowers, and vegetables mainly in southern and central Indiana, with a little time in central Texas and northern Illinois.

As always, I must caution readers to be positive of the identification of any herb you plan to ingest, either as food or tea, or to use in skin, bath, or other body products. Avoid plants that have been grown with harmful chemicals, and do not harvest plants grown near roadways or other problem-laden areas for food or body use.

Herbs are magical, mystical, and marvelous additions to our gardens and lives. Use them wisely and harvest their blessings.

Carolee

Herbal Beginnings

by

Carolee Snyder

authorHOUSE®

AuthorHouse™
1663 Liberty Drive, Suite 200
Bloomington, IN 47403
www.authorhouse.com
Phone: 1-800-839-8640

First published by AuthorHouse   5/30/2008

ISBN: 978-1-4343-9043-1 (sc)
ISBN: 978-1-4343-9042-4 (hc)

Library of Congress Control Number: 2008904554

Printed in the United States of America
Bloomington, Indiana

This book is printed on acid-free paper.

Dedication

To my best friend, Beth,
whose support and editing were essential.

To my family for their love and patience.

And most of all, to my husband David,
the magic man, who makes things happen.

Chapter 1:

JANUARY

A cold nose touched her hand. Buried deep beneath the covers, Callie drew a deep breath and enjoyed her warm cocoon for a few moments more, pretending that she was still asleep. The patient black lab sighed and lay down again next to the bed. Minutes passed as Callie let her mind come awake. A stiff breeze rustled the few remaining leaves outside her window. The temperature had dropped deeply during the night.

"OK, lazybones. Better get moving," her mind argued. Her body was content to stay put. She knew the moment she opened one eye to check the morning through her bedroom window she'd have to get up. Wicca would notice even a flutter of an eyelash. Slowly Callie stretched her body, and just as quickly the lab was on her feet, tail wagging in eagerness.

"Morning, Sweetie-girl," Callie crooned, as she stretched her hand to rub the lab's head. The warm brown eyes responded to her voice and the dog's body trembled. She slipped her feet into a warm pair of slippers. Wicca already knew the routine and raced down the stairs ahead of her mistress, who had stopped at the wide windowsill on the stair landing to pinch a leaf from the big pot of rose-scented geranium. Together, they walked into the old-fashioned kitchen. Callie put a kettle of water on the stove and reached for Wicca's bowl. The lab raced around the kitchen island in anticipation, making little leaps of joy at the sound of dog food hitting the bowl. How a dog as intelligent as her Wicca could consistently be so excited when every meal was the same dry dog food, morning and night, month after month, was still puzzling. Callie could barely make the same recipe twice without changing one ingredient or another.

Quickly Callie rinsed her hands at the sink and collected her teapot, tea canister, a big mug, and the honey jar. When the kettle began to boil, she rinsed the pot with a bit of the boiling water to warm it, then added tea and the rose geranium leaf, and filled the pot. The aroma of the rose geranium leaf immediately permeated the air. Normally, Callie drank rosemary and green tea in the morning to stimulate her body and improve her memory. Today she needed the soothing, calming effect of the rose geranium. She popped two slices of whole grain bread into the toaster and reached for a jar of gooseberry jam.

She used the few moments while the tea steeped to judge the weather through the kitchen window. Gray clouds skidded across the sky. There was a thick layer of frost on the roof of the gazebo and the surrounding lawn. It was too cold to do her Tai Chi routine outdoors today.

Callie poured the fragrant tea into her mug, covering the teapot with one of her hand-embroidered cozies. She smeared jam on the toast and then sauntered into her studio. It was her favorite room of the big, rambling 100-plus year-old house. Facing south, the windows had deep sills that were home to a number of delicious herbs that needed warm temperatures during the winter. Old clay pots held lemon verbena, fruity sage, patchouli, and variegated basils. Callie needed to be surrounded by these old friends, just as she needed her loyal Wicca at her side.

Three of the walls of the studio were filled with bookshelves containing hundreds of old herbals, gardening books, plant references, and garden guides, as well as a few miscellaneous treasures. These books were old friends as well. Awards from garden club shows, photo albums of trips to famous gardens, and bits of memorabilia filled any bare space on the shelves. The fourth wall contained her grandmother's old treadle sewing machine, which Callie planned to use to make sachet bags and tea cozies over the winter for her new shop. Beside the sewing machine was a large desk, rescued from an old high school. Above the desk hung a large corkboard with colored pushpins, holding newspaper clippings, to-do lists, bits of poetry, photos of gardens, and story ideas.

Callie set her honey-laden mug of tea on the desk and leaned back in the old rocking chair. Like the old sewing machine, it had been her grandmother's. Pieces of the dark veneer were missing, but the creaking chair comforted her in a way that padded recliners did not. Today, the creaking of the chair brought memories of her mother, grandmother, and great-grandmother. All were strong women who had remained solid and calm through adversity.

As Callie rocked, her mind recalled the story of her great-grandmother, Rhoda Jane Shaw. Callie remembered her as a petite, strong-featured woman with white hair pulled into a bun at the nape of her neck. She had never seen her without a sturdy, simple apron over a long-sleeved, high-necked, below calf-length dress. A sturdy farmer's wife, Rhoda Jane was alone, milking the cows when a tornado suddenly churned through the flat fields of Indiana and brought the barn crashing down around her. She lay squeezed between two cows, which were killed by the massive beams that fell and pinned her under a giant mound of timbers and hay. Two days later, neighboring farmers came in their horse-drawn wagons and cleared the debris enough to free her. When Grandfather Lewis Shaw arrived home he asked why she hadn't taken shelter in the basement. Grandmother just replied, "The cows needed milking. If it was my time, God would take me no matter where I was." And that was that.

"Enough stalling," she said aloud, setting her empty tea mug on the desk. Facing the herb-laden windowsill, Callie began the warm-up exercises and moved into the Tai Chi routine that kept her supple. It was a private program. No one had ever watched as she moved smoothly from one position to another. Callie had never felt graceful. She envied many of her friends, who were liquid on the dance floor. She had always felt self-conscious about movement. Give a speech in front of hundreds? No problem. Carry a one hundred pound sack of feed? Easy. But go out on a dance floor? Never.

Today, however, she was not focusing on the meaning behind the traditional Chinese movements. Her wrists were not flat against the imaginary mirror, and her hands did not compress the imaginary ball, so at the end of the routine her body still felt tense, and she had not put forth enough focused effort to work up a sweat. Forty minutes wasted.

She showered, donned an old T-shirt printed with herbs surrounding a bee skep, worn jeans, sturdy boots, and a warm Old Navy fleece. Passing through the kitchen, she emptied the second cup of tea into her mug and rinsed the pot. She grabbed a pen, a new notebook, and a tape measure before heading out the door with the lab romping at her side. Wicca dashed ahead of her, sniffing the trail of bunnies, deer, and other wildlife that had passed through the gardens and over the lawn during the night.

It was a short walk to the farm where she unlocked the Cottage and started a fire blazing in the antique woodstove. Two weeks ago, when she'd first moved to the farm, Callie had stocked a jug of water and a tin of teabags at the Cottage. That was after she and Wicca had convinced a groundhog and a few other small critters that they would have to find new accommodations. Then she'd nailed pieces of tin over any holes she could find to prevent their return. She'd spent a couple of days clearing out trash, sweeping and mopping the floors, ceiling, and walls and washing the windows to cleanse away years of grime. A small table and chairs that she'd used on her patio in her old life were the only present furniture. Callie poured water into a kettle and set it on the woodstove where it quickly began to bubble. It was a comforting sound, and she'd be able to refill her tea mug as needed.

Callie was starting a new adventure, a new life, but traditions must be continued. She settled herself at the table and opened the new notebook. Every New Year's Day morn since her first year in junior high school, Callie had written a summary of the past year. The entries were short and succinct. Each one was followed by an arrow pointing up, indicating a "thumbs-up" or good event, or by a downward arrow that marked a goal not achieved or a disappointment. She paused occasionally to ponder as she made the list that summed up the past year. The entries were written in a precise but artistic hand:

Won Outstanding 4th Grade Teacher Award (arrow up)
Quit job (arrow up)
Read 25 books (arrow up)
Got a black lab, named her Wicca (arrow up with asterisk)
Bought farm and old farmhouse (arrow up with asterisk)
Big mortgage (arrow down with two asterisks)
Sold car (arrow up)

4

Dad gave me his old pick-up truck (arrow up)
Ordered hundreds of seeds (arrow up)
Lost Daniel (3 arrows down)

The next page was always her New Year's Resolution. She carefully penned in bold letters, "Be courageous." Brushing her long hair aside, she stared at the falling snow, added a tail to the period changing it to a comma, and wrote "but cautious!"

On the following pages, Callie always entered her proposed schedule and plans for the New Year. Major school projects for the next semester, vacation plans, important family dates, and crucial events or appointments were entered in ink. Minor, changeable plans were added in pencil.

The next page was always a list of books Callie wanted or needed to read. In recent years these were usually herb gardening books, plant propagation texts, garden design books, cookbooks, books related to teaching or child education, biographies of famous women gardeners, and historical novels. Customarily, she listed fifty-two as a goal. Since college, when she'd simply listed the required reading for each class, she hadn't managed a check mark by fifty-two titles. Teaching was too demanding to read a book a week, especially if you gave it your all, as Callie had. Once she discovered herbs and gardening, there was little time in the summer to read. As she gained experience, Callie's initial little plot by the back door of her rented house in southern Indiana had grown to include the entire back yard, and eventually most of the front as well. Soon, she was selling bunches of herbs from a card table at the local farmers' market. By that time the final page of her New Year's journal was always a list of plants she wanted to grow in the coming year.

Callie's passion for herbs had an innocent beginning. She often haunted used book stores picking up lightly used children's books to be used as prizes in her classroom, old cookbooks, cheap travel guides, and other books that caught her eye. One spring day she passed by a display of gardening books. A bright yellow cover attracted her attention. That copy of <u>Herb Gardens of Delight</u> simply changed her life. The author, Adelma Grenier Simmons had started an herb farm in Connecticut in the 1920's. She championed "the useful plants" describing their uses, characteristics, form, and scent in such a descriptive manner that Callie was intrigued. After reading the chapter on herbs used for teas, Callie knew she had to try some of these flavorful plants. A call to information soon gave Callie the phone number, so she was able to have a brochure sent to her. Within a few days, she had selected orange mint, which Ms. Simmons rated as one of her favorite tea plants. A rose scented geranium was the second item written on the order, because over the years Callie had seen several recipes in old cookbooks that required that particular plant. The final plant was lemon verbena. Callie had been mystified by the description of lemon verbena years ago when she had read about it in <u>Gone With The Wind</u>. In that celebrated novel, Scarlett's mother, Ellen, left the scent of lemon verbena trailing behind her as she passed through a room. Callie felt a plant that fragrant had to be included in her first order. Those three plants were still a treasured part of her herb collection, a collection that had grown to include hundreds of varieties.

Returning to the task at hand, Callie started penciling in a proposed schedule. It was an ambitious plan, especially since she had so little experience in running a business. She had moved to the country to start an herb farm. The Cottage would be the focal point and provide space for a shop to sell herbal products, dried wreaths, garden décor, and whatever else she chose to offer. It would be surrounded by gardens to both attract visitors and to provide a place to grow stock plants for propagation. She would also sell plants, just as she had at farmers market for the past four summers, but this time she'd be on her own, without the benefit of other vendors, advertising, and a city's sponsorship. It was a huge undertaking, but she needed to plunge deeply into something new, in a new place to forget about Daniel.

She decided to concentrate on the tasks that obviously had to be done right away rather than try to do the whole year at one sitting. Her schedule and job lists were certain to need constant revising, so nearly everything was in pencil this year.

She labeled a page "January" and wrote down everything she could think of that would get her off to a good start. "Attend a major gift show to purchase items for the Cottage Shop" was the first entry. Maybe she was being overly optimistic, purchasing inventory when the Cottage was not even ready to be a shop yet. She'd have to search on the internet to see where the major gift shows were held. She wrote "Find a good carpenter, get Cottage repairs done" above her first sentence. "Write a newsletter to promote the new farm" came next. Fortunately, she had been collecting the names and addresses of her farm market customers so she had a base list, but most of them were in southern Indiana, hours away. She'd need to start compiling a list of locals. She wrote "Search internet and at library for area garden clubs." "Get the seeds planted" was added but was quickly erased. It was replaced by "Purchase bulk potting soil and pots, shop lights, and shelving". Then came "Find a sign painter." "Get legal forms for a new business completed" followed "Mark out parking lot and get stone ordered."

"Price greenhouses." "Water lines?" "Have well checked for capacity, and have electric pump installed, if possible." "Electric capacity of Cottage wiring?" "See if local newspaper has a garden writer" followed in quick succession. "Plant all those seeds" returned to the list, as well as several other items that popped into her mind. Callie rose to stretch her legs, staring out at the snow-covered ground. Wicca raised her head briefly to check to see if Callie was leaving. Once assured that was not the case she resumed her nap near the woodstove.

"Maybe I should look for an herbal recipe to heal a broken heart", she muttered to herself as she peered out the window. The world outside the Cottage looked cold and bleak. The snow-covered earth was spiked with tall weed stalks right up to the door.

"Daniel would hate this," she thought as she gazed at the lonely landscape. Her heart lurched at the thought of him.

"Enough," she warned herself. "There's work to do."

She wandered around the one-room Cottage, making notes of repairs that were required immediately. She took measurements of the windows for curtains. A quick sketch proposed a floor plan that included shelving, a small table and chairs, a work table, sales counter and a daybed. A small alcove by the chimney would become a storage closet for cleaning supplies and other items. She'd need more electrical outlets for a cash register and a phone line for credit cards. She debated over color schemes, finally settling on cream-colored walls and pale sage green trim around the windows and door.

The Cottage had been the reason Callie had purchased this piece of land. Late last November, she and a newly-acquired realtor had been driving to inspect a property north of town when they passed this land. Callie gazed at the flat field surrounded on 3 sides by woods, saw the little dilapidated Cottage, and fell in love. She ordered the realtor to stop the car and jumped out. Callie waded through the waist high weeds and scrub brush to peek into the grimy windows. She could hear the sound of a nearby creek and noted a neglected patch of iris, daylilies, and an old lilac bush. Returning to the realtor's car, Callie asked her to find out who owned this little piece of heaven. When the realtor showed her a big old farmhouse nearby, Callie was certain she'd found her new home.

Things moved quickly. Papers were signed, boxes packed, a resignation was given to her principal, and over the Christmas holiday break she and Wicca had moved into the farmhouse. She was determined to start a new life, in a new place, with a new occupation.

She worked for several hours making lists of tasks, another page of questions, and a sketchy timeline. The fire was dying down, so she gathered her notebook and the empty water jug and strolled toward the farmhouse with Wicca dancing at her side. Callie loved walking outdoors where she could observe the clouds and the black lacy outline of trees. It was windy today and the branches were "clicking like skeletons' elbows and knees" as an old poem once described. Callie stopped at the mailbox on the way to the house and laughed at herself for not remembering that it was New Year's Day, so no mail would arrive. Since she'd moved to the farm, she had not had the same sense of each day that she'd had when she was teaching. Of course, then it was required. Art class on Mondays, spelling quizzes on Friday, etc. She laughed again as Wicca tried to catch an elusive squirrel. The lab believed that squirrels belonged in trees, not on her turf. It was surprising how quickly Wicca understood where her new property lines were located and began patrolling whenever she was outdoors. Callie observed the dog's valiant but useless attempts to catch the speedy squirrels. When Wicca attempted to run up the side of a tree in pursuit, Callie bubbled with laughter.

Actually, Callie was greatly surprised to find that she could laugh again. When Daniel had left, she had been completely sure she would never laugh again.

Suddenly the moment was shattered by the sound of a gunshot. Callie turned to look toward her woods where the sound had originated. Wicca rushed to her side, quivering and leaning against Callie's leg.

"Easy girl, it's okay." Her calm voice portrayed much less nervousness than she felt. She hadn't given anyone permission to hunt on her land, and she didn't like the idea of someone with a gun wandering around on her property. She looked around carefully but didn't see anything unusual. She debated whether to walk into the woods to see if she could find the trespasser, but decided it might not be wise. Anyone hunting with a large rifle this time of year was already a lawbreaker since the gun hunting season for most game had passed. It was probably still rabbit season, but any reasonable person would use a small caliber rifle or shotgun for that. Her father had taught her to shoot a .22 caliber rifle, so Callie knew this sound came from a large gun. She called Wicca to her side and hurried indoors.

Once settled inside her comfortable old farmhouse, Callie checked her answering machine. There was only one call from her best friend, Beth. Beth was such a good friend that she knew Callie really wouldn't want to talk to anyone. So, she'd simply left a warm message on the machine, reminding Callie that she was right there if she needed to talk, and wished her a "Wonderful New Year". Beth was the best.

"She would probably handle this much better than I am," Callie murmured. She stood by the phone trying to decide if she should call the local sheriff about the trespassing hunter. Since she hadn't seen a vehicle parked along the road, whoever it was had probably walked in from the east. Maybe it was a neighbor. She wasn't even sure the gunshot had come from her property. Sounds could echo on cloudy days. Wicca no longer seemed concerned. She had already settled on her rug in front of the fireplace. Callie decided not to pursue the matter.

She threw a scrubbed potato into the microwave and pulled a tiny container of minced basil and garlic in olive oil from the refrigerator to make a late lunch. She'd frozen several containers of the basic basil "paste" late last summer and had pulled one out to thaw before bedtime last night. Now she added a bit more olive oil, some parmesan cheese, slivered almonds, and stirred the fragrant mixture as she inhaled deeply. It always made her think of summer and sunset suppers on her back porch with Daniel. He loved her miniature pesto meatballs and her famous layered pesto cheese torta.

"Stop!" She couldn't let her mind go there, but it was hard to keep out someone who had been her life for over five years. Her love, her fiancé.

The microwave dinged, so she was saved by the bell. She poured a tall glass of milk and took her pesto-covered potato to the table near the big window that overlooked the backyard and the gazebo. Unfortunately, the old farmhouse did not have a back porch. There was a small patio off the back door and a sidewalk leading to a square gazebo with screened windows. Callie could already picture the scented garden she would plant around it, using exceptionally fragrant plants in her favorite colors. She'd sit in there on inclement days listening to the sound of raindrops on the roof and enjoying the scents. Across from the gazebo, Callie had already placed a big wooden bench with a back in the shape of a sunburst that she had painted a warm apricot color to co-ordinate with the plants she'd use. Her father had made it from her sketch years ago, and she cherished that bench. In the two weeks since she'd moved here, she'd often brushed away the snow and sat there watching the sunrise. She had planned this garden, which would be dug in the shape of a sunburst, with the colors she saw in the sunrise each day—bright yellows, oranges, corals, and apricots, with touches of lavender and rose. During the summer, it would be filled with "Sunspot" roses, "Sungold" buddleia, orange calendula and cosmos, apricot cockscomb, golden lemon balm, bright gold yarrow, daylilies, and dozens of other plants that lifted her spirits. It was here that she would sit in solitude writing the day's job list on her ever-present clipboard. The Sunrise Garden would link with the scented garden around the gazebo, which would connect to another garden around the small deck that would be filled with culinary herbs. She had it all planned. She was a good planner.

As Callie ate, she flipped through the local phone book yellow pages to find a source for the stone she'd need. She'd already rethought the priorities of the list she'd made at the Cottage. It would be good to have an adequate parking area for the carpenter, electrician, and plumber that she would need for the Cottage repairs, so they wouldn't get stuck. She made a note of the phone number and then began filling out the legal forms she'd requested for establishing a business.

Callie had spent hours and hours debating the name for her new herb farm as she'd unpacked and organized the farmhouse. She'd thought about using the location to help people locate the farm. "Heartland Herbs" came to mind, but her farm wasn't really in the nearby town. "Pumpkin Vine Herb Farm" had a certain ring since the farm was bordered on one side by Pumpkin Vine Creek. However she'd finally settled on "Joyful Heart Herbs".

"Heaven only knows I need a joyful heart," she murmured as she filled in the blanks of the legal forms. She liked the sound of it and the images the name evoked.

Suddenly her mind pictured shutters on the Cottage windows, each with a heart in the top center. She made a notation in the notebook in a section she labeled "Cottage Plans" and returned to the forms. Before she knew it, darkness had fallen.

She hurried to the kitchen to make New Year's Day Salsa. Traditionally, black-eye peas are served to bring good luck to the coming year. Some folks cook corned beef and cabbage, some cultures eat doughnuts, and in other countries people consume pork for luck on New Year's Day. Callie preferred the southern custom of eating black-eye peas, but she liked them made into a tasty salsa. Once the salsa was completed, she grabbed a sack of chips and a glass of wine. She and Wicca would spend the evening unpacking more boxes, watching football, and eating black-eye pea salsa for luck. She'd need all the good luck she could get this year.

Callie awoke early the next morning even though the sun had not yet made an appearance. She was eager to make progress on her extensive job list. She hurried through her morning routine and rechecked her lists. As soon as it was time for stores and offices to open she bundled up and headed to town. Wicca bounced happily on the truck seat beside her. That dog just loved riding shotgun!

Callie dropped the business forms at the post office, bought additional stamps, and exchanged greetings with Sharon, the local postmistress. Sharon knew everyone in the area, where they were going and what they were doing.

"I need a good carpenter. Know anyone that might be available right away?" Callie asked.

"I'd try Trev," Sharon replied. "He's usually pretty busy, but he might be willing to take on a quick job."

"What's Trev's last name?"

"Carpenter, of course!" Sharon laughed.

"You're kidding!" Callie said, laughing as well.

"Nope, I'm serious.

"OK, how about a good plumber? I need someone who knows about wells and pumps," Callie explained.

"Well, then I'd call Jesse," Sharon advised.

"And I suppose his name is Plumber," Callie joked.

"You got it!" Sharon nodded.

"No joke?"

"Nope, just check in the phone book. They're both listed."

"If you tell me the best electrician around is Joe Electricity, I'm going to faint!" Callie exclaimed.

"Nope, you're safe there. Best electrician around is Josh…..Sparks!" They both burst into giggles, eliciting the curious looks of several people who were by now waiting in line. Before she left, Callie asked for information on bulk mailing procedures, received a pamphlet, and left the post office still laughing.

Next stop was the local hardware to purchase "No Hunting" signs, fluorescent shop lights, a bundle of dowel rods, and some metal shop shelves. Jake Wilson pouted as he rang up the sale.

"Old Doc Hyde always let people hunt in that woods," he grumbled. "I'd hoped to bag that big buck that roams through there someday."

"Well, after he passed away, his wife Elizabeth didn't, and I don't intend to allow hunting on my land either." After Callie bought the property, several neighbors had stopped in out of curiosity. Many were eager to share the history of the old farm. Around 1910, the local veterinarian had purchased the farm as a summer and weekend place. Doc always rented the fields, but his wife Elizabeth had planted lots of flowers around the Cottage. During the summer weeks, Elizabeth would stay in the Cottage working on her world-famous wood carvings and in her flower beds. Doc would join her in the evenings and on weekends if he didn't have any emergencies. Some of the neighbors had even shared newspaper clippings and photos of Elizabeth's carvings, which were now in museums and galleries around the world. The carving of an entire stagecoach with six horses, complete with harness and driver made from a single block of wood, had completely amazed Callie. She'd love to see it in person someday if she could discover which museum owned it.

During the Depression, many people could not afford to pay Doc Hyde for his services, so he often took items in barter. One local dairy farmer with a big bill offered to pay with a load of black walnut logs. Doc didn't really need them, but he took the logs in trade and stored them in a lean-to shed. Later, when he became one of the first automobile owners in the county, he had the logs cut into planks and hired a carpenter to build a garage out at the farm. As a result, Callie owned a solid black walnut building that she planned to convert to a potting shed.

"Sorry, Jake. I've decided it would cause too many problems. No hunting."

Callie picked up her bag and headed for the door, hoping her firm tone had ended the issue. Jake pushed the cart containing the boxes of shelving and lights out the door and loaded them into her truck.

"You'll change your tune once the deer start chewing on all your pretty plants," Jake argued. "There's way too many deer in this area, especially in those woods of yours."

"We'll see, but right now I don't intend to allow any hunting, not even for mushrooms!" Smiling, Callie waved at Jake as she pulled away from the curb.

The next day, Callie called Trev Carpenter and arranged to meet him at the Cottage. She made her usual breakfast, tea and toast with gooseberry jam.

"I wonder if I can grow gooseberries here?" she wondered aloud to Wicca. She made a note on the clipboard, on the page marked "Research."

After the customary Tai Chi routine and a quick shower, she pulled on a warm sweatshirt and worn-jeans and braided her hair into one long braid down her back. She stared into the mirror, still not quite used to seeing the face that looked back. She was much thinner now, and it accented her eyes. She was not beautiful. Her nose was a bit too "Roman" and her mouth a bit thin. But, she had an interesting face that was pretty when she smiled. When Daniel had said he was leaving, Callie had wildly thought if she changed enough, he might stay. Her long hair was usually just pulled into a bun or a pony tail. So, she got an expensive, stylish haircut, new clothes, and new make-up. Of course, it hadn't prevented him from leaving for the Oakland office as soon as the transfer came through. Thank goodness her hair was still long enough to braid although the layered strands around her face insisted on freedom and curved around her face. Callie hoped they would soon grow long enough to stay in place.

She bundled up, grabbed a hammer, the bundle of dowel rods, the water jug, and a roll of leftover red Christmas ribbon to take to the farm. Wicca bounded along beside, ever alert to the possibility of scaring up a rabbit along the way.

Once at the Cottage, Callie lit a fire, put the kettle on, and returned outdoors. After studying the terrain and the area carefully, she pounded a dowel rod about fifty yards south of the Cottage. She paced off another fifty yards to the South, and pounded in another rod. Fifty yards west the third rod went into the ground followed by the final rod placed fifty rods north. Then she walked to the road and surveyed her work. It looked like an ample parking lot for now, but she decided that people would not like having to walk so far to shop. She moved all four rods closer to the Cottage front, using additional rods to mark a pathway to the Cottage door and a driveway from the road that could easily handle two cars passing. Then she tied bright red ribbons to the top of each rod.

She was still admiring her work when a worn blue pick-up truck with massive tool boxes on each side pulled into the rough lane that had served as a driveway for the Hyde family in years past. The driver seemed oblivious to the small saplings and weeds that had grown up in the lane, and pulled up near the Cottage. Callie could just make out faded black lettering on the truck's door. "Carpenter & Sons" it read.

The driver emerged from the truck wearing a fleece-lined denim jacket, worn leather boots, and a bright orange cap. Callie guessed he was in his early-thirties with bright, crinkly brown eyes and leathery skin.

"Trev Carpenter!" he stated as he thrust out his hand.

Callie's own hand was caught in a warm, firm grip as she responded, "Just call me Callie."

"All right, Callie. What kind of project do you have in mind?"

Callie led him into the now warm Cottage with Wicca scampering in just as she closed the door.

"And who is this little lady?" Trev inquired.

"This is Wicca, and it looks like she is happy to meet you!" Callie said as Wicca pushed her nose into Trev's hand. The lab let out a sigh of contentment as Trev rubbed her ears.

"Well, I'm always happy to meet a pretty lady," Trev replied, looking at Wicca and then at Callie.

Callie felt a blush rise to her cheeks. She had never taken compliments easily, maybe because they came so rarely. Her family had not been a gushy, affectionate bunch.

"Would you like a cup of tea? The kettle's already hot."

"No thanks. I'll probably need my hands, and I'm on a tight timeline this morning. What exactly do you want me to do?"

"Well," Callie began, "Obviously the walls and floor must be repaired where the critters gnawed to gain entry. There's some exterior damage as well where a ground hog chewed through the wall and several woodpecker holes outside, too. The floor seems uneven around the chimney, so I need that leveled. I'll need some shelving units on this wall and a sales counter built. I'd like the counter on little wheels, so I can move it easily, but they need to lock, so it won't roll if customers lean against it. And I want some shutters made for the windows. I have the designs sketched here for the shutters, the shelving, and the counter.

"Hmmm," Trev murmured as he pulled out his pencil. "This interior work is all original beadboard. They don't make this anymore. That could be a problem."

He paced over to the chimney, and lightly bounced on the balls of his feet. "Floorboards are poplar and in pretty good shape, but they do obviously slope toward the chimney, and the one damaged by the ground hog will have to be replaced. I'll have to check the foundation. That could be a big problem, if the joists are rotted."

While he talked, Trev took measurements and made notes on his clipboard. He glanced at the sketches of the shutters and counter, and clipped it under the metal spring clip. His eyes seemed to sparkle with humor as he glanced at all the bits of metal nailed here and there on walls and floors.

"Seems like you evicted quite a population here," he chuckled. "So, this is just a fix, not a restoration?"

"Sorry. To be truthful, I'd love to totally restore the building, but I just can't afford it. I just need it to be functional and welcoming."

"Let me take a quick look under the building, and I'll check the roof as well. I should be able to pull together a couple of estimates and get back to you in a couple of days." With that, he headed for his truck where he pulled out a pair of coveralls and a flashlight.

While she waited, Callie brewed a cup of tea and realized that Wicca had deserted her for Trev's company. She could hear scuffling sounds coming from under the Cottage as well as a few hammer taps echoing under the floorboards.

"Well, we've got some good news and some bad news," Trev announced when he returned. "The perimeter foundations are in pretty good shape, but the area around the chimney has rotted. Sometimes happens when no one keeps an eye on the flashing and sealing around the chimney. Rain starts leaking in, runs down the stonework, and eventually rots out the wood nearby. We'll have to jack up that section and replace the foundation. I'd suggest using some steel plates that we can attach to the good wood and then into brick pilings over a concrete footing."

"You've got quite a bit of damage on the exterior from woodpeckers, rot, and critters. It will cost more to fix all those spots than to recover it with new siding. If you were doing a restoration, you'd need wood siding. Since you're not, you can use vinyl or aluminum. Have a preference?"

After a bit of discussion on the merits of each, Callie decided she'd need to make a trip to the local building supply firm to look at samples. Trev was willing to do estimates using both materials and took her phone number so he could call when the estimates were finished. They were just leaving the Cottage when a large dump truck rolled in.

"Looks like you have more company," Trev stated. "I'll be in touch." As he climbed into his truck, he waved at the incoming driver.

"Hey!" a perky blonde shouted as she climbed out of the enormous cab. "How ya' doin', Trev?"

"If I were any better, I'd be dangerous!" he responded, as he turned the pick-up truck around and headed out the lane.

"Hey!" the blonde called in Callie's direction.

"Hi!" Callie replied, as she took in the petite form of the truck driver. "Probably a size two, and never has to diet," thought Callie as she strode over to the truck.

"Suz Stone," she greeted, extending a tiny hand with a muscular grip.

"I should have guessed," muttered Callie, thinking of the area's tendency for descriptive names.

"What?" Suz queried.

"Oh, nothing," Callie answered. "I'm just surprised to see a woman driving this monster."

"Yeah, you and lots of other people. I've just always loved big trucks, so when I graduated I found a job driving for Mathews Trucking. Had to prove myself, of course, but they were happy, and so was I. Then when Mr. Mathews retired, I bought one of his trucks and went into business for myself."

"Woman power," Callie smiled. "I'm all for it!"

"Yeah, we gotta stick together." Suz smiled back. "What ya' got in mind here?"

"Well, I need a parking lot and a driveway to the road. You can see I've marked out the dimensions already."

"Looks good. Have you measured to make sure you've got enough room for cars to come in and out when other cars are already parked? How many cars to do you expect to have at one time? Do you plan for just cars, or heavier traffic?"

"Good questions! Got time for a cup of tea?"

"Sure, just let me grab my pager."

Over cups of steaming tea, Callie and Suz worked out the requirements for the new parking lot. Since Callie would be expecting large delivery trucks and later on big propane trucks bringing fuel for the greenhouses, Suz planned for a sturdy base. The top layer would be a mixture of crushed stone and filler that would pack hard and level so customers could comfortably walk to their cars. Suz also explained that some grading would be required so the parking lot would drain away from the Cottage. Some leveling and filling would be necessary to make the driveway blend smoothly into the road. She also suggested that they use the old lane for the exit to make traffic flow better. The good news was that Suz could start hauling stone immediately and could also arrange for her brother to do the grader work. Callie should have a parking lot and driveway by the end of the week, if the weather held.

The two women seemed to click, and by the time Suz left, Callie felt as if she had made her first friend in her new community.

Later that evening Callie gathered her tools and empty water jug, put on her hat and gloves, and with Wicca bounding beside her, walked through the deepening shadows to the farmhouse. The sky looked heavy. Tonight there would be snow. Daniel always loved snow.

Callie flipped on the light as she entered the kitchen. Wicca was already salivating in anticipation of her supper, so Callie filled her bowls with food and water, then quickly sorted through the day's mail that she had picked up from the box at the end of the lane. Nothing important, so she threw it into the basket on the counter. Not really hungry, she fixed a quick supper of scrambled eggs, adding a few snipped chives from the pot on the kitchen windowsill, leftover mushrooms, and a bit of grated cheese. She sipped a glass of Corbett Canyon chardonnay while she cooked the simple dish. Daniel would have been appalled at such an inexpensive selection. "Only the best for the best!" was his pet phrase.

"So, I guess I know I'm not the best," Callie mumbled.

She would never forget the day Daniel announced that he was moving to California. Callie had been stunned, shocked into silence. Her mind had gone numb. Her heart had stopped and her hands had turned cold.

His voice had sounded relaxed. Part of her mind had wondered at the time, how he could sound so at ease. Then she realized that it was his "sales pitch" voice, the one that reassured and convinced customers that they really needed that big insurance policy.

At first Callie had thought he meant they were both moving to California and she panicked, wondering how she could give up her teaching job and leave all her friends and family here in the Midwest.

Then her whirling mind caught the assurances that "this was for the best", and that someday she would thank him for realizing their wedding would be the biggest mistake of their lives.

She had stared at him in bewilderment. What was he saying? There would be no wedding next month? He was leaving? This was, "for the best"? He had left her then after a brief hug. There was no mention of Mariah, his co-worker at the insurance office. Two months had passed, but the memory was as vivid and the wounds as fresh as they had been that pretty November day.

Her hands were still cold. Callie suddenly realized the eggs she was cooking in her grandmother's skillet were the same black color as the cast iron. She slid the skillet off the burner and poured another glass of wine. "What went wrong?" Callie wondered. She hadn't had a clue that Daniel was unhappy or straying. She'd thought they were the perfect couple. Everyone said so.

Her appetite gone, she readied for bed, gave Wicca a hug, and tossed and turned the entire night.

The next morning dawned bright and sunny. Wicca was delighted to discover that a thick blanket of snow covered the land. Callie made her morning tea, choosing peppermint and green tea. After a toss and turn night her brain was sluggish. She hoped the peppermint would perk her mind up a bit.

She did her Tai Chi series, trying harder to focus and make the workout a worthwhile effort. Stroke the bird's tail, feel the bubbling well. Afterwards she checked her e-mail, fixed her usual breakfast, fed Wicca, and let her out to patrol the property. Once in the studio she placed a call to Josh Sparks. Obviously, the electrician could not do much until the carpenter had completed the necessary work, but Callie thought he might need to order supplies, or she might need to get on a waiting list for his services.

When she reached Mr. Sparks, she was treated to a deep rumbling voice. She'd always been a sucker for low basses. It was probably from all those years listening to her dad's favorite Statler Brothers' music. Mr. Sparks agreed to do the work and said a few electric lines and a phone line should not be a problem. He'd stop by sometime when he was in the area to look over the existing wiring, fuse box, and outlets so he'd know exactly what to bring.

Then she called Jesse Plumber, who agreed to come over to check out the well. The Cottage was equipped with an outdoor hand pump, stiff with rust. Callie had not been able to budge the handle to see if she could get water from the well. She had no idea if the old well could provide water for the greenhouses she planned to build, or if there were an existing casing for an electric pump to be installed easily. Unfortunately, Mr. Plumber was backlogged with work and could not come for a couple of weeks. Callie could live with that since she really did not have a great need for water at the Cottage until spring. She had all her current inventory of plants housed at the farmhouse and in its attached garage.

She put check marks beside those items on her job list that she had completed, and made entries in both her journal and her calendar. Next she called to book a flight to Atlanta for the gift mart in mid-January. An internet search had indicated that mart would be best for garden-related products. Callie was happy she had not delayed in checking. The days were flying by, and the job list seemed to be growing, not shrinking! She checked the list again and decided she needed to do some research. Not knowing how long she'd be gone, Callie left the black lab at the farmhouse. She gave the pouting dog a treat and a stern admonishment to stay at home and be good. The dog was not happy, looking at Callie with sorrowful eyes, but she seemed to understand and sat watching by the corner of the farmhouse as Callie headed the truck toward town.

She'd spend some time cruising around looking at business signs. Callie needed a sign painter that could put some emotion and welcome into his work. She also needed a printer to do the newsletter, some flyers, and postcards for a special preview party once the shop was open. A check of all the local stores' inventory before her buying trip was also essential. It would be foolish to order items that everyone had already seen in other shops!

Callie drove around the square looking at signs. A right turn pointed the truck up Highway 3 to the nearby community of Roll and back, but there was nothing that captured the look she wanted so she returned to town. She stopped at several stores and wandered through their aisles picking up a few essentials like scotch tape, some birthday cards, and more notebook paper for her clipboard and notebook. She made notes of gift lines that each shop carried when she returned to her truck, so she would not be tempted to order them for her shop. So far, the stores she'd visited were heavy on "country" and "primitives". That's what Callie expected in this rural community.

She maneuvered her pick-up truck into an empty parking space in front of Dinah's Diner across from the courthouse. She'd already discovered that next to the postmistress the "geezers" who met every morning at Dinah's were the best source of information in town. The "Geezers" were a local group of retired professionals and businessmen, who met for coffee and energetic discussion, solving all Heartland's as well as the world's problems with typical conservative politics.

Callie wasn't foolish enough to pull up a chair at the Geezer's official table. Just pausing nearby was enough to draw their attention.

"How's the herb farm coming along?" one of the geezers asked. Jim Peters was the retired dentist who had asked exactly what kind of herbs she intended to grow. This occurred at the first local chamber of commerce meeting Callie had attended. Mr. Peters had been standing next to the sheriff, whom he had elbowed in the ribs with a chuckle.

"Now Jim," the sheriff had drawled, "Miss Callie is a law-abiding citizen who's going to have a straight business. You don't see any of those silly decals promoting making marijuana legal on her pick-up, do you?"

Privately, Callie had been surprised that not only did the sheriff know her name since they'd never been introduced but that he also knew which pick-up truck was hers. Especially since this was a rural county in which nearly everyone drove pick-ups.

Thinking of the sheriff reminded her that she had not yet put up the "No Hunting" signs around her property, so she moved her watchband from her left hand to her right to remind herself. As she did so, she answered Jim Peter's question.

"Just fine, Mr. Peters. I'm making real progress."

"Well, that's just fine, just fine. Have all of you met Miss Callie?" Jim asked. Around the table graying heads bobbed up and down even though Callie did not recognize half of them.

"I'm in need of a good sign painter though. Anybody know of one in the area?" Callie questioned. Callie knew she was taking a risk. If they gave her a name, and she didn't use them, there would be talk. No doubt at least one, maybe more of the men sitting at the table would be related, however distantly, to any painter suggested.

"Doesn't that part-Cherokee gal over by Fowlerton paint signs?"

"Yup, I think she still does."

"Can't recall her name, can you?"

"No, can't recall. How about you, Fred? You know her?"

"She related to Mabel, over at the water office?"

"No, that's the gal that does wallpapering. You need any wallpapering done; she's the gal to call all right. You need any wallpapering?"

"Not at the moment," Callie replied. She had been following the conversation with difficulty, since it had occurred between sips of coffee and bites of Dinah's famous pies with animated fork gesturing that contradicted the slow tempo of the words themselves.

"Talk to Cecil over at the printer's."

"Thanks for your suggestion. Have a good day, gentlemen," Callie called over her shoulder, as she moved away. The "geezers" seemed relieved to return to their political discussion although Callie noted a couple of whispered comments and lowered heads shaking as she glanced in the mirror over the counter.

"Mornin' Callie!" Dinah greeted warmly.

"Morning, Dinah." Callie answered. "Could I have a piece of your wonderful butterscotch pie and a cup of decaf to go?"

"Sure thing. How's it going out there? Plants happy?" Dinah had the plump figure that most really good cooks share. She loved to cook and loved to have people around her table. Her restaurant was not gourmet but served up good, wholesome food and plenty of it. Callie had already sampled several hearty soups, chicken and noodles, and salads in the days before she had her kitchen unpacked and organized. She'd learned that Dinah had moved back to her hometown of Heartland two decades ago after a tour of cooking on cruise ships.

"So far, so good. We've had sunshine some days, so the ones near windows are happy. I've got lights on timers on all the shelves and tables in the garage, so they're okay. Not growing, of course, but I don't expect much in January. I just seeded lots of perennials and a few really slow annuals this week."

Callie took a sip of her coffee, thanked Dinah, paid her bill and left, turning toward the printers' storefront down the street.

The bell over the door jingled as she entered. The store smelled of ink and paper. Shelves were filled with an array of printed mugs, books, calendars, key rings, baseball caps, and more. Colorful printed tee-shirts were displayed on the opposite wall. An energetic woman with a bright smile hurried to greet her.

"Can I help you?"

"I'm going to need a newsletter printed, and I wondered what your size capabilities were, the types of paper you can use, and a general price structure. I also need some pre-printed postcards, but I want to use my own artwork. Can you do that?"

"Oh, my goodness. Sounds like you are going to be a busy lady. You'll need to talk to Cecil for a special project like that," she beamed. "I'll be right back," she said as she scurried down the hallway to a back office. Callie could hear voices as she stood there imagining what Cecil would look like. No doubt his name was Cecil Printer.

"You go right on back, Miss," the saleslady directed.

Callie stopped in surprise as she entered the tastefully decorated office. As the leather chair swiveled towards her, she drew in her breath in another surprise.

"Cecilia Hutchins," the woman grinned as she rose and extended her hand.

"Nice to meet you," Callie stammered.

"Ellen says you need some printing done. Tell me what you have in mind."

The next forty-five minutes were spent looking at paper types, dimensions, print styles, and samples of Cecilia's work. Callie selected a cream colored paper, dark green ink, and a simple but flowing type face for both the newsletter and the postcards. They discussed turnaround time, so Callie would know when to set deadlines for herself. Cecilia promised to e-mail estimates for both projects by the following day. Callie then asked if Cecilia could recommend a sign painter.

"Oh, yes! Did you see the lettering on our walls? And the paint colors? Inspired! Just inspired! I can set typeface in a printer, but I certainly could not paint it on a wall. You need to meet LouAnn. She's an artist, just a true artist. I wish she could stop painting signs and just paint landscapes. She's so talented. Let me give you her number. She loves flowers, too, so you two should get along just fine!"

Callie left Cecilia's office feeling as though she had just gained another friend. She felt she was finding acceptance into her new community. Most people were happy to have a new business that might employ some local people and hopefully attract some out-of-towners into the area, whatever business it might be. She had soon discovered that she gained even more acceptance when she made it clear that she wanted to use local suppliers and talent. She was forming quite a support team, and happily, many of them were women. If she could have found a female carpenter, plumber, and electrician, she'd have been thrilled. After Daniel, she just wasn't ready to trust any man.

She crossed the street to the courthouse to drop off yet another sheaf of papers that were required to form a business. As she passed the notice board, she saw there was a meeting at the courthouse with the governor's Secretary of Agriculture and the county commissioners scheduled for next week. As much as she didn't want to be around people right now, the fight to keep huge Confined Animal Feeding Operations, or CAFO's as they were more commonly called, out of their tiny county was important to her. She had read about it even before she moved to the area.

Callie didn't object to the relatively small confinement operations owned by families that had farmed in the county for generations. However, the new operations that had filed for zoning changes were owned by foreign corporations seeking permission for thousands of confined dairy cows. It just didn't make good environmental sense, especially since the location the corporation had selected was in a flood plain, just a mile and a half from the county seat, Heartland.

This particular corporation had already been cited for several environmental violations. Their CAFO's were polluting streams with manure in nearby states. Neighboring farm families of those operations were complaining of health problems, noise pollution, the thousands of starlings that were attracted to the manure lagoons, and the destruction of local roads. Callie didn't want to see the same things happen here, so she had joined the movement to oppose the zoning change within days of moving to the area.

She'd spent hours studying environmental reports and soil sample research, and then she wrote a letter to the editor that had been published in the local newspaper. She knew that was taking another risk. She

24

could alienate future customers before she even opened. It was a conflict charged with emotion on both sides. So far, all the big money was with the foreign corporation, who seemingly had unlimited funds for lawyers and "environmental experts" who gave glowing speeches. The current governor was strongly in favor of these giant animal factories feeling that it would help the state's economy, and put Indiana on the map for "progressive" agriculture. The overall plan was to incorporate huge CAFO's into agricultural "parks" that would include bio-fuel factories as well. All of this didn't sound too "park-like" to Callie. Somehow creating twenty-million-gallon manure lagoons across the county had little appeal. She could just picture one in the field across from her fledgling herb farm.

Daniel had thought her passion for the environment and family farms was foolish. He teased her about being a throwback, a sixty's flower child. Daniel was all big business, regardless of any environmental impact, full speed ahead. Callie had thought that was the one area on which they didn't agree. Apparently there were others.

She made a note of the meeting time and place in her pocket calendar, dropped off the forms, and headed toward her truck. She still had to post those "No Hunting" signs and assemble the shelving and lights for the spare bedroom.

As Callie strode toward her pick-up, she noticed it seemed to be leaning to one side. Puzzled, she quickened her pace. One tire was flat. She was opening the door to put the sack with the pie and decaf inside before she notice the crude lettering on the windshield. "Get out! We don't need you here!" Callie stepped back and carefully looked around. The street was deserted.

She'd been warned. Some of the other people in the community who were opposing the "cow factories" had already had warning letters or signs stuck in their yards. Callie had seen some dark looks and suspected a few people crossed the street to avoid meeting her, but she'd never really expected any action. Perhaps her recent letter to the editor advising people to have their wells tested and certified before the dairy opened had put her in the spotlight.

She pulled the heavy floor jack from behind the seat, set the parking brake, and located the lug wrench. At least it wasn't raining or snowing.

Prying off the wheel cover and slipping the wrench over the lug nut, Callie bent over and applied all her strength. The nut didn't budge.

"Darn.....darn, double darn!" she exclaimed. Returning to the cab, she pulled out a can of W-D 40 from behind the seat and a long, hollow metal bar.

"Daddy would be proud," Callie thought. Her father had not been well-read or highly educated, but he'd been one of the smartest men she'd ever known. She'd followed him around, passed him tools, and learned to treasure his common sense and self-taught skills. She smiled as she sprayed each nut. Callie slid the metal bar over the handle of the wrench, and placed it on a bolt so it was parallel to the ground. Gripping the side of the truck bed, she jumped up and landed with her full weight on the bar, grinning as her weight slowly lowered the bar to the pavement.

"That's one thing Mariah couldn't do. Tiny, petite, delicate Mariah wouldn't recognize a lug wrench, let alone a cheater bar," Callie thought. One nut loosened, seven to go. Once they were loose, she placed the jack under the axle and pumped the handle until the tire was off the ground. The rest of the job was easy, and she finished it quickly. She was just replacing the jack when someone came up behind her.

"Looks like you've done that before," growled a nearby voice.

Callie turned to see a stocky, dark-headed man wearing a deep green jacket with a DNR patch on the shoulder.

"Let me give you a hand," he stated, as he smoothly tossed the flat tire into the bed of the truck.

"Thanks."

"Glad to help." He sauntered to the front of the truck to study the lettering on the windshield. "Looks like someone left you a love letter," he chuckled.

"Hardly. I guess the locals just don't like newcomers to the area," she said, "or someone objects to my stand against the big foreign dairies."

"Or both," he chuckled again. "They might think you're a drug dealer."

"Hardly," Callie replied.

"Well, don't you own that herb farm south of town? Some people might think you grow some funny plants out there. I've heard that back in the 60's and 70's lots of the so-called herb farms grew a pretty interesting range of herbs!"

"I assure you I don't grow anything questionable. Culinary and fragrance herbs are my passion although I plant Biblical herbs, dye plants, and many others."

"Whatever the reason, it looks like someone's giving you a warning. You'd better get that tire fixed soon. Maybe you'll need a spare again," he called over his shoulder as he walked away. His voice had not sounded friendly, not friendly in the least.

Callie stood for a moment wondering if she'd just met the author of the warning. She looked up and down the street again, but there were only a couple of guys lounging against the hardware store window nearby. She didn't recognize either one although that was not unusual. After all, she'd only lived in the area for a little over two weeks and had spent most of that time cleaning, unpacking, and making plans. She noted they were both wearing hunter orange caps but that was not unusual in this rural area.

She had to acknowledge the good advice of the DNR officer though, so she dropped the flat tire at the local tire store to be repaired. She didn't like being without a spare, so she purchased a new tire just to be on the safe side.

Back at the farmhouse, she glanced at her watch, realized it was on the wrong arm, and remembered she needed to put up those signs. It was already mid-afternoon, so she brewed a pot of lemon balm and peppermint tea to lift her spirits. She crafted a sandwich of arugula leaves, picked from the plants she'd seeded the day she first arrived, and mozzarella cheese slices on crusty whole grain bread. Wicca sat patiently in the doorway between the kitchen and dining room but with longing eyes and salivating mouth. Callie tore the crust from her sandwich, gave it to the lab, and finished her pie, feeling only slightly less guilty than she would have if she'd eaten the entire sandwich.

No messages blinked on the answering machine, so she moved her watch to her left wrist, gathered her staple gun, a supply of heavy-duty staples and the "No Hunting" signs. Wicca was delighted to go on an adventure outdoors and romped ahead, looking back occasionally to make sure Callie was following. It was a lovely afternoon although the ground underfoot was slightly slippery from the now-melting snow.

Callie missed the songs of the summer birds. Winter birds seemed content with a sharp single "Chirp!" She needed to put out some bird feeders, which were still packed away in boxes in an unused bedroom. As she walked past the Cottage, she saw several birds feeding on the stalks of weeds that grew waist high over the entire area. She would need to get it mowed early in the spring, just as soon as the ground was dry enough and someone was found to do it. She wondered how long it would take to have grass growing again in the areas that would not be planted in gardens. She certainly could not afford to have it re-sodded.

She posted signs on all the fence posts along the road and on several of the larger trees along the property line on the south edge. Now, she followed the faint trail that curled through her woods. Her woods. Callie couldn't wait to find and identify all the wildflowers that were sure to be there come spring. She had read many books that advised new property owners not to hurry to clear or make major changes until all four seasons had passed. In that time, she would be able to identify all the good plants that already existed on her property, learn where the land did not drain well, find where the micro-climates were, and discover lots more. She had already started mapping existing trees and the plants that she recognized.

As she walked and worked, her mind drifted to plans for the herb farm. She'd decided to start working on new recipes, and to focus on appetizers.

"Herbal beginnings," she mused. It seemed appropriate since she was on an "herbal beginning" herself. Maybe she could even turn it into a booklet, or a real cookbook that she could sell at the farm. Perhaps it would even go into bookstores, and maybe she would be asked to attend book signings, or to give talks. That would be good promotion for her herb farm. She was just making a mental list of her favorite types of appetizers when she heard Wicca give a low growl and rush towards the creek. Callie hurried to follow, dropping her signs and staple gun next to a large tree, so she could move more quickly.

Her stomach turned as she saw what Wicca had discovered. Halfway emerged in the creek was the corpse of a whitetail deer. Callie assumed it had been a buck since the head was gone. No one would go to the trouble of removing a head unless it had a nice set of antlers. It had been a large animal, but now the hind haunches were gone. The severed legs had floated down the creek but had caught on branches. Since there were no footprints leading down or from the body, Callie assumed the deer had been killed in the woods, butchered, then the remnants thrown into the creek. She called Wicca to her side, reassured her, and clipped the leash she carried in her coat pocket to the lab's collar. She walked back up the creek bank, and let Wicca lead her to the spot where, in fact, the deer had been killed. Blood spattered the leaves, and footprints in the soft earth of the woodland floor led toward the hardened path that wound through her woods. She looked around carefully and finally spotted a crude wooden structure in the crotch of a large tree. Someone had constructed a hunter's "stand" up in an old oak tree that overlooked the faint path made by animals coming to the creek for water, and that someone was big enough to carry a deer's head, two big haunches, and most likely a gun quite a distance. From this spot, it was a long trek to either the road or through the woods and off her property.

Unbidden, her mind returned to Jake's comment about the big buck that roamed through her woods that he someday hoped to bag. Had he already killed it and made the comment to throw her off? When was that? Was it two, or three days ago?

"No," Callie thought, "the light rain that turned to snow would have been enough to wash the blood away. It was recent. Probably very early this morning."

Callie attempted to follow the footprints, but when they moved away from the deeper woods, she could no longer find them in the harder ground of the paths that intersected randomly throughout the property. She did not find any blood trail and suspected the hunter had come prepared with bags and a pack to make carrying easier.

She returned to reclaim her signs and staple gun, and tacked one of the big white, black, and orange "No Hunting" signs on the trunk of the large oak that held the tree stand. She'd come back later with tools and a ladder, so she could tear it down. After stapling signs all along the last edge of her property line, she returned to the farmhouse.

Callie gave Wicca a treat, and went to her studio desk to look up the number for the local DNR officer. She realized with a start that although she'd met the man that very morning, they had not exchanged names. As soon as the voice came on the line, she recognized the deep voice.

It did not sound friendly, and she had not even spoken into the phone yet!

Callie spent most of the evening sulking and feeling sorrowful over the deer's lost life. She was not totally opposed to hunting really, but she thought guns gave men an unfair advantage over the wildlife. Callie had heard all the arguments that the deer in Indiana no longer had natural predators to control their populations. She'd once attended a seminar explaining that deer were starving because they will not leave the relative area they were born in, even to find additional food. This made them more susceptible to diseases. She understood that all of Nature was a balancing act, and that problems arose when things caused that balance to tip. The deer were being wedged between housing and shopping developments, reduction of woodland and changing crop practices that reduced desirable crops. The only natural predator seemed to be the endless stream of vehicles that roar down the roadways. Insurance companies were always complaining about the increasing deer population. Daniel's company had even supplied free "deer deterrent whistles" for the company vehicles of the corporations he called on.

"Gads!" Callie exclaimed, pacing back and forth across the living room. "Does every thought process in my mind have to lead back to HIM?"

Wicca cocked her head to one side and then walked to the kitchen where she pushed the pantry door open and surveyed the shelves.

Callie stopped pacing to look at the lab. "You're right. We should bake!" Cooking and gardening were the two activities that soothed her soul quickly. Since it was winter gardening was not an option, so she would bake. She decided upon rose-geranium rice pudding and within the hour the meringue-topped concoction was browning in the oven.

The following morning her thoughts were as gray and fuzzy as the day as she moved like a robot through her morning routine. Even Wicca seemed subdued and lethargic.

"And this is what we get for eating pudding at midnight," Callie told the dog. As she poured her second cup of tea, her eyes roamed over the day's job list. She moved to the office and fired up the computer.

While she waited, she studied her calendar. Only ten days until she left for Atlanta. She'd been planning to sow all those seeds she'd ordered in such a frenzy right after she'd purchased the farm. Then she'd been stalled because she had no place to put the flats once she'd sown them. A plan to put shelving in another spare bedroom had evolved, and she'd even purchased the shelves and lights, but now she realized that no one would be here to care for the fragile seedlings while she was in Atlanta. Better postpone that task to immediately after she returned.

She went over her lists and determined that if she wanted to get a newsletter out to her future customers she'd better start collecting ideas and writing. Callie had given it quite a lot of thought, and decided that she should start sending a monthly newsletter now even though it was only January. She did not plan to open until April, but her farm market customers were not even aware that she was starting a new business in another area. She had moved after the market had closed. Only a few local people, her immediate family, and of course, Beth, even knew of her plan to open an herb farm. She'd also send the newsletter to her former fellow teachers, former neighbors, and church friends in her old town, but she needed to start collecting the addresses for area people as quickly as possible. The sooner she had a newsletter to distribute, the faster her mailing list would grow.

She'd also been going through catalogs and websites, making lists of possible products for her shop. As she sat, she tried to envision the interior of her future shop, with its new shelving, sales counter, and walls all filled with beautiful gift and garden items. It would be a small shop by today's standards, but stocked with special items. Soft music would always be playing in the background and fragrant herbs would waft from one lovely display to the next, all bathed in glowing light. Light? Callie suddenly realized that she had not told Josh Sparks that additional lighting would need to be installed! And, she hadn't done any research on how to get a credit card machine, or what kind of system it required. There was still the problem of how she was going to label each of the plants offered for sale! She groaned as she reached for her trusty notebook and started making additions to her job list.

Her computer dinged, announcing that she had mail. Her favorite cousin, Eve who lived in Atlanta, had responded to Callie's e-mail that she was coming her way. Callie knew her time would be limited, and that she needed to stay focused on purchasing, but she knew how hurt Eve would be if she found out Callie had been in town but had not visited. Besides, she always enjoyed her time with Eve.

Eve was delighted that Callie was coming and said she'd plan a special evening for them. Callie hesitated, knowing that her time was short, but the gift mart showrooms were not open every evening, and she'd have to eat sometime, so she agreed. Callie promised to call once she was in Atlanta. Of course, Eve knew the wedding had been cancelled, so she didn't question Callie's upcoming trip. Eve had always been intuitive and patient. She'd wait until Callie was ready to talk.

Callie and Eve had grown up on adjoining family farms. Both had learned how to work hard, how to stretch a dollar, and how to make do with little. Eve was a few years older and had left the farm right after graduation to eventually become an important executive with Bell South. She had traveled all over the world, both with work and skiing vacations. Unlike Callie, Eve had learned the art of make-up, fashion, and sophistication. Callie had simply gone to college to earn a teaching degree. She'd had her fill of shoveling manure and loading hay wagons. Life on the farm was boring. She had always envied her "townie" classmates who never had chores to do when they got home from school. They could go to the local soda shop or get together to do one another's hair and experiment with make-up. Her town friends always knew the newest dance steps and the words to all the cool songs. She was certain she'd love city-life, with a ranch-style home in the suburbs, stylish clothes, and clean hands. Not one of her cousins had stayed on the farm. Callie's generation had moved to big cities like Atlanta, Los Angeles, Milwaukee, and Tucson to become graphic designers, electricians, engineers, and business owners.

That was part of the attraction to Daniel. Daniel was going to be a lawyer. He'd be a corporate lawyer in a big, exciting city, not some small-town paper pusher who only handled land transfers and wills. Daniel had been the smartest kid in his high school class with a full scholarship to college.

They'd started dating in college. Daniel was the most wonderful person in the world, so tan and sleek from spending hours at the pool. And, it wasn't a farmer's tan like the other boys' but an all-over, entire body tan. He was smart, confident, talkative, and polite. When Daniel asked Callie to marry him, she didn't hesitate.

It had been the perfect plan, at least in Callie's view. They'd work and save money so they could start out right. She'd teach, and Daniel would go to law school. When they had enough money saved, they would buy their dream house, and have the perfect wedding. Somewhere along the line, law school slipped from the plan. After graduation, Daniel decided he couldn't stand another semester in college, let alone law school, so he took a job in the insurance industry. Callie didn't complain. With both of them working, their savings would grow even faster.

Her thoughts were interrupted by the sound of heavy equipment coming slowly down the road. As Callie looked out the window of the studio, she saw a large truck pulling a trailer loaded with a bulldozer and another smaller tractor drive into the farm. She grabbed her coat, hat, and gloves and ran to meet the driver. Just as she arrived, Suz pulled into the farm with a load of stone.

"Are you ready for some progress?" Suz called as she waved a greeting.

"Can't wait. I'm really glad to see you". They were both shouting over the noise of engines. The driver of the trailer truck was already busily unhooking the straps on the tractor and lowering the ramp.

"That's my brother, Flint," Suz explained. "We're going over the parking lot with a bush hog to clear out some of this brush. It'll make the ground easier to level, and make the stone lay better. You might want to think about having him go over any future lawn areas while he's here. Wouldn't cost much, and it'll make the place look almost livable!"

Callie was so excited that she almost bounced. While Suz and Flint unloaded the truck, she paced around the Cottage picturing the future gardens, paths, and lawn. As she and Suz conferred, guided, and pointed, the bush hog quickly swept through the waist high wilderness. They even cleared the area for the future greenhouse and a swath from the well to the road and the greenhouse site. That would make running power lines and water lines a lot easier. Within an hour, the bulldozer had scraped away the debris and leveled the future parking lot. In another hour, Suz had dumped the first load of stone, and Flint was merrily spreading it. Callie didn't even want to keep track of the number of loads Suz brought, but it took the entire day. When Suz told her she was going after the final load, Callie ran back to the house to get her camera and to put on a pot of coffee. They'd celebrate the first real progress toward her new herb farm. She grabbed a loaf of her special Bishop's Bread from the freezer and popped it into the microwave to slowly thaw. Then she ran back to the farm to capture the creation of her parking lot. What a difference it made to be able to see the Cottage from the road! It gave Callie a burst of energy. Joyful Heart Herbs was really going to happen!

After the final load of stone had been spread, Suz and Flint joined Callie in her kitchen for a hot cup of coffee and thick slices of the fruitcake-like bread.

"This is really, really good!" Suz exclaimed. "I've never had fruitcake with chocolate chips before! And there are flavors in it that I can't identify. Did you make it?"

"It's my adaptation of an old, old recipe. In the olden days, farmwives would make a fruited bread containing raisins, dried or candied fruit, and nuts for the visit of the circulating preacher. No one ever knew exactly which day he might show up, so it was important for the cake to be able to keep well. In later times, when supplies were easier to obtain, bits of chocolate were added to make it more special. I make mine with maraschino cherries and chopped orange mint and drizzle it with orange mint syrup to keep it moist," Callie explained.

"You should enter this in the county fair," Flint nodded somberly.

Until that moment, Flint had been silent. Callie thought he was in his late twenties, about her own age. His sandy hair stuck out at odd angles from being pressed under a cap and being in the wind. His muscular build was obvious, even beneath the flannel shirt and heavy sweater. He had Suz's laughing eyes. It was easy to see the family resemblance although Flint was much taller than his sister.

Callie realized that with Suz around, there probably wasn't much need for conversation on his part. It was easy to see that they worked well together, with few words but complete understanding.

"Well, if we want to stay in business, we'd better get rolling. Call us if you need anything else," Suz called as she and Flint donned their jackets.

"I will, and thanks so much for all your help. It looks terrific!"

Callie watched as they climbed into the trucks and lumbered off down the road. It was only after the noise had died away that she started to laugh.

"Flint Stone! What a town for crazy names!" she giggled.

Rain started the following day. It was dark and gloomy, so Callie did what she always did to lift her spirits. She baked! With an old Mills Brothers CD playing in the background, she mixed up her great-grandmother's recipe for coffee cake. Just as she was placing the bowl of dough in a pan of warm water to rise, Callie's phone rang. She was pleased to hear the sound of Trev Carpenter's voice on the line. He'd finished the estimates and would bring them over after lunch.

Callie planned to spend most of the morning writing short articles, intending to take samples of her writing to the local newspaper. She'd checked the paper daily for nearly three weeks, and there was no sign of a garden column. If all went according to plan, the editor would agree to let her write a weekly column. It would be a good way to introduce herself to the community, and to spread the joy of gardening. She'd already had her letter to the editor published concerning the foreign dairies, but she had not met the editor himself. The Upcoming Events column had listed a local group, The Heart and Soil Garden Club. Callie had made a note of their next meeting and the contact number. She liked the name, linking Heartland and the soil that is essential for gardening and growing. It sounded like an interesting group to join. However, it was taking place while she would be in Atlanta, so she'd have to wait until the February meeting to attend. She began by making a list of possible article topics, things she felt comfortable discussing and speaking on with authority that would not take a lot of research.

The timer went off in the kitchen, so she went to roll out the dough, liberally sprinkling it with a mixture of brown sugar and cinnamon, dotting it with butter, and covering it all with thick cream. She poked the handle of a wooden spoon down into the dough, to allow the creamy, sugary mixture to permeate here and there, popped the cake into the oven and reset the timer.

While she'd finished the cake, Callie mulled over the process of writing the articles. She decided that if the editor did not want her articles, she could use them in her newsletter, so the time and effort spent writing them wouldn't be wasted. Then she had a moment of brilliance! She'd be wise to put them on a website! She hadn't really thought about a website for Joyful Heart Herbs until that moment, but now that she had, it seemed like a stellar idea. She spent the morning making notes, sketches, and outlines for the website. She'd need to decide upon a tone for the articles. Did she want to be the chatty neighbor passing on tips with folksy humor? Or, make them more seriously educational, including scientific names and data? Callie enjoyed the informative articles by the famous English writer, Vita Sackville-West, but they were a bit dry for all but the extremely keen gardener. Callie doubted that many of her future customers would live and breathe gardening the way she did. She'd give it more thought before she began the articles. How much spirituality could she include in her column? Callie was often overcome by the connection of nature and spirit. Should she include recipes? People were more inclined to grow herbs if they could feel confident about using them. She'd learned that quickly from attending the farmers' market. Should she write about gardening and flowers in general or stick to her beloved herbs?

Before she realized the time, Callie heard the sound of Trev's pick-up coming up her driveway. Instinctively, she ran her fingers over her hair and checked her appearance in the entry mirror before she answered the door. Trev was wearing a deep brown jacket that enhanced his deep brown eyes. Without his hat, Callie noticed thick wavy hair that crept over his collar. Daniel would never have let his hair get so unruly. He'd have gotten a haircut long ago. Callie's thoughts had wandered, and it was a moment before she realized Trev's outstretched hand held a stack of papers.

"Am I too early?" he asked.

"No, no. It's perfect timing. I'd just finished...er...,"Callie stammered. She was flustered to discover her mind comparing Trev to Daniel. Daniel was no longer a part of her life she admonished herself, so there's absolutely no reason to compare.

"Something smells good!" Trev exclaimed with a smile.

"It's my great-grandmother's coffeecake. It will be out of the oven soon, so you can sample if you have time," Callie responded.

Wicca had already sidled up to Trev acting like he was her long-lost friend. Before he could move, she had sat on his foot, leaned against his leg, and stretched her head up under his hand.

"Looks like I'll have trouble going anywhere," he laughed as he vigorously rubbed the lab's head and ears. "Sorry, girl, but we have some business to discuss," he said as he made an exaggerated show of the effort required to move his leg.

"Let's work at the kitchen table, so I can keep an eye on the oven," Callie suggested. They moved into the warm kitchen, where framed botanical prints covered one wall. Floor to ceiling cupboards nearly filled three walls surrounding a large refrigerator, huge stove, and a sink with a window overlooking the gazebo. The old-fashioned table and chairs sat next to a huge picture window on the same wall as the sink. A shelf at the base of the window held an assembly of clay pots squeezed together. Each pot held a fragrant, healthy herb plant. The curtains had narrow stripes of cream, buttery yellow and sage green. A center island provided lots of workspace as well as three narrow shelves of cookbooks below. A counter near the stove held a set of canisters in an herbal design, and an herb-painted crock held a variety of wooden spoons and whisks. A gleaming yellow tea kettle was already bubbling on the stove, and a collection of teapots flowed across shelves above the doorways and windows. Woven rag rugs in cream, sage green, and butter were scattered in the work area over the warm brown tones of a well worn wooden floor. A matching placemat was in the center of the table, holding a large clay pot of flowering rosemary.

"Nice room," Trev observed.

"Isn't it? I just love old houses, so much space and so much character," Callie replied. Just then, the timer rang, so she offered Trev a chair, and set a trivet on the table. She pulled the coffeecake from the oven and placed it on the protective trivet, gathering mugs, spoons, forks, and the honey pot as she poured hot water over tea leaves in a Brown Betty pot.

"I saw your parking lot as I came in. You're making some good progress," Trev said as he laid the stack of papers to one side.

"It's exciting. I'm finally beginning to believe that it's really going to happen. But, it also makes me realize exactly how much work there is still to do," she added.

"Well, I'm ready to do my part as soon as you okay the plans." Trev assured.

They spent the next hour going over the estimates, discussing Callie's options, and enjoying the delicious cake. Callie was dismayed to see the estimate for re-doing the interior. The costs were much higher than she'd budgeted.

"I knew I wouldn't be able to find beadboard to match that old pattern, so patching isn't an option. It'll take an entirely new interior. You could do drywall, plaster, or paneling. Or, you could camouflage. Hang pictures over some of those patches you put up. Maybe wallpaper a couple of the worst walls. If the exterior work is completed well, and I guarantee it will be, then the building will be solid. You could always re-do the interior later," Trev advised. "Who knows, you may even find you need some changes once you've worked in there a while."

"Hmmm. Maybe you're right. The wall of shelving will cover one whole end. And the south wall with the two windows only has a couple of patches," Callie mused. "I think you're right. Let's fix the foundation, patch the floor where required, and do the new exterior."

"One thing I should point out, Callie. That old floor won't hold as much weight as you might expect. If you plan on any heavy inventory, like cement statues or fountains, or there are several customers in there at once, you might have a problem. Here's the second estimate for the floor where I've included additional support work under the floor joists. I don't really think you have an option, and while I'm down there leveling up the floor and replacing the rotted supports, it wouldn't be that hard to add the new ones. It'll be cheaper then trying to go back and fix it after the floor caves in!"

Callie's eyes grew big as she studied the additional costs, but she agreed with Trev's concerns. She hadn't thought ahead to the shop being filled with customers, and she hadn't seen the lack of solid support under the Cottage that Trev had witnessed. She could almost hear the floor groan before the old boards sunk in protest. She could picture the chaos if a few of the larger women she'd seen around town all showed up at once. It was not a pretty picture.

She took a deep breath and agreed to the additional repairs. They spent a few more minutes going over the timeline and plans, and then Callie walked Trev to the door. He'd promised to begin work on the foundation as soon as he could get the materials. Hopefully the rain would end. The ground would need to be solid enough to haul heavy supplies from the parking lot.

The week passed in a flurry of activity. Jesse Plumber, the plumber and area's well-drilling expert, spent an entire day disassembling the rusted pump and investigating the well before he sadly determined that the existing casing would indeed support an electric pump, and the well appeared to be one of the deepest and best supplied in the area. His sad demeanor as he announced this led Callie to believe that he'd hoped for a chance to use his new drilling rig. He suggested Callie get the water tested, and reminded her that he could not hook up a pump without a new electrical box and wiring. He promised to order the pump and required fittings, and Callie promised to call just as soon as the electrician had finished. Jesse left a list of electrical needs, and mumbled about the ruination of a perfectly good hunting area as he stomped through the muck to his truck.

Josh Sparks, the electrician, stopped by to look over the space and suggested Callie go to Muncie to look at light fixtures and options. He checked out the existing wiring, which was minimal to say the least, and said that since this building was intended to be open to the public, entirely new wiring that met existing codes would be required. Callie had anticipated this so she was not alarmed. He took the plumber's list of needs and promised a completed estimate by the time she returned from Atlanta, reminding her that this was his busy season with furnaces and all.

Mid-week, Callie dressed more carefully than usual, actually put on some make-up and carefully braided her hair. She gave Wicca her usual treat and instructions before she climbed into her pick-up and headed for the meeting with the governor's agricultural representative.

As she entered the courthouse, she recognized several faces of county residents who opposed the giant dairies. There were also several "suits" with highly polished shoes and fat briefcases. It looked like it was going to be a long meeting, so Callie chose a seat near a window, near the front, so she could hear any details and figures clearly. She was soon joined by Sandy Saunders, the reporter for the local Heartland Banner. Sandy, ever the reporter, had recognized Callie as a new face at the first meeting she'd attended. They'd sat together and chatted briefly, until Sandy became engrossed in taking copious notes and firing questions. Afterwards, Callie had hoped to invite her to join her for coffee at Dinah's, but Sandy had remained after the meeting to complete interviews and questions. During their brief chat, Callie had discovered that Sandy shared her passion for plants and rural lifestyles. Today, they exchanged quick greetings and smiles before the meeting was called to order.

After many presentations by the corporation's lawyers and supporting economic data given by the governor's man, Sidney Lawton, Callie thought her nerves would pop. Lawton continually gave the local commissioners reproving looks and made comments that Bradford County should join the governor's team. The phrase "backward Bradford" became a refrain before the morning session ended. Callie took pages of notes, picked up copies of all the handouts that were available, and wished she'd brought some lavender essential oil along. She felt a headache coming on.

Finally, the meeting adjourned without an opportunity for questions or comments from the audience. Callie exchanged frustrated glances with Sandy, and left the courtroom. She knew it was hard for Sandy to write an unbiased article in this particular case, but she was a professional and would manage to give both sides of the issue even though only one side had been presented.

She didn't linger although she knew it would be prudent to meet other supporters of her own views. She felt she would be unable to make small talk, and she was not in the mood for more CAFO controversy at the moment. She ran a couple of errands, picked up a few groceries, an extra bag of dog food, and drove to the farm. Trev's truck had been there when she'd left that morning, and she was eager to see what he'd accomplished. He'd been working long hours the last two days.

On the first morning, he hauled in a gas-powered generator so he could have a light under the Cottage and use his power tools. Trev also brought a small concrete mixer and a slip bucket that was small enough to fit under the Cottage. Although there was no way to tip it, Trev could slide the flat "bucket" of concrete underneath, then use a trowel to slide the mixture into the forms he'd built. Callie was delighted to fill the bucket with concrete and guide it through the opening as Trev pulled on his end of the rope. When he'd emptied the bucket, Callie pulled her end of the rope to bring it back outside for refilling. It saved Trev from having to crawl back and forth, and it saved Callie the cost of an extra employee.

Callie had found she really enjoyed Trev's easy-going manner. She'd grown up working with her dad, who generally worked in silence. Trev was a constant stream of banter, jokes, and mock-criticism.

"Is that as fast as you can shovel concrete?" he'd tease. "Say, if your pudding is as lumpy as your concrete, I'm bringing along false teeth next time I come to dinner!"

"Next time?" Callie bantered. "You haven't even been invited the first time, so how can there be a next time, Graybeard?" She'd called him that the first time he had crawled out from under the Cottage, his face covered with gray cement and dust. The name had stuck.

When Trev was finished with the concrete, there was still half a mixer of cement left. Callie checked to make sure he had no need for it. When she heard he was just planning to dump it, she ran to the house and collected some empty boxes and a roll of duct tape. She threw a bucket of peat moss and a bucket of vermiculite in the truck and headed back to the Cottage. Within minutes, she had tossed the contents of the buckets into the mixer. While it churned, she reinforced the boxes with duct tape and lined them with plastic bags from the dry cleaners that she kept behind the truck seat for emergencies. One never knew when you might have to crawl under a truck or find a promising plant by the roadside. Plastic bags were always good to have at hand. She fitted a smaller box inside each slightly larger box and packed the space in between tightly with the concrete mixture. By the time she was finished, she had four lovely hypertuffa troughs, or at least they would be lovely once they'd dried.

Since the concrete had to set before he could add the steel supports and brick pillars, Trev started removing the exterior siding. This task revealed a mass of squirrels nests, chewed wiring, and stored nuts. Callie spent part of one afternoon collecting all the debris and sweeping the area between the studs. They'd agreed that while the exterior siding was off, a layer of thick insulation should be installed.

Callie missed being able to go in her Cottage, but until Trev's work underneath was completed, it was not sensible. She spent time marking out where garden beds would go and shuttling hot coffee from the farmhouse to the worksite. Luckily, even though it was January, the weather was not below freezing. Wicca was delighted to have a constant "outdoor" companion while Trev worked. When he was under the Cottage, Wicca peered into the opening and whined. When he pushed wheelbarrows filled with stone or sand, Wicca danced by his side.

Today, Trev had completed jacking up the floor joists and was inside the Cottage with the longest level Callie had ever seen, checking to be sure the floor was perfectly level. He smiled as she poked her head in the door.

"Hey, stranger," Trev called, "got any coffee?"

"Just so happens I made a quick stop on my way home."

"Lucky me!"

They moved to the two lawn chairs Callie had brought from her garage, and used the boxes of siding for a table.

"Wow! Doughnuts, too! What's the occasion?"

"I survived the CAFO meeting," Callie responded, "but I'm not sure how well the commissioners fared. Talk about pressure!"

"Pretty intense, huh?"

"That's putting it mildly." Callie and Trev had discussed the subject at length while they tore off siding one afternoon. Trev had begun with the usual complacency common in most areas. People generally felt "progress" was a good thing, and that the "powers that be" were too powerful to stop anyway. Few people fully understood the impact on the environment that such large operations truly exerted immediately and in the long term. Once she'd explained how CAFO's were negatively impacting other counties, Trev's initial reservations evolved into real concern.

"I really need to think about something besides CAFO's right now. Tell me what's next on the Cottage," Callie requested. She really wasn't in the mood to hash over the details of the frustrating meeting yet.

"Anything I can do to help you?" she asked.

"Sure, you can pass me bricks and supplies once I'm under the house."

"Great! I'll just change into grubbies and be right back"

The afternoon passed quickly. Soon after sundown, the floor was perfectly level. In Trev's opinion it was now sturdy enough to support an elephant, or perhaps two.

That evening, Callie treated herself to a long soak in the tub utilizing a bath tea she'd made up of herbs for sore muscles. She mixed juniper berries, sage, strawberry leaves, burdock root, and mugwort together, placed the herbs in a washcloth closed with a rubber band, and hung it under the hot water as she filled the tub. Once the tub was filled, she used the cloth to scrub the areas of her body that ached. Afterwards, she finished packing for her trip to Atlanta. One problem had been solved. Since Trev would be working on the Cottage every day, he offered to take care of Wicca, collect the mail, and keep an eye on the house while she was gone.

The next morning, she loaded her bag and briefcase into the truck, gave all the plants a good watering, turned down the thermostat a bit, and gave Wicca a tearful hug. It would be the first time they were apart since Callie had impulsively decided to get a dog. She had just felt so alone after Daniel left, and needed someone to love. One look at those lovely lab eyes, and Callie's frozen heart had begun to melt. Wicca had been her constant companion since, so it was hard to leave her.

The drive to the airport seemed long, since Callie was impatient to get there. The flight was non-stop, and so were the days in Atlanta. Each was a whirlwind of frenzy. Every morning, Callie took the train downtown to Peachtree Center and entered the jam-packed aisles of one of the three huge buildings. Each building had twenty or more floors of showrooms. There were over four thousand temporary booths in addition to all the permanent showrooms. Searching through four million feet of display booths was not an easy task. Since many showrooms contained hundreds of lines, it was an absorbing task to look at each item and decide if it belonged in her new Cottage Gift Shop. Of course, she selected all the herb related products she could find. Mid-week, she expanded her picks to include some items that would appeal to any gardener, whether they grew herbs or not.

As a novice to the show, there was much for Callie to learn. Many showrooms had an alarmingly high minimum order. Callie's tiny shop could not hold a thousand of any one item. Others carried products that would be too expensive for her prospective customer base. At the end of the week her feet were sore. Her budget was spent. She couldn't wait to leave the masses of people to return to her quiet farmhouse. And, she missed her dog!

The only time she took away from the business of ordering inventory and collecting relevant catalogs was the evening spent with her cousin. As she'd promised, Eve had selected a special place for dinner. Knowing how much Callie had enjoyed "Gone With the Wind," Eve made reservations at Aunt Pittypat's Porch in downtown Atlanta. There, the two cousins caught up on one another's lives while sipping "Scarlett's Passion" cocktails. They discussed their goals and activities as they sampled the array of traditional southern dishes on Aunt Pittypat's sideboard. Later, the cousins reminisced over classic Georgia peach cobbler with cinnamon ice cream. They sat on the balcony and rocked in old-fashioned caned rocking chairs, surrounded by history and memories of shared childhoods.

Eventually, Eve asked how Callie was doing and if there were any single men in her new town.

Callie assured her that she was too busy to notice and too heartbroken to want to think about men, but a slight blush crept up her neck.

"You know the best way to fix a broken heart is with a new romance," Eve suggested.

"Well, the carpenter that's working on the Cottage is pretty cute," Callie admitted, "but I just don't want to get involved again. It's too soon. I'm too bruised."

Eve promised to come see the farm once it was up and running and Callie promised to schedule more time to visit if she returned next January.

"I'd better see you before then!" Eve demanded with a farewell hug. "And, give yourself a little TLC, Cuz. Maybe you should give that hunky carpenter a chance, too!"

Callie just gave her a warm hug and thanked her for a great evening. At her hotel, she struggled to get all the catalogs and the cash-and-carry items into her suitcase. Next year, she'd know to bring an extra bag. She had an early flight the next morning, but she found it difficult to sleep. Now that she'd bought her inventory, she worried that she had made the wrong choices. What if nothing sold? What if she'd totally misread her clientele?

On the flight home, Callie went over all the invoices that she had entered into her laptop. She'd grouped her purchases by displays, with some based on a theme, others on color, and some on use. When that was completed, she finished the article on parsley that she intended to take to the Heartland Banner's editor.

She was waiting for her luggage when a tall, dark man in a black trench coat asked for her help. The man had a slight accent, so she was having some difficulty understanding his question. He showed her a slip of paper with some numbers on it. Before she could react, someone grabbed her purse from her shoulder. Instead of helping her, the man in the black coat actually blocked her view and continued to talk to her. Callie tried to push past him, yelling "Stop! Stop that man! He stole my purse!"

People turned to stare, but everyone seemed frozen. By the time Callie reached the pavement, she only caught a glimpse of a burgundy-colored sedan squealing away. When she ran back to the baggage area, the man in the black coat had disappeared. She found an airport employee and asked where the police office was located. When she walked into the office, she found four officers sitting around a box of doughnuts having coffee.

"I've just been robbed!" she said quietly. Now that it was over, her knees had begun to quiver and turn to jelly. "Someone grabbed my purse and ran. I think there were two of them, because a strange man distracted me."

"Yeah, there's a ring working the airport," an older officer replied. "We'll have to fill out a report."

Callie's mind screamed, "If you know there are thieves in the airport, why are all of you in here eating doughnuts?" There was no sense in voicing the comment. It wouldn't help the situation to vent. She just wanted to go home as quickly as possible.

One of the officers led her over to a desk, where he slowly typed up a report using only his two pointer fingers. He told her to sign it, and gave her a copy.

By the time she was finished, her luggage was not on the carousel. It had been moved to the airline's storage room. She finally found someone to help her, but of course she had no identity to prove that the luggage was hers. Since she was able to describe several of the items in the outside pocket and had a copy of the police report, the employee finally released her suitcase. Callie dragged it over to a phone. Naturally, somewhere along the line, her suitcase had lost a wheel. This was just not her day. She opened the suitcase, pulling out the emergency credit card and bank phone numbers she always put in before traveling. Once her cards were cancelled and the bank was alerted, she caught the shuttle to long term parking. Fortunately, her truck keys were in her pocket, as well as enough cash to pay the parking bill, so she was able to drive home.

Callie arrived at the farm after dark, but she drove over to the Cottage anyway. She parked the truck so the lights would illuminate the path and gasped with delight. The Cottage was a beautifully sided building in soft beige. Pretty green shutters with hearts cut into the tops outlined each window. The dark brown roof sloped down to shining new guttering, and a wide gravel pathway curved from the doorway to the parking lot. All the mess from construction had been removed. Callie ran up the path and saw a note fastened to the new screen door.

"Welcome Home, Stranger!" There was a gray cement thumbprint below for accent. After the day she'd had, it was just the lift she needed.

The next day turned bitterly cold. January was finally showing some teeth. The sun was not even up before Callie was at work. It was a good thing she was home to fire up the kerosene heater that would keep the plants in the garage warm. She skipped her Tai Chi program, figuring after walking through showrooms for five days she'd exercised enough. Instead, she assembled all the shelving she'd purchased weeks ago and set up two more rows in the garage. She fastened the lights below each shelf, and hoisted a bale of potting soil onto her potting bench.

Callie intended to keep extremely busy to forget being robbed. She picked up the large box of seeds and her seeding notebook. The warm humid air in the garage was filled with the scent of soil and plants. She paused beside a five-foot tall rosemary that was in full bloom. The tiny blue flowers covered stem after stem. She plucked a few to drop into her tea. Holding one between her fingers, Callie remembered that rosemary flowers have been called "fairy cradles." If one looks carefully at the shape, it resembles a tiny baby carriage without wheels, and lore says that fairies often put their babies inside a rosemary bloom to nap. The thought made Callie smile.

She moved to the potting bench to fill several flats evenly with moist soil, smoothing out any lumps and setting them in stacks. She loved working with soil, and most of all she loved propagating plants. Taking cuttings was her favorite work, but seeding was a close second, and that was the task for today. She'd figured Thanksgiving week was the time to seed flats of pansies so they would be in bloom for the farm's Preview Party the end of March. Callie checked the seeded flats of "Chalon Rose" and was happy to see the small plants were growing nicely. She could picture the very frilly, ruffled pansies in multiple shades from soft rose to deep burgundy that would rise from the deep green, scalloped leaves next spring. Even after years of sowing seeds, she was still amazed at the miracle of planting. A speck of brown, sprinkled on soil, gently covered and watered, splits open and sends a root out the bottom. It pushes a stem out the top, and becomes a pansy plant. Not a squash, or a tomato, or an aphid, or an elephant, each seed knows exactly what it is supposed to be. A rose-colored, ruffled Chalon pansy. A miracle. A certainty. If only all of life could be so certain. A pansy seed will always be a pansy. A corn kernel will always become a cornstalk. A fiancé will always become a husband.   "Well, we know that doesn't always happen, don't we?" she mumbled to herself. Daniel's face floated through her mind. Callie slumped onto a stool, and put her face in her hands.

Suddenly, she was aware of a scratching sound. Wicca was home! Trev had left a message on the answering machine that Wicca was so lonely he'd decided to take her home with him each night. He'd promised to bring her home right after breakfast.

Callie opened the door and gave the happy dog a big hug.

"Say, can I have one of those?"

In her thrill at being home, at seeing her dog, at having her Cottage transformed, at being in the midst of the task she most loved, she whirled and happily wrapped her arms around Trev's neck.

She immediately pulled away, when she realized Trev was not returning the hug. In fact he had become awkwardly stiff.

"Sorry, I meant can I have one of those?" Trev indicated the beautiful blue-flowered rosemary that earlier she'd admired herself.

"Oh…er…uh…sorry, it's a stock plant. I wouldn't dream of parting with it. I've had her for years," Callie mumbled as she retreated to her workbench. Wicca moved to Trev's side and looked up at him in puzzlement.

"I was just kidding," Trev apologized. He looked around appreciatively taking in the rows of plants on tiered metal shelves. "So this is where you hide out. Quite an operation. Looks like you could start selling plants tomorrow."

"Most of these plants aren't for sale. They are stock plants. They'll go into my own gardens so I can propagate from them. Only the newly seeded flats are sales material. Of course, they're just babies now."

Callie returned to work to hide her embarrassment. She was surprised to find she had finished seeding the entire packet, so she made the labels for the flats of "Columbine, Grandma's Bonnet." The flats were covered with plastic domes, and moved to the heated mats on the tables at the end of the garage.

"Guess I was on automatic pilot," she thought. Funny how the mind works. Sometimes when she was picking flower bunches for farmer's market, she would get lost in thought. She'd find herself at the end of the row with bunches and bunches of flowers that she barely remembered picking, But, when she counted each bunch, she'd find exactly 50 stems. Somehow, her mind was counting even if she wasn't. Automatic pilot. She seemed to be on automatic pilot a lot these days, working through the job list but not really focused on the task.

The silence between them grew, and even Trev, who generally had a funny comeback, seemed subdued.

"Well, I'm sure Wicca is happy to be home. Did you have a good trip?" he questioned.

Callie was so deflated that she did not want to explain how stupid she had been at the airport. She'd been tired, anxious to get home, and had not been alert to trouble. Plus, she was just a person that generally trusted others. Someone who would stop to help a stranger. She'd assumed the man in the black coat was a foreigner needing directions for something. Now, she felt embarrassed all over again, so she gave only a brief answer.

"Busy, exhausting. I managed to spend my budget before I made it through all the buildings"

"Hope you didn't spend all your money in the big city. I brought my invoices along. I'll need to pay my suppliers," he added hesitantly.

"No problem. I'll write you a check immediately," Callie offered as she turned toward the door. She paused as she suddenly remembered that her checkbook had been in her stolen purse.

"No, you're busy. Just drop it in the mail."

"Okay," Callie answered with relief. "Thanks again for taking care of Wicca while I was gone. I'm sure she had a great time."

"No problem. The kids loved having her. I'll put your mail and the dog food in your truck on my way out. See ya!"

Before Callie could respond, he was gone.

She stood there blinking, forgetting to breathe. Her mind kept circling around and around the phrase "the kids loved having her." What kids? His kids? In all the hours they'd spent together, there had never been mention of kids! Her mind sifted through their conversations. They touched on families. Trev had mentioned brothers and a sister, but never any children.

The day passed, and at its end a list of the number of flats of each variety of perennials was entered into the year's seeding journal following the entries of earlier seedings of pansies and violas. She added the usual notation of the day's weather and the high and low temperatures both outdoors and in the garage. After storing her supplies Callie washed up and began preparing a "welcome home" supper for her dog.

All evening, Callie chided herself for her stupidity. "Men! You just don't know how to pick them," she ranted. Or maybe, she concluded there were simply no men worthy of trust. She still hadn't decided by her second glass of wine.

Much of the rest of the week was spent getting a new driver's license, new bank account numbers and new business checks. Fortunately new credit cards came in the mail, but it took most of a day to call all the companies from whom she had ordered merchandise in Atlanta. She'd paid for all her inventory by credit card, so she could get frequent flyer miles and didn't want the shipments to be delayed. She also had to get a new library card, a new grocery store discount card, and all the other items that normally were in her purse. It was all time-consuming, and Callie was feeling extremely short on time these days.

It was nearing the end of January, and unknown to any of the locals, Callie's birthday was approaching. She decided to celebrate and accomplish a few goals at the same time. She'd been mulling over some recipes while she watered, exercised, or did household tasks. Now it was time to test them. She'd need some guinea pigs, so she made a list of the local women she'd like to get to know better. Before she lost her nerve, she e-mailed the invitations.

This would be her first party, so she cleaned all the rooms she actively used and locked the doors to the others. No sense having someone barge into piles of boxes in a spare bedroom while searching for the bathroom. Then she planned her menu.

The evening of the party was crisp and clear. Callie had some of her favorite Celtic music playing softly in the background. She'd made a big bowl of her version of Tabouli to serve with pita triangles and crackers, invented several different miniature meatballs, and concocted a new herbal cocktail using cinnamon basil syrup. She'd made lots of different herbal syrups at the end of the growing season. They were sealed and stored in a spare refrigerator in the garage.

The group of women seemed to be a great mix with conversation flowing easily and equally from one to the other. It turned out that Cecilia Hutchins was happily married, and while she ran the print shop, her husband was on the road handling the sales work. Sandy Saunders was merrily single and informed Callie that there seemed to be a number of eligible bachelors in the area. Callie assured the group that she was not interested at the moment.

"Just been burned, huh?" Suz spit out. "Been there myself. I feel your pain, sister," she intoned as she raised both arms over her head in a mock revival blessing.

At the mention of bachelors, LouAnn had closed her eyes and refilled her cocktail glass.

"Change of topic, ladies! So, just what is in this divine mixture, Callie?" she asked, as she took a large sip. That led to a general discussion of the foods they were enjoying, which then turned to gardening, the weather, recent books they'd enjoyed, and multiple other topics.

As the women prepared to leave, Sandy said she didn't know when she'd enjoyed an evening so much and wondered why she didn't do something like this more often. Cecilia added that if Callie ever had another batch of recipes and needed tasters, she'd be happy to help out. Everyone else added their pleas to be included, so Callie offered to host another tasting in February.

After everyone left, Callie realized that she now had the first batch of successfully tested recipes for her proposed book. Even better, she'd gone an entire day without thinking of Daniel, at least until Sandy had mentioned men as a topic. As she cleared the dishes, she also realized that she'd missed the opportunity to find out if indeed Trev Carpenter was one of the "eligible bachelors" Sandy had mentioned. Callie flipped off the kitchen lights and trudged upstairs. Maybe she didn't really want to know.

Parsley

A member of the "Carrot" family, related to dill, fennel, cilantro, and Queen Anne's Lace, parsley is a well-known and much-used culinary herb. In olden times, a sprig was laid upon the plate. This was to be eaten after the meal was finished because parsley is a natural breath freshener. It also aids the digestive system. Its fame spread after the publishing of the <u>Tales of Peter Rabbit</u> when Peter eats too much produce from Mr. McGregor's Garden and goes to find parsley for his upset stomach.

A biennial, parsley is often slow to germinate unless pre-treated by placing the seeds in a freezer for a week. Sow them sparsely in good soil, barely covering the seeds, and water well. Parsley grows best in cool weather, with a side dressing of fertilizer mid-season. Harvest the large outer leaves, allowing the center to continue to produce new shoots. Most plants will go dormant over winter. In the following spring, the plants send up new growth. However, this second year growth will be much less tender and the flavor is more bitter than in young plants. Very quickly the second-year plants will produce tough flowering stalks followed by clusters of seeds, so it is best to start with new plants each spring. Parsley should be grown in full sun with adequate water. Drought will cause the leaves to yellow and turn bitter. However, too much water can cause the carrot-like root to rot if the soil does not drain properly. Attempting to grow parsley in a small pot will cause the plant to bolt and flower rather than producing lush, useful leaves. If growing in containers, picture a large carrot root and give it plenty of depth. Although related to carrots, the parsley root is white rather than orange. Note that the parsley root used commonly in German dishes is a special variety, grown for its especially large root. The variety name is often called "Berliner" or "Hamburg." However, one can substitute the substantial root of a standard second year parsley, if desired.

Many chefs claim to prefer the flavor of the flat-leafed Italian parsley to the frilly curled parsley. Both are productive, have a deep green color and are filled with vitamins and flavor. The flat-leaf is easier to wash and stack for chopping, but the curled parsley is prettier as a garnish.

The flavor of crisp green parsley goes well with almost anything. Sprinkled on salads, vegetables, or even fresh fruit dishes, parsley adds not only color and nutrients but flavor as well. Added to soups, stews, or sauces just before serving parsley brightens the flavor of other ingredients. It is a staple ingredient of Tabouli, the famous Middle Eastern dish.

Parsley dries well in a low microwave, keeping its green color and flavor if handled properly. Simply place leaves (discard the stems) on a paper towel. Cover with a second towel and place in the microwave on its lowest setting. Zap briefly. Replace the now damp towels with new layers, and repeat until the parsley is crisp. Allow to cool before storing in an airtight container. Protect the dried herb from heat, moisture and light which will cause the essential oils to deteriorate.

Chapter 2:

FEBRUARY

The warmer than normal temperatures of January had given away to bitter cold by the end of the month, and February began with a snowstorm that kept workers away and Callie indoors. She spent many days working on the collection of articles she planned to take to the newspaper, chiding herself for taking so long. Spring was just around the corner, and that was when people would be most interested in reading about plants and gardening. Spring was also when she was most likely to be swamped. She'd be trying to get the shop off and running, all the gardens planted, and sales benches organized for plant sales. She needed to accomplish as much as she could before her time was taken with customers, too.

Today, Callie just couldn't seem to put words on a page, so she decided to work on another batch of recipes for her book, or booklet, whichever it turned out to be. She planned to organize her "Herbal Beginnings" by the calendar. Each month would feature a type of appetizer and a cocktail or two. She'd worked on little meatballs and Tabouli for January. February would be cheese balls and spreads, and probably a "red" cocktail for Valentine's.

She'd already finished a cheese spread and a chick pea spread. She'd just put a cheesy mixture with dill, clams, shredded carrots with a crumb topping under the broiler when someone knocked on her door.

"Morning, Ma'am," the deputy nodded. "Heard you had some trouble at the airport."

Callie nodded, "Won't you come in out of the cold? I've got something in the oven, so I need to go back to the kitchen."

The deputy sheriff followed her into the cozy room, sniffing appreciatively.

"Looks like you're expecting company," he observed.

"No, just working out some new recipes. Want some coffee?" After her experience with the officers at the airport, the cliché of policemen and doughnuts had been affirmed. "Sorry, I don't have any doughnuts!"

The deputy laughed, a deep smile spread across his face. "Contrary to public opinion, not all lawmen live on coffee and doughnuts," he chuckled.

Once again Callie felt embarrassed, disguising it by busily pulling some crackers from the cupboard, finding a couple of spreaders, and filling two cups with coffee.

"Well, here's some coffee just in case. Is there some problem? Am I in trouble with the law, or did you come about the deer?"

"You have a problem with a deer?" he asked.

"Someone has trespassed on my property and killed a deer even though I've posted it," Callie explained.

"Have you reported it to the Conservation officer at DNR?"

"Yes, but he says it pretty much takes catching them in the act to stop them. And, I'm not sure I'm ready to pull a stake-out in the woods to try to catch someone with a gun who is already breaking the law," she explained.

"Hmmm. Know where they are coming onto your property, or how they are leaving?"

"Not really. I could follow the tracks for a while, but I lost them when they hit the main path."

"Warren's overworked, since he has the entire county to patrol. If you have another problem, call me. I'm Deputy Morgan Wright. I patrol this part of the county, so I pass by here fairly often. I'll keep my eyes open," he stated, handing her a card.

"Thanks, Deputy. I'd really appreciate it," Callie said gratefully. She had pulled the cheese spread from the oven, and set it on a mat. "Feel like being a guinea pig?"

"Well, since I have a few minutes, and especially since you don't have any doughnuts," he teased, "I guess I'm game."

Callie laughed, then asked, "Is there a special reason you stopped by?"

"Sure is, Ma'am. We got word that the Indy police recovered your stolen purse. No money or credit cards left, but if you want to go retrieve it, here's the precinct information. Just take the copy of your police report and some identification."

"Oh, thank you! The purse was a gift from my best friend, so I really hated to lose it. I'll go to Indy as soon as the weather settles."

"You cook like this often?" Deputy Wright asked, as he sampled the third dish.

"I'm developing some recipes to use when I open my herb farm. I'll be doing some cooking classes and demonstrations. So, I'm always experimenting. Right now I'm working on appetizers," Callie explained.

"Well, I'd rate two of these as winners!" he exclaimed. "the first one seems a little bland, but the other two sure perked up my appetite! Let me know if you need a guinea pig again."

"I appreciate your constructive criticism, officer. I just might ask you to taste-test again. And I certainly will call you if I have another deer problem."

"You do that," he replied as he sauntered toward the door. "Ma'am," he said politely, touched the brim of his hat, nodded, and disappeared out her door.

The days passed too quickly. Callie had kept seeding on schedule, transplanted baby seedlings as they needed more space, and clearing boxes out of the spare bedroom, so she could add more shelving for plants. As she transplanted each variety, she made a sales sign using colored photos from seed catalogs. Adding her distinctive script to describe each variety's attributes and growing requirements gave them a personal touch. She'd have them laminated at Cecilia's print shop on her next trip to town.

The roads had been plowed and the weather had moderated a bit, so Callie was able to go to Indy to retrieve her purse. Unfortunately, the officer explained as he passed her a large brown envelope, some carpet layers had found it lying outside next to a dumpster. It had been out in the weather, lying in melting snow for several days before it had been discovered. The workers turned it in to the local police, where it had been a simple task to find enough information to locate her. The purse was ruined, but she recovered several items that were still useful. She thanked the officer, and headed to the south side of the city. As long as she'd made the long drive to Indianapolis, she might as well make it worthwhile. At the greenhouse supply store, she purchased two more cases of flats and several boxes of blank plant labels.

Once home, Callie phoned LouAnn to discuss the farm's sign requirements. LouAnn e-mailed sample styles and suggestions that evening. Callie selected those she preferred, and made an appointment to meet later that week.

The two women met at the Cottage on a sunny, crisp afternoon. LouAnn exclaimed over the Cottage, admired the proportions of the new sales counter and wall shelving and made suggestions for decorations. She even offered a couple of her landscapes to hang over the offensive metal patches.

They discussed the merits of each of LouAnn's proposals, selecting final designs for the "Joyful Heart Herbs" sign for along the road, a sign for "Callie's Cottage" and a banner head to use on the newsletter. As soon as Callie saw the sketches, she agreed with Cecilia's earlier assessment that LouAnn was truly an artist. Callie asked LouAnn if she would be willing to paint a floral "garden" on the front of the sales counter. LouAnn readily agreed to start as soon as the weather warmed a bit.

"When's the merchandise due to arrive?" LouAnn inquired.

"Shipping dates are March 1st," Callie informed her. "I know I'm cutting it close, but the light fixtures have to be installed, and there's just no storage space left at the house for more boxes. Plus, I don't want to have to heat the shop every day and night just so bottles of lotions and vinegars don't freeze."

"Well, then, we'll just have to hope it warms up soon. It normally does sometime in February, but then it'll turn nasty again in March around high school basketball tourney time."

They finished details on the designs over cups of lemon verbena tea. LouAnn was an optimistic woman, full of creativity and energy. Callie looked forward to working with her in the coming weeks. Before she left, LouAnn promised the sign would be finished and installed before Callie's opening day.

Callie made arrangements for a phone line to be installed at the Cottage and ordered a credit card machine through her local bank. Josh Sparks had already finished the basic wiring in the Cottage, and was waiting for the power company to install a new transformer and to run a line from the road.

She'd drawn an accurate floor plan of the Cottage shop area and completely organized all the merchandise she'd purchased into displays. She'd already painted several pieces of furniture and other items in colors that blended or accented the displays. Her dining room looked like a disaster area, divided into grouping of colors, with yards of fabric, tablecloths, lamps, mismatched chairs, and pillows stacked next to small shelves, little tables, and display cases. There was also a card table that held her seed box, seeding journal, the new cash register, boxes of extra register tape, the box of credit card slips, and still another box with all her completed plant sales signs. A box of ragged seed catalogs that she was cutting up to make signs and posters sat beside the sofa. Callie was normally a neat person with a tidy work place, so this chaos was beginning to get on her nerves.

The garage was so packed with plants that she could barely squeeze between the aisles to water. And now that it was so full, and the temperatures remained cold, she was fighting an outbreak of botrytis.

Callie bundled up, scraped the ice off the windshield, and opened the door to let Wicca into the truck. Her first stop was the hardware store where Jake greeted her with a lopsided smile.

"Need some more of those "No Hunting" signs?" he asked in a hostile tone.

"No, today I need some fans," Callie replied calmly.

"Fans? In the middle of winter? You're out of luck. We only stock those in the summer time. Too hot for ya', or what?"

"Never mind. Thanks for the help, Jake," Callie called cheerfully as she sailed out of the store.

Back at the truck, Callie wasn't quite as cheerful.

"Okay. Plan A was a bust, what's Plan B?" she asked the lab. Wicca cocked her head to one side, and seemed to ponder the problem. A bit of drool escaped her bottom lip.

"Right you are! Plan B. When in doubt, start with pie!" Callie crowed, as she eased the truck around the square and slipped into an empty space near Dinah's.

As usual, the place was packed, and Dinah didn't seem at all surprised when Callie ordered a luscious piece of coconut cream pie before 9:30 a.m.

"How's it going out there?" Dinah asked.

"Got a minor problem," Callie replied.

"Any way I can help?" Dinah offered, as she slid a huge chunk of pie onto a plate.

"I need some fans, and the hardware only sells them in summer," Callie explained.

"What kind of fans?" Dinah asked, "Big ones, little ones, exhaust fans, circulating fans, or what?"

"Just a standard fan. I need to keep the air moving around some plants to help prevent mold and to move the heated air from the ceiling back down to the floor."

"Hey, Jim!" Dinah yelled over the counter to the table filled with "geezers".

Several gray heads turned her way as the room became silent.

"Callie needs a couple of fans. I move we loan her some from the fairgrounds. Any objections?"

Jim Peters had just cleared his throat when Dinah banged her fist on the counter, causing several saucers and cups to shake. "Hearing no objections, the motion passes. Barney, grab your coat. Go over to the fairgrounds and load a couple of those fans we use in the hog barn into Miss Callie's truck."

As she passed the sack, containing the pie over to Callie, Dinah winked.

"Pays to be president of the Fair Board once in a while," she whispered.

Callie had just set up the fans and plugged them into a grounded extension cord when the garage lights flickered, dimmed, and then went out.

"Now what?" she grumbled, as she pushed her way through the shelves to reach the fuse box.

"Be courageous, but cautious!" she admonished herself as she peered at the dusty box. Sure enough, a fuse had popped. Callie gazed at the old-fashioned round fuses. She'd only seen modern breaker panels since she'd left her folks' farm. It looked like she'd be making another trip to town since she didn't see any spare fuses in the area. She unscrewed the glass and metal cylinder, placing it in her pocket so she'd get the correct size. She studied the fuse box, noticing that the one labeled "Laundry" was the same size, so she unscrewed it, knowing that doing laundry was not on the immediate job list. She unplugged the extension cord before screwing the fuse into the circle labeled "Garage". The banks of lights on the shelves returned to life.

Before she made the second trip into town that day, Callie collected the articles she'd finished for the newspaper. Although she hoped to have three month's worth of articles all finished before the farm opened, she felt one month's material should be enough for the editor to judge her work. Sandy had encouraged her to submit some sample articles but warned her that the editor was tight with his budget, so there might not be any financial reward.

Jake proved to be only slightly more helpful when Callie stopped at the hardware store. He snickered when he saw the fuse she'd brought in.

"Lucky we still have these old antiques in stock," he nearly sneered as he made change.

"Lucky for me that you sell them in winter," Callie sang as she breezed out the door clutching the sack.

Callie pulled her truck up to the newspaper office, checked her hair, and applied a bit of lipstick before she went inside. She'd taken the time to place her articles in a folder and clipped a business card to the front just in case the editor was not in the office. Inside, she was greeted by a young woman sporting a butterfly tattoo on her shoulder, with the words "Live Free" printed underneath. Callie wasn't old, but she was admittedly a bit old-fashioned. She failed to see how a rhinestone in the middle of one's tongue improved either one's appearance or one's ability to communicate clearly.

"I'd like to see the editor, please," Callie stated.

"Have an appointment?" the girl countered.

"No, but Sandy Saunders suggested that I talk to him," Callie responded comfortably. Sandy had assured Callie that she would be happy to be a referral.

"Just a moment, I'll see if he's available," she said with exaggerated sweetness.

"Hey, Pop!" she bellowed toward an open door. "Are you available?"

Everyone in the building could hear the sound of a book or something just as solid being thrown against a wall. The pictures on the wall facing the entrance actually shuddered, and one portrait of someone's esteemed forebear slipped to a forty-five degree angle.

"I guess he's in. Go right on in," the daughter nodded.

Before Callie could reach the door, a red-faced man in his mid-fifties stomped into the doorway.

"Lucille McKenzie, this office has a perfectly good intercom system, and I expect you to use it!" Before she could respond, the editor turned his back and stomped to his desk. Had he turned back quickly, he would have seen a rhine-stoned tongue stuck out in his direction.

"Sorry about that. Can't seem to do a thing with this younger generation, especially if they happen to be your daughter! Mac McKenzie," he stated with a nod toward the nameplate on his desk.

"Just call me Callie," the young woman stated. She quickly took in his appearance. A fringe of graying hair surrounded his head. Wire-framed glasses perched on the end of his nose, and he had already pushed them into place twice during this brief period. His wrinkled shirt sleeves were folded up nearly to his elbows, and a pocket protector held several pens of various colors.

"I'm interested in producing a garden column for your newspaper," she stated concisely. "I've noticed that your paper does not currently publish one. I have a degree in education from Indiana University, and I've completed the state's Master Garden Program. In fact, I've taught sections of the course in other counties. I'm now a professional grower with several years of gardening experience. I think I have a lot to offer your readers." Callie had added the remark about her degree from Indiana when she noticed a framed degree hanging above the editor's head from the same school.

"Always happy to meet a fellow alum. Most college folks around here are from Purdue," the editor stated glumly.

"Go Hoosiers!" Callie replied with a smile. "I've brought some sample articles that I can leave with you. I've written in two different tones. You, as editor, will no doubt know the proper voice for your local audience. I'll be happy to follow whichever style you select."

Callie felt it wise to indicate she assumed that he would choose one or the other. As a teacher, she'd found that setting a positive tone and outlining a very brief course of action normally produced positive outcomes.

"Unless you have questions, I realize that you are very busy, and I did come without an appointment," Callie said as she rose to leave. "My name and phone number are on the cover, or you can e-mail if that is more convenient. I can start immediately once you give me guidelines on length and tone. It was a pleasure meeting you, Mr. McKenzie."

Mac McKenzie was already absorbing the top article in the folder.

"Hold on, hold on, Miss," he requested. "I think we may be able to work out something right now. What were you thinking in the way of payment for an article of this length?"

Callie had checked on the average pay scale for articles in a newspaper of this size, and quoted the amount. "However, Mr. McKenzie, I'm willing to work on the barter system if you'll trade advertisement space for my weekly columns."

"Well, Hoosier lady, I think we speak the same language," he smiled, as he held out his hand. "Yes, indeed, always nice to meet a fellow alum."

While she was in town, Callie mailed all of the forms that were required to place a sign on the road. She'd barely begun her small business, and already she was tired of red tape and bureaucracy. She'd also had to spend phone time with the local utilities. "Dial before you dig" wasn't just a slogan. She'd been amazed at the number of gas line, oil line, phone line, fiber optic line, cable line, and other company officials that had to sign off on her forms before she could put up her business sign. And, of course there was a form and a fee to purchase the little license plate that had to be placed on the sign itself.

The following day brought sunshine and warmer temperatures although there had been another light snow during the night. Callie had managed to balance the power load by running the extension cord into another part of the house to run the fans, so they weren't added to the already overloaded garage. She just couldn't do laundry or plug the vacuum into an outlet in any bedroom, the living room, or the dining room. She'd have to unplug the fans to vacuum before her evening of recipe testing at the end of the month.

Callie took advantage of the slightly warmer weather and sunshine to get out of the house for a while. With Wicca circling around her, she headed over to the farm. The snow was already melting, and Callie sniffed the air for smells of spring. Nothing yet, no swelling buds on the maples or greening of the willows even hinted that spring might be on the way. She knew it was too early for winter to end, but she could hope. There was just so much to do before April 1st.

She peeked in the Cottage, but didn't want to track mud inside. She moved her watch to her right wrist to remind herself she'd need a couple of sturdy floor mats for the Cottage entrance before she opened for business. She retreated a few steps to snap a few shots of the Cottage decorated in winter snow with her digital camera, and turned toward the woods. Wicca bounded to the edge of the woods, spotting a rabbit that had popped from under a shrub. The race was on, and Callie laughed as the rabbit lead the lab on a merry chase of loops and circles before sliding down a burrow to safety. At first, Wicca tried to dig, but the ground was too frozen, so she quickly gave up and began searching for another bit of sport.

Further into the woods, Callie veered off the path to find the old oak. She'd brought along a crowbar to tear down the illegal tree stand as well as a small folding stool slung over her shoulder. She could see the giant tree in the distance. With the leaves all gone and the heavy snow pressing smaller brush toward the ground, its majestic outline was clear against the whiteness of the snow and the clear sky.

"Fairies always live in the oldest tree in the wood," she reminded herself. She smiled with conviction, picturing a happy group of fairies ensconced in the interior of the old, old tree.

Her smile quickly vanished when she was close enough to make out the obscenities that had been scrawled on the "No Hunting" sign she'd gently tacked to the tree. Below it, under a large rock, were all her other signs, torn into pieces. Someone wanted to emphasize that her signs were totally ineffective. To accent the obvious, another deer carcass hung from the tree. This one was a young doe, and again, only the rear haunches had been taken.

Wicca was growling and running in circles around the tree, leaping to try to pull the carcass from the branches. "Come, Wicca, Come!" Callie commanded. The obedient lab came quickly and sat at Callie's feet. She clipped the leash on and unfolded the stool. Her legs were shaking so badly she needed to sit. After taking several photos of the deer and the sign, Callie moved the stool closer to the tree and stood on tiptoes to lever the crowbar under the boards that formed the hunter's stand. When they were all free, she angrily threw each one into the creek.

"How dare you desecrate my fairy tree!" she shouted with each throw. "How dare you!" With the melting snow, the creek was running fast and the old wooden boards quickly floated away.

The beautiful morning was spoiled. As she returned to the house to call the local DNR officer again, she remembered Jake asking if she had come to buy more "No Hunting" signs. Had he already known she would need them?

The DNR officer did not answer, so Callie left a message on his machine and dialed Deputy Wright. She knew it would be too late to capture anyone, but maybe he knew how to contact the DNR guy directly.

"Wright here," the voice said crisply. Callie could hear a motor running in the background, so she assumed he was in his patrol car.

"This is Callie at the herb farm. The old Hyde Place? You told me to call if I needed you," Callie stammered.

"Are you cooking again?" he laughed

"No, I have another deer problem. I just found a doe hanging in a tree. They left some threats this time. I called the DNR, but no one answered. I thought maybe you could contact him," Callie said hopefully.

"I'm three minutes away. Stay put."

True to his word, in less than three minutes the patrol car pulled into the parking lot.

"How far is it?" he asked.

"About halfway back in the woods. I took some photos while I was there."

"Better if I see it in person," he advised. He walked back to his car and spoke into his radio.

"Ready?" he called as he strode toward the woods.

Wicca caught up to the officer quickly, and Callie wasn't far behind. When they reached the deer, Deputy Wright pulled out a notepad and started taking notes. Then he slowly started walking in a circle around the tree, looking for footprints or clues.

"Sorry I tramped around so much while I was here," Callie apologized, "but I was just so darn mad! I tore down their stand and threw it into the creek."

"Was it a metal model? New?" he queried.

"No, it was wood. Old wood. Looked like it had been up there forever."

"Too bad, if it were new, we might have been able to trace it to a store. It probably was old. People have been hunting on this place for years. I used to play here when I was a kid myself. School friend of mine lived across the creek. There was a huge sycamore back there that was hollow. Big enough five or six of us could sit in there. We used to camp there overnight sometimes."

"It's still there! It's dying, and has lost lots of branches, but it's still like a cave. Wicca and I found it soon after I moved here," Callie exclaimed.

"Well, I don't think we can track them. It snowed after they were here. I'll drive around on the other side of the woods and see if there are any tracks where they pulled off the road."

They had started walking back to the parking lot, but this time he walked slowly enough that Callie had no trouble keeping up. She was not petite, nor out of shape, but she'd had difficulty keeping up with those long legs on the way in.

Callie broke the silence as they walked. "Should I be worried about those threats?"

"They're probably just trying to scare you off. This farm was abandoned for several years, and some folks got used to treating these woods as their own playground. May just be some kids. Just be observant. I'll contact DNR. He'll need to write up a report, too. We'll try to put a stop to this, but it may take some time," Deputy Wright assured.

"Well, thanks for your help. I hated to call. I know you're busy, but this time seemed even more serious than the last time." They had reached the patrol car, and Callie could hear the dispatcher's voice on the radio.

"No problem, Ma'am. Part of my job. You call again if you find another deer," he smiled, "or if you start cooking!" He climbed into the patrol car, started the engine and was already on the radio before he reached the driveway.

The days were flying faster, and February was a short month. Each day, watering the plants and checking for insects or mold took a little longer because each day Callie was transplanting seedlings into individual pots as well as seeding additional flats. Flats with dwarf strawflowers, annual statice, snapdragons, hot peppers, and asarina were added to the shelves. As soon as a seeded flat germinated, it was moved from the heating mat to a place under the lights. Callie had pushed the kitchen table nearer the picture window, covered it with plastic, and moved most of the larger stock plants from the garage to free up more space there for flats of seedlings to grow. She'd added two ladders with boards placed across the steps to form shelves in front of the living room window and filled it with flats of transplanted babies. She was starting to feel like she lived in a jungle, but she loved being surrounded by green, growing things. Each one was a miracle.

She'd replaced all the "No Hunting" signs, watching Jake for any signs of guilt when she made her purchase. He seemed nonchalant and observed that a lot of folks had to replace their signs. "Winter winds and critters, you know," he'd offered as explanation.

During a warm spell, LouAnn called to say the road sign was finished. Flint Stone would bring his tractor and auger to drill post holes and help hang it that afternoon, if that was convenient. Callie could hardly wait. She put a batch of butterscotch brownies in the oven and made a thermos of hot chocolate. This would call for a celebration!

While she waited for the brownies to bake, she put the finishing touches on the first edition of the farm's newsletter. This one had been easy to write. The front top half page announced the future opening of "Joyful Heart Herbs," giving a brief account of what the shop intended to offer, including a lovely photo of the refurbished Cottage exterior. The bottom half was an invitation to the Opening Celebration on April 1st, giving the time and schedule for the day's events. Callie planned to give a couple of talks on the best varieties to plant in this area and the newest trends in culinary herbs. She'd give a "Cooking with Fresh Herbs" demo and pass out free recipes. Inside on page two, she briefly introduced herself and told about her experience at the farmer's market, just to remind those former customers who she was. She included the fact that she was the garden writer for the Heartland Banner and encouraged garden clubs in the area to send information regarding their meetings or special events to her. Page three was a glowing report of many of the herbs, perennials, and flowers that would be available next spring. She had emphasized easy-to-grow plants, deer resistant plants, and fragrant plants. Other categories would be covered in future issues. The final page again emphasized the opening date, gave her e-mail address in case someone needed to book an appointment for a group visit to the farm, wanted her to speak, or had a question. It included a few topics that Callie had used for presentations in the past. The slides were already in the trays, and it would be simple to review her notes for a speech. The last segment was a short article on the joys of gardening with fragrant herbs. She e-mailed it to Cecilia at the print shop, along with a short note saying how delighted she was that the process had been so painless. She'd really enjoyed the times they'd gotten together to discuss the layout and format for the newsletter. Now Callie was looking forward to seeing the final proof.

While she was at the computer, she checked on the status of her order for honeybees and hives. When she'd first started reading about the history of herbs and herb gardens, she'd quickly learned how closely herbs and bees were connected. Honey had been essential in olden times, not only as a sweetener, but also as a preservative. The beeswax was just as valuable since it formed the base for many salves and ointments, was used for candles, furniture wax, and helped to keep leather from cracking. Many herbs attracted bees and provided a long season of nectar and pollen. All of the old monastery gardens had had hives. Herbs and bees just seemed a natural fit. She was especially fascinated by the story of Brother Adam and the famous bees of Buckfast Abbey in England. Brother Adam was a Benedictine monk who spent his life studying and breeding honeybees. Eventually, he developed a disease resistant strain of highly productive honeybees that became famous throughout the world.

When Callie was a vendor at the farmers' market, she'd thought having bees would be an excellent idea. They would not only pollinate her flowers so she could harvest more seeds, but the honey would be a product she could sell early in the season before it was really time to plant and late in the season when frost had put an end to the garden harvest. However, having bees in town had not been a reasonable idea. As soon as she'd found the farm in Bradford County, she'd attended a class sponsored by the Indiana Beekeeper's Association and made arrangements to purchase bees from a member. Callie was ecstatic when she discovered his bees were actually descendents of the legendary Buckfast bees that Brother Adam had developed. She'd ordered hives from a trusted company in Kentucky and was eagerly waiting for them to arrive so she could get them assembled. She wanted her hives and bees to be in place as soon as spring arrived.

The brownies came out of the oven, but she still had a couple of hours until LouAnn was expected. She'd already finished the watering and decided to do some reading. Callie tried to read every night before bedtime. Right now, she was reading books on operating a small business, promoting on a shoestring budget, and attracting sales through amazing displays. The ladies at the library had been extremely helpful in getting copies of things she wanted on interlibrary loan. She was so absorbed in her reading, she didn't realize LouAnn's truck had pull into her driveway until Wicca barked and ran to the door. She grabbed her coat, and they both ran outside.

"I can't wait to see my sign!" Callie yelled as LouAnn climbed out of the cab.

"I think you're going to like it," LouAnn grinned. "I just passed Flint bringing the tractor about a mile back, so he'll be here soon. How are all your babies?"

"Growing, growing, and wanting more space! I've ordered a small portable greenhouse, but it hasn't arrived yet. It's too cold to be able to keep most of the plants warm enough in it even with a heater, but I'm hoping to move some of the perennials into it soon. I'm going to need space in the garage to seed all the annuals in two weeks. I just can't believe how fast the time is going. Can you believe "Joyful Hearts" is going to open in only six weeks?"

"Well, I hope the weather cooperates. We can still get some snow in April. Will the greenhouse handle that?"

"I sure hope so. It's designed so the snow slides off easily. Keeping the plants from frost damage should be the only problem.

"That and wind," LouAnn added, as a stiff breeze blew off her hat and carried it across the parking lot. Wicca dashed after it and proudly brought it back.

"Thanks, Wicca. I'm impressed!"

"I'm impressed, too," Callie laughed, "I've never seen her retrieve anything before. Usually when I throw a stick or a Frisbee, she just grabs it and plays 'keep-away, you can't catch me'!"

"Well, labs are natural retrievers. You chose a good breed."

"Yes. I debated a lot before I decided on which breed of dog to get. Knowing I was going to have lots of customers around, I knew I needed a dog that was basically friendly and quiet. I can't stand those yappy little lap dogs. And labs were bred for 'soft mouths'," Callie added.

"Soft mouths?" LouAnn asked.

"Right. Labs were bred to quietly sit in boats until the duck hunters made a shot. Then they'd jump out, swim over, grab the duck and bring it back to the boat. They just hold the duck firmly enough to keep it in their mouths, but they don't try to penetrate the skin. Labs have soft mouths, as opposed to something like a German Shepherd or a Scottie that historically were trained to really bite," Callie explained.

They were interrupted by the arrival of Flint and his tractor. Callie had already measured the required distance from the road and placed dowel rods to mark the location for the posts. With the three of them working together, the sign was installed quickly. It looked terrific with bright green lettering on a beige background, with roses and lavender twining along the sides. A heart identical to those in the Cottage shutters had been cut into the top center. Callie captured the moment with her camera, then invited LouAnn and Flint to the house for hot chocolate and butterscotch brownies to celebrate.

70

That evening, Callie printed out the photos from the camera and started a photo album that would chronicle "Joyful Heart Herbs". The first photo was herself, pulling up the "for sale" sign that had been in front of the farmhouse. The second was of the dilapidated Cottage surrounded by waist high brush. The third showed her truck piled to the top with boxes and furniture with a U-Haul trailer hooked behind that was filled with her beloved herbs. She added the photos of Flint on the bulldozer creating the parking lot and Suz in her big truck dumping the first load of stone. Next were shots of Trev nailing up the new siding on the Cottage and Trev standing beside the cement mixer with his gray "cement" beard. Trev. She hadn't heard from him since the day of the awkward hug. She hadn't really expected to, but she found she missed the lighthearted banter they'd engaged in while they'd worked companionably together. She missed the company of a man. She really missed Daniel.

She sat unmoving for several moments. A tear ran down each side of her face, and she was filled with longing. Daniel had been so perfect. Everyone said they were the perfect couple. "What went wrong?" Callie wondered. She hadn't realized that Daniel was unhappy. And she certainly had been totally clueless about Mariah.

She thought about all the things Daniel had said he loved about her. He thought she was funny, praised her dedication to the children in her classroom, and admired her honesty. He'd teased her about being so good with tools, and although he wasn't the least bit interested in gardening, he'd praised her many experiments in cooking with fresh herbs. He'd said he was marrying her for her outstanding, flakey, mouth-watering pies.

"Apparently all those attributes were not enough to keep Daniel's heart," Callie mumbled thoughtfully. She wondered what was missing. Where had she failed him? Maybe there was something about her that just did not appeal to men, at least not the right men.

"I wonder if Mariah bakes pies?" flitted through Callie's mind. For a moment, the picture of Mariah flashed through her mind as well. Mariah tossing stylish dark hair, with a sleek body, sophisticated clothes. Mariah gesturing with perfectly manicured hands and a delicate gold chain around her ankle. Callie had seen her leaving Daniel's office one day and had felt large and lumpy by comparison. Mariah worked in claims, so she often had meetings with Daniel and the other insurance salesmen. Callie hadn't given it a second thought.

Callie slumped in the rocker, feeling her spirits sink. "To bake, or not to bake. That is the question."

Lemon balm, or *Mellissa officinalis* was the herb of choice for the next morning's breakfast tea. Callie was still feeling melancholy and lacking in self-worth. Lemon balm was reported to "maketh the heart cheerful." She'd done her Tai Chi and all the watering, and was still waiting for the benefits of the tea to kick in. "Maybe I need another cup or two," she pondered, and added two slices of chamomile nut bread to her saucer. The answer last night had been, as usual, to bake. She still had butterscotch brownies, and now two loaves of fragrant chamomile-walnut bread sat on her counter as well. She'd be a butterball before long if she didn't cheer up.

She showered, braided her hair, and pulled on a warm lavender sweater that was actually imbedded with lavender in the fiber. It had come from Norfolk Lavender in England, a gift from her fellow teachers at her "farewell party." The lavender dispersed from the warmth of the body and was supposed to make the wearer feel comforted, secure, and calm. She'd give it a test run today.

Callie packaged some of the nut bread and brownies into boxes and called Wicca, who eagerly jumped into the truck and gave Callie a look that said, "Where are we going today, Boss?"

"We're going to pick up the newsletters at Cecilia's, and drop some of them at the library. Then we're taking this week's herb article to the Heartland Banner. And if you're very, very good, we'll get some dog food. You're almost out!"

Wicca seemed to understand the entire conversation, nodded, and sat still as a statue for the entire trip.

Cecilia was out of the shop, but her assistant, Ellen, bubbled with enthusiasm while she made out the invoice for the newsletters.

"Didn't they just turn out so well?" Ellen gushed. "I just can't wait to visit your little shop. I bet it will just be sweet as sugar. And I hope I can attend some of your classes. Will they be during the day or in the evenings? Are you going to be open every day? I only have Sundays and Mondays off, you know."

Callie realized that Ellen had brought up some good questions and quickly made a note on a scrap of paper. "I need to give scheduling some thought," she responded. "You've given me some things to cover in the next issue of the newsletter. Thanks for pointing out things I missed!" She left a plate of goodies with Ellen.

She loaded the bundles into her truck. Then she stopped at the library to drop off a plate of goodies and a few issues of the newsletter, and ordered the next books she wanted on interlibrary loan. She especially looked forward to reading Hattie Ellis's history of honeybees and honey production titled <u>Sweetness and Light</u>.

Lucille McKenzie had spiked her hair and dyed the tips bright pink. Today she sported a sweatshirt that said, "Enjoy the quiet before the storm!" Her dangling bright pink earrings looked like tornadoes made of spiraling wire.

Callie had given the girl her column and turned to leave when Lucille yelled, "Hey, Dad, the garden lady is here!"

"He told me this morning that he wants to see you," Lucille confided, as she blew a bright pink bubble.

"I didn't think teens today chewed bubble gum," Callie observed.

"Dad won't let me smoke in here. Too many fumes from the presses and such. Said it would be dangerous, so I have to do something else," she said as she rolled her eyes. "Go on in, he's waiting."

Callie entered Mac's office, which seemed even more cluttered than on her last visit.

"Have a seat, Callie," he offered. "You going to the garden club meeting tonight?"

"I planned to."

"Good. Take some notes. Gloria can't go, so I need a reporter to cover it." Callie had learned earlier that Mac's wife, Gloria, was secretary for the Heart and Soil Garden Club.

"I've never really worked as a reporter before," Callie responded.

"You're a writer aren't you? Just listen and write. You don't have to glorify it like Gloria does. Get it? 'Gloria, glorify?" Mac laughed at his own joke.

"Ok, I'll do it. But, I get an extra large ad before my big opening in exchange, right?"

"You drive a hard bargain, Hoosier lady," Mac chuckled, "First thing I know, I'll owe you an entire special edition!"

"Sounds good to me," she laughed.

Callie spent all afternoon addressing newsletters, and sorting them by zip code as the postmistress had instructed. The minimum for bulk mail was 200 identical pieces, so there was no problem reaching that number. She placed them in the official mailing trays Sharon had provided and stacked them by the door. It had not been a fun job and had taken lots longer to finish than Callie had anticipated. Although she preferred the personal touch of a handwritten address, she'd need to look into printing the labels on the computer. She wouldn't have time to do it by hand during the spring rush, especially if the list grew.

She just had time to re-braid her hair, put on some make-up, and down a carton of yogurt as her supper before she needed to leave for the garden club meeting. She put a stack of her newsletters into a carry-all, grabbed a pen and notebook, and headed into the library where the meetings were held.

A group of twenty-five ladies and five men were milling about the public meeting room when she arrived. On one table stacks of seed catalogs and garden magazines were laid out in neat rows under a sign that said "Swap N Trade." Another table held a coffeemaker and plates of refreshments. A third table held several used gardening books.

"All right, everyone find a seat," a woman called. There followed a brief welcome by the president, Maxine Barnes, the treasurer's report, and several committee reports. Ellen, from the printers' shop, stood to explain that, as everyone knew, one of the club's life long members had passed away, and her collection of gardening books was available for "adoption."

"There should be at least one book for each member," Ellen explained, "and I know each of you will want a volume to remember Wilma by."

"Wilma did love her garden books," one man nodded.

"Wilma was the glue that held this club together," a woman wearing an "I Love Dirt!" sweatshirt added.

A five minute mini-lesson was given by a man on building a cold frame, accompanied by printed instructions for each member. Then a slide show of Mr. and Mrs. Jackson's late summer trip to see Thomas Jefferson's garden at Monticello followed. They passed out pamphlets from the Heritage Seed Foundation that resides on the Monticello grounds and showed several packets of heirloom seeds they had purchased there.

Maxine urged everyone to begin planning what they would bring for the club's annual plant sale in June. "I know it seems far off right now, but once spring comes, we'll be busy in the fields and gardens. I hope some of you men are making those lovely bluebird houses again. I know Merle grew a bumper crop of gourds last year, and he'll need some help cleaning and painting them next month. And remember, we need all the old boots and purses you can come up with. Denver, how are those hen and chicks coming along?"

Denver grunted something that must have meant affirmative, because Maxine nodded and continued. "Now I see a couple of new faces, so does anyone have a guest to introduce?" Callie suddenly felt as if she might have made a mistake. Maybe the club was by invitation only and she certainly hadn't been invited.

One lady stood and introduced her cousin, who had just moved into the area from out of state. Then Ellen stood and said, "I want to introduce a wonderful new addition to our community. Callie, stand up, please!" Callie stood and smiled at the group. There was a little round of applause.

"Callie is opening a new plant business south of town. It's called "Joyful Heart Herbs," but she'll have lots of other plants besides herbs. She's going to have a lovely little shop and offer classes and everything, and I just know you are all going to love it and make her feel real welcome," Ellen said breathlessly, as she started clapping. A flurry of applause joined in.

Maxine called for a motion to adjourn, which was made, seconded, and passed, and everyone moved toward the refreshment table, the memorial books, or the "Swap" table.

Callie sat for a moment completing her notes, before Ellen came over and sat beside her.

"Thanks for that great introduction," Callie said gratefully. "Are you supposed to be invited to join, or can anyone come?"

"Oh, Heart and Soil is open to the public. We just don't get many new members. We're happy to have you come," Ellen assured her.

"Mac McKenzie asked me to report on the meeting for the newspaper. Could you fill me in on a couple of names," Callie inquired. They spent the next few minutes discussing the role Wilma had played in the birth of the club, and Ellen explained how the "Swap" table worked. Callie promised to bring some duplicate catalogs to add to the exchange at the next meeting and asked if leaving her newsletters on the table would be appropriate.

"Of course," Ellen said, "Now, let's get some of those refreshments before they're all gone! Most of these gardeners are good cooks, too!"

Before the evening ended, Ellen had introduced Callie to most of the members. Several ladies said they would look forward to seeing her new shop and the Jackson's asked if she'd be selling any heirloom plants.

Driving home, Callie smiled. It had been wonderful to spend an evening with other plant lovers. She had met several interesting people and enjoyed the presentation. It appeared that the club sponsored several worthwhile activities and contributed a great deal to the local community. She looked forward to being a part of the Heart and Soil club.

The following week, the power company finally put in the transformer and the new electric line to the Cottage. Josh Sparks came to hook everything up, including the new water pump Jesse Plumber had installed. Callie was delighted as she flipped on the light switch for the first time. The new fixtures bathed the Cottage walls in a soft glow. She plugged in the new cash register, turned the key, and was relieved when the monitor glowed. She lifted the phone and heard a dial tone. Progress! She loved it!

Since she had lights, she could put in a couple of long days painting. The sun was shining, but it was still below freezing. She built a small fire in the woodstove, filled the kettle, and cracked a window for ventilation. She'd just finished painting two flat walls and the wall of shelving when the UPS truck arrived. The driver unloaded two huge cartons and one small rectangular box.

"So, looks like you're starting a new business here," the driver smiled. "Mike Shipley," he stated as he extended his hand.

"You're right," Callie answered. "I imagine I'll be seeing a lot of you starting next week. All my inventory shipments are scheduled to arrive the first two weeks of March. I'm expecting lots of boxes!"

"Well, these three big guys should get you off to a good start," he said.

"Oh, these aren't merchandise for the shop. These are my new hives. I'm going to keep honeybees!" Callie said enthusiastically.

"Sounds interesting, but dangerous," he teased, backing away in mock fear. "Guess I'll be seeing you soon then," he called, as he threw a handful of mini dog biscuits to Wicca. "I like your make-up!" he yelled as he pulled away.

"My make-up?" Callie wondered.

She returned to the Cottage, removed the precious cash register to a small table and covered it with an old tablecloth for protection. She finished painting the final wall and put the first coat of paint on the sales counter before she stopped for a late lunch. She'd planned to eat a sandwich she'd brought with her while she worked in the Cottage to save time, but decided she'd better get the truck to move the big boxes over to the farmhouse.

Once the boxes were safely in the living room, there being no other space left in her house for them, she went to wash up. When she looked in the mirror, she saw streaks and smears of cream paint across her face.

"Yeah, nice make-up!" she thought. She'd buy a mirror for the Cottage on her very next trip to town.

Callie worked until nearly midnight painting the second coat on all the walls and the sales counter. She'd brought over a CD player and several of her favorite opera CD's after lunch, so the time had gone quickly as she painted to the rhythm of the music. Although she was used to hard physical work, loading potting soil, pushing wheelbarrows and such, several muscles complained about having to endure twelve hours of brushing. She was sitting on the floor, cleaning out brushes and singing loudly along with Pavarotti when the door opened.

"Taking advantage of your new lights, I see," said Deputy Wright, "Sorry, didn't mean to startle you," he added when Callie jumped.

"Didn't hear anyone drive in," she choked.

"I'm not surprised," he quipped, "Nice music. Surprised though, thought you'd be more the George Strait type."

"I'm not any type," she answered a bit testily. Daniel had never liked her love of opera, either.

"Sorry, again. That wasn't criticism, just an observation," he stated.

"I'm sorry. I didn't intend to snap. It's been a long day."

"Well, I saw lights on over here, and wasn't sure who was messing around, so thought I'd check. Just passing by on my patrol. Glad everything is okay, and congratulations on getting your power on." Before Callie could respond, he touched his hat brim.

"Ma'am," he nodded politely as he exited into the inky blackness.

Callie had been so upset with herself after Deputy Wright had left that she'd eaten all the remaining butterscotch brownies while she soaked in a hot tub laced with lavender oil. It had been over four months, and Daniel was still affecting her emotions and her behavior. This had to stop!

The next morning, she made a pot of tea, and fed Wicca her usual breakfast. She watered the ever-growing number of flats, slightly changed the angle of the fans so the air moved in a different pattern, fixed a sandwich and poured the remaining tea from the pot into a thermos. She was too stiff from painting yesterday to do Tai Chi.

It was a glorious morning, and Callie's spirits lifted as she observed one of the best miracles of Nature. Every blade of grass, weed, and branch was covered in a layer of white hoarfrost. The entire world sparkled and glittered. Bright red cardinals chirped greetings to one another as they plucked bittersweet berries from the vines near the gazebo. Callie returned to the house to get some colorful twine and wrote herself a big note to find the birdfeeders. Back outside, she tied pieces of the bright pink string onto all the vines that had berries and blue string on the few that showed no sign of clusters at all. When spring finally came, she'd be able to tell which vines were females and which were males. She'd propagate some of each, since people would need to buy both a male and a female bittersweet plant in order to get berries.

She paused to admire her new sign and imagined the plantings she would add under it when the season allowed. She turned in a slow circle, enjoying the beauty of the morning as the sky streaked with apricots, pinks, and bits of lavender. Once in the Cottage, she built up the fire, filled the kettle, and began the slow process of taping the walls so she could paint all the trim. She was about half-finished doing the window trim when the phone startled her. Her first official phone call at the Cottage!

It was LouAnn calling to see if the sales counter was ready for her to start the artwork.

"All ready and waiting if you don't mind a few paint fumes. I'm still working on the trim."

"What's a few more fumes to a painter?" she laughed, "I'll be over in a few minutes with some sketches and my paints"

By lunchtime, Callie had the sage green trim painted around all the windows and the door, as well as the moldings and a couple of small wall cupboards she intended to hang in the fairy corner. LouAnn had made good progress on the sales counter. Daylilies, lavender, rosemary, thyme, lambs ears, beebalm, penstemon, and larkspur "grew" across the front of the counter in beautiful colors.

"It looks marvelous!" Callie exclaimed.

"Wait until I'm finished with the shading before you get excited," LouAnn laughed appreciatively.

"I think we deserve a break. I can whip up a quick omelet if you're hungry."

"My muse is starving," she chuckled. They chatted all the way to the farmhouse and through a simple lunch of omelet with sautéed mushrooms, melted cheese, and a sprinkling of fresh herbs. Thick slices of whole grain bread were toasted and spread with jam.

LouAnn ooh'd and aah'd over all the plants and how nicely they were growing before they returned to the Cottage. By evening, Callie had given all the trim a second coat. LouAnn had finished the details on the plants and added a realistic monarch butterfly to the "garden" she'd painted on the counter.

"My customers are going to love it. You have to sign it," Callie instructed. So, LouAnn painted her name on the corner with a flourish of black paint, and gave Callie directions for sealing the artwork once it was completely dry. Callie took LouAnn's photo with the counter before her friend packed up her paints and departed.

Callie cleaned up all the drop cloths, rags, and brushes. The Cottage was ready for inventory. Tomorrow, she'd bring over the display props and items she had in the dining room and hang the curtains she'd sewn on her grandmother's treadle machine.

The last week in February was a flurry of activity. Callie caught up all the plant work, and filled the space where the shop things had been in the dining room with flats of plants. She seeded "Victoria," "Coral Nymph," and "Blue Bedder" salvias, perfumed nicotianas, and the first basils in narrow rows. Tiny pinches of dill and cilantro seeds were sprinkled on flats of peat pots. If that greenhouse didn't arrive soon, she'd have plants on every horizontal surface in the house, including her bed!

She'd attended yet another meeting about the CAFO, this time at the zoning board. Unfortunately, it looked as though their permits were moving forward.

It had taken two afternoons to assemble the bee hives. When Callie opened the first box, she found what appeared to be hundreds of flat "Lincoln Logs!" Fortunately, the instructions were clearly written and easy to follow. However, each frame required four slender pieces to be fitted together and required lots of tiny nails. Ten frames fit into each super. When they were complete, she gave each super two coats of cream paint, as well as the hive tops and bottom platforms. The smaller rectangular box contained sheets of pure beeswax. Each frame would hold a sheet requiring a slender wood strip to be nailed in place to secure it. Callie would wait until just before the bees arrived to add the beeswax sheets.

The articles for the newspaper column for the entire month of February as well as March were complete and already delivered to the office. Callie suspected she'd be glad they were finished since March would be even busier.

She was congratulating herself on completing her February job list when Josh Sparks called to say her pressure tank had arrived.

"Pressure tank?" she asked.

"Yeah, you need a pressure tank if you're going to pump water on a fairly steady basis. I looked at your water test and you're going to need a filter, too. Lots of rust in this area. Wife says it's bad for plants. I'll be over to hook it all up tomorrow. By the way, you'll need to do something to keep that tank from freezing. Most people build a pumphouse," he said just before he hung up.

Callie sat for a moment in stunned silence. Of course. How could she have forgotten something so basic? She recalled the pumphouse at her parents' farm, except they had always called it the milk house. Originally, it had been used to store the cans of milk until the dairy truck picked them up. At the far end of the small building stood the pump and a large pressure tank. It was a well-insulated little shed. Inside, the temperatures never went below freezing. She hesitated for a minute, and then reached for the phone book.

The next morning, Trev's beat-up blue pick-up truck pulled into her driveway. Callie was in the garage striking cuttings of scented geraniums. The stock plants in her windowsills throughout the house were getting a bit leggy. Since she needed to cut them back, and there was room on the heating mats until she started seeding annuals, the timing was perfect. She stripped the lower leaves and placed them in a bowl. Then she pushed each stem into sterile potting soil in a plug flat. Once the flat was filled, she draped plastic wrap over the top and placed them on the heat mat. The air around her was filled with the luscious scent of roses, ginger, lime, and peppermint as she processed each variety. If things went well, the new plants should be rooted and ready to sell by Mother's Day.

She stopped work when she heard the truck and met Trev at the back door.

"Morning, Stranger," he greeted.

"Morning, Graybeard," Callie replied.

Trev stepped into the garage and surveyed the rows of green plants.

"Looks like everything is growing on schedule," he observed.

"I'm running out of space, that's for sure," Callie answered.

"Still waiting on that portable greenhouse?" Trev asked.

"Yes, I keep calling, and they keep promising, but so far it hasn't appeared."

"Well, maybe it'll show up soon. I was able to get all the materials for your pumphouse. Fortunately, they still had siding that matches the Cottage. I think there were enough shingles left from the Cottage repairs to roof it, too. Remember I laid those packages of shingles in the crawlspace, so you'd have some for repairs if ever the roof were damaged?"

Callie had been lucky. Normally, Trev had jobs lined up, but the house he was scheduled to start had a problem with the building permit, and he was waiting for some special-order woodwork for another. Since her project was small, he'd been able to fit it in.

Callie rode over to the Cottage in Trev's truck with Wicca wedged between them. They discussed the dimensions, and Trev explained that since there was already a concrete pad around the old well, he wouldn't need to pour footings. That would speed up the process, so he'd probably be able to have it finished enough to keep the pump and pressure tank from freezing by the end of the day. If needed, he could do the finish work later. Callie offered to help, but Trev said he'd be fine for a bit. He'd call her if he needed someone to hold up a wall.

Callie returned to the garage to finish her cuttings. There was still room available on the propagating mats, so she did a flat of rosemary and another of lemon thyme and placed them on the warm surface to root. Then she put a kettle of minestrone on the stove and stirred up a batch of bread. She told herself that she wasn't doing it to impress Trev, or anything like that. She was just hungry for homemade soup and baking always made her feel better.

She worked on recipe ideas for the "Girls Night In" while the bread was rising and made a shopping list. She checked her e-mail. A few questions and some messages had resulted from her initial newsletter. Callie decided it was a good time to start her website, so she did some preliminary work and set things in motion. She had a little experience with websites since her class had had one at school. It was amazing what fourth graders could do on a computer these days. She'd had to take several special classes and seminars to be able to keep up with their skills and interests. At her school, each class had a website that was linked to the school's webpage. Parents could check on homework assignments, look up special events, and find out what projects the class was tackling. She'd learned to upload photos and documents and most of the basics.

The phone never rang, so she started writing the newsletter that would go out in March. Finally, in late afternoon Callie walked over to the Cottage. The pumphouse was standing tall. A plywood roof was on, and the wall studs were stuffed with insulation on the inside. Another layer of Styrofoam insulation lined the outer walls. Trev had apparently left, but Jesse Plumber was just unloading a large blue barrel-shaped object onto a sturdy cart.

"You're just in time, young lady. Normally, I'd drive right up to the spot to unload this thing, but I didn't want to make ruts close to your Cottage. I know you'll be opening pretty soon," he stated.

"Just another month, so it is getting close," Callie responded. "What can I do to help?"

"Grab that tool box. I got everything else on the cart," he puffed as he pushed the cart toward the pumphouse.

Together, they unloaded the pressure tank and placed it in one corner of the pumphouse. He flipped the breaker switch, so the pump could not run, and started disconnecting fittings. Callie stood and held a light as evening fell. By the time they'd finished, the well was connected to the pressure tank, and the pressure tank was connected to the filter. The filter was connected to a fitting with a shut-off valve. Hopefully, soon, the fitting would be connected to a water line.

The next day, Callie took her truck into Muncie. She had arranged to rent a Ditch Witch to dig the trenches for water lines. When she pulled into her parking lot, Trev's truck was already there, and she could see that the pumphouse now had shingles on its roof.

"Morning, Stranger," he called.

"Morning, Trev," she answered.

"Looks like you have some major work planned."

"Gotta take advantage of this weather," she called back. The last week of February had turned out to be lovely. She'd already checked the condition of the soil with a shovel and found, to her relief, that the ground was not frozen below six inches. They'd had a fairly mild winter so far.

Trev walked over and began helping unchain the large piece of equipment. "You know how to run one of these things?" he asked.

"I grew up driving a tractor, and the guys at the rental store gave me a crash course. Looks pretty straightforward to me."

"You're the boss," he laughed. "If you run into trouble, just yell."

"You bet I will," she replied.

Trev watched in admiration as Callie started the engine, released the clutch and brakes, and backed the machine off the trailer. Before she left that morning, she had run stakes and a string line where the water lines would run. Then she had poked a hole in a bag of flour, and slowly shaking it, had marked a white line across the ground directly under each section of string. After removing the stakes and string, she'd rechecked her lines. They looked good, so she'd headed to town.

Now, she carefully guided the trencher over the white lines. The machine worked like a dream, and within an hour she had trenches over three feet deep. She turned the trencher off and climbed down to check the depth with a tape measure. She'd have to dig the trench next to the pumphouse by hand, since she couldn't get the trencher close enough to do it all the way.

Trev walked over to meet her. "You made that look easy," he remarked.

"Piece of cake," she replied, refusing to admit how nervous she'd been.

"That sounds good, too!" he joked.

"No cake, but I've got homemade bread, and I can heat up some minestrone," she offered.

"Be still my heart! A lady that knows how to dig ditches and bake bread! I'm ready to stop if you are," Trev said as he unbuckled his tool belt.

As they finished lunch, Trev said, "You know, I'm no expert on garden centers, but don't most of them have some sort of roofless building where they put plants? I've seen those black covers stretched on top. You gonna have something like that?"

"A shadehouse. Yes, I'd planned on putting up one later in the summer. They help protect the plants from scorching sun, and reduce water needs. That reduces labor costs as well, so they are cost-effective in more ways than one," Callie stated.

"I was thinking. Since your greenhouse hasn't arrived, and you really need space for plants right now, what if we build a shadehouse and cover it with two layers of plastic? You could move plants into it now, and then you'd already have it when you need it this summer. We could make it so it'd be easy to add on additional sections later if you want it bigger."

"Hmmm," Callie pondered the idea, but quickly saw its merit. "That would also give my customers a place to shop for plants out of the wind or rain. I think it's a great idea, but do you have time to do it now?"

"I think I can squeeze it in. Let's go pick the site. You'll need to run a water line to it, so we'd better get the trench dug before you have to take the Ditch Witch back! When you return, I should have the siding on and the door built for the pumphouse."

As Callie stood looking at the new shadehouse, she knew Trev's idea had saved her lots of headaches. They'd been able to get it up quickly, and Suz had brought a load of stone for the floor. While Trev was building the shadehouse, the pipe for the waterlines had been delivered. Callie had spent hours crawling in and out of trenches, cementing pipe connectors and elbows. She'd put a hydrant near the Cottage, one at each end of the proposed greenhouse site, one at each end of the shadehouse, and six more where the major gardens were planned. When she was finished, and all the lines had been tested for possible leaks, Flint had brought over his Bobcat to spread the stone in the shadehouse, and fill in the trenches.

Now the plastic layers were on, and she had formed benching with cement blocks and wooden pallets. They weren't as glamorous as the benching she'd picked out, but the pallets were free for the hauling and her budget was straining. Once the pallets were covered with wonderful plants, she hoped no one would notice. She'd purchased fans and returned the borrowed ones to the fair grounds. Eventually, the fans would be permanently mounted in the greenhouse, so it was not an extra expense. She couldn't wait to start moving plants inside. She took photos for her album and grinned with pleasure.

The "girls" were coming this evening for another evening of recipe testing. She'd revamped the one cheese ball that Deputy Wright had said was bland and added several other new candidates. She'd made a syrup of the rose-scented geranium leaves she'd removed when she'd done the cuttings a few days ago. Mixed with a blackberry liqueur and other ingredients, it became a stunning cocktail punch. She'd decided to hold this tasting in the Cottage. It was empty while her house was so full of plants one could barely move. She'd moved some comfy lawn furniture and some odd chairs inside as well as a wrought iron coffee table that she intended to use for an outdoor display later. And, her new bee hives would serve as end tables! The sales counter was filled with an array of appetizers, plates, glasses, tea cups and saucers. Everything was ready for her guests.

Sandy and Cecilia arrived in the same car. Suz and LouAnn pulled in just behind them in their separate trucks. They all paused to look at the glistening shadehouse and the network of brown earth that ran from one building to another.

"Looks like you've kept busy since we got together last," Cecilia commented. "I can't wait to see the Cottage." Once inside, everyone exclaimed over LouAnn's beautiful artwork on the sales counter. She blushed with pleasure and pointed out Callie's curtains and bee hives.

"You two make me feel like such a slug," Sandy moaned.

"Sure, like the rest of us could run around soaking up the news and turning it into scintillating stories the way you do," Suz commented.

"Speaking of scintillating stories, sounds like you've had some excitement, Callie," Sandy probed. Everyone looked at Callie expectantly. "I was down at the sheriff's office reading the daily reports, and your name came up a couple of times. Tell me more about the threats and the dead deer."

"Threats!" "Dead deer?" the other women exclaimed.

"It's nothing. Some hunter is trespassing on my property, and killing deer out of season. I keep putting up 'No Hunting' signs, and he tears them down. Last time, he scrawled some obscene threats on one and left it for me along with half a dead deer hanging in a tree," Callie explained.

"That doesn't sound like nothing to me," Suz said.

"And did they find out who stole your purse?" Sandy asked.

"Stolen purse! When did that happen?" the others cried.

"Help yourself to some food, and I'll tell you all about it," Callie urged.

By the end of the evening, everyone had exchanged news although no one else had had as much excitement as Callie in their lives. Sandy filled everyone in on the latest developments with the CAFO issue since she had attended another commissioners' meeting. The county road superintendent had been asked about the impact it would have on road budgets, if existing culverts could handle the weight limits, and other questions along those lines. The issue seemed to be dividing the county.

The woman laughed, ate, and pronounced all but one of the recipes winners. Soon the pitcher of blackberry & rose geranium cocktail punch was empty. Cecilia had brought a caramel apple pie from Dinah's Diner, which they enjoyed with steaming cups of Apple Geranium tea. As the evening ended, they all waddled to their cars, hugging, laughing, and counting the days until their March get-together.

Scented Geraniums

Scented geraniums are a delight to the nose as well as the eye. They have been cherished by homemakers since the 1600's when sailors brought them home as gifts from the shores of South Africa. Since they are so easy to grow, so useful in the home and such a delight to the senses, they have continued to be popular over the centuries.

Experts have developed hundreds of varieties from the original rose and lemon parents. Now we have dozens of scents with intriguing names such as "Clorinda," "Joy Lucille," "Prince Rupert," "Chocolate Mint," "Velvet Rose," and "Pretty Polly." The scents are generally divided into categories; rose, citrus, mint, spice, and pungent. There are scented geraniums that mimic the fragrance of pine, southernwood, lime, strawberry, nutmeg, and endless other aromas.

Scented geraniums grow well outdoors during the summer and are wonderful houseplants indoors during the months where frost threatens. They prefer well-drained soil with adequate nutrition. Water potted plants after the surface of the soil becomes dry. Diseases may occur if plants are over-watered or forced to sit in a water-filled saucer. Good ventilation and proper watering usually prevent disease. Bright sunlight is desired, especially during the winter months. Those varieties with large leaves, especially the "hairy" ones, will appreciate some light shade outdoors during the hottest days of summer.

The plants easily "cross", so if more than one variety blooms at the same time, seeds will not come "true." This is how so many varieties of scented geraniums have come into being, by crossing and re-crossing different types. To get a duplicate plant, one must take cuttings, which is also fairly easy to do with most types of scented geraniums.

Scented geraniums are delightful in the landscape, and useful in containers. Because there are tall columnar types, mounding forms, and prostrate ones, the perfect candidate for any requirement can be found. The variety of leaf texture, size, and shape offer foliage for blending in the flower border or an accent for a quiet spot. Since they are fast-growing, they are useful to hide dying foliage of spring bulbs or to fill in blank spaces in the border quickly. Varieties such as "Apple," "Endsleigh Oak," and "Nutmeg" are wonderful in hanging baskets.

Scented geranium leaves were a staple in the stillroom in medieval times, where they were dried for teas, potpourris and sweet bags. Rose geranium is an especially popular and soothing scent that helps relieve stress and anxiety even today.

While rose, lemon, lime, peppermint, or ginger scented geranium leaves are abundant in summer, make batches of geranium sugar. Simply layer one inch of white sugar with a layer of leaves, repeating until the container is full. Seal tightly, and allow to age for several days, shaking the container daily. The sharp edges of the sugar crystals will rupture the microscopic oil sacs and absorb the flavor and scent. Remove the leaves once the sugar is well-flavored. If the desired intensity is not there, add another batch of fresh leaves and repeat the aging process. The resulting sugar will flavor delectable desserts, teas, frostings and more. Experiment!

Instead of cinnamon rolls, make rose-geranium rolls, using rose-geranium sugar and substituting finely chopped leaves or rose-geranium flowers for raisins. Rose geraniums have long been used to flavor cakes. Simply place leaves between wax paper, weighted with a book for a few hours to flatten the leaves. Then place the leaves in the bottom of a buttered and floured cake pan. Pour your favorite cake batter over the top, and bake as usual. After cooling, turn the cake out, and remove the leaves from the bottom.

Scented geraniums also make delightful tea. Use either the fresh leaves, or the dried ones. Simply place in a pot, pour boiling water over, and allow to steep. Adding a leaf of lime, ginger, rose, mint, strawberry or lemon to a cup of black or green tea is a sensual treat. Small leaves, such as "Prince Rupert," "Fingerbowl," or "Gooseberry" can be frozen in ice cubes and added to iced tea or lemonade.

Rose geranium jelly has long been a staple in the herbal panty. A small amount on a sugar cookie turns it into a special dessert. A bit added to whipped cream makes a lovely addition to puddings. Spread a thin layer over a warm apple pie, and the result is amazing.

The more one grows scented geraniums, and experiments with the variety of flavors and scents that are available, the more uses one will find.

Chapter 3:

MARCH

March came in like a lion, with blustery winds, heavy snow, and single digit temperatures. Callie had been watching the weather forecasts, and decided not to risk moving plants into the new shadehouse after all. She crossed her fingers that it would mellow in another week, counseled her plants to be patient, and told them to quit crowding one another. She was growing weary of carrying watering can after watering can throughout the house to keep the plants happy. She spent several hours a day watering, rotating pots to receive sunlight more evenly, raising the lights on the shelving as the plants grew taller, and keeping accurate records. If things worked, she'd be happy for all these notes next season, and if things were too small, she'd simply make an adjustment to the seeding schedule. Of course, next year she would have a greenhouse, but she'd probably still need to use the garage as well.

Callie made more plant signs and labels. She added material to her website, pleasantly surprised by the number of hits it had already received. She was working on an article called "Using Herbs for Spring Cleaning", and one on the "Herbs of Shakespeare" that she hoped to upload soon. She filled twenty-five hanging baskets with potting soil and planted nasturtiums seeds in them. She was out of space, so she hung them from the garage rafters. When they germinated, she'd have to move them somewhere to get light, but they'd be okay for now.

Earlier, she'd located the box with her birdfeeders. Since she couldn't get her shepherds' hooks into the frozen ground, she hung the feeders in nearby trees. Within minutes the birds had located them, and spread the word. Callie enjoyed watching the variety of birds that came to her feeders. When she noticed woodpeckers, she started spreading peanut butter on the bark of an old cottonwood tree near the house. In the evenings, she used a large needle to run yarn through stale bread, rolls, and bits of leftover fruit. Each morning, she'd hang the offerings in the tree and refill the feeders. As a reward, even more types of birds started visiting her yard. She knew that every bird that settled in her gardens meant fewer bugs next spring, so she did everything she could to encourage them.

Callie figured she had the first week of March to do other things before the merchandise started arriving. She pulled out her grandmother's old sewing machine and spent one entire day sewing tea cozies that would co-ordinate with the lovely teapots she'd ordered. At night she did the hand finishing, while watching college basketball on television.

She finished the March edition of the "Joyful Heart Herbs" newsletter, and e-mailed it to Cecilia to be printed. She'd included an article on chives since they'd be up and growing the instant the snow started melting. Her favorite cheesy sauce with chive and parsley was included with an explanation that it was delicious as a dip or poured over baked potatoes, steamed broccoli, or asparagus. A reminder of the Opening Day festivities, the farm's schedule and business hours as well as a registration form for the April classes were included. There was also an announcement about the new website. An article on the importance of fragrance plants and another on plants that attract butterflies filled page three. This issue also included directions to the farm and a photo of the interior of the Cottage along with a brief teaser about the tea corner.

Flint had stopped one afternoon after the wind settled and plowed her driveway and the new parking lot. He explained that his sister was worried that the UPS might not be able to make deliveries. Callie tried to pay him, but he refused saying he was "just doing what good neighbors do." The very next day, Callie was grateful for good neighbors when she heard the UPS truck rumble in.

Wicca beat her to the door, and was frantically scratching to get out. Callie grabbed her coat and ran to the Cottage just as Mike Shipley was giving the lab a handful of mini treats.

"Ready for some boxes?" he called.

"Ready and excited," Callie answered as he pulled up the back door of the truck. "Some of these are pretty heavy," Mike worried. "Sorry I couldn't get closer to your building."

"I found my sled," Callie laughed as she pulled it from behind the pumphouse. "It should slide pretty easy in this snow." She stacked the first two boxes on the sled and pulled it to the Cottage door. Mike followed carrying a third box. She unlocked the door and they stacked them inside.

"Wow, this place looks different. You've put in a lot of work since I brought those bee hives," Mike observed.

"I'm surprised you remembered since you deliver hundreds of boxes every week." Callie beamed.

"Did you do this artwork?" he asked, pointing at the sales counter.

"Oh no, a talented friend painted that for me."

"I'd say she's talented," Mike agreed. "Well, we'd better get the rest of those boxes." Two more trips completed her order, so she signed the electronic scanner, and Mike was on his way.

Since it was obviously going to take hours to unpack, Callie built a fire in the woodstove. She started opening boxes, checking packing slips, and learning to use her new pricing gun. When she had finally emptied the last box, she flattened the cardboard, stuffed the packing materials into a big plastic sack, and placed all the packing slips and invoices in a folder. The tea corner already looked distinctive with several teapots, teacups and saucers, tiny spoons, and strainers. A small kitchen area now had cutting boards, recipe boxes, tea kettles, spoon holders, rolling pins, and colanders all with herbal designs decorating the shelves and counters. The wall opposite the kitchen area was hung with wreaths containing colored eggs, artificial bird nests, and spring flowers. Small shelves contained sweet bird figurines that held votive candles, and right next to it she'd hung little bird themed wind chimes. There were goldfinches, wrens, bluebirds, and robins. LouAnn's landscapes covered two metal patches, and added a lovely sense of scale to the display. The other metal patches on that wall were successfully covered with birdhouses. It was coming together already.

The following week brought warmer temperatures and a good forecast. As the snow melted, Callie found there were some low spots on the shade house floor, so she hauled several wheelbarrows of stone onto the paths between the benches so her customers would not have to walk through standing water.

Afterwards, she began moving some of the hardier perennial plants into the shadehouse. Some of them already needed dividing, so she set up a workspace, moved bales of potting soil inside, and opened a carton of pots. Callie kept a clipboard handy to make notes of labels required for the plants she potted. When the plants were finished, she set up two kerosene heater in the aisles, breathed a prayer, and crossed her fingers. Even though they were perennials, since they hadn't been exposed to below freezing temperatures, they were susceptible to frost damage. While the weather was good, she'd better get more kerosene and bird feed.

Callie left Wicca in the truck while she stopped at the hardware for the wild birdseed and sunflower seeds.

"Haven't seen you in a spell," Jake stated. "Thought maybe you decided country life was too hard and left."

"Oh, no. I love country life. I've just been too busy to come to town."

"Really? I heard you'd had some more problems out there," he said looking puzzled.

"Oh? Other than that wind blowing away my 'No Hunting' signs, there hasn't been anything major," Callie replied innocently.

Jake actually offered to carry the bags to her truck, and she decided to let him feel macho thinking she might get some information.

"By the way, Jake, do you know anyone who does fencing?" she asked.

"Fencing? What do you need fencing for?" he asked suspiciously.

"Well, I think I'll get some sheep to keep the grass mowed. Maybe get some goats to thin out the brush in the woods. Environmentally correct, you know. I've read about those new high-strength five-wire fences. What do you think?"

Jake snorted in disgust, as he threw the first bag into the truck. "Goats! Fencing. Ruination of a perfectly good hunting area if you ask me!"

"Well, as I told you, I don't plan to allow hunting, but the land should be productive in some way. I can't afford to just keep it as a nature preserve although that would be great."

The second bag landed with a thud. Jake slammed the tailgate and stomped into the hardware.

Callie filled her kerosene cans at the local gas station and stopped at the print shop to pick up the March newsletters. She'd ordered a few more than last time to cover the requests coming through the website and the calls from folks who had picked it up at the library. She'd also asked Dinah if she could leave a stack at the restaurant and she left a few copies at her dentist's office. Next week she'd been invited to speak at a garden club in a near-by town, so she'd need a stack to take along there, too.

She dropped the newsletters at the house, put the birdseed into storage cans in the garage, and took the kerosene to the shadehouse. Melting snow was running off the Cottage roof making a merry tinkling sound in the new guttering. Just as she unlocked the door she heard the phone.

The beekeeper was on the line asking if he could bring the bees first thing in the morning. Callie had talked to him previously to discuss proper placement for the hives. After their talk she'd walked around the farm, finally selecting a sheltered spot that faced south. The creek ran behind it providing plenty of water for the bees. The sight was well away from customer areas, so she wouldn't have to worry about people being in the direct flight-path to the hives. Branches were trimmed away so the hives could sit in the shade during the heat of summer. Brush and tall grass were cleared from the area where the front of the hives would face. Then she had placed cement blocks levelly on the prepared ground and sat the hive bases on top. She assured the beekeeper that tomorrow would be fine, and that she would have her hives all prepared.

When she hung up the phone, the UPS truck rumbled in for what was becoming a daily delivery. Mike unloaded the boxes, and paused a moment to look over what had come in the prior shipment.

"My mom would love these teapots," he stated. "Will you keep one back for her birthday next month? She loves violets. It's her sorority flower."

"I'd be happy to save it for you, Mike," she promised. "I have a question for you since you go all over the county. Is there anywhere in the area that I can recycle all this cardboard? I don't want to burn it, but I'll have an entire Cottage full of cardboard if you keep bringing all these boxes!"

"Sure, there's a box factory in Eaton that takes cardboard for recycling. Let me draw you a map," he offered.

"That's great," Callie said thankfully, walking him to his truck. She waved as his truck left the farm, already planning a trip to Eaton.

Callie was deeply engrossed in unpacking boxes when she heard an odd sound. Wicca growled, walking toward the farmhouse uncertainly. Callie grabbed her jacket and followed. Just before she reached the road, Wicca started barking frantically and streaked toward the house. Suddenly a car came shooting out of her driveway. Callie was startled, but managed to see two men in the car. One had dark shoulder-length hair and a scruffy beard. The other man was blonde with glasses. She didn't recognize either one, but as the car sped past she noted the license plate was out of state.

Her television sitting in the middle of her driveway was the first clue that something was seriously wrong. The front was smashed. "That explains the odd sound," Callie thought as she entered the back door.

Her house was a disaster. Kitchen drawers had been dumped on the floor. A quick glimpse into the living room revealed slashed and tipped over furniture. Callie ran into the studio and dialed "911."

"I've been robbed!" she told the dispatcher. "Two men in a gold car just trashed my house. They headed south on Center Road. It was a blocky looking small car with out of state plates, gold with red lettering. I don't know what state."

The dispatcher told her to stay on the line, relayed the message, and took her name and address. "We'll send a deputy right out," he promised.

Callie went outside to wait. She just didn't feel comfortable remaining in the house. Once again she felt stupid and blamed herself. She should have locked the doors after she'd unloaded the birdseed but she'd intended to come right back after she unloaded the kerosene. She paced back and forth, stopping by the broken television set.

"Darn, darn, double darn!" she vented. She could hear the sound of a distant siren coming closer. Within minutes, Deputy Wright's patrol car screeched to a halt beside her.

"Are you okay?" he asked as he jumped out of the car.

"Yes, I'm fine. I was over at the Cottage when Wicca let me know something was wrong. We heard the television drop and I started jogging toward the house, so I saw them leaving. The house is a mess," she added.

Before the deputy could respond, a call came over his radio. He picked it up, listened, asked the dispatcher a question or two, and then turned toward Callie. "Think you could identify the car?" he asked.

"I think so. I got a pretty good look at them," she said.

"Climb in. We're going for a ride," he ordered.

"Stay, Wicca. I'll be right back. Right back," she assured the lab.

She climbed into the car and fastened the seatbelt as Deputy Wright hit the gas. As they were shooting down the road, he explained.

"A Ball State canine policeman that lives in Heartland was on his way to work. He had his radio on and heard the call. Looked around and realized a car matching the description had just crossed the road in front of him. He pulled them over and back-up has already arrived"

They'd just crossed Highway 28 when she saw half a dozen patrol cars parked in the driveway and along the road in front of a brick ranch house.

"That looks just like the car I saw," Callie observed.

"Don't say anything unless I ask you to, okay? Stay right by my side," he requested.

They climbed out of the car and walked toward the assembled group of officers. Deputy Wright exchanged several greetings as they approached. The two suspects were lying on the driveway, face down, wearing handcuffs. The man with long, dark hair turned his head toward Callie. In that moment, she understood the phrase, "If looks could kill...."

"Do you recognize anyone here?" the deputy asked.

"Those are the men I saw leaving my house," she stated calmly.

"Okay, officer, you can open the trunk."

"Hey you can't do that!" the man shouted.

"We have probable cause," the officer answered.

"We were just helping a friend move some of his stuff," the man argued.

"Step over here, Callie. See anything familiar?" Deputy Wright asked.

"That's my stereo. It looks like my power tools. That's my suitcase."

"I tell you those are my friend's things. We're just helping him move," the tattooed man argued.

"If you turn it around, you'll see that one wheel is missing. And if they didn't take it out, there's a paper in the inside pocket giving emergency phone numbers for the credit card office and my bank," she instructed.

One of the officers turned on a video camera and recorded the actions of a second officer as he turned the suitcase around, opened it, and pulled a paper out of the inside pocket. The officer held it up, so the video camera could record the writing on the paper.

"Read them their rights, Bill," Deputy Wright suggested. "That's all we need for now. I'll take you home," he said softly.

Nothing was said on the trip home. Deputy Wright seemed to sense that Callie needed some time to process and recover. When they arrived, he contacted the dispatcher and asked for a crime scene officer to meet them at the farmhouse.

When they went inside, Deputy Wright whistled. "Wow, looks like they were looking for something," he surmised. He pulled over a chair with the words, "Sit for a minute. I'll look around."

Wicca came over and laid her head in Callie's lap. Stroking the dog seemed to calm her nerves and organize her thoughts. By the time the deputy had returned to the kitchen, she had filled a kettle with water and put tea leaves into a teapot.

"It's pretty messy. I need you to stay in this room until the crime scene officer arrives. Normally, I'd have you look around to start listing what's missing. In this case, it looks like everything they took was still in the car, so you should get it all back in a day or two," he explained.

"Why did they tear everything apart? Dump all the drawers? I don't have anything that's really valuable," she wondered.

"They were in a hurry. Probably looking for things they could sell quickly, or pawn-jewelry, guns, computers, small electrical stuff. Hoping for some cash, of course," he stated.

Callie had just poured the tea when the crime scene officer arrived. Callie could hear the two officers conversing as they moved from room to room. When they returned twenty minutes later, the officer photographed the kitchen.

"Just one question, Callie. Could you come upstairs a minute?" Deputy Wright asked.

Callie followed him up the stairs noting with dismay the slashed sofa, the empty studio desk, and every floor littered with her belongings. When they reached her bedroom, Deputy Wright indicated the dresser.

"That yours?" he asked, pointing to a huge shiny knife. The blade was ten inches long and curved to a point. It was thick with a heavy looking handle. Callie took a step backward and shook her head.

"I didn't think so," he nodded.

Callie looked around the room. The mattress had been flipped over, all the drawers had been dumped, and her closet had been ransacked. The door to the spare room had been opened, but nothing seemed to be out of place there. At least one room had been spared.

As she passed the bathroom, she could see broken bottles in the sink and on the floor.

They returned to the kitchen. "Not hers." Deputy Wright stated. The other officer returned upstairs, and came back with the knife inside a plastic bag. He attached a label before he placed it in a briefcase.

"We're finished here. You'll need to call your insurance agent. I'll write this up as quickly as possible and send them a copy of the report. Don't change anything until your agent gives you the okay. You did a good job. Good description, stayed calm. You should be proud of yourself, Ma'am,"

Callie thanked the officers. After they left, she put a can of soup, a can opener, some crackers, and a saucepan into a bag. She took a sleeping bag from a closet, grabbed Wicca's bowl and some food, and loaded them into the truck. She filled a jug with water and picked up a couple of books. She'd already decided to spend the night in the Cottage.

Callie spent a restless night in the Cottage. She'd tried to read but couldn't concentrate. Her small CD player was still under the sales counter, so she put on her favorite arias and made chamomile-lavender tea. Eventually, the music, the tea, and the devotion of her lab comforted her. At some point she dozed, but woke well before sunrise to put her restless energy to use by putting the beeswax foundation into each frame of her beehive supers. She stopped mid-project mid-morning to meet her insurance agent to survey the damage at her house. He took some pictures, took some notes, and said she could start cleaning. If she wanted to have a professional service come, she should supply two estimates. Callie thanked him, closing and locking the door after he left. She leaned against it, surveying the chaos, and feeling drained when the phone rang.

"I just heard," Suz's voice came over the line. "Oh, Callie, I'm so glad you weren't in the house when those robbers came! Can you just imagine? You might have been stabbed!" Suz's voice had risen higher with each word.

"Calm down, Suz," Callie suggested. "I'm fine, but my house is an absolute mess. My karma must be really messed up. That's twice I've been robbed in three months!"

"Well, don't you worry about a thing. You just relax. I'll be right over with breakfast."

Suz arrived only moments later bearing Styrofoam cups of hot chocolate and a box of Dinah's muffins. After giving Callie a long hug, she clucked like a mother hen. "You need a hot shower and a good night's sleep, girl," she stated, pulling the cups and paper plates from a bag.

"Well, I can't do that now. The beekeeper is on his way with my bees, and I still have some sheets of foundation to put in. Besides my bathroom is a health hazard at the moment," she moaned.

"Okay, first things first," Suz stated. "Just show me what to do." Callie smiled for the first time since she'd found her television in the driveway. She got a second hammer from the tool box in the garage and led the way to the Cottage. They finished nailing the final sheet of beeswax into the last frame just as the beekeeper arrived. He'd brought a trailer and a large cart. After removing the straps from the hives, he slid the first one onto the cart. Together, the beekeeper and Callie wheeled the hive to the site she had selected.

"It looks perfect," he stated. "If you don't mind, we'll swap bases so we don't disturb the bees so much."

"That's fine," Callie agreed. She could see a piece of wire mesh stapled across the space between the super and the base.

"You'd better move back just in case I drop them," the beekeeper advised. Callie had not thought to put on the new bee suit and veil she'd ordered.

She needn't have worried. He slipped the base onto her cement blocks so smoothly that the bees in the hive barely murmured. They were slightly more disturbed when he quickly removed the temporary top, which he replaced with one of Callie's new supers. He added her new top with the protective metal covering. The process was repeated with the second hive, during which Callie was able to gather further information. She was instructed to leave the mesh on until lunchtime, so the bees would have time to settle from their trip. They would be exploring their new space and making plans to expand into her new supers, he assured her.

Callie thanked him. He loaded his equipment and departed with the check for the bees in his pocket. Callie felt it had been a good investment. Because he was interested in seeing her succeed with his bees, he would be a good resource.

She looked for Suz at the Cottage but there was no sign of her. She locked the building, sighed, and trudged toward the house. She'd better start the clean-up process. It was going to take days.

When she reached the house, she saw two familiar trucks and a car in her driveway. As she entered, the soundtrack from "The Big Chill" was blaring from a stereo. Inside, she saw Suz bouncing to the rhythm as she loaded solid dishes and tableware into the dishwasher and placed broken dishes into a box on the counter.

"Knowing your crafty notions, I thought you might want these for mosaics," she yelled above the music, nodding at the broken pieces of china.

Callie looked around the room. There were already several boxes sitting along one wall, and one large trash bag leaning against the table leg.

"Go on upstairs and hit the shower," Suz advised. Two big tears rolled down Callie's face as she hugged her friend. Then she went upstairs as instructed. The bathroom was spotless although the medicine cabinet was now empty. Two unfamiliar towels, a washcloth, shampoo, and a bar of soap were lying beside the sink. Cecilia came to the door, wearing a pair of overalls, a scarf tied around her head, and rubber gloves.

"Suz called and said she needed some help. Gave me a list of things to bring. I hope we have everything," she said soothingly. "Take a long shower, and then you can supervise the troops."

Callie peeled off her clothes and stepped into the gleaming shower. She let the hot water and suds wash away her worries. She silently gave thanks for her good friends. By the time she came out, LouAnn was coming up the stairs.

"These just came out of the dryer," she stated. "I know I wouldn't want to wear anything those rascals touched, so I'm washing everything that doesn't say 'Wool' or 'Dry clean only.' That okay with you?"

"Fantastic," Callie replied. Within minutes, she had dressed, braided her hair and joined Lou Ann in the bedroom. Together they remade the bed with clean sheets, wiped out drawers and re-filled them with Callie's cleaned clothes. Cecilia brought in a basket of books.

"Did you have these in alphabetical order, or anything?" she asked.

Callie shrugged, "Don't worry about it. Just get them off the floor for now. I'll sort them later."

"You might want to check in with Sandy. She has the greenest thumb, next to you of course. She's trying to repot all the plants that got dumped but she's not sure which label goes with which," Cecilia added.

"I can finish up here," Lou Ann assured her.

Callie joined Sandy in the dining room where her friend was gently picking up plants from the floor.

"Some of them have great root systems, so they are in good shape. A few got broken and one flat of babies is a mess. I did the ones in the living room first. They're resting in the garage, but I'm not sure I got everyone grouped back in the correct flat," she said sadly.

"Hey, however they are they're better off than they were this morning lying all over the furniture and the floor," Callie said. "Let's finish these, and then we'll check the ones you did. Thank goodness they didn't tip over the shelves in the spare room or the garage, or I'd be out of business."

"That's right. Look for the positive and move on from there," Sandy advised with a hug.

"Sounds like something my grandmother would say, and it sounds like good advice," Callie smiled.

They finished potting the plants that could be salvaged. Callie saved some broken branches, hoping to save a few cuttings that would root. Once the ladders and shelves were standing upright again they replaced plants and moved to the next room. The sound of the vacuum mixed with Suz's singing floated in from the kitchen.

As Callie and Sandy carried plants to the garage to recover, Suz announced that the kitchen was finished, and she'd phoned for take-out. Cecilia said she was ready to kidnap the vacuum and did. Soon the great sucking sound was coming from the study. The smell of pine and lemon cleaning products filled the air.

"I know a woman in Montpelier that does great upholstery if you want to do the sofa. Sometimes it's just cheaper to get a new one, but maybe this one has sentimental value," Sandy offered as they re-labeled the plants she had potted.

"I don't know yet. My mind seems to be frozen. I just feel so violated, so vulnerable," Callie admitted.

"That's common in victims. Your security blanket has been ripped off. You probably feel like it's your fault, but you shouldn't. Criminals are going to find a way to get what they want. If you'd locked the doors, they would probably have broken a window. It will take some time to feel solid again. I deal with victims all the time, nearly every day, so believe me," Sandy advised.

A voice came through the back door. "Pizza delivery!" he called.

"I've got it," Suz yelled. "Come and get it while it's hot!"

The five friends gathered around the table in the now spotless kitchen. Everyone ignored the boxes of broken dishes, lamps, and pictures. There would be time to sort them later when Callie was ready.

"I don't know what I'd have done without you," Callie said as she looked around the table at each one.

"You'd do the same for any of us," Sandy said.

"I don't want you to give up and move," Cecilia teased. "I need your business!"

"Yeah, you have to teach me how to keep a plant alive," said Suz. "I figure we'll just trade my cleaning for some free lessons some day."

"Hey, we had to clean up the place so you'd have time to test this month's recipes," LouAnn stated. "This pizza's not bad, but it's not as interesting as the dishes you think up." Everyone laughed, and chatted.

It was after four o'clock as they cleared up the lunch dishes. Callie had already begun to think how silent the house would be when they'd all gone home. She wasn't sure she was ready to stay in her violated home alone. She needn't have worried.

"We're having a sleepover!" Suz announced.

"I've got the movies and the popcorn," Sandy added.

"Our spare television and DVD player are in the back seat of my car," Cecilia answered.

"Before we do anything, we're having a house cleansing ceremony," LouAnn announced. "We have to get rid of any lingering evil spirits. Remember I'm part Cherokee. We believe in those things," she said solemnly.

"You didn't think we'd let you spend your first night here alone, did you?" they smiled.

Callie was overcome with emotion. She and LouAnn walked over to the shadehouse to gather some bits of white sage from one of her stock plants. They checked the bee hives and Callie apologized to the bees for being late as she removed the screen mesh. The two women retreated, watching as first one bee and then another cautiously left the hive.

"Those are the scouts. They'll locate water and come back to the hive to tell the others," Callie explained.

They stopped at the Cottage to get packages of frankincense and myrrh. Callie had ordered these resins as well as several other traditional herbs and spices for potpourri and incense making for the shop.

When they returned to the farmhouse, Suz, Sandy, and Cecilia had all had showers and were dressed in their nightwear.

"LouAnn said the ceremony would be more effective if we all wore clean clothes," they explained.

"Right," LouAnn nodded. "You shower next, Callie, while I get the rest of the things together."

With the others' help, LouAnn located salt, a wooden bowl, a glass bowl of clear water, and a small metal plate. She wove stems of white sage with some sweet grass she'd brought with her and tied them with cotton thread. By this time, Callie entered the room carrying a white candle and matches.

"Your turn," Callie said to LouAnn.

While they waited, Callie drew a kettle of water and put it on the stove. She added a large handful of marjoram, another of rosemary, and a third of bay leaves. She added seven cinnamon sticks, a cover, and said, "We'll have to wait for this to come to a simmer." She pounded equal parts of frankincense and myrrh to a powder. A charcoal disc was placed on a metal plate. The powdered resins were sprinkled on top.

Callie put a white cloth on the coffee table and arranged the white candle, the bowl of salt, the bowl of water, and the metal plate around the center. When LouAnn came down, she poured the fragrant infusion from the kettle into five small bowls. Callie opened the front door and several windows. They all move to stand around the coffee table.

"We're lucky there's a waning moon. Too bad we're not all wearing white, but we have good hearts and positive energy, so that should help," LouAnn stated.

Callie lit the white candle and the charcoal. Soon the pungent scent of incense filled the air. "Everyone think positive thoughts, and picture all the evil spirit and negative energies flying out the windows," she instructed. She passed her hands slowly over the elements on the table, repeating three times, "I charge you, tools of the elements, to sweep my house clean of all ill." After the third time she added, "This is our will, so mote it be!"

LouAnn lit the smudge stick she'd constructed of sweet grass and white sage. When it caught, she blew out the flame, leaving a trail of slowly curling smoke. She repeated a Cherokee chant in a low voice as she led the group from room to room. The other women each carried a bowl of infusion. As they entered each room, they sprinkled all the pieces of furniture with droplets from their bowls. As they left each room Callie said, "I banish evil and negativity." When they had finished each room including trips to the garage, attic, and basement, they sprinkled the windowsills of the open windows and solemnly closed them. Everyone went outside, pouring the remaining infusion from their bowls around the door's framework and over and around the front steps. When the group returned inside, Callie pulled the door shut and smiled.

"That should do it," LouAnn said.

"Thank you, all of you," Callie said, with tears glistening in her eyes.

They popped corn, made hot chocolate, and watched sappy, romantic movies. They helped Callie fold, staple, address, and organize her newsletters by zip code.

"Boy, that sure went faster than when I do it by myself," Callie observed.

"I thought it was fun," Cecilia said.

"Me, too," Suz agreed, "Why don't we help Callie with her newsletters every month while we do our taste-testing? Seems like a fair trade for all the cooking she does and groceries we eat."

The others agreed. Callie brought out ice cream, and they ate and talked until the candle burned out. Then they all slept soundly in sleeping bags on the living room floor.

A brilliant sunrise had occurred hours before as Callie rose and put the kettle on. She'd started making omelets when Suz came in to pop bread into the toaster. "Do I smell coffee?" Sandy said hopefully as she entered the room.

"Only in your imagination," Cecilia countered sleepily from the doorway.

"I'll start the coffeemaker," Callie offered. Cecilia moved to the counter and finished grating the cheese Callie had started.

LouAnn came bouncing in the back door, her cheeks rosy and her eyes glowing. "Come on out, you sleepyheads. You gotta see this!" The women slipped on shoes, grabbed their coats, and followed LouAnn around the house to the front door. They all gasped in pleasure. All along the front steps where they'd poured the last of their protective infusion were clusters of bright gold, deep blue, and purple crocuses.

"They're beautiful," Cecilia cried.

"That stuff's more powerful than I thought!" said Sandy. They all laughed, hugged one another, and hurried to the warm kitchen and a hearty breakfast.

After the women left, Callie checked her bees. All seemed well although none were leaving the hive since the temperature was not above fifty-five degrees. In the shadehouse, she spot-watered the few plants that needed it and checked the Cottage.

She returned to the house, made a list of all the plants that had been destroyed, and then seeded peat pots of arugula. Flats with rows of chamomile, parsley, cardinal climber, calendulas, ammobium, gomphrena, and lots of varieties of basils followed. As it always did when she was working with plants, the hours flew. When she watered the plants in the garage, she noticed that some of the primroses, pansies, and violas she'd seeded were getting buds. "Hurry girls," she told them, "it's only two weeks until the party starts!"

The following day was filled with a trip to Indianapolis for another load of pots and potting soil. She met her best friend, Beth, for lunch at their favorite restaurant. Callie filled Beth in on everything that had been happening. They'd talked regularly on the phone, of course, but Callie had waited to tell her the most upsetting aspects of all the events in person. She didn't want Beth to worry. She and Bob were expecting their first child in mid-summer. Beth filled Callie in on all the news from her old town. Since they had taught at the same school, Beth could tell her how some of her favorite students were faring.

"Everyone misses you," Beth said. "Maybe you should think about coming back. I know the school board would hire you for the first opening. You might even take my class if I decide not to go back next fall. I'd love to stay at home with the baby, plant a big organic vegetable garden, and start quilting more."

"I miss our quilter's group and all the other ladies at church," Callie admitted. "But, I've invested so much in my new place. It's MY baby. I need to watch it grow and to nurture my little business. I can see it all in my mind and I have this strong urge to make it happen."

Beth understood, and they parted with hugs and promises to meet more often. Before she left the city, Callie visited a couple of wholesale plant businesses to replace as many of the plants that had been destroyed as possible. She wished she knew what kinds of plants her customers wanted. When she'd started looking at property in the area in November, gardens were already finished. Of course, she could see stalks of departed sunflowers, hollyhocks, and brown mounds of mums, but that didn't tell her if people wanted fragrant plants, everlastings, the common, or the unusual. She had decided to grow the plants she wanted for her own gardens, the plants she liked best, and some that industry newsletters said would be featured in the spring gardening magazines. She just hoped her new customers wanted some of the same things.

She also picked up a few beautiful Rex Begonias, some flats of fragrant stock, and ivies. Callie loved combining pansies, primroses, and sweet alyssum in early spring planters. Fragrant stock would provide height and survive frosts as well as the others. It came in luscious pastel colors that would compliment the pansies and primroses. The begonias would make wonderful houseplants until the weather was warm. Then they would be perfect for shady patios or porches. Ivy would trail and help soften the stiff effect of the begonias' red, green and silver splotched leaves in combination planters.

Her final stop was at two garden centers to see what they were offering and their price ranges. She mentally compared "Joyful Heart's" new displays with theirs and felt satisfied that hers were well-designed and thoughtful. All in all it was a successful day, and it had taken her mind off all the problems at her new home.

The following days were filled with opening cartons and pricing merchandise. She found herself looking forward to the rumble of the UPS truck. Not only did it feel like Christmas every day, but she enjoyed the brief visits with Mike Shipley. She observed that Wicca seemed to be able to hear the truck before it hit the intersection over half-mile away. Wicca could be sound asleep in front of the woodstove, but she'd suddenly jump up, and run to the door begging to go out. Callie found that if she moved quickly, she had time to run a comb through the front of her hair, add a bit of lipstick, and pour a cup of tea for Mike before he arrived. They'd unload the boxes together, joking and laughing. Every day, Mike would tease, "Isn't that little Cottage full yet?" He was amazed at how much inventory it could hold.

When the boxes were all inside, he'd walk around the Cottage drinking his tea and marveling at the displays Callie was putting together. "You really have a good eye," Mike observed. "When you did all this shopping, could you take items from one showroom to another to match the colors?"

Callie laughed, "Nope. They won't let you do that. I just try to remember and cross my fingers. I did take a few paint chips with colors I thought I wanted to use. Problem is, I couldn't find merchandise to go with some of them, so I had to start over for some displays."

"Well, I think it looks great. By the way, my mother loved the newsletter I gave her. She asked if she could have some more copies for her garden club," Mike stated.

"Absolutely," Callie assured him. There was silence for a bit as Callie placed a stack of newsletter in a bag. Then Mike said, "It does look like the Cottage is about full. I suppose soon I won't need to stop. You won't be getting more boxes forever."

Callie thought she detected a note of disappointment in his tone. "Oh, I'll still be getting some shipments now and then. I ordered a few deliveries for the next four months, so there'd be something new for customers to come to see. I'll also need to re-decorate the shop once spring is past. You know, take out the daffodils and bird nests and put in some mid-summer décor."

She refilled his tea cup, and then added shyly, "I know you have a schedule to keep, but if you have time, you could always stop in for tea. And we'll be adding cookies or something herbal every day once we're open. Wicca would miss you and all those treats you give her if you stop coming."

"I'll keep that in mind," he smiled. He took the bag of newsletters and his tea, whistling as he walked back to his big brown truck.

Mike had been correct in his assessment that the Cottage was full. Callie placed a few final touches on the displays, added some nicely lettered signs, and stocked the little closet with disposable cups, napkins, small paper plates, and trash bags. She had a basket with give-away prizes for her first customers ready and newsletter sign-up sheets already printed.

Her parents had visited to see how things had progressed. Callie was thankful that her house was spotless, although overwhelmed with shelves and tables filled with plants. Her mother was amazed at the number of plants she had produced. They admired the merchandise she'd stocked and the artistic displays. Her father inspected the pumphouse, the changes to the Cottage, and agreed that Trev knew what he was doing. Before they left, her father surprised her with a lovely plant cart he'd made, completely equipped with lights. She could use it in the Cottage to display a few culinary herbs and tender plants that would be good houseplants. Other than getting change for the cash register the shop was ready to open. Now she needed to concentrate on the plant sales area.

Today was March 21st, the official first day of spring. Callie seeded peat pots of larkspur, poppies, Job's tears, flax, and cotton. Then she seeded rows of sheep phlox, borage, cleome, mignonette, and tithonia into flats.

The temperature was fifty-six degrees and it felt almost balmy. The bees were out and about. Since the sun was shining so brightly the shadehouse, covered in two layers of plastic with an insulating layer of air in between, was so warm that Callie didn't need a jacket. She propped the door open and soon the few blossoms that had appeared on the earliest primroses and pansies were being visited by honeybees.

She was placing stakes containing her carefully made signs into their proper pots when she heard the shot! It sounded so close, reverberating through the air that Callie was certain it had been fired on her property. Wicca ran into the shadehouse leaning her quivering body against Callie's leg. Callie patted her head and spoke softly to assure the lab. Then she ran to the phone in the Cottage.

Deputy Wright answered almost immediately.

"Someone just fired a gun in my woods," Callie told him.

"I'm four miles away. I'll be coming past your woods on the other side, so I'll look for vehicles. Stay put," he ordered.

Callie shut Wicca into the Cottage, and skirted along the edge of the woods as it followed the creek. She would have a good view of the creek in case some one crossed it, and also of part of the path to the south if someone used it. She moved silently, watching her footing so she wouldn't trip or snap twigs, repeating her mantra, "Courageous… but cautious," over and over. When she'd found a good spot, she pressed her back against a tree. No one would see her silhouette against the light. She waited and waited, but she heard no noises and saw nothing.

After what seemed forever, she heard a vehicle and saw Deputy Wright's patrol car coming across the driveway that led into the woods. She stepped out of the trees and walked over to meet him.

"I thought I told you to stay put," he stated.

"I was careful. I thought maybe I could spot them leaving. Did you see anything?" she asked.

"No vehicles on the highway. Stay here. I'll go take a look. And this time, I mean it! Stay put," he warned.

"Be careful, Deputy," Callie said worriedly.

He touched the brim of his hat and headed down the path into the woods.

Several minutes later, she saw him return, talking on his cell phone and folding something that he placed in his back pocket.

"I called the conservation officer. There's another dead deer lying back there. They may have heard my car come in because they ran. Looks like two sets of prints going from your woods to your neighbors on the south. They didn't take time to gut the deer, but your signs are down again," he informed her.

"You stay at the Cottage. I'll be back," he said as he climbed into his car.

Callie returned to the Cottage as ordered, and made another pot of tea. She had not met the neighbors whose woods connected with hers. She knew that Little Joe Creek, which edged her back field, flowed through their woods and connected with Pumpkinvine Creek, which meandered through her woods. Pumpkinvine Creek formed her north boundary, flowed under the road just north of the farmhouse, and connected with Licking Creek. Their township was named Licking. She'd always wondered where the name originated. Maybe an old salt lick? She'd have to check some day at the local historical museum. Or, maybe the ladies at the library would know. She should probably read a local history of the country, just so she'd be able to answer questions for her out-of-county customers.

While she waited, she started a list writing the words "county history" at the top. Then she added chalkboard paint, plywood, screen door, and small bucket in a column. At the side, she sketched a wreath, making a list of materials she'd need. She planned to hang pretty spring wreaths on the Cottage and shadehouse doors, and place a bucket of flowers under the welcome sign. She wrote, "Create a vignette by the shadehouse to encourage plant sales" in a second column. "Add bows, maybe balloons? To the road sign" followed. She was surprised her mind was working so well under the circumstances.

She moved over to the window, relieved to see the deputy's patrol car pulling into the parking lot. Wicca rushed past her as she opened the door, heading for the woods. Callie called to her, but she did not stop. By then Callie had reached the car.

"Find anyone?" she asked.

"No one was home at the Parkers'. I didn't see any strange vehicles or fresh tracks," he said. "Let's go into the Cottage. I need to talk to you."

"Sit," he ordered.

Callie sat.

"I was actually headed over to see you when you called," he informed her. His voice had a serious tone that made the hairs on Callie's neck tingle. She looked at him expectantly.

"The fellow that robbed you? The one with the long hair and tattoos?" he started, "Well, he comes from a bad family, a big family in the next county. We pulled his rap sheet. He'd only been out of prison for five weeks when he robbed you. He's been in and out of jail all his life. Drugs, theft, battery. Problem is, he's kind of the big brother in his family. Lots of younger kids that look up to him; want to be just like him."

Callie swallowed the lump that was forming in her throat, and waited for him to continue.

"The knife we found? That changes the charge from simple robbery to theft with intent. Bringing a weapon into the residence indicates they were prepared to harm. Means a longer term, a lot longer term considering his record. The family isn't happy about it. They might not want you to testify," he paused letting Callie absorb his words.

"I don't want to alarm you, but you need to be watchful. Be careful, lock your doors, don't let strangers in, that sort of thing," he cautioned. "Maybe you could take a little vacation till the hearing."

"Not let strangers in? In nine days, I'm hoping to welcome LOTS of strangers in here!" Callie exclaimed. "I've just invested every penny I have into this business. I can't go on vacation. I've got to push every

112

minute till opening and pray for a hoard of strangers to come through that door," she said, her voice rising with each word.

"Ma'am," the deputy said quietly, "Take a breath, a real deep breath."

Callie sat, her hands clenched, and forced herself to take a few deep, cleansing breaths. "Deputy," she said quietly, "do you think there's any connection? I mean between the deer killings and the robbery?"

"I doubt it," he answered. "Of course, until we find out who's killing the deer, we can't be sure. But, the deer problem started right after you came here, right? And the robbers have a long history of being in trouble, but not for poaching. They are townies, so I doubt the incidents are related."

"We'll do our best to protect you, of course," he stated, "but our county just has a small force. I'll do some extra patrols past your place, and I'll ask the night officer to do the same. You have a cell phone?"

"No," she answered.

"Might be a good idea to get one. I don't suppose you have a gun for personal protection?" he asked, his eyes searching her troubled face.

"No."

"Lots of small business owners, especially those out in the rural areas do," he reported. "Might be something to think about."

"I don't think I could shoot someone," she admitted.

"Then better not get one," he counseled. "Sorry to bring you bad news. You've had a lot to handle in the short time you've lived here." The radio on his shoulder started crackling. He left the Cottage, and Callie could hear faint parts of a one-sided conversation.

Deputy Wright stuck his head in the door. "Gotta go, Ma'am. Keep your eyes open and try not to worry." He touched the brim of his hat politely, nodded as always, and climbed into his car.

Callie sat there for several moments until she realized she'd been wishing for the feel of Daniel's arms around her sheltering her from the world. Even though Daniel had never been the macho type, she'd always felt protected in his arms. She sat there longing for that feeling again. To feel safe and trouble-free, the scent of his aftershave filling her senses, the warmth of his body comforting. Her thoughts were interrupted by the sound of Wicca scratching at the Cottage door.

When Callie went to let her in, she discovered an orange hunter's cap dangling from her lab's mouth!

She took the hat from Wicca's grip, and searched it for a label. She hadn't really expected the hunter to write his name inside like a child going to camp, but she felt disappointed anyway. It was standard fare from any discount store. She laid it aside to give to Deputy Wright.

She'd just locked the Cottage door when the UPS truck roared into the parking lot.

Before she realized what she was doing, she ran to the truck and threw herself into Mike's arms.

"What's wrong, Callie" he asked worriedly.

"Oh, Mike, everything, just everything!"

"It can't be that bad," he said as he wrapped his arms around her. He rested his chin on the top of her head. Several moments passed before Wicca began whining and pushing against their legs.

"I think your dog is jealous," he stated.

"I think she's getting impatient for her treats," Callie managed a smile.

"Okay, Wicca, I'll take care of you first and then I'll take care of your mistress," he stated as he gave the lab a handful of treats. He grabbed Callie's hand and led her to the Cottage. Once inside, he hugged her again, asking her to tell him what was wrong.

Slowly, with lots of pauses to brush away an escaping tear, Callie explained first about the possible threat from the robber's family, and then about the third deer.

"Wow, that's a lot to handle at once," he said. "What can I do to help?"

"I don't think there's anything you can do. Just keep your eyes open as you drive past the area." Callie requested.

"I've been doing that since I first found out about the poachers," he informed her. "Do you have any family that can stay with you for awhile?" he asked.

"No, and I don't want to expose anyone else to trouble," she answered. She took a deep breath, "I'll be fine. I have Wicca."

"Yeah," he laughed, "Wicca, the ferocious guard dog. She's a lover, not a fighter."

They were interrupted by the sound of a vehicle. Mike looked out the window, "It's the conservation officer," he told her.

Mike had to continue his deliveries, but he promised to call her that evening and suggested she get a cell phone.

The conservation officer that had thrown her flat tire into her truck bed climbed out of a dark green SUV with a DNR logo on the door.

"Trouble again," he stated without preliminaries. "Point me in the right direction," he stated as he slid the straps of a pack onto his back.

"I didn't see the deer this time, but if you follow the trail north of the creek, you'll probably find it. Somewhere past the huge oak tree," Callie offered.

"Morgan gave me some general directions, too," he growled as he stalked off.

"Wow, that guy has an attitude," Callie told Wicca. She'd clipped the dog's leash on when the DNR officer had arrived. The lab was eager to go with him, but Callie doubted she'd be welcome, and might even get in the way. They went into the shadehouse where Callie could finish putting plant labels into newly potted plants. She'd be able to see the officer return easily through the clear plastic.

It was nearly an hour before he returned packing a deer in the framework on his back. He lifted the back door of the SUV and leaned backwards to drop the carcass into the vehicle. Then he pulled the pack straps from his shoulders and straightened.

When Callie and Wicca reached him, he squatted and took the lab's head in his hands.

"Beautiful animal," he said.

"Yes, she is. My best friend, too," Callie stated.

"That deer was a beautiful animal, too. Pregnant," he sighed. "As the landowner, I need you to sign this report. It simply states that you did not kill the deer yourself, and that you did not allow anyone on your property to hunt. Sign and date at the bottom," he instructed.

"Any clues?" Callie asked.

"Several footprints. The ground is getting soft. Looks like they left in a hurry. I followed them to the property line fence. Saw where they climbed over. Looks like they had an all-terrain four-wheeler waiting. Tracked the muddy tire tracks for a bit, but lost it in the creek. Parker kids have a four-wheeler course that they've laid out on their farm. Goes in and out of the creek. Poachers could have used any of the trails. I'll talk to the Parkers, but I'm sure they're not responsible. Nice people," he added. "Need to get this deer to the processor," he stated. "Nice, fresh killed. They'll make summer sausage for the poor."

"Didn't know you could do that," Callie said.

"New program," he answered. "Here's my cell phone number. Call me if you hear something. You get your tire fixed?"

"Same day," Callie answered.

"Glad to hear it. Old boy scout saying, 'be prepared,' still holds true," he offered as he departed.

Since two people had expressed the same plan of action, she decided getting a cell phone was a good idea. She closed the Cottage, got the truck, and drove into town. Wicca was delighted to ride shotgun as usual.

After getting the cell phone, she purchased the other items she'd listed earlier as well as more bird feed. Jake had the day off at the hardware, and she didn't recognize the older man that ran the register. She stopped at the library and checked out a copy of the "History of Bradford County". She stopped at the discount store to purchase some wired ribbon and paper lunch sacks for customers' small purchases. She wandered through the men's clothing section and just as she'd expected, found the same orange hats on display that Wicca had brought from the woods.

"We've had a rough day. We deserve a treat," she told the lab. She stopped at Dinah's for a piece of pecan pie to go. It was mid-afternoon, so the "geezers" had long gone, and the restaurant was nearly empty.

"Why don't you eat that here," Dinah asked. "I have a few minutes to spare, and I could use a break," she said as she slid the pie onto a plate. She poured two cups of coffee and led Callie to a table.

"Been hoping for a chance to visit with you," Dinah said. "Heard you had some more excitement today"

"How did you know?" Callie asked.

"Mike dropped a big carton of supplies off a little while ago. He seemed pretty concerned. Sweet guy. You could do worse," she eyed Callie speculatively.

"Oh, we're just friends," Callie protested.

"Really?" Dinah said doubtfully.

"I barely know him," Callie assured her.

"Sometimes it only takes a New York minute," Dinah countered. "I've known Mike for years," Dinah continued. "Never heard him sound so worried except when his dad took sick and eventually passed away."

Callie bent her head and took a big bite of pie before responding. "This is the best pecan pie I've ever tasted! Do you use corn syrup?" She was successful at changing the subject. Dinah launched into the merits of blending molasses and dark corn syrup rather than using just one or the other and the subject of Mike was dropped.

Back at the farmhouse, Callie sanded the edges of the plywood pieces she'd purchased and sprayed them with chalkboard paint. They would be great for announcing specials, giving planting advice, or posting daily schedules. Once they were dry, she painted decorative sprigs of lavender and floral designs around the edges that echoed the design LouAnn had used on the road sign.

She grabbed a pair of nippers, called Wicca, and headed into the woods, checking on the bees again as she passed. As she walked through the woods, she saw a few early wildflowers poking through the melting snow. She could see that the buds on many trees were swelling and Pumpkinvine Creek bubbled merrily on her left.

When she reached the oak she'd name her "Fairy Tree," she paused, noting that the melting snow had eradicated the last traces of blood from the second deer. She continued on and realized that once again her "No Hunting" signs had disappeared.

After snipping several branches of various lengths and textures, including a small branch of pine, she returned to the shadehouse. She set the pine aside, and wired several of the twigs into two branchy circles. Their fat buds added texture and interest to the basic structure. She added some light green stringy moss and a small bird nest to each. Then she glued some artificial pansies left from a Cottage display onto the wreath. A fat, luxurious bow and tiny colorful eggs glued into the nests complete the wreaths. Callie laid them aside. She'd fasten them to the doors on opening day.

She finished all the plant work for the day. By now the sun was setting and she wanted to be safely home before dark. She was not as comfortable walking back and forth from the Cottage to the farmhouse after sunset as she'd been before the deputy's warning.

Callie picked up a few supplies from the Cottage and returned to the house, carefully locking all the doors. She fed Wicca, and mixed up a kettle of chicken tortilla soup. While it simmered, she checked the plants in the garage, dining, and living rooms. She poured herself a glass of wine as she passed back through the kitchen and went to check her e-mail. There were several requests for newsletters and two requests for presentations in other towns. She responded to those e-mails needing replies, and pulled a reference book from the shelf. It took quite a while to find it since her books were no longer grouped by subject. She'd need to spend some time after supper re-organizing her reference library at least. All the fiction could just wait, even until next winter if need be.

She returned to the kitchen retrieving the sprig of pine she'd placed in her coat pocket. She carefully removed the needles and placed them in her mortar. It was a lovely old marble one Callie had found at an antique shop. She flipped through the pages of Magical Herbalism by Scott Cunningham until she found the list she wanted. Cinnamon bark, frankincense, myrrh, and sandalwood chips came next. She added leaves of mugwort and rose geranium that she pinched from plants on the windowsill. By the time she had pulverized the mixture, the soup was ready. She'd just finished eating when her phone rang.

"Joyful Heart Herbs", Callie stated.

"And just how joyful are you at the moment?" Mike's voice came over the line.

"More joyful than a second ago. Thanks for remembering to call," Callie responded.

"I've been worrying about you all day," he said. "All your windows and doors locked?"

"Yes, and I'm thinking of digging a moat around the house, just for insurance," she laughed. Callie was not sure whether she was feeling so much better because of the glass of wine she'd drunk on an empty stomach, or if it was the sound of Mike's voice. She was definitely feeling better.

"Did you get a cell phone?" Mike inquired.

"Sure did," Callie answered.

"That's good. Have you had anything to eat? Are you taking care of yourself?" he asked.

"Just finished a bowl of chicken tortilla soup with fresh cilantro," she lied.

"Sounds good. So you like Mexican food?" he probed.

"Love it," Callie replied.

"Want to go try out the new Mexican restaurant that just opened in Heartland sometime?" he asked.

"I'd love to," she said without hesitation.

"How about tomorrow night?" he invited. "I should be done fairly early. Pick you up at seven?"

"I'll be ready," she responded. She suddenly realized that she was responding very well indeed. Whether it was because she'd been so stressed out lately, or missing Daniel so much, or Mike's sweet, rumbly voice, she didn't know at the moment. Whatever the reason, her body was becoming warm and moist in all the right places.

They exchanged cell phone numbers before they hung up. Callie's mind said she was crazy for "wasting an evening out" when there was so much to do. Her business opened in only nine days! But even while her mind was arguing, her body was warm with anticipation.

Afterwards, she divided the herbal mixture she made earlier into one small portion and one very large portion. She placed the small portion into a white cloth and tied it with a red thread. The large portion was ground into a fine mixture. She added a bit of orris powder and rosewater to make a paste, and then shaped dozens of little cones. The cones were placed on waxed paper to dry.

She bowed her head and asked God for his guidance and protection from evil. She tucked the herbal amulet into her pocket. Some people might view it as a kind of witchcraft mumbo jumbo, but Callie believed God had placed all the plants, flowers, and especially herbs on earth for mankind to utilize in one form or another.

She'd done all she could for now. She spent the rest of the sleepless night organizing the books in her studio, with the white amulet of protection tucked safely into her pocket.

Later in the week Callie attended the Heart and Soil Garden Club monthly meeting. This time she felt more comfortable, paid her dues, and became an official member. She had taken copies of duplicate seed catalogs that had come in the mail and traded them for two she had not seen before. The business meeting was filled with the usual reports and another plea by the president to plan ahead for the club's plant sale in June. The local county extension leader gave a presentation on the Master Garden program and asked for the club's help in organizing a junior gardening program for area kids. After the meeting, Callie introduced herself and offered to help. She missed teaching and children, and if she could pass on the passion she felt for plants and gardening to someone else, she'd be pleased.

Throughout the following days, Callie was surprised at her level of uneasiness. She found herself listening intently to every vehicle that passed to detect if it were slowing down. Every unusual noise made her heart jump. Her mind replayed the deputy's warnings. She forced herself to do her usual Tai Chi routine hoping its rhythm and stretching of muscles would help her relax and focus on the things that needed to be done. She fixed breakfast and forced herself to eat even though she wasn't really hungry. She watered all the plants, and then potted primroses that were crowded in tiny pots into roomy four-inch pots. She gave the pansies and violas a watering with "Bloom Booster" fertilizer to encourage them to flower. She made signs for the new begonias. She called Josh Sparks to install better lighting around her front and back doors, including motion detecting lights for the house and Cottage.

One morning while the sun was shining, she worked outdoors mixing up a batch of hypertuffa and forming it into small mushrooms. Callie stuck a nail into each mushroom, burying the head into the stem and allowing the remaining two inches to stick out the bottom. The rest of the day was spent making the front of the Cottage look more presentable. Wheelbarrows of stone were added to make the path look better. Some of the pieces she'd prepared for an outdoor vignette were moved to the front of the shadehouse. The day of the opening baskets filled with flowering pots would go on the old laundry tub stand. The concrete birdbath would be filled with bloomers as well. She painted three wooden birdhouses in colors to match the primroses that were already blooming: bright purple, vivid yellow and deep rose. They'd hang on the shepherd hooks she'd bought for her birdfeeders earlier. That would add some height and a punch of color that would mimic the primroses. She pulled a purple gazing ball from the carton Mike had delivered earlier and added it to the display. It was stainless steel, so she didn't have to worry that the wind would knock it off the stand and break it.

Mike hadn't stayed long today, since he wanted to finish his deliveries as quickly as possible so he wouldn't be late picking her up for dinner. He'd teased her about the Cottage being full but she'd explained that these boxes actually were destined for the shadehouse. Bird feeders and small birdhouses like the ones she'd painted were hanging with the "Native Plants" sign and native plants inside. Several hummingbird feeders were suspended over the plants that attract hummingbirds. Whimsical fat frogs perched amid the tiarellas, lungworts, and hostas in the area designated for shade plants. Bumpy concrete toads hid beneath the pots of toad lilies. Interesting wind chimes made of various antique-looking kitchen items hung with flattened silverware that tinkled together in the breeze created by the fans hung over the culinary herbs. The weather had been good enough that she'd been able to move some hardy perennials outside to harden off. A deer made of grapevines stood next to one display, holding a sign that read "Deer Resistant Plants." Things were looking good and Callie felt confident that any customers who came would be happy.

She'd purchased several buckets, tubs, and old planters at the local antique shop in town. It was really more of a "Trash to Treasures" shop than expensive antiques, of course, but that was just what Callie had been looking for, trash that she could buy cheaply and turn into treasures with a bit of ingenuity, paint, and colorful plants. She'd filled old lunchboxes, cake pans, coffee pots, and saucepans with cooking herbs. Old buckets and even old children's toys had been planted with colorful pansies and primroses. Several tool boxes, old tins, and a small wagon had been planted with a mixture of succulents that were placed in the display of sun-loving, drought tolerant plants. She still had to put price tags on planters and make several more signs, but things were progressing nicely.

Next year, the Cottage would be surrounded by gardens. There would be rose bushes starting to leaf, daffodils in bloom along the path, and lots of perennials showing new growth when April 1st came again. This year, she had to be satisfied with things the way they were.

Although the lawn wasn't really a lawn yet, since the grass she'd seeded had not shown signs of sprouting, at least it was more or less mowed level by Flint's bush hog.

She hung a terra cotta "Green Man" on the pumphouse door. A tiered stand next to it would hold fairy plants. Realizing that if it were muddy customers would not be able to see the plants on the stand clearly, she extended the path to the front of the stand. Then she attached some bins to the side of the pumphouse that would hold fairy furniture and tiny trellises. Her batch of mushrooms would fill one bin once they'd dried and cured. She'd made a wonderful fairy house to sit on the stand along with a sample fairy garden. Hopefully, people would want to buy all the plants and furniture to make their own.

Callie had been checking her watch all day, and it was finally time to quit. She had decided to curl her hair. It would be the first time..... the first time since Daniel had left. Daniel hated her braid or a ponytail. He loved being able to play with her long curls, he'd said. "I love long hair, blowing freely like this," he'd told her one day as they'd walked along a lake. Mariah had short hair.

"Go figure," Callie thought. She was out of practice, so curling her hair would take more time than a quick braid. She locked the Cottage, fastened the door of the shadehouse, and headed for the house. Wicca romped ahead of her making the squirrels run up the tree trunks.

She was nearly to the back door when she saw something fluttering near its base. A piece of brown grocery sack was stuck to the ground with a knife. Callie paused and looked around, calling Wicca to her side. The dog ran up, nosed the knife, and looked at Callie as if to say, "This is new. Is this a new display, Boss?"

Callie walked over to the piece of paper. In black marker were the words "Don't show up at Cort!" Her knees shook as she leaned her back against the door. She reached for her cell phone and punched in Deputy Wright's number.

"Don't touch anything," he advised. "I'm on my way."

Callie walked over to the sunrise bench that her father had made for her. She breathed deeply and tried to feel his strength and wisdom. Nearby remnants of the former owner's flower bed were coming to life. Bright yellow daffodil buds were just ready to open in the next day or two. Normally, Callie would have bent down to study each one.

122

Now she just sat woodenly on the bench, her hands clasped around her protective amulet releasing a cloud of pungent fragrance.

Ten minutes later the patrol car pulled into the end of her driveway and stopped. Deputy Wright was talking into his radio as he emerged. He walked directly to her and joined her on the bench.

"Ma'am" he said, nodding as usual.

"It's over there," she said without preliminary greeting, nodding toward the back door.

"Are you okay? You look a little pale," he said. "I've got some coffee in my thermos." He reached down and touched her skin. "Your hands are cold," he added.

"I'm all right. It was a surprise. I thought I'd been listening so carefully all day," she frowned as she spoke.

"A little jumpy today?" he asked.

"A lot jumpy every day since you warned me about his family," she admitted.

"Well, let me look for tire tracks. You had your truck out today?"

"No, I walked over to the farm. I went to town yesterday," she replied.

"Anybody else come to visit you, deliveries or anything?"

"Not that I know of," she said thoughtfully.

"Did you come over for lunch?" he inquired.

"No, I worked at the farm all day. Skipped lunch," she told him.

"Then they could have been here any time," he surmised. He walked over to her truck to look at the tread. "Think you have another problem," he called.

Callie looked toward the Deputy, who had bent down to inspect a tire. It had been slashed. In fact all four tires had been slashed. Callie moaned in dismay. She couldn't afford four new tires at once. There were still eight days until she opened, so she couldn't expect any income until then. And, it was early in the season. She couldn't reasonably expect people to buy lots of plants the first part of April. Here in Indiana it sometimes snowed the first week of May! Well, at least she could walk to work! "Think of the positive and move on from there," her grandmother and LouAnn always said.

Deputy Wright had slowly walked down the driveway and back peering at the driveway. "Looks like a small car with old tires drove over your truck prints. Tops are pretty dry, so I'd guess it was sometime this morning," he estimated.

He walked over to the knife and placed it and the note in a large plastic bag he'd pulled from his pocket. "We'll have these dusted for prints, but they probably wore gloves," he stated. "Won't learn anything from the note. Looks like a standard grocery sack and marker."

"Well, we learned one thing," Callie observed.

"Yeah. They don't know how to spell 'court'," he replied.

They sat for several minutes on the bench. Deputy Wright had convinced Callie to drink some coffee. He filled out a report, and took pictures of the truck tires and the tire prints in the driveway. She'd asked if he knew if a court date had been set, but he hadn't been informed of one.

As they were talking, Callie's hands began to shake.

"They knifed my tires," she said shakily. "Do you think they would really hurt me, or Wicca, or do you think this is just scare tactics?" She was trying to remain calm and be strong, but a tear rolled down her cheek.

Surprisingly, Deputy Wright reached out to brush it away, his thumb remaining on her cheek.

"Probably just scare tactics, Ma'am," he said softly

"Guess I'm early," Mike called from the driveway.

Callie and the Deputy both jumped in surprise.

"I couldn't pull into the driveway. Your squad car's blocking it," he stated. "Something happen?"

"She's had some trouble," the deputy answered. "You staying for a while?"

"Mike is taking me to dinner," Callie answered before Mike could respond.

"That's good," Deputy Wright said slowly. He looked at Mike, then added, "Probably best if she has some company for awhile. I'll be going to finish my rounds, and then I'll file this report. Ma'am" He tipped his head in farewell, and touched the brim of his hat, as always.

Callie watched him lope down the driveway in that long, long stride of his.

Mike cleared his throat to gain her attention.

"What happened?" he asked. "Want to talk about it?"

"Would you mind if we didn't? I'm so sorry. I haven't even had time to change," she apologized.

"You look fine to me, Callie. I'm sure the restaurant is casual," he added.

"Just give me a few minutes," she requested. "I need to feed Wicca and wash my hands at least."

"Take your time. I'll bring my car in."

The food at the restaurant was delicious, and Mike coaxed her into having a marguerita made with fresh pineapple. He led the conversation, asking about the preparations for her big opening, telling her funny stories about things he'd delivered, and telling her about the vacation he was planning for next summer.

"I've always wanted to see the Rocky Mountains," he explained. "I haven't taken a vacation since my dad died. Always hated to leave mom alone, and she refused to come with me."

"The mountains are always gorgeous in the movies. I'd like to see them in person some day, too," she replied.

"You like movies?" he asked. This led to a long discussion of their favorite movies, favorite musicals, and favorite actors and actresses. Before they realized it, the employees were starting to stack chairs on the tables, all of which had emptied except theirs.

"I think they're hinting that they'd like to close," Mike said with a laugh.

"I can't believe how the time flew. You sure know how to make a girl forget her troubles," Callie smiled.

"That was my intention. Glad I was successful," he smiled back. He held her coat, and then put his arm around her shoulders protectively as they walked to his jeep in silence.

He took her home, parking so his headlights shined brightly on the back door. They could see Wicca looking through the window. He walked her to the door, saying reluctantly, "I'd asked to come in, but it's already pretty late. I have an early pick-up tomorrow, and I know you're on a tight schedule preparing for your opening. I had a great time, Callie"

"It was just what I needed. I had a great time, too, Mike," she answered.

He put his had under her chin, and tipped her face up for a brief kiss.

"I'll call you tomorrow. Take care, Callie," he said softly before he left.

Wicca's face was looking directly into hers when Callie opened her eyes the next morning. Sunlight was already streaming through the windows. She could see the branches swaying rhythmically in a blustery wind. She'd had a toss and turn night that hadn't included much sleep. Puffy bags and dark circles jumped from the mirror when Callie looked at her face. She fed the lab and let her outside to patrol for vagrant squirrels.

She used green tea bags for her morning cup of tea, and then lay on the sofa with the cooled bags on her eyes until Wicca scratched at the door She'd been thinking that at least she'd made the trip to Indy for potting soil and replaced the damaged plants before the truck was sabotaged. That was good. She had stocked all of the supplies she thought she'd need before opening. Of course, she'd still need some groceries to do all the baking for the big opening.

She let Wicca in, gave her a big hug and then checked her e-mail. Several more newsletter requests and an invitation to speak at the Master Gardener's group in Delaware County were mixed among her "spam alerts."

Since it was blustery, she dressed in several layers before she headed to the farm. She checked the Cottage, and everything looked beautiful. She listened to messages on the answering machine, made notes of calls she'd need to return, and pulled her CD player from the sales counter. Once in the shadehouse, she turned off one kerosene heater and set a kettle filled with water on the other. Callie rationalized that with the wind blowing she wouldn't be able to hear anyone sneaking around anyway. She'd have to trust Wicca to let her know if someone came. She plugged the CD player in and placed a disc inside. She'd chosen the soothing but complex music composed by the famous 12th century mystic and herbalist, Hildegard of Bingen. St. Hildegard was one of the first known women to write about the usefulness of herbs. In fact, Callie had a reprint of her text on healing plants that she was studying. Hildegard had not only written about plants but theology as well even though at that time only men were allowed to study that subject, let alone write about it. A special dispensation from the Pope was required before she was allowed to study and write. Hildegard's music was amazing as well. Composed for female voices, it was filled with joy and praise. Callie always felt uplifted and calmed by the lyrical phrases even though she couldn't understand a word of German! St. Hildegard believed that one should surround oneself with as much of the beauty God had provided as possible, and that one should sing every day to remain healthy.

While she listened, Callie put together the spring planters she'd planned. Fragrant stock in the center for height, pansies and primroses surrounding it, then sweet alyssum and ivy tucked around the edges to drape and trail. The color combinations were delightful, and she was soon lost in the music and her work.

"Hey there!" a voice shouted, "Nice music!"

Callie jumped at the unexpected voice and was relieved to see Sandy standing in the doorway. "Hey, yourself," she waved, as she leaned over to turn down the CD.

"I tried to call, but I guess you can't hear the phone out here, especially with the music," she explained. "Wow, it looks wonderful and smells terrific." Sandy wandered up and down the rows, reading signs and looking at the displays.

"Thanks! It's good to have another person's opinion. Think you'd have any trouble shopping here?" she asked.

"Only problem is that I'd want everything, and I'm not even a gardener," she laughed. Then she looked around. "So where are the shopping carts?" she asked.

"Shopping carts," Callie muttered. She'd been so engrossed in having things people would want, she hadn't thought about how they'd actually get them to the Cottage for check-out, let alone getting them to their cars. Suddenly it was clear that there would be traffic problems in the narrow Cottage door. A whole new set of problems entered Callie's mind. And only four days to solve them!

"Sorry, I didn't mean to criticize," Sandy said worriedly.

"Oh, Sandy, it was constructive criticism, and I appreciate your pointing it out. I hadn't even considered how people were going to handle their purchases," Callie declared. "I should have taken the time to pretend to be a customer myself. Maybe I would have noticed it," she said dejectedly.

"Better now than April 1st," Sandy offered cheerfully.

"You're right, of course. I just don't know a quick fix," Callie responded.

"How about buying some little red wagons? That's what some of the other garden centers have," Sandy proposed.

"That would help, and at least I could get them in and out of the Cottage door, but I think they are about sixty dollars each," Callie stated.

"We'd take them into the Cottage? Up the front step? There's not much room in there for people with wagons, Callie," Sandy said hesitantly.

"I know. You're right," Callie admitted. "I'll have to think of something else."

"What about having the cash register out here? Then the wagons wouldn't need to go inside," she questioned.

"I just don't know. I'd be hesitant to be out here, when the more expensive and breakable items are in the shop. One bottle of chamomile essential oil slipped into someone's pocket, and there goes my profit for the week," Callie speculated. "Plus the credit card machine is hooked up for the Cottage."

"Well, you'll think of something," Sandy assured. "The reason I phoned is that Mac thinks we should do a story on 'Joyful Heart's' grand opening. He assigned me to interview you and take some photos. We need to do it soon if you want it to appear before you open. And he needs your copy for your ads. Wants to know if you want to do some kind of coupon."

"I can get a couple of good shots in the Cottage, maybe one of the exterior with your pretty displays out front, too," she continued. "Then maybe one of you making these planters. Anything you'd really like to see in the newspaper?"

They spent the next half hour sipping tea and discussing the article. Sandy took several notes and started taking some photos while Callie returned to the house to tidy her hair and put on some make-up. Sandy had suggested she wear a plain top, to contrast with all the merchandise and plant material. Unfortunately, the Heartland Banner still only used black and white photos. Once the interview was finished, and the photos completed, Sandy departed with a promise to return the following day to "pretend shop." She'd go through the shop looking for missing price tags and see what kind of questions she might have about merchandise. Then she'd go through the plant sales area and do the same. Callie had already seen what a help another pair of eyes could be, so she readily agreed.

That evening, Callie worked on the handouts she'd have available for customers. She'd purchased some clear plastic containers made just for the purpose that she could hang in the shadehouse or in outdoor displays. A list of plants that attracted and fed butterflies was composed first. She rewrote a list of common culinary herbs with a few recipes that she had passed out at farmers' market. She pulled up the "basic guide to herb gardening" handout that she used in a recent talk for a garden club. The final sheet was suggestions for plants that repelled deer, or at least the deer ignored. She printed twenty copies of each one, and slid them into the containers. Then she printed an easy-to-read label and attached one to each lid.

She pulled up the menu she'd planned for opening day and made a list of the groceries she'd need. Since she had no clue how many people might come, she wanted to have plenty. If there were leftovers, she'd serve them to lucky customers the second day. If no one came, she'd put things in the freezer and use them up as she could. She planned to feature violas, those sweet little blooms that looked like miniature pansies. Every one of the colorful flowers had a tiny face. Folklore said the spring fairies painted each one. The spring fairies were called "pillywiggins." Callie thought they must have the most fun job ever, flitting around tapping the trees and shrubs with their wands, calling "Wake up! It's spring and time to grow! Wake up!" They did the same to the underground bulbs and all the other plants, until the world was filled with green and colorful blooms.

Callie's thoughts returned to the plans for opening day. She reviewed her schedule of talks, checked her notes, and made a list of supplies she'd need to gather together ahead of time. She'd placed a small table, and a few picnic benches at one end of the shadehouse. She wished it would be warm enough to have the makeshift classroom outside but she couldn't count on good weather. Better to be prepared for the worst even though it meant giving up valuable sales space. Hopefully, the talks would generate sales enough to compensate.

She completed a new job list for the remaining three days and started a list of problems that she must solve. It was overwhelming, with the stress of all the other troubles in her life. Dead deer, slashed tires, threatening notes, knives. What would be next? It was hard to concentrate.

Three days until April 1st. April Fools. She was feeling like a fool. Why had she assumed immersing herself in a new, complex, demanding life would make her forget Daniel? It certainly hadn't worked so far. She'd thought being in a new area where her mind wouldn't expect to see him sitting at the local coffee shop, smiling in the seat next to her at their favorite theatre, or waiting for her in the school parking lot after work would make him disappear. He still danced across her thoughts. She still ached for the sound of his voice, his laughter, and even his sarcasm. It seemed that the more problems she had, the more she wanted Daniel.

She forced herself to return to the plans for opening day. The menu would feature violas. Their traditional folk name was "Heartsease." That's just what she needed. Something to ease the pain in her heart. How appropriate.

As promised, Sandy came the next day to be a pretend shopper. Callie was surprised at the number of good questions she raised.

"Is this dish safe in the microwave?"

"Can I order four more of these, so I'd have a set of eight?"

"I like the blue, but can you get it in green?"

"Are the batteries for these candles hard to find?"

"Is this rug machine washable?"

"Are these fairies safe to put in a garden outside?"

"Are any of these plants poisonous to pets?"

"If I decide it doesn't match, can I bring it back?"

"I really like this. Would you take less for it though?"

Callie took notes of all her questions, adding a few of her own. What kind of policy should she have if a customer broke an item? Should she try to do special orders? Running a small business was more complex that she'd estimated.

They stopped for lunch, walking over to the farmhouse to wash up and fix sandwiches.

Sandy stopped in the driveway. "What's wrong with your truck, Callie? Oh, my goodness, your tires are flat. All of them!" she exclaimed.

"Yes, I know. It happened two days ago," Callie sighed.

Over lunch, Callie explained how the tires had been slashed. Sandy said she was sure the local tire store would be happy to bring new ones.

"I'm sure they would. But they might not be so happy when I couldn't pay for them," Callie sighed. "My emergency fund is getting low, and I have to keep enough in there for the next few mortgage payments, utilities, and kerosene for the heaters. I can't let my plants freeze just when it's time to finally sell them."

"Don't you think this is an emergency?" Sandy questioned. "You need transportation."

"I know. I'm just hoping I sell enough on Saturday to cover the tires. I think I can make it three more days. That's if I can get to the bank to get change for the cash register and to the store for the groceries I need."

"Consider it done. I can shuttle you around a bit. Or, I'm sure the tire store would be willing to set up a payment plan. You should at least check with them. They might even need to order them since you need four. It's a small store, you know," Sandy added.

"Maybe you're right," Callie admitted. "I'll call them."

The man, who came the next morning, driving a truck with the words "Heartland Tires" painted on the side, was one of the scruffy men she'd seen lounging outside the hardware the day she'd had the first flat tire accompanied by the writing on her windshield. Callie had nearly forgotten about that incident with everything else that had transpired. He wore an orange hat identical to the one Wicca had found.

"Looks like you have some enemies," he grunted as he knelt to read the size of Callie's tires.

"No, I just can't get my dog to stop chewing on them," Callie replied with a bit of sarcasm.

"Humph!" he said, as he spat a stream of tobacco juice onto the driveway. He walked around and inspected all four tires.

"Might be able to fix that front one for a spare. Rest of them are shot," he informed her.

"More like stabbed," Callie muttered under her breath. "Fine," she said aloud. "How much for two new ones?"

"Two? You can't run a truck on two tires!" He spat again.

"Well, if you fix one, and I put on the spare I have, then I can get by with two for now," she explained.

"I'll have to check with the Boss. He'll call you," he said with a glare, before he sauntered to the truck.

Callie shivered as she returned to the house. That guy was creepy. Wicca must have thought so, too, because she hadn't been friendly at all. She'd stuck to Callie's side like glue.

She finished the watering and gathered all the plants that would go into the plant cart in the Cottage together on the kitchen table. Lemon verbena, apple geraniums, patchouli, French lavenders, pineapple sage, and other beloved herbs filled the kitchen with delectable fragrance. She made sure each plant had a label, then made a sign that read "Delectable Houseplants....enjoy them now, treasure them always!"

She checked her closet to make sure she had the outfit she intended to wear for the big day ready to go. She went through her mail, checked her e-mail, and browsed through garden center supply websites for a solution to her plant moving problem. She had one standard nursery cart that she'd been using to haul plants from her truck into the shadehouse but it was too big to fit through the Cottage door. There was no easy answer.

Finally, she decided that since it was so early, people would not be purchasing that many plants on Saturday. They could carry a flat into the Cottage to check out. She'd come up with a solution within a week or two, but she didn't see any way she could solve the problem in two days. Even if she ordered something, it probably wouldn't arrive tomorrow, and most places didn't deliver on Saturday. None of the garden center supply places were nearby, and besides, she didn't have a truck with tires.

That afternoon Sandy came by to take her into town. First, she dropped Callie at the newspaper office to drop off her articles for April.

Lucille's hair had touches of yellow added to the pink and tiny yellow lemons hung from her ears. Today's T-shirt had a big lemon on the front with the words, "Squeeze me!" emblazoned in citrus green.

"Hey, Miss Callie," Lucille greeted her. "Dad's not in today."

"That's okay, Lucille, I just need to drop these columns. He'll need the first one on Monday," Callie said.

"Call me Lucy," the girl smiled. "Say, I've been wondering. I was reading the ad in today's paper. You're giving some interesting talks on Saturday. But, I was wondering who's going to watch your cash register while you talk?"

"Oh, my gosh, Lucy. I hadn't even thought of that. You're absolutely right!" Callie exclaimed.

"I could do it. I run the register here all the time and I know how to process credit cards, too," she offered. She seemed to sense hesitancy on Callie's part. "I could ditch the tongue stud, if that would help."

Callie considered her options for a moment then decided she really didn't have any.

"Can you be there by 8:30? Do you have transportation?" Callie asked.

"You can count on me," Lucy promised.

Callie walked to the bank for change, and then to the grocery. By the time she had checked out, Sandy's car was parked in front. As soon as Callie and her groceries were inside the farmhouse, Sandy said she had to run. Callie thanked her, and said she was looking forward to seeing Sandy's article in tomorrow's edition of the Heartland Banner.

Mike called that evening. "How's it going?' he asked.

"I'm elbow deep in cookie dough," she laughed. "I made my timeline and decided I'd better start tonight. I wish I could have sold tickets so I'd have an idea how many people to expect."

"Well, I've been telling everyone I've seen. Don't forget to set that violet teapot back for me," he added.

"It's already tucked away under the counter," Callie laughed. "I'm looking forward to meeting your mother and her gardening friends. Are they still planning to come Saturday?"

"You bet. Well, since you're busy, I won't keep you. I just wanted to ask if you'd like to go out Saturday night to celebrate your grand opening."

"Oh, Mike, I'd love to, but I'll probably be too tired to be good company if it goes well and I'm really busy. If I'm not busy, I'll be so depressed you wouldn't want to be in the vicinity."

"I'm willing to take my chances," he persuaded.

"All right, but let's keep it casual. No fuss, okay?"

"Your wish is my command," he said grandly. "Expecting any deliveries tomorrow?"

"Not that I can think of at the moment. I think everything has come except the lavender tea from England and the little music boxes that play 'Happy Birthday'" she mused.

A bing sounded in the background.

"That's my oven timer, Mike, I really have to go," Callie stated.

"I understand totally. Happy baking, Callie"

"Thanks for calling, Mike. Bye." Callie held on to the phone for a moment after Mike hung up. He really was a very sweet, very caring man. She found herself looking forward to Saturday night.

Friday was overcast, with a bit of sleet in the morning and a blustery wind in the afternoon. Other than checking things at the farm, replying to messages on the Cottage answering machine, clipping some chives, and grabbing the mail from her mailbox, Callie spent the entire day in the kitchen. She made an array of appetizers featuring asparagus, shredded carrots, and chervil. The chives were snipped onto canapés covered with spicy cream cheese. She decorated cookies, cheese balls and canapés with perky viola blooms. She baked tray after tray of chamomile nut bread, purple viola shortbread, and mint-laced brownies.

When everything had cooled, she arranged them prettily. She'd have to start carrying the platters over early the next morning. Without her truck, it would take a while. Everything was ready. Now she prayed for customers and good weather.

Chives

Sometimes when things are too easy or too common, we tend to take them for granted. Such is the case of the lowly chive plant. Since they are so trouble free, easy to grow in nearly any condition, and extremely abundant, we tend to overlook the contribution they can make to everyday meals. Maybe if they had been included in the Simon and Garfunkel hit as "Parsley, Sage, Rosemary, and Chives," they would be more often-remembered and respected members of the herb family!

Actually, chives are the most delicate flavor in the allium, or onion, family. They have been used throughout history and should be included in any Biblical garden. In addition to their flavorful leaves, chives should be valued for their lavender-rose blossoms which appear in late spring. These eye-catching spheres of color are wonderful when torn into little bits and added to salads or sauces. The whole blossoms can be steeped in white vinegar. After a week, the vinegar will turn a lovely rose-pink color and have the subtle flavor of chives. It is very tasty in salad dressings or stir-fry. The blossoms can also be dried for use in arrangements and culinary wreaths. Be sure to pick them just as soon as they are fully open but before seeds have formed for best color.

Chives are extremely hardy and easy to grow in average soil and full to part-sun. They are 12" perennials that self-seed easily. The leaves can be harvested at any time during the entire growing season. Simply select a few "strands" and clip them off near the base of the plant. They will soon re-grow. Clipping the leaves higher will result in brown tips, so it is better to harvest at the base.

Snip the harvested chives into small pieces with scissors over sour cream, yogurt, cottage cheese, cream cheese, or salads. Add them to salad dressings, over baked potatoes, steamed vegetables, or broiled meats. Toss them into stir-fried vegetables or over fresh-sliced tomatoes. Stir them into your favorite biscuit or bread dough, or add them to cornbread batter.

Chives are especially good with egg dishes, such as omelets or deviled eggs, or to brighten the bland flavor of macaroni and cheese or plain hamburger patties. Put two tablespoons of snipped chives into a stick of softened butter and freeze to use throughout the winter on rolls, meats, or freshly popped popcorn.

And just when you think you've tried everything, give another member of the allium family a try. Garlic chives! Also known as Chinese chives, these flat-leaved wonders have a mild garlic flavor. These make our favorite herbal vinegar and are fantastic in stir-fry. As easy to grow as common chives, these beauties are two feet tall with starry-white blooms in September. Just when the rest of the culinary garden is looking a little dull, the flowers burst into bloom. They can be used in the kitchen in similar ways as common chives. Garlic chives are a hardy perennial and self-seed easily.

Give both of these useful plants a space in your garden. Mine is planted near the back door where I can snip them quickly and return to the kitchen. They are so versatile you will want them nearby. Keep a pot on a sunny windowsill in winter, too!

Chapter 4:

APRIL

The wind blew the clouds away overnight, so the morning dawned clear and bright. The temperature was fifty-four degrees and sunny as Callie watered all the plants in the house, garage, and those in the shadehouse. She loaded the "Delectable Houseplants" from the kitchen table onto her big cart and pushed it over to the farm. The pretty plant cart her father had made was already in the Cottage, filled with blooming plants on both shelves. The touch of bright green plants with the sage green trim on the woodwork was perfect. She'd clipped some mint from a pot in the kitchen and rubbed it inside the cash register, a ritual that was supposed to promote good sales and prosperity. She hung a bunch of mint over the door as well. The practice probably came from shop keepers hanging mint in doorways and windowsills in the days before screening. The scent of the mints would repel flies and other critters. Callie imagined that those shops without insects to bother customers indeed did a better business and had more appealing merchandise than those without.

She carried the platters of food from the kitchen, filled the coffeemaker with water, and added jasmine tea to the percolator basket. She put out the small cards that identified each food and taped a sign that read "Jasmine tea, decaffeinated" to the coffeemaker. She garnished the buffet with small bouquets of pansies, tiny early fern fronds, and bits of ivy. The food area looked beautiful. Carefully wrapped extra platters of food were stored in the closet.

By eight o'clock, Callie was dressed in a lavender shirt with tiny lavender sprigs embroidered around the neck. Her cream colored overalls had lavender sprigs painted on the pockets. She added a darker lavender cardigan, a pair of lavender embroidered socks, and even a bit of purple eye shadow.

She plugged in the coffeemaker and reviewed the notes for her talk. At eight-fifteen, a bright yellow Volkswagen bug still sporting brown reindeer antlers with bright red bows on each side pulled into the parking lot. Lucy emerged wearing a subdued outfit of blue jeans and a navy blue sweatshirt that simply said "Peace". Her hair was covered by a pretty floral scarf and matching flowers dangled from her ears. As promised, her tongue was stud less. They spent a few minutes going over the basics of Callie's cash register and credit card procedures. Callie showed her where the small bags, larger bags, and bubble wrap for delicate items were stored under the counter. She also showed Lucy where the extra cups, napkins, plates, and platters of food were stored. She explained the newsletter sign-up sheets and told the girl to encourage everyone to sign up, including their e-mail address, if possible.

They went to the shadehouse, so Lucy could see where the price was printed on the plant labels. They were just emerging when LouAnn's pick-up truck pulled in.

"Great day for a Grand Opening!" she called. "Hey, Lucy, are you shopping early?"

"Lucy is here to watch the shop while I give my talks," Callie explained.

"That's a good idea," LouAnn agreed. "Can you two give me a hand?"

Callie and Lucy walked to the back of the pick-up. Sitting in the bed were four shiny green wagons, each with the words "Joyful Heart Herbs" painted on the side.

"Oh, LouAnn, they are beautiful! How did you know I needed them? They're wonderful," Callie gushed as she hugged her friend.

"Sandy gave me a call earlier in the week. Suz picked them up in Fort Wayne and dropped them off. Cecilia cut a stencil and I painted the lettering. It was a group effort," she laughed.

"They're perfect. I can't thank you enough," Callie said.

"Look! We have customers," Lucy crowed as a van pulled into the parking lot.

"Looks like I got them here just in time," LouAnn said as they lifted the wagons from her truck.

The day passed in a blur. There was a steady stream of cars coming in and out of the parking lot. The first van had turned out to be Mike's mother and her garden club friends. They were the first to arrive and the last to leave, having attended all of Callie's talks and picked up every handout available. Callie barely had time to exchange introductions with Mike's mother. She appeared to be a very pleasant, enthusiastic lady, and her friends happily chatted and fussed all day.

Callie answered questions as quickly and effectively as she could throughout the busy day. She was grateful for the prep work Sandy's pretend shopping had provided. Several people promised to return for plants they liked as soon as the weather settled. Lucy was a blessing, managing the cash register when Callie was talking, carrying bags to customers' cars, and sacking purchases during the few moments Callie ran the register. She also proved invaluable for the dozens of phone calls that came from people who were lost on country roads. Since Lucy had grown up in the area, she was able to direct people from whatever landmark they named.

When the final customer had left, they both fell onto the daybed, which earlier had been filled with garden-themed pillows.

"You were a wonder," Callie told the girl. "I couldn't have managed at all without you."

"I haven't had that much fun in ages," Lucy smiled. "I think you did really well. All those ladies loved the shop. I just wish I knew more about the plants. People kept asking me if this was an annual or a perennial, and I always had to look at the tags. And some people asked if perennials were the ones that came back, or if annual meant it comes every year. It's kind of confusing."

"We probably need a sign to explain it. Did you get anything to eat?" Callie asked.

"There wasn't any time. I put the last platter out at 3:30. I think the tea's all gone and that's a hundred cup coffeemaker. Everyone raved about the food," Lucy said with awe. "I had to empty the trash cans twice. The bags are hidden out behind the lilac bush."

Callie groaned with the effort to become upright and walked to the cash register. She opened the drawer and looked inside. A puzzled expression crossed her face.

"It doesn't look as full as I'd hoped," she said dejectedly.

"Oh, I hid all the big bills and checks in a box under the counter," Lucy explained. "With your luck with robbers, I decided we shouldn't take any chances. Besides the drawer was too full to close!"

"You are a blessing!" Callie said as she hugged her.

"Tell that to my dad," Lucy responded.

Callie paid the girl, asking her if she was available to come each Saturday. Lucy was delighted and practically skipped to her car.

Callie ran the day's report tape, breathing a sigh of relief. There would be money for tires and a good amount to deposit as well. She was too tired to examine what had sold best at the moment. She slipped the cash drawer inside a bag to disguise it. Hopefully, there were no robbers lurking outside to grab her cash, but she wasn't taking any chances. She loaded the empty platters, the coffeemaker, and the cash drawer onto the cart. After carefully locking the door she pushed the cart back to the farmhouse. It had been a great day.

She'd just finished washing the platters when Mike called.

"Ready to celebrate? I heard your Cottage was overflowing with customers," he said proudly. "Mother said the place was wonderful, and she can't wait to come back."

"I'm glad she likes it, Mike. I'm exhausted. Would you mind if I cancelled? I just want to soak in the tub and get some sleep. I've been so worried about today that I haven't slept well in days," she admitted.

"That's okay," he replied. "We'll celebrate another time. You get some rest. You deserve it."

Callie fed Wicca, who had been so busy being the official greeter she hadn't had a chance to nap all day. After hiding her money in the bottom of the dirty clothes hamper, she took a long, soothing bath. Then she slept well for the first time in weeks.

The next morning, she hurried to the farm with her clipboard. She spent the next two hours making lists of merchandise in the shop that had sold. All of the little pastel pillows with inspirational sayings that had filled the daybed were gone. About half the teapots and most of the cups and saucers had been sold. The herbal items in the kitchen area were nearly all gone, and the tubs containing herbal soaps were nearly empty. Several framed herb prints and wreaths had sold, so some of the offending metal patches were visible again. The plant cart had two plants left, both of which looked like they had been "touched and sniffed" too many times. "Poor babies," Callie crooned. "You can go back to the house for some R&R. You deserve it."

The spring corner looked like all the birds had flown away, and the candle shelf was down to two scents rather than the eight original offerings. The only areas that still looked full were the gourmet herbal foods and the fairy wall. "Maybe after all the free appetizers and cookies they consumed, food just didn't sound good," she mused.

She did the same exercise in the plants sales area, noting that basically only the cooking herbs and blooming plants had sold. That seemed reasonable since it really was too early to plant outdoors. All of her funky containers had sold. Nearly all the fragrant spring containers, the baskets, and pots of primroses were gone. About three-fourths of the pansies and violas had been sold, too. She'd have to come up with some color quickly for her outdoor displays. There were plenty of "Delectable Houseplants" growing happily in the living and dining room to refill the plant cart, so that wouldn't be a problem. Several of the shelves in the spare bedroom were filled with culinary herbs that could be up-potted and ready to sell in three or four days. She was thrilled with Joyful Heart's first day.

As she took notes, her mind wandered over the previous day. She recalled greeting several of the Heart and Soil members and some ladies who had attended the speech she'd given out of town mid-month. Most of the ladies who worked in the library had come and she'd recognized a couple of neighbors. Other than that, she hadn't recognized anyone. The advertising must be working!

She made a new job list that included calling the tire store first thing Monday morning. Then she called Wicca to join her in a walk in the woods. The spring beauties, hepaticas, and a few wildflowers that Callie could not identify were blooming. She was delighted to see the variety of trees in her woods. Now that the leaves were beginning to unfurl, she found maples, beech, hickories, sycamores, cottonwoods, and even redbuds. She began planning a woodland walk for her customers to enjoy. Finally, she found the giant sycamore that was hollow and went inside to look at it more carefully. Over the years, many people, probably kids, had carved their initials inside and outside as well. The interior was smoky from campfires and the ground was hard-packed and smooth. She dubbed it "The Teepee", since that is what it resembled, placed her hands on the huge trunk and thanked it for all its years of service. From the looks of the many dead branches, it might not last many more.

Wicca romped ahead as Callie returned to the farmhouse by way of the creek. She detoured once slightly to check on the bees. She'd need to put on her suit and open the hives to make sure the queen was laying eggs. The beekeeper had told her to remove the mouse guard once the hive seemed strong enough but to replace it before winter threatened. She made a note to check the hives soon.

She pulled her cart to the lilac bush, adding the bags of trash Lucy had hidden there to the sacks she'd emptied the full wastebaskets into earlier. Callie was delighted to see patches of sweet woodruff appearing around the lilac bush. Several clumps of daffodils were appearing nearby and she could see the beginnings of several hosts, lungworts and violets along the edge of the trees. Elizabeth must have had a flower bed here. Now that the brush and weeds had been mowed, Callie could see the faint outlines.

Back at the farmhouse, she found the folder of shop invoices so the phone numbers were handy to re-order the items that had sold. She marked a few additional items from the companies that had sold best and hoped she was making the right decisions. On the computer, she read many e-mails that were compliments from people who had shopped yesterday. A few wanted to order additional items. While she was at the computer, she typed in all the names and addresses from the newsletter sign-up sheets that had been filled. Cecilia would need to print more copies of the April newsletter than they'd planned. Callie started a new data base for an E-newsletter that she planned to start sending out on a monthly basis. Once the office work was finished she spent the rest of the day happily up-potting plants.

Monday was a gray day, so Callie didn't mind spending it making phone calls, writing a couple of articles, and making a list of the supplies she'd need for the workshops she'd scheduled for April. If Saturdays were busy, and she scheduled workshops for Sunday afternoons, she'd need Mondays to go to the bank, run errands, and catch-up from the weekend, so she'd decided to be closed on Mondays. She checked the mail. A few people had mailed in the workshop registration form from the March newsletter, a few had e-mailed their registration from the posting on the website, and several more had signed up Saturday at the farm. She entered the names into the proper dates and found that she had enough to justify doing each workshop. The "Cooking with Herbs" class was nearly filled. Most of the afternoon was spent making outlines and timelines for the classes, which were all to be held on Sunday afternoons. She'd scheduled one class for a Saturday afternoon, just to see which day was more popular, and found that it was the smallest class. She had decided not to have evening classes since there really was not enough space in the Cottage. She was debating the wisdom of building an addition to the Cottage someday when the phone rang.

"Trev Carpenter here," the rumbly voice stated.

"Hey, Graybeard, been mixing any concrete lately?" she teased. Callie had found that having money in the bank had improved her mood greatly.

"Nope, I save that job for my employees," he laughed. "I'm working on a remodeling job at the moment. Building a big riding stable out west of town. There's a few things they're going to throw away and I thought of you. Have time to take a look? I'm heading out your way as we speak," he said.

"What kind of things?" she asked hesitantly.

"Oh, come on. It's a surprise," he encouraged.

"Okay, I'll be at the end of the driveway," she surrendered.

By the time she'd run a comb through her hair, put on a touch of lipstick, given Wicca a treat to compensate for leaving her, and hurried to the road Trev's old blue pick-up was pulling to a stop.

"Hop in," he instructed, pulling a pile of paperwork, tape measures, flashlights, and a thermos from the passenger seat to the center. "Sorry for the messy office," he laughed. "I haven't had time to call the cleaning lady."

They bounced along the road with Trev pointing out the houses he'd built, the barns he'd restored, and bits of information about who lived where. Twenty minutes later, they pulled into a driveway with concrete pillars topped with a rearing horse placed on each side of the wide opening. Ornate metal gates that opened electronically swung open as Trev pushed a remote.

"Wow, this is quite a place," Callie remarked.

"Local lawyer. Wife is the one that loves the horses. She wants a riding stable for the kids," Trev explained. He parked the truck near piles of lumber, pointing to a stack of what appeared to be old board fencing.

"It's beautifully weathered and the boards are solid. I tried to talk her into using it for some of the interior rooms, but she wasn't interested. I thought it would look great as paneling in the tack room, the office, in the restrooms, or the groom's quarters. She says to toss it, so I thought maybe I'd toss it your way," Trev offered.

"It is beautiful, Trev," Callie pondered.

"It would certainly cover those metal patches. Has a nice silver patina. Some of the smaller pieces could be made into shelving and the smallest into picture frames. You could use some of it to make some shelving in that black walnut garage of yours or even build a small tool shed. I just hate to see it go to waste, get burned, or go to a landfill. Doesn't make sense."

"I'll take it, with gratefulness," Callie smiled brightly.

"Great. I thought you'd like it. Now look at this," Trev said as he grabbed her hand and pulled her around the corner of a shed. "Can you picture this on top of your garage?" he said as he pointed to a large weathervane. The design was a large crowing rooster. Beside it were a wrought iron gate and two sections of fencing.

"She said to throw this away, too," Trev stated.

"Just throw it my way," Callie assured him with a laugh. "This is must be my lucky day!" she exclaimed.

"I think you deserve some luck from all I've been hearing," Trev said solemnly. "I'm really sorry you've had so much trouble since you've moved here. I've lived here all my life and never had a problem. This is a good community, nice people. Hard-working, church-going."

"Maybe I just brought bad luck with me," she laughed. "I told myself just this morning that surely I'm over the hump, and there must be good things ahead. And just look. Now I have a weathervane and a bunch of possibilities in a woodpile. Things are looking up already, thanks to you."

"Glad I could help, Callie," Trev said as he looked into her eyes. "Yup, I'm truly glad I could help." They stood for a moment, looking at one another searchingly. Callie couldn't help remembering the fun they'd had repairing the Cottage. She couldn't help noticing the hair curling around his collar, the muscular build under the denim shirt and jeans, and especially the crinkly eyes that were smiling at her right now.

"Er, I'd better get you back. Your dog will be wondering if you've been kidnapped," he stammered.

"Yes…I imagine she will….be wondering, I mean," Callie stammered in reply.

They returned to the truck. Trev offered to have his crew load the treasures onto one of his flatbed trucks and bring it over mid-week. Callie gratefully accepted since she still didn't have tires. Hopefully, the tire store would be out this afternoon with two new tires and the repaired spare.

"Well, I'll be seeing you, Callie," Trev said as she hopped out of his truck.

"Yeah, be seeing you. And thanks again for sending all those things my way," she answered.

"Hey, I had this all thought out," he teased. "You're going to need someone to make something with that wood, and it had better be me!" He pulled away before she could reply.

The tire store did indeed send out the scruffy tobacco-spitter just before lunchtime. Accompanied by much mumbling and obscenities, he eventually put the two new tires on the rear, and the two spares on the front. He tossed the three remaining slashed tires into the store's truck and pounded on her door.

"Here's the bill," he grumped. "Due now."

"And here's a check," Callie replied as she wrote out the amount indicated. "I appreciate your help."

He stood for a moment and glared at her expectantly.

"Twenty dollars due for a service call," he stated, holding out his hand.

"I see that listed on the invoice," Callie said frowning. "Maybe I should call the store and see if there's been a mistake."

"Yer mistake," he spat as he stomped toward the truck.

Callie watched until he disappeared out of sight. Then she grabbed her purse, keys, and her box of money. She'd already gone over the checks and added all the names and addresses that hadn't appeared on the sign-up sheets to her mailing list. She'd sorted out the credit cards slips and balanced her cash register tape with the income. All of the data had been recorded in a new Excel spreadsheet on her computer. She was so happy to finally have categories labeled "Plant Income" and "Shop Income" to join the "Speech Income" column. The "Expense" categories had seemingly unlimited columns already!

She made her first deposit at the bank, where she was given an official deposit bag so she could make after-hours deposits. She had the teller check to ensure her credit card deposits had gone through correctly. Happily, the system had worked perfectly. The Joyful Heart Herb account had grown overnight.

She stopped at the hardware for yet another batch of 'No Hunting' signs.

"Don't have any left," Jake informed her almost cheerily. "Only order one box a year and we never sell the whole box."

"Well, maybe you need to order another box," she responded, smiling sweetly.

She stopped for more kerosene, disposable cups, napkins, and two more boxes of sugar cubes. She'd learned from Saturday that her customers apparently preferred tea with lots of sugar.

She stopped at Dinah's to treat herself to a piece of black raspberry pie. Dinah was busy but took time to congratulate her on the opening of Joyful Heart Herbs.

"I've heard lots of comments about how pretty everything was," Dinah confided.

"Thanks, Dinah. Fortunately, I had a good day. Pretty weather always makes people more willing to spend, especially when it comes to plants," Callie replied.

"By the way, a group of ladies were in for breakfast," Dinah added. "Heard one of them say the local congressman's wife and a couple of her friends are coming out to see your place on Thursday. She was all in a tizzy. Owns the antique store down the street. Been trying to get that type of clientele at her place for years and can't understand why Mrs. Lacey is going to your place instead."

"Thanks for the heads-up, Dinah," Callie said, already thinking of all she needed to replace before Thursday. She needed to make a good impression, and it wouldn't do for the congressman's wife and her friends to be greeted by empty displays. Wouldn't do her cash register any good either. "The pie is terrific, as always. Do you ever make gooseberry?"

"No, I haven't, but my rhubarb custard pie is to die for," Dinah said proudly, "You come back in a week. By then my rhubarb should be big enough to make a couple."

Callie skipped out the door and hurried home. There was shopping to be done!

Callie unloaded the truck, gave Wicca a treat, reminded her to be good, and left for Indianapolis. The greenhouse supply clerk loaded cartons of peat pots, flats, and pots into the truck. She also purchased more fertilizer and plant labels. Then she stopped at both plant wholesalers and filled the truck with more pansies, primroses, stock, ivies, and Rex Begonias. At the floral supply warehouse she selected a few plastic stakes that said "Happy Easter" and another package of stakes in a heart-shape with "Happy Mother's Day" printed inside. She purchased bolts of ribbon in colors to match the pansies and a dozen large wicker baskets.

It was nearly sunset by the time she arrived home with her treasures and began unloading the plants into the shadehouse. She was surprised when she saw Wicca slinking around the corner of the garage, her tail between her legs. "What's wrong, girl?" Callie called, kneeling down and extending her arms. Wicca paused, and then came bounding toward her mistress. When she was ten feet away, Callie jumped up in alarm.

"Wicca! You smell like skunk!" she shouted. "Where have you been?" The poor dog immediately slunk back to hide behind the garage.

"Oh, I'm sorry, girl. It's okay. We'll fix it," Callie called remorsefully.

She finished unloading the plants and drove to the house where she unloaded the remainder of her supplies. By the time she'd finished, Wicca was whimpering by the back door.

The internet reported that tomato juice, vinegar, and strong soap were successful at removing skunk odor. She pulled a large washtub that she'd intended to use as a planter from behind the garage and filled it with a layer of warm water. Then she coaxed Wicca into the tub, poured tomato juice over her coat and worked it in with gloved hands. She followed with a rinse of more warm water, a vigorous shampooing, and a vinegar rinse. Fortunately, one or more of the treatments seemed to have worked, and Wicca smelled acceptable. The dog was not too thrilled, but she was happy for all the attention, and by the time she was towel-dried and had received another treat, she was ready for a nap.

"I wonder where she found that skunk," Callie pondered as she dragged the washtub outside.

The next day, Callie was up before sunrise to sweep the Cottage, fill in the outdoor displays, and finish the watering at the house before the first customers arrived. She began making more fragrant spring planters, filling the beribboned wicker baskets with pots of primroses, and finding more odd containers to plant with pansies. Sadly, she was only interrupted a few times by customers.

Mike rolled his UPS truck into the parking lot, happily announcing that the lavender tea from England and other small cartons had arrived.

"Looks almost as good as it did before you opened," he observed.

"Almost?" Callie said worriedly. "What's different?"

"I liked all those buckets and tubs full of flowers that you had in front of the shadehouse. It looks kind of empty there now," Mike observed.

"I put in some planters," Callie pointed out.

"Yes, but the old things were more interesting and held my attention more. And you'd painted a bunch of the buckets so it was really colorful," he added.

"You're right, Mike. Standing here in the parking lot, it doesn't attract as much attention as it did before. Thanks for pointing that out," she smiled at him.

"Always glad to help my girl," he responded, putting an arm around her shoulders. "Should we stack all these small boxes in your cart? There's a bunch of them," he informed her.

Callie's mind got stuck at "my girl", so she was several steps behind as Mike moved to the back of his truck.

"I'll get the cart," she mumbled. By the time she positioned it behind the open door, Mike had rummaged through his load and located all her boxes.

"Wow! This is great. I just ordered some of these things on-line yesterday," she exclaimed happily.

"So, when can we celebrate your big success? I was thinking dinner and a movie on Saturday night," Mike suggested.

"Oh, Mike, I have my first workshop on Sunday afternoon, and I'll have a full morning getting all the watering and set-up done," Callie declined.

"Okay, how about Friday night," he tried again.

"Saturday should be another really busy day. I'd like to get to bed early Friday because I'll be up before the sun to get everything ready," she explained.

"Thursday?" he tried hopefully.

"Okay, Thursday, but maybe just dinner without the movie. I just have so much to do," Callie apologized.

"Guess I'll have to settle for whatever time I can get," Mike chuckled. "Maybe I'll have some more boxes for you tomorrow, too."

After the UPS truck disappeared, Callie unpacked the cartons, priced the merchandise, and filled in the empty displays in the Cottage as best she could. The lavender tea made a beautiful display when paired with some white and purple teapots on a lavender embroidered tablecloth. The herbal rolling pins had arrived along with some new hot pads and oven mitts in the same design. The music boxes that played "Happy Birthday" were small, but when they were placed with a box of filigree tussie-mussies holders on a lace doily, and a few tiny bouquets of silk flowers were added, they looked terrific. Callie remembered a pair of white silk gloves that she had tucked in a drawer in her bedroom. She'd stuff them with lavender, tie the wrists shut with ribbon, and add those as a Victorian touch to the display. Feeling pleased, she paused before preparing all the cardboard boxes for recycling.

Suddenly, she became aware of an odd sound. Investigating outside, she found Wicca trying to pull the siding off the bottom edge of the Cottage.

"Stop that, Wicca. Bad dog!" she cried, as she ran over to grab the dog's collar. Wicca was pulling and growling, trying to free herself from Callie's grip. "What's wrong with you? You can't tear up my Cottage!" Callie pulled the lab's leash from her pocket and clipped it on, dragging the unwilling dog from the scene.

"If you can't behave, you'll just have to wait in the truck," Callie told her as she opened the door and ordered the reluctant dog inside.

Callie returned to the corner of the Cottage to inspect the damage. As she knelt on the ground, she saw a pair of golden eyes looking back at her from the crawlspace grid nearby. Backing away, she suddenly noticed the faint scent of ......oh, no, it was....skunk!

There was a skunk under her Cottage. And the congressman's wife and her friends were coming day after tomorrow! Callie knew she shouldn't try to scare the animal, or it would release its scent, and her Cottage would smell for weeks, maybe months! Walking around the Cottage, she found a small hole had been dug in the loose earth where the electric conduit had been buried earlier.

"How do you get a skunk to leave?" she wondered in a panic.

She locked the Cottage door and drove to the house. She looked up the number for the DNR officer. Shouldn't they handle all wildlife, not just deer?

"Officer Pease here," the grumpy voice answered.

"This is Callie, from the herb farm," she started to explain.

"Someone shooting at your place, I'm on my way," he said.

"No, no, it's not that. I have a skunk. I mean, there's a skunk under my cottage. Can you come and get it?" she begged.

"Wait a minute. You called me to come and get a skunk? Sorry, that's not my job," he said crankily.

"Well, what should I do? I just can't sit and wait for it to waltz out. I have customers coming. If a skunk decides to unload under my shop, it will keep customers out for weeks," she wailed.

"Call Bill Ketchum, the local trapper. If anyone can lure a skunk out, old Bill can. Not cheap though, but you don't have many alternatives," Officer Pease said, reciting the trapper's phone number by heart.

It was almost five o'clock before a rusty black van pulled into her parking lot. If she hadn't known to expect him, Callie would have been nervous to see the wiry man in worn clothes step down. His face was smeared with mud, as were his boots and pant legs.

"Sorry, I'm late," he said. "Took longer to catch some crappie than I expected. Fish just weren't biting this afternoon. Normally would have caught them this evening. Lot easier in the evening. But, you said this was an emergency."

"Yes, it is. I appreciate your coming so quickly," she said.

"Where's the little troublemaker?" he said, pulling a large black-painted metal container from the back of the van. He had put on a pair of gloves, and carried a small tin can.

"It's under my shop. There's an air grate at one end, that's where I saw it, but I think it went in on the other side," she said as she led the way to the newly dug hole.

"Yep, skunk prints," Mr. Ketchum nodded as he looked at the ground. He dumped the tin can's contents on the ground, revealing several small fish. Callie gasped when he tore one in half and put the two pieces in a small holder inside the rectangle. He slid the open end of the rectangle until it fully covered the hole, and wedged it securely in place with a brace.

"Don't touch it. I'll be back in the morning to get it. Payment in full on capture. Forty dollars per animal," he said flatly.

"I open at ten, so I hope it's gone before then," she said hopefully. "Will there be lots of odor? I can't imagine it will be happy to be stuck in that box."

"Specially designed. Top of the line," he called over his shoulder as he climbed into his cab.

Wednesday dawned with a panorama of color in the sky. It was going to be a beautiful day. She'd spent all last evening writing out check to pay bills and making plant labels. After the slow sales yesterday, she'd decided to postpone any more orders. She'd better save the last of her money.

Following her usual Tai Chi routine, watering, and a quick breakfast, Callie hurried to the farm leaving an unhappy Wicca at the house. Callie didn't want her to disturb the skunk trap. She carefully unlocked the Cottage door, stuck her head in for a sniff, and was relieved to find only the sweet fragrances of mint and lavender mixed with a few other scents from potpourris and herbal soaps.

She worked in the shadehouse, watering, and re-arranging empty flats until she heard Bill Ketchum's van. She hovered in the background as he checked his trap.

"Hmmmm, nothing. Crappie always works. Guess it was just too fresh, or we got ourselves a finicky eater," Mr. Ketchum joked. "We'll just try something else today, and let that fish age a bit in the sun." He pulled the trap from the building, removed the fish and threw it into the tin can. He replaced the fish with marshmallows covered in peanut butter.

"Maybe this little fellow has a sweet tooth. Never met a skunk that could resist marshmallows and peanut butter. We'll get him today," he said confidently. "I'll be back tonight to pick him up."

Callie was dismayed that the skunk was still under the Cottage. She found herself praying for no customers who might tromp on the floor or slam the door. It might frighten the skunk into action. Some businesswoman she was, hoping for no customers! She ran to the house and grabbed the rag rugs from her kitchen and bedroom since they most closely matched the décor of the Cottage. Maybe more rugs on the floor would soften the sound of footsteps and the skunk would sleep all day.

Luckily, only a handful of very quiet customers visited. Callie was torn between relief and anxiety that so few people had come on such a lovely day. If this was going to be the normal customer flow, Joyful Heart Herbs was in big trouble.

Just before sundown, Bill Ketchum's van rolled in. Unfortunately, the trap was still empty, but the marshmallows were gone. "I don't understand it," he said, as he checked and oiled the spring mechanism. "This trap always works fine. Well, at least we know what he likes now," he nodded as he replaced the peanut butter-coated marshmallows.

Her stomach was in a knot all Thursday morning as she waited nervously for the congressman's wife and her friends to arrive. There were a few other customers in the morning, but they spent most of their time in the shadehouse looking at plants and only came into the Cottage briefly for their free cup of tea and to check out.

Soon after lunch, a group of ladies arrived that Callie suspected were the expected guests. A pretty redhead seemed to be the center of attraction, so Callie correctly guessed that she was married to the local congressman.

The ladies were drawn to the fragrant spring planters, and the redhead gestured for Callie's attention.

"Can you tell us about these wonderful flowers?" she requested.

Callie spent the next few minutes identifying the frost-resistant flowers and their scents. After a few moments one of the group asked where the culinary herbs were located. "I don't suppose you have Thai basil," another lady asked.

"Oh yes, in fact we have three varieties," Callie replied. "We're you looking for the regular Thai basil, the sweet Thai basil, or Meng-luk?"

"All three," exclaimed the lady, "My husband loves Thai food. His parents served in the Peace Corps there." By the time they finished shopping in the shadehouse, each of the ladies had selected a flat of plants.

Callie placed their flats in a wagon as the ladies headed toward the Cottage. Once inside, they helped themselves to tea and chatted merrily as they moved from one display to another. They admired the teapots, sniffed the big tub of lavender flowers, and handled nearly every item in the shop before they made their selections. Callie checked them out, encouraged them to sign up for the farm's newsletter, and pulled the wagon to their car. It wasn't until they'd left, that she realized she'd been holding her breath. She gave a big sigh of relief. So far, so good. Their visit was the high point of the day, sales-wise. A few times Callie tip-toed out to the trap to listen for any noise, but all was silent.

Just after dark, Bill Ketchum finally came to check the trap. Callie had been moving a load of plants from the house to the shadehouse in her truck, keeping Wicca in the cab, when he arrived.

"Success!" he bragged, "I knew it couldn't resist my marshmallows. Always work, those marshmallows."

Silently, Callie wondered if the marshmallows were so fool-proof, why had Mr. Ketchum baited the trap with crappie first? She removed forty dollars from the register and asked for an invoice, which he quickly filled out. He put the trap in his van and rolled out of the parking lot.

Callie nearly jumped for joy as she hurried to the house to change before Mike arrived. She did feel like celebrating this evening!

They had a talk-filled dinner at a local family-owned restaurant known for its breaded tenderloins. She had just finished telling Mike about her harrowing week with the skunk problem when her cell phone rang.

It was Bill Ketchum on the line. "'Fraid you still have a little problem, Ma'am," he said without preamble. "Your skunk was a female."

"So, you think her husband might still be under the Cottage?" she asked.

"Nope, but her babies probably are. She was nursing," he explained. "I'll be out tomorrow. Dead skunks could smell just as bad as a mad live one," he finished.

The dinner ended on that note, so Mike drove Callie home and left her to ponder the joys of country living most of the night.

Bill Ketchum was at the farm before Callie had finished the watering. He crawled under the Cottage and reappeared pulling a box behind him. "Wanna look?" he asked. "They're real cute at this age," he stated with a big smile.

Callie looked into the box to see five little black "kittens" with white stripes down their backs. They were indeed "real cute."

"What are you going to do with them?" she asked.

"Oh, I know lots of people that like to raise them as pets. They eat bugs, grubs, and such, you know. It's pretty easy to remove those scent glands at this age, and once you don't have that problem, it's almost like having a cat around," he told her. "I can find homes for them. Unless you want them," he added.

"Oh, no! I really don't need any more pets. Besides, I can just see my customers running for their cars the first time one of them waddled from under a plant bench," she assured him.

"Well, in that case, that's two hundred dollars. I'll write out your receipt," he said with a smile.

"But they're just babies!" Callie cried.

"Ma'am, the deal is forty dollars per animal, and there's five animals in this box," he stated calmly.

"Will you take a check?" Callie asked dismally.

After he left, she tried to find the bright side and decided that two hundred and forty dollars had been a reasonable price to pay to save both her Cottage and the farm's reputation. She might have had to spend that much on a fumigating service to get rid of the smell. Someday, she'd look back on the whole thing and laugh, but right now, it was difficult.

The UPS truck rolled in soon after, and Mike hurried to the Cottage.

"I couldn't wait to hear what happened, so I came here first," he explained. Callie poured him a cup of tea, added the two cubes of sugar he liked, and briefly told him what had occurred.

"Well, I have something that will cheer you," he said. "I've got six boxes for you in the truck. And, I found out that Beatrix Potter movie you've wanted to see is playing over in Marion this weekend. We could go over on Sunday evening after your workshop, have dinner and see it."

"Oh, Mike, that's great. It's just what I need," Callie bubbled. "Thank you. You've really brightened my day."

"That's my job," he laughed. "Speaking of jobs, if I want to keep mine, we'd better get those boxes."

Friday was so quiet at the farm that Callie wondered if the road had been closed, or some disaster had occurred. She turned on the radio just to check, but all seemed well. She groaned as she looked around the shop. The place did look fantastic, if she did say so herself. She wandered out to the shadehouse where she noted many more pansies and violas were coming into bloom. The redbuds were coloring the edge of the woods in bright rosy-pink, and her lilac was coming into bloom.

She spent the day mapping the clumps of Elizabeth's daffodils and labeling them by color and height. Callie was delighted at the variety of shapes and colors. Elizabeth must have been as fond of them as she was herself. Of course, it made sense, especially in a garden near the woods. Nothing ate daffodils, not even deer or moles.

She could see several clumps further into the woods and tied plastic twine to mark the edge where she needed to clear back further. Maybe there were more garden plants there as well as the daffodils. As she worked, she began thinking about Selma Steele, the wife of famous

Indiana artist, T.C. Steele. Selma had loved daffodils and had planted thousands around their home in Brown County. In fact, she became noted world-wide as a daffodil hybridizer who shipped bulbs all over the world. At a time when few women worked, she employed many workers to tend the beds, harvest, clean, and package the bulbs for shipping. Callie made a note on her clipboard to see if the library had Selma's book, House of the Singing Winds. Somewhere, in the boxes she had yet to unpack she had a print of her favorite T.C. Steele painting, "Selma in the Garden." Someday, when she had extra cash, she'd get it framed.

It wasn't until she was eating a supper of stir-fried vegetables with fresh Thai basil in front of the television that she understood the lack of customers. The announcer mentioned that this was Good Friday. She was amazed that anyone had signed up for the workshop scheduled on Easter Sunday. She'd totally forgotten to check a real, printed calendar. The computer generated one she'd used hadn't given her a clue.

Before she opened in the following morning, she drove into town for some chocolate bunnies and foil wrapped eggs to put in a Cottage display. She found the "Happy Easter" stakes she'd purchased and put them into various planters and baskets, adding pastel bows everywhere to give things a festive look.

Lucy showed up early wearing a pastel outfit and white bunny ears. Her sweatshirt said "Hop to it!" and the reindeer antlers on her VW had been replaced by furry bunny ears that matched Lucy's. They were both busier all day than Callie had expected, but not as busy as she'd hoped.

The following week passed in a blur of activity. Some days the weather was warm and beautiful; some days it was blustery with sleet or snow. Callie finished the April newsletter announcing the arrival of the lavender tea, music boxes, other new items, and included an article about fairy gardens. Since that area had hardly been touched since opening, she knew she needed to educate her customers on the joys of fairy gardening. She planned a special weekend in May for Fairy Days and outlined the event in the newsletter. This time, she asked people to make reservations, so she'd know how much food to prepare. She e-mailed the copy to Cecilia and made arrangements to pick up the newsletter the following Monday. Then she called her friends to invite them for a recipe-testing and newsletter folding evening.

Stuffed eggs and canapés would be this month's trials. She made notes of several combinations that sounded tasty and completed a grocery list. If Callie continued developing and testing recipes on a monthly basis, her book could be finished by the time the farm opened next spring. It was a motivating thought.

When there were no customers, she spent the days at the farm removing weeds and scraggly shrubbery from the areas around the Cottage. She marked the proposed beds in front of the shop with a garden hose to make the curves and then edged the beds with a straight bladed shovel. She shook the loose soil from weeds she removed, carefully working around clumps of perennials that she found. Until they bloomed, she had no idea what color scheme would emerge. Maybe Elizabeth had followed a color scheme, and maybe it would just be a riot of color. Callie couldn't wait to find out.

Soon there were beds along the tree line and beside the pumphouse. She cleared a circular path in the woods that looked over Pumpkinvine Creek for shade-loving plants, and staked out a formal garden behind the black walnut garage. Trev's workers had delivered the load of treasures, and one sunny day she climbed on the garage roof and installed the proud rooster weathervane. Shortly afterwards, Callie noticed an unfamiliar bird perching on the weathervane nearly every morning and evening. It sang several different calls. On her next trip to town, she borrowed a bird identification book from the library. It was a mockingbird! According to the book, a male could learn over three hundred songs! Callie started whistling the first two lines of "You Are My Sunshine" whenever she saw him and, amazingly, by the end of the week it was part of his daily repertoire! She loved nature and loved the feeling that working outdoors always gave her. That connection to the earth, the rhythm of the seasons that sang to her soul soothed her in a way nothing else did. Being with the plants and nature worked magic.

Callie worried that children today were not getting enough exposure and experience with the natural world. She read many reports that concluded that working with nature or even closely observing nature results in healthier, happier people. Reportedly, today's children were developing a multitude of problems which many researchers believe is connected to "nature deficit disorder". Instead of soul and body satisfying contacts with nature and the outdoors, children spend the majority of their time in front of computers or televisions. Even in England, that bulwark of gardening, researchers report that children and young adults are no longer interested in plants or the environment on a personal level. Oh yes, they can explain about global warming and threatened species, but few have ever spent time actually looking at or touching a tree. Callie worried about the kind of detached stewards of the environment that would soon be looking out for the Earth's future. They had little understanding of the relationship between the earth and the food supply. She hoped programs at Joyful Heart Herbs could help encourage children to enjoy and respect nature. Hopefully, they would gain the same sense of peace and belonging that Callie felt when she worked with the earth. She finished the trail through the woods, made a list of the plants that would go there and whistled duets of "You Are My Sunshine" with her mockingbird. Afterwards, she watched the sunset while making notes of possible children's programming that she could add to the farm's offerings.

The tasting evening rolled around quickly. Callie had spent most of the day making a selection of stuffed eggs and pretty canapés that featured pansies, violas, and other herbs. She also tested a viola quiche and another herbal cocktail. She placed a basket filled with blooming pansies on the coffee table as a centerpiece and turned the lights down low. Hopefully her friends wouldn't notice the dust. She just didn't have time to do a thorough cleaning.

Fortunately, her friends were true friends who didn't mind a little dust and wouldn't have mentioned if they did. They were too busy chatting, spending a delightful evening sharing news and information. The newsletters were folded, addressed and sorted, although with additional names, the process took longer than last month.

"We're either going to have to learn to write faster or add a couple more women to our group to help," Suz laughed.

"Hey, we just have to write faster. I'm not sharing this pitcher of peachy-rum whatevers with more people!" Sandy exclaimed.

"That cocktail did turn out pretty well. I still have to come up with a good name for it," Callie smiled, "but we'll be pulling all-nighters if my mail list keeps growing."

"I'd hoped to have figured out how to print mailing labels on my computer by now," Callie apologized. "Just sticking a label on wouldn't take so long."

"I do mailing labels all the time. Just show me your computer," Cecilia directed. A few minutes later, she had determined the type of label that would be required and promised to set it up before the next meeting.

"Good," said LouAnn happily. "I like our group just the size it is."

"Me, too," the others chimed.

The third week in April found temperatures nearing seventy degrees. The farm was busier as people were feeling the urge to plant now that spring seemingly had arrived for real. Callie stayed up most of one night seeding the varieties she planned to use in her own gardens. She was putting in very long days, watering, sweeping, and re-stocking before the farm opened, and up-potting, labeling, and tidying after the farm was closed.

Wicca was in seventh heaven greeting each and every customer. She was obviously the farm favorite, and many returning customers started bringing the lab treats. Along with those from Mike, even though she ran many miles a day chasing squirrels and patrolling both the house and farm, Wicca was getting plump. Many people asked for an explanation of her name. Callie wasn't hesitant to explain that the word "Wicca" signified a pre-Christian religion that had celebrated the vital relationship between humans and the plants that surrounded them. It seemed appropriate for a dog that lived on a plant farm, especially if most of those plants were herbs, the useful plants.

Callie decided that from now on, she would have one Sunday a month without workshops. Had she been more aware, she would not have scheduled Easter Sunday, but instead this coming Sunday was her free day. She had decided she needed a holiday at least once a month. Lucy promised to spot-water at the farm on Sunday morning after church and to take Wicca to her house. For her first day off, Callie was going to the Cincinnati Flower Show!

She left just as soon as the farm closed on Saturday. Callie enjoyed the rural scenery since she'd decided to take smaller highways. She'd return on the interstates, but she wanted to enjoy the beautiful drive. Spring was well underway, as she traveled south, with the magnolias already beginning to fade. She saw a flock of wild turkeys feeding in a meadow, and quaint small towns. One little town especially appealed to her, and when she found a motel with a vacancy, she checked in.

Callie couldn't vacation the entire time, so she spent the evening in her motel room outlining articles, sketching displays that would replace those currently in the shop, and making a new job list. She also started working on ideas for June workshops, deciding that there might be more registrations if her customers knew the topics and dates further ahead of time. Then she started reading a book on advertising and promotion. Business had not been as good as she'd hoped, so maybe she did need to advertise more after all. The big question was how and where. By the time she quit reading, Callie had pages and pages of notes.

That trend continued as she walked through the Flower Show the following day. She took lots of pictures of elaborate displays and beautiful show gardens. She made notes of varieties that caught her eye or that seemed to be favorites of the other spectators. She studied and sketched floral arrangements and talked to vendors about their products. By the time the day ended, she was more than ready to return to her motel room.

After a quick supper, she studied the map and worked on her route home. She hoped to stop at a few shops during the trip, to compare prices, look at displays, and possibly find some interesting merchandise lines. There was a noisy thunderstorm in the night, but Callie barely noticed it as she dreamed of beautiful gardens.

The next morning, she packed the few belongings she had brought, turned in her key, and walked to the parking lot. "Wow! Someone really tossed out a bunch of litter," she thought as she walked toward her truck. Suddenly, she realized it wasn't litter, but sheets of notebook paper. Callie hurried to her truck and saw with dismay that her window had been broken out. Those were her sheets of notes floating in the puddles and blowing across the blacktop! She threw her bag through the window to weigh down the remaining papers, and then ran to capture all the pages she could find. Those sheets represented hours of work. Unlocking the door, she piled the wet sheets on the floor, and looked inside. Her opera CDs were on the floor, but the country ones were missing as well as her large floor jack from behind the seat. The glove compartment was open, but there had been nothing else of value in the truck.

Callie closed the door and returned to the motel office to phone the police. It was two hours before a squad car pulled up.

"Probably looking for a gun," the officer explained. "In Ohio, you can't carry a weapon in a vehicle. In Indiana, you can. Makes you a target here, especially if you drive a truck. Thieves think a truck probably means a man, might mean a gun. With the storm last night, no one would hear breaking glass. We've been real busy this morning because of it," he continued. He wrote a report and gave her a copy for her insurance company. Callie was getting used to the procedure and took it without comment. The motel owner loaned her a hand vacuum, to clean up all the broken glass as well as a piece of plastic and a roll of duct tape. Callie wondered if he found need of these supplies often for just this purpose.

Of course, the storm had brought much cooler temperatures. Before she had driven many miles, the plastic she'd taped over the window was coming loose. As she crossed the Ohio-Indiana border, fat snowflakes were starting to fall. She stopped for hot coffee and put on all the clothes she had packed and tried to re-tape the window. Within a few miles, the plastic blew away and icy wind filled the cab of the truck. Although she turned the heater as high as it would go, by the time she reached home, her fingers were stiff with cold. She hurriedly checked the shadehouse and Cottage. All seemed well.

At the house, Callie warmed her hands around a mug of hot buttered rum and spread all the pages of notes across the kitchen table and counters to dry. She took a long, warm bath and tried to banish negative thoughts. Three robberies in four months. She should have made a protective amulet for her truck as well.

Of course, she'd barely made the appointment to have the glass repaired in her truck before the phone started ringing. Cecilia had heard the news of Callie's ordeal when she'd stopped for coffee and muffins at Dinah's before going to her print shop. Sandy had heard it as soon as she arrived for work at the newspaper. Suz had a call from Flint, who had heard all about it when he filled up the dump truck at the gas station. LouAnn heard it at the library, where she was hanging some of her paintings for a one-woman show in the public meeting room. Callie was amazed at the efficiency of the Heartland grape-vine. They didn't really need a newspaper at all to hear the news!

Mike stopped in just as she was opening the shop, his screeching tires announcing his arrival.

"Are you all right?" he said as he grabbed her by the shoulders and looked into her face. "It must have scared you to death to be held at gunpoint like that! Oh, Callie, when I think what might have happened," he said as he pulled her into his chest.

"I'm fine, Mike, really," she assured him. "What's this about being held at gunpoint?"

"Oh, the guys on the shipping dock at the feed store told me all about it," he told her. "How you were held at gunpoint and all."

"I wasn't held at gunpoint. I wasn't even there when it happened. I found the window broken out of my truck the morning I planned to leave. I was never in any danger. I was a little cold on the drive home, and bummed that I got robbed yet again, but I'm safe and sound all in all."

"That's three times you've been robbed. That could be a new record. Have you checked the Guinness Book of World Records yet," Mike said with an almost straight face.

"Oh, I'll do that at the library right after I take my truck to the auto glass repair shop," she said, as she punched him in the chest lightly. He pulled her close, and was looking into her eyes when Lucy's VW bounced to a stop nearby.

"Callie, are you okay?" she shouted as she jumped from the car. A happy Wicca nearly knocked the girl over in her eagerness to greet her mistress.

"I'm fine," Callie repeated as she knelt to give her lab a big hug. "Did you miss me, girl? I sure missed you!" Lucy gave Callie a hug as soon as she released the lab.

"I'm so relieved that you are okay. So, where are the bandages? Did the bullet go clean through? You look pretty good for someone who was shot!" she exclaimed.

Callie laughed. Okay, so maybe the town did need a newspaper to report the news accurately after all.

The final week of April had been a good one. A fairly steady stream of customers flowed through the sales area. Although plant sales weren't large, many people promised they'd return in mid-May when it was safe planting time. The frost-free date for central Indiana was May 10th. Cottage sales were holding steady, and the inventory she had ordered to be shipped May 1 would be arriving soon to fill in displays.

Callie received a few more invitations to speak at area garden clubs, and the reservations for her special Fairy Day weekend were mounting. She decided to schedule workshops for the other two Sundays of the month. The remaining Sunday was Mothers' Day, so that would be her free Sunday for the month. She planned to visit her parents that day. Callie had not seen them since their visit although they'd talked on the phone each week.

She spent the final Monday in April running errands, getting supplies for her up-coming workshops, and paying bills. At the rate those frequent flyer miles were piling up, she'd be flying to the gift show in Atlanta for free next year! She also rented a tiller and started tilling up the new formal garden. She hauled a load of topsoil and added it to the newly tilled space, along with compost and fertilizer, then tilled the beds again. She returned the tiller, making notes of its manufacturer, size, and performance. Before she spent her hard-earned money on a piece of equipment that costly, she intended to rent every model available to compare their ease of use, best features, and problems. Her final stop that day was for a load of mulch, to cover the newly tilled beds. Her plan was to do one garden area a week until she had six gardens this year….the Cottage's garden, of course would be an abundant mixture of old-fashioned flowers, fruits, vegetables, and herbs, just as the traditional cottagers would have planted. The shade garden would fill the area along the tree line west of the Cottage. The circular path she'd made in the woods would house the fairy garden within the "Enchanted Forest". The formal garden behind the garage would be traditional herbs divided into beds of medicinal plants, dye plants, repellant plants, and cosmetic plants. The largest garden, composed of two long parallel curved islands just north of the parking lot, was labeled "Butterfly & Hummingbird" Garden. The final garden was the

"Cook's Garden" east of the plant sales area. Callie knew since she spent all her time at the farm, there was no time or energy to have a vegetable garden at her house. She'd broadened the original plan to include her favorite and essential vegetables as well as the customary cooking herbs. This garden would be all raised beds, using the thickest of the boards Trev's crew had brought to build the rectangular, triangular, and square beds. Her design for this garden was inspired by the lovely Kitchen Gardens of Villandry, in France.

Fortunately, the weather that final week of April was balmy. Callie spent every night after the farm closed on the new gardens or up-potting plants for the sales area. Lucy worked a couple of evenings after school to help move plants or to transplant seedlings. She was a good worker and always kept a lively stream of conversation going that made the time fly. Callie made the offer of part-time work all summer and Lucy quickly accepted, declaring that working at the farm was lots more fun than at her dad's newspaper office.

Saturday was May Day, so Callie and Lucy spent the evening before constructing a May Pole of PVC pipe. Since Callie still had lots of work to prepare the refreshments for the following morning, Lucy offered to make the floral wreath to top the pole, and attach the ribbon streamers. Callie left the farm with a springy step even though she knew it was going to be a long, busy night ahead.

She had just turned on the oven to preheat and buttered two jelly roll pans when she heard a knock at the back door.

"Come on in, Lucy," she called.

"I'm not Lucy, Ma'am," Deputy Wright's voice answered.

"Oh, come in, Deputy," Callie invited.

"Heard you had some trouble again," he stated, his gold-flecked brown eyes searching her face.

"Yes, I'm starting to feel like a magnet for trouble," she answered. "It would make a really funny story, almost unbelievable, if it were happening to someone else."

"Hmmmm….I guess I see so much trouble every day that I have a hard time thinking it is funny no matter who it happens to," he said.

"You're right. It's not a humorous matter anytime a crime is committed."

"Well, I can see you are busy, so I won't waste your time. I just came to tell you they've set a court date for the two suspects that robbed your house," the Deputy stated. "It's in two weeks, May 12th. You'll be getting a notice in the mail, but I thought you'd need as much advance warning as possible. I know you run your business by yourself, so you'll need to decide whether to close or find someone to fill in."

"I appreciate your thoughtfulness," she replied. She had been watching his face and thought she saw a shadow cross his features. Those were extremely handsome features, too, she couldn't help thinking!

"Anything else, Deputy," she asked.

"Well, Ma'am," he said, taking a step closer. "The suspects will be informed of the upcoming trial, too. They'll be passing that date on to their family. You might want to be more vigilant, take some extra precautions for the next two weeks."

His serious tone sent a shiver down Callie's back.

"Lock that back door when you come in. I noticed it was open when I arrived. Your truck doors were unlocked, too. And, you'd be wise to add some lighting between it and your back door.

"Locking my truck didn't keep it safe before," she said.

"Still, it's good practice. Make them work for it, at least," he advised. "Sure you can't take some time off and go visit some relatives or something?" he asked.

"I'm sure, Deputy. I have to be here. I'll be careful," she promised.

"I'll drive by as often as I can. You keep my number handy," he told her.

"I have it programmed in my cell phone."

"Where's your cell phone right now?" he asked.

"Oh, let's see. I think it's in my jacket, maybe with the cash drawer in the dining room," she said thoughtfully.

"If I had bad intentions and was turning the door knob right now, how long before you could find that phone and call me?" he said sternly. "How long before your brain kicks in? How long before you give up trying to remember where you put it and run into the studio for the house phone. What's your plan of action?"

"I haven't really thought about it," Callie admitted.

"Well, think about it now," he ordered. "I told you this is a bad family, and you could be dealing with kids that think they are 'saving' their big brother. Kids aren't known for making good choices or for thinking through the consequences. But, you're not a kid, Callie." He had closed the distance between them.

"No, you're definitely not a kid!" he said as his lips claimed hers.

Callie's feet left the floor as his arms tightened around her slim body. Her mind was blank; she let herself float away. Her brain registered the faint scent of aftershave, a mixture of musk and the complexity of bay. She felt heat surging from the center of her body radiating toward her extremities.

"Wow!" Callie thought she must have spoken, but her lips were otherwise engaged. Suddenly, her feet touched the floor as the deputy withdrew his grip.

"Wow!" Lucy said again in awe.

Silence filled the room, so quiet that the only sound was Wicca's soft panting as she looked from one person to the next.

"You remember what I said, Ma'am. Think, and be cautious," he reminded her, as he picked up his hat and left the house.

"Wow!" Lucy breathed as she stared at Callie's glassy, wide eyes.

Violas

Much loved and praised, the Viola is an easy-care plant for many types of gardens. It belongs in the fairy garden, is at home in a shaded spot, makes a delightful edger in perennial gardens, and some varieties belong in the fragrance garden. For cooks, the viola is prized for not only its flavor but for the delightful colors it adds to salads, desserts and main dishes. The candied flowers have been used for centuries to garnish elaborate confections. The flowers themselves have added flavor to sugars, jellies, custards, and more. Floating atop May Wine or topping tiny canapés or tea cakes, the viola is a treat for the eye as well as the palate.

The traditional Johnny-Jump-Up, also known as Heartsease or *Viola tricolor*, is as essential to cottage gardens as roses and dianthus. While technically they are perennials, they often do not survive harsh winters. However, since they are emphatic self-seeders, once planted in a garden they reappear year after year. Hybridizers have worked over the years to broaden the color spectrum to pure white, yellows, blue, orange, lavender, purple, nearly red, and various combinations. One can also find panolas, which are crosses between pansies and violas that offer the color range and size of pansies but the hardiness and better heat-tolerance of violas.

For best results plant violas in partial shade since they detest the hottest days of summer. Plant them in containers that can be in full sun during the cooler days of spring but moved to partial shade when summer heat arrives. While they will grow in average soil, they will appreciate a bit of fertilizer once they begin to bloom. Removing faded flowers will prolong bloom. If spent flowers are not removed, the plant will form a seed pod. The pod explodes when ripe, shooting the seeds quite a distance in all directions, thus giving the name "Johnny Jump Up" because the plants will appear here and there in the garden.

If you plan to use violas in cooking, be sure to grow them without harmful chemicals, fungicides, or insecticides.

Violas are commonly used fresh as a salad ingredient (both leaves and flowers) or floated on punches, teas, and lemonades. Fresh flowers are also frozen in ice cubes as a pretty garnish for beverages, or used on canapés.

Layering flowers with sugar or grinding flowers with sugar will produce a delightfully flavored sugar which can be used in cookies, pound cake, custards, teas, etc. Flowers are often candied by painting the flowers with beaten egg white (use dried egg whites, made according to package directions to avoid the possibility of salmonella) and coating with fine sugar to decorate cookies, cakes, and other desserts.

Chapter 5:

MAY

It was May 1st. Callie had just assembled most of the ingredients for a mock May wine into a box. It had taken several attempts to locate the punch bowl and ladle that had still been packed away in one of the many boxes that still filled a spare bedroom. She was running behind schedule. The watering took more time each day as the days grew longer and the plants' roots were filling their pots. Plus, she'd just finished another round of seeding into peat pots which dried out faster than plastic ones. Plants that resent having their roots disturbed will transplant directly into the garden or large containers without adverse effect when grown in peat pots, so Callie liked to use them. However, they did take more attention until they were planted into the garden or containers, so her hours of watering were increasing.

She loaded the box into her truck and added several platters of flower-shaped cookies with pastel-frosted petals, cupcakes that were decorated with the petals of scented geranium blooms, and a lemon thyme cake whose center held a bouquet of violets.

She'd had to scrape frost off the truck windows this morning. It was a chilly day for prancing around a May Pole. She wondered how many people would brave the cool temperatures. Hopefully the day would warm up quickly.

Once the food was placed and ready for customers, she filled the punch bowl with a container of sliced fresh strawberries. She added white grape juice that she had infused with sweet woodruff last spring using the leaves and flowers from her own garden. Daniel had teased her at the time, saying the green stuff in her basket had no smell let alone flavor. She had explained that the scent and flavor of vanilla and new-mown hay developed as the plant dried. The juice had spent the winter in her freezer. She'd also infused a bottle of brandy and some white wine, but she wouldn't serve that at the farm. She'd save that for the newsletter folding/tasting party this month. A few sprigs of fresh sweet woodruff that she'd plucked from the plantings under the lilac and viola blooms garnished the punchbowl.

Daniel! She hadn't thought about him in days. Maybe eating so many violas as she tested salads, cheese balls, canapés, and such was working after all. Her heart did not feel as broken as it had. Still bruised, definitely, but she could breathe when she thought of Daniel now. The tears did not automatically begin to flow. Quite possibly, "Heartsease" was an accurate folk name for the pretty little plant. Or, possibly it was that potent kiss from Deputy Wright. She was too swamped to analyze it right now.

She cleared up the food area, stored the box in the closet, and hurried to the plant sales area. It was only May 1st, but it was time to put the "Happy Mother's Day" stakes into rosemary topiaries, miniature roses, and planters to stimulate thoughts of buying for mother.

Pots of double apricot and white "Angelique" tulips and Callie's favorite lily-flowered "Marietta" tulips bloomed brightly in the area by the shadehouse. She'd dug the bulbs from her old gardens and planted them in pots right after she'd decided to quit her teaching job and start a farm. They'd been sitting behind the garage since she'd moved. When the new growth reached four inches, Callie had moved them to the shadehouse and lightly applied fertilizer. Now they were glorious. If they didn't sell, she'd plant them in her own gardens.

She also moved several varieties of spearmint onto her cart along with a few hanging baskets of the fragrant plant. A sign showing a race horse and giving the recipe for mint juleps was attached to the front. It was Derby Day down in Louisville, but she suspected she was not the only who celebrated the day with an annual mint julep.

The CD player with a lively Celtic disc was already sitting on a small table near the May Pole. Josh Sparks had advised her to add several outdoor outlets to both the Cottage and pumphouse exteriors and she was glad she had taken his advice. The music gave a cheerful atmosphere to the farm, and she decided to make it a daily occurrence. She had recently read a study that said music improved customers' moods and could increase sales. Plus, it just made her happy!

Lucy showed up in, of all things, a dress! It was a flowing white creation with silk flowers hot-glued around the neckline and randomly over the skirt. A wreath of silk flowers with ribbon streamers that matched the May Pole sat atop her head. "I made a crown for you, too," she beamed. "Don't you own a dress? You can't lead a May Pole dance wearing overalls!"

Callie looked down at her own outfit of worn overalls, a sweatshirt, and a pair of seen-better-days tennis shoes. "You're absolutely right," she called. "I'll be right back."

She hurried to the house, unlocked the door, and flew to her closet to rummage for anything suitable. Suddenly, she remembered the wispy pink dress she'd worn as maid of honor at Beth's wedding. She pulled the garment bag from the depths of the spare bedroom closet and shook it out. It took some digging but she found a rose-colored long-sleeve top to put on first, pulling the dress over it. After all, there was still frost on the ground. There weren't a lot of choices, but she finally settled on a pair of green slippers that matched yet another bridesmaid outfit she'd been forced to wear. One thing was certain. Her bridesmaids had been able to select sensible dresses that they'd be able to wear often, if they chose. She and Daniel had easily agreed on lovely shades of green for their wedding. They would look luscious with all the holiday colors of Christmas.

It would be the most wonderful wedding.

"Well, it could have been," she muttered to herself. "It should have been."

She pulled herself together, surprised to find tears running down her cheeks. She threw some water on her face. No sense in taking time to braid her hair. She grabbed a green sweater and ran back to the farm just as the first customers arrived.

The morning passed quickly, highlighted by Ellen's arrival with a vanload of young girls. "My granddaughter's Brownie troop," she explained. "I saw in your newsletter that you were going to have a May Pole. I haven't danced around a May Pole since I was their age," she continued. "So, last week, I taught the girls how. By the way, I told Mac what we were going to do and he's sending a photographer. Figures all those girls' parents and grandparents will want to buy a paper to get a picture of them dancing."

"Great planning, Ellen. Thank you so much," Callie beamed. "Take the girls inside for some cookies and punch until the photographer arrives," she instructed with a smile.

The sun broke through shortly afterwards and the number of cars increased. Lucy pulled another crown from her car for Ellen, who wore it proudly as she led the girls through a practice dance.

Quite a crowd of smiling faces were watching the dancers by the time the photographer arrived to capture the event for the newspaper. He took a few shots of people in the crowd, interviewed some of the Brownies, and popped into the Cottage for a sample of May wine.

"Mind if we give the recipe in the paper?" he asked, holding a copy of the free recipe Callie had placed in a basket beside the bowl. Callie had anticipated a brisk sale of sweet woodruff plants which she had placed in the plant cart near the check-out, and she'd been correct, especially since the sign over the flat explained that it also removed stale odors indoors and was a beautiful groundcover in shaded areas outdoors.

"Can I get a shot of you and Lucy next to the food table?" the young man asked, blushing slightly. Callie noticed that Lucy was also sporting a rosy blush that Callie suspected was not from dancing.

The day ended with a full cash register and two slightly exhausted young women wearing flower crowns sitting on the daybed. A plate containing the last of the cookies sat between them.

"I'd love a cupcake," Callie said wishfully, "but the table is just too far away. My feet are killing me. I was crazy to wear these slippers all day."

"But you look like a princess," Lucy said admiringly. "Too bad Deputy Wright couldn't have seen you today!" she said knowingly.

Callie's hair clouded around her face and shoulders, and her cheeks were rosy from rushing around in the cool air all day. She'd made a hundred trips from the shadehouse to the Cottage, to people's cars, to the May Pole, and back to the shadehouse.

"You were a wonder again today, Lucy," Callie praised. "I don't know how you stay so focused when people ask dozens of questions while you are trying to ring up prices. And that one lady kept changing her mind about what she wanted a dozen times. I'm not sure I would have been so patient myself!"

"I've been working at the newspaper since I was a kid," she said, "so I've had years of practice running a register while people change the wording of the ad they're placing over and over. Mrs. Davis never could make up her mind then, either. I hope I didn't make any mistakes, but I put a pencil mark by the register tape when her sale stopped, and I wrote down the things she actually did buy on the pad by the register after she left. You can check it later. It can tire a person out though," she said as she stretched her arms and legs. "I could sleep for hours," she yawned.

The phone rang and Callie groaned.

"I'll get it," Lucy offered.

"Bless you, my child," Callie grinned as she reached for the last cookie.

Lucy blushed and turned her back to Callie as she murmured into the phone.

"That was Time," Lucy nearly shouted as she jumped up and down. "He asked me to go out tonight!" she told Callie gleefully.

"That's wonderful, Lucy. Time?" she asked, "Isn't that an odd name?"

"Oh it's short for Timothy," Lucy informed her. "His dad always got teased about his name, so he said he was given his son a normal, distinguished name from the Bible."

"Timothy is a distinguished name but how did it become Time?" Callie asked.

"Oh, you know. It just happens in school. Besides, I think it's kind of cute. He's kind of cute, too. Time was the photographer that was here today. Didn't you get introduced? Time Pease" Lucy said dreamily.

"Cute, real cute," Callie agreed skeptically. "What's his father's name?"

"Warren!" Lucy called as she raced to her car.

Callie continued to chuckle as she closed up the shadehouse, collected the day's earnings, loaded the soiled platters and punch bowl into the truck, and locked the Cottage. Funny how a girl that said she "could sleep for hours" was suddenly energized by an invitation for a date! Callie could barely walk. She probably had blisters. A good hot shower and a soothing footbath was all she longed for at the moment. Wicca raced ahead of the truck. Darkness was falling.

She pulled to a stop and filled her arms with platters topped by the punch bowl and struggled toward the house. She'd followed Deputy Wright's advice, adding a row of solar lights along the walkway to the back door and a light by the corner of the house that came on when it detected motion. It was already gleaming brightly, having detected Wicca streaking by ahead of her.

The glass platters nearly fell from her hands when she saw the door was already open. She set them on the ground and ran to the truck to climb inside, letting Wicca jump in first. Callie locked the doors with one hand and reached for her cell phone with the other.

No pocket! She had neglected to get her cell phone when she'd changed into the dress. She backed out of the driveway and drove directly to the sheriff's office.

Several appreciative glances followed her as she walked to the duty desk.

"Someone broke into my house again. I didn't go in. They might still be there," she explained breathlessly.

"You're the herb lady," the officer at the desk stated. "Figures." He reached for the phone and spoke to the dispatcher. "Patrol car is near your place. He'll stop and check it out. Have a seat over there," he pointed to a stiff chair with cracked plastic seats.

Callie took a seat and wondered if there was a fine for driving to the sheriff's office to report a crime without having ones driver's license. It was in her wallet in her jeans, too.

Better not to mention that, she mused. She sat with her head in her hands, not wanting to think what the open door might portend this time. Another trashed house? Another nasty warning? Another knife?

A hand touched her shoulder. She jerked her head up to see Deputy Wright standing before her. She almost didn't recognize him without his uniform. He was dressed in a light blue shirt and nicely, oh, yes, very nicely fitted jeans. His damp hair was combed back from his face, and he smelled of soap.

"Ma'am," he said quietly, nodding his head toward her. "Your house is clear. I just got off duty, but I'll follow you home. You look a little shaky."

"I am a little shaky, I guess. I don't know why. I've been expecting something to happen. I shouldn't be surprised. You warned me," she babbled.

They walked to her truck where he helped her climb into the cab. "I'll be right behind you," he said. "Take it slow."

The officer who had checked her house was waiting in the driveway. Deputy Wright looked at him for a moment and suggested Callie wait in her truck. He conferred with the other officer for a moment and then returned.

"Let's pull your truck over to the side, so Deputy Thomas can continue his patrol," he suggested. He had parked his car far over to one side when they'd arrived. Deputy Thomas waved and backed his patrol car onto the road.

"You can relax," he said. "The house is all in one piece. This time." He guided her into the house, one hand firmly on her elbow to steady her.

One kitchen wall was covered with a spray-painted message, "Stay out of cort!" Below it, stuck to the wall with a knife was her favorite photo of herself and Wicca sitting in her old garden. Beth had taken the photo just before Callie moved. The frame was lying on the floor in pieces along with the shattered Mary Engelbreit print that normally hung on that wall. Only someone who had seen the photo before would have recognized it as being Callie and Wicca. Both their heads had been cut out of the picture.

Callie slumped into the chair the deputy had guided her to, pulled Wicca to her side, and buried her face into the dog's fur. Wicca whimpered in sympathy, not sure what was happening, but certain that her mistress was upset.

"I'll make you some tea," he said softly. He filled the kettle and put it on the stove.

"I would have taken that down before you came home, but I thought you needed to see it. You have to understand and to take these threats more seriously," he said, kneeling before her. He reached for her hands, grasping each of her small ones in his large, muscular ones.

"You're going to have someone stay with you for the final week before the trial," he stated. "Since I doubt you can afford to hire a body guard and the county can't hire one, I'm taking a week of vacation. Say hello to your new best friend," he stated.

It took a few moments for his words to sink into her befuddled brain. "But you can't," she said in a startled voice. "What will people think?"

The deputy continued to hold her hands in silence.

"You can't use your vacation days. I'm sure everything will be fine." Callie said softly.

"Callie, look at the photo. Really look at that photo. Think about the fact that the next time they come, you could be in the house alone. Think about Wicca. They're threatening her to get at you. Even if you had your cell phone, which I point out you don't, we might not get here before something happens."

Her hands began to shake. Two fat tears rolled down her cheeks as she looked into his eyes, the dimple on his chin, his strong hands holding her own. Moments passed in silence as she stared at his face. His jaw was set. His eyes said he would not take "no" as an answer. Callie felt as if she were melting.

"So, this is what it feels like to be afraid," she thought. Forcing herself to break the electric shock that seemed to be connecting her eyes with his, she looked into the face of her wonderful Wicca. The lab's gold-flecked brown eyes looked back with devotion. She swung her eyes back, and for a nano-second she thought she glimpsed the same in Deputy Wright's eyes.

It was settled. Callie was too tired and too emotionally fragmented to argue. She drank the tea which she discovered the deputy had laced with rum. She didn't argue about that either or the suggestion of a long hot soak in the tub.

When she'd inquired about his clothing, personal gear, and such, he answered simply that he always kept a change of clothes and a shaving kit in his trunk. He'd turn in the patrol car and gather a few more things tomorrow during her workshop. It was doubtful that anyone would attempt anything while there was a crowd of ladies around. She could keep Wicca safely at her side.

Callie soaked in a lavender scented tub, hoping the herb would work its magic, help her relax, plus relieve the headache that was beginning to pound at her temples.

Unknown to her, while she bathed upstairs, the phone rang. Deputy Wright sprinted to the studio and caught it on the second ring. He didn't want Callie to interrupt her bath.

"Yes," he growled into the receiver.

"Sorry. Guess I have the wrong number," said the caller and hung-up.

Deputy Wright waited by the phone. It rang again immediately, and this time he picked it up during the first ring.

"Yes," he growled again.

"Er...sorry. Is Callie there?" a male voice asked.

"She's taking a bath," the deputy informed the caller. "Who's calling?"

"Who are you? Let me talk to Callie," the caller barked back.

"I said the lady's busy," the deputy countered. "I'll take a message."

"Never mind." Mike Shipley said as he hung up the phone.

Callie dressed in a soft apricot sweat suit, slipped her feet into a pair of flip-flops, and braided her hair into a tight braid down her back. She went to the closet to pull a blanket, sheet, and pillow from the upper shelf.

"Sorry, there's no spare bed right now. I've filled both rooms with plant shelves and boxes," she apologized.

"No problem. I'd intended to sleep here on the sofa, so I could keep an eye on things," he stated.

She looked at the sofa. She'd covered it with an old blanket to hide the slash marks and keep the stuffing in place. Callie hadn't called about having it reupholstered because frankly, the house and its furnishings ranked way down the line in terms of budget right now.

"It'll be fine," he said, as if reading her mind. "You get some rest. Wicca and I will be right here. I don't think they'll be back tonight, and a patrol car in the driveway is a pretty good deterrent."

Callie thought, "Seeing a patrol in my driveway all night is something all right. Something else for the local grapevine to talk about!"

Although Callie was up before sunrise, she could already smell coffee before she descended the stairs. She'd dress in grubbies since she had to do all the watering and set up for her workshop. Today's topic was hypertuffa troughs, a messy production anyway. She'd warned the participants to dress for mess.

"Want some breakfast to go with that coffee?" she asked as she entered the kitchen. Deputy Wright was seated at the kitchen table reading her Sunday newspaper. "I could throw an omelet together. No trouble. I'd do one for myself anyway since I won't be getting any lunch," she babbled like the proverbial brook.

"Sounds good. Can I help?" he said, rising and stretching. Callie wondered if he'd been able to get any sleep at all on the lumpy sofa. She suspected there might be places where the stuffing was missing entirely, right down to the wood support. She'd try to do something to fix that before tonight.

"Sure, dice up this ham," she said, tossing a small package onto the counter. Within minutes the kitchen smelled of gently sautéed onions, peppers, and mushrooms in butter. As soon as the ham was diced, quite efficiently she observed, Callie poured in the whisked eggs and seasoned them with freshly ground pepper. She walked over to the kitchen window where she snipped tiny branches of winter savory and tarragon. She quickly removed the leaves from the stems, rolled the leaves into a cylinder shape, and snipped them over the eggs. A layer of grated cheese covered the entire mixture.

"No salt?" he observed.

"That's one of the benefits of using herbs. They add lots of flavor, so the dish doesn't need salt. Healthier. If one can call eating a skillet filled with eggs, ham and cheese healthy!" she laughed. He'd popped two slices of thick, homemade bread into the toaster.

"Jam's right above the toaster," she told him.

"Jam. Right. That's real healthy," he said dryly.

"One of my vices," she informed him.

"Got any other vices I should know about? Smoking, drinking, gambling, carousing, sleepwalking?" he said, almost teasing.

"Not that I care to share," she said with a chuckle.

Breakfast passed quickly with the deputy sharing bits of interest from the Sunday paper. He was surprised at her passion for college basketball.

"I would really go into depression once the NCAA tourney is over if the plant work didn't come on so strong right then. Fortunately, gardening and plants pretty much take over my world as spring starts and basketball ends," she explained.

"You don't seem like the depressed type to me," he stated. "You seem to take a positive attitude toward things. I think a lot of people would have buckled under the load of things you've had to handle recently."

"On that compliment, I think I'd better get to work. The watering has to be finished before the workshop starts," she stated.

"You did the cooking. I'll do the dishes," he said, beginning to clear the table.

Callie paused a second, then replied, "Okay. I'll let you, deputy!"

The next hours passed quickly as Callie watered the plants in all the rooms in the house and garage, gathered together some workshop supplies, and announced she needed to go to the farm.

"Right by your side," Deputy Wright stated. He paused, staring at the box of supplies. "Sorry, I can't offer to carry your box. Need to keep my hands free."

At that moment, watching his hand poised over his holstered gun, Callie truly recognized the seriousness of the threat posed. A chill ran through her body. She didn't want anything to happen to Wicca. She didn't want anything to happen to herself. And, the thought flashed through her brain like lightning, she truly did not want anything to happen to the tall man now standing in her kitchen.

The workshop went smoothly. All the ladies were delighted with their troughs. As Callie had hoped, they purchased an array of plants from the succulent display after she had shown them her finished planter. It contained a delightful mixture of colors and textures, all done in plants that loved dry heat. She'd told them the planting could withstand drought and three-week vacations without watering. That seemed to bring out the shopper in those more reluctant to open their purse strings. Several of the ladies had such a good time that they signed up for the next workshop before departing.

Callie had finished the shadehouse watering before the workshop started, so she only needed to clean up the mess, hide the cash drawer, turn off the coffeemaker, and close up the Cottage. By the time she'd finished, a black convertible had pulled into the parking lot.

"Don't they see the 'Closed on Sundays and Mondays sign'?" she muttered irritably, as she peered out the window. Then she gasped. It was an older car. It had tires that were definitely smaller than those of her pick-up truck. That fit the description of the tire tracks after her truck tires had been slashed! She hid behind the curtain and opened her cell phone.

Before she could push in the final digit she saw the long, lanky frame of Deputy Wright unfold from the car. She was so lost in amazement at his being able to fit into the sporty car that she didn't realize her thumb had pushed the button. She saw him reach for his cell phone as he walked toward the Cottage.

"Wright here," came a faraway voice. Callie suddenly became aware of what she had done. "Er.." she stammered, "Just checking my phone. I see you are indeed right here!" she said lamely. "Sorry, I didn't recognize your car."

Wicca was straining on her leash begging to be allowed to run. She'd been hooked to a table during the entire workshop and forced to stay in the Cottage while the ladies shopped afterwards. Callie wasn't taking any chances.

As Deputy Wright approached, Callie waved and called, "Wicca's going stir-crazy. We need to go for a long walk and let her get some exercise."

"Lead on," he smiled, shortening his long stride to match hers. They walked into the woods with Wicca dashing in circles around them.

"Nice piece of property," the deputy said. They'd been walking in silence only broken by the sound of scolding squirrels for several minutes.

"Yes, it's beautiful. I've already recorded forty varieties of wildflowers growing in these woods. There are probably lots more," Callie responded.

"The previous owner told me it hasn't been logged or pastured in over a hundred years."

"I believe it. There are some really large trees in here," he added.

"Giants. Especially the old oak about halfway back. Then there's the Teepee," Callie said.

"The Teepee?" he echoed.

"Wait till you see it. Then you'll understand," she smiled.

Indeed, he did when later they stood inside the hollow old sycamore. Callie was surprised that he could remain upright if he stood directly in the center. They spent a few minutes studying the carved initials inside the cavity.

"Looks like this has been a popular place over the years," the deputy stated as his fingers traced some of the dates carved into the wood. "A very popular place," he paused with his hand next to a heart surrounding two sets of initials. Callie glanced at the heart and felt her own heart do a somersault. Morgan closed the small distance between them, pulling her into the circle of his arms. His lips found hers in a searching kiss. Her heart continued to somersault for the next several minutes.

The week before the court date passed without further incident. After the kisses in the Teepee, Deputy Wright seemed to have gone back on duty, at least in terms of his actions around Callie. They were polite, and at times even warm, but there was a wary distance between them. Conversations were animated and always interesting. The days sped by with Callie attempting to get the gardens planted, keeping the displays filled, and the farm running.

Several customers gave Callie knowing looks as she helped them with plant selections or bagged their purchases. Deputy Wright, dressed in denim shirt and jeans was always lounging nearby, his holster barely hidden under a leather jacket. Sometimes he read, usually westerns, history or biographies of historical figures. Sometimes he worked Sudoku puzzles. After Callie demonstrated "her" mockingbird's echoing her whistling of "You Are My Sunshine," she heard him whistling the first line of "From the Halls of Montezuma" over and over whenever the bird perched on the weathervane. The deputy never complained although Callie was certain he must have planned a more exciting way to spend his limited vacation days.

They spent evenings cooking together, washing the dishes, and taking Wicca for walks. Sometimes they sat in the darkness of the gazebo and talked. One evening, Morgan taught her several new card games. The week passed quickly. Callie was surprised at how comfortable she grew with Morgan's constant presence.

On the day of the trial the weather was drizzly and cold. Deputy Wright insisted that she ride with him. Callie assented but insisted they take the truck, so Wicca could ride along. There wasn't room for all three in his little convertible.

He had described the courtroom procedure, so Callie was prepared. She'd never appeared in court before, but she'd seen a few courtroom scenes in movies.

"They aren't really that intense or scary," he'd assured her. He wore his uniform, since he would be called to testify along with the crime scene officer that had photographed the damage to her house, the Ball State canine officer who had stopped the car, and the officer who had video-taped the opening of her suitcase.

"It should be a slam-dunk," he said, trying to help her relax as they entered the courtroom.

While it wasn't exactly a slam-dunk to Callie, it was not as difficult as she'd expected. The only time she was really nervous was when she first took the stand. The defendant with tattoos and long dark hair, now shaped into a tidy military cut and dressed in a conservative suit that hid all his tattoos, gave her a murderous look. It was cut short by his attorney's elbow to his ribs. She spoke slowly and clearly, keeping her answers short and to the point, as the county prosecutor had suggested. The trial seemed to take a lifetime to Callie, but when she checked her watch as they were leaving, it had been less than forty minutes. Later the judge sentenced the dark-haired defendant to nine years in prison. The younger blonde man was a minor. However, since it was not his first offence, he was tried as an adult and received four years in jail.

It was over. The prosecutor and the sheriff both assured Callie that she could relax. Although several of the defendant's family had attended the hearing, the officials felt no one would risk capture now that harming her would no longer keep their relative from jail. Callie asked if they might not just do something out of meanness or seeking revenge. The sheriff smiled as he informed her that it was doubtful.

The worst of the lot had been arrested earlier in the week on a burglary charge, so they would be out of circulation for a while. She could indeed relax.

Deputy Wright collected his belongings from her house and stashed them into the tiny trunk of his convertible. Callie thanked him for his kindness, assured him she could never repay him for giving up his vacation, and placed the last loaf of homemade bread she'd made the day prior into the empty passenger seat.

After his departure, Callie wandered about the house which still smelled like paint remover and fresh paint. All the graffiti had been removed from the cabinet, appliances, and furniture. The wall had been repainted. The house looked perfectly normal and entirely too empty without the lanky deputy.

LouAnn filled in at the farm the day Callie was in court. She wanted to hear every detail of the hearing, so the two friends remained at the Cottage long after closing. Mike had brought a shipment of merchandise earlier in the day, so they unpacked and priced it as they talked.

"I'm surprised I haven't heard from Mike all week," Callie said.

"Oh really?" LouAnn looked speculatively, noting the tone in her voice. "Do you hear from him often?" she teased.

Callie stood looking at her friend. Then she laughed, "Look, I know everyone in this town knows Mike and I have had dinner a few times. You probably even know what movie we saw!"

"Oh, movies, too?" LouAnn giggled, watching the blush rise up Callie's neck. "Is there more that the local grapevine hasn't discovered, friend?"

"Nothing I care to discuss," Callie replied haughtily as she raised her head in mock severity and glided across the room before she burst into giggles herself.

LouAnn joined her on the daybed. "Seriously, Mike did seem pretty stiff today. Not his usual joking self. I'm sure he heard that Deputy Wright was staying at the house. It wasn't exactly a secret. In fact, as quickly as word got around, I wondered if some of the officers hadn't told folks on purpose hoping word would reach all the way to the bad guys so they'd think twice about coming out here."

"I'm just grateful that the week was trouble-free. Even though Morgan was here, I heard every sound, every car that drove by," Callie stated.

"Oh, now it's Morgan, is it?" LouAnn said in her speculating voice. "More news for the grapevine, Callie?" The blush was repeating itself, rising to include her entire face.

"No comment," Callie said turning away in embarrassment. "We'd better finish these boxes. I still have to work on those invoices tonight."

Callie fixed a simple omelet for her supper, noting that it was not nearly as much fun cooking this evening as it had been while Morgan was there. She wondered to herself when he had stopped being Deputy Wright in her mind. He was strong, fairly quiet, and private compared to Mike, who was talkative, teasing, and outgoing. Mike was more like Trev. Big teddy bear types that you just had to love and enjoyed having around. None of them were like Daniel. Daniel was......Daniel was warm, loving, tender, thoughtful, giving. Callie paused. Was he really, really all those things, or were those just characteristics she had projected onto him? Had she seen him through the rose-colored glasses of first love? Was she a judge of character at all, or were her perceptions easily skewed by emotion? Were Morgan, Mike, or Trev really who she thought they were? She'd thought Daniel was a man of character who truly loved her. Yet while she thought they were in love, he'd fallen out of love and into the arms of the persuasive Mariah.

Had he needed persuasion? Indeed, had Mariah seduced Daniel, or had he persuaded her? Callie did not have a clue. "That's me in a nutshell," she told Wicca. "Clueless."

She couldn't trust her own judgment. Heavens, she didn't even know if Trev was married, but she now suspected he lived with kids. None of the men in her life ever mentioned a wife, or even girlfriend, but then neither had Daniel.

"Stop!" she ordered her mind. "There are no men in my life. I don't have time. My heart is not healed yet. I don't need any men complicating my life." She forced herself to process the invoices and headed to another toss 'n turn night.

Chicory and sorrel leaves were big enough to harvest as well as the first lettuces, cilantro, spinach, snow peas, and radishes in the cook's garden. Callie had decided to gamble during the week Morgan had been protecting her. Although the frost-free date not been reached, the soil was warm enough to plant early beans, salad burnet, skirret, red-veined sorrel, smallage, summer savory, and calendulas. She put in borders of alpine strawberries, winter savory, lemon thyme, dwarf sage, and colorful violas. The cook's garden was not only cutting the grocery bill, but attracting lots of attention. "If they like it now," she thought, "wait till the opal basil, lemon marigolds, and hyacinth beans are showing-off!" She added a trellis in the center with a hops vine to cover the arches.

A simple wooden bench at the end held big pots of rosemary, bay, and colorful gallon jugs of herb-studded vinegars.

She'd worked evenings after the farm closed to plant shade lovers along the circular path in the woods. It was decorated with tiny, brightly colored bird houses, little wind chimes hung with bright ribbons, and colorful mushrooms made of resin or concrete. Fairy houses were spaced randomly along the path with little stone paths to their entrances. Miniature garden tools sitting on tiny benches hinted that the fairies had done all the gardening. Sweet alyssum, violets, primroses, and other small beauties were tucked near each house. Lily of the valley, sweet woodruff, golden babies' tears, and small ferns were scattered throughout the plantings. Hand-painted slates with fairy sayings were tucked here and there leaning against the trunks of trees, many of which sported tiny fairy sized doors and windows attached to their bark at fairy height. Nodding flowers of columbines swayed on tall stems in the breeze. It was indeed an Enchanted Forest that visitors to the farm loved.

The Joyful Heart Herbs "Fairy Days" had been a great success. Over a hundred little girls wearing wings had accompanied their mothers, grandmothers, aunts, or troop leaders on fairy hunts. They had enjoyed fairy tea and cakes, fairy stories, fairy crafts, and made fairy gardens. The local newspaper had sent Time Pease out to photograph the fairy parade. Even Lucy's VW, wearing colorful butterfly wings sprouting out each window had made the newspaper. LouAnn and Sandy had both been called into service to help that day. Each wore wings LouAnn had designed and painted.

Twice more, she'd rented tillers to work up the shade garden and the formal garden before she started planting there. Her tiller evaluation file was filled with comments. She was on a first name basis with the family that ran the local mulch business, having mulched not only the gardens and the planting she'd installed under the road sign, but also the paths in the Enchanted Forest.

The Cottage Garden was gradually filling with plants. The hanging baskets of nasturtiums planted in early March were beginning to have enough flowers that Callie could experiment with new recipes using the peppery blooms. The girls were scheduled to come this week to taste more recipes, so she'd need to dream up some new creations.

That also meant she had to get the newsletter e-mailed to Cecilia, and although Callie had done some preliminary notes, it was far from being ready to go to the printer. She found herself hoping that there would be few customers today, so she'd have time to work on it, but looking at the clear sky and listening to the birds sing sweetly, she doubted it. In any case, she loaded her laptop into the truck, the back of which was entirely filled with plants again. She'd been moving plants that were hardier from the shadehouse to pallets set up on cement blocks at the east end of the parking lot every day this week. Then she filled the shadehouse up again with plants from the house. The living room, dining room and one spare bedroom were actually empty now! Callie felt like she was living in a mansion, compared to the cramped quarters she'd been in all winter. She took down the temporary shelving and moved it to the farm for additional displays, storing the lights in the space above the rafters in the black walnut garage. She'd need them in the greenhouse or shadehouse this winter.

She finished unloading the truck, filled the coffeemaker with water, and opened a new variety of tea for her customers to sample. As she worked, she noticed dust on a few items in the store and sighed, knowing that she had to dust immediately. Customers, consciously or unconsciously, saw dust as a sign that the inventory had been there a long time and therefore must not be desirable. That was one problem with a gravel parking lot; the dust traveled and settled in minutes. She was sick of dusting although it did provide a chance to see what merchandise was moving well and what orders she needed to place. She still didn't feel she had a good handle on ordering. Some weeks anything blue sold, but the next week everyone wanted red. She just couldn't tell what her customers would buy, and that was frustrating.

Callie was tired. She worked fifteen hours a day doing physical work at the farm. At night she did bookkeeping on the computer, answered the constant stream of e-mails, and updated the website. She worked on handouts, sample projects, descriptions, and pricing for workshops or plans for special events. The books on promoting one's business had been correct. Without special events Callie felt her business would be doing half the current sales. Special events were crucial to success, but they took a lot of planning and hours of extra work and promoting.

She loved her plants. She loved her Cottage. She loved her gardens. She loved her business, but two hands were just not enough to do the ambitious schedule it was requiring to get it off the ground. She needed another pair of hands and another pair of eyes. Lucy was here on Saturdays and was looking forward to working more once school was out, but Callie needed someone now!

Callie flipped the pages on the calendar she'd added to the wall behind the sales counter. This Sunday was Mother's Day. Callie planned to go visit her parents. Her mother had a keen instinct where her children were concerned and she could read paragraphs into a sigh, a change of tone, or even the speed or number of pauses. She'd be plied with questions and worried looks unless she could put on a very good front. Could she get through the day without letting her parents know the troubles she had? Could she convince them she was just tired and working too hard? Although the robbers were now in prison, there were still the questions of who had been killing deer on her property, and who had left the message on her windshield along with the slashed tires.

"Speaking of tires...." Callie remembered. She still had the two worn tires on the front of her truck, which meant she had no spare. She'd better not drive to her parent's without good tires. Her dad would notice that in a minute and she'd hear his soft voice express worry. If the tire store were open, he'd probably insist they drive right in and get them replaced. She reached for the phone and made an appointment to get two new front tires before the farm opened the next morning.

Since she had to go to town tomorrow, she decided that evening after she finished the newsletter, she'd finish the column for the newspaper, too. She'd intended to always be writing a few weeks ahead, but she'd been so busy in May that she had not kept up. Now she was writing each week's column as it was due. She pulled some of the handouts that she had used to promote sales at farmers' market from her filing cabinet. Since she had done these before she had the laptop, she couldn't just pull the handouts up and edit them. She had to type them in first. Too bad she didn't have a scanner. She added that to her wish list.

The newsletter fell together nicely. She wrote about National Herb Week, which the farm would celebrate a week late since Callie had forgotten all about including it in last month's newsletter. She wrote about arugula, a tasty herb commonly used in Italian cooking and listed the workshops for June. She'd do one workshop on lavender, since that was one of her favorite herbs, and one on herbal topiaries. The third would be "Herbs of the Bible" she finally decided. Then she changed it to "herbal cheeses" since June was National Dairy Month. She could do "Herbs of the Bible" anytime. It was already too late to promote any sales for Mother's Day, so she did a brief article about plants that men might like and offered a sale for Father's Day on "Dad's Favorite" dianthus, a ruffled white beauty with burgundy edges and streaks.

She wrote about nasturtiums for the newspaper since she had been thinking about them in terms of recipes throughout the afternoon. The baskets in the shadehouse looked beautiful. If someone read her column and wanted to give them a try, they wouldn't be disappointed at the plants they found at Joyful Heart. It was nearly dawn before she slipped between the sheets.

The alarm went off and was truly alarming. Callie looked at herself in the mirror and thought she wouldn't even need a mask if this were Halloween. Her hair was a tangled mess. She didn't just have bags, she had suitcases under her eyes. They were sunken into her head and were surrounded by dark shadows. She hurried through her morning routine, skipping Tai Chi as she had most of the week. It was probably a mistake. Although she was working hard physically, she wasn't using all her muscles equally. Tai Chi also gave her a sense of calm that she was definitely lacking these days.

At the tire store, she encountered the surly employee who'd asked for the "service fee." She felt his eyes following her as she went to the sales counter. The man at the counter was cheerful and helpful, calling "Hey, Joe, put two more new tires on this lady's truck!" He turned to Callie and said, "You remember Joe? Joe Suggs? He put on the first two at your house."

"Oh, yes, I remember Mr. Suggs," Callie said sweetly. Out of the corner of her eye she saw Joe Suggs spit a stream of tobacco juice on her new tire. As Callie flipped through magazines in the waiting room she noticed a Christian radio station playing in the background. The music was uplifting and she found herself feeling immensely better by the time she paid the bill and headed to the grocery. She needed some ingredients for the Strawberry Tiramisu she intended to take to her parents' home for Mothers' Day and a few things for the Mothers' Day refreshments on Saturday at the farm. She thought about stopping at the library to order a few books on interlibrary loan, but then decided she really didn't have time to read. She was still trying to finish knitting the tiny blanket for Beth's expected baby in her spare time.

She had a busy sales day at the farm since it was officially time to plant tomatoes, peppers, basil, and annual flowers outdoors. Callie planted some in the Cook's Garden during the lunch-time lull, filling one bed with rows of green beans and another with zucchini and yellow crookneck squash. She edged a bed with deep purple basil and another with the tiny mounding "Spicy Globe" basil. She filled one rectangular bed with "Genovese" basil with its heady fragrance and succulent large leaves. The last bed was edged with pretty "Serrata" basil. Its lacy, serrated edges made it one of Callie's favorites. She could almost taste the pesto she'd make!

Surprisingly, she heard the UPS van come at the end of the day as she was tidying the Cottage and closing out the register. Mike's route usually brought him by in mid-morning. Wicca took off like a shot, anticipating a handful of treats. She checked her hair in the mirror and wished she looked better than she did.

"You look tired, Callie," were his first words.

"And it's nice to see you, too," Callie said sharply. "I'm sorry," she quickly apologized as she saw his face crumple. "You're right. I am tired."

"You have some boxes," he nodded toward the back of the truck.

"Great. You're running late today. Have a problem?" she asked as she pulled the cart over to the truck.

"No, I saved your boxes until last. I thought maybe we needed to talk. I knew you'd be busy with customers earlier, so I waited until closing time," he explained. He took one of her hands and looked at her face. "I've missed you, Callie."

Callie tried to think of a reasonable response. "I've missed you, too," would be the most expected, but she found the words just didn't come out of her mouth. "Sorry, but I've decided men are just too confusing" was another possibility, but she didn't think Mike would understand that one. She finally settled on the trite, "I've just been too swamped here to think about anything but my job list, Mike. I'm sorry."

Mike looked at her face then at the horizon. "I see."

There was an awkward pause.

"I thought maybe Morgan was still at your place, but I haven't seen his car when I've gone by," Mike said hesitantly.

"Oh, no," Callie said quickly, "he was just there the week before the trial for my protection. There were all those threats….." her voice trailed off.

"So, you two aren't an item?" he asked quietly.

"No, we're not," Callie answered. Silently, her mind said "Darn it."

"Let's get these boxes unloaded," she said aloud.

"I've got a tube for you, too." he said, passing her a thick brown cylinder.

Callie popped one of the ends open and withdrew a sheaf of blueprints. "It's the greenhouse blueprints, Mike! Look! It must finally be on its way!" Callie was jumping up and down in delight. "Oh, thank you, thank you!" she exclaimed as she hugged him joyously.

"Now that's more like it," Mike smiled as he hugged her in return.

They unloaded the boxes of summer merchandise that Callie had ordered in Atlanta. Afterwards, they drank glasses of iced tea as Callie showed Mike the drawings of her new greenhouse. It was the most beautiful thing she'd ever seen. She could already picture herself happily transplanting inside in the warm space with snowflakes whirling outside in the dead of winter. She'd finally cancelled the order for the small, portable greenhouse. This one was a full-sized commercial structure.

Mike commented that it looked pretty complicated, but Callie explained that her father was coming to help construct it. He could build anything, and she was really looking forward to the time they would spend together. She'd take the blueprints over on Sunday, so he'd have a chance to study them before the greenhouse materials actually arrived.

It was after dark by the time Mike left. He had extracted a promise to have dinner with him early the following week. Neither of them noticed the slowly moving patrol car that went by just before sundown.

The rest of the week flew. The Mothers' Day refreshments looked as good as they tasted, and the few people who sampled the goodies complimented them. Most people were in a hurry. They just wanted to get mom a gift and get going. Sales were much slower than Callie expected, but it meant that she had not given away as many free flowers as she'd anticipated, so she guessed that was the positive aspect.

She visited her parents on Sunday and they enjoyed the strawberry dessert she took.

Callie's dad poured over the blueprints like a kid with a new toy and started deciding which tools he'd need to bring. Callie's mother filled her in on all the old neighbors and happenings both in the community and at their little country church. Although Callie saw the worried look in her eyes, her mother did not lecture her on taking better care of herself.

After Callie left, her mother told her father, "That girl is just pining away for Daniel. Did you see how thin she is? Those circles under her eyes! I could just shake that boy!"

Callie checked her schedule on Monday and noticed the Heart and Soil meeting was that evening. She'd given a speech to a church ladies' group in a nearby town on "Herbs of the Bible" so she had missed April's meeting. She wrote this week's column so she could drop it off in town when she ran errands. This time "Cardinal Climber" was the topic. Callie loved the delicate serrated foliage of the sturdy annual climber. During the summer, right up until a hard freeze, it produced masses of scarlet trumpet-shaped blooms that hummingbirds loved. After she finished the article she made a note to hold a "Climbers for Pots and Privacy" workshop in July.

She dropped the article at the newspaper office, picked up some supplies she needed for her workshop next Sunday, and went to the bank to transfer the CD she'd been saving to pay for the greenhouse into her checking account. She stopped at the hardware to pick up some plastic tubing and copper wire for some fountains she intended to make.

"Got a plumbing problem in that old house of yours?" Jake Wilson inquired.

"Not at all," Callie responded.

"What are you gonna do with all this tubing?" he asked.

"Oh, I have a project I'm working on," she said evasively. It wasn't any of Jake's business what she bought. "Have any 'No Hunting' signs come in yet?"

"Yeah," he said sulkily, "they're in the back."

"I'll take twenty," she said cheerfully.

Back at the farm, she did the essential watering, moved more plants from the garage to the plant sales area, and paced off the area for the new greenhouse. She couldn't wait for it to arrive. The letter accompanying the blueprints said it was being shipped that week. Callie didn't know how many days it would take the semi to make the trip from Iowa. She'd phoned Flint Stone and made arrangements for him to bring his bobcat over as soon as the semi came. The forklift attachment would be a lifesaver to unload all the pallets and the auger attachment would dig the holes for the main poles. He was also bringing his bulldozer to make the ground perfectly level. Callie would need to rent a transit and a cement mixer. Suz was scheduled to bring a load of crushed stone.

After Callie told her about the greenhouse project, Lucy discussed it with Time Pease. He and three of his football teammates were willing to help pour concrete and "fetch and carry" as required. Callie's dad was a skillful builder, but it would take more muscle than he and Callie could generate to put this giant tinker toy skeleton together. Those large sheets of Plexiglas would not be easy to hold in place in a breeze, let alone in the winds that blew across the central Indiana flatlands.

The more Callie anticipated building her greenhouse, the more she began to worry. With her father here she'd have to cook regular meals, rather than skipping most because she was busy. She'd be working with him on the greenhouse, which would make it difficult to manage the shop and aid customers. Her eyes traveled around her gardens, noticing the magenta bloom of money plant along the woods. She needed to move some into the Butterfly Garden. Elizabeth's irises were just beginning to unfurl. Old-fashioned dark purple ones, some in a pinkish lavender, and some that were almost brown were crowded together. Clumps of coral bells held their airy stems aloft for the hummingbirds to sip on the tiny bells. Suddenly she pictured weeds taking over her gardens. There was no getting around it. She had to hire some help. The big question was where she would find it.

By the time she'd finished at the farm, spent an hour on paperwork, and grabbed a sandwich, it was time to go to the garden club meeting. Most of the business meeting was again centered on the plans for the June plant sale. It was part of the town's "Heritage Days" celebration, so lots of people were expected to attend. The program was given by the gourd-grower, Merle, and his wife Arlene. She did the crafting and talking; Merle did the growing. Arlene gave a lively presentation on twisting the stems of long-handled gourds into odd shapes using pantyhose. They asked for volunteers to help clean more gourds to be made into birdhouses for the plant sale, and several members raised their hands. Afterwards, Callie was visiting with Ellen when a petite, very primly dressed woman approached.

"Oh, I'm sure you two know one another," Ellen exclaimed.

"As a matter of fact, we haven't been introduced," the well-dressed woman stated. "I'm Gloria McKenzie, Lucille's mother."

"How nice to meet you," Callie said warmly. "Your daughter has been a godsend. Lucy's a real jewel. I can't tell you how much I enjoy having her at the farm."

"Thank you. Lucille has told me she enjoys her time there," Gloria said somewhat coolly. "I hope she isn't too much trouble."

"Oh, she's no trouble at all. In fact she's just the opposite. She has amazing people skills. Just seems to be able to zero in and helps them find exactly what they want even if they weren't sure when they came in," Callie added enthusiastically. "She has so much artistic talent as well. She's doing most of our color planters and making all the succulent wreaths now. She really has a good eye for color and style."

"Yes, she does have a certain amazing style," Mrs. McKenzie said blinking rapidly.

"She's a bundle of energy, that's for sure, and so much fun," Ellen added.

"I just wish I could find another person just like her. I'd hire them in a flash," Callie said wistfully.

"Well, I'm not exactly like Lucille, but I think I would enjoy working at your business," Gloria stated.

A lengthy silence followed. Callie's mind was whirling. What would Lucy think about her mother working at the farm? Had they discussed it? Gloria seemed so cool and prim. Would she work well with customers? Be willing to weed and drag water hoses?

"Gloria does have beautiful gardens, Callie. You should see them. And she knows her plants," Ellen offered, breaking the awkward silence.

"Well, it would be seasonal work. Mainly just part-time in June and July until the greenhouse is finished. Then I may have to re-evaluate my labor needs," Callie said, hedging her commitment.

"That would be lovely," Gloria said. "I can start whenever you would like me to come."

"Then I'll see you tomorrow morning. Shall we say around nine, so you have time to get acquainted with the shop before we open," Callie suggested.

"It will be my pleasure," Gloria said as she glided away.

Callie watched her go, wondering if she had just made a huge mistake.

By the end of the week Callie had totally re-evaluated her impression of Lucy's mother. She was poised and graceful but willing to tackle any garden chore. She came to work dressed in stylish clothes designed just for the lady gardener, usually floral slacks with a matching jacket of durable cloth over a coordinating knit shirt. She had trendy garden clogs in a never-ending variety of colors to match the outfits as well as stylish, but practical hats. Callie discovered that Gloria was perfect for the customers that were serious gardeners and wanted to flout Latin names. She was equally good at patiently helping beginning gardeners to avoid serious mistakes. And best of all, she loved to dust!

With Gloria's help three days a week and Lucy on Saturdays, Callie was starting to get a handle on the job list. Gloria managed the farm whenever Callie needed to leave early to give presentations. And with two people weeding or watering between customers, Callie was able to squeeze in other jobs during the day. Occasionally, she now made it to bed before midnight. She even allowed Mike to persuade her to have dinner with him once a week.

Feeling optimistic and having finally found the time to weed the garden around the gazebo, Callie decided to have the May recipe-testing evening outdoors. She moved a small table into the gazebo and filled it with tiny vases of flowers and candles. The evening was great fun. Callie had chosen appetizer dishes using nasturtiums and fruits. The cocktail for the month was a mint julep made with a variety of mint syrups, sugars, and mint varieties.

"Did this come from your new still?" Suz asked, twirling the icy glass in her strong fingers.

"My still?" Callie repeated questioningly.

"Word around town is that you're building a still," Cecilia nodded. "Isn't that illegal?"

"I'm not building a still," Callie protested, although as soon as the words went through her mind it leaped at the possibilities! A still! She could distill her own essential oils! She could make her own hydrosols as a by-product! She was lost in thought when Suz poked her in the ribs.

"So, what was all that copper tubing for if you aren't building a still," she repeated now that she had regained Callie's attention.

"Oh, I'm going to make some wonderful fountains. Possibly for a workshop," she explained.

"Sign me up," said Suz. "Me, too!" the others chimed.

The newsletter was folded and true to her promise, Cecilia had developed sheets of computer printed address labels that allowed the women to finish in record time

One day, Callie took time to wander along the edge of the woods replacing the 'No Hunting' signs. Wicca was delighted to be covering some new territory. She spent most of her days greeting customers and soaking up all the attention they gave her. Callie brought a basket with her to collect elderflowers, more commonly called "elderblow". She made some of the flower clusters into traditional fritters, spiked with peach schnapps and dusted with confectioner's sugar. The bulk of the flowers were dried for a future "Herbal Cosmetics" workshop.

The wildflowers were gone in the woods now that the canopy of leaves blocked out the sunlight. Ferns grew in colonies near the creek in places and Callie found some patches of garlic mustard. She'd need to come back and destroy the invasive before it seeded. Garlic mustard would spread exponentially and smother out the more desirable native wildflowers.

She revisited the Teepee, where she noticed a new heart had been carved with the initials "LM + TP" inside. "Hmmm," Callie wondered aloud to Wicca. "What do you make of that?" Wicca just grinned and wagged her tail knowingly.

The days were getting much warmer, often in the upper seventies. Callie ordered shade cloth for the shadehouse, thinking how great it would be if it arrived while the football players were still here to help hoist it over the rafters and tie it down. She had already removed the plastic from the sides of the shadehouse to allow breezes to blow over the plants and to help keep the building cooler. May was nearly over.

It rained the last Saturday in May, buckets and buckets at a time. It was Memorial Day weekend, and Callie suspected business would be slow or non-existent. It proved to be the latter. Since there were no customers, Callie and Lucy spent the day in the Cottage removing the spring daffodils, cast iron baby chicks, bird nests, bunnies, and other obviously spring décor. They packed it into a carton labeled "Easter/Spring" and stored it in Callie's attic. The spring green and soft yellow tablecloths and ribbons were replaced with more summery whites and blues. When July rolled around, they'd add some red.

They put up a new display that featured lavender. Callie had found some lovely linens with a lavender motif and several body products that featured the heavenly scent. They draped lavender tulle over a table and Lucy made some beautiful tassels to tie at the corners. They moved the big tub of lavender to the center of the display and surrounded it with embroidered sachet bags. The display would also help promote the "Crafting and Cooking with Lavender" workshop the middle of the June.

The second display for summer featured butterflies. Callie had scheduled a butterfly event in late June. There were a few books on butterflies, some butterfly houses made by a local woodworker, signs, dishes, candleholders, and flags with butterfly motifs.

As they'd worked, Callie brought up the subject of Lucy's mother working at the farm. "It's okay with me," Lucy said. "She really loves plants, and she is very good with people. We just have different styles. She's a little old-fashioned, you know, but some of your customers like that!"

Callie hid a smile as she responded, "Well, God made everyone just a little bit different to make the world more interesting. Just think if we only had one kind of plant or one kind of bird."

Since business was so slow and it was Saturday night, Lucy left early. The rain had finally stopped, so Callie took a mug of tea outside. Her mockingbird flew out of the trees onto the weathervane and began singing, happy that the storm had passed.

Callie listened with enjoyment then felt her heart lurch as he began singing "From the Halls of Montezuma". Pictures rolled through her mind like an old movie reel. Deputy Wright cooking with her in the kitchen or laughing as they played cards. She remembered the way his eyes never stopped surveying the area for possible danger even as he helped her move plants. She saw him playing with Wicca or leaning against the fender of his convertible. She recalled the way he combed his damp hair back after a shower and the smell of the oil he used to clean his pistol. She hadn't heard a word from him since the day of the trial.

"Men!" she shouted, causing Wicca and the mockingbird both to jump in surprise. "They show up out of the blue and just when you start to feel something, they disappear! Take my advice, girl. Don't trust them. Don't trust any of them." Wicca nodded in agreement as she moved to Callie's side. Together they locked the Cottage and went to clean the spare bedroom for her dad to use during his stay.

Arugula

A traditional Italian salad ingredient and herb, arugula came to colonial America better known as "rocket". The French call it "roquette". Whatever the name, this dark green leafy herb is filled with flavor. Some describe it as tasting like smoked turkey with a bite, others call it spicy. Arugula is an annual. It is easy to grow from seed and will self-seed to provide continual harvests. The seeds germinate in early spring, while the ground is still cool. In fact, arugula prefers to grow in cool temperatures and bolts when the weather turns hot. One can begin harvesting the lobed outer leaves as soon as they are finger-length. Eventually, the plant will produce a tall (18"-28") stalk bearing small clusters of beige flowers. These flowers are delicious when added to salads or used to decorate small canapés.

The leaves will become more biting and less tender once the flower stalk is formed. At that point, many people prefer to use them cooked in soups and stews rather than raw. They can be used in any way that spinach or other greens are cooked, although their flavor is rather spicy. Left to self-seed, another crop will germinate in late August as the evenings begin to cool, and provide leaves through the light frosts of autumn. Arugula is a good candidate for cold frame gardening since it can survive cold temperatures. It also grows nicely in containers.

Chapter 6:

JUNE

June arrived on a cloud of soft air. The grass was a luxurious green. Mock orange shrubs and clumps of peonies Elizabeth had probably planted filled the air with perfume. Callie moved other plants around as they appeared in Elizabeth's old beds into the new ones she had made, so colors blended better. She'd already found valerian, dairy pinks, white columbines, pink toadflax, and clumps of aromatic Sweet William. She spent the time until the greenhouse arrived weeding, mulching, labeling plants, and rescuing more of Elizabeth's old varieties from the encroachment of the woods. As the ground received sunlight and the weeds were removed, more clumps of perennials kept appearing. She discovered bluebells, campanulas, daylilies, and even a scraggly rose bush or two. Those she pruned and fertilized, waiting eagerly to see what type of rose they turned out to be. She suspected one was an old moss rose since the stems bristled with fine thorns.

Business was steady, and she had full workshops this month. She potted some plants for the Heart and Soil plant sale, so they'd have time to settle in by mid-month when "Heritage Days" were held. She rented yet another tiller and worked up some ground behind the shadehouse for additional raised beds that would hold lavenders she had ordered from growers all over the country. These lavenders would be stock plants that she intended to use for propagating.

Finally, the freight company called saying her greenhouse would arrive on Tuesday. She called her father and then phoned Flint to arrange for the bobcat. The days passed in a tornado of activity. Her father arrived with his new truck loaded to the top with tools. He also had a big box of food and a picnic basket of treats that her mother had sent, "Just in case you're too busy to cook properly," the attached note read. "Take good care of your father and don't work too hard. Love, Mother"

Callie and her father used the rented transit to check the grade as Flint's bulldozer scraped and leveled the earth. It took much longer than Callie had envisioned, because her father correctly insisted that the ground slope ever-so-slightly from the center to insure good drainage.

When the semi arrived, Flint unloaded the huge inventory of materials, forming what looked like a barricade at one end of the parking lot. There were pallets of boxes containing bags of screws, plastic washers, and long bolts. There were bundles of short, medium, and long metal poles. There were pallets with fans and furnaces strapped tightly. Huge rectangles of Plexiglas and an enormous roll of double poly were too heavy for the bobcat, and had to wait for the assistance of the football players. Every box and package was stenciled with a code that matched the inventory parts list. Sometimes Callie spent hours searching through the stack of boxes to find the part that was needed next.

Flint dug the holes for the structural poles using the bobcat's auger attachment. The next morning, they were totally filled with water so Callie had to rent a pump in addition to the cement mixer. Time and his fellow football players earned their pay unloading the heavy pallets, carrying parts, pushing wheelbarrows filled with cement, and helping connect the long metal poles. Each day was filled with new challenges. Many evenings after supper she helped her dad assemble mechanisms to be installed the following day. It was a very special time, the two of them working together as they had when Callie had been a girl on the farm. As the greenhouse grew, customers and neighbors would stop to watch the progress. Whenever the UPS truck rolled in, Callie could count on Mike to take time to praise her father's skill. Some days he brought parts that had not been shipped originally. A couple of evenings he came back after work to help attach Plexiglas to the walls, staying to share the supper Callie had prepared.

One day, Callie and her dad took a short break while they waited for a part they needed. She wanted him to see the Teepee, so they walked into the woods.

"This is a beautiful piece of woods," her dad observed. "Lots of wonderful trees."

"Aren't they?" she sighed happily. "The former owner told me the place hasn't been logged or pastured for over a hundred years."

"That's not necessarily a good thing," her father replied. "Oh, if you want it to be totally natural, I suppose it's the thing to do, but it seems like a waste to me. A woodlot needs to be managed to be productive and healthy. You've got some big black walnuts over there that are beginning to show some signs of old age. Shame to let them just fall down and rot after they've worked for decades to grow tall and straight."

"You think so, Dad?" Callie said as she considered his words. "I just don't want to see my woods ruined. Loggers always seem so destructive. They tear it all up, damage other trees."

"My granddad always brought the logs out with a team of horses. Didn't have to cut a big road, no heavy equipment required. Hardly even knew any trees had been removed. Except, most times, those heavy stumps dragged along the ground, mixed the soil up a bit, and made a little furrow. Next spring, you could follow a trail of wildflowers right along the path those logs made. Always seemed magical to us kids. Then, where it was a little brighter, because a big tree had been taken out, we'd always find the biggest berries growing the next summer. Nope, taking out a tree is not always a bad thing, Callie"

"And," her father continued, "you'd get a decent price for those trees. I know that greenhouse cost a pretty penny or two. If you don't need the tree money for bills, put it aside for a rainy day. You never know when the cow might die."

Callie laughed. The story of the cow dying was one she'd heard over and over as a child. When the Depression first started, her father's grandfather lived on the farm where Callie's parents now lived. They'd only had one cow to provide milk for the family, and one day it died unexpectedly. For days afterwards, grandfather and grandmother debated whether to buy another cow or to purchase milk from the neighbors. It was a big decision because buying a new cow would take all their savings. Finally, they decide to buy a cow so grandfather hitched up the team, and went into the bank to withdraw all their money. The next day the banks closed in the panic that hit the country. The family didn't buy a cow but instead hoarded their meager savings to pay taxes and buy crucial items that saw them through the Depression. While many families around them lost their farms because they had no cash to see them through, Callie's forbears had not only survived, but thrived. By the time Callie's grandfather had married, each son in the family had his own farm. The story pressed home the family's belief that one should save for the unexpected, not trust banks, and that it wasn't always bad when the cow died or some other disaster struck. If you waited and had faith, there was usually a silver lining to every cloud.

When the greenhouse was finally completed, Callie threw a party for all those who had helped, including the football players and their families. Suz and Flint Stone came, of course, as well as Josh Sparks, who had done all the wiring. She invited Lucy and her parents. Everyone had a wonderful time, eating and inspecting the new greenhouse. The boys proudly pointed out all the things they had accomplished, including putting the new shade cloth on the shadehouse. As evening fell the automatic shutters closed just as they should, and everyone cheered. After everyone left, Mike helped her load the leftover food and dishes into boxes while her father packed his tools into his truck.

"Now that the greenhouse is finished, maybe you'll have a little more time to socialize," Mike said thoughtfully.

"Yes, tonight was fun. I'd forgotten how much fun a party can be," Callie smiled.

"I wasn't exactly thinking of parties and lots of people," Mike said as he pulled her into his arms.

"Mike, dad's here," Callie warned.

"Do you think he'd object?" Mike asked playfully.

"Maybe not, but now's not the time. I have to clear up this mess and get the leftovers into the refrigerator. It's getting late," Callie observed.

"You're the boss," Mike said sadly.

The next morning, Callie hugged her dad as he prepared to return home. He'd been there over two weeks. He needed to get home to prepare his combine for the upcoming wheat harvest. Besides, her mother would be getting lonely. Callie sent a few items from her shop that she thought her mother would enjoy, along with pictures of her father building the new greenhouse and the completion party.

"You're wonderful, Dad. The greenhouse is perfect, and how you figured it all out was amazing. You're the best," Callie said as she hugged him again.

"Take good care of my old truck," he smiled. "Glad to see you got new tires. Didn't think the old ones were all that bad, but it's probably best to get new ones with all the loads you haul from Indianapolis."

Callie waved as he pulled out of the driveway. She'd never tell him how "bad" the others had looked, slashed and flattened. No need for her parents to worry.

When her father returned home, Callie's mother plied him with questions about his stay. He gave brief one-word answers without much comment. However, just as they were settling in bed that night he said, "I don't think Callie is pining over Daniel any more." Then he rolled over and went to sleep. Callie's mother stared at the ceiling in frustration, wondering what his comment meant. "Men!" she thought, as she made plans to call her daughter first thing the next morning.

Callie and Wicca both moped around the house the evening after her father left. The house seemed really empty even though her father was a quiet man. She pulled the sheets from the bed in the spare room and threw them into the washer. She checked her e-mail, made a new job list, and sat down to work on the blanket for Beth's baby. It was a soft green. Once Callie heard from Bob, she'd embroider little pink flowers on the edge if it was a girl, maybe a row of little train engines if it turned out to be a boy. As she worked, she mentally went over the "herbal cheeses" and "herbal topiaries" workshops that were scheduled for this month. There were still some supplies to get and some timing problems to solve. She needed to make another trip to Indianapolis for greenhouse supplies. Many of the plants were outgrowing their little pots, and she needed window boxes and big containers to make additional patio planters. The bee hives would require another super soon, and she still had to mulch the new lavenders she'd planted in the raised beds with a layer of crushed stone. She was glad school would soon be out, so Lucy could work more days.

She had taken her father's advice and made arrangements for a logger to buy the big, aging black walnuts. A nearby breeder would bring a team of Belgian draft horses to drag the logs from the woods. The local woodworker, who made the butterfly houses for her shop, would take the larger branches for woodworking projects. The small branches would be left in the woods to add humus to the soil. Callie decided to have a big garden party at the farm so people could watch the beautiful horses do their job. She announced in the June newsletter that it would happen on the Saturday before Father's Day. Callie thought it might be an event in which the men in the family would be interested enough to accompany their wives to the farm. The newsletter included the workshop topics for July and a reminder for Butterfly Day the end of June. She included an article on one of her favorite plants, Monarda, and a recipe using it. The newsletter also announced a party to celebrate the birthday of author Beatrix Potter on Saturday, July 28th.

She'd have to get the newsletter in the mail quickly to promote the Father's Day event. So, she called her friends to assure an evening that week would be possible for recipe testing and processing the newsletter. Unfortunately, June was a busy month with graduations, weddings, and anniversaries. Sandy had lots of committee meetings for Heritage Days since Mac had roped her into filling in several of the spots where the newspaper participated. LouAnn was in charge of the art show at the fairgrounds that was part of Heritage Days, too. Suz was "stoned" she reported. She had so many jobs backed up that she and Flint were thinking of renting another dump truck and pulling her father out of retirement. Cecilia was just as busy. She'd fallen a bit behind in May with all the political posters that had to be printed for Election Day in the county, and now everyone wanted flyers, party invitations, and scholarship applications copied "yesterday." She could get them printed as soon as Callie e-mailed her the copy, but she couldn't help fold and label either. Callie crossed her fingers and hoped Lucy and Gloria could help with the task this month.

Callie had just hit "Send" when the first clap of thunder roared. For most of the night a huge thunderstorm rolled through. Lightning flashed and struck a tree near the house. The wind blew shingles off the roof. Callie saw her trash barrels at the farm rolling across the parking lot. Wicca snuggled against her legs, quivering.

In the morning, Callie surveyed the damage. Flats had blown away. Plants were floating in puddles; their plastic pots were nowhere to be seen. Signs had disappeared, and some of the ties on the shade cloth had broken, so it was flapping in the wind. A few shingles were missing on the Cottage, and display shelves and pieces of outdoor furniture were lying on their sides far from their proper locations.

When Gloria arrived later than scheduled, she apologized, explaining that a tornado had touched down in Heartland. The roof had been peeled from the grocery store, and several other businesses had been damaged.

"Was anyone injured?" Callie asked.

"No word of anyone, at least not at the newspaper when I left. Mac is swamped trying to get all the information before today's deadline. Lucy is helping him since school was cancelled. Lots of debris in the streets and some power lines are down, so the buses couldn't run," Gloria explained.

They worked together to retrieve pots, replace displays, and drag the trash barrels back to their proper spots. Callie couldn't help noticing that Gloria had called her daughter "Lucy." She thought it was a good sign, a very good sign.

Callie called Cecilia to see if she could pick up the newsletters, but the power was out on her side of the square, so they weren't finished. The power line crews were there working, so Cecilia would call as soon as they were ready.

Callie left Gloria to mind the farm and returned to the house to run the address labels on her printer and finish the handouts for her workshop on Sunday. Later that day, Cecilia called and she was able to pick up the newsletters. Gloria helped her fold and label until closing time. Callie finished sorting them into the official mail trays a little after midnight.

The week flew. Since she'd decided to hold a birthday party in honor of author Beatrix Potter next month, she was inspired to plant a Children's Garden, complete with a realistic scarecrow Mr. MacGregor that Callie made using stuffed pantyhose, stitched with life-like features and dressed in a plaid shirt and denim overalls. With a fluffy moustache and straw hat he looked ready to chase the nearby concrete statue of Peter Rabbit. She added a white concrete cat looking over a little pond containing a goldfish, an antique watering can, and edged the beds with parsley. After an evening spent painting slates with quotes from Miss

Potter's books, which were placed in appropriate locations, Callie was satisfied with the completed garden. She planned to serve carrot cake and chamomile tea in Miss Potter's honor.

Suddenly, it was Father's Day and time for the logging party! The weather was perfect, the horses well-behaved, and everyone stood in amazement as the huge Belgians followed their owner's commands so precisely. Children climbed up on the thick logs after they reached the parking lot, counting the rings on the exposed trunks. Fathers and grandfathers stood admiring the bark and talking about the "good old days" when every farm had a woodlot, and quail and pheasant roamed the fencerows in abundance. Everyone enjoyed the simple refreshments Callie had provided. There were grilled brats with buns and pots of herbal mustards, chips, and big pitchers of minted lemonade. All of the "Dad's Favorite" dianthus went home with lucky fathers, filling the departing cars and truck cabs with their spicy fragrance. Callie grinned and phoned her father when she saw the size of the check from the logger. It was a good day.

The rest of the month was extremely busy with three workshops and fighting the weeds that suddenly seemed to pop up everywhere. Callie hauled and applied more loads of mulch. Lucy and Callie spent hours up-potting hundreds of plants. Gloria, whose handwriting was beautiful, wrote labels for each pot whenever there were no customers in the shop. Lucy put together dozens of colorful annuals into combinations planters for decks and patios, with Gloria's input on which plants like sun, or which needed more water and shade. Callie was happy to see them working so well together. She'd had the strong impression from Lucy that Gloria had spent very little time with her in the past.

Callie thought about her own childhood. She'd spent a lot of time helping her dad outdoors or in his workshop, but she'd also spent lots of quality time with her mother. They washed the dishes together every evening. They worked together canning and freezing all the produce from her mother's huge garden. And, she spent time with the other women in her family as well.

She'd missed seeing all the cousins, who came home for Thanksgiving. She'd been too upset about Daniel's announcement that he was leaving to see anyone. Now she thought about her family. It was funny how the cousins had spread across the country. Her father's brothers & sisters had all lived within a mile of one another all their lives on adjoining farms, sharing large equipment and the workload of farming. Everyone got together to make hay, harvest the corn, or bale straw, moving from one farm to the next. Male cousins began driving tractors by the time they were six and were proficient at backing a trailer by age ten. The wives and daughters would prepare massive meals in one another's kitchens wherever the men were working in the fields.

Between meals, the women would often work together to preserve food for the winter. Callie recalled the time they'd made applesauce from the big "Transparent" apple tree at Uncle Bill's. The young girls collected the apples and washed them. Teenage girls peeled and sliced, trying to achieve the skill that Grandma Miller displayed. No one could peel an apple or a potato faster than Grandma. The aunts ran the kettles to cook the apples, put the cooked fruit through the food mill, filled the jars, and operated the water bath and pressure canners. For some reason that afternoon, Callie couldn't recall why, everyone had gone outside.

Suddenly, there was a loud whoompf. When they looked into the kitchen, applesauce was dripping from the ceiling, the kitchen cabinets, and running down the walls. Applesauce covered the floor, everything on the tables, and the light fixtures. One of the canners had exploded. It was one of the funniest things Callie had seen, but no one laughed. It took days to get the sticky applesauce removed from every surface of the kitchen. Mothers were haunted by what could have happened if anyone had been in the kitchen. And hours of work on that batch of apples had been wasted. It was not a subject for laughter, but later the cousins often recalled the day and how the applesauce had dripped from the ceiling onto their mothers' heads.

Callie had loved that feeling of closeness, the bonding that occurred while all ages worked together. She loved the sense of accomplishment everyone felt as they loaded the boxes of cans or freezer cartons into their vehicles at the end of the day. The little kids were as proud as the adults. They appreciated the food because they had participated in the work. No one wasted food, because they knew the amount of time and work it had taken. There had been lots of play time, too, and they had all grown up knowing who their cousins were and how their family was connected to the others. It saddened Callie to realize that it was doubtful her own children would feel connected to their cousins in the same way.

Her own children. Well, that was putting the cart before the horse, as her great-grandmother would say. She could not even understand a man, let alone think about trusting one enough to vow to love him forever.

Speaking of children, she'd better get that baby blanket finished. She expected Bob to phone any day now announcing the birth of their child. She was so happy for Beth and couldn't wait to hold that new baby.

The Saturday of the garden club plant sale, Callie loaded the selection of plants she'd decided to donate into cardboard boxes and placed them in the back of the truck. Gloria and Lucy were both working until noon, so Callie would have the opportunity to see "Heritage Days" firsthand. Then she'd be at the farm all afternoon. After lunch, Gloria was scheduled to help with the club's plant sale, as well as appearing with Mac, who was the emcee for several contests and events that were being held. Lucy was marching with the school band in the parade that evening and needed to help her committee finish the float the band was sponsoring.

Callie located the garden club's booth easily since a big green sign with yellow daisies saying "Big Plant Sale!" hung across the top. Under the booth and on tables lined up on all sides were pots of plants. Signs lettered "Annuals," "Perennials for Shade," "Herbs," "Perennials for Sun," "Veggies," and "Groundcovers" were taped to tables. Garden club members wearing pale green T-shirts with a red heart and letters that said "Heart and Soil Garden Club" scurried around answering questions, helping customers box plants, and taking money. Ellen wore a pretty yellow hat covered with flowers and gave a leaflet to each customer that announced the club's normal meeting time and place, as well as a list of its annual activities. Callie had not seen it before and was interested to note that the club organized all the Christmas decorations for the Historical Museum, maintained the flower beds around the library, and did the big planters around the town square. She spent several moments admiring the gourd bird houses and interesting planters Merle and Arlene had brought for the sale. There was a table of gently used garden tools, gardening books, flower vases, and envelopes of seeds for sale. It looked like they were doing a brisk business.

After depositing her plants on the proper tables, Callie wandered through the other booths. There were several food booths, of course, and several others that were selling flea market objects. A few displayed locally done pottery, handmade soaps, crocheted or knitted items, jewelry, and even artwork in various media. She picked up a few business cards, thinking she might contact them about having a booth at a farm event or possibly carrying their work on consignment in the shop later. She purchased a pretty pair of earrings for her mother and a painting on a circular saw blade of a John Deere "A" tractor, her father's favorite.

She was heading to checkout the sidewalk sale, being held by the local merchants in front of each store, when Deputy Wright joined her.

"Deputy Wright!" she greeted him warmly, "how nice to see you again."

"Ma'am," he touched his hat brim and nodded.

"It looks like a nice crowd has come for 'Heritage Days'", she observed. She followed his long strides across the square, giving up her plan to see the sidewalk sale.

"We're lucky the weather is so perfect. Especially after the big storm earlier this month," she continued. "Did you have any damage at your house?" Callie had no clue where Morgan lived, or where Mike lived, or where Trev lived actually. It flew through her mind that she didn't know exactly where Daniel was now either. Certainly not at the house they'd searched so long to find. A shadow passed across her face.

"Trouble?" Deputy Wright finally spoke.

"No, just thinking," she replied.

"Anything in particular?" he questioned.

"Not really. Well, actually, I'm hungry," she announced. "Are you on official duty? I have to be back at the farm to relieve the troops at noon, but we could have something quick."

"Thanks, but I am on duty," he replied. "Are you coming back for the parade this evening?"

"I hadn't planned on it," Callie hesitated, "but maybe I should since Lucy is participating."

"All of us have to pull double shifts this weekend," the deputy said. "But, I have some time off next week."

"I have Butterfly Day on Saturday and a workshop all Sunday afternoon," she said sadly.

"How about supper on Wednesday night? I know a place out by the reservoir," he invited.

"I'd love to. You still have my number? Call me," she smiled as he tipped his hat and left her side to cross the street where a group of teenage boys were getting rowdy.

She barely had time to grab a bowl of chicken and dumplings from a local church's booth before she had to hurry back to the farm. She immediately began to help several new customers who had driven into town for the festival, waving to Gloria and Lucy as they rushed off. When Callie finally had a break, she refilled the coffeemaker with water, opened another box of tea for customer sampling, and read the note from Gloria telling her they were out of scented geraniums in the shadehouse.

Instead of going in for the parade, Callie moved geraniums from the garage to the shadehouse and refilled shelves in the shop with more inventory from boxes hidden under the draped tables. After devouring a salad of greens from the garden, she decided to catch up her photo album, adding the photos of the new greenhouse, each theme garden in bloom, the display of patio planters that Lucy and Gloria had done, and the shadehouse sporting its new shade cloth. Her favorite photo was of her father balancing with a hammer raised in one hand while he walked across the very top metal beam of the greenhouse. He had climbed over the structure as nimble as a monkey. She filled a page with shots showing the beautiful horses dragging out the first log, and a photo of the trail the logs had left across the woodland floor. She'd go back next spring to see if there was a trail of wildflowers instead.

She had just finished labeling the final photo when the phone rang.

"It's a girl," Bob told her, bubbling with excitement. "She's beautiful, and Beth is doing fine, and her mother's coming to help for a few days, and she has a whole head of curly black hair, and we've named her Penelope!" he ended, finally taking a breath.

Callie congratulated the new father and promised to come see little Penny, as the baby would be called, as soon as she could. She put the photo album away and went to search for pink embroidery floss.

Since her friends had not been able to test recipes this month, she decided to ask Morgan Wright. He'd seemed to enjoy her cooking when he'd stayed in her house, and although these dishes would be experimental, she expected them to be good enough for company. She proposed the change in plans when he called and was relieved that he didn't seem upset. She couldn't explain it, but she wanted to see him in her kitchen again. She needed to know if some of the feelings she'd experienced when he was here before were just because she'd been so terrified by the threats, or if they would still be there now. After all, he'd been her knight in shining armor, her protector from all evil. He'd taught her to be more vigilant and to take the precautions anyone living alone in a rural area should take. She had felt grateful for his presence and filled with emotions. Had fear heightened the attractions that she hadn't been able to dissect or analyze well at the time? Maybe some of those electric currents had been her imagination. Or, maybe she'd felt a lot more than she wanted to admit.

Trev Carpenter pulled into the parking lot the following day, calling "It's Monday, Princess, isn't this your day off?" He pulled a brown envelope from his cab.

"Hey, Graybeard, long time, no see!" she called back gaily.

"There's not a gray whisker in this beard," he laughed and she noted with surprise that he was indeed growing a beard.

"Is that for 'Heritage Days'?" she laughed, pointing at his chin.

"No, I'm getting ready for Christmas. I'm going to spray paint it white," he teased.

"Christmas in July?" she asked.

"No, I figure it'll take me six months to get it long enough to cover the jelly belly I'm supposed to have."

"Are you serious?" she said.

"Yep, I'm going to play Santa in the town Christmas parade this year. I'll need a Mrs. Claus, interested?"

"No, I think I'll apply for the elf job instead," she laughed.

"You're too tall," he teased.

"And you're too skinny to be Santa," she teased back.

"You could help fatten me up," Trev replied. "I haven't had a good peach cobbler since I finished your pumphouse. And I hear I missed out on a killer bread pudding when your greenhouse was done."

"You could have come around. Lots of other people did. I did lots of cooking while my dad was here. Where have you been keeping yourself?"

"That horse stable project just kept growing into one thing after another. I got so far behind on everyone else's jobs that I barely slept nights," he growled.

"I know that feeling," Callie commiserated. "Want some coffee? There's no bread pudding or peach cobbler, but I have some lavender shortbread and a lavender-lemon balm pound cake left from the workshop yesterday."

"I'll take anything you make, Princess," he said, following her into the Cottage. He placed the brown envelope on the counter. "I'll help myself. You look at this."

Callie opened the envelope to see a photo of a beautiful old barn. "What's this?"

"It's a picture of a barn," Trev teased.

"Duh! Whose barn and where is it?"

"Your barn, if you want it. It's about twelve miles from here. I'm supposed to tear it down and build this big lah-de-dah mansion. I figure I could hire an Amish crew to help me. We'd number the main framework logs, haul it over here, and reconstruct it. You could quadruple your shop space, have plenty of room for classes, and maybe even put in a little tea room. There's a lot of beautiful stonework in the cow stanchions. The sloped shed you see on the side is worthless. Too rotted to bother moving but the rest is in good condition. Some of the siding I hauled over here from the horse stable job could replace the few boards that are rotted. Of course, you'd have to pay to have it moved and put on a new roof. It'd need wiring and plumbing, but you'd have something really wonderful when it was done."

"Oh, Trev, it is beautiful. But I don't even know if I have enough business to justify that expense. I haven't run any numbers. I was waiting until the end of June. That would be three month's of data and give me something to go on. I'm not sure I need a classroom unless the number of workshop attendees increases."

"Give it some thought, Callie. I'd love to take you out to see it. We'd have fun working on another project together," he said between bites of pound cake. "And with your cooking skills, you really should think about a tea room or something. Didn't you say something about herbal weddings once?"

"Yes, I said I'd never, never, ever do another one," she laughed

"You'd have room to put up a quilting frame and start a quilting group like you talked about. Heck, you could even have quilt shows. There'd be enough space. You could do anything you want. Dry bunches of herbs upstairs in the loft. Store all those boxes that fill up your house," he argued.

"You could scratch the whole herb thing and fill the barn with dairy goats. You could turn it into a day-care center. I know you love kids. You could start a Christian school and start teaching again. Callie, you could do anything with this barn! Come with me and have a look. Please?"

How could she resist the boyish pleading? Trev Carpenter was certainly a charmer. Adding her curiosity and interest in the barn, she could not refuse.

"Can Wicca come along?" Callie laughed.

"Sure, as long as she takes a window seat," he laughed, pulling Callie through the door. With Wicca happily sitting next to the window, Callie was pressed against Trev in the cab of his old blue truck. As always, they found plenty to talk about during the trip. Trev regaled her with stories of local history and old objects he'd found while digging foundations. Quickly, they arrived at the old barn.

"It is beautiful," Callie breathed as Trev helped her out of the truck. Wicca had already jumped out and was checking out the variety of new smells in the knee-high grasses that surrounded the barn. Here and there Callie recognized common barnyard weeds like burdock, lambs-quarters, and agrimony.

"Was there a farmhouse here, too?" she asked.

"Years ago. It burned down, and the family moved away. A neighbor bought the place but didn't build a house on the property since he already had one. He used to keep cattle here, but he died recently. Now his kids are splitting up the land into lots."

"This is a lovely site, sitting on this little rise. Trees in the background. Is there a creek over there?" Callie asked.

"Actually, it's the river," he replied.

"This is a beautiful place. I can understand why someone would want to build a house here. I just don't understand why they don't want to keep this beautiful old barn," Callie sighed.

"They want to spend all their money on a big house, not restoring a barn. They think it's a fire hazard, would attract wild animals, and raise their insurance costs," Trev explained. "Come on. Let me show you some fantastic beams. They're all hand-hewn and notched. Original peg construction everywhere, except in the grain bins that were added later. All the wood on the cow stanchions was hand-carved," he said admiringly.

Trev led her on a tour of the building, pointing out which kind of wood was used where and why.

"Couldn't they sell these old beams and planks to places that specialize in restorations?" Callie asked.

"They probably could if they wanted to, but they're in a hurry to start building. They've hired me to haul it away, and fast," Trev said. "If I could, I'd take it apart and store it where it wouldn't deteriorate until I had time to rebuild it myself. I'd make it into a house with a big stone fireplace at one end. Can't you just picture those old beams running across a great room? You just can't get logs this size any more with the price of lumber now."

They had returned outside, and Trev walked to the truck. He pulled a large picnic hamper from the back along with a blanket. "Come on, it's a beautiful day, and we have to have lunch anyway," he said, leading her to a nearby tree. "Just look at that barn with the view behind it. Then think how it could look at your place with pretty windows, maybe shutters with hearts on them, and flower beds filled with color in front. LouAnn could paint a beautiful sign to hang over the big doors. You could have storage in the loft. You could host graduation parties, even dances. Did you see what good shape that floor is in?" Trev practically bubbled.

While he was talking, he'd spread the blanket under the tree and started removing an array of items from the hamper. There was a broasted chicken and cole slaw from the grocery's deli, two large pieces of pie that Callie recognized as coming from Dinah's Diner, a bag of apples and fresh pears, a huge bag of potato chips, a lovely piece of butterkasse cheese, and a bottle of white wine complete with two glasses.

"Wow! This took some planning," Callie remarked.

"Well, I thought this whole idea might take some persuasion," he laughed. Then in a more serious tone, he added, "This is a wonderful opportunity, Callie. It's the kind of thing that won't happen again in your life. You can save this big beautiful old piece of history. Do you know how many barns like this are falling down all over Indiana? We have a rich farming heritage, and we're letting them fall down or tearing them down all over the state!" Trev said passionately.

"Yes, I do know. LouAnn is part of a group of Indiana artists that have been traveling all over the state painting lovely old barns just like this one. They hope to establish a traveling art exhibit to help make people aware of what we're losing," Callie told him.

"In Vermont, and some other states, owners actually get a big tax break to keep old barns like this. Those states realize that it adds to tourism, in addition to their historical value," Trev added as he poured the wine. "To beautiful barns made of huge old virgin trees, the likes of which we will probably never see again, and to the craftsmen that built them with simple tools and bare hands," he toasted. "No power tools in those days!" he added raising his glass to salute the old barn.

Callie sat reflectively as she sipped the excellent wine. She appreciated the wine, the picnic, the old barn, and especially Trev. He had more facets than she'd first seen. He certainly was more than just a small town carpenter. He had a passion for fine wood, nature, old trees, history, and craftsmanship.

"I won't pressure you any more. But, I did run some numbers that I'll give you when I take you home. There's no one else that I'd rather see have that barn if I can't have it myself," he said somberly.

"Aren't there any historical societies or agricultural museums that could save the barn?" Callie asked.

"There are more barns, some with more historical significance than this one, than they can afford to save, Callie. There are just not enough people that care. It's all big business and the bottom line," Trev said sadly as he shared a piece of chicken with Wicca.

They finished their picnic accompanied by the songs of birds and an occasional visit by a butterfly or two. They leaned against the tree and watched the pastel shades turn into a brilliant red sunset as they finished the last of the wine.

"What is so rare as a day in June," Trev quoted, "then if ever, come perfect days." Callie sighed. She couldn't remember when she'd had a more relaxing or enjoyable day. It had been entirely perfect.

However, Callie felt pressed for time the rest of the week, having accomplished nothing at the farm on Monday. In addition to all the preparations for Butterfly Day, she cleaned the house in preparation for Morgan Wright's coming to test recipes. Her mind kept returning to the barn, and she had no trouble at all picturing it on her property. She had made pages of "pros" and "cons". The "pros" listed all the possibilities that the barn would give her in terms of special events, storage, sales space, classes, displays and more, in addition to the fact she'd be saving a beautiful building and valuable resources. Of course, the biggest "con" was the fact that she really couldn't afford it. She'd definitely have to take out a loan, assuming she could get one, or a second mortgage. It would increase her insurance payments, utility bills, and probably force her to increase her staff as well. She'd have to increase traffic flow, and that meant increased advertising costs. Callie would love to believe, "If you build it, they will come," but she couldn't count on that. With that kind of investment she'd have to be open year-round. So far, she wasn't convinced that this community would support a year-round business here so far out in the country. Gas prices kept creeping up, and the acceptance of on-line shopping by even the most average consumer would affect her sales. Joyful Heart might have to go to on-line sales itself eventually. She just hadn't been able to convince her business self that buying the barn was a sound business decision. But, her romantic self loved the idea of having a barn, especially saving a beautiful structure like that one from destruction. She'd been having trouble staying on-task since seeing it. Next Monday, she had an appointment with her accountant and another with her bank. She really couldn't make a decision without more information. She'd thought of sending a picture of the barn to her dad. He would love the old structure as much as she did, but she didn't really need to have a second opinion on the barn. She trusted Trev's evaluation that the wood was solid and that it could be moved. Her parents didn't have the kind of money she would need, so why worry them that she might "bite off more than she could chew" as her grandfather would have said.

By Wednesday evening, she was still in a tizzy as she prepared a selection of new appetizers. These featured lavender, not something that most men really were thrilled about so she was taking a risk. However, she thought the miniature meatballs in lavender jelly were especially good and most men liked meatballs. Stuffed dried apricots and dates were on the menu, as well as some fruit kabobs with interesting sauces. She didn't expect a big man like Morgan to make a meal of appetizers, like her girlfriends did on tasting night. So, she'd fixed a big salad and had marinated steaks ready to go on the grill. She made her "killer" bread pudding since it had been such a hit at the greenhouse party.

Morgan showed up right on time, bearing a beautiful bouquet of daisies. "Like coals to New Castle," he said. "I know you have lots of flowers already, but I wanted to bring something."

"They're just lovely, thank you," Callie smiled, as she stretched to reach a crock sitting on a high shelf.

"Here, let me get that," Morgan moved closer and easily reached the crock without even stretching. They were barely an inch apart and Callie could smell his usual aftershave. It was a scent she had missed after he'd left her house. She had almost purchased a small bottle one day while shopping, just so she could have that scent of him near, then stopped herself just in time. "Don't be so silly," she'd chided herself. "You're not some love-sick teenager!"

She took the crock from his hand and turned to the sink to fill it with water before arranging the daisies prettily.

Wicca had been wiggling in delight from the moment Morgan came into the kitchen. Now she sat on his shoe and leaned against his leg begging for attention.

"I didn't forget you, girl," he chuckled as he pulled a treat from his pocket and let the dog take it from his hand. Wicca pranced over to her favorite rug with her prize.

"Something smells good," he stated. Callie started to respond, "Oh, yes you do!" but caught herself in the nick of time.

"I hope you are feeling adventurous. I've experimented with some new ingredients, so I'm not entirely sure how they'll turn out."

"Well, I don't think they can taste too bad if they smell that good," he assured her.

Callie poured them each some iced tea and busied herself arranging the appetizers on a tray. "I thought we'd eat in the gazebo," she said. "I've been so busy since I moved here that I've rarely spent any time out there."

Morgan picked up the tray and followed her out the back door. "Seems a shame to be so busy that you can't even find time to sit in this pretty spot," he observed. "Did you plant all these flowers since I was here?"

"Most of them. The roses were already here. The lilies came up unexpectedly. They should be fabulous next month. I can't wait to see what color they are, but they are Orientals so they'll be fragrant. I suspect they'll be yellow or white. A lot of the other flowers that belonged to the former owner have turned out to be in those colors. It makes sense. Most farm wives are so busy that they really couldn't enjoy their flowers until everyone was in bed. White, light blue and yellow show up well after dark by the light of the moon. It's been exciting to see what comes up and what colors they are, both here at the house and over at the farm. I've had lots of wonderful surprises," Callie bubbled.

"And some not so nice," Morgan added. "Sorry, I shouldn't have brought up the bad side of things. You're probably trying to forget all the negative things that have happened since you've moved here."

"Yes and no. I try to forget the worse things but to remember all the things you taught me about being vigilant. I tell myself I don't have nearly the things to worry about that the pioneer women who first settled here had. They had wild animals, Indians, crop failures, and a lot of health issues in addition to the occasional robber. And, they probably didn't have close neighbors or any law enforcement driving by on a regular basis. I've got it pretty easy!" she laughed. "And, I suspect you are talking more than usual because you are scared to test these new creations, Deputy Wright," Callie teased.

Morgan looked at the platter suspiciously.

"Okay. I'll take the first one, just to prove they aren't poisonous," Callie offered.

They talked easily about things that had been happening in the community and at the farm. Morgan asked about the mockingbird.

"He's still here. And you'll be happy to know you were successful. He still has 'From the Halls of Montezuma' in his repertoire," she smiled. "Were you a Marine?"

"I am a Marine," he replied seriously. "Once a Marine, always a Marine." Since he didn't continue the conversation, Callie decided a subject change was needed.

"Well, you need to rate the appetizers. Be honest. I can take it," she challenged.

"Well," he said slowly, "I thought they were all really good. Really small," he added, looking at the empty tray, "but really good. I liked the meatballs, kind of sweet and rich. The stuffed apricots and dates were a little girly for me, but I bet the ladies would love them. I liked the one with the tuna and black olives, and that really spicy sauce for the fruit sticks was good. Could have been hotter, though."

"I'm impressed! That was a helpful critique. I can't believe you want the sauce hotter though. I made it with Thai peppers, and they are really high on the Scoville chart. Frankly, it was too hot for me. I was thinking I should tone it down," she said thoughtfully.

"Maybe for the ladies, Ma'am," he agreed.

"And I'm glad to hear you are still hungry because there's salad chilled and steaks to be grilled. Mind doing the grilling while I make the salad dressing?" she asked. Callie felt comfortable asking Morgan to grill, since he'd gladly assumed the task a few times during the week he had guarded her house.

"Sure thing. Are they ready to go?"

"All set, and the coals should be ready too."

Callie mixed a dressing of poppy seeds, celery seeds, balsamic vinegar, honey, chopped shallots, and olive oil which she poured over fresh greens she'd picked from the cook's garden. As they were eating, Morgan said, "I came by on Monday, but you weren't here. Worried me since your truck was still parked in the driveway. I figured maybe you had gone for a walk in the woods or were working with your bees since Wicca wasn't around either."

He paused, but Callie didn't respond immediately. "Checked back on my later rounds, and you still weren't around when I went off duty."

"I went to look at a beautiful old barn," she said. "It's going to be torn down and I have the opportunity to buy it for Joyful Heart. It's a big decision, and I'm having a big debate with myself over it."

Morgan noted that she hadn't said exactly who had taken her to see the barn, but he could guess and chose not to pursue it.

"It would be an enormous commitment, financially, and it would really change almost every aspect of my business," she continued. "I'm not sure I'm ready to tackle it all."

"Sounds like you intend to stay in the area though if you're thinking of expanding," Morgan observed.

"Oh, I think I'm taking root pretty fast," she laughed. "Are you ready for dessert?"

They lingered over coffee although most of the time was spent in comfortable silence. The soothing sounds of crickets and night birds filled the air. A big moon was on the rise, and the scent of roses mingled with Morgan's aftershave as they sat side by side on the wicker sofa.

"If I ever have to come back to protect you again," he broke the silence. "I might just sleep out here," he added contentedly.

Callie found it difficult to sleep after Morgan departed. She sat at the kitchen table in her old white nightgown, embroidering the last of the pink flowers on Baby Penny's new blanket. Finally, she finished. Her hands were aching from holding the slender needle. She stared at the crock of daisies. The crock had been her great-grandmother's. She wondered if her great-grandfather had ever brought her daisies, if indeed whether the crock had ever held flowers before. She did not come from romantic stock.

She recalled a visit with her great-grandmother, one day while Callie was still in college. It was the day Gran had given Callie the crock as well as a few other items from the old cedar chest. Her granny had decided it was time some of her possessions were passed on to her relatives.

"You're the most interested in gardens and flowers of all the young ones," Gran had told her. "You should have this crock. And, my garden tools when I'm gone. I want you to have seeds from these cockscombs," she said as she pointed to the row that edged her driveway. They've been passed down in our family for generations."

"Thanks, Gran. I'll cherish them because they came from you," Callie assured her. "It's a lovely present," she said, caressing the crock. "What was the best present great-grandfather ever gave you?" Callie asked.

"Oh, let me think. Well, when we were first married, we moved into the little log cabin back by the woods on the home place. It was long gone, even before your father was born, so you wouldn't remember it. John Henry and his wife had built a new house up by the road. It sat behind the house your folks live in now, where the orchard used to be. So, they gave us the cabin to live in right after we married. I was tickled to death to have my own place right away," Gran said.

"That first autumn, I was expected to help in the fields just like the other womenfolk. We'd get up before light to do our chores so we could be in the fields as soon as the sun came up. We'd walk behind the wagon drawn by that old mule. Begeesuz, he was called. It used to rile John Henry's wife whenever he called to that old mule. 'That sounds like blasphemy,' she'd say sourly. So later on when he could afford another mule, darned if he didn't name it Blasphemy!"

"Well, to get back to your question," she chuckled a bit before continuing. "We'd walk behind that wagon, and we had a thing called a corn peg that strapped onto your hand. It was leather and had a sharp little metal blade attached. You'd pull an ear of corn away from the main stalk and slice it off with that little blade. Then you'd toss the ear into the wagon. You had to work pretty fast, mind you, especially if it was a pretty good year and the stalk had two or three ears. And I had to work faster because my legs were so short. Still are, I guess," she paused to chuckle again.

"And, since my arms are a bit on the short side compared to most, I had to toss those ears farther. It was a job, I can tell you, keeping up with that wagon. And you had to do two rows, one on each side of where you walked. And those rough corn leaves crossed over the path and would scratch your cheeks till they'd bleed. You couldn't push them aside cause that would take too long, and you'd either have to call to the wagon to stop or miss some ears. Since I was the newest and trying to prove myself to be a good wife, I wouldn't have called for that wagon to stop on my account if I'd lost my shoes! And I wasn't going to miss any ears either. No, sir. I wanted my George to be proud of me and to show his family he'd chosen well."

"That night, I was so tuckered out I fell into bed as soon as the supper dishes were washed. I didn't know when your great-grandfather came to bed, but it was late. He'd told me he needed to mend some harness."

"When we started to the field the next morning, he pulled me aside and gave me a little bundle tied in a red bandanna. I opened it up and there was a corn peg, made just to fit my hand."

"Your hands are so little," he said. "I saw that leather was just sliding around, cutting into your hand so I made this for you. It'll fit real snug and keep your hand from getting more blisters and such."

"I looked at his face, and I saw tenderness there I'd never seen before. That was the best present I ever had," she finished with a faraway look in her eyes. "Still have it in my cedar chest. Every autumn when it's harvest time, I take it out and rub it with beeswax, and I recall all those times we walked side by side harvesting our crops. George had to replace the leather every so often, and once he said he ought to just throw that old thing away and make me a new one, but I wouldn't let him."

She rocked a few moments. "I think that pleased him. Yes, I think it did."

Callie pulled a daisy from the crock and walked out to the gazebo with Wicca at her side. The moon was high; the air was sweet. Callie sat on the wicker sofa, her feet tucked under her, and wondered what her great-grandmother would have thought about a man who'd brought her daisies.

As soon as her workshop on herbal cheeses was finished, she packed a few things in her truck, whistled for Wicca, grabbed some of her favorite opera tapes, a box of the cheeses left from the workshop, and the gift-wrapped baby blanket. She was heading south!

The three-hour drive passed quickly, and she felt her pulse quicken as she drove past familiar buildings once she reached Owen County. There was the school where she used to teach. There was Grace Methodist church where she'd sung in the choir and taught Sunday school. The church where she was supposed to have had her wedding. She clenched her jaw and turned past the church and past the library where she had spent so many hours reading about herbs and gardening. She'd often gone to the library after school if she had choir practice or another meeting rather than going home to the empty house. She loved libraries.

She took Pottersville Road because it was more scenic than the highway, and before she knew it, she'd arrived at Bob and Beth's home. They'd bought an old farmhouse and Bob was planting an entire hillside with blueberry bushes. Once he retired from teaching he'd have a ready made business, he told Beth. He also planned to make maple syrup since their woods was filled with sugar maples.

Bob bounded out of the house, grabbed her suitcase, and gave her a big hug.

"You've been burning wood," Callie observed, as she caught the scent of wood smoke on his clothing.

"Yes, I've been out cutting firewood for the winter. Had a dead tree come down over by the blueberries. I'm burning all the brush, making more space for more blueberries," he explained.

"Smells wonderful!" Callie exclaimed, "Any blueberries left?"

"You're too late. Picked the last of them last week. Any I missed, the cedar waxwings finished," he said. "Next year I'm going to add some later varieties to extend my season."

"Are you two going to stand out there and talk farming all day," Beth called from the doorway, laughing. "Lunch is waiting!"

"Come see our shiny new Penny," Bob laughed as he pulled her along to the back door. "There's never been a better baby. I'm going to get her a pony."

"Not anytime soon," Beth told him with a mock-frown. "That man is going to spoil her rotten," she laughed.

Callie had already reached the basket that sat between two chairs by the kitchen table. "Oh, Beth, she's beautiful. So tiny, and look at all that hair!"

"She's tiny, like Bob's mom," Beth agreed, "but she has a good pair of lungs."

They enjoyed a tasty lunch. Callie pulled a jar of honey from one of her boxes and they spread it on Beth's warm biscuits. After Penny had been held, changed, fed, and was taking another nap, Beth and Callie went out to sit on the front porch swing. Beth filled her in on all the school gossip and community news. After a while, they sat in comfortable silence, the way good friends can.

"I miss the hills, almost as much as I miss you," Callie said finally, squeezing Beth's hand.

"I miss you, too." Beth replied. "I don't think I could adjust to be a flatlander."

"Oh, it has its charm. You can see storms coming from miles away," Callie said.

"I think I'd rather have them hidden by the hills," Beth responded.

"There's a good view of the sunset on the horizon."

"There's nothing to stop the wind," Beth countered.

"You have a point there," Callie admitted. "Some days, I can barely stand upright and I constantly have to go into the woods to retrieve pots and signs. I think lots of them end up in Ohio."

"You could come back," Beth said wistfully. She paused before adding, "Daniel did."

Callie bolted upright, spilling the glass of tea she'd been holding down the leg of her jeans.

"I wasn't sure I should tell you," Beth said, searching Callie's face. "He's been back about a month. He's living in the house you two picked out."

"Alone," she added after another pause.

Callie stood up and began to pace across the porch. Her throat felt tight and tears rolled down her cheek. Her hands began to shake and her heart felt squeezed.

Just then, the baby began to cry.

"You go check Penny," Callie said quietly. "I think I need to take a walk."

As soon as she stepped off the porch, Wicca came to her side and stayed there as they followed the winding tractor trail into the woods.

They passed Bob's sugar shack, tall woodpiles stacked on two sides. They passed a small abandoned rock quarry. That had been one of the big selling points in Bob's eyes. He taught earth science at the local high school but geology was his passion. Anyplace that had rocks was special to him. The trail stopped at the edge of the White River. Callie sat on a large rock to rest her legs. It had been months since she'd walked a steep slope.

Finally, she let her mind grasp the concept that Daniel was back. Without Mariah. Memories of the sweet times they'd had together flooded her mind. Nearly two hours passed before she was ready to return to the house.

The evening passed quickly, with Callie rocking the baby and giving her a bath. Wicca was jealous of the attention the newborn was getting from her mistress, but was compensated by Bob's petting while he read.

Beth pronounced the pretty green blanket, "Heavenly!" and showed Callie the special quilt that the quilting group they had once both belonged to had made for the new baby.

"I miss being part of that group," Callie said. "I loved the fact that there were such diverse ages and interests. I learned so much from the older ladies and not just about quilting."

"I know. Since both my mother and Bob's mother live out of state, I'm happy for their advice with a new baby," Beth added. "And I know I'll appreciate one of them being in the baby nursery each Sunday, so I can attend service without worrying."

Before she had heard that Daniel was back, Callie had planned to attend her former church to see her old friends again. She'd thought she was ready to face everyone, most of whom she hadn't seen since Daniel had announced he was leaving for California.

Now, she wasn't so sure. Would he be there? Finally, she asked Beth if Daniel usually attended services.

"I haven't seen him, but we haven't gone since Penny arrived. The doctor said he'd like her to be six weeks old and have her first shots before we take her out around lots of other people," Beth explained. "I could make some calls."

"No, don't bother," Callie decided. "My time is so short. I think I'd rather just spend it with you this trip."

"So, I am a coward," she thought to herself as she lay on the antique bed in Beth's guest bedroom upstairs. Her window looked out over the tidy rows of blueberries, across the river and on to the hills in the distance. The full moon that she and Morgan had watched was now shrinking. "Why did Daniel come back? Why did he choose to live in 'our' house?" she wondered before falling into a fitful sleep.

She left her friends after lunch the following day. Lucy had promised to water while she was gone, but there were things Callie needed to do. Watering was taking more time again as the days grew hotter, so she planned to move some things into bigger pots. She had appointments with the accountant and bank the next day. Lots of plants in her gardens were ready to propagate and she had noticed that the black raspberries that grew in the fencerows were nearly ripe. Since the farm would be closed for July Fourth, she'd have time to pick and make jam. She hoped to put some in the freezer, too, to make pies this winter. She had not yet started the July newsletter, and she needed to update the website.

Wicca was glad to get out of the truck when they arrived home. "Tired of riding shotgun at last?" Callie teased her. She grabbed her mail from the box, skimmed the newspaper, and saw that the county fair would be held toward the end of the month. There was a pile of bills, so she decided she'd deal with those tonight and stuck them on the desk in the studio. The answering machine light was flashing. She listened to messages and made call-back notes. She finished unloading the truck and decided to drive over to the farm. Her calf muscles were still sore from walking down to the river, and even more so from walking back up! She really did need to get back in the habit of doing Tai Chi!

A quick check at the farm told her that sales had been lower than she'd hoped on Saturday. Most of the butterfly display was still in the Cottage although most of the plants for butterflies in the outdoor display had sold. She noticed that Gloria must have come to dust while Lucy watered today because everything sparkled. There were no messages on the farm answering machine, so she walked back to check the bee hives.

The front of one hive was covered with bees. This was not good. Callie recognized the signal that they intended to swarm. She remembered the old saying "A swarm in May is Aye, a swarm in June is none-too-soon, but a swarm in July will surely die."

She hurried back to the house, donned her bee suit, put a base board, two framed supers, and a top in the back of her truck and hurried back to the farm. She stopped to add three cement blocks to her load and drove as close to the hives as possible without disturbing the bees. She placed the cement blocks next to the worrisome hive and placed the base board securely on the blocks. The bees were not happy as she puffed smoke around the hive and into the opening. She pulled the lid off and leaned it against a tree. They were really angry as she removed the top super and put it on one of the empty supers nearby. She removed the next super and placed it on the new base board, covering it temporarily with the lid.

She gave each hive another short puff of smoke, since the level of buzzing had started to increase. After inspecting the frames, she pulled out one with queen cells and exchanged it for one filled with honey. She added a few frames of larvae to the new hive, and closed it. It took a few minutes to locate the old queen and to ensure that there was a young queen still in the hive. Sadly, she destroyed the old queen and closed the second hive. Now both hives would thrive. The new hive's workers would quickly raise a young queen and busily build their new home. The hive that had threatened to swarm because it had two queens would now have room to expand and only one young queen to serve. That was enough for one day. She gathered her gear and left. She'd only gotten two stings from bees that were caught in her pant leg as she removed her bee suit. Not bad. She'd have to remember to close the Velcro strips tighter next time.

Lavender

One of the most popular and well-known herbs is lavender. Few other plants can claim such a wonderful, refreshing aroma. A traditional strewing herb, lavender also has an historical use in cosmetics, medicines, teas, and magic. Perfumes, soaps, and sachets are always associated with lavender, but it is also used as an insect repellent, smelling salt, antiseptic lotion, sedative, and cough suppressant.

Lavender is commonly used in love potions and protective charms. Many believe it induces sleep and imparts a feeling of well-being. Lavender may also contribute to long-life, chastity, and happiness. Even the purple color of its blooms would indicate power and healing qualities.

It is no wonder that many people want to grow this special plant in their own gardens. However, not all lavender varieties are hardy, so some care must be given in making selections for the landscape. While many can tolerate intense cold, they will not survive a winter if their roots are subjected to soggy soils. The keys to growing lavender are excellent drainage, high light levels, and sufficient lime. If soils are heavy, drainage can be improved by constructing raised beds. Even a "sweet potato" ridge technique will increase the chances of survival. Mixing quantities of crushed stone into the planting area will also help. Lavender loves lime, so mix ¼ to ½ c. of garden lime into the planting soil for each plant. Place plants at a minimum of two feet apart for good ventilation. Some larger varieties may require additional space. Applying a mulch of crushed stone will improve ventilation, and also reflect light to the undersides of the leaves. This also discourages weeds and will make an astounding difference to plant growth and general health. With attention to these factors, many lavender varieties can be successfully grown in cold climates.

The number of cultivars of lavender seems to grow each year. In central Indiana, where temperatures can reach twenty degrees below zero, there are fifty different kinds that grow outdoors in the field with little attention except harvesting the flowers each year. There are short lavenders through very tall lavandins. There are varieties with greenish leaves and those with pure white leaves. Bloom colors range from pure white through pink, palest lavender, blues, and lilacs to the deepest purple. Flower stem length can vary from two to twenty inches!

Most chefs feel that *L. angustifolia* has a sweeter, better flavor for cooking. Some even insist that only the white or pink forms should be used in cooking. The lavandins and French or Spanish lavenders tend to have a stronger camphor flavor. Whatever variety one chooses to grow, be sure to pick a few blooms to enjoy fresh. Tuck them into a pocket, add them to bath water, or toss them on a salad or over ice cream. Add them to iced tea or even scrambled eggs! Experiment, and enjoy this magical plant.

Chapter 7:

JULY

July turned hot and steamy. Record heat waves hit the area and Callie was glad that Jesse Plumber had apparently been correct in his assessment of her well's capability. They were spending hours watering the plants in the sales area as well as all the gardens planted in the past weeks.

She picked black raspberries as fast as she could in any time she had and was delighted to find a patch of wild gooseberries back near the Enchanted Forest. At least they were wild now. Callie wondered if Elizabeth had planted them, or maybe some earlier pioneer woman. She'd like to research the history of her land someday to see who had lived here in the past, before Doc Hyde and Elizabeth.

She hung some black plastic in the greenhouse to form a fat tent. It was so warm in there that bunches of herbs Callie harvested from the gardens dried overnight. She planned to hold an herbal harvest workshop next month, but she was uninspired for other topics. When Gloria arrived for work the next morning Callie asked her for ideas.

"Maybe the heat has just fried my brain," Callie lamented, "but I'm just not coming up with any creative ideas beyond the harvest workshop. I need as least two more workshop ideas. I was considering one on making natural herbal cosmetics. What do you think, Gloria?"

Gloria sat in her designer garden clothes with nary a hair out of place. Her manicured nails, always protected by gloves when gardening, tapped lightly against her mug of tea. A few moments passed as she pondered her reply.

"Callie, you know I admire you and what you are building here. And I love my job and all you've done for Lucy, but dear," she paused, looking up from her mug, "you really are not a walking advertisement for the benefits of herbal cosmetics. I hope I don't offend you, dear, but I feel we are becoming friends. I have to tell you what I think. Just look at your hands, Callie."

Callie looked at her hands. They were browned by the sun, cracked, scratched, and looked like they'd never seen a jar of hand cream. Her nails were broken short and chipped, and she hadn't had a manicure in her life. She knew if she looked in a mirror, her face would not promote any sales either. "You're absolutely right, Gloria. I can't try to sell people on the idea that herbs will make their skin smoother, or softer, or healthier when I look like I just crossed the Dead Sea without a boat."

She scratched herbal cosmetics off the short list on her clipboard. "I'll just have to come up with something else."

"What about one called 'Growing and Blending Herbal Teas'?" Gloria suggested. "You have a lot of plants that are used for tea, and you already have a beautiful selection of tea pots and accessories."

"Perfect!" Callie agreed immediately. "The Monarda is blooming now, and I can dry the petals and leaves. I already have jars of chamomile, mints, thyme, and rosemary. I'll clip some sage this morning. One more!" she stated as she scribbled on her clipboard.

"How about 'Homemade Herbal Paper'?" Gloria said, as she nodded toward the clipboard. "With all the interest in scrap booking and homemade greeting cards, it seems like a natural."

"I've never made paper, but I suppose I could read a book and give it a try," Callie replied hesitantly.

"I learned in an art class in college. I could teach it. Lucy could help," Gloria volunteered.

"You, my fair lady, are a lifesaver," Callie crowed. "What Sunday next month works best for your schedule?"

They spent a few more minutes trying to come up with a good special event for August, but the creative juice seemed to have evaporated. The first car drove in, and they prepared for customers.

The mini-van held four young girls, probably college-aged, Callie surmised. They immediately headed toward the butterfly and hummingbird garden, chatting with animation, and photographing several plants as they strolled between the beds. Callie walked up to welcome them to the farm.

"Are you the owner?" a slender girl with owlish eyes asked.

"Yes, I'm Callie, and welcome to Joyful Heart. Have you been here before?"

"No, our journalism professor listed your farm as a possible resource. We have to do a story on a business for our class," a dark-haired girl with Asian features explained.

"Well, welcome to the farm. If I can be of any assistance, please let me know," Callie smiled.

"What's this wild plant? I love the shaggy red things, and those little birds seem to like it, too" a chubby girl said, shooting the plant in a close-up with a chunky Nikon.

"That's Monarda, or beebalm," Callie told them. "It's a favorite of the hummingbirds and butterflies, too. Taste a petal and rub a leaf," she advised them. "The Native Americans taught the colonists to use it for tea. We have Hummingbird Cake in the Cottage today and Oswego Tea. They are both made with Monarda. I hope you'll enjoy them when you visit the Cottage."

"Wow! That's good!" they exclaimed later as they sampled the goodies. Callie spent the next hour showing them plants, answering their questions, and introducing them to the magical world of fragrant herbs. All four girls were filled with enthusiasm and promised to send Callie copies of the articles they wrote for their class. They all had more tea and cake at a picnic table outside the Cottage where they worked on their notes. After asking Callie several more questions and taking more photographs, they signed up for the newsletter and took copies of the June issue so they'd have her website address. By the time they'd left, the Asian girl had purchased a flat of culinary herbs. The dark-haired girl carried a bag filled with lavender products, and the other two had purchased books on beginning herb gardening.

Callie smiled as she watched them leave the farm. "Oh, the joy of youth," she sighed. "I wish Lucy had been here to meet them."

That night before she left the farm, Callie gathered a basket of ripe tomatoes from the vines, added some hot peppers, and some heat-resistant lettuce that was just starting to show signs of stress. Her tiny rows of green beans were already producing but she'd need to plant a new crop next month. The spring crops of spinach, arugula, snow peas, and radishes were long gone, but the summer squash and beets were growing nicely. She'd have tomatoes by the bucketful next month. Suddenly, inspiration struck. She'd host a "Salsa Day" and use those tomatoes and peppers to advantage. The farm could sponsor a contest, have a display of hot peppers, and a demonstration on making fresh salsa. Most of the locals were accustomed to eating salsa from a jar. Callie couldn't wait for them to taste salsa from the garden, with fresh cilantro and interesting ingredients. The tomatillos would be ready then, too. It was brilliant!

She hurried to the house and began writing the next issue of the newsletter. She posted the new workshop dates she had fixed with Gloria and an article about Salsa Day on her website. It was the wee hours before she ran out of steam and went to bed.

Her meetings with the accountant and the bank had not been as glowing as she'd hoped. The accountant pointed out some things Callie had not considered and felt it was a little too early to think of expansion. She felt Callie should do some intensive market research before even considering such a costly project as moving the barn. The bank simply felt she did not have enough business history to justify a large loan. She hated to let the barn go, but she didn't really have a choice. She knew Trev would be disappointed, too.

The heat continued all week, making everyone grumpy and irritable. Mike invited her to the "Symphony on the Prairie" Patriotic Concert at Conner Prairie on July 4th since the farm would be closed. Callie was ready to do anything besides water plants and pull weeds. It was still a mystery to her that weeds could thrive in the heat while her cherished flowers withered and pouted. Sales had been pitiful. Callie wasn't sure whether it was the holiday, with lots of people going on vacation, or the heat. She'd happily let Gloria and Lucy take the week off since there was no business. It was the one week a year that Mac would take off, so traditionally it was their family vacation. They were going to Charleston, South Carolina to visit some of Gloria's relatives. Consequently, Callie was dragging hoses and doing all the watering alone. She was certainly ready for an evening away.

She'd e-mailed the newsletter copy to Cecilia and tried to schedule a time for their monthly gathering, to no avail. It looked like she'd be processing the newsletters alone again. The county fair was this month. Everyone was involved in committee work, manning booths at the fair, or going on vacation. She stayed up past one a.m. on three evenings to get the newsletters processed.

At least she only had one workshop this month. There was no sense in trying to hold one on the weekend of the Fourth or on fair week. She planned to attend an herb conference one weekend, so only the Sunday following the Beatrix Potter party would be filled, assuming anyone signed up for the class So far, there had been little enthusiasm for anything scheduled at the farm in July.

She spent an evening gathering elderberries and processing half into juice for jelly. The other half of the berries were dried to be used in muffins and pancakes. Elderberry jelly was one of her favorites. If she had time to gather more before the birds ate them, she'd make elderberry-apple jelly, too. Surprisingly, when mixed half and half, the juices combined to make a beautiful ruby red jelly. Callie was thinking of giving jars of various jellies and some of her precious honey as Christmas gifts. Several jars already lined her pantry shelves, and there was plenty of time to make additional kinds. Maybe she should think about herbal jellies as a topic for a workshop next year. She wasn't sure many people made homemade jellies anymore but maybe it was worth a try.

The daylilies were coming into bloom. Callie labeled and mapped the existing clumps. Several were the tall, old-fashioned roadside orange variety. However, since they were excellent culinary ingredients, she kept them. This fall she'd move them into a bed along the woods and replace them with varieties that fit her color schemes better. She preferred daylilies with ruffled petals, fragrance, and extended bloom periods. Breeders were making great improvements, developing tetraploids, expanding color choices and forms so the variety was endless. She pickled daylily buds and dried petals to use as a thickening agent. She experimented with fresh daylily petals in cheesecakes, puddings, and stir-fry.

The Fourth of July was hot and humid. She and Mike had agreed to split the duty of making a picnic. Mike would bring the main course and drinks; Callie would make a dessert and appetizers. It would give her a chance to test a couple more recipes. Once she finished watering, she made her favorite pesto loaf and put it into the refrigerator to chill. As soon as she put the mixing bowl in the sink, she realized she'd made a mistake. In this heat the loaf would turn into a puddle by the time they spread a picnic blanket on the ground! She pulled some ingredients from the panty and stirred together a tapenade instead. No worries about melting there. A cherry-berry pie was soon in the oven, with a flag design cut into the top crust. It seemed appropriate for Fourth of July to have bright red cherries and blueberries. And she knew Mike liked pie, as most men do. Just before she showered, she made a bowl of fresh salsa and tucked a bag of blue corn chips into a basket.

Mike's jeep pulled into the driveway a little early. Callie was just finishing braiding her hair. Unfortunately, the jeep didn't have air-conditioning so it would be a windy ride down I-69. He placed her basket beside another in the back. There were also lawn chairs and a small citronella candle bucket. They chatted companionably during the drive down to Conner Prairie. Callie was impressed by the number of people that were attending when traffic came to a stop over two miles from the entrance.

"It's one of the most popular concerts of the year," he explained. "Families make it a tradition. They honor the veterans, and the fireworks are terrific." He picked up his basket and the little bucket in one hand, pulled the lawn chairs onto one shoulder, and grabbed her hand.

"It may be tricky to stay together in this crowd, but if your basket gets too heavy, let me know and I can take it, too," he said. They moved slowly through a massive crowd, all flowing in the same direction. Men pulled big coolers on wheels, while women carried baskets and blankets. Boy scouts pulling wagons were available to help older citizens or people with small children move their picnics from their cars to the hillside. Everyone seemed in a festive mood.

Mike found a spot on the hill overlooking the band shell. Children pulling balloons or eating ice cream ran through the crowd. Older ladies sat under umbrellas for shade as they chatted with one another and sipped iced tea. The smell of barbequed chicken and hot dogs filled the air. Some families had elaborate picnics, complete with tables, wine glasses, and candelabra. Others had KFC boxes on a blanket. There were thousands of people ready to enjoy a beautiful summer evening and inspiring music.

Callie and Mike enjoyed their picnic, with Mike expressing approval of both appetizers and especially the pie. He confessed that his mother had made the fried chicken, but he'd made his special German potato salad recipe as the side dish. He'd brought a bottle of sparkling apple cider and a thermos of coffee to have with dessert. The citronella candle was appreciated. Its lemony fragrance was delightful and kept the mosquitoes at bay.

The symphony was excellent, and Callie's heart swelled as the veterans proudly stood and saluted the flag as each military service's theme song was played. Tears filled her eyes as she thought about all the sacrifices that had been made so that Americans could celebrate freedom on this day. When "From the Halls of Montezuma" rose from the orchestra, Callie's heart thumped again as she thought about a special Marine. She felt a bit guilty that she wasn't totally focused on the man beside her at the moment. Mike was such a sweetheart and good company. It was obvious that he was fond of her, maybe more than fond.

They remained on their blanket allowing the crowd that was in a hurry to depart once the elaborate fireworks were over. The live cannon fire punctuating the strains of "The 1812 Overture" had been a fitting finale. Parents carried sleeping children. Senior citizens moved stiffly after sitting on the ground so long. The air smelled of the powder used to fire the cannons.

"Aren't the stars amazing?" Mike asked.

"This whole evening has been amazing," Callie said happily. "I love a good symphony orchestra. It's so rich, so uplifting."

"Maybe we can make it an annual event," Mike said softly, taking her hand possessively.

"Maybe we should invite your mother to come along," she said quickly. "After all, she did cook the chicken."

Mike looked at her through the fading light for a few moments before he realized that the groundskeepers were herding everyone out of the area. "I guess we need to pack up."

"Why do I feel like I just dodged a bullet?" Callie thought to herself as she drew a deep breath. To Mike, she said aloud, "At least the baskets will be a lot lighter!

The drive north was lovely. The air had cooled a bit, and the stars were gorgeous. Mike tuned in a radio station that played old standards from the 1940's, and they teased one another about how much they actually enjoyed the sounds of the old-time big bands. At one point, a silly song called "Huggin' and Chalkin'" by Indiana's own Hoagy Carmichael came on, and Callie broke into laughter over the lyrics that described two fellows who meet unexpectedly while they are hugging their overly chubby girlfriend from opposite sides .

"Can you imagine the uproar if someone sang a song like that today?" Mike queried. "The weight-challenged folks would be up in arms."

"I actually have the sheet music for it somewhere," Callie laughed. "My great aunt once had the sheet music for the song on her piano. When I saw the picture of the two guys holding chalk in their hands, I asked her what the song was about. She played it for me, and we both laughed and laughed. I inherited all her sheet music and even had some of the best ones framed to hang over the piano. They're actually in a box somewhere in the spare room."

"I'd love to see them sometime, if you ever find the right box," Mike teased.

Callie was delighted to discover that Mike actually knew the lyrics to most of the old Perry Como and Vaughn Monroe hits, except he often changed the words to make them hilarious. By the time they reached Callie's farmhouse her sides were sore from laughing. She invited him in for coffee, but he said he had to go to work extra early the next morning, and it was already after midnight.

After he left, she poured a glass of white wine flavored with a bit of her homemade lemon verbena liqueur and sauntered out to the gazebo. The pale blossoms around the gazebo shimmered whenever the moon peeked from behind fast-moving clouds. It was a gorgeous evening, the kind just made for romance. Callie had enjoyed herself so much tonight. Mike was good company and could nearly always make her laugh. Was that enough to be the foundation for a lifetime relationship? She was still wondering as she fell asleep.

The lavenders Callie had planted in raised beds behind the shadehouse were nearly finished blooming. The heat changed the flowers almost overnight. The fragrance was indeed heavenly and she spent several hours harvesting the flowers before they faded. It was one of the most pleasant jobs she'd ever had, surrounded by the satisfied hum of worker bees as they collected nectar from the purple blooms. She couldn't wait to taste the first lavender honey that would come from her hives.

She hung bunches of lavender on a drying rack in the Cottage where the scent encouraged sales. A new notebook was begun, purple of course, in which the color, fragrance, size, hardiness, and other characteristics of each variety were recorded. Callie also noted customer preferences, intending to increase the number of plants they liked best for next season. She not only loved the colors and scents, but the history of lavender. And the names were enchanting. "Sleeping Beauty" was a variety that bloomed later in the season. "Lullingstone Castle" and "Hidcote" were named for castles in England. "Baby Blue" was a small plant with intensely dark flowers. "Marge Clark" was named for a well-known Indiana herb writer. It was all fascinating to Callie, who dreamed of planting an entire field of lavender. It would be her own bit of purple heaven.

The heat still continued to beat down upon central Indiana all through fair week. Callie recognized the fans she had borrowed fighting a losing battle in trying to keep the show hogs cool. One morning the headline of the Heartland Banner was "Three Ribbon-Winners Die in Extreme Heat", with the article following explaining how even running sprinklers on the hogs had not been enough to save them. The following day all of the livestock was released from the fairgrounds.

The carnival people complained about low attendance, and Callie heard from her friends that several of the churches were worried about their budgets for the remainder of the year. Many organizations depended upon the profits they made at the fair to support their causes the rest of the year. Callie felt badly for the groups and felt better about the low sales at the farm. At least she wasn't the only business that was feeling the heat.

She had attended the fair one evening with Mike, who insisted on throwing balls to win her a gigantic teddy bear, which she had now named "Comfort". She saw Lucy and Time twirling around on death-defying rides together. "Oh, to have a stomach young enough to think that was fun," she laughed. She studied the entries in the garden vegetable and horticulture categories, noting several of the garden club's members had won ribbons. They spent an enjoyable hour viewing the artwork and crafts. She was not surprised to see that LouAnn's still-life had won the grand champion ribbon. Mike wanted her to see the quilt exhibit since his mother and several of her friends had entered the competition. Afterwards, they ate homemade ice cream at one of the church booths. It had been a long time since she'd been to a fair, and she'd enjoyed it.

The lilies around her gazebo came into bloom, releasing their powerful fragrance. Indeed, as Callie had predicted, they were a glistening white with dark freckles in their centers. Unfortunately, in the intense heat the blooms were short-lived. The roses dropped their buds. The birds rarely sang during the day.

Callie made a big display of heat-resistant succulents using a big brightly painted plywood sun as the focal point. She created a wreath out of a coil of bright green garden hose and lettered "You can retire your hose, or go on vacation with these plants!" on a sign to hang above it. Old kettles, pails, tea kettles, a child' dump truck, terra cotta bowls, and anything else she could find were filled with a mixture of the interesting plants. She moved as many big flowering planters as she could into the shade. Then she moved all the benches and chairs under the trees. No one was interested in sitting in the sun. She purchased all the used umbrellas she could find at flea markets and put them in a container marked "Help yourself to some Shade!" to encourage people to stay in the plant sales areas a little longer.

She set up an area in the shade of her black walnut garage for the plug flats of scented geraniums and lavenders she was trying to propagate. It was too hot in the greenhouse. The butterflies hovered over the shallow dishes she'd filled with sand. As soon as she poured in a little water they began puddling, drawing moisture from the damp sand. She gave up trying to keep the hummingbird feeders filled. In the heat, the syrup turned sour in hours. They'd just have to sip nectar from the abundant plants in her gardens. Even Wicca gave up trying to keep the squirrels in trees. She lay panting in the shade. It was, indeed, the "dog days of summer."

The dates for the Herb Conference approached. Callie was packed and ready to head to the airport days ahead. Wicca would have sleepovers with Lucy while she was gone. She and Gloria would take turns working at the farm. As slow as traffic had been they wouldn't have a problem handling the few customers that might appear. Callie had laid out the lists of the merchandise she expected to arrive while she was gone, so Gloria would know which went where. By the time she returned there should be a corner of the shop with Peter Rabbit items and another with a hot chili theme. She'd picked up a sombrero and some fiesta-looking fabric to cover a table and to drape over one wall. It should be bright and festive, accented with red pepper salt shakers, chip dishes, and a string of bright red chili pepper lights.

She'd had coffee one morning with Trev at Dinah's Diner where she'd explained she just couldn't take the barn. He hadn't tried to argue at all and although he was disappointed, he accepted her decision gracefully. The only awkward moment had been when Mike, dressed in his official brown shorts and baseball cap, had come in carrying a large carton for Dinah. He nearly dropped the carton when he saw Callie and Trev's heads together bent over a piece of paper. Callie hadn't noticed him enter, so she was surprised when he stopped at their table on the way out.

"Morning, Callie," he said stiffly. "I have some boxes on the truck for you, so I'll be out later. Will you be there, or shall I leave them at the house?"

"Oh, hi, Mike," Callie said in surprise. She glanced at her watch saying, "I should be back there by your usual delivery time."

"Oh, by the way you left your sunglasses in the jeep," he said, watching Trev's face.

Callie was watching, too, and noted that Trev didn't even blink. He was busy placing the papers they'd been looking at in a folder.

"I'll give them to you later when I drop the boxes," he said. "Morning, Carpenter,"

"Morning, Mike," Trev smiled. "I need a refill," he said as he rose taking both his and Callie's cups.

"Business meeting?" Mike queried.

"As a matter of fact, yes," said Callie. She didn't offer any more. Mike started to say something more but just turned and stalked out.

"Well, that seemed a bit awkward," Trev laughed when he returned, placing both cups of steaming coffee on the table between them. "Am I stepping on someone's toes? Bruising any egos?"

"Of course not," Callie smiled. "So, Santa, how DO you manage to drink coffee without staining your beard? I've always wondered."

Trev laughed, "That's a secret, little girl." He laughed again, "However, I can tell you there is a little magic involved."

Before she could reply a shadow fell over her. Deputy Wright's long form appeared from behind her.

"Ma'am," he said quietly as he stopped by the table. "Had any trouble with skunks lately," he said softly, giving Trev a piercing stare before he continued on.

"Now, that was interesting." Trev chuckled. "If I weren't Santa Claus, I just might take offense!"

Yes, Callie was happy, almost relieved to be heading out of Heartland. Not only was she looking forward to a few days in an air-conditioned hotel, but she was excited to be able to attend educational sessions and do lots of networking with other herb business owners. She hoped to get new ideas for workshops and displays and find more suppliers of herbal products for the shop. She might even discover a good speaker that she could bring to the farm for a special event. And, she hoped to go home with a few new herb books tucked into her suitcase.

She checked her suitcase, and keeping a firm grip on her purse, headed for the proper gate to await her flight. She changed planes in St. Louis, and while she was waiting, she noticed a woman wearing a jacket decorated with herb designs and carrying a briefcase. The woman took the seat next to Callie, noticed that she was reading a book on herb garden design, and started a conversation. Both women were headed to the same conference, of course, so they talked about the speakers and sessions they planned to attend. The time passed quickly, as did the flight to Portland, Oregon.

The International Herb Association Conference was all that Callie had hoped it would be. She attended sessions given by notable experts and spent every possible moment networking with other herb business owners. She learned techniques from professional growers and listened to reports and research from university professors. During meals, she sat at tables where discussions revolved around websites and self-publishing. She bought so many books and gathered so many catalogs that she was certain she'd fill the empty suitcase she'd packed for that purpose. She even attended a workshop on herbal skin care and making cosmetics. Gloria would be pleased, especially if Callie actually started to implement the ideas and recipes.

She went with a group of fellow herb lovers to visit a beautiful family-operated herb farm called "Blue Heron" outside of Portland where she saw new varieties of plants, including actual tea plants. They also went to the famous gardens and nursery at Joy Creek, where Callie saw exotic plants she wished would grow in Indiana. However, Portland and Seattle had the tempering effect of the ocean and could grow a much broader range of plant material than the Midwest. A visit to Nichols Herb Nursery was inspiring and Callie was able to purchase dozens of seed packets of new varieties. She bought another carry-on bag to hold a collection of miniature plants from a specialty nursery.

When the official conference was over, she took a side trip to Sequim, Washington, to attend the famous Lavender Festival. Dozens of small lavender farms dotted the area along the coast, with shuttle buses providing transportation on various routes. She took lots of photographs to document the varieties of lavender she liked best and was even able to purchase a few plants. The shops and booths provided lots of ideas for lavender products. Callie was able to sample lavender margueritas and lavender ice cream. She couldn't wait to tell Gloria and Lucy about her trip and show them all the catalogs and ideas she'd gleaned. She felt revitalized and renewed, ready to pour even more energy into her dream farm.

Returning to the farm, there was more reality than dream. Callie was disappointed to find the heat wave had continued in her absence. It was nearly impossible to keep the gardens watered in addition to the sales area with only two people working. Gloria and Lucy had tried their best and even called a couple of garden club members in to help, but some things were wilted. The candle inventory had begun to melt in the shop, so Gloria had taken them home to her air-conditioned house. Callie called Josh Sparks to see if the wiring in the Cottage could handle a window air-conditioner.

There was no time to unpack other than putting all the new plants she'd brought back with her onto an empty windowsill in the dining room. She hurriedly prepared for the Beatrix Potter birthday party. The recently planted garden had grown more lush and abundant while she was away, only because of Lucy's faithful watering. She gave it a quick tidy and returned to the kitchen to start the refreshments. Happily, Dinah's Diner would supply the carrot cake. Gloria and Lucy had made a charming display in one corner of the shop using the new "Peter Rabbit" merchandise that had arrived. Lucy had pulled a few bunnies from the box of spring leftovers to add to the mix and the over-all effect was delightful. While Callie organized the books and handouts, Lucy hid two dozen little resin rabbits in the gardens for a "Find Peter Rabbit" game. Gloria covered the food table with a pretty Peter Rabbit decorated tablecloth that she'd found at a party shop and added a centerpiece made of colorful pots filled with parsley. Lucy had to tie weights to the corners of the tablecloths on the outdoor tables they'd set up for customers to enjoy the birthday cake. The wind was picking up, and everyone hoped that it would eventually bring some rain.

Thankfully, the breeze made it seem a bit cooler so all the participants had an enjoyable day. For many families it was a last fun day together before frenzied preparations to begin the new school year. Everyone enjoyed Callie's presentation on Beatrix Potter's life while they savored carrot cake and iced chamomile tea. Several kindergarten teachers came to relax before they had to organize their classrooms. Callie made arrangements with two of them to do a program on gardening for children using the Beatrix Potter stories as a theme. She had done a similar program in her own classroom, so it would not take long to pull it together.

Just as the day ended the wind picked up sharply, and dark clouds pushed on the horizon. Customers picked out the last of their purchases and hurried to their cars. Gloria and Lucy quickly gathered things from the outdoors and moved items under cover. The women hurried to close up and get home before the approaching storm arrived. Callie and Wicca barely made it to the house before the first fat raindrops fell. The rain would be a blessing. Callie's lawn was a beige carpet, and there were cracks in the ground so wide she could put her hand into them. Any moisture would help, and this storm looked like it could last for several hours. Lightning cracked as Callie stood in the doorway sniffing the welcome scent of rain.

"Guess I won't be checking my e-mail for a while, girl," she told the lab, "but I can sort through this pile of mail and unpack the suitcases." After finishing those tasks, she spent the rest of the evening pouring over the new books she'd purchased at the conference, adding notes to her folders for workshops and events that she'd gleaned while networking with other herb business owners. Then she read the catalogs she'd picked up at the trade show and made a list of websites to browse.

Outside, the storm raged with brilliant flashes of lightning and winds that bent the trees in curves. A few more branches fell from the ancient cottonwood near the house, and Callie saw some shingles fly past the window. Once the storm was over, she'd have to investigate to see how much damage was done to the house's roof. Needless to say, she'd have to comb the woods tomorrow to recover the signs that had blown away from the plant sales areas and probably a few "No Hunting" signs had blown off, too.

Hopefully the storm not only brought much needed rain but maybe some cooler temperatures as well.

Callie slept in the following morning. She was more tired from traveling to the herb conference than she'd thought and was still adjusting to the time change. After breakfast, she put in a load of the laundry she'd unpacked and checked her e-mail. She entered new customer information into her data base and started working on the newsletter that would go out in August. It was hard to believe July was nearly over.

Luckily, the damage at the farm was minimal. The only major casualty was Mr. MacGregor, who was lying on the ground missing his hat. His face was fairly lop-sided and part of his moustache was gone. She carried the soggy body into the greenhouse and laid him across the plant benches to dry. For over an hour, she sat pots back up that had blown over and retrieved signs. A quick tour of the Cottage told her that sales had been minimal on Beatrix Potter day. She'd need to run some numbers to see if they'd sold enough to justify the expenses for refreshments and decorations, plus all the advertising she'd bought. She emptied all the trash barrels, amazed at how much had accumulated from yesterday's small crowd and loaded the bags into the back of the truck.

She'd been disappointed while she was in Oregon to hear that only four people had signed up for today's workshop. Gloria had called her on the deadline date for reservations and they'd decided to cancel it and refund the four fees. Now, she was elated to have the afternoon free. The rain in the night had already disappeared into the parched soil and the day was unbearably hot and humid. Anyone attending the workshop would have been miserable, and she was too tired to teach effectively or enthusiastically. Perspiration ran down her back as she drove the truck to the roadside and put the bags out for Monday's trash collection.

It was too hot to cook lunch, and she wasn't hungry anyway. She made a big pitcher of lemonade and took a stack of new books out to the gazebo. If she could stay awake, she'd read. She opened the first book and began to skim the table of contents.

"Callie! Callie! Wake up!" a voice yelled in her ear.

Callie opened her eyes and tried to bring things into focus. She must still be dreaming. She thought she saw Lucy with bright purple hair, wearing a lime green bikini.

"Callie! Get up! There's a dead body at the farm," the girl yelled again, pulling on Callie's arms in an attempt to get her into a sitting position.

"Lucy? Is that really you? Why are you wearing a bikini?" Callie stammered.

"Callie, didn't you hear me? There's a dead body at the farm. First dead deer, then robbers, and now they've actually killed someone!" Lucy said hysterically. "I called 911. And I called my dad. He's sending out a reporter right away." Callie could hear a siren in the distance.

"Calm down, Lucy," she told the girl. "Where did you see the body?"

"He's in the greenhouse. I saw his feet sticking up and his arm is hanging funny. I didn't want to go any closer," Lucy cried.

Callie began walking down her driveway, still fuzzy-brained from deep sleep. Lucy was dancing at her side, her purple dolphin earrings flashing in the sunlight.

"Do you have on sun screen?" Callie asked her. As soon as the words were out of her mouth, she knew how odd it must sound to the teenager.

"Callie, are you crazy? Someone is dead, and you're thinking about sunscreen!" Lucy had begun to cry in earnest. Tears streamed down her face, carrying lines of purple eye make-up.

"Sorry, I just can't help thinking you're exposing a lot of skin," Callie replied, shaking her head in an attempt to clear it.

"I've never seen a real live dead body before," Lucy declared. "Wait until I tell Time. Maybe I should call him to come and take a picture." She reached for her ever-present phone, but of course, the bikini had no pockets. "I left my phone in my car," she wailed, running across the road to the parking lot. Her VW bug was sitting with the driver's side door still open.

Callie had just crossed the road when the patrol car pulled in. It was quickly followed by the sheriff's unit, Sandy Saunder's sedan, and a police car from town.

"Are you okay?" Deputy Wright called through the window. "Where's the body? What happened?"

"I have no idea," Callie told him. "I was sleeping in the gazebo. Lucy woke me and said she saw a body at the farm." The deputy nodded and pulled up to Lucy, who was standing next to her car talking on her cell phone with much arm waving and tears.

By the time Callie ran up to the girl, Deputy Wright and the sheriff had already left her and were jogging toward the greenhouse. Sandy jumped from her car and ran over to Callie asking the same questions the deputy had voiced.

"Oh, no," Callie said. "Oh, no," she repeated as she started to laugh.

"She's hysterical," Lucy diagnosed. "Someone should slap her to bring her out of it. I saw that in a movie."

"Lucy, it's Mr. MacGregor! No one died," Callie told her, still laughing. "It's the body I made for the Peter Rabbit garden."

By this time, the deputy and the sheriff were returning to the crowd that was beginning to form in the parking lot. Several off-duty volunteer firemen had heard the call go out on the radio and responded.

Some passers-by stopped to see what was happening, and a couple of neighbors had seen the patrol car go by with its siren wailing.

The sheriff raised his arms, asking for silence. "There's no problem here. No one died. Everyone go about your business." A few people returned to their cars, but several milled about waiting for an explanation. Those who were left turned to look as the coroner's van pulled in.

"I think you can handle this," the sheriff said, looking at Deputy Wright. He walked over to the coroner where a brief conversation took place before they both drove away. At that point, the crowd decided there really was nothing to see, so most of them departed.

Sandy was still trying to get an explanation that made sense, and Lucy had become silent with embarrassment. When her father pulled in, screeching to a halt next to the VW, Lucy rolled her eyes and begged Callie to hide her somewhere.

"It was a reasonable mistake, Lucy," Callie told her, hugging her tightly.

"I'm so sorry," the girl began. "I really, really thought someone had died. I didn't want to go touch him. With everything that's happened out here I just assumed someone was dead."

The deputy was leading Mac toward the greenhouse. They paused at the edge of the parking lot, talking and shaking their heads. Sandy walked up to join them but returned quickly to Callie and Lucy.

"Lucy, I swear if I had seen that body lying there, I would have freaked, too," Sandy assured her. "It really looks like a corpse. In fact, if I took a photo, I don't think any of our readers would question it."

"Oh, Sandy, you wouldn't," Callie frowned.

"Of course not, but it does look real with his boots sticking up and his arm dangling down," she told them.

"Young lady," Mac called to his daughter.

"Don't be too hard on her, Mac," the deputy cautioned him. "She was probably scared to death. She was crying when I arrived."

Callie put her arm around Lucy's shoulders as the two men approached, and Sandy wrapped an arm protectively around the girl's waist.

"Mac McKenzie, you be nice to this girl," Sandy ordered. "She's just been through an ordeal. Anyone could have made the same mistake, so don't you give her a rough time."

"Well, that was some prank," Mac said, shaking his head.

"I'm sure it wasn't a prank," Callie replied. "Lucy truly believed she'd seen a body."

"I'm sorry, Dad," Lucy said meekly.

"Well, it does look pretty dead," he smiled. "Now, young lady, what are you doing out in public in that outfit? You get yourself home this minute and put on something respectable!"

"But Dad, I'm meeting Time at the reservoir. We're going swimming with a bunch of our friends! I just stopped here because I left my camera under the sales counter yesterday. I went to get it from the Cottage, and that's when I saw the body," she explained.

"Has your mother seen that swimsuit?" he asked. "You're not wearing that anyplace. We're going home right now, young lady." They departed in a cloud of dust. Callie was surprised that the parking lot was so dry, despite last night's drenching rain.

"I'm going, too," Sandy said. "I think I'll give Gloria a call and warn her that Mac and Lucy are butting heads again."

"Probably a good idea," Callie muttered.

"Well, that was pretty exciting," Morgan chuckled. "I almost thought it was a corpse, too, until I saw the button eyes."

"I carried him in there to dry out after last night's rain. I never dreamed anyone would mistake it for a body," Callie smiled apologetically. "Sorry it caused so much trouble."

"I'm just glad it's not a real body," Morgan replied.

"Well, if it were, it would be fully cooked by now. The temperature in that greenhouse is easily a hundred and twenty degrees," she laughed. "Have you ever known it to be this hot?"

"Not in recent years," he said, wiping his sleeve across his forehead. "I'm just about off duty. By the time we drive to your house, I will be. Have anything cold over there?"

"I'm pretty sure the lemonade I made earlier will be warm by now, but I think I can come up with something," she offered. "Go on over and I'll close the gate behind you."

When Callie reached her house, Morgan had exchanged his uniform shirt for a light-weight cotton tee. He followed her into the house unbuckling his gun belt on the way.

"How does iced tea sound? I put a jug on the deck earlier, so it should be steeped by now."

"Anything with ice will be perfect," he answered. Callie went out to get the jar while Morgan pulled two glasses from the cupboard and filled them with ice.

"Want to sit in the gazebo? It's a little cooler there than here in the house," she asked. "Did you have lunch? I have the makings for shrimp salad, and there's marinated tomatoes."

"With fresh basil and garlic?" he asked, smiling.

"Absolutely," she laughed, pulling a loaf of Italian bread from the pantry. "It's been too hot to bake bread, but I picked this up for the Beatrix Potter party yesterday. I served it with an herb, carrot, and parsley spread that turned out pretty well. There's some leftover carrot cake for dessert, too."

"Sounds like my lucky night," he smiled, raising his glass in a salute. "What can I do to help?"

Monarda

One of the most striking plants for the herb garden, Monarda has all the features required to be called a great herb! Native to North America, it is easily grown in full sun or light shade. While it prefers moist, rich soil it adapts to average soil and only suffers when conditions are extremely dry.

Monarda has been a popular plant for centuries. It has acquired several names in that time. It is often called beebalm, or bergamot. The name bergamot comes from the scent of the leaves, which is similar to the fragrance of the small orange fruit used to flavor and scent Earl Gray tea.

Visually, Monarda's vibrant crimson, shaggy blooms attract humans, hummingbirds, and butterflies. There are also varieties with white, pink, magenta, lavender, rose, or deep purple blooms. Both the leaves and flowers of the Monarda are delightfully fragrant and edible in salads, cookies, or breads. The leaves and flowers have been dried for centuries to make "Oswego Tea", a very popular beverage during the American Revolution. A jar of its dried red petals and deep green leaves in layers makes a pretty and appreciated Christmas gift. Many people dry the flowers for winter bouquets and potpourri, too. Medicinally, Monarda has been used for nausea and insomnia.

Another native, *Monarda fitulosa*, has a pale lavender bloom and a pleasant scent. It grows in abundance in wayside places, but is prone to powdery mildew.

Another variety, *Monarda citriodora*, is a special favorite. Its tall spikes carry eight to ten pinkish purple blooms stacked on a single stalk, making a very striking accent. This one seems to do best in full sun and moist soil. Plant it close to paths where passers-by can brush its lemon-scented leaves. A short-lived perennial, this "Lemon Bergamot", as it is also called, self-seeds readily so its short lifespan is not a problem. Grow it for the butterflies that will cloud around it!

Monarda may be grown from seed for mixed plantings. To guarantee a specific color or variety, a cutting roots easily in moist soil. Or mature plants can be divided in spring. Height varies with color, variety, and soil fertility. Generally, the white-bloomed plants are usually shortest, along with the patented "Kim's Knee-High," "Petite Delight," and "Petite Wonder." Some of the deep purples planted in the same location reach nearly five feet! The purples and magentas bloom first, usually mid-June. Then the pinks, lavenders, and rose varieties flower in succession. The white plants blooms next followed by the reds in mid-July. If plants are kept picked, the bloom period is extended. This is easy to do since Monarda is a nice cut flower. We use them in "patriotic" bouquets for the Fourth of July along with white feverfew and blue cornflowers. Cutting the plants back to eight inches after the first bloom promotes a second bloom in September.

There are many named cultivars developed to resist powdery mildew, or to have double blooms, or reduced height. All of them are easy to grow. Look for "Cambridge Scarlet," "Jacob Cline," or "Gardenview Scarlet" if you want good reds. "Croftway Pink," "Marshall's Delight," and "Aquarius" are good pinks. "Purple Mildew Resistant" and "Prairie Night" are excellent deep purples. "Raspberry Wine" is a deep wine-red. And, the tell-tale square stems of Monarda remind gardeners that they are related to mints and can be vigorous spreaders when given good conditions.

Few herbs can compare with Monarda—easy to grow, great visual impact in the landscape, wide color range, nectar for butterflies and hummingbirds, edible blooms and leaves, colorful blooms for fresh or dried bouquets, a medicinal tradition, and a delightful scent. Monarda is truly one of the great herbs!

Chapter 8:

AUGUST

Callie started the morning with iced green tea. The thermometer already read eighty-one degrees at seven a.m. The heat of summer would be blasting again today, so she fixed a large cooler of tea, packed some fresh fruit, and a washcloth. She grabbed her hat and headed for the sales area. Before leaving the farmhouse she made a tour around the structure and noticed a half dozen shingles had blown off during the storm on Saturday night. Other than a few fallen branches there wasn't any other significant damage.

At the farm Callie left the cooler and fruit in the Cottage and headed to the woods with a basket and her big staple gun. Wicca walked along beside her lethargically. It was too hot for romping. Before Callie had gone very far, Wicca abandoned her. Callie could hear the lab splashing in the creek ahead. Callie wished she could join the dog, but there was so little water in the creek that it was now a series of stagnant puddles and not very appealing. She picked up plant signs and pots all the way from the edge of the woods to the creek, along with a few "No Hunting" signs. Those she replaced on posts and trees with the staple gun. She placed the pots and plant signs she found into her basket. As she walked, she let her mind drift over the prior evening that she and Morgan had spent. They'd had a good time fixing the shrimp salad and watching the sunset. Eventually, she felt she'd found all the signs in the area, and knew she needed to start watering. It had taken much longer than she'd planned already. When she reached the Cottage the phone was ringing. It was Monday, so she let the machine get it.

There was watering to do outside which would take most of the day. She wouldn't have time to run many errands. Callie was looking forward to a quiet day at the farm after all the excitement yesterday. Morgan had stayed after dinner, helping to wash up the dishes and also helping her move some boxes in the storeroom. Then they'd sat and talked in the gazebo while the sun set. She'd unpacked the boxes they'd moved until the wee hours. And, she was still tired from the trip and trying to adjust to the heat again. Maybe this afternoon, she'd work on the plant list for the new moonlight garden. She'd already staked out the beds using the sketches she'd drawn on graph paper as a guide. A full-moon circle filled the center surrounded by curving paths. On the south and north sides matching crescent moon shapes were created with paths on all sides. Two narrow rectangular beds extended on those ends with openings on each side balanced the plan. Very long rectangular beds on the east and west sides connected all the paths and completed the area. She envisioned the entire garden surrounded with a white picket fence, each picket having a moon shape on top. Iron archways with moons and stars would provide entrances and space to grow fragrant moonflower vines. She could picture the entire garden in her mind. The white stone paths would be lined with furry gray lambs' ears, silver veronica, gray santolina, and ghostly artemisias. The beds would be filled with white cleome, hydrangeas, pale daylilies, fragrant woodland nicotianas, and sweet alyssum. White petunias, cosmos, and phlox "David" would weave among silvery centureas and rattlesnakemaster. Spring bulbs in pure white would begin the season with white mums, boltonia, and asters completing the year. Evening primrose, night-blooming jasmine, night-blooming daylilies, white mirabilis, and jasmine primroses would fill the night with fragrance. It would be a magical place to stroll by moonlight and she couldn't wait to start planting. Someday, she'd put a lacy, white gazebo on the southwest corner. It would be a romantic place. She could picture herself sitting out there on a white wicker sofa, sipping wine, and listening to Morgan's rumbly voice. Or maybe Mike's voice humming old show tunes. She was delighted that Daniel had not been her first vision. He'd dropped to third place, but he was still there in her thoughts causing her heart to throb in pain.

Despite the recent rain, it had been an unusually dry summer, and the big cottonwood by the driveway was already dropping crispy leaves. The black walnut trees in the front yard were turning yellow and their leaves were fluttering to the ground in any breeze. As she walked back to the sales area she noticed many butterflies sipping nectar in the Butterfly Garden. There were swallowtail caterpillars munching on fennel and monarch caterpillars hanging upside down on sturdy milkweed plants. She stopped to run a small stream of water into the puddling pan and was rewarded by several tiny blue butterflies as well as half a dozen yellow sulfurs drifting over to suck moisture from the moist sand. The ironweed was swarming with butterflies and beneficial wasps, its deep purple flowers towering above her head. She made a note on her clipboard to deadhead it as soon as it finished blooming. It was a wonderful plant in the garden and for the butterflies, but each flower cluster produced hundreds of seeds which could quickly take over much more space than desired. The "Gateway" Joe Pye Weed was breathtaking, with huge ten-inch rosy-pink balls of bloom. Nearby on the iron trellis, the cardinal climber she'd planted was twining upwards with dozens of scarlet trumpets. Already, three hummingbirds were enjoying a breakfast of its sweet nectar.

She'd only been watching for a few minutes before the phone rang again. "Maybe it's someone wanting to come to the next workshop," she thought hopefully. The class was not filled, and another attendee or two could help the bottom line. As she unlocked the Cottage, she could hear her mother's voice talking to the machine, her voice choked with strain.

"Mom, I'm here," Callie said as soon as she'd grabbed the phone.

"I'm so sorry to have to call you, but Dad had a stroke. I knew you'd want to know. We're at the hospital in Wabash, but they're transferring him to Fort Wayne. I know you have a workshop this afternoon, and there's nothing you can do here. I thought maybe you could drive up afterwards," she said, her voice trailing off to a whisper.

"Which hospital? I'm coming now, Mom," Callie said quickly. Tears were already running down her face as she wrote down the information. As soon as she hung up the phone, Callie pulled the workshop folder from the counter and called all the workshop participants to cancel the class. "One thing about gardeners," Callie thought to herself for the umpteenth time, "they are basically really nice people." No one had protested or even asked if the fee would be refunded. There was only one person that she could not reach, so Callie called Gloria's house and left a message on the machine. The McKenzie family would be at church for another hour but Callie was sure Gloria or Lucy would handle everything.

She grabbed the suitcase she had just unpacked recently, threw some clothes inside, added a couple of books, and her Bible. She'd be spending lots of time in waiting rooms. Once the bag of dog food and Wicca were in the car, she was ready to leave.

The hour's drive seemed to take forever. Her mother's words spun through her head over and over. Her father had collapsed in the kitchen. His left side was immobile and he could not speak. The paramedics had arrived only seven minutes after her mother had placed the call and administered medication. They'd taken him to the local hospital and quickly determined that surgery was required. Callie found it difficult to process. Her father was so strong and nimble. He had always been wiry and thin, never overweight. He didn't smoke or drink. He should live forever.

Her throat was tight, and she had to blink continually to clear her eyes. Beside her, Wicca sensed the emotion and laid a paw on Callie's thigh. "You're right, girl," Callie said to the lab. "Dad's tough. If anyone can come through this, he will." She whispered prayers until she pulled into the hospital parking lot.

After locating her mother, listening to the nurse's explanation of the procedure, and visiting the chapel, Callie settled in to wait. She held her mother's hand, fetched coffee, and maintained a positive outlook. Periodically, she returned to the parking lot to take Wicca for a quick walk and refilled her water bowl.

The surgeon finally came to the waiting area. A frown creased his face. Callie found herself stiffening, her breath stopping. He explained that the surgery had gone well. All of the blockage in the carotid arteries had been cleared, but before they had finished, Dad's heart had stopped. All attempts to restart it had failed. He was gone.

Callie's mother took the news with stoic grace. "He would have wanted to go quickly," she said quietly. "He would not have wanted to be stuck in a bed or a wheelchair or to go to a nursing home. If he couldn't drive his tractors, he wouldn't want to be here." She lifted her head and said, "Thank you, Lord, for sparing him pain and suffering."

Then she turned to the surgeon, took his hand, and thanked him. "I am sure you did all you could," she said, "God just wanted him to come home to Him."

The next few days were a blur to both Callie and her mother. There were phone calls to make, services to plan, food to organize, and a host of legal matters. Callie stayed with her mother, except to make a quick trip back to the farm. Lucy met her there and promised to take good care of Wicca until Callie could return.

"If there's a problem, just put the cable across the gate and tape a big 'Closed for Family Emergency' sign on the gatepost," Callie advised her.

"We've got it covered," Lucy assured her. "Some of the ladies from the garden club have volunteered to help out. You've got a pile of messages here already. I put your mail in this box," she said reaching under the counter.

"You are an angel," Callie told her. "I don't know what I would do without you and your mother."

"Dad said not to worry about your column for this week. He still has two left from that first day you came to his office."

"Tell him I'll e-mail him something as soon as I can. I just don't know how many days I'll need to stay. Mom is doing great, but there are still legal matters to attend to, and all the dishes to be returned to the people that brought food. Dad's family has lived there for generations so everyone knew him," she choked. "I still can't believe he's not coming back."

At the farmhouse, Callie checked her e-mails and grabbed several folders. She pulled a few items of clothing from the closet and threw out the spoiled food in the refrigerator. Lucy had already watered the plants at the house. She checked her calendar and made a list of things that were high-priority. She read through the phone messages and listened to those on the house machine. Mike had called a dozen times. There were several business-related calls and some from neighbors, too.

As soon as she had everything loaded into the truck, Callie returned to her mother's house. It seemed odd to no longer call it her parent's home.

The days passed quickly, but the nights were long. Callie found she couldn't sleep, but she couldn't concentrate enough to read or write either. Everything was a painful reminder that her father was gone. She helped sort through her dad's clothing, taking it to the local mission sponsored by the church. She made dozens of phone calls and tried to get her mother to eat and rest. She talked to bankers, insurance representatives, and lawyers.

Her mother had written all the "thank you" notes by herself although Callie had offered to help. She had allowed Callie to return all the neighbor's dishes and the items that belonged to the church women's group. They had made trips to the lawyer's office, the bank, and the funeral home. Callie had made copies of death certificates, and filed insurance claims. It seemed a never-ending process

At the end of a week, Callie's mother encouraged her to return to the farm. "I know you have mountains of obligations," she said. "I'm going to be fine and I don't mind being here alone. I'll have to get used to it eventually, so I might as well start now."

"Take any of his tools that you can use, Callie," her mother told her. "Dad would want you to have them, especially the ones that were his father's and grandfather's." Together, they sorted through the tools and loaded them into the truck.

Callie made her mother promise to call if she needed anything at all. She left knowing her mother was a strong, strong woman, surrounded by friends and family that would keep an eye on her.

August was nearly half over, and Callie had accomplished little on her schedule. Gloria and Lucy, with the help of a Heart and Soil member or two had kept the farm running beautifully. Sales had been dreadfully low. Callie did not know if that would be normal for August, or if people had heard of her father's death and stayed away, assuming the farm would be closed.

She found it took a few days to return to her routine, to feel normal and know what she should be doing. She had trouble getting everything organized on her job list. Her mind just seemed to be stuck in low gear. The moonlight garden project was abandoned. She did not have the energy or the funds to do it. The mundane tasks that required no thought were what drew her. Weeding, watering. After countless revisions, Callie finally finished an article on dividing irises. She soothed her soul by digging up all Elizabeth's old iris plants, cleaning them of borer, trimming the leaves, and replanting them in gardens where their colors would fit best.

She planted a late crop of green beans in the cook's garden, ordered hard-necked garlic, and hoped it would arrive to plant in early September. Gloria helped her get all the gardens weeded before two garden clubs came to visit and taught the papermaking workshop as planned. Callie was thankful that the two groups actually came since several scheduled groups had cancelled during the prolonged record heat of July and early August.

She forced herself to work on the herbal teas workshop plans but passed off much of the planning of "Salsa Day" to a willing Gloria. They worked together on ads to promote the day, and Gloria offered to give them to Mac.

Callie felt guilty for wanting to isolate herself. So many people had sent cards, left messages, and other expressions of sympathy. Mike continued to call, but she had a hard time holding up her end of the conversation. She deflected offers to spend time with anyone by pleading a backed-up calendar. Everyone was very understanding, so Callie had blocks of time alone. She just wasn't accomplishing much during those blocks.

Beth called and they had long talks. Beth had lost her father a few years before, so she knew what Callie was facing. She talked to her mother frequently, often to discuss insurance problems and legal matters. Her mother was working in her garden for solace, still canning and freezing all the harvest it produced.

The heat continued. School was back in session. Customers were few and far between. Callie harvested the silver artemisias, hanging the bunches on the rafters of both the garage at the house and at the black walnut structure at the farm. She collected seeds from the plants in the gardens, filling envelopes and filing them alphabetically in plastic shoe boxes. She made culinary wreaths of dried mints, oreganos, sage, savory, chive blossoms, thymes, and lavender then decorated them with nigella pods, poppy pods, dried hot peppers and garlic bulbs. They looked beautiful on one wall of the Cottage.

She picked annual statice, starflowers, strawflowers, ammobium, and cockscombs, hanging the bunches under the black plastic in the greenhouse to dry. In the heat, they dried overnight. Then she was able to create colorful swags and garlands of everlastings to hang inside over the Cottage door and windows. August was a good time to propagate lavenders and scented geraniums. Callie spent hours taking the cuttings, stripping the leaves, and sticking the stems into plug flats. Over time, the aromatherapy of the herbs began the healing process. She was able to sleep. She was able to smile, and finally, she was able to think. The herbs had worked their magic.

The morning dawned with the promise of yet another blistering day. Callie forced herself to do her normal Tai Chi routine and watered all the pots around the house and on the patio. She fixed a tall glass of iced tea, grabbed her calendar, the farm schedule, and headed for the gazebo. It was already too hot to work in the studio, so she positioned the laptop on a small table and began making a new job list. There were still a few days until "Salsa Day," but she needed to select the recipes she would demonstrate, make the grocery list, timeline, and write the handouts. She also needed to complete this week's column and finish the lesson plan for the children's gardening class she'd promised to teach so the teachers could purchase supplies.

She spent a productive two hours, stretching when it was over and feeling that she was finally over the hump in terms of accomplishing something. Once the sales tax and employee withholding tax forms had been filled out and mailed, she could spend the remainder of the day catching up at the farm. Some of the cuttings that she'd struck and placed in the shade of the garage were rooted and needed to be put in their individual pots. She also needed to check the flats of seedlings that were tucked in the shade under the greenhouse benches.

Calling Wicca to her side, Callie gathered her basket of supplies and walked to the farm. The "Joyful Heart Herbs" sign looked pretty with the flowers in full bloom below. A few butterflies were having lunch on the blossoms. She didn't have a joyful heart, but it was healing, and she knew her dad would counsel her to savor each and every day. "Every day has a miracle, if you just take time to look," he'd say, quoting his grandmother. Callie had been forgetting to look. She paused to continue watching the miracle of the butterflies, God's "flying flowers".

Wicca was impatient, so Callie continued to the Cottage, checking the messages and emptying the wastebaskets. Then she watered the displays and mentally listed the plants that needed to be moved into new displays for September. It would be time to feature Asters, Boltonia, and other early autumn varieties. She'd need to use a new color scheme, one that featured deep reds, purples, and yellow. In October she'd add orange pumpkins, bittersweet, and colorful mums.

As Callie entered the greenhouse to water the seedling flats under the benches, Wicca ran to the far end of the greenhouse. Thinking that Wicca was after a mouse or possibly a squirrel, Callie followed the dog in back of the black plastic "tent" that she'd hung to protect the drying flowers from sunlight. A bit of green caught her eye.

"What plants are those?" she wondered. They were tucked between the end of the greenhouse and the wall of black plastic. "That's an odd place to put anything. I wonder what Gloria or Lucy were thinking. Why not put them closer to the hose?" She stood over the row of pots, nine in all, and looked at them carefully.

"Who are you?" she said to the plants. She picked up one pot and absently rubbed a leaf. Immediately a distinctive aroma filled the area. "Oh! Oh, my word," Callie exclaimed. She recognized the plant from the program the state police had given to teachers to help them recognize drugs. It was marijuana!

"How did you get in my greenhouse?" Callie's mind was in a whirl. Whose plants were they? Surely they weren't Lucy's. Although the girl was a little wild with her hair and dress, Callie did not believe Lucy would be experimenting with "pot". Then who?

One of the garden club members that had helped while Callie stayed with her mother after the funeral? She didn't have a clue but she knew she could not leave the plants on her property. Should she ask Gloria or Lucy? Should she just destroy them and not say anything to anyone? She sat on the ground staring at the plants, trying to decide on a course of action.

Finally, Callie walked slowly to the Cottage and dialed the phone.

"Wright here," the voice stated flatly.

"I wish you were right here," Callie stated soberly.

"Callie?"

"Yes. Morgan, I need you to come to the farm when you have time. It's not an emergency, but I need to show you something."

"I need to finish some paperwork on an arrest I made this morning, but I can be there in twenty minutes."

"That's fine. I'll be waiting."

While she waited, Callie tried to think of anyone who had access to the greenhouse that might have brought the plants. It would be easy for anyone to walk in through the back door. It was never locked and with the black plastic hanging, blocking the view, it would be unlikely that anyone would notice. Of course, they'd have to carry them from the parking lot, crossing open space.

"Unless," Callie pondered, "unless they came through the woods. Then no one would be likely to see them at all." She was tempted to walk to the back of the greenhouse to see if there were tracks but decided to wait for Deputy Wright.

He arrived after nearly half an hour, pulling his patrol car to the front of the greenhouse where Callie was waiting.

"Sorry, it took me longer on that paperwork than I expected. What's wrong?" he asked, his eyes searching her face.

"When I came to the greenhouse this morning, I found something," she stated as she led him to the back of the building.

Deputy Wright looked at the row of plants. "Not yours, I take it?" he stated flatly.

"Certainly not," Callie assured him emphatically. "I don't know how long they've been there, but a while. There are pill bugs tucked under the pots and you can tell they've been there awhile. They would be attracted to the shade, coolness, and moisture under the clay pots."

"Anything unusual that you can spot? Are those your pots? Soil the same as you use?" he asked.

"I don't have any clay pots that size and the soil doesn't have the same perlite granules that the brand I use contains," she answered after inspecting the pots more closely.

"Have any idea who they belong to?" the deputy said searching her face again.

"I'd hate to make any unfounded guesses. Gloria and Lucy McKenzie work here part time. And several members of the Heart and Soil Garden club helped out off and on while I was away."

"Yes," he said softly. "I heard your father passed away. I'm sorry for your loss. I know how hard it is to lose your dad. Lost mine five years ago, and it still hurts."

"Thank you. It is hard, but it's getting better every day. Although, being in the greenhouse is painful. He helped me build it, you know, and I see him climbing over the structure, or carefully placing the panels on the wall, or building the benching every time I look at it. I wouldn't have it if it weren't for my father. His coming to do the work for free meant I had enough money to put the greenhouse up. I couldn't have afforded to hire a crew to build it."

"I'm sure he loved doing it for you, Callie," he stated quietly.

"Oh, yes, Dad loved a project," she smiled. There was a pause in the conversation and Deputy Wright noticed a slow tear escape from her eyes. He cleared his throat and looked away briefly.

"I think I'd better have a look around outside. Did you touch anything? The door handle? I'll call the station and they'll send someone out to dust for prints if you didn't."

"No, I came in through the front. I thought you might need to look around so I didn't even walk around back," she answered.

"I'll be a few minutes. Maybe you should make some coffee or tea," he smiled.

"I've got a thermos of iced tea in the Cottage. It's already getting too hot for coffee," she responded. "I'll be there when you finish."

A few minutes later Deputy Wright came into the Cottage, returning his cell phone to his pocket. "There'll be an officer out in half an hour. Meantime, I need a list of anyone that you know of that has access to the greenhouse."

"That's difficult since I really haven't been here much. And I have to admit I haven't been very observant recently. Should I talk to Gloria or Lucy to see if anyone unusual has been around?"

"I'll be speaking to them. Don't mention this to anyone else right now. I need to do some checking. The officer will remove the plants when he leaves, after he takes some photographs. Right now, I need an official statement."

"Should I be worried? Am I going to be considered a suspect? Do you think it's just some kids?" she worried aloud.

"I don't think you'll be a suspect, Callie. It could be kids. Hard to tell right now. Keep an eye out. As a business owner here in the middle of nowhere, you always need to be vigilant, Callie. Someone is breaking the law and whether it's kids or someone else, it's a crime. Or, it could be someone put the plants here hoping to get you into trouble," he said quietly.

"Oh, Morgan, I hadn't even considered that!" she exclaimed, a whole new range of possibilities opening up in her thoughts.

"Any enemies that you know of?" he asked.

"Well, the family of the guys who robbed my house might be happy to cause some trouble for me still, I suppose," she proposed. "Or, maybe whoever was killing the deer in my woods is trying a new tactic."

"Feelings are still running hot on the CAFO matter, too," Morgan replied

"Not that I know about. I've been too busy and preoccupied to attend any of the recent meetings. I'm not even sure where all that stands now," she answered.

"Warren Pease told me you had a flat tire and a message on your windshield."

"That was months ago, right after I first moved here and sent a letter to the editor," she said. "I doubt anyone is holding a grudge that long over an opinion in the newspaper."

"You never know," he stated, taking the glass of iced tea she passed him. "Haven't seen you around for a good while," he continued.

"I went to a conference in Oregon in July. Then I was behind here at the farm, trying to get ready for an event. Of course, I stayed with my mother after Dad died. There was all the legal stuff and things to work out. When I came back, I was overwhelmed, and I just wasn't ready to be around people much. I'm perking up, but now I'm behind here at the farm again," she explained.

"Any chance you'll get back to testing some recipes soon?" he smiled quizzically.

"Are you volunteering, Deputy?" she asked.

"Just thought you might need some expert help. I could bring the wine," he said tentatively.

"As a matter of fact, I do need to experiment. This month I'd planned to complete some recipes for new salsas and some pickled things. The dill is perfect right now. The month is nearly over and so far I haven't tried the first thing!" she smiled shakily.

She checked her calendar and they set aside an evening later in the week. Just as they finished their iced tea, another patrol car rolled into the parking lot.

"He'll take over now. I need to finish my patrol. See you on Thursday night," he said, caressing her cheek. The now familiar gesture of tipping his head and touching his hat brim accompanied a farewell as he left the Cottage and strolled over to speak to the crime scene investigator.

Callie watched him from the window, realizing that her pulse was beginning to slow. She hadn't even realized it was quicker than usual. A glance in the mirror showed high color on her cheeks. "Must be hotter than I thought," she mumbled. She certainly felt hot.

During the week, Callie tried to spend more hours at the farm watching any customers that came, and even watching to see if Gloria or Lucy ventured behind the black plastic curtain. Although she really didn't suspect either of them to be the culprit, she was relieved that neither of them attempted to sneak back there to water the now missing plants. Just out of curiosity, Callie had fastened a thin thread to the back door, duplicating something she had seen in an old movie. Each morning she checked it and on the second morning after Deputy Wright had investigated, the thread was broken, indicating someone had opened the back door.

The knowledge did not make Callie rest easier. Since the pot grower now knew the plants were gone, he or she had no reason to return. She hoped that they would just stay away forever. However, in the back of her mind, she also recognized the fact that now they knew that she knew the plants had been there. They might want them back. If they had wanted to get her into trouble, they had failed. Callie doubted that was the purpose. Wouldn't anyone who had wanted her to get caught with the plants on her property have tipped off the authorities? And they wouldn't have needed to put nine valuable plants there just to get her into trouble. One or two would be plenty unless there was some quantity possession law that would raise the stakes. She'd check on that. So, why else would someone have put them there? It was still early enough in the season that there was no danger of frost. They could have been hidden safely anywhere, even outside this time of year. She just couldn't come up with a good explanation.

The heat broke mid-week with another storm, although this one was not as violent as the last. Gloria filled in at the farm while Callie taught the children's gardening classes that week. Lucy was back in school, so she'd only be available to work on Saturday mornings and early afternoons. The band played at all the high school football games, so she had to leave early for rehearsal before the games.

The customer flow was still so slow that Callie could handle the farm easily alone. She seemed able to focus now, so jobs were being completed. She made some herbal vinegars from the abundance in the cook's garden and continued harvesting everlastings for wreaths and swags. During the day she let her mind ponder flavor combinations that might work, using the crop of basils, dill, shallots, and rosemary that spilled over the raised beds. By the time Thursday rolled around she had a stack of recipes to test and several sacks of groceries on the counter.

She got up early to prepare an array of vegetables so they'd be ready to grill. She made some herbal syrups for experimental marguerita-type cocktails and put them in the refrigerator to chill. Then she tidied the area around the gazebo and cleaned the grill. By the time the farm opened that morning, she was nearly prepared for the evening to come.

Business was slow at the farm again, so she was able to close and leave at five o'clock on the dot. Wicca seemed to sense that company was coming and took a look-out post by the back door. Callie showered, braided her hair, and put on a comfortable sundress in pastel blue, white, and apricot stripes. She had just begun chopping some tomatoes for fresh salsa when Morgan's car swung into the driveway. She wiped her hands and went outdoors to greet him.

He stooped to give Wicca's head a good rub, speaking softly to the lab and smiling.

Callie couldn't help noticing the stretch of fabric over taut shoulder muscles and biceps. The jeans were stretched nicely in all the right places, too. Morgan Wright was all man, a man's man, with straight

266

planes on his face. There was no softness, no flab. She felt her heart thump as he straightened his frame and walked toward her. The sunset was reflected in the dark sunglasses he wore causing flashes of light to spark from the lens.

"You look good," he stated without preamble.

"I was just thinking the same thing about you," she said without coyness in her voice, just a statement of fact.

"That's the first good news I've had all day," he said dryly.

"Rough day," she said without making it a question. "Then you deserve a good night."

"It already is," he said, removing his glasses. A touch of smile reached his lips. Callie started as she realized a moment had passed while she'd been studying those lips.

His smile grew as he took a step closer. "I brought the wine."

"If you don't mind, we'll save it for later. We're experimenting with an herbal marguerita if you're game," she laughed.

"Sounds like a girly drink to me, but I'll give you my unbiased opinion," he assured her. "What can I do to help?"

"We're testing some salsas, so you can help chop if you'd like," she answered, leading the way to the kitchen.

"Now, salsa sounds like something worth testing!" he laughed. "The hotter the better."

"We're not looking for heat; we're looking for flavor and eye-appeal," she retorted, but with a smile.

"You may not be looking for heat, but I am," he said, sweeping his eyes over her trim figure before turning toward the counter. Callie suspected that the subject just might not be salsa anymore.

The evening passed quickly with Morgan again skillfully manning the grill for the veggie kabobs. The herbal margueritas were given a good rating although Morgan suggested that since they were sweet, a ring of sugar might be substituted for the traditional salt. Callie filed the suggestion in her mind, thinking herbal sugars could be perfect. The salsas were tasty and colorful, needing only minor adjustments to improve their flavor. Of course, none of them were hot enough for Morgan's taste buds, which Callie teased him were probably too burned out to be reliable by now.

Morgan told her they had not been able to lift any good prints on the greenhouse door. She told him about her thread being broken indicating that the culprit had discovered the plants were gone. He announced the plants had been analyzed, and that they were a premier variety, extremely high in active ingredients. That might indicate that it was not just high school kids but someone who had access to more potent, highly prized, and expensive seed. Callie wondered aloud that if that were the case, why would anyone risk putting them in her greenhouse where they were likely to be discovered? Why not put them where they'd be more hidden? Morgan didn't have the answers she wanted.

"You know Indiana is a major drug thoroughfare, Callie," Morgan told her. "It's in the center of the country where lots of major interstates meet. Indiana is not called the "Crossroad" without reason. Much of the marijuana comes from Mexico and is carried north over the interstates to Indiana. A lot of it is headed for Detroit, or Chicago, or points further east. Then you've got all the places on Lake Michigan where a boat can come in from Canada without detection. The federal government set up a special drug task force in Lake County just to try to cut down on stuff coming in by boat. So, north or south a lot of marijuana comes through the center of Indiana by interstate. Heartland is just off I69. It's a quiet place where anyone can park without being bothered. Bags can be moved to other vehicles without notice. Last year Indiana law officials seized nearly 400 kgs of marijuana, and that doesn't count all the wild crops that were destroyed.

"Wild crops?" Callie asked.

"Sure, back during the wars Indiana produced lots of hemp to make rope to use on ships. Afterwards, there was no market for rope in those quantities so farmers switched back to corn, wheat, and soybeans. But marijuana seed drops and lasts for a long time. Patches would come up on the edge of a field, along a fencerow, or by a woods. Farmers ignored it. It was just another weed. So, year after year it would drop seed and new crops would grow. You can find it growing along creeks all over the state. Of course it isn't very potent, but the state can get federal funds if they destroy marijuana. There's not a lot of stipulation on whether it was planted by people or not."

"So the wild isn't as effective as what was in my greenhouse," Callie said.

"Not nearly. Yours was grown by someone who knew exactly what they had. It was a special hybrid from Asia, but it's grown in Mexico now because they know they can get a premium price for it. It's a better quality than the growers around here normally use," Morgan explained.

"The growers around here?" Callie questioned.

"Well, I can't say there are any growers in the neighborhood, but Indiana has a problem just like every other state. Just a few plants can produce a lot of cash. People grow it in hidden areas, usually small plots hidden in wooded areas, National Forests, public lands, or near riverbanks. They used to hide plots in corn fields, but with our new technology airplanes flying over can detect it from miles away. Of course, sometimes they grow it in buildings under lights, but that's more risky for them. You've probably noticed a small white and red plane flying over," Morgan continued. "Well, he sweeps several counties every week during the growing season. The plane carries technology that can spot outdoor marijuana plants in a flash and equipment that notices even small changes in the landscape. We got a report when you put up your greenhouse. Suspicious construction."

"You're kidding!" she exclaimed.

"Nope, Indiana is really trying to crack down on all kinds of drug growing, traffic, and use. Drugs lead to other kinds of crime. Our state ranks twenty-ninth out of fifty in violent crime. A lot of the robberies, murders, traffic accidents, and physical abuse are often drug related. People are usually on it, or want it," Morgan continued.

"I hadn't told you, but the younger of the two guys who robbed your house finally told us the whole story. They thought they'd been cheated by their drug dealer so they decided to make him pay. Borrowed a car and headed north out of Muncie with no destination in mind. Just thought they'd look for a place that would be easy to rob. They saw your house sitting back off the road, so they didn't think they'd be seen. Saw your truck and the 'No Hunting' signs. Figured you were a hunter that wanted to keep all the deer for yourself, so they thought you'd have guns. Saw flowers around the house and figured there was a woman living there. Women usually mean jewelry and they needed stuff to sell easy, so they could buy more drugs, or a gun to use to even the score with their dealer. The young kid came to the door to see if anyone was home. If someone had answered, he'd show them the magazines he had brought with him and say he was selling them for a club at school. No one was home, so they went in. They were really disappointed not to find guns, or jewelry, or a stash of cash. The more frustrated they got the more they trashed the place. Finally, they decided to take what they could and get going. They were just trying to get the television into the back seat when they saw you walking over at the farm. They thought you saw them, so they just dropped the television, jumped in the car, and left."

"So, it wasn't premeditated, and they didn't pick me as a target," she mused.

"No, it was just your lucky day," Morgan chuckled.

"Yeah, I've been having lots of lucky days since I moved here," Callie frowned.

"Well, I'd think you're due for a run of good luck. You have had more than the normal share of trouble since you came here," Morgan agreed. "Maybe you need a four leaf clover, a rabbit's foot, or at least a horseshoe over the door. Maybe a lucky penny."

"Oh, I could use a lot of lucky pennies. Maybe I should have just sold those pot plants and paid off the mortgage," she laughed.

"I don't think you have the connections to pull off a deal like that," he laughed in return. "Besides, then I'd have to arrest you. You look pretty good in the stripes you're wearing tonight, but I can't say you'd look that good in prison stripes.

"I thought inmates wore hunter orange jumpsuits nowadays. I think you're teasing about the stripes," she nodded sagely.

"You're right. They do. But I'm not taking back the part about you looking good in these stripes, Ma'am," he chuckled again, as he wrapped his arms around her.

Later they sat in the gazebo and watched the moon rise, sipping wine, and enjoying one another's company. Callie leaned against his chest, his chin resting on her head now and again. The feel of his arm across her shoulder gave her a sense of security. The same feeling she'd had when her dad took her hand or put his arm around her shoulders. Yet it was not exactly the same after all she thought, giving it more consideration. There was the same feeling of security, but the sense of peace was not there. Instead, there was a heightened sense of being as well as a light tension in her body. She hated for the evening to end, and it didn't until the wee hours.

It was a glorious sunrise, and Callie felt wonderful. She was back on schedule, and she smiled as she pushed her muscles through the Tai Chi routine. Her green tea was liberally dosed with honey since she intended to skip breakfast. All those chips she'd had with the salsas last night would float right to her hips if she didn't watch it.

She made the changes to her recipes based on last night's testing. They'd need to be made again before she could put them into her book. Hopefully her friends would be able to test next week. She hadn't been able to send out an August newsletter so the September issue needed to go out early. Of course, the Labor Day Holiday would come into play, too, so maybe it wouldn't work out for her friends to come. She'd call them later in the morning.

She was putting the finishing touches on the plans for tomorrow's "Salsa Day" when the UPS truck rolled in.

"You're early!" she smiled as Mike climbed out of the truck. "What did you bring me?"

"Only my sweet little self today," he laughed. "No boxes for Joyful Heart Herbs. I wanted to stop early to see if you have any plans for Labor Day. You won't be open or have a workshop, and I don't have to work either. I was hoping we could get together. I haven't seen you since, well," he hesitated, "well, since your dad passed on."

"I know, Mike, and I hope you got my note thanking you and your mother for the flowers. They were beautiful. It was so thoughtful of you both," she said expressively.

"I wish I could have done more. Maybe been with you, helped out in some way," he stated wistfully.

"There really wasn't anything you could have done. I hadn't realized how complex all the legal and insurance matters would be. It's taken lots of time, and frankly, I just haven't felt like being with people until recently.

"That's what you said every time I called. I've been waiting," he said, looking into her eyes, "but now I think you need to get out. Do something fun. Hopefully, with me!"

"What did you have in mind," she asked, "for Labor Day, I mean?"

"I thought we'd drive over to Geneva. Gene Stratton Porter's old home, 'Limberlost' is there. It's a state historic site. I know how you love books and strong women. Gene Stratton Porter was both an author and a woman with vision. She cared about the environment, nature, and preservation long before it was a popular cause."

"That sounds too interesting to pass up. I'd love to go," she smiled.

"I was hoping that would appeal to you," he said warmly. "I'll call you and work out the details. Later tonight?"

"I'll be home all evening prepping food for Salsa Day tomorrow," she replied.

"Well, I'd better get moving. Talk to you tonight. I'm really glad to see you, Callie. I've missed you," he said, giving her a quick kiss before he left.

"Hey! Bring me some boxes next time," she yelled, laughing as she waved good-bye.

The crowd for Salsa Day was enthusiastic, and Callie was grateful that she could indeed call it a crowd. Gloria brought extra folding chairs from the newspaper office, and when those were filled, she called Mac, who brought a few more from their church. The salsa-making demonstrations were well attended with lots of lip-smacking and favorable comments during the sampling after each session. There was interest in the posters explaining the various heat levels of different hot pepper varieties and in the diagram of how a pepper was constructed internally showing the heat points.

The display of hot pepper varieties was inspected by many, and several people picked up the handout and bought pints of the hot peppers that Callie and Lucy had picked from the cook's garden. All of the culinary wreaths Callie had made earlier sold off the walls, along with several of the swags and garlands. Sales out of the "Fiesta" area in the shop sold well, and every child present enjoyed a turn swinging at the piñata before it exploded, showering them with sugarless candy and colorful stickers.

Lucy had appeared in a bright Mexican skirt with a white peasant blouse. Red chili earrings hung from her ears, and a necklace of plastic hot peppers that blinked off and on circled her neck. She had borrowed a few "salsa" CD's from the school's music library, so music vibrated through the sales area. While Callie had been with her mother, Lucy and Gloria had made planters that each held five different varieties of hot pepper plants. There were combinations of plants with tiny purple peppers, orange Scotch Bonnets, long thin cayennes, chunky black Anchos, delicate oval Serannos, and bright red Thai peppers. Gloria had wrapped the pots in shiny red foil, and they filled a display near the Cottage door along with jars of salsas. Before the day ended, all the planters had sold. Lucy had explained her idea to put them in large pots was stimulated by the fact that they were requiring water three or four times a day in their little packs. It had turned out to be a very profitable decision, and Callie made a note on her calendar to plant combination pepper containers again next year. She also gave Lucy a bonus for her thoughtfulness in making the planters. After running the register tapes, it looked like Salsa Day should be an annual event.

After the customers were gone, they cleared up the Cottage, and Callie urged Lucy to take home some of the leftover chips and salsas. While they worked, Callie told Lucy about the plants she'd found in the greenhouse.

"Really?" Lucy asked, her eyes wide and round. "Wow! I didn't see them, or I would have told you. Not that I would have known what they were, but I would have wondered why there were plants there by themselves, rather than with all the others. Any clue who put them there?"

"No. None at all. I thought maybe you could keep your ears open at school. Or maybe you knew of someone who had come to the farm and acted strangely," Callie stated. "Deputy Wright said not to talk about it so don't mention it. Just listen for anything that might be interesting."

"We didn't have many customers the Saturday I worked, so I think I'd remember anything weird. I was in school most days, so Mom was here most of the time you were gone," Lucy recalled. "Mum's the word. I won't breathe a thing to anyone," she promised. "I know there are drugs in most schools. Some of the kids brag about it, but you never know if they are just pretending to be cool or if they really use them."

"Drugs of any kind aren't cool, but I know you know that," Callie smiled. "They just lead to trouble eventually," she said as they walked to the parking lot.

"Thanks again, Lucy, for all your help today. You are a special young lady. Joyful Heart really benefits from you being a part of it," Callie said with a hug.

Callie spent a quiet evening, much of it in the gazebo. The growing season was coming to an end, and it was reflected in the fading greens of the trees and the browning of the fields. She sat reflecting on her life and her goals. She'd already reached many of the ones she'd set for the farm's first year. Her father's passing had made her think more about her personal goals and her personal life. Ten months had passed since Daniel had dumped her, and yet some nights she still found herself longing for him. Maybe it was all the crises she'd had. Life certainly had thrown her some curves since then. She'd left teaching and her old life to push memories of him into the far corners of her mind. She'd started a whole new demanding life to keep her too busy to think of the life they might have had together. She'd been robbed three times in four months, had her house ransacked, and her life threatened. She'd found deer killed on her property, had skunks under her shop, tires slashed, and financial worries. Then, when she thought things couldn't get worse, her father had been taken away. No wonder she was feeling fragile. No wonder her mind kept going back to the happy times with Daniel when life was so good.

"Or, at least I thought it was good," she reminded herself. She had believed in Daniel and trusted him completely. She thought she knew him inside and out after all the time they'd spent together.

"Girl, you don't know enough about men to rub elbows with them, let alone rub anything else," she admonished herself.

August ended with continual heat. When the humidity reached nearly one hundred percent, and the temperatures climbed, even the schools were closed for two days. Callie was busy trying to keep the gardens and plants in the sales area watered and gave daily thanks for the farm's good well. The cleome, zinnias, anise hyssop, cockscombs, and cosmos in the gardens were more brilliant than ever. She made more herbal wreaths to replace those sold on Salsa Day and harvested big bunches of southernwood, tansy, and mugwort to make insect repellent mixtures for closets. She designed an herbal tee shirt, thinking that the farm needed more things to sell now that the planting season was waning. Callie had looked at the marts in Atlanta for interesting shirts with herbal motifs but had not found anything appealing. So, she'd decided to design one of her own. She met with Cecilia to discuss the printing.

"I didn't know you could draw, too," Cecilia exclaimed as she looked at the design.

"Not nearly as well as LouAnn, but if I keep it simple, it's not too bad," Callie replied. "I need to understand more about the silk-screening process so I can refine the design. I've never had any experience with it."

"It's really very simple. Come on back," Cecilia said leading the way to the back of the print shop. They passed several big presses spitting out colored newspaper inserts and one that was printing a catalog for the local corn seed company."

"You really have a diverse operation," Callie said with admiration.

"Sometimes it's too diverse. I put in some really long days. And now, so many of our jobs come in on the computer that I spend days in front of a screen trying to make formats match and giving quotes. It used to be a lot simpler. The jobs are so much bigger now. All the small, easy jobs we used to do are being done by people on their own home computers. It's getting more competitive every day," Cecilia sighed.

"Isn't that the case for all business?" Callie agreed sympathetically.

"Here's the silk-screening room. Each color has its own plate, so you can use up to five colors. The shirt goes over this form and the first plate comes down from overhead. You can see there are five plates so the color goes on one layer at a time. You'll have to have a separate drawing for each color, making sure they are perfectly aligned so it comes out right. When all the colors are on, it goes through this little heater to set the ink and they come out here," she said pointing to a moving circular belt.

"I think I need to see a color chart to know what inks are available," Callie posed.

"Oh, I can mix any color you want. You just draw it the way you want it, breaking down each color onto a separate sheet. We'll make the plates, mix the ink, and run a test shirt for you to see before we do the entire run," Cecilia assured her. "Let me show you the selection of shirt colors and styles that we can do."

They spent the next hour going over styles and looking at color and fabric swatches. Callie placed an order for one hundred shirts in various sizes and pastel colors, and promised to have the revised design ready right after Labor Day.

Since she was already in town, Callie decided to treat herself to lunch at Dinah's Diner. Then she'd go to the used book sale sponsored by the Friends of the Library. She walked the short distance from the print shop even though the day was already a scorcher. As she passed the large windows of Second Hands, a store sponsored by a local charity group, she saw three large bookcases for sale as well as several items that would make good planters.

"Can't pass those up," she mumbled to herself as she ducked inside. She went directly to the bookshelves to see if they were sturdy and to check the price. No one appeared to be in the store, but she soon heard voices coming from a back room.

"I can understand your concern, Alma," a woman's voice carried to Callie's location.

"After all, she is a stranger to this area. You really don't know anything about her."

"Yes, and she just seems to be a magnet for trouble," a second woman's voice replied.

"Oh, yes. I've heard all kinds of stories about the goings-on out there," the first voice stated with authority. "Why, that deputy was out there day and night for weeks. Who knows what all went on then. My Walter has seen that convertible of his out there at all hours. Why, last week he said it was still there after midnight!"

"That's not all. Junior Matthews said he saw her lying on a blanket with Trev Carpenter, drinking from wine glasses right in the middle of the day. They were out at the old Garner barn. Junior was mending a fence in his back pasture and saw them plain as day."

"Well, that tells me everything I need to know. No morals whatsoever, out there with a married man, drinking and all, and in broad daylight," the first voice exclaimed.

"I know, Noreen. I'm just so upset. I just don't know what my Mike sees in that girl," she sighed.

"Well, I wouldn't wonder if she wasn't using some kind of herbal magic or something. Maybe some love potion. There has to be some reason she has men flocking to her like flies on a carcass. And something powerful, if she can get a nice boy like Mike sniffing after her," Noreen replied indignantly.

Callie's cheeks were burning, as she realized she was the topic of the women's gossip. She left the store, returning to her truck. She had too much to think about to enjoy lunch or the book sale now.

Elder

There is something wonderful about the elder, this common roadside plant. Since colonial times, people have picked the ebony-purple berry clusters, washed them, removed the berries from the burgundy stems, covered the berries with water in huge kettles and cooked them until soft. Then the berries were poured into a clean pillowcase hung over another large kettle and the juice was squeezed out. From that juice, jars and jars of deep purple elderberry jelly were made. Sometimes, elder juice was mixed with equal parts of apple juice to make a jelly that was bright cherry-red with a totally different flavor. It seemed magical that two very different jellies came from one plant.

Another popular product from the elder's berries was elderberry wine. It's a rich, deep, fruity wine—used for medicinal purposes, of course! Often the berries were dried for winter, to be added to muffins, scones, pancakes, or fruit pies. Elderberries should always be cooked before eating. Never eat them raw.

Elderbloom, or elderblow, as the clusters of fragrant white flowers of the elder have been called, also have a wonderful flavor. Dipped in a liqueur-laden batter and deep-fat fried, then dusted with powdered sugar, they make a delightful dessert fritter.

The elder has always been considered a magical tree to be treated with respect and honor. To the Welsh, it is sacred. A piece of the tree carried on the body is thought to cure most ailments. In Scandinavia it is believed that the tree has prophetic powers. Many European cultures follow the custom of standing under an elder on Midsummer's Eve in order to be able to see the fairies dance. In England, elder was used to compel witches to undo their evil spells. In Germany and many other countries, no one dared cut an elder tree without first begging the tree's pardon. For centuries it has been a source of fruit, flower, medicine, and even music! Its hollow stems have long been carved into flutes.

The large clusters of white, fragrant bloom have been used as food and as an ingredient in many beneficial cosmetic products. In Egypt, where the elder originated, elder flowers were used not only as an ingredient in many facial cosmetics, but also as a cooling wash for sunburn. The "elderblow" is often dried to be used in beneficial salves and ointments.

The inner bark, roots, and leaves of the elder have been used in teas, poultices, and to cleanse wounds. This often made the patient very ill, since elder has many purgative properties. Now scientists have learned that the elder's leaves, wood, and roots contain harmful, potentially poisonous substances. Therefore, use only the flowers or cooked berries.

The elder is a small tree, or large shrub. It grows well in sunlight with adequate moisture or in lightly shaded areas if the soil is average. It spreads aggressively by underground stems. Generally, it reaches six to ten feet in height. The American elderberry, *Sambucus Canadensis* has naturalized throughout much of the United States. The pointed leaves are generally dark green. However, over the years plant breeders have developed beautiful varieties of *Sambucus nigra* with variegated cream and green, gold and green, or deep burgundy leaves. Some newer varieties also have finely cut foliage that adds an interesting texture to the flowering shrub border. All are hardy in zones 4-9. Most will not bloom until they are at least three years of age.

Chapter 9:

SEPTEMBER

The early days of September continued to be hot, but fortunately, the evenings were beginning to be a bit cooler. Callie worked in the gardens during the cool of the evenings, pulling weeds, collecting seeds, and harvesting flowers and herbs for drying. There could be a frost by the end of this month, so she needed to get as much done as possible. She'd been propagating plants and even ordered a second heating mat for rooting. All the varieties of hard-necked garlic had arrived and been planted in the cook's garden in separate beds. She'd made a note in next year's schedule to have a "Garlic Day" near the end of August or early September.

After dark when it finally cooled off a bit more, she could work in the studio without baking. She spent hours on the computer. She threw herself into her work on her book to avoid thinking about the fact that she was probably the major topic of gossip in the county. And to avoid thinking about the fact that Trev was married. Now she regretted being too cowardly to come right out and ask him. She'd told herself that maybe the children he had mentioned were nephews and nieces or neighborhood children. Surely he wouldn't have acted so sweet and flirted so pointedly if he were married. She should have asked Cecilia, or Sandy, or Suz. In a way, she was surprised none of them had said anything. After all in a small town like this, they had no doubt heard the gossip, too.

night, sleeping with windows open Callie found the insects'
relaxing, a soothing music, the rhythms of nature that are balm
...n's soul.

"Or, I should say woman's soul," Callie said tossing and turning.
...this point, I'm not even sure men have souls," she grumbled. She
...t very alone. She'd thought she had made some real friends here, but
...turned out that no one had her back. No one was truly watching out
...or her. Even her women friends had not warned her.

"It's just you and me, girl" she said to the black lab that lay beside
the bed. She turned over again, pounding her pillow into a bigger lump,
so she could look out the window more easily.

"So, Mike's mother is upset that he spends time with me. Should
I call him and cancel our trip to the Limberlost tomorrow? Or, should
I go just to spite the old gossip?" Callie asked the dog. Wicca daintily
crossed her front legs in front of her, rested her head on top of them,
and looked at Callie with expectant eyes.

"You're right, always be a lady. Where are my manners? It's too late
to cancel. And, I really do want to see Gene Stratton Porter's home. I
loved reading her books as I was growing up. She liked to draw, too.
And she loved roaming in the woods and swamps," Callie said to her
canine friend. Wicca seemed to nod in approval.

"Mike is a grown man. If he wants to spend time with me, despite
his mother's opinion, he's old enough to make that decision," Callie
argued. A low moan came from Wicca's throat.

"Okay, okay. You have a point," Callie chuckled. "I have to decide
if there's any future with a guy, even if he is really sweet, funny, and
really, really cute but has a mother that has decided she hates me."
Wicca lifted her head, eyes bright, and licked her long tongue across
her mouth.

"You don't get to vote even though I know you think Mike is
the greatest because of all the treats he brings you." Wicca gave an
exuberant yip, thumping her tail against the floor.

"And, he lets you ride in his truck. I know, I know," Callie laughed.
"And he's dependable. If he says he'll call, he calls. He's always on time
or even a bit early. Very dependable. That's Mr. UPS."

She paused, turning over again and rubbing the labs ears. "He
reminds me so much of Daniel. Strong, efficient, thoughtful, energetic,

sweet. I would say loyal, but that didn't turn out to be true in Daniel's case. I think Mike is loyal though, don't you?"

Wicca wagged her tail emphatically. "Yes, I think he is, too," Callie responded. "But, maybe he'd be torn between loyalty to his mother and loyalty to me." She pounded the pillow again, tossed, turned, and finally gave herself up to sleep.

Labor Day dawned with streaks of dark pink and lavender on the horizon. Long, narrow wisps of clouds crossed the sky.

"Mare's tails," Callie said as she pointed them out to Wicca. "Daddy always said the mare's tails were pulling rain clouds after them. I hope he's right."

She hurried through the watering, showered, and dressed in a yellow short-sleeved top and matching Capri pants. She'd hand-painted little sprigs of herbs on the front of the top. Little leaf-shaped earrings in gold dangled from her ears, and she'd swept her hair back in a chignon on the back of her neck. She stuck a comb and a hair band in her purse just in case. They'd have the windows down in Mike's jeep in this weather, so doing her hair had probably been a waste of time. She added a bit of make-up including a touch of green eye shadow wondering just what her motives were. She really didn't know. She wanted to look nice, but was she really trying to tempt Mike? Trying to convince him that she was worthy of his attention, even if his mother objected? She'd decided on a conservative outfit, no shorts, no sundress. She really didn't know how she felt.

Hurt, of course, that people were thinking she had no morals.

Hurt, that Mike's mother didn't think her son should be with her.

Rebellious. "How dare they judge me, when they don't have any real facts?"

Competitive? Deep down, did she want to "do battle" with Alma for Mike's affection? Was that a normal female competition thing, she wondered? Doubtful. She'd loved Daniel's mother, and in fact, felt that Mrs. Lyons had been as hurt to lose Callie as a future daughter as Callie had been to lose Daniel. They'd often had lunch, shopped, and belonged to the same quilters' group at church. Mrs. Lyons had even come to help Callie set up her classroom each year before school started and helped with the class Christmas party. She had been intimately involved in the wedding plans since Callie's own mother was so busy on the farm and farther away. There was certainly no competition there. They'd agreed on almost everything. She would have loved having Daniel's mother for a mother-in-law. She doubted she'd feel the same about Alma Shipley.

"Hey! We're not talking marriage here. Let's just see how this day goes," Callie said to the mirror as she heard the crunch of tires in the driveway.

"Wow, you look great!" Mike's first words greeted her.

"You picked a perfect day for an outing. It's gorgeous this morning," she smiled back.

"Not as gorgeous as you are," he said, putting his arm around her shoulders and planting a kiss on the top of her head.

"Thanks. You're certainly in a good mood," she observed.

"Get to spend an entire day with a beautiful girl. Who wouldn't be in a good mood?" he laughed.

"Well, I'm looking forward to it. I've never been to Geneva or anywhere in the area east of Heartland," she replied.

"You'll love it. Lots of Amish in the area. This is Monday, so you might even see clothes hanging on the line outdoors," he told her as he held the door to the Jeep.

"I'm glad I brought my camera," Callie said enthusiastically.

They drove through Heartland, past the town limits into rolling fields of various shades of beige and olive greens.

"The harvest will start soon," she said.

"Already has in some areas. They cut the corn at this stage and chop it for feed for the big operations. Can't afford to wait to just harvest the grain separately. Corn prices are up with all the bio-diesel fuel plants going in. Eventually that will impact meat prices, too," Mike explained.

"I didn't know you knew so much about farming," Callie observed.

"Oh, I learn all kinds of interesting things on my route. People tell the UPS driver everything, and we know who gets what, who needs what," Mike replied.

"That's probably true," Callie said thoughtfully. "Do you ever wonder what's really in some of those boxes? I mean, do people ever try to ship illegal things? Like drugs or something?"

"Sometimes. Once we had some boxes of Mexican pottery. Turned out the pieces had false bottoms stuffed with marijuana. The dog found them though," Mike said. "I was surprised. Didn't know a dog could smell through pottery."

"Mexican pottery is very porous. Doesn't stand up to weather, especially in winters like ours. That's why it's a lot cheaper than Italian or Vietnamese pottery, for instance. Those are made from a more dense clay, and they are fired at higher temperatures. Plus the glazes are more likely to be lead-free. That can be a real problem with Mexican pottery. But, you mentioned a dog?" Callie inquired.

"Yeah. Law enforcement brings in drug-sniffing dogs sometimes. We also have some technology that helps detect drugs. UPS wants to be in the shipping business for a long time, and they want to keep their good reputation. Plus, transporting illegal drugs for criminals would not be the safest occupation. The company hires good drivers, and they want to keep them safe."

"I'm sure some drivers do have to go into some questionable areas though. Big cities, slums, places that could be dangerous," Callie said.

"We hire street-wise people from the area in those cases. And we have great training. We're vigilant," he assured her. "Look!" Mike pointed to a field in the distance where a group of Amish men were stacking corn stalks into large teepee-shaped bunches. "They cut the stalks and stack them together to help keep the ears dry. Then they'll haul them to the barns and have big shucking parties where everyone pulls the ears off the stalks. They chop the stalks for feed and put the ears in bins until they need to shell it. They save the biggest ears for seed to plant next spring."

"Oh, look! There's a row of laundry on the line just like you said," Callie exclaimed. "Look at all those blue shirts. It must be a big family."

"Probably is. Lots of homes house three generations, maybe more. It takes lots of willing hands to do all the work in their old-fashioned way. And they generally just do laundry one day a week, so there's lots to hang," Mike said.

"I wonder if they are any happier than we are? If they get more satisfaction from doing things the old ways, living closer to nature, more simply," Callie sighed.

"I'm not sure it is more simple in reality. Seems pretty complicated to me. You pretty much have to know everything and how to do it. Can't call in a specialist or order a part on the internet," Mike said seriously. "And, they have to pay taxes just like we do, so coming up with cash can be a problem, I'd think. That's why so many of them have farm stands. There's one coming up on the right that sells all kinds of fruit, vegetables, and baked goods. They often have craft or sewing items the women have made. Sometimes there are even quilts and such."

"Oh, can we stop? I'd love to see it. It would remind me of my farmers' market days," Callie exclaimed.

"Your wish is my command, Princess," Mike said, flipping on the Jeep's turn signal.

Mike's jeep was not the only vehicle to stop as the small parking lot was filled with cars and trucks. The aroma of freshly-baked bread filled the air. When they got closer, Callie could also detect the fragrance of apple pies and ripe melons.

"Oh, look, it's a 'Grandmother's Flower Garden' pattern," Callie bubbled as she strode toward a quilt hanging on a clothesline that was sagging with the weight of other colorful patterns. "Just look at the workmanship, those tiny stitches! This must have taken forever to make."

"Look at the size of those watermelons. Must be all that horse fertilizer that goes on the fields," Mike pointed at the small mountain of large green melons piled nearby.

They wandered around the various tables, drooling over sparkling cans of apple butter, peach jam, and black raspberry jelly. In addition to the bread, pies, cookies, tarts, and cinnamon rolls filled a bakery table. Wooden rocking chairs, rocking horses for children, quilt racks, and spice racks showed the touch of someone who understood the grains of various woods. Another table filled with patchwork hot pads, crocheted doilies, and hand-knitted hats, mittens, and socks caught Callie's attention. A flatbed wagon parked in the shade of old oak trees was crowded with baskets of fresh garden produce and a smaller table to the side held jars of honey and beeswax candles.

"Oh! Look, Mike," Callie said tugging on his arm, "they must keep bees, too!"

"Yes, I deliver boxes from an apiary in Kentucky every spring to the Hostetler's. I can tell you those boxes that buzz are not my favorite things to haul," he laughed.

They selected several items that were just too wonderful to resist.

"I wish I could afford this one. I'm sure I'll never have the patience or the time to make one that beautifully stitched. Whoever put it together had a marvelous eye for color," Callie raved as she touched the fine stitching of a "Wedding Ring" patterned quilt. "I wonder where they find such wonderful fabrics."

"Now that I can answer," Mike smiled, putting his arm around her waist. "I don't know if she'll be open on Labor Day, but there's an Amish fabric store that my mother loves right in downtown Geneva. We'll stop if she's there."

"This day just keeps getting better and better," Callie said appreciatively as they walked arm in arm. Mike stowed her treasures in the back of the Jeep. It was a short drive into the small town of Geneva.

The Limberlost Museum proved to be everything Callie had thought it would be. The lovely old log cabin had a patina and charm that held her spellbound. She was captivated by Gene Stratton Porter's drawings of birds, complete with real feathers attached to the wings and tail. The collection of butterflies was interesting, including some species that had lived in the swamps of the area before they were drained. She purchased two volumes from the gift shop, which she studied closely for display ideas and customer flow before leaving. Mike picked up a schedule of events, telling her that his mother always attended the annual formal tea that was held on Ms. Porter's birthday each August.

"Oh, I'm sorry I missed it," Callie lamented.

"There's always next year," Mike laughed as he picked up her bag of purchases. "Speaking of tea, I'm hungry. We need lunch, and I know just the place."

They drove downtown where a family-owned restaurant that specialized in home-cooked meals was located. Mike ordered a huge plate of chicken and dumplings, mashed potatoes, cole slaw, and hunks of freshly baked bread. Callie selected a wilted spinach salad with toasted pecans, slices of fresh pears, and blue cheese crumbles. All the food was served by quiet, modest women dressed in traditional Amish long-sleeved, high-necked dresses, and white caps. They finished the meal by sharing a piece of shoo-fly pie topped with freshly whipped cream.

Afterwards, they walked around the downtown area looking at the shops until they came to the fabric store. It was filled with hundreds of bolts of calicos, muslins, cotton blends, and denims. Callie had never seen such a variety and was delighted to find a bolt with an herbal design. She purchased ten yards, wishing she could afford more. When she spotted a pretty blue cotton printed with charming little kittens, she bought three yards.

"I understand the herbal print," Mike said, "but why cats? Why not the one with the black labs?"

"I have a lot of customers that buy cat grass and catnip plants for their pets. I've got bunches of catnip hanging in the garage to dry. I thought I'd make up some catnip mice for the shop. They'll make great stocking stuffers, and most cat-lovers can't resist a little treat for their pets," Callie explained.

"You're always thinking, aren't you?" Mike smiled in admiration.

"Small business owners have to look for every advantage," she replied.

The day passed quickly, and as it had progressed, the clouds had gradually begun to build and billow.

"Looks like it could rain," Mike said as they put the bags of fabric into the back of the jeep. "I'd thought we might stay longer but maybe we should head back."

"I left Wicca outside. I'd hate to have her caught in a storm, so we should probably go home," Callie said reluctantly as she looked around at the unexplored storefronts.

Mike noticed her forlorn expression, and grabbed her hand. "Hey, we can come back, Princess. It's not like it's hours away, Callie."

"I know. But, today just seemed so special. I feel like a child who was only allowed to open half her birthday presents! Isn't that silly?" she laughed.

They drove back the same route they'd used coming to town. Callie noted happily that the parking lot at Hostetler's produce stand was still crowded with customers.

"I wish I had that kind of traffic at my farm," she said quietly. "I think people have a fascination with the Amish, their lifestyle, and their traditions. Maybe I should start wearing caps and long dresses."

"I'd be real unhappy to see that, Callie," Mike chuckled as he reached for her hand. "You look real cute in your herb tee shirts and shorts. Besides, I think people could spot an imposter. And, you wouldn't feel right about a charade. You're too honest, too good."

"And I probably can't bake bread that delicious, either," she laughed.

"Are you fishing for compliments? I know how well you can cook and bake," Mike challenged. "Why I told my mother about that coconut cream pie you made and all those recipes you've been testing. She was really impressed with all the ingredients you use."

"And speaking of testing recipes," he continued, "why haven't I been invited to be a guinea pig lately? Has someone else stolen my job?"

"I haven't had as much time for cooking. And it's been too hot to cook," Callie responded slowly. "Maybe when the weather cools, I'll be more inspired."

"Well, then I can't wait for the thermometer to start dropping," he laughed.

"Speaking of your mother, how is she? I haven't seen her at the farm since our opening day last April. Did she run out of room for plants? Or is she buying what she needs at another garden center?" Callie asked innocently.

"Oh, Mom's fine. She's got a bigger garden than usual. Had me till up another whole section of the yard. I'm surprised she hasn't been over. She volunteers at Second Hands in Heartland two days a week and I thought she'd been out to your farm afterwards a few times. She loved the teapot with the violets that I gave her for her birthday, and she raved about your shop after she'd been there," he said cheerfully.

"Well, maybe she's been there when I've been away. I have given lots of presentations, and I've been away from the farm more than I expected to be," Callie reflected. Privately, she suspected that Mike's mother had not returned. "Interesting," Callie thought to herself. "If

289

my son were seeing someone, I think I'd use coming to the farm as an excuse to get to know her better."

Mike might have been thinking along the same lines. Presently, he added, "I should get you and mom together soon. You have so much in common. You both like to cook and garden. And you both sew," he paused. "And, you both really like me!"

"Now who's fishing for compliments?" Callie laughed.

They pulled into Callie's driveway just as the first rumble of thunder filled the air. Wicca danced around the car, racing back and forth to the front door trying to get both humans to hurry. They pulled Callie's purchases from the Jeep and managed to get into the kitchen just as the skies burst.

"Wow, this looks like a real duck drowner!" Mike exclaimed, looking out the rain-covered window toward the gazebo. "We made it just in time!"

"Perfect timing. I'll put the kettle on, and we'll have some of those gooseberry tarts I bought at Hostetler's. You won't want to go out there until the storm passes," Callie said reasonably. After filling the kettle and putting it on the stove, she joined Mike at the window.

"I don't think I've ever seen it rain this hard. It's coming down in walls of water," she observed. "Look, there's already a little creek running past the gazebo."

"Yeah, it looks like it's really setting in. What shall we do until it stops, Callie?" he said pulling her into a bear hug. His warm kiss brought the speculation to an end. The kettle bubbled on the stove and the windows steamed over. Wicca finally gave up waiting for some attention, and dejectedly went to sleep on the rag rug.

"That was quite a storm we had last night," Cecilia said brightly as Callie entered the print shop the following morning.

"Yes, Pumpkinvine Creek has overflowed its banks at my place," Callie responded. "At least I don't have to worry about doing any watering today. I left Gloria replacing sales signs and standing pots back up. I asked her to work this morning, so I could get the newsletter finished. I would have e-mailed the copy to you, but since I wanted to bring in the revamped design for the tee shirts this morning, I just brought it on a disc."

Cecilia studied the sheets of tracing paper containing Callie's drawings of herbs. "This should work. The tee shirts all arrived on Friday, so we're ready to do a test as soon as I mix the inks. Which has your top priority, the newsletter or the shirts?"

"The newsletter. I need to get it out right away since I couldn't do one in August. I put the farm schedule on the website but lots of people forget to access it. They need that reminder in their hot little hands. And, even after you get them printed, I still need to fold, staple, label, and sort by zip code. That address label program you designed and installed for me is a godsend. Saves me three or four hours at least. And with the frost coming I need every hour I can get."

"Hmmmm. Especially if you take an entire day off," Cecilia said speculatively.

Callie looked at her questioningly.

"I tried to call you all day yesterday to tell you the shirts had arrived. You didn't answer. I finally quit trying when the storm hit since the lines were popping."

"You didn't leave a message on the machine," Callie observed.

"No, I kept thinking I'd get you in person. Figured you'd be hard at work at the farm, getting it ready for the big Harvest Special this month. By the way, we can have the tee shirts printed well before then, so don't worry," Cecilia stated.

"I've decided to move it to the first weekend in October. I found out the big football game is on the weekend I'd picked. Everyone will be glued to their televisions, and I doubt a sale at the herb farm will be enough to pry them away," Callie told her.

"Oh, really? I would think that would be a good time for the women to come. Leave the men folk getting eye-strain and beer-bellies at home while they come to a pretty shop filled with flowers and good smells," Cecilia proposed.

"Maybe you have a point. I'll keep that in mind in the future, but I've already changed the schedule on the website and here on the disc, so I think I'll try the October weekend. I can use that extra week to prepare, and I still have merchandise that hasn't arrived, so pushing it back may make a big difference."

"You still haven't said where you were all day yesterday," Cecilia teased. "A little bird told me you had quite a busy day."

"Really? Wow, the grapevine in this town is even more extensive than I thought," Callie said in amazement. "Who's the little bird?"

"Jenny Carpenter. She said she saw you with Mike Shipley at the Hostetler's yesterday. Said you were looking at a 'Wedding Ring' quilt together and just maybe that had some significance."

"Jenny Carpenter? I don't think I've met her," Callie said slowly.

"Trev's wife. Surely you two have met with all the work he did at your place. She's such a sweetheart. Doesn't get out as much now since the twins were born, and that Tristan is a handful by himself. Looks just like his daddy and is just as full of mischief. He's going to be a heartbreaker some day."

"Just like his daddy," Callie thought to herself.

Another customer came into the shop claiming Cecilia's attention, so Callie left the disc and made her escape. Cecilia would call or e-mail just as soon as the newsletters were ready.

She headed toward the library, head bowed and deep in thought. So, it was really, really true. Trev was married, and the children were definitely his. Happily married, Jenny probably thought, especially if they had newborn twins. Cecilia had told her they were little girls, Tina and Tara. Thinking back, Callie recalled seeing a pretty brunette pushing a dual stroller at the produce stand. She didn't remember ever seeing her before and wondered how Jenny Carpenter had recognized her. And, she wondered why Jenny had bothered telling Cecilia about seeing Callie and Mike together. How many other people had recognized them? Of course, everyone in Heartland knew Mike, and he knew everyone in return. And everyone probably thought of him as a friend and took an interest in his well-being.

Once at the library she studied the gardening section to see if any new books had been added. Then she spent a few minutes at the computer looking for reference material for her column. She was running out of "top of her head" ideas and was going to have to dig a little deeper for interesting material, especially as the garden season was coming to a close. She wouldn't just be able to walk out into the garden and see what plant caught her eye to write about each week. She found a couple of books that looked helpful and took them to a reader's desk. The lingering effects of black walnut trees on plant growth and soil were the subject of her search. She'd noticed some of the plants in the folklore garden were not doing as well as she expected. Several of the nearby trees were black walnuts, and she'd heard they were toxic to some plants. She scanned several pages and was just finding some pertinent information when she heard whispers coming from a nearby stack.

"Oh, yes, I just heard it while I was having my hair done at Clip and Curl. That herb lady and Mike Shipley were picking out bedroom linens. They were looking at a "Wedding Ring" quilt. She must have her claws sunk deep," the voice said sharply.

"Poor Alma. She must be devastated. To have a woman like that snag one's only child," a second voice hissed.

"Oh, she's more than devastated. She's about to go on the warpath, I'd guess," the first voice bragged.

"If she's settled on that sweet UPS man, then maybe Jenny Carpenter's marriage will be safe. I'd heard all kinds of stories about her luring Trev to her place on various little projects. And him with those brand new little girls."

"Well, Jenny had a rough time before those twins arrived. Bed rest for months. And you know men. They have their needs. You can't really blame them. And he is such a man. Quarterback, high-school king, army hero. Full of testosterone and all."

"There's no excuse for a home wrecker like that woman though. Oh, speaking of home, look at the time. I've got to get Orville's lunch started. He's driving grain wagons to the elevator today, so he'll be in early."

Callie could hear their movements as they scurried away through the stacks and breathed a sigh of relief that they didn't come her way. She sat for several moments absorbing the information she'd just heard. The venom in the whispers was hard to miss. Obviously, one was not innocent until proven guilty in this small town.

She checked out the books she needed, flipped her cell phone open, and punched in a number.

"Sandy Saunders, Heartland Banner," the voice answered tiredly.

"Sandy, it's Callie. Are you totally snowed under?" she asked.

"Hey, stranger. Haven't seen you in forever. Are you at the farm?" Sandy asked.

"No, I'm here in town. If you're not busy, I'd like to buy your lunch," Callie offered.

"You're in luck. I just sent my last article for today's edition to the editor. I don't have an assignment until two o'clock. Can't remember the last meal I ate, so let's make it a good one. Dinah's in fifteen minutes?" Sandy proposed.

"I'll be there," Callie answered.

She selected a small table as far from the center of activity as she could find. Callie didn't recognize the waitress who came with glasses of water on a tray. "I have a friend joining me. There will be two of us," she smiled.

"I'll just bet," the waitress said smugly as she banged two glasses on the table and flounced away.

"Hmmm. I wonder what that was all about," Callie puzzled as she saw Sandy coming through the door.

"This was a great idea," Sandy smiled as she hung her jacket on a nearby rack. "Of course, it won't do the diet a bit of good, but I really needed to get out of that office. Mac is on a rampage today, and we're all getting ulcers in our turn. Presses threw a bolt and apparently it's in some place that's almost impossible to reach. Our maintenance guy is in the hospital having his gall bladder removed, so Mac is trying to squeeze under there himself. It's not a pleasant workplace although I'm learning lots of new words," Sandy chuckled.

"I can just picture Mac trying to fix it himself. He's not exactly the engineering or mechanical type," Callie giggled.

"No, he's the bossy 'I want it done yesterday, don't bother me with anything but the story' type," Sandy agreed. "He wants this issue to hit the stands on time. Seems there's a move to fire the high school football coach, and the school board is meeting this evening. Won't sell papers if everyone hears all about it before they can read all about it."

The waitress returned to take their orders, all sweetness for Sandy's benefit.

"Who's the waitress?" Callie asked after she'd left with the menus.

"Joanna Snipes. Would you like to be introduced?" Sandy asked.

"No, it's just that she wasn't very friendly when I sat down, but she seems to like you," Callie explained.

"Everyone is nice to me. Power of the press and all," Sandy chuckled. "I write almost all the local stuff, interviews, business column, all the area news. No one wants a bad review."

"I understand. That's why I'm paying for your lunch," Callie teased. "Joanna Snipes," she mused. "I'm sure I haven't met her or seen her at the farm. I wonder why she was so hostile," she said bewildered.

There was a long pause while Sandy toyed with her fork. Callie finally broke the silence, "Okay, spill. What do you know that I need to know, that you don't want to tell me?"

"Joanna is Jenny Carpenter's little sister," Sandy said bluntly.

"Oh," breathed Callie.

"Yeah. Oh!" Sandy replied looking at Callie levelly.

"So you've heard the same rumors I've heard," Callie said raising her chin and looking directly in Sandy's eyes.

"Well, I can't say I've heard the same rumors. There's quite a variety of them going around. Let's just say I've heard some rumors, but maybe not all," Sandy smiled sympathetically.

"There was never anything between us. Just business," Callie asserted.

"Picnics in the middle of nowhere? His truck parked at the farm long after dark but no sign of either one of you?" Sandy relayed. "He never mentioned having a wife?"

"We never really talked much about personal things. And, no, he never, ever mentioned a wife. He did mention kids that like to play with Wicca, but I assumed he had nephews, or nieces, or neighborhood kids. Why didn't any of you girls tell me while we were folding newsletters? Or just give me a heads-up that he was married?" Callie questioned.

"I hadn't heard anything until recently. And it was my understanding that you were pretty man-shy after all that heartbreak with your fiancé. I guess we just didn't think you were contemplating getting involved again," she explained.

"Well, I'm not involved with Trev. Everything was totally innocent on my part," Callie said defensively.

"Methinks the lady dost protest too much," Sandy quoted. "And he is a charmer. You're not the first woman to stray his way, and you probably won't be the last."

"I didn't have a clue. I guess this is just another confirmation that I'm a poor judge of character," Callie lamented.

"You were hurt, vulnerable, and lonely. Trev took advantage of that," Sandy offered.

"I'm becoming more certain that you really can't trust men," Callie said firmly.

"No farther than you can throw them," she chuckled. "And if you like them big and hunky like I do, that's not very far!"

"Okay, so enough about Trev Carpenter," Callie said softly. "What else do I need to know that's whipping through the grapevine about my sterling character?"

"Well, you must be more ready for involvement than I'd guessed, because to hear it told, you're a mighty busy lady," she chuckled. "Alma Shipley is about to have a heart attack because her little Mikie is straying from home and mamma. Every single woman in town is afraid you'll take Morgan Wright off the market, and half the single guys I know are about to take up gardening!"

"I haven't noticed any increase in men shopping at my place. In fact, part of the reason I wanted to talk to you today was to see if you thought people were avoiding the farm because of the rumors about me," Callie said hesitantly.

"Oh, I doubt that," Sandy said confidently. "In fact, I'd think some people would come just out of curiosity. I think it's the terrible weather we've had since July. No one wants to garden in this heat, and people are struggling to keep what they have already planted watered. The town board is even thinking about starting some watering restrictions."

"Besides," Sandy continued. "Now that you and Mike are a couple, the fuss about Trev will die down."

"But, we're not a couple," Callie whispered emphatically.

"Really? Alma Shipley will certainly be glad to hear that, but how does Mike vote? I've heard you two are spending a lot of time together."

"To spend as much time with all the men I've been linked with would take more energy and hours than I've got," Callie assured her.

"That may be true, but I'd sure like to have that problem," Sandy nodded wistfully. "Why are all the big, hunky guys attracted to little skinny girls like you?"

"I think they want my money," Callie said in mock-seriousness.

"Yeah, gardeners and reporters. We make the big bucks all right," she laughed.

The cloud of birds swept across the sky and then landed as a unit in nearby trees. The air was filled with their chatter.

"Those must be practice runs to correct formations and placement of each individual before they begin their southern migration," Callie told an attentive Wicca. "I imagine that they have lengthy discussions. Whose turn is it to lead this round? Can we go back to that lovely maple tree near the creek? The mosquitoes were so plentiful there, and I'm hungry! Are we there yet? Is that what they are saying?"

Wicca seemed to agree with her assessment of the birds' conversations. Callie had loaded her bee equipment into the back of the truck. It was a little cooler, and she needed to put mite treatment in the hives and check on their honey stores. Wicca jumped into the truck, unaware that this would be a very short journey.

Callie climbed in, noticing that the poison ivy in the trees at the edge of the woods was already turning ruby-toned. The cornfields were completely beige now and the soybean leaves were golden.

"The colors of the flowers in the gardens always intensify as the night-time temperatures drop lower," Callie explained to the lab. "The flowers seem determined to attract the few remaining butterflies to their blossoms. A last attempt to be pollinated and reproduce before the frosts come. It's a sexual thing."

Wicca looked impressed with Callie's wisdom and watched as a butterfly veered to avoid the truck. As they passed behind the greenhouse, Callie noticed that some of the lavender varieties were reblooming. She'd only have a few more weeks to propagate any plant material for the next season. Once frost came none of the material would be usable. She needed to start moving the tender plants on her patio nearer to the house and get the greenhouse benching cleaned and ready to hold frost-sensitive plants from the sales area. That meant she'd have to get all the dried flowers and herbs hanging under the black plastic boxed and moved to the garage soon. She wished she had been able to afford the barn Trev showed her. Then she'd have a loft to store all those boxes and plenty of workspace for making wreaths. Now that fall was coming, she'd planned on having booths at nearby small town festivals to promote the farm. She'd need to stockpile wreaths and other products to haul to the shows. Right now she had boxes stacked in her garage, along with all the out-of-season leftovers from the Cottage. She wondered if she'd ever have room to put the truck in its rightful place.

They arrived at the hives. Callie was careful to park the truck out of the flight path for either hive. She cracked the windows in the truck and told Wicca to wait inside. Bees do not like black shapes, which is one reason beekeepers always wear white. Callie supposed it reminded bees of bears, who loved honey and could be destructive to hives, but she doubted any of her bees had ever seen a bear. "It must be some kind of programmed memory leftover from centuries ago," she mused as she pulled her bee veil into place and lit the smoker.

The hives were in great shape and Callie was able to remove a shallow super from each hive. She was surprised at the level of production. She'd thought as hot as it had been, more workers than usual would have been required for fanning to keep the beeswax from melting and to carry water to the hive. However, it looked as if there had been plenty of worker bees to gather pollen and produce honey. The worker bees would still be making goldenrod and clover honey until the hard frost came, so she slipped a couple of empty frames into each one, making sure that there were no larvae on the frames she removed.

When cold weather arrived, the drones would be forced from the hive and would die. Only the female worker bees would be left to manage the hive over winter. They would tend the queen, raise the larvae, and keep the hive as clean as possible. When really cold weather hit, they would cluster together to keep the queen, eggs, and larvae warm. As spring approached, new drones would be allowed to grow to maturity to mate with the Queen on her spring flight.

Callie's thoughts were intent on keeping the bees as calm as possible as she placed the pads of thyme oil in each corner of each super. Researchers had discovered that essential oil of thyme helped reduce the mites that threatened the life of honeybees. She wondered if the beekeepers of old, who often placed their hives near beds of thyme, understood that, too. She finished installing the treatment, closed the hives, and returned to the truck.

She had just removed her bee suit when she heard the sound of a vehicle echoing through the woods. It sounded like a motorcycle and seemed to be heading away from her. "Should I check it out?" she debated. "Well, wasn't our New Year's resolution to 'Be courageous'?"

she asked the lab. Wicca jumped up and wiggled and then crouched like she was ready to start a race.

"I guess we should at least look around back there," Callie agreed. She finished covering the supers of honey with a tarp and drove the truck away from the hives into the shade of a tree near the greenhouse.

On instinct, she took her camera from the truck and stuck it into her jeans pocket. She'd been planning to photograph some of the flowers to use on signs and to make into slides for talks, so she'd put the camera in the truck. Wicca bounded beside her as Callie pulled on her old hat and rubbed some insect repellent on her arms. Together, they headed to the woods. She hadn't walked in her woods all summer. There had just been too much to do. And without the lure of the spring wildflowers, there'd been little to tempt her there. As she passed the creek, she chided herself for not returning to pull the last of the garlic mustard before it dropped its seed. Now she'd have another crop to contend with next spring.

She saw shelves of fungi growing on the sides of trees and looked around, so she could return to the spot later. They would make beautiful steps into the fairy tree she intended to add to the Enchanted Forest. She could picture the little door she'd attach to the tree along with tiny windows with yellow cellophane panes.

Crops of hickory nuts were already falling from the shagbarks. "Probably due to the dry weather," she muttered. Although they'd had a few big storms, overall rainfall had been well below normal. Pumpkinvine Creek was a series of puddles separated by spots of smooth sand and gravel. Without a flow, the stagnant puddles were a mosquito paradise. Another reason she'd avoided the woods this summer.

She passed the trails left by the horses that had pulled the logs from her woods. Now they were covered with leaves. She wondered if there would be a line of wildflowers next spring. Eventually, she could see her Teepee tree. The old sycamore had lost a few more branches. Only three remained that still had leaves attached.

As she stood surveying the silhouette of the old tree, she became aware of the faint smell of engine exhaust. Slowly, she studied her surroundings as she moved toward the giant tree. She was almost to its trunk before she noticed the tire tracks. She could see where foliage had been matted down by the treads. She listened intently but she could no longer hear any vehicle except the distant rumble of a train. The rail line was two miles to the east but sometimes, when the wind was just right, it sounded as if the engine were coming right down her driveway. Sounds traveled a long distance over the flatlands in this area.

Callie moved toward the opening in the massive trunk, but Wicca was first inside. Instead of running back out to circle around her mistress, the lab remained inside the hollow tree. When Callie peeked inside, she saw Wicca poking and pawing at a parcel wrapped in brown packing tape.

"Here, girl," Callie called. When the dog didn't respond, Callie grabbed her collar and pulled her to her side. "Wicca, sit."

Callie stood and looked at the package. She could see no writing on the outside. She started to pick it up, but hesitated. Instead, she pulled her camera from her pocket and photographed the box from as many angles as she could without moving it. She wished she'd brought her cell phone, but it was in the truck. She had nothing to use as gloves with her. She decided to return to the truck. Calling Wicca to heel, they moved as quickly as possible to her vehicle.

Once there, she dialed Morgan's number and waited. There was no answer. She debated. Should she call the sheriff's office and ask the dispatcher to send a deputy? What if it were just a present some kid had left for his sweetheart? After all, she'd seen Lucy and Time's initials carved into the tree late last spring, and from the abundance of carvings it appeared the tree had seen more than its share of romance. She hadn't really expected to be able to keep out all trespassers. The woods was too big and she couldn't patrol it or pay to have it all fenced. Besides, she wanted the wildlife to be able to come and go as they had for centuries. She decided to return to the house and keeping trying to call Morgan for his advice.

As she approached the truck, her attention was drawn to a steady stream of honeybees arriving and departing from under the tarp on her truck's bed. The bees were trying to recapture the honey she'd taken from their hives. She needed to get it safely to the house. She planned to store it just in case the winter was a hard one, and she might need to put it back in the hives later on.

By the time she'd covered her counter with a sheet of plastic, carried the hives into the kitchen, and cleaned any sticky spots off her truck she'd forgotten about the parcel. She put the honey into jars and set the frames aside to return to the hive area tomorrow. The bees would clean any remaining honey from the frames.

Clouds were collecting on the horizon, so Callie decided to check the weather forecast. She turned on the computer as she thumbed through her calendar. There was a reminder to do the ads for the harvest special and to order bulbs to plant next month. She'd need to go to Indy to get more wreath bases, and she needed to find a pumpkin supplier since she hadn't grown any. She had plenty of gourds, and she was picking gomphrena, strawflowers, starflowers, and statice every day. The yarrow and cockscomb crops had been good, but she'd need some preserved babies' breath, too. After checking the weather, which predicted scattered rain for the next two days, Callie checked her e-mail. There was a query from an Indianapolis morning news television show wanting her to do a segment on windowsill herbs for the winter. And there was an invitation to appear on a Christian radio show in Fort Wayne to talk about herbs of the Bible. Maybe things were looking up! She had not finished replying to the inquiries before the telephone rang. Cecilia announced the newsletters were finished and ready to be picked up.

By the time Callie returned from town and had folded only half the newsletters, she was too tired to stick on the labels or sort by zip code. She fed Wicca, scrambled a few eggs which she ate with honey-spread toast, and called the day done.

The gentle rain began in the night, and Callie smiled to think that she would not have to water in the morning. There would be few customers, so she could probably get the newsletters finished, too. She wished she had the wreath bases, so she could start making the dried flowers and herbs in the greenhouse into wreaths. The more she got processed, the less she would have to box and move.

The dampness in the morning air made it feel chilly. Callie searched through the bureau to find a light jacket and jeans. She'd need to bring her autumn clothes into her closet and start putting away the shorts and sleeveless tops she'd worn all summer. She watched out the window for a few moments, seeing the stiff breeze pulling leaves off the trees.

A movement caught her eye. A bit of rusty red fur appeared from the edge of the woods near her bedroom window. It was a red fox.

He sat down at the lawn's edge, yawning widely and shaking his ears. Then he rose and stretched each hind leg behind him like a runner before a race. He sat again, surveyed his surroundings, and then delicately licked each front paw. After another long stretch he trotted along the edge of the lawn, setting a leisurely pace. Callie stood in wonder at the beauty and grace of the animal. Another miracle in her small world. It was going to be a good day.

The steady drizzle did indeed keep the customers away. Callie kept a kettle going over a small fire in the wood stove, put her favorite opera on the CD player, and spent a productive day folding the rest newsletters and making catnip mice. She'd brought her grandmother's old treadle sewing machine to the Cottage after she'd purchased the kitten printed fabric. She'd just been waiting for a rainy day to start working with it. She felt creative, vibrant, and peaceful for the first time in weeks. As the rhythm of the sewing machine matched the music, her mind explored one idea after another. As always, she kept a clipboard at hand, jotting down workshop topics, recipe ideas, tasks for the coming day, jobs for the week, and goals for next year. A shopping list started to grow as well as a list for her upcoming trip to Indianapolis. She needed more potting soil, seeding flats, wreath bases, and preserved babies' breath. Then she began adding supplies to make herbal Christmas projects. Maybe she'd hold an herbal Christmas workshop with a wonderful afternoon tea and fragrant holiday crafts. She listed the colors of mums to purchase at the wholesalers. Having investigated the steps it took to grow healthy mums with their propensity toward spider mites, rust, and various other problems, she'd decided to let someone else deal with all the spraying and continual clipping. Maybe some year she would have the staff and time to do it but certainly not now.

She thought about the patchwork hot pads she'd seen for sale at the Amish produce stand and about the boxes of fabric she had left over from her quilting days. She could make patchwork hot pads, placemats, pillows, and even Christmas stockings. Since she had to be at the farm on rainy days just in case a customer braved the weather, she might as well produce something for sale. She might even make patchwork curtains for the Cottage to put up for the autumn season. That would really change the look and ambiance of the shop. It would seem more cozy and warm, and it could pull the entire autumn color scheme together. With spiced cider simmering on the stove, pumpkin cookies for customers to nibble, and all the dried wreaths, pumpkins, and gourds it would look quite festive. She made a note to cut out and paint some wooden pumpkins and to construct some wooden block candlesticks. She wondered if Heartland was ready for a "Witching Herbs" workshop or presentation for Halloween. Maybe not, since apparently some locals already suspected her of using love potions. Although, maybe that could be a whole new product line! Joyful Heart Love Potions? She'd have to give that more thought, too, she chuckled.

Eventually she had made a pile of fabric mice that were ready to be stuffed with catnip. She grabbed an umbrella and went to the greenhouse, slipping under the black plastic to locate the row of catnip bunches. The fragrance of the rows of drying flowers and herbs was overwhelming, a mixture of sweet, pungent, and spice. Callie decided that once she had the mice finished she'd start snipping the herbs for a moth repellent mixture and an autumn potpourri. She'd seen a sweet gum tree in the woods, and the spiky balls would add their deep brown color and interesting texture to the mixture. Deep red rose hips, golden calendula petals, cinnamon sticks, and the pretty chartreuse mountain mint would make a nice combination. She'd have to ponder the rest of the herbs to add to make it an interesting fragrance. It would look wonderful in the big rectangular wooden dough bowl. Maybe she'd add some shagbark hickory shells and acorns. And little bunches of bittersweet would look pretty, too.

When she returned to the Cottage, the answering machine light was blinking. The wind and rain had obliterated the ring of the phone while Callie had been in the greenhouse. It was Cecilia, reminding her that they were ready to do a test tee shirt whenever Callie could come in to approve the ink colors. Gloria was scheduled to work tomorrow, so Callie could go to Indy. Callie called the print shop and arranged to meet with Cecilia before she went to the city. She added "autumn toned candles" to her shopping list and surveyed the shop. Where and how would she display the tee shirts once they were finished?

She spent a busy evening working on various lists and finished her weekly column for the Heartland Banner. Her topic was entitled

"Preserving the Basil Harvest". With frost possible at any time the entire basil crop needed to be harvested. Basil leaves would get brown spots and start falling off as soon as the night-time temperatures fell to thirty-eight. It was time to harvest, and there were so many ways to preserve it the article nearly wrote itself.

At bedtime, she began reading Digging Deep, a book about developing one's creativity through gardening, written by Fran Sorin. Callie didn't realize how late it was getting until she had finished the last chapter. She was going to have a short night, but the message of the book had been worth it.

The next morning at the print shop Callie quickly approved the ink colors Cecilia had mixed and promised to come to see the finished shirt as soon as she returned from Indianapolis later in the day. She couldn't wait to see her design articulated. Wicca would stay at the farm with Gloria since Callie thought she would need the space in the front seat for purchases, and she didn't know how long she'd be. It was another drizzly day, and Callie was happy to discover that Gloria loved to sew, too. Callie left the box of fabric scraps at the Cottage, and Gloria planned to spend the day creating sample projects. She'd even suggested they make some small patchwork bags in autumn colors to use as sachets for lavender flowers or autumn-scented potpourri. And together, they'd come up with the idea to make small pumpkins out of the piece of orange corduroy they'd found in the box. Stuffed with a spicy potpourri, it would be a perfect fall item to put by the cash register for impulse sales.

Callie was feeling particularly pleased as she drove south on I69 into the city. Although sales had been sluggish during the extensive heat wave, she had high hopes that cooler weather would bring new customers. She loved the autumn season with its bright colors and crisp leaves. It had its own sense of vitality. Not the electric energy of spring, but an energy nonetheless. Squirrels bustled with the task of burying nuts for the winter. Birds congregated in excited bunches before their migration. People debated the merits of this football team and that one, making tailgating plans for the next game. Children started planning for Halloween. Farmers were busy with all the harvest and the landscape changed every day as crops were sheared from the fields. It was an exciting time of year. In rural communities, the harvest also meant farmers had income from the grain they were selling. For centuries, storekeepers' spirits lifted in autumn, and now that Callie was a businesswoman, her spirits lifted as well.

Quickly, the truck was filled with bales of potting soil and boxes of seeding flats. At the floral supply warehouse she selected cartons of preserved babies' breath, several bolts of autumn toned ribbons, and candles to match. She bought wreath bases in several sizes and all the supplies for testing some Christmas projects. At the wholesale greenhouse Callie selected the mums she wanted and made arrangements to have them delivered by the end of the week. Having depleted her checkbook and checked off all the items on her list, she turned the truck towards Heartland. The wind was increasing. Dark clouds skidded across the gray sky, and her wipers were struggling to keep up with the raindrops covering her windshield. She decided to stop for gas and a cup of coffee. Maybe by then this little storm cell would pass and the rain would become a drizzle again. It didn't.

By the time Callie neared home, it was already five o'clock. She had tried to call Cecilia to tell her she'd been delayed, but the storm had blocked the signal from her cell phone. She unloaded the soaked cardboard boxes into the garage at the farmhouse, but left the potting soil bales on the truck. Then she drove to the farm, which had already closed. Gloria had left a note about the day's activity which had been surprisingly good. Several farm wives who had been busy helping their husbands and sons in the fields had been relieved of duty because of the rain. Apparently, they had felt they deserved a treat and had come to the Cottage to shop and enjoy the hot tea and scones Callie had prepared for customers. Gloria had been able to complete a dozen small projects that were lovely. In fact, she'd sold four to the farm wives! That was wonderful news and looking at Gloria's work, Callie formed ideas for additional projects. She'd have to look through her boxes for more fabric! Maybe she'd return to the lovely fabric shop in Geneva soon, she thought, as she unloaded the potting soil. She spent the evening at the farmhouse sorting through the boxes still piled in one spare bedroom. While the thunder rolled, she looked for additional fabric or items she could use in autumn displays.

The trial tee-shirt was perfect so Callie gave Cecilia approval to complete the entire order the following morning. The rain finally stopped after five soaking days. It would be a long while before the farmers could get their heavy equipment back into the fields. The ground was also too saturated for Callie to do any tilling or digging. Instead, she spent most days creating wreaths, cleaning the greenhouse, and evenings working on her book. When Lucy worked on Saturdays, Callie demonstrated wreath-making techniques, which the girl quickly mastered. Lucy was soon producing wreaths as quickly as Callie. Her color combinations were entirely different from Callie's selections, but they were both delighted to discover there were customers who preferred each style. Callie's were more "Williamsburg" in tone, while Lucy's creations were much less conservative. They had the boldness and sense of vitality of a youthful eye. Gloria combined Lucy's wreaths with some interesting pottery, bright candles, and whimsical wind chimes in one corner of the shop. Callie's wreaths were on an opposite wall with Victorian tussie-mussies, lace shawls, and vintage hatpins. The customers were delighted.

Once the weather cleared and the moisture had dried away, Callie completed the basil harvest. She spent several evenings packing basil in oil, making pesto, and stripping leaves from dried stems. The house was filled with the distinctive scent, and Callie's mind was filled with new recipes to use the fragrant harvest.

The space in the greenhouse that had held catnip was now filled with rows of garnet cockscomb and annual statice in bright rose, sky blue, deep purple, and white. There was a second cutting of Artemisia, starflowers, and sunflowers drying as well. As Callie stood gazing up at the colorful rows she wished the Cottage had higher ceilings so she could hang them there. The customers would love it! But, the ceilings were too low. As soon as they were dry, they'd have to be boxed and stored in her garage. The shelves that formerly held plants now held boxes and baskets of wired strawflowers and bunches of purple, red, orange, rose, and lavender gomphrena. Blue Bedder and Mexican Bush sage bunches lined its rafters. Fortunately, everlastings had grown well in the summer's hot, dry conditions. The gourds were collected and stacked on pallets to cure. Bittersweet was gathered into bunches and hung from small drying racks Callie made from dowel rods. She hadn't had time to make the patchwork curtains for the Cottage, so she hung sprays of bittersweet from the curtain rods, storing the lacy spring curtains away.

Outdoors, the pumpkins and mums had arrived. Gloria and Callie had spent two mornings making attractive displays, including a scarecrow and several black crows that Callie had cut from plywood and painted. Her father's tools were coming in handy. The displays looked so pretty that Callie decided to take some photos for the album that chronicled the farm's progress.

She made one last sweep of the gardens collecting seeds and trimming back faded plants. There were envelopes filled with seeds of cardinal climber, jasmine nicotiana, Queen Anne pocket melons, moon lilies, cleome, cosmos, and more. Nearly every day, flats of cuttings from the perennials in the gardens were added to the propagating mats. She still had lots to do, but things were progressing on schedule.

After her discussion with Sandy, Callie had decided to throw herself into her farm. Of course, she hadn't been in love with Trev Carpenter, but she was very fond of him, and she'd thought maybe something might have developed in their futures. She certainly loved the time they had spent together. He made her laugh and feel good about herself. He tolerated her teasing and teased her back. He had made her feel lighthearted and desired. After the ego-killing, confidence-shattering experience with Daniel, she had needed that to start healing. She had thought what she had with Trev might grow into love someday. But, once again, her evaluation of the situation had been faulty. "No, not just faulty, disastrous," she told herself.

She wasn't even going to try to evaluate her relationships with Mike or Morgan. Trev's had been the simplest, at least in her mind, and she'd totally blown that, so she wasn't going to attempt the others. No, she had her dog, her work, her farm, and that was plenty to keep her busy. Besides, Sandy had suggested she let the rumors cool off, and that was exactly what she was doing. She'd told Mike she was swamped with work. After all, she had all the preparation for the fall season including setting up a booth at several festivals. Plus the radio and television appearances must be planned. Her column was taking more time, and she was desperately propagating before frost came. She had not made it to a Heart and Soil meeting since June! Mike understood. They talked on the phone frequently, but she wasn't going out with him. Maybe the rumor mill would find another target.

It was a crisp morning, and frost covered the roof of the gazebo. A scratching at the door reminded Callie that Wicca was ready for breakfast, so she filled the dog's dish with water and a second dish with the proper measure of food. She pulled out a loaf of whole wheat bread, a jar of gooseberry jam from England, and located the toaster. She selected jars of orange mint, whole cloves, and calendula petals from her pantry, put those ingredients into a teapot with boiling water, and set it aside to steep.

The toast popped. Callie smeared it with jam, grabbed a cup and the teapot, placed it all on a tray, and headed to the cozy breakfast nook. Bittersweet orange placemats were on the antique oak table. Comfy stuffed cushions in an autumn leaf pattern covered the sturdy chairs. Callie had decided that her home needed to reflect the autumn season as well as the shop, so she'd made a few changes. She'd purchased some deep brown and gold rag rugs for the floor in front of the woodstove. The windowsills were once again lined with tender herbs that would not survive frost. Callie poured the fragrant tea, looking out the large picture window that overlooked the gazebo and gardens. Several birds were visiting the feeders located on numerous shepherds' hooks. She'd need to get more bird feed stockpiled. The sun was rising over the horizon in vivid shades of orange, apricot, lavender and rose. A few purple clouds scurried across the sky.

As she sipped her tea, redolent of the familiar Earl Grey flavor and scent, Callie suddenly realized that she was totally relaxed for the first time in months. The killing frost meant she could no longer propagate. Of course, the gardens would need to be trimmed and mulched eventually, but there was no rush. The dried flowers, wreaths, and other products were all boxed in her garage, ready to take to the first festival this weekend. So many people had wanted to take Gloria's papermaking workshop that they'd scheduled a repeat for Sunday. That meant Callie did not have to prepare for a workshop herself. The next two week's columns were already in Mac's hands. The outlines were finished for both the radio and television spots next month. Amazingly, there was nothing really pressing on her job list.

She decided to spend the two hours until she'd need to open the shop in the studio. Things had piled up a bit there. Catalogs had arrived and been put in piles, but not studied. All the important mail had been sorted and processed, but the rest was in a basket on the desk. As she sat down, her eye caught the photo album of the farm. She flipped through the early pages showing the dilapidated Cottage and then flipped to the middle to see it in its summer glory surrounded by flowers and merchandise. That reminded her that she had not printed the photos of the autumn displays that looked so pretty in front of the Cottage now or the fall displays inside. She hooked the camera into the laptop and started clicking on the thumbprints, selecting the shots to print for the album. Suddenly, she recognized the photographs taken in the Teepee. She had completely forgotten about the mysterious parcel! She wondered if it was still there.

Within minutes Callie and Wicca had entered the woods. The frost had been too light to penetrate into the canopy of trees, but the air was crisp. As they passed the hives, Callie made a mental note to stack some hay bales in front to help protect them from blasts of winter winds. The squirrels were busy with their breakfasts, and Wicca was busy sniffing tracks of various creatures that had visited the woods during the night. Callie recognized raccoon and deer prints in the soft ground. They'd had a spell of off and on rain. Callie hoped the weather would be good for the festival this weekend. Her booth was a canvas and metal pole affair that would offer only minimal protection. And, she knew from her farmers' market experiences that it was no fun to load and unload in bad weather. Not to mention how it affected attendance and customer spending!

They had reached the Teepee, and the first thing Callie noticed was a set of muddy tire tracks. It looked like a four-wheeler of some sort had made them. She peeked inside the trunk but didn't see anything. The parcel was gone. Wicca came inside and sniffed in earnest. Suddenly, she lifted her head and stared at the ceiling of the enclosure. Callie followed her gaze and saw what had drawn Wicca's attention. There was another parcel. This one was similar in size to the one she'd seen before, but the tape was different. Like the first, it was entirely wrapped in layers of tape. Loops of tape at each end were fastened to nails that had been put in the trunk. If Wicca had not noticed it, she never would have seen it in the darkness wedged into the pointed top of the teepee's interior. She'd brought her camera and took photos of this parcel. Then she called Morgan, who told her to meet him at the Cottage.

She walked back to the parking lot, hoping that she had not just wasted the deputy's time. A nagging feeling pulled at her thoughts. She doubted that some romantic teen had gone to so much trouble to hide a gift for a sweetheart. The weather was not very conducive to having a girlfriend trudge through mud and cold to retrieve a gift. No, this was something very different, and she was pretty sure Morgan would feel the same.

Callie waited in the parking lot, pacing back and forth, watching for the patrol car. It was nearly twenty minutes before Deputy Wright pulled into the driveway. As soon as the Deputy emerged, Callie started explaining what she'd seen. She struggled to keep up with his long stride as they walked briskly toward the Teepee.

"It's fastened inside at the very top," Callie told him as he ducked his head to go inside. "Do you see it?"

"Come inside, Callie," Deputy Wright instructed.

Callie walked into the trunk and looked up. "It's gone. I swear it was there."

Deputy Wright studied the ground and then walked outside and studied the area around the old tree. Callie could see lots of footprints.

"Morgan, I tell you there was a package. Look, I took photographs," she said urgently as she pulled the camera from her pocket. "Look, here's the one that was there today. You can see it in the top of the trunk." She pushed the previous button several more times.

"And here is the first package. It was just lying on the ground. And, you can see it didn't have loops of tape on the ends," she showed him.

"I believe you, Callie," the deputy said, looking at the photo on the camera's screen. "Let me see the bottom of your shoe." Callie lifted her foot showing the shoe's tread.

"Someone else has been here recently. Wait here. I doubt anyone will be coming back since they got what they wanted," he told her.

He was gone less than five minutes but it seemed like an eternity.

"The date on that first picture was two weeks ago. Why didn't you call me then?" he asked when he returned.

"I just thought some kid had left a package for his sweetheart. All these carvings and initials. I just assumed kids have been meeting here," she said softly.

"It's probably too late to find whoever took this package now," he said, looking at his watch, "even though they came in on foot."

"Someone obviously came in on a four-wheeler of some kind earlier. They probably brought it," Callie observed.

"We don't know that for sure. Could have just been some kid out riding. Maybe the Parker kid. I'll check with them next," Deputy Wright said.

"So, what should I do? Try to keep an eye out for incoming packages?" Callie asked.

"Let me check with the sheriff. See how he wants to handle it. I'd advise staying away from the area, but keep an ear out for any vehicle. Keep an eye open for anything unusual."

"I really don't like the idea of all these trespassers using my farm. I'm thinking maybe its drugs. Do you think it's related to the pots we found hidden in the greenhouse?" she said nervously.

"Too soon to tell, but we'll get to the bottom of it eventually," he assured her. "How have you been, Callie? I haven't seen you around."

"I've been keeping busy at the farm. Trying to get everything done in the gardens before it frosted. You know," her voice trailed off. "Morgan?"

"What?"

"That day when you passed my table at Dinah's, when you made the comment about 'having any more trouble with skunks'. Why didn't you just tell me Trev Carpenter is married?" Callie asked in a troubled voice.

"Figured that was his responsibility to tell you and maybe yours to ask," he said stiffly. "I'd better report this and swing over to the highway. Check with the Parkers. You take care, Callie." Deputy Wright climbed into his car.

"Wait!" Callie cried. He rolled down his window. "So, are you married, Morgan?"

A slow grin filled his face, "No, ma'am, I'm not. About time you asked though!"

311

Callie didn't have time to think about disappearing parcels. She was up before four a.m. to drive to Pendleton to set up her booth for the weekend. Fortunately, the weather was good, and sales were brisk. It was an exhausting weekend, and by the time she'd returned to the farm on Sunday evening, unloaded the truck, and checked the notes Lucy had left at the farm, she was ready for bed. She was glad she had Monday to put all the merchandise she'd pulled from the shop back into the Cottage displays and to enter all the names she'd collected for her mail list into the computer. She was happy that she'd made the effort to do the show. Pendleton had a very active garden club, and she could tell by looking at the numerous well-tended gardens around town that she would gain some customers. She'd also picked up information from several crafters who might like to put items into her shop or possibly set up booths at her Harvest Special next weekend. She wished she'd ordered some sweatshirts with her herbal design. Now that it was cooler, few people were interested in tee shirts, even die-hard herb lovers.

The cool temperatures of late September brought a changing landscape. At the end of the month the hummingbirds left. Callie missed all their antics at the feeders and in her gardens. Often during the summer, they hovered right along with her, sipping nectar from the flowers on flats of plants as she carried them from the sales area to the check out counter. She'd put out several feeders and spaced them far enough apart so a male could not defend them all. Although the female did most of the work raising the young, the males drove them away from the feeders if they could.

"Men!" Callie sputtered, as she took down the feeders for cleaning. She'd store them for the winter and make a note on her calendar to put them out again the end of April next spring.

She had not heard any more from Deputy Wright, except for a request for her to e-mail copies of the photos of the two parcels to his department's office. Another officer had come to take photos or imprints of the footprints. Callie wasn't sure which since she had left the Teepee as soon as she'd shown the officer the location. She'd been watchful the past week but had not seen or heard anything that was suspicious.

Besides, she was totally occupied trying to prepare for the Joyful Heart Herbs "Harvest Special". The ads had been running in the newspaper all week. She'd even taken the plunge and recorded a commercial for both the local radio station and one in the next town. One was a country music station, the other was the area public radio station located at the college. It would be interesting to see which gave the best response.

She had the plants in the greenhouse all organized for winter and had a lovely selection of herbs and houseplants on the plant cart in the Cottage. There were additional pots all ready and priced in the greenhouse to refill it if sales were good.

The butterfly garden, children's garden, and shade gardens had all been trimmed and were just waiting for the ground to freeze solidly before they'd receive a thick blanket of mulch.

It was fairly calm today, which was a welcome relief from the blustery winds that had been common lately. Callie decided to get the Cottage's garden trimmed. She pulled the wheelbarrow from the black walnut garage and began trimming off the dead stalks of annuals and the bedraggled leaves of perennials. By the time she was finished, the garden looked neat and tidy with asters, anemones, and mums adding color. She emptied the wheelbarrow into the compost pile and dug the dahlia and canna bulbs. She still needed to order more fall bulbs, so there would be even more color next spring. If she'd been smart, she'd have them now. Then she could just plant them in the holes she was making as she dug the dahlias, thereby accomplishing two jobs with one effort. She made a note on her clipboard so she could do it better next autumn.

Lucy was coming after school this afternoon, and together they would take the shade cloth off the shadehouse. The weight of even a light snowfall could damage the cloth, so Callie wanted it safely stored away before that possibility. On Saturday morning, they would hang brightly colored paper lanterns and bunches of Indian corn across the shadehouse rafters. Callie had made several comical scarecrows to tie to the posts, each holding signs to promote the sales of perennials and pumpkins. Next year she'd have lots of painted gourds to sell as well, but the ones she'd grown were not cured enough to paint for this season.

Tomorrow she would make the refreshments for the Harvest Special scheduled for Saturday. In addition to Callie's pumpkin cookies, there would also be doughnuts and persimmon pudding from Dinah's Diner. A local popcorn grower was bringing a portable popper and giving out samples of the kettle corn he would make on site. An orchard from the next county was bringing hot spiced cider and a wagonload of apples and cider jugs for sale. A local country music group was going to perform and Callie was giving three presentations. Gloria would handle the shop, and Lucy would work the outdoor displays. Sandy had offered to come and be a "gopher", "You know, go fer this and go fer that!" she'd laughed. She could refill the plant stand and bag purchases if Gloria needed help. It should be a good day if the weather held.

Basil

Nothing says summer more than the unforgettable fragrance of basil, filling the air with its heavy, sensual perfume and promising taste buds a memorable experience. A sprinkle of fresh basil turns any dish into something special! Pasta becomes a gourmet's dream. And pesto.... ahhh, pesto! There is nothing on earth that compares to pesto—served on pasta, dolloped on baked potatoes, or spread on Italian bread. It is one of those flavors that grows on one slowly. Its flavor haunts, drawing one back until suddenly, it's a full-fledged craving! Impatiently, one waits all winter for spring and then for the soil to reach at least seventy degrees so the basil can be safely planted. Then it feels like an eternity, watching the tiny leaves grow to become large enough to harvest the two cups required to produce the standard batch of pesto. The first batch of pesto of the season deserves great ceremony and marks the true beginning of summer.

There are two basic forms of basil, Sweet and Bush. The Sweet Basil group originated in Far East Asia and the Middle East. It is a tall growing plant with large, smooth leaves. Sweet, Genovese, Opal and most of the "flavored" basils belong to this large group. The Bush Basils that hail from Chile have smaller leaves and a more rounded, compact form illustrated in varieties such as Fino Verde and Spicy Globe. The name basil comes from the Greek *basilikon photon*, or kingly herb.

In Eastern Europe, basil is traditionally planted on St. Basil's Day (January 1st). That would be too cold for most of the United States. Basil seeds require warm temperatures to germinate, and soil must be warm before transplanting into the garden as well. They cannot tolerate even the slightest hint of frost or the leaves will drop from the plant. All varieties of basil develop fullest fragrance and flavor in full sun, average to good soil, and adequate water. Since they are heavy feeders, they appreciate light applications of fertilizer or compost during the summer as well as at planting time. In most areas, basil is grown as an annual.

The number of varieties of basil seems to increase each year. They range in size from tiny-leaved Miniature Opal basil to the East Indian Tree basil, which may reach over five feet in height! Each basil has its own distinctive flavor. Some are fruity, sensual, and robust. Others are earthy, sharp, or spicy. Scientists have worked to develop plants rich in specific oils for the perfume and tobacco industry.

Within the basil family there is variety in leaf size, height, and also in leaf color and texture. Dark Opal basil was first introduced in 1962 and became an instant hit because of its deep purple leaves and pretty pink blooms. A descendant, Purple Ruffles basil, is a cultivar with beautiful purple color and ruffle-edged leaves. All of the purple-leaved basils produce luscious ruby-toned herbal vinegar.

Cinnamon, Clove, Lemon, and Anise basils all have distinctive flavors that can be explored. Dry them for teas or grind the dried leaves for use in cookies and pound cake. Their flavors are unmistakable. There are several cultivars of Lemon basil, such as "Mrs. Burns" and "Sweet Dani." Some have very small leaves, some larger and both cultivars are slower to bolt than standard lemon basil.

Lettuce Leaf basil has a bright, light green color and fancy leaves. Mammoth basil is, as the name implies, extremely large often bearing leaves as large as a human hand.

For more adventure in flavor, try Thai basils, Peruvian basil, Mexican basil and some of the small-leaved Greek varieties. Aussie Sweetie is small-leaved columnar basil that is extremely slow to bolt.

In the landscape, try African Blue basil, which can make a shrub four feet in diameter. It becomes covered in purple-tinged flower stalks, and its purple-veined leaves are an attractive addition to any garden.

One of the newest introductions is Pesto Perpetuo basil, a beautiful cream and green variegated plant that is columnar in form and extremely slow to flower.

In Italian folklore basil is the herb of love. If a woman puts a pot of basil outside her door, she is ready to receive a suitor. Basil has also been known to tell if a husband is faithful. If a match is applied to a leaf held in his hand catches fire and burns him, he has been philandering!

Basil has a tradition of medicinal use as well. It has generally been used for intestinal complaints, stomach cramps, and vomiting. In some cultures it is used for headache or anxiety. Mixed with honey, it is said to relieve hoarseness and scratchy throats. It has also been used as a tonic for the kidneys. Leaves were crushed to put on insect bites or stings, or to repel mosquitoes and flies.

In India, necklaces made of basil wood were worn to protect the wearer from electrical shock and lightning. It is also believed that wearing them improved blood circulation and brain activity.

Placing basil leaves in the four corners of a bedroom is reputed to help induce sleep. Placing basil sprigs in the four corners of a house is said to protect and purify the home.

Chapter 10:

OCTOBER

The weather held for the first annual Joyful Heart Herb Farm's "Harvest Special." It was typical October weather for central Indiana, crisp and with skies so blue it could make your heart ache. Many of the trees had prematurely lost their leaves. According to an interview of the district forester written by Sandy Saunders in the Heartland Banner, it was due to the unusually hot and dry conditions the area had experienced over the summer. Those trees that still had leaves were shades of brown with just a few yellows. So, the autumn foliage was not spectacular. Callie was accustomed to hordes of people from the cities flocking to southern Indiana hill country for the fall foliage. She worried that few would be enticed to come to the flat areas of central Indiana especially with no fall color, but thankfully people flocked to the farm. Cars filled the parking lot and overflowed into neat rows across the adjoining field.

The scent of wood smoke, popcorn, and apples filled the air. Customers seemed to be in a festive mood, and attendance at Callie's presentations was excellent. It was a busy day and the farm did well. The patchwork display of the products she and Gloria had sewn was nearly empty as well as the big basket of moth repellent potpourri and the catnip mice area. The customers loved the new handmade items.

Callie asked Gloria, Lucy, and Sandy to quiz customers so she'd know which advertising medium had been most effective. At the end of the day the women sat in the Cottage eating the few remaining doughnuts, discussing the event, and analyzing the results of their survey. They couldn't decide if having "outside" vendors come had helped or hurt sales. Gloria felt that many people had purchased the orchard's apples, the farmer's popcorn, and crafts from the potter and jewelry-maker that had come and therefore had less money to spend in the Joyful Heart Cottage. Sandy felt that having all the other vendors enhanced the shopping experience and made people happier, and therefore they spent more. Callie wondered if there had been any retail research on the topic. Lucy observed that since the Cottage was so small, and not all the customers could get inside at once, it was nice to give them other things to look at. The vendors outdoors kept them at the farm until they could get inside. It was something else to think about. The number of customers who said they'd heard the radio ads seemed to be small. Most came as a result of word-of-mouth, the newsletter, the road signs, or the website. Callie would have to evaluate her budget for advertising carefully before her next event.

The "Harvest Special" had gone well, but Callie barely had time to think about it. She spent a few hours later that night entering all the new names from the sign-up sheets into her mailing list and was pleased to see that the majority of the new customers were from other towns. When she had more time, she'd plot the addresses to see where her advertising had worked best. The next morning she did a quick inventory and decided with Halloween still more than three weeks away, she'd need more mums and pumpkins. A quick phone call to place an order solved that problem. If only all problems could be solved so easily, she wished silently.

Monday was Beth's birthday, and the two friends had not seen one another since Callie had gone to see newborn Penny. As soon as the watering was finished, Callie packed a few goodies from the shop that she knew Beth would like. With Wicca riding shotgun they made the trip to southern Indiana in record time.

When she arrived at the farmstead, Beth rushed out the door to greet her. The two women hugged and bubbled with happiness. As soon as they entered the back porch, Callie could smell the aroma of fresh-baked bread. Soon they were in the kitchen sharing a pot of tea, thick slices of bread spread with homemade apple butter made from the huge apple tree in the backyard. Callie could not believe how much baby Penny had changed in the four months since she'd seen her. The two friends had much to tell one another even though they talked often on the phone, and e-mails zipped through almost daily. Beth had regained her figure and somehow managed to totally fill her pantry shelves with sparkling jars of produce from her garden over the busy summer. In addition, Bob had purchased two dairy goats to eat the brambles and poison ivy in their woods, so Beth was learning to make cheese. Bob promised to let Callie do the evening milking.

"I wish you'd move back here," Beth said wistfully after the supper dishes were washed and they were sitting by the fire. "You could have an herb business here, you know."

"And my mother thinks if I had to move to a farm, the least I could have done was move to her area, or maybe even take over a few acres on one corner of the family farm," Callie laughed.

"Do you really like the Heartland area so much?" Beth asked, searching her friend's face.

"I've fallen in love with my land, my Cottage, and my old farmhouse," Callie told her. "You know I told the realtor I wanted to locate near a large city to ensure a good customer base. But land near big towns was just too expensive for my limited budget. Then I saw the listing for the farm near Heartland. Its motto is "Heartland, the Little Town That's All Heart," you know. That somehow reached me in my frozen, shattered emotional state. As soon as I saw the land and that poor little cottage, I felt I belonged. And when the farmhouse across the road turned out to be for sale, too, I knew it was meant to be. You, Bob and Penny must come for a visit. The photos I've e-mailed you just don't do it justice."

"Well, as soon as we can find someone to do the milking, we'll come. I promise," Beth said with a hug. "I just worry about you being up there all alone."

"Oh, I'm making friends, as you know. In fact, the girls are all coming for recipe testing and newsletter folding one evening soon. I don't know how I'd manage to do it all without them. And they were all so good to me when my father died," she added. "Besides, I need to prove to myself that I can manage on my own."

"I think it's just because that town seems to have an abundance of single men," Beth teased.

"Well, it's true that there are several bachelors in the area," Callie laughed. "And they all look like brawny outdoorsmen, too! Must be something in the water!"

"Callie, do you still think of Daniel?" Beth asked quietly.

"All the time. I keep telling myself I'm over him, and then some little thing reminds me of him. A snatch of music, the sunset, when I cook something he used to love," Callie admitted. "When I feel lonely or insignificant, or worried, I wish he were there to hold me and make everything go away for a while. He was my first real love, and I was totally prepared to spend the rest of my life loving only him. It's still hard to know that won't happen."

"It might happen," Beth said, taking her hand. "Daniel asked about you again. He looks terrible, Callie. He looks like he never sleeps or eats properly. Of course, he's just as dapper and cool as always, but he certainly doesn't look happy."

Callie sat quietly, a tear rolling down one cheek. Wicca rose and put her head on Callie's lap.

"Wicca thinks it's time to go, and she's right. I didn't realize how late it is getting. It's a long drive home," she said.

Brightening she added, "Don't forget, you promised to come for a visit. Try to make it soon before the roads get bad. The farm will be closed from mid-December until March 1, you know, so I'll have time to spoil you and that precious baby.

"What about me?" Bob laughed, bringing an armload of wood to place in the wood box near the stove.

"I promise to spoil you, too," Callie laughed.

The dates for the radio and television appearances were fast approaching. Callie spent a little time each day reviewing information on herbs of the Bible. At least she didn't have to worry about what to wear for a radio show. Gloria had already asked what she intended to wear on television. Callie suspected she didn't approve of anything she'd seen in Callie's wardrobe. She'd need to unpack some of her "teacher wardrobe" and find something appropriate. The show's producer had suggested solid colors.

She spent one afternoon using her father's table saw to cut out wooden ghosts and pumpkins. The ghosts were three-dimensional so they could hold a large mum plant. She made a big "Happy Halloween" wooden banner to hang across the shadehouse and put Halloween masks on the scarecrows.

For the October e-newsletter and the newspaper column, she wrote an article entitled "Herbs for Halloween!" For centuries, it was believed that Halloween was the evening when all the evil spirits of the world moved about the countryside looking for a warm home for the winter. Those folk who were wise in the way of herbs placed bunches of protective plants around all the openings to their home and kept a good blaze in the fireplace to keep spirits from entering through the chimney. Evil spirits were thought to search for unprotected homes, knowing it would be simple to move in and rule where the occupants were ignorant, unsuspecting, or lazy. Wise folks also hung bunches of protective herbs in any buildings that housed their valuable livestock.

To be sure a home would not be occupied by evil spirits in winter Callie suggested folks hang bouquets of rue, mugwort, southernwood, elder, and dill around doors and windows. Rue, elder, and dill seed heads are especially effective against witches. A little silver Artemisia and the dried heads of teasel, which are also protective, make the bunches especially pretty. Callie made bunches for her house, the black walnut garage, and the Cottage. She hung a bunch tied with a big orange ribbon on the pumphouse for insurance. With the luck she'd been having, she wouldn't take any chances. Many mornings now, the ground and branches were covered in frost. On mild days, when the sun shone and the wind was still, Callie trimmed gardens and tidied for the winter. Some days, she worked in the greenhouse, trimming the topiaries that would go with her to the television studio. On two weekends, she packed the truck and sold plants and herbal crafts at nearby festivals. There were never enough hours or days to do all that she wanted or needed to do.

As she checked her calendar, Callie realized that Wicca was nearly a year older. She needed to find a veterinarian to get the lab's shots and annual check-up. She'd heard good things about the local vet, so she called for an appointment. Wicca was delighted to ride in the truck and to be the center of attention once they arrived.

"This is a beautiful lab," Dr. Tyler said admiringly. "And, you've kept her in good condition. Not overweight. That's essential for larger dogs that tend to get hip problems."

"She's my best friend," Callie assured him. "And she does lead a very active life. Wicca has a whole farm as a playground and a huge woods full of squirrels that she insists on keeping in the trees."

"They are great dogs," the vet said as he checked Wicca carefully. "Good companions, loyal, quiet, sensitive to your moods."

"She's all that and lots more," Callie said. "She's so smart. I swear sometimes she knows exactly what I'm thinking, and she lets me know it!"

"Well, keep her this fit and she should be around for a long, long time," he smiled.

Dr. Glenn Tyler was about Callie's age with strong hands, wide shoulders, and a quick smile. His reddish-blonde hair was slightly wavy with a mind of its own in terms of direction. It curled this way and that over his collar and around his face. His mother had probably forever been licking her fingers to try to smooth his cowlicks down. Serious blue eyes noted every detail of Wicca's condition. His soothing voice calmed and assured both the dog and Callie as he administered the necessary injections.

"You're a new patient, Wicca," he said to the dog. "Where do you live?"

Wicca cocked her head at the vet and nodded in Callie's direction, seeming to give Callie approval to answer.

"I have the herb farm south of town," Callie said. "Joyful Heart Herbs. Maybe you've seen our signs along Highway 3 or the ads in the newspaper."

"Yes, I have. I do a little gardening myself. Recently, I attended a seminar on treating animals with a holistic approach including using medicinal herbs," he smiled. "I've been thinking of planting a few of the plants they suggested."

"I'd be glad to help you get started," Callie said. "I think there's a real place for herbal treatments in some cases. Of course, that doesn't mean I think herbs can do everything. There's no herbal substitute for a rabies vaccine."

"Not that we know of," he laughed," but who knows, there might just be something out there. I just read a report that researchers have discovered a frog that secretes a substance that stops HIV virus in its tracks. Trouble is, the frog is becoming extinct. They are going to try to duplicate its natural habitat and establish a program to breed them so we don't lose their gene pool."

"Wow, that's fascinating," Callie responded. "I'd like to read more about it. I try to encourage frogs and toads to live in my gardens, but I didn't realize they could provide more than insect patrol and 'toe of frog for Shakespeare's witches' cauldron'."

"A foundation is being established to finance the habitats and hire researches to go into places to rescue all kinds of frogs and toads that are threatened with extinction. Right now there's over four hundred endangered species. Over one hundred have already become extinct," he said solemnly.

"Maybe after I learn more about it, I can give the readers of my newsletter the information, in case they'd like to contribute," Callie said seriously.

"You have a newsletter?" Dr. Tyler asked.

"Yes, a monthly letter giving information on special events, workshops, sales, recipes, and gardening information. Sometimes I just write about the wonderful things in nature. Just whatever is on my mind, especially if it will bring customers to the farm," Callie explained.

"Sounds interesting. Put my name on your list," he requested. "I think I'll come by and get some herb plants if you don't think it's too late to plant."

"I'd be happy to do that. It is getting a bit late to plant, but I have some catalogs of reliable herbal suppliers, so you could start doing some trials using dried herbs." Callie smiled.

"I think I need to do a little more studying before I try any experiments, but I'll come by for those catalogs," he laughed. "I think we're finished here. You and Wicca need to wait in the outer room until the test results come back. Should be about fifteen minutes."

Callie and Wicca waited until the technician brought in a good report. Just as she was leaving, Dr. Tyler emerged from the office.

"My office is closed on Wednesdays. Could I come by in late afternoon for the catalogs? I'd really like to see your farm. Maybe we could have dinner in town afterwards?" he asked.

"It would be my pleasure, Dr. Tyler," she smiled. And she was still smiling all the way home.

The Heart and Soil meeting was that evening. Callie had arranged for Lucy to come after school to watch the shop, so she could run errands in town before the meeting. She stopped at the DNR office to get a list of the hunting season dates. This year, she wanted to have the 'No Hunting' signs up early, before any season started. Warren Peace looked harried and worn with his usual gruff personality. Callie wondered if he just didn't like her or the fact that she didn't allow hunting on her property. Or, was it because he hadn't caught the poachers killing deer out of season on her land that made him short with her? Or, maybe he was just grumpy with everyone. She really should ask Sandy or Cecilia, or maybe Mac knew him well enough to know. Regardless of his gruffness, Callie needed those dates, so she put on a brave front, lifted her chin, and marched into his office.

"Good afternoon, Mr. Pease," Callie said cheerfully.

"Hello," he answered without looking up from his computer screen.

"I need to know the hunting season dates so I'll know when to get my signs up," she pushed on.

"You're already late. Archery season opened for deer on October 1. Fox and coyote are already in season, too," he said without expression. "There's a folder on the counter in the rack. Help yourself."

"Thanks for the information. I don't suppose you've any more information on the shootings at my farm," Callie asked hopefully.

"Nope. Hear you have other problems. Pot, suspicious packages. You run a busy place," he said with a tone of sarcasm.

"The farm has been busy, thank you," she said. "I do hope you catch the poachers so I don't have any further problems." There was no response, so Callie pulled the appropriate brochure from the rack and headed to the hardware store. As she left, she wondered how such a dour man could have produced a bubbly son like Time. She'd like to meet his wife.

"Good afternoon, Jake," Callie called as she entered the store. There was a new display of electric heaters in one corner and a new glass case filled with ammunition. Next to the case was a bright display of hats, vests, and gloves in hunter orange. A stack of boxed tree stands stood on the floor below. A case of hand warmers and "hot seats" were placed on each side.

"Looks like you're gearing up for hunting season," Callie observed.

"Yep. If you came for shotgun shells, I'm already out. And, skunk season opened the fifteenth," he teased.

"No, I came for signs, as usual. Hopefully, they'll stay put this year. I'm attaching them with new glue that's guaranteed to be weatherproof as well as using extra long staples this time," Callie laughed.

"Guess that'll keep them up there," he said skeptically.

"I want twenty 'No Trespassing' signs as well, just in case someone thinks they can roam around the woods if they aren't hunters," she told him.

"There must be a lot of hunters in this area," she stated, looking at the large display of gear.

"Not as many as there used to be. Old days, every dad taught his son how to hunt. Rabbit, squirrel, raccoon, fox, quail, deer. Kept the grocery bill down, and it was good quality time together," Jake reminisced. "Now all kids want to do is stay in the house staring at a computer. Kids aren't learning anything about how to manage outdoors. Pretty soon, there'll be robots to cut the grass. Heck, they even play football indoors now. It's a sorry state when a kid spends all his time indoors."

"I imagine the wildlife is a little healthier," Callie chuckled.

"You'd like to think so, but it's not always the case," Jake shook his head. "Hunting helps keep things in balance."

"I suppose there are arguments for both sides. I'm not totally opposed to hunting. I just don't want shooting on my property. Could scare the customers, stray bullets could puncture my greenhouse, not to mention what it does to my blood pressure," she smiled.

"Well, I ordered an entire case of signs just for you," Jake said, "but when you get overrun with deer, and they eat all your plants, you keep me in mind. There's always been good hunting out at your place. Lots of deer bed down in those woods."

"If I ever change my mind, you'll be the first person I'll think of," Callie said.

"Well, now, that's good to hear," Jake nearly smiled, as he rang up the price of the signs. Callie didn't bother to add that although Jake would be the first person she'd think of, he'd be the last person she'd invite to hunt on her farm.

Callie dropped her column at the newspaper office and her November newsletter copy at the print shop. Ellen was manning the counter and smiled brightly as Callie entered the store.

"Are you coming to garden club this evening?" Ellen asked.

"I'm looking forward to it," Callie replied. "I've missed going to the meetings, but my schedule has been a killer lately."

"Too bad you missed the summer meetings. We always tour one another's gardens. Help the beginners identify their weeds, give suggestions, and such. It's always fun to see everyone else's plants and how they use them," Ellen bubbled.

"Oh, I am sorry to have missed that," Callie answered, "but I'm sure tonight's meeting will be worthwhile, too. The club seems to have good programs."

"We do. And, we'd love to have you give a program sometime in the near future, too," Ellen added. "Tonight we're discussing our plans for the Veteran's Garden that is going to be installed on the other side of the town square, and of course, it's our annual seed exchange."

"Yes, I saw that in the newsletter. I've got mine in the truck," Callie assured her. Callie had sorted some of her favorite seeds and put them in small labeled envelopes. They were in a shoebox in the truck.

"Well, then, I'll see you later," Ellen waved as Callie left the shop.

She stopped at "Second Hands" to look at the two bookshelves that were still in the window. An unfamiliar woman was standing at the counter, but she smiled and called a greeting. Callie was glad Mike's mother wasn't working. She was not ready for any kind of encounter.

"I'll take those two bookshelves if we can get them loaded into my truck," Callie told the clerk.

"Oh, they aren't as heavy as they look. I think the two of us can load them," she said breezily. "I hate to see them go. They can hold a lot of merchandise, but I guess they do rather block the view." Silently, Callie agreed. After all, she'd been completely hidden the day she'd overheard Alma and Noreen talking about her.

"Well, I'm delighted they are still here. I looked at them a few weeks ago, but I didn't buy them that day," Callie told her as she paid for the shelves. Within a few minutes, the two shelves were loaded into the bed of her truck. A coat of exterior paint and they would be perfect at one end of the shadehouse to hold watering cans, small statuary, pots, and other merchandise that could be displayed outdoors. The Cottage just wasn't large enough to hold all of the inventory Callie needed to carry.

She picked up a few groceries and more dog food. There was still time to do some research at the library before the meeting, and she had a list of books she wanted to check out. Several cars filled the usual parking spaces, so Callie parked on a side street in the next block near the Eikenberry Funeral Home. She paused after locking her truck, chuckling at the funeral home sign, thinking how appropriate the name was. This area seemed to have a lot of fun with their interesting names. Tucking her notebook under her arm, she hurried to the library where she worked until time for the meeting. There was a good crowd, and Callie chatted with several interesting people. The program was "Planting for Songbirds" by a representative of the Backyard Habitat organization. Afterwards, Maxine Barnes made announcements and reminded everyone to visit the seed exchange tables. Plans were made for the group to have a table at the annual Christmas craft show at the local armory to earn money to purchase plants and mulch for the new Veterans' Garden. Other organizations in town were donating a flagpole, flag, memorial plaque, and benches. Callie was delighted that the town had chosen to honor its veterans with a beautiful, serene garden of living plants that everyone could enjoy.

The seed exchange was interesting, and Callie picked up several heirloom flower varieties and a new climbing nasturtium she was eager to try. The members enjoyed a delicious apple cake and hot chocolate before they adjourned. As Callie left the library, her arms filled with books and the shoebox of seeds, she noticed the moon slipping behind clouds. The lighting on the street was minimal, but even in the darkness before she had reached her truck, she could see white writing on the windows.

"Some kids must be out soaping windows. It is almost Halloween," she chuckled, thinking her windows needed washing anyway, and this would push her to do them. However, when she was close enough to read the words, she decided it might not be kids after all. The words "Drug pusher" and "Pot grower" were scrawled across her windows along with a few obscenities. Callie carefully looked around her surroundings but did not see anyone. She placed the library books and box containing seeds in the truck and removed a water bottle from her cup holder. Using a glove, she wiped enough soap from the window to be able to see clearly and then returned home, a bit shaken.

Someone certainly knew about the pot plants. As far as she knew, only Lucy, Morgan, and the deputy who came for the plants knew about them, besides whoever put them there. Probably more law enforcement authorities had been informed. Then she remembered Warren Pease had mentioned that she had problems at the farm. Had Lucy told Time, and he in turn told his father? Or, did he know because it had been in a legal report? Did the sheriff's office connect with the DNR on a regular basis? How many other people knew? She needed to talk to Morgan and maybe to Lucy as well.

Callie called Morgan the next morning, but the dispatcher told her he would be in court most of the day. After her Tai Chi routine, she showered and dressed in a long-sleeved tee that had autumn leaves printed in fall colors accompanied by dark brown overalls with a matching leaf motif on the bib. She pulled her hair into a ponytail low on her neck and grabbed a brown sweater. It was chilly and dreary outside, so she decided to make mulled cider for the customers.

The morning passed without a single car, so Callie spent it pouring over seed catalogs preparing her orders for pansy and viola seeds. She was looking for fragrant ones as well as a broad selection of colors and styles. Personally, she loved the ruffled "Chalon" series, and they had sold well this spring. Lucy had urged her to plant some of the pure black pansies, explaining that Heartland High School's official colors were black and red. Lucy was certain that planters filled with black and red flowers would sell well during May as centerpieces for all the graduation parties. Callie was willing to try them. It was hard to keep her order within budget because there were so many appealing varieties to grow. She decided to order more stock seed and some new varieties of perennials, too.

Lucy came after school to help transplant all the scented geranium cuttings Callie had struck in August. They were well-rooted and needed individual pots. Callie hoped they would be good sellers as houseplants now that the outdoor gardening season was over.

As they worked, Lucy chatted about all the happenings at school and forecast a good outcome for the football game on Friday night. It was against their arch rival in the neighboring county, so the stands would be full. The band had prepared a special half-time show, and Lucy encouraged Callie to attend.

"I haven't been to a high school football game in years," Callie laughed.

"Then it's time you go again," Lucy argued. "Besides this is the last home game and you've never seen our band march. We're really good."

"Oh, all right. But I'm leaving right after your show because I have to leave at four a.m. Saturday morning to drive to Noblesville. I'm doing that charity benefit show and set up is Friday afternoon. Assuming I get the booth set up and back home in time to load the truck again, I'll come. Of course that means I have to drive a fully loaded truck and leave it parked at the football game. Maybe that's not a good idea," she wavered.

"Maybe you could get a ride to the football game," Lucy posed. "I'd come to get you, but I have to be at band practice before the game. Maybe mom could come out and get you. I'd really like for you to see our show."

"I'll try, Lucy," Callie promised. "By the way, is Time in the band?"

"No, he never took music lessons. Besides, he's on the team. But he takes photographs at the game from the sidelines for the school newsletter and the annual, and sometimes Dad uses some of them in the newspaper. Time's hoping to get a new camera soon that is faster, so the action shots aren't blurred. The camera the school supplies is ancient and the one dad gave him to use for the newspaper isn't much better," Lucy explained.

"Lucy, you didn't happen to mention the pot plants we found growing in the greenhouse to Time did you?" Callie asked.

"Oh no, Callie. You said not to mention it, so I didn't tell a soul, not even Time," Lucy said emphatically. "I've been listening for anything relating to it at school, but I haven't heard anything. Just the usual stuff. There seems to be more joking around about marijuana than ever though. Lots of kids think it's so cool. Their grandparents smoked it in the sixties, and they survived. In fact, they are the pillars of the community so most kids think it can't be all that bad. They say it makes them forget all their troubles and helps them focus."

"Well, there's lots of controversy over pot. It definitely has its benefits when used properly by cancer patients and other people in pain, but kids don't generally use it properly. And as long as it is illegal, everyone without a medical prescription should avoid it. It can be just as bad, or worse, than alcohol," Callie expounded.

"Hey, you don't have to preach to me. I saw a film at school, and I'm not even interested in trying it," Lucy assured her.

The last baby scented geraniums were in their pots, and Lucy had just left when Morgan's convertible pulled into the parking lot.

"Heard you've been trying to reach me," he said without preamble.

"It's nothing urgent. I just had a few questions that have been bothering me," Callie replied. "I'm just closing up. There's still mulled cider left if you'd like some."

"Looks real festive in here," Morgan said as he took in all the decorations and displays. "All ready for Halloween. Are you having a party?"

"No, just trying to induce customers to part with some coin," she laughed as they walked together toward the Cottage.

Once inside, Callie wiped her hands and poured two cups of cider. She pulled some herb motif pillows off a nearby bench and offered Morgan a seat.

"I had my windows soaped Monday night during garden club," Callie began.

"That's not unusual around here. It's almost Halloween and kids are out roaming around at night. Weather's been pretty good, and the big football game is coming up, so kids' energy levels are high," Morgan replied.

"I realize that, but the message indicated someone knew about the pot plants. It said 'Pot grower, drug pusher' and had a few obscenities thrown in for good measure," she told him. "I've been trying to figure out how someone would know other than the person who put them there. I asked Lucy if she told anyone, and she assured me she didn't."

"That doesn't necessarily mean they knew about the pots. Didn't you have someone write something similar on your windshield right after you moved here? When you wrote the article about the CAFO controversy?" he reminded her.

"That's true. I suppose some people might assume I could be growing more than just parsley, sage, rosemary, and thyme. I can't believe normal people would think that though. There's no way that I would risk all I've put into my farm by growing anything illegal," she ventured. "So you don't think there's a connection?"

"I can't be sure," he offered, "but don't worry. It's probably just some kids. Maybe if you'd checked, they'd written the same thing on other vehicles in the area."

"I didn't think of looking. I just wanted to get home and lock my doors," she admitted. "Speaking of locking doors, it's after five, so I can close up shop. Want to come over to the house for potluck. It appears you are off-duty."

"Yes, Ma'am, I am," he smiled.

It was comfortable, cooking together in the kitchen. Callie prepared eggplant parmesan, while Morgan sliced and diced a salad of tomatoes, fresh mozzarella, and baby spinach with balsamic vinaigrette. While the eggplant baked, they sat by the fireplace where Morgan had a welcoming fire started. Soon the aromatic smell of baking marinara sauce filled the house.

Callie talked of her visit for Beth's birthday and Lucy's request for her to attend the football game on Friday night. Morgan told her of a recent canoe trip he'd taken with some fellow officers down Sugar Creek in Montgomery County.

"There's beautiful scenery and some of the best canoeing in the state," he told her. "This is a great time of year to go. Leaves are off the trees, so you can see the wildlife. Since travel by canoe is so silent, you often see deer or fox or other animals drinking at the river's edge. The river is up with the fall rains, so the speed is good. And, there's no mosquitoes this time of year," he chuckled. "You should go sometime. It's fun shooting the rapids."

"Sounds lovely, but I'm not much of a water person. Nearly drowned one time at church camp, so I've never really felt comfortable on the water. Plus, I get seasick in a bathtub," she admitted sheepishly.

"Isn't there some herbal remedy for that?" he teased.

"Well, actually ginger root works well for car and airplane motion sickness. I've never tried it for water travel, but maybe I should," Callie responded.

Over the delicious dinner, conversation flowed easily. Morgan told her about the court cases he'd had that day. Some had turned out well, but a few had ended in the release of the suspects due to legal technicalities.

"It must be frustrating especially if you are convinced the suspect is guilty," Callie sympathized.

"Yes, it's one of the worst parts of the job. Appearing in court is so time-consuming. Some days, you sit around forever, only to find out the case is postponed," he nodded. "Of course, it's not as bad as being shot or working a death scene. I don't think I'll ever get used to the mangled bodies in car accidents or kids that have been beaten up by their parents."

"I know I couldn't handle it. You must be a very strong person and truly believe in what you are doing to be in law enforcement," Callie said.

"Some days, I think I have to be truly crazy," he smiled. "Then other days, when things click, I can't imagine ever wanting to do anything else."

"And does your family feel comfortable with you being a deputy?" she asked.

"I don't have any close family anymore," he answered quietly. Then he stood to put another log on the fire. "You know, I could pick you up Friday night. Then you wouldn't have to take your loaded truck into town."

"You don't have to work traffic detail for the game?" she asked.

"No, Ma'am. I have to work double shifts the rest of the weekend, so I get Friday night off," he answered.

"Are you sure? I really do need to leave after half-time, so you'd miss part of the game," she stated.

"I can be back before the end. Who knows, if it's a lopsided score, I may be ready to call it a day anyway."

"Then I'll be ready. And, if there's any problem, if I'm running late, I'll call you so you won't miss the opening kick-off," she said.

"Hopefully, the set-up will go smoothly, but I won't know until I see where my booth is located. Sometimes, I have to carry everything clear across the county, and sometimes they let vendors drive right to their booth space."

"Well, we'll hope this is an easy one, so you get home early," he said. "Speaking of early, I have the sunrise shift in the morning, so I need to get going." He rose from the sofa and extended his hand to help her rise, pulling her into his arms.

"Still have that sofa, I see," he observed. "Thought you wanted to toss it after it was sliced to shreds."

"Yes, I thought I would. Then I decided to reupholster it, but I just haven't had time to select fabric and find a shop to do it," Callie told him. "Besides, it has sentimental value." In her mind, she was recalling the picture he made sleeping there, feet extending over one end.

"I was kind of hoping you'd trade it for a longer model," he said, "just in case I have to come play bodyguard again."

"I'm not sure my reputation can stand up to another assault by having you stay here again," she teased him. "I may just have to risk bodily harm next time."

"Don't even think it," he growled huskily. "This town gossips about the smallest thing and blows it up like the Hindenburg. Safety first. If you need protection, I'll be here."

"That's good to know, Deputy," she sighed as his lips set off flames hotter than those in the fireplace. Her body melted into his. Her mind whirled. She felt safe and protected and set adrift on a piece of flotsam in an angry sea, all at the same time. She couldn't breathe, but she didn't want their lips to part. She could feel the heat in his body matching her own and suddenly imagined them both bursting into flames. She let her mind float away as one kiss followed another. She caught a ragged breath between kisses as Daniel's face floated behind her eyelids. Suddenly, Morgan pulled his lips from hers, searching her face.

"Who is he?" he asked fiercely.

"What?" she said breathlessly, forcing her eyes to open.

"Who is Daniel?" he said tightly. "You said 'Daniel'"

Callie tried to pull her spinning mind back to reality. "Daniel," she whispered.

Morgan held her shoulders tightly, staring into her face. "Who is he?"

"Daniel was my fiancé. My first love," she said, lowering her head.

"And," he said the word slowly, expecting her to continue.

"And," she said, pulling away, "he left me at the altar. Well, almost. Actually it was a few weeks before the wedding. We had time to notify the guests. I'm sorry. I didn't realize I'd spoken."

"Hard on a fellow's ego to have the girl he's kissing whisper another guy's name," Morgan said quietly.

"Harder on a girl's ego to be dumped for a petite little dark-eyed co-worker," she retorted.

"I'm sorry," he said softly, as he pulled her back into his arms, "he was a fool. You're better off without him."

"That's what I keep telling myself, but it's obviously taking more time to process than I'd hoped," Callie said sadly. "The heart is apparently stubborn and slow to heal."

"No quick herbal remedy?" he murmured into her hair.

"Apparently not. I've tried heartsease and lovage, which are the traditional choices. I think I'm over it all, and then something triggers the old feelings," she said softly.

"Sorry I pulled that trigger, Ma'am," he teased her. "Maybe you just need some stronger medicine." The next kiss was longer, stronger, and more intense than any Callie had ever experienced. The arms around her were strong, muscled, and hard, not at all like Daniel's. The scent was entirely Morgan's.

Wednesday was one of those perfect October days that make you think summer is still a possibility. Callie spent her time between customers planting the orders of spring bulbs that had arrived. There were guinea flowers and dwarf blue irises for the Cottage Garden, bright yellow holy moly bulbs for the Biblical garden, and stately purple fritillarias and blue scillas for the Enchanted Forest. She also planted "White Fire" tulips, with narrow red and gold stripes on pure white petals. Callie thought they looked like a fanciful candy, something the fairies would love. Nearby, she planted "Cherry Vanilla" double tulips. And, she had treated herself to some gorgeous "Ballad Dream" lily-flowered tulips for the garden around the gazebo at her house. Even though they weren't fragrant, their deep purple petals edged in gold insured them a place of honor. By the front door she planted the species tulip "Pallida" with deep blue centers and pure white petals. They would bloom in early April and spread quickly. Callie intended to divide them and move clumps to the Shade Garden as soon as they were plentiful, mixing them with blue crocuses. When the planting was finished, she mapped the new additions in her garden journal. Over the winter, tags were lost and squirrels could dig bulbs. Sometimes they ate the bulbs, sometimes they just buried them in a location of their own choosing. It was always wise to have a map. She spent the rest of the afternoon taking thyme cuttings. There were luscious lemon thymes, redolent caraway and oregano thymes, Pennsylvania Dutch Tea thyme, miniature fairy and elfin thymes, silver thyme, creeping lime thyme, orange spice thyme, and many more. She did one flat of each, promising herself to finish the job after the farm closed for the day.

It was nearly closing time when a panel truck pulled into the parking lot. Callie was just about to close out the register for the day but stopped when she heard the crunch of tires. She checked her hair in the mirror and put on her best "is there something I can help you with" smile, even though inside her tired muscles were begging for the day to end and a hot bath to be on the immediate schedule.

She stepped out of the Cottage and recognized Dr. Tyler striding in her direction. Wicca was already bounding by his side. Callie had completely forgotten that he had asked to stop this afternoon. She smiled and walked toward him, extending her hand. "Welcome to Joyful Heart, Dr. Tyler!"

"This is quite a place," he said looking at his surroundings in admiration. "You've done a lot with this old place. Last time I was by here, the house was falling down, and the place was waist high in scrub."

"Yes, and not so long ago, either," she laughed. "I have the blisters to prove it!"

"Just look at all these flowers. Surely not all these plants are herbs?" he said as he moved closer to the displays.

"No, there's a lot of different things. I suspected when I moved here that I wouldn't be able to survive as a business on just herbs.

337

I grow old-fashioned flowers, lots of fragrant plants, things that attract hummingbirds and butterflies, and unusual perennials, too. Anything that interests me or that I think will please my customers," she explained.

"I had no idea you offered things like this," he said, pointing to a large mixed planter designed to survive frost. "I don't even recognize most of these plants."

"That's 'Amber Waves' Heuchera. This is a trailing purple-leafed sedum. That's a miniature evergreen, and the little beauty with the blooms is a special toad lily."

"Ahh, I recall you said you tried to attract toads to your garden. Is this what you use?" he asked.

"No," she laughed, "I'm not sure why they call it a toad lily, other than all the little spots that are sprinkled on some blooms maybe resemble the spots on a toad. This particular one, however, is spotless, and it's also unusual because the color is a deep purple. Generally, they are white with maroon or purple spots. They are at their best this time of year, and I love them."

"They look like miniature orchid blooms," he observed.

"Exactly," she smiled with pleasure. "You do know something about plants, Dr. Tyler."

"Not as much as I'd like," he smiled in return. "Now, where are those medicinal plants?"

"As I said, it's a little late to plant, but you can see several traditional medicinal herbs in the greenhouse," she said leading the way past other colorful displays. They stopped at a bench filled with happy plants.

"Most of the hardy perennials are stowed away in the shadehouse. After they freeze, I'll put a protective cover over them to keep them frozen all winter. But, these are plants I'll take to herb conferences and shows over the winter. Some of them will be used in my speeches, and some are going to go on television with me next week," she said happily.

"I'm impressed. Which are the medicinals?" he said as he fingered leaves and sniffed.

They spent the next hour looking at traditional herbs, discussing the information he'd heard at his conference, and talking about various books they'd read on herbal pet care.

Suddenly, Dr. Tyler looked serious. "I'm starving! I just realized I haven't had a thing to eat since five o'clock this morning! All these wonderful smells are making me hungry. Are you ready to find some dinner?"

"Absolutely," she laughed as she led him to the Cottage. "I thought you said you had Wednesdays off. Why such an early morning with no lunch?"

"Well, the prize mare at Eichmann's Thoroughbreds decided it was the perfect morning to give birth," he began. "Unfortunately, her little one decided to make things difficult and tangled things up a bit. It was touch and go, but he should be fine and his momma, too. I'd just felt comfortable leaving them and had stowed my gear when I remembered I was supposed to be here."

"Well, congratulations on your successful delivery," she said. "There's some ginger cookies and mulled cider to hold you until we find dinner. Did you have someplace in mind?" Dr. Tyler had been moving about the Cottage, looking at one display and then the next.

"Do you do all the decorating?" he asked, nodding at a corner filled with dried floral arrangements and wooden pumpkins."

"No, but I made the dried arrangements and the wooden pumpkins and crows," she said with satisfaction, "Gloria McKenzie puts a lot of our displays together. She has a great eye for color and texture. Do you know her?"

"No, but I've met Mac. Nice man, a little intense," he answered. "Well, whichever of you is responsible, this shop is pretty. Very appealing, even to me, and I'm not much of a shopper. I'm glad you didn't tear the old place down."

"I couldn't. The moment I saw it, I fell in love with the place. It's too small, of course," she added, "but I'll always use it for something special. I hate to see old buildings torn down. Guess I'm old-fashioned that way."

"Well, then I am, too, because I love old buildings. Speaking of old buildings, the old bank building has been turned into a bistro, but I haven't had a chance to try it. We could go there or the new Mexican place in town if you like fiesta food," he turned toward her.

"I like Mexican food. Haven't you heard I'm the Salsa Queen?" she laughed.

"Salsa Queen?" he asked.

"We held a 'Salsa Day' at the farm. I demonstrated making fresh salsas using a variety of ingredients and recipes. The local newspaper dubbed me the 'Salsa Queen,' so I've had some people call me that when they come to the farm," she chuckled.

"Well, I hope the restaurant's salsa is up to your high standards," he added between bites of spicy ginger cookies. "I think I'd call you the 'Cookie Queen'. You are a woman of many talents."

"Thank you, kind sir," she laughed. "But, if you don't really mind, I'd like to try the new bistro. I've heard good things about it from Gloria. I can be ready to go as soon as we put Wicca in the house."

After a few moments admiring the old farmhouse, Dr. Tyler handed her into his van.

"Not very luxurious travel, but Gilda holds a lot of equipment and instruments. Even hauls a patient or two on occasion," he said patting the dash fondly.

"Gilda? I don't think I've ever heard of a vehicle named Gilda," she laughed.

"Well, it was all I could afford after college and vet school. I had to purchase all the equipment for my practice and buy a building, which of course, had to be remodeled," he explained with a smile. "The van was rusted out and lopsided, but I sanded it, primed it, and painted it a shiny black with the gold veterinarian symbol on the side. I was so proud of it." He paused to check the intersection and shift gears, which produced a grinding rumble.

"Then I took it to show my grandfather. He said 'You can gild a sow's ear, but it's still just a piece of pig,' Dr. Tyler laughed. "My grandfather was never one to mince words or opinions."

"Of course, my heart was broken and I kept remembering what he said about 'gild a sow's ear', so she became Gilda," he chuckled. "That was six years ago, and she still runs like a top!"

"Except I think her clutch is about to go out," Callie laughed.

"So, the expert gardener, cookie-baking, decorator Salsa Queen is also a mechanic?" he laughed again.

"Guilty. I grew up on a farm working with my father. He could and did fix anything, and if he needed something, he made it," she said. "He believed everyone that drove a vehicle should know how to fix basic things. Didn't matter if it was a man or woman. So he taught me. I've replaced water pumps, distributor caps, and who knows what else over the years. It's come in handy. He was a wise man," she said softly.

"You miss him," he stated as a fact, not a question.

"He passed away this summer, and yes, I think of him every day. He built my greenhouse and had planned to come over to do some repairs on the farmhouse once the crops were in," she added. "I was a lucky girl to have him as a father."

"I lost my dad when I was young. My mother and grandfather raised me. Grandpa always wanted me to take over the family farm, but I wanted to go to college and be a vet. He died soon after I showed him my van. I think he was still hoping I'd take over the farm. Mother is cash renting it now. I still go over and help out, driving grain trucks to the elevator during harvest when I can," he added. "Well, we're here. Let's see if I can find a parking space, so I don't have to back out."

"Don't tell me. Gilda doesn't like to go backwards," she laughed.

"Well, she's a little temperamental when you want to shift into reverse. Just a bit stubborn at times," he added defensively.

"She's a woman," Callie added mischievously. "We're all a bit that way at times. I think she's just begging for some attention from a sweet mechanic with steady hands."

"Sorry, I grew up on a farm, too, but these hands are made for surgery, not mechanical tools," he laughed, leading her into the restaurant. "Want to give it a try?"

"Sorry, transmissions and clutches are just a bit beyond my expertise," she laughed. "You'll have to find someone else to do Gilda's surgery."

They had a quiet table, complete with candlelight. The menu was surprisingly diverse, and the food was exquisitely cooked. When they returned home, Wicca was happy to join them in the gazebo to watch the full moon rise.

"I had a great time tonight, Callie," Dr. Tyler said quietly, as he rubbed the lab's ears.

"It was fun, and the bistro was an excellent suggestion," she told him.

"Can we try it again, sometime? Maybe it was beginner's luck," he said.

"Oh, I doubt that. I'm not that great in the luck department," she chuckled.

"Well, I'm feeling very lucky," he said. "Lucky, that you brought Wicca to my office. Lucky that you went to dinner with me tonight and lucky that the moon is full and the evening is so mild."

"Lucky that Gilda made it all the way here," she teased.

"Now, it's not nice to tease a man about his first love," he teased in return.

"I apologize. A good van is like a good woman. Once you find one, you should never let it go," Callie said, thinking of Daniel again.

"I don't intend to," Dr. Tyler said, looking into her eyes.

Cecilia brought Callie's November newsletter to the farm for the tasting-folding party. Callie had been cooking all afternoon, while Gloria watched the shop. The girls had also promised to help her select an outfit to wear on her television debut, so it would be a busy evening. The November newsletter was an important one because it would announce the Christmas Open House and the Herbal Christmas workshop schedule, as well as inform her customers about her television appearance. Hopefully, it would also stimulate a lot of holiday shopping in November and December.

Once everyone had arrived, Callie set out an array of dips and chips. The cocktail for the evening was called "Tarrasette", a French tarragon infused vodka concoction that Callie had invented. She'd also prepared a pasta salad and a lavender crème brulee for dessert.

They'd barely filled their plates when Sandy said, "Okay, Callie, tell us how you do it."

"Do what?" she asked innocently.

"Capture every hunk in the county. First Mike, then Deputy Wright, and now Dr. Tyler," Sandy said in mock dejection.

"Dr. Tyler?" chimed a chorus of voices. Callie looked at her circle of friends, slightly embarrassed.

"We just had dinner," she said quietly.

"I've been trying to get him to ask me out for two years," Sandy complained. "I even had to go out and get a pet to have an excuse to see him. Now I have cat hair on every outfit I own. How did I know I needed a big lovable black lab to snare him?"

Everyone laughed, as Sandy pulled a face to show Callie she'd been joking.

"You're right," she said seriously, "he fell in love with my dog, and now I just can't keep him away!" She joined her friends in giggles.

"Well, you must have some sort of charm. Did you discover some secret herbal love attractor?" Suz questioned. "If so, I think it's only fair that you share." Everyone else chimed in.

"Hey, Cecilia, you're happily married. Why are you agreeing with them?" Callie challenged laughingly.

"Never hurts to have a little insurance," Cecilia laughed, "Mike and I are old married folks, fifteen years now. You never know when a man might get a little mid-life crisis, so it would pay to be prepared."

"Your Mike would never give another woman a second glance. He's totally devoted to you and your family," LouAnn assured her.

"I know," Cecilia nodded, "but I've seen it happen so often. You just can't take love for granted."

"Amen," the other women chimed solemnly.

"Change of subject!" Callie announced. "It's time to rate the recipes. What needs work?"

"This one has too much hot pepper for my taste," LouAnn said licking her lips. The others agreed.

"I don't know what the herb is in this one, but I really like it," Sandy said, pointing to the half-eaten miniature Reuben on her plate.

"That's a mixture of traditional caraway and a little dill weed," Callie explained.

"I think everything else is just heavenly," Suz stated. "I wish I could cook like that. You should offer classes, Callie."

"Right, I should fit that into my schedule. I doubt there would be enough interest to fill a class," Callie sighed.

"You might be surprised. Especially after you become a big television and radio personality," LouAnn teased.

"Right, one appearance and I'm a star," Callie said dramatically.

"Stranger things have happened," Sandy suggested.

"Not in Heartland," Callie countered.

"Oh, strange things happen in Heartland, let me tell you," Sandy interjected. "I've seen lots of crazy things in this town."

"Don't get her started, or we'll be hearing horror stories all night," Cecilia laughed.

"Okay, Callie, time for the style show. You go change into whatever you've chosen to wear on the set, and I'll serve dessert," LouAnn proposed.

Callie came out in her favorite herbal outfit, the lavender cardigan and slacks.

"Too pale," Sandy said. You either need solid white or solid dark. With your light hair, I'd go for the dark."

"I thought maybe I needed to wear something light to contrast with the topiaries when I work on them. They have dark leaves and I want people to be able to see the shapes clearly," Callie explained.

"Good point," Cecilia declared, "but I think you need a stronger color."

"Everything solid in my wardrobe is dark brown or green, and the leaves won't show up against the green," Callie moaned.

"How about your denim dress? You look nice in that," LouAnn offered.

"I look fat in that, and you know they say television adds at least ten pounds," Callie replied.

"You could add ten pounds and still look great," Sandy moaned as she puffed out her cheeks. "I could lose ten pounds, and no one would notice."

"How about that sage green pant suit you wore to the CAFO meeting last January? That was the first time I'd ever seen you, and I thought 'who's that lovely woman?'" Cecilia recalled. "It's not too dark in tone, very becoming, and not too flashy to distract from what you're showing. Go put that on."

When Callie returned, the dessert plates were empty. Suz was serving tea and coffee while the others folded newsletters. They all agreed that the outfit was perfect and assured her that even Gloria would approve.

"What's that lovely scent?" Cecilia asked.

"It's my rose beads," Callie replied. "My grandmother used to make them every year with the last of the rose petals. I just finished these last week."

"They look stunning with that suit, against your white blouse," LouAnn assured her.

"I thought it might give me something else to talk about if I didn't have enough material on the topiaries. It would be a good lead-in for plugging my Herbal Christmas Workshops," Callie explained. "All the small business magazines say you must constantly think marketing."

"Good idea," the others agreed.

The evening passed quickly although everyone had to leave before the task was completed. Callie's mailing list had grown. They either needed more hands or another evening. Cecilia suggested she look into using a bulk mailing service and gave her two names of companies in nearby Muncie that specialized in such jobs.

"But we still get to come to test recipes, don't we?" Sandy asked.

"Until I get my book finished and quit doing the newspaper column and newsletters. Till then, I'll still need to develop new dishes," Callie laughed as she waved good-bye to her friends.

"And at the rate the book is going, I'll be old and gray and ready for a home," she told Wicca as she began clearing up the kitchen.

The next day was spent sorting, boxing, and loading inventory into the truck for the show in Noblesville. Gloria came at noon to tend the store while Callie set up her booth, which she was happy to find located in the hog barn at the fairgrounds. She could drive her truck right up to the space to unload. After getting her shelving in place and unpacking all the inventory she'd brought, she was able to leave right on schedule. Once she was back at her house, Gloria helped her load boxes of dried arrangements and sewn items from the garage into the truck before she left for the day. The farm had had little business in Callie's absence, but Gloria had been able to produce lots of patchwork sachets for her to take to the show. They still needed to be filled with potpourri, but Callie could do that once her booth was set up, and in between customers if the show wasn't always busy.

She just had time to shower, braid her hair, and change into brown slacks, a beige pullover, and a warm fleece before Morgan pulled into her driveway. She grabbed a pair of gloves, gave Wicca a treat, and locked the door behind her.

"All ready for an exciting evening of Heartland Panther's football?" Morgan asked, as he opened the car door for her.

345

"Ready to give my all cheering for the home team," she replied with a smile.

As they drove into town, Morgan asked about her day and her set-up at the show. Callie asked him about his day, and if he'd made any progress on a problem case or two. They found seats near an aisle about halfway up the stands. Several people greeted them and waved. Lucy stopped to say "hello" on her way to the section reserved for the band. Mac and Gloria joined them just before the game was about to start. Watching the game brought back memories of her high school days when she had played in her high school band. Memories of sitting at college games beside Daniel also flooded her mind. She tried to focus on the game. Next to college basketball, a good football game was her favorite spectator sport. A brisk, chilling wind played havoc with the quarterbacks' passing game. The running game for both teams stalled as each defense was able to stop the opposing offense. As often happens, special teams changed the momentum. Heartland's punter was having a difficult night, giving the opponent good field position. On the last drive before the half, the rivals scored a touchdown and ran the ball in for a two-point conversion. The home crowd groaned. The band members streamed down from the stands to gather for their entrance. The show was a medley of upbeat jazzy songs, played while the band formed one serpentine shape after another on the field. The drum line was magnificent, a featured part of the show. Afterwards, Callie hugged Lucy, who had played a piccolo solo in one segment. Gloria and Mac beamed with pride as their daughter ran down the steps to join Time for a soda before the second half began. The concession stand was doing a brisk business in hot chocolate, gooey cheese nachos, and hot dogs as Callie and Morgan left.

Once at the farmhouse, Morgan walked her to the door. Wicca pushed the curtain back and watched through the window as he kissed her goodnight before returning to the game.

When Callie went inside, Wicca pushed her nose into her hand for attention. "Oh, you're jealous, are you?" Callie smiled as she rubbed the dog's head and ears. "Maybe, just maybe, you have a right to be." Wicca sighed deeply and laid her head against Callie's thigh. "He is a special man. That's for sure." Callie checked her money box and the list of supplies she needed to take to the show. She laid out her clothes and tried to go to sleep. Four o'clock was going to come too quickly. Unfortunately, sleep avoided her. She tossed and turned, listening as the wind increased, crossing her fingers that it wouldn't rain. Sales at the farm had been really slow since the harvest special. She really needed good sales at the show tomorrow, and rain would not help.

She woke to a loud clap of thunder and a black lab's nose in her face. The clock said three-thirty, so Callie decided she might as well get up. At least there was still power, so she took a quick shower and dressed to go. She gave Wicca a treat and a big hug and promised her she'd be back. Lucy was scheduled to work, so she'd take Wicca to the farm for the day.

Rain continued as Callie drove to the festival and unloaded her truck. By now, the hog barn was filled with booths, so she had to carry everything from her truck, which was parked in the distant vendor parking area. Puddles of rain and areas of mud made the task even more difficult. She was glad she'd put an extra pair of shoes in her bag at the last minute. When her booth was finally complete, she poured herself a cup of hot tea from the thermos she'd packed and ate the sandwich she'd made. If the show was busy, she wouldn't get a lunch break. Several vendors, some of whom she had met at previous shows, stopped by to chat and commiserate on the poor weather. Although the show was technically indoors, customers would have to walk from one building to another in the rain. Vendors in the hog barn worried that customers might give in to the weather and leave before venturing that far since the hog barn was the farthest building from the entrance.

Just before the opening time, festive music came over the loud speakers as the show chairman announced that the doors were opening. The vendors scurried to their booths in preparation. However, it was nearly an hour before the first customer bustled into the building, umbrella dripping and shoes covered in mud. It was going to be a long, disappointing day. Callie finished filling the last of the patchwork sachets before noon. She spent much of the afternoon working on job lists and sketching ideas for additional products for the shop. She was also trying to figure out how to get two truckloads of merchandise and shelving into her truck since she had not sold anything. It was a two-day show, but the forecast was not promising for Sunday either. She'd have to take one load home and come back for the second load afterwards. She visited with other vendors and picked up a few more business cards. She wished she'd brought her laptop or at least, a book. When the loud speaker finally announced that it was fifteen minutes to closing, Callie pulled the sheets from under her tables, carefully covered her merchandise, and then put on her muddy shoes for the trek to her truck.

The rain had turned the puddles into a lake. She waded through ankle high water to her truck. Show organizers always gave the best parking to the customers and the vendors got whatever spots were leftover. She was shivering by the time she climbed inside, wishing she'd packed another thermos of hot tea. The drive home was slow due to periods of rain so heavy her wipers could not keep up with the flow. When she finally pulled into the driveway, she was surprised and nervous to see lights on in the farmhouse.

She opened her back door cautiously to the fragrance of herbs, simmering spaghetti sauce, and an exuberant black lab.

"Welcome home!" Morgan called, waving a spoon in greeting.

"This is quite a surprise," Callie said haltingly. She was stunned by the sight of Morgan standing at the stove, wearing one of her aprons over his uniform.

"Rugged weather today. I figured you had a tough one, too, so I decided to cook something hearty," he informed her, as he tasted the sauce.

"Taste this. I'm not sure it's right. You know, you really should label those jars of dried herbs. One little dried up leaf looks just like the other. I didn't have any trouble with the bay. It's big, but I'm still not sure that what I put in here was oregano and basil," he frowned.

"We're lucky. You guessed right. It's definitely basil and oregano, although I think it could use a little more basil since you asked me to taste," Callie replied, licking her lips. She hadn't realized how hungry she was.

"The water is almost boiling for the pasta, but I didn't put it in until you actually came in the door. Nothing worse than overdone angel hair," he stated with authority.

"I thought you had to work all weekend," she said, hanging her dripping coat on the peg by the door and removing her muddy shoes.

"I patrolled all day, and I'm on call tonight. One blast from this beeper and you're on your own," he smiled. "So, how was your day? Any customers?"

"Don't even ask," she groaned. "Two sales the entire day, and those were catnip mice. I won't even cover my booth rental, let alone ten hours of gas from going back and forth, and I ruined a perfectly good pair of shoes."

"I thought it might be disappointing. I'm sorry, Callie," Morgan said. "But, all is not lost. There's still tomorrow." He put the pasta in the water and opened a bottle of wine, pouring a glass for her.

"And more rain in the forecast. I'll be lucky if I can get there. In some places there was already water in the road," she brooded.

"Well, cheer up. You'll feel better after a hot meal. The bread is ready to go under the broiler and there's a salad in the refrigerator. Wash up," he ordered.

Soon she was relaxing with an excellent merlot and a crisp salad of arugula, endive, artichoke hearts, and black olives. The aroma of garlic bread filled the air as Morgan dished up the pasta.

"This is my secret recipe," he said, "taught to me by my Italian grandmother. She was a war bride, you know. Grandfather said he saw her leaning over a balcony as he marched through their village, and his life was never the same."

"How romantic," Callie sighed. "The arugula is wonderful. Not many people use it around here. Where did you find it? I never see it in the stores."

"My grandfather always grew a patch even after grandmother died. It self seeds, you know, so I just let it do its thing. In the fall, I throw a cold frame over it so it doesn't freeze right away," he explained.

"Deputy Wright, you constantly surprise me. I had no idea you were a closet gardener," she teased.

"Just carrying on a family tradition," he said, somewhat embarrassed. "Of course, the sauce would be better with real prosciutto. I had to use regular bacon."

"It's perfect. I've never had anything better," she praised.

The dinner was excellent. They had just finished eating, and Morgan was insisting on clearing the dishes when his beeper went off.

He listened to his radio and headed for the door. "Sorry, weather like this there's more accidents than usual," he said, putting on his slicker.

Callie had followed him to the door where she gave him a warm hug. "Thanks for the lovely dinner. I was totally surprised. Be careful out there; it's really pouring," she said as she gave him a goodbye kiss.

"Always, Ma'am," he replied, tipping his hat as he hurried out into the deluge.

Callie tidied the kitchen, tried to scrape the mud off her shoes unsuccessfully, and finally took a hot bath. She wouldn't have to leave as early tomorrow since the booth was already set up, and there was no need to restock, but it would still be an early morning. If the rain continued, she'd need to allow more time in case she had to detour due to high water on some of the country roads between her house and 169. Before she went to bed, she packed more fabric scraps and thread in her bag. If she had to sit all day, she might as well accomplish something. There was still plenty of catnip boxed in the garage to turn into mice.

It took nearly two days to get the inventory from the show home, unloaded, and back into the shop. After the show closed, Callie had loaded one truckload and took it home. It was too dark and drizzly to unload that night, so she did it first thing Monday morning. Then she had to drive back to Noblesville for the second load. Gloria used most of Tuesday between customers putting things back into displays, and repairing the things that had been damaged. Bumping around in a truck always damaged something, squashed bows, or broke off flower tips. It had been a very expensive show.

While Gloria dealt with boxes and customers, Callie was appearing on the radio show. It was an educational experience and one she thoroughly enjoyed. The show host asked excellent questions, and the call-ins showed a lot of interest. Near the end, the host was kind enough to ask lead-in questions that allowed Callie to promote the farm's upcoming events and workshops, and the host encouraged listeners to visit the farm's website. It was a rewarding experience; one Callie needed after the disappointing show over the weekend.

Since she didn't go to Fort Wayne often, she took the opportunity after the radio show to visit large bookstores and the Botanical Gardens. Then she investigated two garden centers to see what inventory they carried, how they displayed it, what their pricing schedule seemed to be, and what their customers were buying. She returned to the farm just as it was closing, exchanging information with Gloria about the day's meager sales and answering multiple telephone inquiries about the herbal Christmas workshop she'd mentioned on the radio. Results from her appearance were already apparent!

Buoyed by her radio success, Callie prepared for the television appearance later in the week. The topiaries looked wonderful, despite the lack of sunshine the last several days. Some of the rosemary and jasmine plants were just coming into bloom, and the lavender topiary was already in flower. The timing couldn't be better.

She made a list of supplies she'd get while she was in Indianapolis. They needed more potting soil and pots, and she needed to get Christmas ribbons and candles for the displays they'd planned for the holidays. She hoped to find a nice set of cornucopias and a few Thanksgiving items for one corner and a table display as well. And, she needed some bells to add to some of the metal pieces. It would probably be wise to get a few poinsettias and holly plants, and maybe some small evergreens to decorate outdoors. It would be a full day in the city and a stretch to the tightened budget. She had really counted on good sales at that last show, but she'd have to manage somehow.

Appearing on television was even more fun than the radio although Callie worried that the audience would see her hands shaking. The segment hostess was warm, friendly, and seemed to be genuinely interested in Callie's work. The plants looked great on camera, and the display Callie and Gloria had devised was stunning. She'd brought some milk crates and fabric to make varying heights for grouping the topiaries. Her plan to place a small square of fabric under her workspace was ideal. Once she'd demonstrated snipping and potting, the area was pretty messy. While they went to commercial, Callie simply whipped the cloth carrying all the debris away, allowing the camera to do a beautiful close-up of the finished topiary on a tidy table. The graphic at the end, showing the farm's logo, phone number, and website was actually correct. And the entire crew crowded around the table to touch and sniff the fragrant plants when the segment was ended, asking questions, and praising her professionalism in front of the camera. Callie thanked them all for making her look good, and for making it so easy. Before she left, the segment hostess took notes on a possible future appearance next month on Christmas herbs. Callie was delighted.

She ran all her errands in the city, keeping the quantities of the things she purchased as low as possible. She decided against getting the poinsettias this trip. It was still early and there might be things the farm needed more. After the bustle of rush hour traffic, Callie was happy to clear the city and return to the rural countryside. Wicca was happy to have her mistress back home, acting as though she'd been gone for weeks rather than one long day.

She'd barely poured herself a cup of tea and looked at the day's sales report when the big brown truck rolled into the parking lot.

"I heard you on the radio," Mike said smiling, as he gave Wicca a handful of treats. "You're a natural! You didn't sound nervous at all!"

He strode toward Callie, giving her a big hug. "Wait till you see all the boxes I've got for you today," he added. "Maybe you'd better get the cart, or I could load them onto the back of your truck."

"Boxes? I'm not expecting anything for at least two weeks. Then the Christmas merchandise should start arriving," she said frowning.

"Well, I assure you. You have boxes!" he laughed, returning to the truck.

Mike pulled up the back door and started passing his scanner over the labels. Callie looked at the return addresses of at least a dozen large cartons.

"Oh, great," she said crossly, "they've shipped early. I don't have room in the Cottage for any of this. We were supposed to pack up all the Halloween and summer stuff that hasn't sold to make room for it before it arrived."

"Whoa, Miss Grump, don't blame the messenger," he laughed, "or in this case, the deliverer. I just bring them. I don't decided when to ship them."

"Sorry, Mike. I didn't mean to bark at you. It's just that I planned everything so carefully and now this," she apologized. She was nearly crying with frustration. She didn't mention it to Mike, but companies billed as soon as they shipped. She'd hoped to put another two weeks of income in the bank before the boxes showed up. There was a group of ladies coming all the way from Kentucky to take the herbal soap making class next Sunday, and she was hoping for good sales in addition to the workshop fees. Pulling herself together and taking a deep breath, she looked at Mike.

"Let's put them in the truck, then. I'll take them over to store in the garage until there's room in the Cottage," she sighed.

"Why don't I just drive over to the house and unload there?" he said reasonably. "It'll save you a lot of lifting."

"Great idea, thanks. I just remembered. My truck is full already with things I got in Indianapolis today. I'll meet you at the house," she replied, thinking dully that she must be more tired than she'd thought to entirely forget her truck was already full.

As they unloaded the boxes, Mike asked about her television appearance. Once the mountain of boxes was in the garage, she offered Mike some brownies and a cup of tea. "Sorry, I need to get rolling," he declined. "Lots of other places are starting to get their Christmas inventory, too. Just as soon as Halloween is over, they put up their decorations."

"I've notice that, too," she said. "I'm putting in some Thanksgiving décor and hoping it's not a waste of time. If you get done with your route and have time, come back for pizza and cookies later. I'm trying a new vegetarian pizza recipe tonight, but I'll be eating late. I still have to unload the truck."

"I've got a better idea. Why don't I bring pizza from town? You've had a long day, and my last delivery is near Pete's Pizza," he offered, "besides, I've never had supper with a television and radio star before!" He laughed, giving her a quick kiss before he rumbled away.

By the time Callie had unloaded her truck, Mike was already back. The aroma of pizza floated toward her as soon as he climbed out of the Jeep.

"Wow, that's some full garage," he said, balancing the pizza in one hand, while he wrapped his arm around her shoulders with the other.

"I'm not even sure I can get the door closed," she said wearily.

"Sure a good thing you're skinny, so you can squeeze between the piles," he teased her.

Callie had checked the packing slips and written the contents in large black letters on each box. Then she had stacked items together by display and category, putting the things that went to the Cottage first closest to the door. Somehow, she still had to find time to open each box to check for damage before the claim date passed, but there was no time tonight. Besides, she had left for the television station before five this morning, unloaded and reloaded the show display, loaded and unloaded the purchases, put the topiaries back into the greenhouse, and moved this mountain of boxes. Appearing in front of the camera had been more tiring than she'd first thought once the adrenalin rush had passed. She suddenly realized she was exhausted. She was grateful Mike had dinner in his hand.

"Let's eat," he said, "I'm starving."

Over the tasty pizza and mugs of milk, Mike told her of all the happenings around the area, and Callie told him about her time on the radio and television. Before they knew it, the clock struck eleven.

"I've missed you, Callie," he said, carrying his plate to the sink. "Haven't seen you since our trip to the Limberlost. That was Labor Day. Now it's practically Halloween." His tone was that of a disappointed little boy.

"I'm sorry, Mike," Callie said. "We've talked often on the phone. You know how busy I've been. Running a small business on your own is a big challenge. There just aren't enough minutes in the day or the night."

"I was wondering if that was all there was to it," he said with skepticism. "I get the feeling there's something else. Or someone else."

Callie picked up her plate, carried it to the sink, busying herself rinsing the dishes and filling the tea kettle.

"All right, Mike. There is something more," she said, turning to look at him. "Let's sit down over here." She led him to the armchairs near the fireplace in the living room.

"Oh, this isn't good. Not good at all," he said with mock fear. "The dreaded armchairs instead of the sofa. No, this doesn't bode well at all. Must be serious."

"It is serious," she said softly.

"Okay, I can take it. Who is he?" he said sadly.

"It's not he. It's a she," Callie replied seriously.

"A she?" he said, a frown filling his forehead.

"Your mother," Callie said flatly. "She doesn't like me. She doesn't approve of me. I heard her talking to a friend myself. She's very upset that you see me."

"My mother," he said puzzled. "But, she likes you. She thinks your shop is adorable."

"She may like my shop," Callie stated, "but I can assure you that she doesn't want her son to date me."

Mike rose to pace the room, pausing in front of her. "Just when did your hear her say something negative?"

"I was at Second Hands, looking at some bookshelves. No one saw me come in, but I could hear your mother and a friend, Noreen Someone, talking in the back room. They had quite a lot to say about my character, or lack of it in their opinion. I was very embarrassed, so I left before they came out," she admitted.

"That doesn't sound like my mother," he said defensively. "She's the sweetest, kindest person in the world. She never says anything bad about anyone."

"I think it might be different in this case. A mother protecting her young and all that," Callie said, lowering her eyes. "And, apparently your mother and her friend aren't the only ones in town who question my character and motives. There's been some gossip, especially about the time I spent with Trev Carpenter. It appears he's a married man with small children. I didn't know that, but it hardly makes any difference. We were just friends. He helped me with several projects here at the farm and offered to move an old barn here. I told you that, I think. Anyway, I decided it was in my best interest and probably yours as well given your mother's feelings that I just pour myself into the farm. Heavenly only knows, it needs every minute I can give it and more."

"I'm not sure what to say," Mike stammered.

"Well, that's a first in itself," Callie chuckled. "But, you really don't have to say anything. I value our time together, but I am still hesitant to form any serious relationships right now. I need to focus on the farm, and I'm still shaky from my experience with Daniel." Just saying his name sent an arrow of pain through her heart and a rush of memories through her brain. The pain showed on her face.

Mike knelt in front of her, took her face in his hands, and kissed her gently. "I'm sorry you were hurt so badly, Callie. I can understand that you're reluctant to risk the possibility of that kind of pain again. But not all men are like him. I don't know him, but I know I couldn't bail on someone I had promised to marry. I'd have to be so darn sure before I made that promise, that there'd be no doubt on my part."

"I'm sure you think that, Mike. I really think Daniel thought that, too. Things happen," she said sadly. "Personally, I really don't think I understand love well enough to recognize it. I thought I did, but now I'm not sure. It's too confusing, and I just don't have the energy or the time to investigate my feelings. I have to keep this farm going, or I'll lose everything I have. I've invested everything. The farm has to be my top priority. I hope you understand."

"I think I understand," he said, kissing her gently again. "But, you have to understand. If there comes a time that I love someone enough to want to spend the rest of my life with her and to make that total commitment, the opinions of other people in town won't matter to me. Not even my mother's." He kissed her again, this time more passionately, as he moved them to the sofa.

The weather was perfect for "Trick or Treating" on Halloween night. The wind was still and the clouds barely moved across the sky. All day, flocks of geese had been moving south in their "V" formations. The masses of grackles and other birds that had filled trees and power lines for weeks had disappeared. Colder weather was definitely on the way, and people seemed to sense it. The shop had been bustling with customers for several days, buying last minute pumpkins, blooming asters, and mums to decorate their homes for parties. Several of the scarecrows Callie had made to decorate the shadehouse front had even sold although she hadn't made them for sale. But, a dollar was a dollar, and she could always make more to decorate next year so she cheerily loaded them into customers' trunks.

Callie was relieved that nearly all the Halloween items in the shop sold. She hadn't invested heavily, but it was good to have it gone rather than having to mark it down so there was no profit. She filled in the few blank spaces with the cornucopias filled with dried flowers from her garage and artificial fruit she'd purchased at the florists' supply warehouse. A few turkey and pilgrim candles and paper foldouts completed the look. She replaced most of the bright orange ribbons and bows on wreaths and swags with deep golds and rich browns or olive-greens, to reflect the tones in the Thanksgiving items she'd pulled from one of the boxes Mike had delivered. The leftover Halloween candy and smallest items went to the house, to hand out that night if any "trick or treaters" arrived at her door.

She remained in the witch's costume that she'd worn at the shop all day in celebration of the holiday as she fed Wicca and fixed herself a salad. After lighting the candles in the two Jack-o-lanterns by the front door, she settled at the computer, determined to enter the pile of invoices into a spreadsheet before she went to bed. With Lucy's help after school one night, they'd finally been able to check all the boxes for damage and accuracy. There were several items on backorder, but that was good. It meant she wouldn't have to pay for them until they were finally shipped. If they arrived. Callie had discovered that many of the things she had ordered at the gift shows never came. When she called, she was told the item was sold out. Larger stores with bigger orders got priority and if an item was gone, her little store was just out of luck. It meant redesigning displays, or finding something to use instead, but so far, she'd managed.

She was lost in concentration when there was a knock at the door. Wicca immediately rushed to look out the window, and when Callie saw her tail wagging in excitement, she knew there must be children waiting. Wicca loved children and nothing excited her more than seeing them arrive at the farm. Callie put on her witch's hat and picked up the basket of goodies as she answered the door. A group of youngsters in various costumes chimed "Trick or Treat" as they held out their bags for goodies. Several of the children reached out to pet the dog, calling her by name. They obviously were customers at the farm. She complimented their costumes as she put candy and treats in each bag and continued to wave until she saw their van pull from the driveway.

She fixed herself another cup of tea, helped herself to a small bag of candy corn, and then returned to her invoices. A few moments later another knock came at the door. She donned her hat and went to answer. A small boy dressed as "Bob the Builder" was waiting by the door. Callie could make out the shape of a parent waiting in the shadows.

"Trick or Treat" the boy cried expectantly as he held out his bag.

"Why, look Wicca! It's Bob the Builder. Have you come to fix my house?" she teased.

The boy looked puzzled for a moment, and then turned to look at his father. "Daddy, did we bring any tools?" he asked seriously.

Callie heard Trev's familiar laugh before he stepped out to join his son on the front step. "No, Bob, I don't think we put them in the van. We'll have to come back another time to do the work."

Callie felt herself smile. She just couldn't resist Trev's warm smile, even if he was a rascal. She put treats in the boy's bag and watched as he petted Wicca's head.

"I know your dog," he said. "We babysat her one time. She's pretty."

"Yes, I remember. Thank you for taking such good care of her. I think she remembers you, too," Callie replied warmly.

"Do you remember me, too?" Trev asked innocently.

"Yes, Mr. Graybeard. Or, should I say Santa? Your beard is really growing," she observed.

"Sshhh!" he warned, looking at his son. "Trev will do. But maybe I should ask if you've been naughty or nice as long as I'm here!" he chuckled.

"Oh, I think that's still under debate," she laughed. "Your son is handsome. He looks just like you. Without the beard, of course."

"Thanks. I hope you don't mind that we came," he added.

"I'm delighted to see you both," she said genuinely.

"Callie, I…" Trev seemed unsure what to say next.

"I'm sure you have lots of other stops to make, and it's getting late. It was very nice to meet you. Tristan, isn't it?" Callie said, stooping to look into his eyes.

"No, I'm Bob the Builder," he said assuredly, pointing to his hardhat. "Can we go get some more candy now, Daddy?"

"Sure thing, Bob, let's hit the road," Trev said laughing, scooping his son into his arms. "Can you say thank you to the nice witch lady?"

"Thank you, Mrs. Witch," Tristan called.

Callie stood watching until the van was out of sight. It must be his wife's van, she thought. She preferred the old blue pick-up. Sighing, she returned to the computer, determined to finish before midnight struck.

She'd been totally focused on her work for over an hour when Wicca sent a low growl of warning and rushed to the front door. Callie heard someone yelling, but she could not understand what they shouted. Suddenly, two shots fired in succession split the air. Upstairs, she heard glass shattering. She threw herself to the floor and crawled to the window nearest the door. Two men, dressed in dark clothing were standing in her front yard under the largest tree. She was finally able to make out some of the words they yelled, none of which she would care to repeat. Several times they yelled "Get out of the county if you know what's good for you!" She suspected they'd been drinking. The scruffiest of the two looked vaguely familiar, but in the shadows she could not see clearly enough to identify him. More shots filled the air and Callie heard another window shatter. She pulled an unwilling Wicca to her side, hugged her tightly, and kept her close as they crawled over to the closet, and crouched inside. "We don't want to be under that window if they decide to shoot it out, too," she whispered to the lab. They waited in the darkness. She heard something solid banging on the front door, and more yelling. She yelled that she'd called the police and that they were on their way. Their shouting ceased, but she couldn't be sure they weren't still there. Eventually, the dog relaxed and Callie suspected the men had gone. She crept from the closet and peeked out the window. Nothing moved, or seemed unusual. Wicca paced around the house and then lay down in her usual spot on the rug near the fireplace. Callie checked the back door and looked out the window carefully, but everything looked normal. She went upstairs to check the damage. Two windows were broken in the spare bedroom, and one in her bedroom. The bullets had also shattered the glass on a picture that hung on the opposite wall and broken a lamp on the bedside table. One curtain panel had two new holes.

Her heart rate was just returning to normal when there was a knock at the back door. Adrenalin surged through her body as she ran down the stairs, following the racing lab to the back door. She picked up a rolling pin as she passed through the kitchen. The curtain barely moved as she peeked through the window. A man's dark silhouette stood on the threshold. Callie tensed, as she peered at the forbidding form. She flipped the light switch, hoping to scare the intruder. The overhead spotlight flooded the area with light. A chuckle of relief bubbled out as she opened the door.

There stood her familiar UPS driver, with a sword bearing the label "FED EX" sticking through his body. Fake blood ran down his brown shirt.

"Can you give aid to a dying man?" he cried dramatically, clutching his chest. "Actually, I think I'm blind now, too," he said, blinking rapidly as he tried to block the bright light over the door from his eyes with a bloodied hand.

"You deserve blindness, Mike Shipley," she laughed. "You nearly frightened me to death. That's quite an outfit."

"Hey, I won second prize at the company party tonight," he informed her as he moved indoors. "I would have won first, but Helga showed up in some very non-regulation shorts."

"Sorry I wasn't there to see that," she laughed, inspecting the sword.

"It was for employees that work out of the Muncie distribution center and their families only," Mike said, "otherwise I would have invited you."

"That's okay. I've been pretty busy here anyway," she said.

"Have you had lots of trick or treaters?" he asked as he removed the sword sections.

"A few," she said hesitantly. "You didn't by chance see anyone as you came in, did you?"

"I met a couple of vehicles on the road, but no one right in the area. Why, did something happen," he asked, noting her tone.

"A couple of guys in costumes, at least I assume they were costumes. Definitely too old to be out asking for treats. Did a lot of yelling. Told me to get out of the county. Shot off guns and broke two windows upstairs," she told him.

"And you were going to take them on with a rolling pin? Are you crazy? Are you all right?" Mike said, taking the rolling pin from her clenched hand. Then he encircled her protectively in his arms. "Were you in danger?"

"I'm not sure," she said, laying her head on his broad chest. "I guess if they'd really wanted to hurt me, they could have broken down the

360

door, or crawled in a broken window. Wicca certainly didn't like them. She began growling even before they came near the door. I watched them from the window until the shooting started. Of course, it was too dark to see them clearly. They tried the lock and banged the guns against it. I yelled that I had already called the police. That seemed to stop them and I guess they left. I didn't see a vehicle leave though. I thought they were still out there. In fact, I thought they were at the back door, when you banged." Callie didn't realize that she had begun to shake until her knees turned rubbery. Mike clutched her more tightly to support her.

"We should call the sheriff," he said.

"No, I'd think they are long gone," she told him. "Just stay with me a bit, so they won't come back,"

"I'll stay as long as you need me," he promised, kissing the top of her head as he led her into the living room.

"You just sit here and I'll tack something over the broken windows," he instructed.

"No, I'll help. It'll be faster, since I know where the hammer is. And truthfully, I'd rather be with someone right now than sitting in here alone," she told him.

Together, they used pieces of cardboard from the stack of flattened boxes in the garage, duct tape, and small wooden slats nailed to hold the cardboard in place to temporarily repair the windows."

"You can take measurements into Heartland Glass on Monday, and they'll cut new panes," Mike explained. "Do you know where they are?"

"I can find it," she said, "and yes, before you ask, I do know how to glaze a window. Piece of cake."

"MMmmmmm, cake," Mike said wishfully. "You don't happen to have any cake do you? I've lost a lot of blood. I need food, woman!"

Callie laughed as she collected the tools and led the way down the stairs. "You happen to be in luck. No cake, but I have leftover pumpkin bread and candy corn. We can make hot chocolate. Will that do?"

Thyme

A favorite of the fairies, the cook, and the gardener, thyme is an easy-to-grow perennial. The two main requirements for success are a sun-filled location and excellent drainage, especially during a wet winter. Thyme is excellent in a raised bed or rock garden. There are dozens of varieties of thyme, but they divide nicely into two main groups, the creepers and the uprights. Creeping thymes are wonderful as a groundcover for sunny areas, and in small spaces, such as fairy gardens. The tiniest leaves are found in fairy thyme, elfin thyme, and miniature thyme. Many of the creeping thymes are used between stepping stones. Taller thymes are used as edgings or low hedges.

There are many varieties of thymes that are just used for ornamental purposes, because they have hairy leaves that are uncomfortable on the palate. Most of these are called wooly thymes. Others have been bred for outstanding flower color, rather than flavor. All thymes are excellent plants for honeybees and have a wonderful fragrance.

Both the creeping and upright types of thyme can have a variety of leaf shapes, from rounded to needlelike. There are thymes with green, golden, silver, and variegated leaves.

Cooks love thyme for soups, stews, biscuits, and seasoning mixes. It is also a staple in many marinades and salad dressings. In general, common cooking thyme, also called English thyme, and narrow-leaf French thyme are most commonly used in recipes. However, many recipes call for lemon thyme, especially those with fish, chicken, or cookies! All of these are good for teas, too.

The adventuresome cook might also try caraway thyme, orange thyme, lime thyme, or rose-scented thyme.

Thyme is antibacterial and antifungal, so it has a long history of medicinal use. A strong thyme tea has often been sprayed on pets to help remove fleas and other insect pests. Recently, thyme oil has become a key ingredient to control mites in bee hives. It is commonly used in mouthwashes, treatments for athlete's foot, and other minor skin ailments. Thyme is often added to sleep mixtures to help prevent nightmares.

It is said that carrying a sprig of thyme, lavender, and mint tied with a ribbon will help one find a sweetheart.

Chapter 11:

NOVEMBER

It was a surprising sixty-eight degrees by lunchtime. Yesterday's high temperature had been thirty-eight. The old saying "If you don't like the weather in Indiana, wait a little and it will change" held true. Callie had just finished sweeping up all the broken glass and was preparing to put in the new panes. With the warm temperatures and sunshine, she'd rather be trimming in the gardens, but the windows had to be repaired before the next cold snap.

"I'll certainly never forget my first Halloween at this farm," she told Wicca as she swept. "You were very brave, girl." Wicca jumped up and ran down the stairs.

The sound of a vehicle pulling into her driveway reached Callie's ears as well and sent her running to the window, then down the stairs, and out the back door.

"Morning, Ma'am," Deputy Wright smiled, then his face turned serious. "Why didn't you call me last night?"

"So, you've heard," Callie said.

"Mike Shipley stopped at the sheriff's office this morning before he started his route. He was concerned and thought we should know someone shot out your windows and threatened you," he reported. "You should have called."

"Yes, I guess I should have," she admitted. He gave her a quick hug, holding her tightly.

"Let's see those windows," he said, releasing her and moving toward the house.

"I've already swept up the glass," she said, trying to keep up with him.

He went directly to the spare bedroom, assessing the scene quickly. He removed the damaged picture from the wall and dug a bullet from the plaster behind it.

"Twenty-two hollow point," he murmured. He looked at her and added, "Pretty common ammunition for a small rifle. Used for squirrel hunting, varmints mostly."

"How many shots did you hear?" he asked.

"I'm not sure, five or six maybe," she told him. "They broke a lamp. I threw it away."

"Where was it sitting?" he said as his eyes swept the room again.

"Here on the bedside table," she pointed.

He knelt near the table, surveyed the room, and then walked over to the rocking chair across the room. Callie had not noticed the damage to the chair until Morgan began removing a second bullet from the headrest.

"Another twenty-two, but different brand of cartridge," he told her.

"Yes, they both had guns," she nodded.

They moved to Callie's bedroom, where Morgan found a third bullet lodged in the woodwork above her closet door.

"You were lucky," he said bluntly. "If you'd been in here, you could have been hit."

He continued searching the room, but no others bullets were found. "Let's go downstairs. Fix some tea."

"I need a description, as much as you can remember. Their size, the sound of their voices, what they wore, where you saw them, what they said, everything you can recall," he told her.

"They were standing under the largest tree in the front yard. In the shadows so I really couldn't see them well," she began.

"Fix the tea. I'll be right back," he told her. Callie filled the kettle and pulled two mugs from the cupboard. Then she moved to the living room window where she watched the deputy searching the ground near the tree she had described. By the time the water was boiling, he was back in the kitchen.

"Two sets of prints. They walked in from the road," he told her as she poured the water into a teapot. The next several minutes were filled with Callie's description of the event and the men.

"One was a little bit shorter than I am, I think, and much stockier. The other one seemed skinny and mostly kept behind the shorter guy. I think they'd been drinking or something. Their speech was a bit slurred, so I had trouble figuring out some of what they were saying, or maybe just one did all the talking. I only remember one voice, kind of whiney, not low-pitched." she continued. "Their clothes seemed scruffy, baggy. At first I thought they were wearing costumes, but now I'm not so sure. The shorter one was wearing a heavy, bulky coat. The skinny one had whitish shoes, maybe athletic shoes. I never saw their faces."

Morgan had been taking notes. "You know the drill by now. There will be a crime scene officer out later to take some photographs and maybe a casting of the footprints. I have to go now. I'll take a closer look along the road to see if I can find the signs of where they parked a vehicle. You didn't hear a vehicle, or see their lights when they left?"

"No, actually as soon as the windows started being shot, Wicca and I hid in the closet until she seemed to know they were gone. I didn't see any lights," she admitted.

"Glad to hear you had the sense to take cover," he said. "I heard you were ready to assault them with a rolling pin!"

"Not really. When I heard someone at the back door, I thought they were coming in. It was the only thing handy to use as a weapon."

"You should have called," he repeated, pulling her into his arms. He tilted her head back and kissed her firmly.

Callie didn't have time to dwell on the incident. Once the windows were repaired, she focused on completing her weekly column and the December newsletter. Her friends were coming this week to help fold and address, so she had to get the copy to Cecilia as well as decide what recipes she'd test. She hadn't had time to check with the bulk mailing services but put it at the top of her job list. There was another meeting with the group opposing foreign CAFO's this week, and she needed to start preparing for her second television appearance. She was also speaking at the "Women's Expo" in Marion this week on herbs for stress. Gloria had said there was a wonderful quilters' museum in Marion as well as a lovely tea room. Callie was hoping to have an opportunity to see one or both after her speech.

The weather forecast for the remainder of the week was not good. Snow was forecast later in the week to be followed by temperatures in the low twenties. Callie needed to check the greenhouse furnaces and the heater in the pumphouse. She'd spent part of one morning storing away the wooden ghosts and pumpkins that had been in the outdoor displays. She couldn't think of anything appropriate, cheap, and easy to do for Thanksgiving so she was letting her mind start to move toward Christmas displays. Too bad she didn't have a beautiful old sleigh or an old red pick-up truck to decorate. She'd have to come up with something that would attract people driving by since she wouldn't have large areas of blooming flowers to draw their eye. So far, she was clueless.

She decided to focus on the column and newsletter, and quickly realized she could use most of her preparation for the "Herbs for Stress" talk in both. That would save lots of time. While she was turning her speech notes into a column, the phone rang. It was an invitation from a near-by college to teach a class on herb-growing as part of their life-long learning program. She quickly agreed to the terms, promising to send an outline and brief description for the three evening classes they requested.

By the time the column and the article for the newsletter were finished, it was lunchtime. She filled Wicca's water bowl and made a salad. Then she mixed up batter and put two loaves of Bishop's Bread in the oven to use as refreshments for customers at the farm this week. Soon the kitchen smelled of baking nuts, chocolate, orange mint, and maraschino cherries. She'd need to think of other things to make that fit the Thanksgiving season. Maybe she'd make cranberry cobbler or black walnut cookies.

While she waited for the bread to bake, she rummaged through her cupboards and panty, trying to get inspired. According to the list she'd made last January, this month's topic was supposed to be hot dips. Her mind roamed through all the hot dips she'd had over the years-- artichoke, spinach, Reuben. She'd need to think of something original.

Maybe a hot cranberry and rosemary dip? Maybe a sage-infused cheese with bits of turkey? Should she invent recipes to use up traditional leftovers, or come up with things that would compliment normal Thanksgiving food? Should she forget Thanksgiving fare altogether and just focus on any hot dip or spread that came to her? Whatever she decided, she'd better come up with some ideas quickly. She'd just put the loaves of bread on a rack to cool when the phone rang again.

"Joyful Heart Herbs. Callie speaking," she said without thinking. She was so accustomed to answering the business phone she'd forgotten that she was on the house line.

"Hey, friend," Beth's voice came over the line. "Happy November! Have time to talk? I just put Penny down for her nap and Bob's gone to bring up another load of firewood."

"You're just the tonic I needed," Callie laughed. "I was spinning my wheels here. Can't seem to get my creative juices flowing."

"Well, fill me in on your projects. Maybe I can help," Beth offered.

"I'm just trying to finish up the newsletter and come up with ideas for hot appetizers that I can test. Before Friday!" she chuckled.

"Hmm. Probably I can't help with the appetizers, but maybe I can make a couple of suggestions for your newsletter," she said. "You'll have an article on your Christmas Open House and the herbal Christmas workshops this month. How about an herbal Advent wreath using lots of thyme, hyssop, horehound, and the other herbs that still look good this time of year? And, you should talk about sedums. Those rusty flower heads look stunning in the garden right now. I just picked a big bouquet of them and even though they are all dried, they look great with some curly willow twigs and a few bittersweet vines. I added some evergreen pieces and a big gold bow and it looks great. I'm using it as a centerpiece in the dining room."

"Great ideas," Callie exclaimed, "you're on a roll. Keep going!"

"Give them some other ideas for decorating. Maybe clear vases filled with acorns or sweet gum balls. Pots of culinary herbs wrapped in burlap or stuck into little pilgrim hats. Maybe give the recipe for a bouquet garni, since lots of people will be making turkey soup later this month. Or talk about using bay leaves to keep the bugs out of the cupboard."

"You're an angel," Callie said, "not to mention a lifesaver. I might just be able to get this newsletter to the printer on time after all. Now tell me, what's happening at your house these days?"

"Well, Penny can sit up all by herself now. Of course, she tips over once in a while, but she's able to sit for longer and longer periods," Beth said proudly.

"I can't believe how fast she's growing," Callie said.

"And, she's getting teeth," Beth added.

"Wow, she'll be crawling before you know it," Callie chuckled. "When are you coming for a visit?"

"Oh, we still haven't found anyone to do the milking while we're gone, but Bob thinks they'll both quit giving milk soon. He's trying to find a registered buck so we can have kids next spring, but we haven't been able to find the right breed yet," she explained. "We do have a neighbor that will feed and water the stock, and keep the woodstove burning, so maybe we can come in December. We might stop on our way to visit our parents over the holidays. Would that work?"

"Anytime you can come, you know I want to see you," Callie assured her.

"You know, it's your year to make the fruitcake. We always do it around Halloween, so there's plenty of time to sprinkle them with sherry every week. Did you remember?" Beth asked.

"I'd totally forgotten. I'll make them this week. Maybe we can meet in Indianapolis for lunch after Thanksgiving, and I can give you your share," Callie proposed. Since their college days, Beth and Callie had taken turns making Christmas fruitcakes. The recipe they used made four loaves and it made sense for just one of the friends to go to the trouble of locating the ingredients and the mess of baking. Each of them got two cakes, which was plenty for entertaining over the holidays and usually a bit leftover to treat themselves occasionally through January.

They visited for a few more minutes, exchanging local news and family matters. As soon as the call ended, Callie wrote the articles for her newsletter and worked out the details for the Christmas season schedule. Before mid-afternoon, the newsletter had been e-mailed to Cecilia and the newspaper column was on its way to Mac's computer. Callie checked two items off her list and began making calls to the bulk mail services. She located one with a good package deal in Yorktown and made an appointment to visit their facility the next week. She spent an hour adding the few names from the Noblesville show to her mailing list, as well as all the requests that had come from her website. Another hour was spent updating the website with the holiday schedule.

By five o'clock, she badly needed a walk, and Wicca was getting restless as well. She grabbed her coat, a warm cap, and gloves, and they headed over to the farm to check the greenhouse and Cottage. Everything was well, so she decided to check the hives. She had a small closure to attach that would help keep mice out. It reduced the area the bees had to defend, making it more difficult for the mice to enter. Once that was finished, Callie hiked around the edge of the woods, checking the signs she had glued and stapled. All of them seemed to be attached securely. She found three of her plant sales signs that had blown away and been missed on her earlier searches and a couple of empty pots that were half-hidden in the fallen leaves. She passed the fairy tree and paused to wish the spring, summer, and autumn fairies a good winter's sleep. The winter fairies would be busy making snowflakes soon if the weather forecast was correct.

Callie continued through the woods to the old Teepee, with Wicca romping ahead. The air was crisp and chilling. The wind was beginning to increase, and clouds skidded across the sky. Here and there she discovered the track of a deer or raccoon as she hurried along the trail. At the Teepee, she found evidence that someone had been there recently. There were several footprints and a couple of cigarette butts lying inside. There were no parcels on the floor or attached to the top, she was happy to note. Wicca ran around and around the old tree, sniffing with interest.

The air was definitely getting cooler, and Callie felt that by the time she walked back to the farmhouse she'd have had sufficient exercise for the day. She still had a long job list waiting. She could accomplish several tasks yet this day if she worked until bedtime. She circled through to the back field and checked the signs along that edge before crossing the creek to check a third side on the way home. The fourth side would have to wait for another day. Wicca waded through the creek, rather than walk along the bank with Callie. When they reached the road, she bounded up the bank, ran up to Callie, and began to shake the water from her coat. Callie shouted and ran to escape the bulk of the flying water drops. Wicca decided it was a new game and ran to catch her. By the time they returned to the house, Callie's cheeks were red with cold, and her eyes watered. She put the kettle on and lit the fire in the fireplace.

"I love this room," she thought as she slowly spun in a circle. Wicca spun in a circle, too.

"Except that sofa," she paused, eyeing the offending piece critically. "I really am going to have to do something about that sofa," she told herself. While she waited for the kettle to bubble, she added "Find fabric and an upholsterer" to her January job list. There really wasn't time to deal with it now. And, her parents usually gave her some money for Christmas. Maybe this year she'd use it to recover the sofa. Callie's hand dropped the pen she was using. Suddenly, she was overwhelmed with longing for her father. She'd thought about him the entire time she'd repaired the windows, using the cat's paw and putty knife from the box of tools her mother had told her to take. She went to the closet, hung up her coat, and put on an old shirt her father had left when he'd built the greenhouse. It still had a faint scent of "Old Spice" aftershave. Life was so hard sometimes.

A pot of anise hyssop tea might help lift her sadness, so she pulled a jar from the pantry and filled a teapot with the correct measurement of fragrant leaves. The kettle was bubbling, so she added water and covered the pot with a cozy. When the tea was ready, she took her mug to the rocking chair in front of her computer.

"I should be working," she told herself, but she sat and rocked and let her mind roam over the past with her father. She remembered the first time he allowed her to drive the tractor alone, and how she'd almost run it into the creek before she'd remembered which pedal was the clutch and which one was the brake. She recalled one time when she was very little. They had gone to town, and she had seen a woman walking a dog on a leash for the first time. She was fascinated by the idea. On their farm, all the dogs were farm animals that ran free. None of them even wore a collar, let alone a leash. And they were far too independent to walk obediently beside someone. Later, while her parents were busy milking the cows, Callie managed to put a loop of bailer twine around one of the barn cat's neck. Of course, the semi-wild animal objected and began howling and pulling with all its might. That resulted in the twine tightening around the animal, which began rolling and encasing itself in a tangle of twine. Callie had just stood frozen, holding one end of the twine and trying to figure out why the animal wasn't behaving like the lady's dog. Her father had come running at the noise and quickly freed the cat using the pocket knife he always carried. He received many scratches and bites in the process. Once the cat had escaped, he pulled Callie onto his lap and asked her what she had been thinking. She tried to explain about wanting to be like the lady with a dog on a rope. Her father laughed and told her that animals that lived on a farm liked to be free. Animals that lived in town had to stay on a rope so they wouldn't get run over by all the traffic. Callie had never forgotten the incident. The smell of the hay in the barn, the feel of her father's arms around her while she sat on his lap came back to her. And, especially the calm way he had talked to her that night even though his hands must have been stinging from the claw marks. Her father had been a special man, too.

She finished her tea and sighed. She must finish the confirmation letters for this month's workshops, look over the schedule, make a list of supplies she'd need, and make a timeline for the month. November was going to be exceedingly busy. She'd thought once the main plant selling season was over and the gardens were put to rest, her season would be easier. So far, it was just as busy as every other month. In fact, she was falling behind on keeping the website updated and the business paperwork filed. She always did the taxes on time of course. The monthly sales, state, and federal withholding taxes were mailed promptly because she didn't want to pay penalties. Of course, she did payroll and paid invoices as they were due, but she was behind entering everything in her computer bookkeeping program. She'd have a lot of catch-up to do later. It also meant she didn't have a good idea where she stood on her budget, and she had not had time to run a profit and loss statement. She wished she were rich enough to hire an accountant to do it all. Maybe some day that would be possible, but not now. It was a part of the business she hated.

It was nearly midnight before she had a list of groceries made for the recipes she'd dreamed up. She'd give them more thought tomorrow while she worked at the farm and revise the list if needed. She was eager for her friends to come. She felt incredibly lonely.

The forecasters were wrong again. Fat snowflakes began falling in mid-afternoon and it was only Tuesday, not the end of the week as predicted. Although it was barely November, Callie put Christmas music on in the Cottage, hoping it would lift her spirits and make her feel jolly.

Her first customer was Maxine Barnes, president of the garden club, looking for a large rosemary plant to take to her mother who resided in a nursing home. Callie had just refilled the plant cart, so there was a plant with deep blue blooms that would be perfect. While the woman browsed throughout the shop, Callie made a note to herself to get short strands of white twinkle lights to decorate a few large rosemary bushes for the holidays. The woman selected one of the large cornucopias and half a dozen knobby chartreuse hedge apples. Callie had collected the knobby spheres from behind her house and placed them on a large pottery plate as a decoration. She hadn't intended them for sale, thinking anyone could collect them along the country roadsides, but if the woman wanted to pay for them, she wouldn't decline the income!

"Now remember, Callie. Friday afternoon we are all meeting to decorate the downtown planters. Everyone is supposed to bring a bushel basket of evergreen branches and large pine cones if you have them," Maxine reminded her. "Will you be able to get away from the shop? We're meeting at one o'clock. After we finish, most of us will go to Dinah's for hot chocolate and pie. I hope you can make it. Oh, and did Mildred pay you for the ribbon you bought for us at the wholesale place?"

"Yes, the check came in the mail just this morning," Callie smiled. "Gloria took the ribbon home with her, and I think she already has all the bows finished and ready to go."

"You know, these hedge apples would look pretty with the dark green evergreens and red bows. Do you think they'd last through the entire Christmas season?" Maxine asked.

"I think they would. I wonder if there might be a problem with kids throwing them around though. They are just softball sized, and it's just so tempting to pick them up. I know I have trouble resisting handling them," Callie added, rubbing her fingers over the light green bumpy surfaces.

"You might be right," Maxine said thoughtfully. "We certainly don't want to be responsible for any broken windows."

After Maxine left, Callie wrote "collect hedge apples" at the top of November in her new calendar for the coming year. She spent the next hour consolidating garden and fairy items together in one small area, and refilling the emptied shelves with snowmen and bright red cardinals. She moved many of the kitchen items into one cabinet and put in a display of gingerbread themed products. Then she added red watering cans to the floor near the cardinals, and a few silver frames to the shelves near the snowmen. The shop was already taking on a festive air. She'd still have to make some major changes to allow room for a Christmas tree. There were boxes of gardening and nature-related ornaments that would require a tree.

The Christmas potpourri was already aging in her spare bedroom in large metal tins. She'd need to sort out appropriate fabrics to make into sachet bags. Maybe they could do some in holiday patchwork, too. There were some small red buckets that would look good filled with candy canes, so she added those to her grocery list and made a note to find her grandmother's fudge recipe.

A few more customers came during the afternoon, interrupting the watering Callie was doing in the greenhouse. As she hurried to the Cottage, she once again noted how bleak the outdoor display areas looked. She really must get some color there, and soon.

After the farm closed, Callie went to town. She needed the groceries on her list and Wicca was nearly out of dog food again. Maybe she should buy bigger bags! As she turned to pull into the parking lot, she saw an old bicycle leaning against a trash can across the street. The tires were flat, and the seat was broken. On impulse, she threw it into the back of the truck.

"It must be trash day," she thought. Instead of going to the grocery, she cruised a few back streets. By another set of trash cans, she found an old ladder, which quickly went into the truck bed. Behind the tire store, she found a stack of old tires. She pulled into the parking lot and went inside to ask if she could have three.

"Normally, we ship them off to be recycled. You know they are making garden mulch with tires now?" the manager told her.

"Yes, I've seen it at horticultural shows, but I haven't ordered it. If you could part with three old tires, I'd really appreciate it," Callie said.

"Well, you've been a very good customer since you've come to this area," he smiled. "I think we can part with the ones you want."

Callie finished at the grocery in record time and hurried home. Since she'd moved some of the Christmas merchandise to the Cottage, there was a little space to work in the garage. She rummaged through the cans of paint leftover from painting the shelves for the shadehouse. It was a soft, soft beige that would work in a pinch. She didn't want to spend any money if she could avoid it. She painted the three tires and leaned them against boxes to dry. She located her dad's wire brush and rubbed the bicycle to remove all the rust. She painted it bright red, then painted two large plastic buckets the same color.

There was no time today to work on the displays. Callie was up before sunrise, dusting, vacuuming, and tidying for her friends. She did as much food preparation as she could before it was time to open the Cottage for business.

A blanket of snow covered the earth, giving the world a magical feel. The scent of wood smoke hung in the air. Callie filled the bird feeders before she left the house. Several cardinals hopped aboard the feeders before she was halfway down the driveway.

It was a beautiful day. Callie filled the little red buckets with candy canes and placed them in the red and white display. She decided to make cinnamon tea to go with the bishop's bread for any customers that might come. Soon the shop was filled with a delightful scent.

She pulled her grandmother's old treadle sewing machine away from the wall and began sewing together small sachet bags, using various shades of green, burgundy, and red. There was a growing stack of rectangles by her elbow when a vehicle pulled into the parking lot.

A group of ladies had come to see her shop, having heard about her on the radio. They twittered and exclaimed over each display, and Callie was happily busy ringing up their purchases and wrapping parcels. After they left, Callie cleared the empty cups and plates they'd left here and there, answered several phone calls, and refilled the teapot.

She'd just backstitched a new sachet when another van pulled in. She recognized the sound even before she stood to look. Sure enough, it was Gilda.

She opened the door wide, and Wicca bounded out to greet Dr. Tyler.

"Hello there," she called.

"Hello yourself," he called in return, stomping his feet before he entered the Cottage.

"You still haven't fixed your transmission," she accused, laughingly.

"Just waiting to find a sensitive mechanic," he laughed. "I can't entrust my girl to just anyone! How have you been? I've been meaning to call, but between my practice and helping out with the harvest, I've been swamped."

"I'm fine. You look well. Would you like some tea?" she asked.

"If that's what smells so good, I do," he smiled. "You know, when I was here last time, we looked at plants, and I looked at your shop. And we went to dinner, but I totally forgot to get those catalogs we talked about."

"Goodness! You're right!" she exclaimed. "I don't have them over here. They're at the house. I can go get them, if you want," she said, pouring the fragrant tea into cups. "Would you like some Bishop's Bread to go with that?"

"Looks good, and it's been a long time since breakfast," he added. "There's no hurry on the catalogs. Actually, it was just an excuse to stop by. I wanted to ask if you'd like to go to dinner again some night. I thought maybe we'd go into Muncie. The symphony has a special holiday concert next week, and it's usually very good. It's on campus. Have you ever been there?"

"No, I haven't. I keep thinking I'll go over to the library, but the ladies at our local library are so good about finding anything I need on interlibrary loan that I haven't made the effort. I'd love to go to the symphony. I always went to concerts at Bloomington when I lived near there," Callie said.

"It's Wednesday evening. We could have dinner first downtown, then go over to campus," he offered.

"Are there plenty of parking spaces that don't require reverse?" Callie teased.

"Gilda will have to stay home alone that night. We'll take my car," he told her. "Can you be ready by five thirty?"

"I'll be ready," she assured him. There were a few other customers throughout the afternoon. Of course, since she wanted to close right on time, four ladies came about twenty minutes until five and stayed until nearly five thirty. Since they made several purchases, Callie was pleased, but she would still have to hustle to have things ready before her friends arrived.

It began snowing again just as LouAnn pulled into the driveway. The others came shortly afterwards, riding in Suz's four-wheel drive truck. Much laughter and chatter accompanied the folding, which they decided to start immediately this time. They took a break after an hour's work and sampled the hot appetizers Callie had prepared.

"I've had something almost exactly like this at Bible study," Cecilia said.

"Really?" Callie said sadly, mentally marking it off her list. She couldn't use something that was previously published, and if someone else was already making it, chances are they saw it in a magazine or on television. She'd have to think of something else.

"This one is really, really good," Sandy said, helping herself to another tiny toasted appetizer. "What is it?"

"It's a smoked oyster and thyme mixture," Callie beamed, as she poured this month's herbal cocktail.

"Did I see Dr. Tyler's van here this afternoon?" Suz asked. "I was delivering a load of stone nearby and went past Joyful Heart on my way home."

"Yes, he stopped to get some herb catalogs. He's thinking of adding some holistic approaches to minor cases," Callie explained.

"Is that a little blush I see? Or, is that herbal cocktail getting to you already?" Sandy teased.

"Well, he did invite me to the symphony next week," Callie admitted.

"Galloping galoshes! Does anyone want a cat? There's no sense keeping that animal any longer," Sandy groaned. "I swear the only single men you don't have swimming around you are Suz's brother Flint, Warren Pease, and Joe Suggs."

"But Warren Pease is married. He's Time's father," Callie interrupted.

"He's a widower," Cecilia said quietly. "His wife died when Time was in grade school. She was sick a long time, in terrible pain. It was really hard on Warren and Time."

"Oh, I didn't know," Callie said quietly. "But, who's Joe Suggs? How did I miss him?" Callie teased.

LouAnn laughed. "You probably know Joe. He's that guy that works at the tire store."

"The one that spits tobacco all the time?" Callie asked.

"That's him," Suz answered. "But you forgot Jesse Plumber and Jim Peters. They're both available."

"No thanks," Callie laughed. "I've met them both, and I've got more than I can handle already."

"You can say that again," moaned Sandy, reaching for more dip.

"How's business been now that the ground is frozen?" LouAnn asked. "I know my sign-painting business suffers once the weather changes."

"It's been really slow," Callie answered slowly. "In fact, I'm thinking that I might have to go put in my application for substitute teaching once the farm closes. I was hoping to bank enough profits to get me through the winter, but it's not happening."

"Most new businesses take three to five years to show a profit," Cecilia stated. "At least those were the figures when we started the print shop. At least you have an option, and most schools always seem to be looking for reliable substitutes."

"All right, girls, back to folding and gossip. We've still got all those labels to stick," Sandy ordered, "and Callie said no dessert till we finish!"

Everyone worked like troopers and soon the newsletters were in neat files, sorted by zip code and ready to go to the post office. Callie served a warm gingerbread cooked in applesauce that had been baking while the women folded. She whipped fresh cream and made a pot of strong tea to go with the dessert.

"Wow, I'm glad I brought the truck," Suz said as she looked out the window. "The snow is really beginning to pile up out there."

"Maybe I'd better get going," LouAnn stated. "Can I have my dessert to go?"

"You can have anything you want, dear girl, after all those newsletters you folded and sorted," Callie said, giving her a hug. "You be really careful going home. Or, you could stay here overnight, you know."

"No, I need to get home. I have a deadline. Still have three paintings to finish before the next show and being around all of you always gives me a big lift," LouAnn replied. "I might paint all night!"

"I have a deadline, too," Sandy added. "Maybe you've heard that the CAFO deal went through. Rumor says they've already filed for a second dairy. This one might be just north of the high school. I've got to check all the legal filings for this week and do a title search on the land first thing in the morning."

Everyone gave LouAnn a goodbye hug and watched as she maneuvered out onto the road, her tires spinning in the snow.

"Maybe we should get going, too," Suz said, finishing her gingerbread. Callie helped everyone into their coats and gave them hugs, as well as parcels of warm gingerbread to take home.

She watched the truck's headlights disappear, then banked the fireplace and poured another cup of tea. Like LouAnn, being with her friends had cheered her immensely. She felt revitalized and ready to work. The tires and bicycle got second coats of paint, a list of materials she'd need to take for her next television appearance was made, and an outline for the first lifelong learning class was on her computer before she climbed into bed.

When she awoke, it was still snowing, and the wind was beginning to pile it into drifts. She did her Tai Chi routine and fixed hot cornmeal mush for breakfast, sweetening it with some of her bees' honey. The farm didn't open until nine, but she doubted any customers would be banging at the door in this snow. Wicca bounded through the drifts as Callie walked to the Cottage, where she taped a note to the door that read "Back at 9:30. Sorry for any inconvenience. Five percent discount on purchases when I return. Callie." She shoveled a path from the Cottage door to the parking lot. Back at the house, she loaded all the newsletters in the truck's cab. There was no room left for Wicca, so she gave her a treat and left her in the house. It wasn't quite time for the post office to open, but Dinah's would already be doing a booming breakfast business, so Callie climbed into the truck and put it into four-wheel drive.

As she'd figured, Dinah's place was busy with folks eager to talk about the snow. Callie ordered coffee and a bran muffin and then ambled over to the Geezer's official table.

"Good morning, Herb Lady," Jim Peters greeted her.

"Good morning, Mr. Peters, gentlemen," Callie said nodding at the group. "I was wondering if you gentlemen could help me."

"Need those fans again, do ya'?" one gray-whiskered man asked.

"No, this time I need someone to plow my parking lot," she said. "Know of anyone who'll do it for a reasonable price?"

"Did she say she has lice?" one bald fellow asked the others.

"No, she wants someone to plow her snow," another told him.

"She needs to talk to Charlie," a man with bushy eyebrows told Jim.

"Yes, Charlie's your man," a fourth geezer chimed in.

"Charlie Porter," Mr. Peters explained. "He's in the phone book. Good man, retired Marine, reliable. If you can get him, he'll do a good job. In demand, though. You might have to wait awhile to get on his list."

Callie wrote the name on her list and thanked everyone for their help. She returned to the counter to pick up her order and pay.

"How's it going, Callie?" Dinah smiled. "I heard you on the radio. We have one in the back where I roll out piecrusts. You did a good job. Maybe you'll bring some folks to Bradford County."

"I hope so," Callie replied.

"Well, if you get some folks out there, send them in for pie," she waved as she moved to answer a ringing phone.

"Sure will, Dinah," Callie assured her, picking up her bag.

She dropped the newsletters at the post office and paid for postage, stuffing the pile of forms into her bag to be filed later. Then she hurried to the farm. Of course, for the first time in two weeks, there was a SUV in the parking lot full of waiting customers. She began wishing she'd left the five percent discount part off the sign.

She parked her truck next to the vehicle and waved merrily as she trotted to the Cottage to unlock the door and turn on the lights. She punched the CD player, which immediately launched into the Christmas music of Mannheim-Steamroller. After turning on the coffeemaker, which she'd filled with teabags, whole cloves, and cinnamon sticks before going to town, she hung up her coat and donned an apron. The ladies came into the shop just as she was turning on the cash register.

"Welcome to Joyful Heart Herbs," Callie said cheerily. "I'm sorry for the delay. I was trying to locate someone to plow the parking lot for me. What are you looking for today?"

The usual murmurs of "We're just looking" drifted over the counter as the ladies turned to look at the displays.

"There will be hot tea in just a few minutes, complimentary, of course, and Bishop's Bread, too," Callie told them, pulling the platter from the cupboard. She unobtrusively moved throughout the shop, turning on battery operated candles and stirring the potpourri.

"Your shop is lovely," said one lady, who was dressed in a stylish suit with a matching coat.

"Is that wreath really made of lavender?" asked another.

"Yes, it's one of my favorite varieties, Royal Velvet," Callie responded. "All the lavender is grown here at the farm although we're about to run out. I'm going to have to expand my plantings for next year."

One lady was busy rubbing the leaves of scented geraniums and sniffing her fingers. "Do you by chance have 'Mabel Gray'? She's my favorite, but one rarely finds her."

"I do. I can bring some in from the greenhouse if you'd like. I haven't had a chance to shovel a path there yet, so I'd be happy to go get them for you," Callie offered.

"That would be lovely," she replied, "and I'd like Apple and Lime, if you have those as well."

Callie put on her coat, picked up a Styrofoam cooler that they kept under the counter for bringing plants in during cold weather and headed to the greenhouse. She returned moments later with the plants to find the ladies enjoying their refreshments. By the time they left, she'd sold an entire flat of plants, an herbal canister set, two herbal teapots, three herbal cutting boards, two rolling pins, and an assortment of other items from the Victorian display. She helped the ladies carry the items to their car and noticed a Michigan license plate.

"We're members of a Michigan herb club," the stylish lady told her.

"We're on our way to a meeting in Ohio. When Helen heard you on the radio a few weeks ago, we looked for your business on the internet. We discovered it was only a few miles out of our way, so we made plans to come to visit," another added.

"Too bad your shop is so small. You have some lovely things, but our group is too large to come for a tour," a third said sadly.

"I'm certain we could work something out if you came during the growing season," Callie supplied. "Part of the group could tour the gardens, some could shop in the greenhouse, and some could visit the shop. We could even do a presentation in the shadehouse if we need to divide even more."

"That's a possibility. We'll talk to our committee," the first lady stated.

"All the contact information is on the website. Thank you for coming and I'll look forward to seeing you again," Callie added. She'd stuck a newsletter into each bag and made sure they'd signed up for future editions before they'd left the shop. It had been a good morning, so it was easy to smile as she waved at their departing vehicle.

Back inside, she looked up Charlie Porter in the phone book and left a message on his machine. Then she consolidated merchandise to fill the voids caused by the ladies' purchases, creating yet another bit of space for more new merchandise. Not all the incoming products were holiday items. She had not been sure how much holiday traffic the shop would draw, being so far out in the country. She'd decided it would be better to bring in new merchandise that could sell next season. There were more items to expand the Victorian corner and several more herbal-themed products. By lunchtime, the new displays filled the shop, and she was back at the sewing machine. This time she was making velvet sachets for lavender and tying them with gold ribbon. They would decorate a small tree and fill a pretty basket placed underneath it.

Mid-afternoon, Mike's UPS truck rumbled in.

"Something smells awfully good," he called, as he dropped several small boxes near the counter.

"You get the last piece of Bishop's Bread," Callie told him as she poured a mug of tea.

"Is that all the reward I get for trekking through the snow," he asked, leaning over to kiss her cheek.

"You haven't tasted the bread," she teased, "It's worth its weight in gold."

"So, what's in these boxes?" he asked, pulling off his gloves and reaching for the mug.

Callie looked at the label and then smiled broadly. "I was hoping these would arrive. Its frankincense, myrrh, and more orris root to make potpourri. Plus some pine, spruce, sweet orange, and other essential oils. This is my lucky day."

"Glad it's someone's lucky day. I've been pushing my way through drifts all morning. The roads have all been plowed now, but the side streets and driveways are still packed," Mike complained.

"I've got someone coming to plow here. Soon, I hope," Callie assured him.

"Oh, I wasn't complaining about your lot. You know I'd come through snow over my head to deliver to you, Callie," he smiled.

"Well, let's hope it never gets that deep," she laughed.

"You're in a very good mood," he noticed.

"Just had a carload of herb lovers from Michigan, and they made my day," she laughed again. "I'm just hoping they come back for plants next spring."

"So, business is picking up? Maybe we should celebrate," he proposed.

"I'd like to, but I have a killer schedule again. That television appearance is lurking just around the corner, and I have three workshops this month," she said slowly. "By the way, did you talk to your mother?"

"I did. It was just as I thought. You must have heard someone else that day. Mother says she'd never criticize someone she barely knows," Mike said confidently. "She really is the nicest lady you'll ever meet."

"I'm glad to hear that," Callie said. Privately, she wondered if there was any chance that another woman named Alma worked at Second

Hands. Maybe she'd do some checking, but she was pretty sure in her own mind that there would not be.

"Well, beautiful, I have to run. Everyone is getting packages this time of year. My truck was so full we had to put a second run out today," Mike told her, putting his gloves back on. He gave her a quick kiss and left, only to stick his head back inside the door.

"I think your parking lot is about to be plowed," he announced. "Charlie just pulled in." Callie grabbed her coat and followed Mike to his truck. He gave her another hug before he jumped inside and started backing up, waving at the incoming truck as he left.

"You must be Charlie Porter," Callie beamed. "I'm so glad you were able to come."

"Got your message when I went home for lunch. I can just fit you in before I have to go to work. How much do you want plowed? The whole lot, or just part of it?" he asked, looking around the space.

"Let's do half, pushing the snow to the south end. Be sure you clear the area around the LP tanks, too. I'm expecting a delivery yet this week. Can I make arrangements for you to automatically plow whenever there's six inches of snowfall?" Callie asked.

"That's what most businesses do. Of course, since you're out here all by yourself, that takes an extra trip. I'll have to charge you a little more than the ones in town," Charlie said hesitantly, naming the fee.

"That seems reasonable to me. We have a deal," Callie said, smiling. "Come in for tea or coffee when you're done if you have time, and I'll have a check ready."

It was bitter cold when Callie was cutting evergreen boughs from behind her house. She returned to add another layer of clothing after she'd piled the fragrant greens in the back of the truck. Gloria was going to watch the shop this afternoon, so Callie could help do the downtown planters. It made sense since there were no evergreens to cut in Gloria's small yard, and she didn't like being out in the cold. Callie cut enough branches for Gloria's contribution as well and put the box of bows in her cab. Wicca would keep Gloria company at the farm.

Callie stuck two large screwdrivers and a couple of hammers into her truck and then drove to the meeting place near Dinah's. Several of the garden club members were already there, wiring large pinecones to bamboo sticks. As soon as Callie brought the box over, they added a large puffy red bow to the top of each stick. They loaded several baskets containing a variety of evergreen branches onto Callie's tailgate. She drove to the first planter, and as she'd suspected, the potting soil was frozen solid. She gave two members each a set of tools, and soon they were pounding holes into the soil, so the branches and bamboo sticks could be inserted. A third member trimmed the branches to the desired length.

Soon Denver, Merle, and the Jackson's drove up, so two more teams started working on the other side of the square. Denver and Merle both had tools in their vehicles, so it didn't take long to complete the job. Then everyone moved to the Historical Museum where planters were filled, and garlands were hung along the porch railing. Big red bows were tied to the posts, and fluffy green wreaths were hung on the doors.

"Looks like we're all ready for Santa to come," Maxine said, admiring the decorations.

"He'll be lucky if he doesn't freeze his nose off," Denver added glumly.

"Oh, you know he's used to the cold," Mrs. Jackson laughed.

"Well, I'm not. If we're done, I'm ready to go inside someplace warm," Denver grunted.

"Okay, everyone pack these boxes into my van, and we'll meet at Dinah's," Maxine directed.

The group gathered at the official Geezer table since the men had left. While they sipped hot chocolate, Maxine held an informal meeting, announcing upcoming events and reminding everyone that no meeting would be held in January.

Afterwards, Callie ran a few errands and made a stop at the library. She returned to the farm just as Gloria was closing out the register.

"You had a pretty good day, surprisingly. One lady came and bought little packets of frankincense and myrrh for everyone in her Sunday school class," she said. "Another couple came for an entire tray of culinary herbs for a windowsill garden in their kitchen. I made a list of everything that sold. You're going to have to order more of those herbal pillows, and I put out the last of the teapots that we had stored under the daybed. I didn't get much sewing done, but I can take it home. Lucy has band practice tonight. They're trying to get ready for their big Christmas concert next month. Mac is attending the county council meeting since Sandy has a bad cold."

"Oh, I'm sorry to hear Sandy is sick. I'll take her some chicken soup or something," Callie said quickly. "If you could take some sewing home, that would be great. Keep track of your hours. You're still available to work the morning I go to Indy for the television show, right?"

"I have it on my calendar. Are you sure you don't need me to come in Saturday?" Gloria offered.

"No, I'd rather you come in Tuesday as we'd planned. I'm hoping we can get more things moved around to make room for a tree, and I have that appointment with the bulk mailing service in Yorktown," Callie assured her.

Saturday went well although there were fewer customers than Callie had hoped. She set a fencepost into the ground in front of the shadehouse and leaned the largest of the tires she'd painted against the bottom. Then she wired a medium sized tire on, topped with a smaller tire. She attached a top hat she'd made from a bucket and piece of plywood for a brim. It was painted black. She fastened a wooden circle on which she'd painted eyes and a mouth, and attached a plastic carrot nose inside the smallest tire. A green and red striped scarf that she'd made of two old sweaters from the thrift store completed her snowman. She filled the bottom of the two larger tires that formed the snowman's body with soil, and stuck evergreen branches and plastic poinsettias into it. It was unique; it was bright and cheery, and it was cheap. She set a second fence post near her snowman and wired the red bicycle to it. After lining the wire basket on the front with moss, she filled it with soil and repeated the evergreen and cheery red flowers. She wired some bells to the handlebars. Two short windowsill planters were attached behind the seat and filled with greenery as well. The two red buckets were placed nearby and filled with matching greenery. Callie looked at the scene and made a note to make some big gold bows to add to the bucket handles and handlebars. It certainly was eye-catching. She looked at her snowman and just had to laugh. It was dark by the time she and Wicca returned to the house for a late supper. She spent a quiet evening preparing for the workshop scheduled for the following afternoon. The workshop would have gone better if there had been more room to work. The temperature in the greenhouse, while warm compared to outdoors, was not close to most people's homes. By the time the workshop had ended, several ladies were too chilled to be in a mood to shop in the Cottage. Unfortunately, there was not enough room to hold workshops in the Cottage, and Callie refused to hold them in her home. It did not bode well for the herbal Christmas workshops later in the month. Space was really going to be an issue now that winter had arrived.

The meeting with the bulk mailer went well, and arrangements were made for them to process the February newsletter. Callie had decided to skip a newsletter in January since the farm would be closed. Postage costs had risen and she'd be stretching her budget to return to the gift shows that month. She stopped in Muncie on the way home for more pieces of fabric and a few grocery items that she hadn't found in Heartland. She loved living near a small town, but if you wanted exotic items like porcini mushrooms or smoked salmon, you had to shop in a bigger town.

That night, Callie went through her wardrobe trying to find something suitable to wear to the symphony and on her next television appearance. She finally settled on a forest green sweater and long skirt with a simple gold chain and earrings.

Looking around the packed auditorium, Callie was satisfied with her wardrobe choice. Dr. Tyler led her to excellent seats, and they both enjoyed the concert immensely. By the time they left, it was snowing lightly.

"Want some coffee and dessert?" he asked, holding the door while she slipped into the seat.

"I'm not a big coffee fan, but a cup of tea would be lovely," she said," I think I'm still too full from that wonderful dinner to eat dessert."

"Then, would it be too presumptuous to ask that we have tea at your place? I could build a fire. Then if the roads start getting slick, we'll be close to home," he said reasonably.

"That's fine with me, and Wicca will be glad to have us back home. I have a new tea we can try, if you like tea. Otherwise, I can make hot chocolate or hot-buttered rum," Callie offered.

"Now you've struck a chord. I haven't had hot buttered rum since I took some sessions in New England," he laughed. "Do you do it with a poker heated in the fireplace?"

"Nothing quite that dramatic," she laughed, "although you're welcome to try it if you'd like. I do have a poker and a fireplace."

They drove to the farm and were given a warm welcome by the lab. Soon, they were sitting in front of the fire with the warming drink in their hands and soft music playing in the background. The conversation leaped from one topic to another. By the time Dr. Tyler left, they'd made a date to go ice skating after Thanksgiving and to attend the symphony's Christmas concert next month.

The second television appearance was easier since Callie knew what to expect. The segment went so quickly that she didn't have a chance to mention the rose beads or the herbal Christmas workshops. Before she left, the producer asked her to generate a list of possible future segments and e-mail them to the station.

Afterwards, she met Beth and baby Penny at a small restaurant near the mall. They had a wonderful visit, and Beth was thrilled to get the fruitcakes Callie had baked promising to take her turn with the baking next autumn.

Callie made a stop for more potting soil and a case of plant sleeves to help protect plants from the cold when her customers took them to their cars. She'd hoped to run more errands in the city, but the skies were turning dark and more snow was in the forecast.

By the time she reached her house, snow was falling rapidly. She quickly changed her clothes and drove the pick-up to the greenhouse to unload the potting soil. It would be easier to get it inside before more snow piled up in her way. The Cottage was dark. Callie glanced at her watch and was surprised to see that it really was after five o'clock. Gloria had already left for the day.

Callie was just unloading the last bale of soil when Wicca began growling and ran toward the woods. Callie called for her to come back, but the dog seemed intent on her mission. Hurriedly, she closed the greenhouse door and climbed into the truck. Normally, she didn't worry when Wicca took off. Usually she was just chasing a squirrel or sometimes a stray dog or cat. However, Callie sensed that this was different. Wicca's growl was deeper, more threatening.

The truck bounced through the meadow, hitting frozen ruts. Callie could no longer see her dog. She stopped the truck at the edge of the woods, pulled on her gloves, and turned off the ignition. She could hear Wicca barking madly at something deep in the woods.

Grabbing the metal cheater bar she kept behind the seat, she set out through the snow, following the sound of Wicca's fierce barking.

Suddenly, a shot rang through the air. Callie's heart froze as she heard Wicca yelp. Her barking ceased. Callie ran as fast as she could on the slippery, snow-covered trail. She could barely make out the prints Wicca had made and almost missed where her route turned off the main path to the back field and toward the Teepee instead. In the distance, she could hear the sound of a small engine. It appeared to be heading east through the woods toward the highway or possibly the Parkers' farm. She had to stop to catch her breath, calling Wicca's name frantically, and listening for any answering sound.

There was only the fading purr of the engine and the distant sound of a freight train. Callie began running again gasping in chunks of frigid air. A few dozen yards from the Teepee, she saw Wicca lying in the snow. She could see bright red spots even though tears had begun to flood her eyes.

Callie knelt in the snow running her hands over the dog's prone body, begging the dog to hold on. She pulled a handkerchief from her pocket and stuffed it into the wound she could see and groped for her cell phone with her other hand. The dog was barely breathing. Callie pulled off her coat, covered the dog as much as possible, and prayed as she made the call. After what seemed to be a lifetime, she finally heard a voice.

"Dr. Tyler here."

"Glenn, Wicca's been shot. I'm here in the woods. She's bleeding badly," Callie sobbed into the phone. "Please come, please!"

"Callie, I'm clear across the county. Can you tell if it was buckshot? Lots of little holes, or one big hole?" he asked calmly.

"I'm not sure. One big hole maybe. There's a big hole. I stuffed my handkerchief in it, but it's still bleeding. I can't see if there are more. I think she's in shock. I'm in shock! What should I do? She can't die, she just can't," Callie sobbed, trying to breathe.

"Stay calm, I'll be there as soon as I can. Did you see who shot her? Are they still around? Are you in danger?" he asked.

"I think they left. I could hear an engine, like a four-wheeler maybe. Just tell me what to do for Wicca. I'm not worried about me. She's not moving. She's barely breathing,"

"Try to keep her warm. Check for other wounds and try to stop the bleeding. I'm coming as fast as Gilda can run," Dr. Tyler told her.

"Hang on girl. I'll be right back. I'm not leaving you," Callie said, running her hands over the dog's body. They came away sticky with blood.

She pulled off her scarf and bound it around the wound as tightly as possible. She buttoned the coat around the dog, moving her as little as possible. By pulling on the sleeves, she was able to slide the dog across the snow. When she finally reached her truck, she was dripping in perspiration, and her muscles screamed from the exertion. She pulled her emergency pack from behind the seat and found a blanket. After checking the wound area again, she called Morgan.

The two vehicles arrived at nearly the same time. Morgan helped Dr. Tyler gently lift Wicca into the back of the van, where Glenn immediately began pulling supplies from the shelves.

"Unwrap the wound, Callie," he ordered her. "Then just hold her head and talk to her."

Morgan left the two working and went to study the area around the Teepee. The snow was falling faster and soon any tracks would disappear. He had no trouble locating the blood-covered snow where Wicca had fallen. He circled the area, until he located footprints, which he followed to a set of tire tracks. The tracks left Callie's woods and entered the Parker property.

Back at the van, Dr. Tyler stabilized Wicca and told Callie he'd need to take the lab to his office for surgery. She followed his van in her truck with tears streaming down her face and prayers emerging from her stiff lips. Callie helped Dr. Tyler carry her wounded pet into the surgical area still using her coat as a sling. He had called his assistant, who had everything prepared.

Callie was sitting in the outer room when Morgan found her. He wrapped his arms around her, saying nothing, but the contact gave her the additional strength she needed. His calming presence was balm to her frazzled nerves. Eventually, he began asking questions, and she was able to answer with the limited knowledge she had of the event.

Time seemed to drag and Callie was reaching the limit of her patience when Dr. Tyler finally emerged through the door.

"She's got a chance of making it, Callie. I won't lie to you. It'll be touch and go for the next few hours. The bullet went straight through, but it did a lot of damage. Her shoulder is broken, there's some internal damage, and she's lost a lot of blood. We'll be with her through the night. You go home and get some rest. Wash up, eat something. I'll call you if there's any change."

"Can't I stay here with her?" Callie begged.

"It would be better for her if you just go home. It will be a good while before she comes out of the anesthesia. You rest, so you can be her support once she wakes up," Dr. Tyler told her. "Callie, I promise I'll call you if there's anything you can do, or if Wicca wakes up. I promise," he said, taking her hands in his.

"Go home. Rest. You look like you're ready to drop," he added.

"I'll follow you home, Callie," Morgan told her.

"Thank you, Glenn. I know she's safe with you," Callie said gratefully.

"We'll do our very best for her. You know that," Glenn assured her, giving her a hug. "Now, I really do need to go back and check her vitals. I'll keep in touch."

Morgan took her elbow and guided her from the office. She was shaking from head to toe.

"Are you sure you can drive?" he asked.

"Yes, I'll be okay," she murmured.

"You're freezing. Here, take my coat," he said, pulling off his uniform jacket. "Let's go before the snow gets any deeper."

At the farmhouse, Morgan sent Callie in to wash the blood off her hands and arms, and to change her clothes. He heated water for tea and rummaged through her pantry until he found a can of soup to put on the stove.

"Are you going to be okay if I leave you now?" he asked. "I need to go over to the Parkers and see where those tracks stop before the snow covers them."

"Yes, I'm fine. Thanks for all your help," she told him, blinking back tears.

"Eat something," he told her. "I'll come back when my shift ends. Glenn is a good vet, Callie. She's got a chance." He hugged her tightly and left. Callie couldn't eat, but she sipped tea as she prowled around the house. Occasionally, she sat in her grandmother's rocker trying to draw in the strength of the women who had sat in it over the centuries. The house seemed so totally empty.

The snow had ended. A sliver of moon showed in the dark sky whenever there was a break in the clouds. Morgan kept his word and returned to the farmhouse when he was off duty. He insisted on making an omelet, toast, and hot chocolate for them to share in front of the fireplace. When Callie finally drifted off to a troubled sleep, leaning against his shoulder as they sat on the sofa, he shifted his body until they were lying side by side. He held her closely throughout the night, murmuring gentle words of comfort when she stirred.

Callie awakened long before the sun rose. She opened her eyes to find Morgan's eyes watching her.

"Thanks for staying, Morgan," she told him.

"My pleasure, Ma'am," he smiled. "But, now that you're awake, I'd sure like to move a muscle or two. This sofa hasn't grown any since I slept on it last time."

"Oh, I'm sorry," Callie said, jumping to her feet. "You must be stiff as a board."

"Yes, Ma'am, you could say that again," he teased. Callie hurried to the kitchen to start a pot of coffee and see what she could find for Morgan's breakfast. She'd just started mixing pancake batter when her cell phone rang.

"She made it through the night, Callie," Dr. Tyler's reassuring voice said. "She's still in rough shape, and I'd like her to rest as much as possible, but you can come see her around lunch time if you'd like."

"I'll be there. Are you sure she'd doing okay?" Callie asked hesitantly. "Is she in a lot of pain?"

"I'm giving her what I can. She's really weak from the blood loss, but she was in very good condition before the accident, and that helps," he replied.

"She's holding her own," Callie told Morgan, smiling for the first time since she'd heard that awful shot. "Glenn says I can go see her at lunchtime."

"That's good," Morgan replied, flipping the pancakes. "Real good. She's a fine animal."

"Why would anyone shoot her?" Callie asked for the fiftieth time. "I just don't understand it."

"I'll find out, Callie," Morgan promised.

During the next two weeks, Callie spent as much time with Wicca as Dr. Tyler would allow. It was hard to focus on the workshops that were scheduled, but Callie knew she could not cancel them. She'd need that income more than ever now with Wicca's surgery bills. The dog had pins holding her shoulder together and could barely stand, let alone jump or manage stairs. Dr. Tyler had made her a leg-splint and harness system that reduced as much of the pressure on her shoulder as possible and put a cast on her shattered leg to help support it. Recovery would be slow, but the lab was young and would eventually be nearly normal. Dr. Tyler wanted to keep her in his hospital until after Thanksgiving.

Callie was filled with emotion when get-well cards and packages of treats began arriving for Wicca. Many of the cards were hand drawn by the children of customers, who often played with Wicca while their mothers shopped. She pushed herself at the farm stuffing the last of the Christmas inventory into the Cottage, seeding perennials for the next growing season, and propagating rosemary cuttings. At night, when the house seemed so very, very empty without Wicca nearby, Callie wrote late into the night working on her book, writing articles for the newspaper, and outlining new speech topics. When she was too tired to write, she read until the wee hours. The days dragged by with dreary weather and few sales.

Callie ordered two dozen Christmas trees. She decorated one in the Cottage and three more outdoors near the shadehouse. She used natural items that could feed the birds on one tree. Strings of popcorn, suet, and birdseed molded into shapes, pinecones spread with peanut butter, and orange halves filled with suet hung from the branches. She mixed water and flour paste and used it to "glue" sunflower seeds to cardboard shapes. More sunflower seeds were stuck into bright red apples and hung on the tree with silver ribbons.

A second tree was filled with old garden tools that she'd painted in bright colors. She stuffed colorful gloves with old pantyhose, and tied the wrists shut with ribbons. An old straw garden hat decorated with red apples and plastic snowflakes and poinsettias topped the tree. Callie had spent several evenings painting small pieces of slate with garden sayings and hung them on the tree with red yarn. Small terra cotta pots topped with bright ornaments dangled from the branches along with miniature watering cans and laminated colorful seed packets.

The third tree was filled with "normal" holiday lights and colorful ornaments. She asked her customers to "vote" for their favorite tree by putting quarters in jars that sat beside each tree. The money would go to help buy warm mittens, hats, and scarves for needy children.

Inside the Cottage, a small tree sat on a table glistening with golden ribbons and tiny golden spoons. China teacups, dried orange slices, colorful foil-covered tea bags, silver infusers, and small teapots hung on its branches.

A large tree stood in one corner hung with hundreds of silk lavender-filled sachet bags, filigree tussie-mussies, Victorian fans, and odd pieces of costume jewelry that Callie had got at a great price. The dealer had appreciated all the odd containers Callie had purchased from her for the succulents display last summer. And, the dealer had promised to watch for more interesting containers whenever she attended auctions and set them aside for Callie to have first choice come spring. Callie tied the last of her lavender flowers into small bunches with purple ribbon and placed them between the branches. She definitely needed to grow more lavender next year. The farm looked ready for the holidays, but Callie was not sure she was.

It was mid-month when Callie received an internet order for packets of frankincense, myrrh, and some bulk lavender from a small herb group in Illinois. She assembled the order and wrapped it for shipping. As she walked to her truck, she automatically studied the heavy skies. It was another in a string of blustery November days. Callie felt a chill even though she had dressed warmly. After checking her lists, she drove into town to mail the package.

"Anything fragile, perishable, dangerous, or explosive in there?" Bob asked. Bob Spencer lived down the road from the farm but worked at the post office part-time. Callie was surprised to see him there since it was deer hunting season. Everyone in the county knew that Bob lived for two things, the opening week of deer season and Purdue football. His two sons, Ben and Bill, were currently on the Boilermaker defensive line. Bob always felt free to give Callie a rough time knowing that she was an Indiana grad.

"No, just some Christmas herbs, nothing toxic or flammable", Callie replied. "Where's Sharon?"

"She's off in Virginia. Get'n a new grandbaby. She'll be back afore Christmas," Bob replied. "Sure was poor timing. I hate being in here during hunting season. Don't know why that baby couldn't come at Easter or Mother's Day when nothing's in season."

"Speaking of hunting, were you out hunting yesterday morning early?"

"Yer kidding, right? Gun season doesn't open till Friday at midnight. Besides, it's too windy. Deer would be spooky. More 'n likely they'd be bedded down in the thick woods. You'd have to walk 'em up. Me, I like to pick my spot and let them walk up to me!" he chuckled.

"Just wondered. I thought I heard a shot in my woods again."

"Well, it was right breezy. Sound coulda carried from a good distance away. Coulda been someone just sighting in his gun shooting at a target getting ready for opening day," Bob said. "You know, I was real sorry to hear about your dog. Glad to hear she's on the mend, but you gotta realize that most hunters are good people. Abide by the law. Whoever shot your dog is a mangy criminal, not a true hunter. I sure hope they catch him. I can understand why you'd be upset every time you hear shooting though."

"You're right. My heart pounds whenever I hear a shot now," Callie admitted. "Well, good luck Saturday morning."

"Oh, I don't need luck. I got my buck all picked out. I might need some of that sage you grow though. Found a new recipe I want to try for venison summer sausage. Got any extra?"

"Sure. I put in a long row this summer. Just give me a call and pick up as much as you need."

"Will do. That's $4.68. Do you need insurance?"

At the library, Callie returned a stack of books and began pulling the books on her list off the shelves. She found an empty table and took off her coat. The farm was closed today, and she intended to do lots of research, including some on the history of Bradford County. She sat for a moment trying to gather her thoughts. She dreaded the opening of hunting season. There would be guns fired all around the area. At least this time they would be legal, assuming the hunters had valid licenses. She knew she'd never hear another gunshot again without thinking of Wicca and all that blood covering the snow. It took several moments for her to redirect her thoughts and to focus on the task at hand, but finally she became absorbed in the books she had selected. She was so engrossed in her reading that before she realized the time, the lights in the library blinked, signaling it was nearly closing time. She gathered her things, stacked the books she intended to check out, and headed for the counter.

"Hello, Callie," the cheery voice of Ellen greeted her. "Looks like you intend to do a lot of reading," she said, noting the stack of books in Callie's arms.

"Yes, that's the plan," Callie smiled. "What are you reading?"

"A new book on succulents. Your display at the farm inspired me, and I think I'm going to put in a little rock garden in the back corner of my yard. It's too far for me to drag a hose out there to water, so I thought plants that like it dry would be the perfect solution," Ellen chatted.

"Just remember that even though they like it dry, you'll need to keep them watered until they get established," Callie reminded her.

"Oh, I know. I remember your talk earlier in the season," Ellen smiled. "Callie, I was so sorry to hear about Wicca. I just don't understand how anyone could shoot such a beautiful animal. Do you think someone mistook her for a deer?"

"I doubt it. We really don't know what happened, but Deputy Wright and Warren Pease are both investigating," Callie told her.

"They're both good at their jobs," Ellen assured her. "Anyway, I'm glad Dr. Tyler was able to save her. When does she get to come home?"

"Not until after Thanksgiving," Callie answered. "And I really miss her. The house seems so empty."

"Do you have plans for the holiday? You're not going to be all alone are you?" Ellen frowned.

"Oh no, I'll be with my family. This will be the first Thanksgiving without my father, so I need to be with my mother," Callie told her.

"My, my. You do have a lot on your shoulders, dear girl," Ellen smiled, "but you know, God never gives us more than we can handle because He's always there to help out. And if there is ever anything I can do, you just give me a call."

"Thanks, Ellen. I'll remember that," Callie smiled in return. Since that day at the library, Callie had spent her time working, writing, and visiting Wicca. The lab was getting stronger, but she could not walk more than a step or two. Dr. Tyler assured Callie that her dog was doing well. With all the damage that had been done by the bullets, it was a miracle that she was still here at all, let alone attempting to walk.

As often as he could, Dr. Tyler had joined Callie during her visits with Wicca. He explained the physical therapy the dog would need and the medications she was being given. Some days, Callie took cookies or sandwiches, which she and Glenn shared at the office. A few evenings, they went out to an informal dinner after his office closed. One evening she rode with him on an emergency call to deliver a calf. They were becoming good friends. Dr. Tyler's gentle, calm manner with animals reminded her of her father, and she admired his skill.

Occasionally, Deputy Wright stopped at the shop during his patrols, but he had little information to report on the investigation except to say that it was continuing. He encouraged Callie to stay out of the woods, especially with deer hunting season now officially in full swing.

Mike Shipley was extra busy on his delivery route with the holiday shipping season beginning. And, since the shop was closing in another month, there were few deliveries at Joyful Heart. He did report that his mother was planning a big Thanksgiving dinner for all his family from surrounding states. He invited Callie to attend, but she declined.

She could no longer delay thinking about it. Thanksgiving Day was only two days away. Callie dreaded facing all the family at a big celebration. A year ago, she had just cancelled her wedding, spent a disastrous week with her emotions in shreds, and decided to change her entire life. Instead of spending Thanksgiving break with her family, she spent it with a realtor locating her farm. Callie was surprised to realize that so much time had passed. An entire year. It seemed like only a few months ago. She still was raw with hurt in places and still just as confused and uncertain as she had been a year ago in many ways. She was not sure she was ready to face all her happily married cousins, some of whom would have been her bridesmaids. And, she was not sure she could handle the holiday without her father. Her mother would wonder why she hadn't brought Wicca. Callie refused to worry her mother with the news that Wicca had been shot. Looking in the mirror at her sunken eyes ringed with dark circles, Callie knew her mother would worry anyway. Maybe she would just have the "flu". Rocking slowly, Callie pondered her options.

If she didn't go, or didn't let someone know she wasn't coming ahead of time, there would be no pumpkin or cranberry pies for the big feast. Callie was famous for her pies. Daniel had laughingly told everyone that he was marrying Callie because of her fantastic pies.

"I wonder if Mariah bakes pies?" flitted through Callie's mind. For a moment, the usual picture of Mariah flashed through her mind as well. Mariah, with the stylish dark hair, sleek body, sophisticated clothes. Mariah, with perfectly manicured hands and a delicate gold chain around her ankle.

Callie slumped into her grandmother's rocker feeling the beginning of another headache and the effects of too little sleep. "To bake or not to bake. That is the question", she whispered. Normally, at this question, Wicca would have raced to the kitchen. Now there was only silence broken by the creaking of the rocking chair, a soothing rhythm. Callie continued the comforting action of rocking. She let her mind drift to past Thanksgivings and happier times.

The phone rang. A startled Callie nearly tipped herself out of the rocker. Had she slept? She certainly wasn't sleeping much at night, with worrying about finances, missing Wicca, meeting the farm's demanding schedule, trying to write her book, and trying to avoid dreaming. She picked the phone up just before the answering machine responded. Had she not been so surprised, she might have had the good sense to let the machine get it.

"Are the pies all done?"

It was her mother's voice, and Callie knew it was not a real question. Her mother knew no one baked perfect pies two days ahead of the big day, especially cream, custard or pumpkin pies. They'd need refrigeration, and the quality of both the flaky crust and luscious fillings would be compromised.

Callie forced a cheery tone to her voice before she responded. "I'll bake tomorrow afternoon. Is everyone still coming?"

"Yes, everyone. Eve is flying in from Atlanta today, and everyone else will be here on Thursday," her mother reported. The conversation was filled with family news and travel plans.

"Callie, could you stay over a day or two? I really need to talk with you, and it's just too complicated to do it over the phone," her mother said quietly.

"Of course, I can if you need me, Mom," Callie answered. It was unusual for her mother to ask for help for anything.

"Well, come as early as you can. There will be lots to do, and it will be good to see you, sweetheart," her mother said.

Callie breathed a sigh of worry when the call ended. Her mother had never, ever called her "sweetheart" before. After hanging up the phone, Callie stood looking out the window over her snow-covered gardens. Her mind swirled with thoughts. Was her mother ill? Were there legal problems with her father's will? Did her mother have financial problems, too? Callie wasn't sure she could handle another set of worries. "I wish I could just get away," she wished, "somewhere warm and sunny where gardens are still in bloom."

Since she was now committed to taking the pies and staying a few days with her mother, Callie tried to project the positive. It would be good to see her family all together. An entire year had passed, and she had survived without Daniel. She wanted to think she had grown as a person, was more independent and stronger. She and her business had a future. Wicca was healing and would be coming home soon. The farm would be open until Christmas, and then it would be closed. She could get some rest and get caught up.

"Unless I have to go back to the classroom," Callie realized with a jerk. She had asked her accountant to do some analysis, but she had not received a report yet. There was money in her bank account, but she was not sure it was enough to see her through until the farm reopened in March. The accountant was checking on small business loans that Callie might be able to get to purchase supplies and inventory for spring. She was not sure how much work she could get substitute teaching in the local schools. She would still need to attend the gift shows in January to purchase merchandise and she already had several speaking commitments. She was not certain she could keep the plant work done and get the farm ready to reopen if she were teaching. One more worry to add to her shoulders.

Thanksgiving dinner at her parents' farmhouse was just as Callie had imagined. Tables and counters were laden with all the family favorites. Animated conversations filled every room, and the laughter of small children bubbled as they chased one another from room to room.

Of course, her family looked at Callie and assumed she was still pining away for Daniel or her father. Her cheeks were hollow; dark circles hugged her eyes. She was too thin, and too quiet. Her aunts told her she must be working too hard. Her uncles teased her that she should have known what she was getting into. Farm life was taxing, even a little farm like hers. Her cousins eyed her with sympathy and privately told one another that she must be crazy to live alone on a farm working herself to death.

Callie and Eve stayed up late that night after helping clear up all the dishes. The two cousins carried mugs of tea into her father's woodworking shop. The rest of the family had gone home, gone to bed, or were watching endless football games. Callie wandered around the shop handling her father's tools and looking at unfinished projects on his bench.

"It's hard, but it will get better," Eve told her as she settled into a worn wooden chair. "I lost my mother first, you know, and that was really hard. The house just wasn't the same anymore. Made it easier to move to Atlanta, that's for sure."

"Everyone says it gets better and eventually quits hurting, but some things just trigger incredible pain," Callie told her.

"Holidays are hard. But someday, you'll create new memories that crowd out the pain. Just the good times will surface, and the pain will become a gentle sorrow," Eve assured her. "Now, tell me. How is the farm doing? The last time we talked sales weren't good except when you scheduled special events. Is that still the case?"

"Yes, and special events require more advertising. It's hard to track every expense and justify it with income. You really can't know if the advertising you did for this event brought them, or the ads you ran two months ago finally penetrated their brains," Callie said. "Running a small business is a lot harder than I expected. In teaching, there are so many guidelines, and you get so much training and classroom experience before you are responsible for a class. And you have a good support network, lots of lesson plans already exist, and there's a set schedule for every day. It was easier," she sighed.

"Maybe you should go back to teaching," Eve suggested.

"I may have to, but I love my farm. I just wish it were so profitable that there wouldn't be so much pressure on each decision. Should I spend the money on ads or save it for merchandise? Should I spend more time out giving speeches and doing shows to promote the farm or stay at home to make better displays and produce more plants? Should I try to do it all myself or should I hire more employees? And where do I find them? And how do I pay them? It's just so complicated. Some days I love every minute, and some days it just seems like too big a challenge for me," Callie admitted.

"I think you've just had an awful lot to handle this year. Starting a new business right on the heels of losing Daniel was difficult enough. Moving to a new community and trying to organize a new house is rough. Add to that all the trouble you've had with three robberies, the slashed tires, and those dead deer, and you've got to be feeling a lot of emotional strain. And that's without losing your father and financial worries. Don't be so hard on yourself, Callie," Eve counseled.

Callie had not told Eve about Wicca being shot, the soaped threats on her windshield, or the broken windows at Halloween. She stood in silence weighing Eve's words.

"Why don't you stay with me for a few days when you come to the gift shows in January? We could have a good time, visit the Botanical Gardens, and go to my favorite fabric stores. There's a terrific used book store that I love, and we could eat at a great Thai restaurant. I know Heartland doesn't have good Thai food," Eve cajoled, urging her cousin with a smile.

"That's true. And, you know I do love Thai food," Callie said, mulling the idea over in her mind.

"There's a wonderful garden center we could visit, too. Maybe you'd get some good ideas. I know the owner. He's been in business for decades, and maybe he could share some valuable advice," Eve persuaded. "I know you've been trying to find another way to do labels. You could find out what system he uses to print his. That could free up hundreds of hours right there to give you more time to do other things. Like rest. You look a little worn, Cuz."

"I'm feeling a little worn, Eve." Callie sighed. "Let me think about it. You've made some good points, but I'd have to find someone to watch the greenhouse and water the plants. That may not be easy in the dead of winter."

"You're going to have to find someone anyway to be able to come to the gift marts," Eve argued. "Just see if they can come two or three more days. You can sleep in my guest bedroom and take the train into the gift mart to save the cost of a hotel, and we could have evenings together. I'll even take a day off, and you know that means I'm serious."

Callie laughed, "You should have been a lawyer, Cuz. You make a strong argument. Okay, if I can find someone to take care of my plants, I'll stay a couple of extra days."

"Great. I can't wait," Eve said. "Now, let's get back inside. There's a piece of your fabulous pumpkin pie that's calling my name."

Eve left the following morning as well as the last of the out-of-town relatives. Callie helped her mother strip beds and launder sheets and armloads of towels. Finally, the house was back to normal, and the mother and daughter sat alone in the living room.

"I'm worried about you, Callie," her mother began. "You are too thin."

"After all the eating I did yesterday, I doubt that will be a problem for long," Callie said lightly. "I'm worried about you, Mom. Are you sleeping okay? Did you overdo with all the family here?"

"No, you know I love having everyone here, and I didn't do anything I haven't always done," her mother stated. "I was happy that everyone was able to come." She paused and added "Especially you, Callie. I wasn't sure you would come."

"To tell the truth, I wasn't sure either, Mom," she said slowly. "But, I'm glad I did. It wasn't as bad as I thought it might be. Just different."

"Yes, your father was a very quiet man. Rarely said much during family gatherings, but I missed him. Even though the house was filled with people, laughter, and chaos, I missed him," her mother said quietly.

"Of course we did," Callie answered, taking her mother's hand. A few minutes of silence followed, broken when her mother continued.

"Callie, there's something I want to do. You know I couldn't handle the farm by myself. The neighbors and relatives stepped in to do the harvest this year, but I've cash rented the place to your uncles for next year. That will give me plenty of income to live on," her mother explained. "I'm going to sell all the farm equipment, and I want you to have the proceeds of the sale."

"Oh, Mom. You should keep it. Maybe you'll need it later on," Callie argued.

"No, I've talked to my accountant, and he says I'm fine. Your father was a good farmer, and we were able to put some savings by in case the cow died," her mother chuckled. "I'd feel better knowing you had it. For your rainy day. Or to use to get your farm over the hump, if you insist on keeping it. I really wish you'd consider coming back home. You could get a teaching job here, Callie."

"I love my land, Mom," Callie replied slowly. "I'm building a life there. I love working with the plants and building my gardens."

"You could have an herb farm here, too," her mother countered. "There's plenty of land, and you could even convert some of the outbuildings."

"I appreciate the offer, Mom, but I've already got a good start there. My greenhouse is up and running. I've invested a lot of time and energy. I don't think I can leave it now. And, I'm making some good friends. Heartland is a good place to live."

"I guess I understand. I had to try, you know. I miss you, too," her mother said quietly. "But, I want you to take the money from the equipment sale. And, I want you to have your father's new truck. I've never driven it and don't intend to. I have my car. Your father would want you to have it. You can sell the old one you have or keep it. Maybe you can hire someone to take a load of plants in it to farmers' market on Saturdays."

"Mom, are you sure?" Callie asked her.

"Yes, it's decided. I've already done most of the paperwork. The equipment is being sold next week. It's time to move on. And, if you could help me sort through some more of your father's things, I'd appreciate it. I think I'm ready to deal with it now," her mother smiled.

A few days later, Callie spent the drive home, all that evening, and the following day thinking about her options. Her mother's generous offer could make all kinds of things possible. Should she bank the money, invest it, or spend it on a barn? Or, should she build an addition onto the Cottage? Should she invest some in more advertising or save it to publish her book? Should she pay off the mortgage instead? It was a big decision and one that she could not make until she knew the actual figure. Of course, she'd seek advice from her accountant, but ultimately, it would come down to her choices. She made notes and lists of things she'd love to do, like travel, hire another employee, hire someone to do the website, and buy a new sofa. She'd thought about Morgan's comment that her sofa had not "grown any," and smiled to think how pleased he would be to see one that was longer. She might still get the old one reupholstered. It would look great in a display in the barn. The barn. There it was again, that vision of a big barn that could serve as expanded shop space, classroom, workspace, storage, and so much more. Her house might actually look like a home rather than a warehouse if she had a barn. When she came home at night, she might actually relax and recharge her batteries if she weren't surrounded by unfinished work and projects spread all over every room.

She started a list of all the complications of building a barn. Building permits, state officials, insurance, plumbing, contractors, and enough money to actually not only build it but put in fixtures and enough inventory to make it appealing. It would take a mountain of planning and lots of energy to see the project through. It would mean higher property taxes and more insurance costs. Could she handle it and still keep her business going, still do the presentations, and writing required?

She'd need to give that more thought. Callie certainly had lots to think about as November drew to a close.

It was a happy day when Dr. Glenn Tyler released Wicca into Callie's care. The dog had learned to walk in her cast and harness system, although still very slowly and with difficulty on uneven surfaces. She could not walk up steps, so Callie had built several small portable ramps and placed them in locations where Wicca would need to go. However, the lab's spirit seemed to be giddy when she realized that she was going to get to ride in Callie's truck. Dr. Tyler carried her to the front seat, while Callie carried the box of medications and special food Glen had prepared. Wicca needed a special diet to rebuild all her muscles and blood supply, and Callie would be certain she got everything she needed.

Once she was home, Wicca settled in her usual spot on the rug in front of the fireplace and quickly fell asleep. The short journey home had obviously exhausted her. Callie settled in front of her computer determined to accomplish as much as she could while Wicca slept. She had lots of e-mails to answer. More requests for her to speak were coming in as well as requests for garden clubs and other groups to tour her farm next spring. She'd already filled in several dates on her new calendar for the coming year. She finished writing another article for the newspaper and made a list of things that would need to be stored away when the farm closed next month. It didn't seem possible to her that Christmas was only four weeks away even though she'd been making holiday inventory and Christmas displays for weeks already. She sat in her grandmother's rocker and worked, watching Wicca sleep peacefully. Callie felt as if she'd already received the best Christmas gift ever. Her dog was alive and healing well. Her house did not seem empty anymore.

Later, she celebrated Wicca's return by bringing a tree over from the farm and placing it in the living room. She placed new strings of lights and her favorite old-fashioned bubble lights on the branches with a big star on the very top. She didn't have time to dig through her boxes for her ornaments. Besides, they were the ones she and Daniel had purchased together. They would have been married at the start of Christmas break, so they could honeymoon between semesters. The joy she had felt that had instigated the tree decorating was suddenly gone. She went upstairs, pulled several blankets from the linen closet, and grabbed her pillow. Until Wicca could manage the stairs, Callie would be sleeping on the lumpy sofa. Hours later, she still lay awake. Several blankets had somewhat cushioned the sofa, but her heart was still aching.

Sage

There are over 900 members of the sage family! Many people are familiar only with the common gray-leaved cooking sage. However many of the sages are among the most beautiful plants in the herb garden. The bright red flowers of pineapple sage are not only gorgeous, scented, and tasty, but they attract hummingbirds to the garden as well. The hummingbirds also love the velvety deep rose blooms of rosy-leaf sage. The beautiful sky-blue blooms of bog sage are loved by bumblebees. The leaves of purple-leaf sage, tri-color sage and variegated sage are pretty through the first frosts. Sages can be found in all colors and heights.

Many sages have scented leaves, such as honeydew sage, fruity sage, Clevelandii sage, tangerine sage, and grape-scented sage. There are many ornamental sages that are not used for cooking, but are delightful in the landscape such as the cultivars "Blue Bedder" and "Victoria," "Purple Rain," "East Freisland," and "Rose Queen." Some sages are annuals, while others are perennials. Many of the sages are treated as tender perennials in gardens where winters are long and cold. Mexican Bush sage and the Greggii sages are tender here in central Indiana, but worth growing for the hummingbirds. Clary sage, a biennial, has long been used in the garden, and as a flavoring for tobacco. It also has been used in various eye treatments, thus its folk name, "clear eye." Silver sage, another biennial, has fuzzy silver leaves and in its second year produces a tall stalk of silver "bells."

Most of the sages prefer full sun and average to well-drained soil. Common sage and pineapple sage are the two most frequently used in the kitchen. Cooking sage has bumpy gray-green leaves, and is most recognized as an ingredient in stuffings, biscuits, and breads. Common sage also has a long history as a tea ingredient. In olden days, the Chinese were willing to trade one pound of black tea for seven pounds of dried sage. Sage tea is thought to aid digestion and increase longevity. It was also used as a hair coloring to cover gray hair and ground to use as toothpaste. Sage tea refreshes the mouth and strengthens gums. It also has the reputation of contributing to good general health, mental ability, and wisdom. Grow sage for good fortune and success in life!

Chapter 12:

DECEMBER

Unexpectedly, December came in with warm and gentle weather. Then it rained off and on for two days, and then the temperature plunged into the teens. Callie worried about her lavender plants. The stems were fully saturated and then frozen before they had time to dry. She expected several losses. After all, Indiana was not exactly the south of France. She was working on plans for a field of lavender, using some of her father's equipment sale money for stone and groundwork. It should be a good promotion tool and would offer something no other herb farm in the state had. A field of fragrant purple heaven. Lavender was one of her best selling items in all its forms. She'd sold every stem she'd grown in her patches and beds this year, so she was confident in expanding her planting. If she had enough, she could offer it U-Pick, and that would result in a free listing in Indiana's direct market publication. Every bit of free advertising, especially brochures that might reach people out of her immediate area, was a help.

Wicca was moving better each day, and Callie tempted her and coaxed her into walking a bit farther according to Dr. Tyler's instructions with tasty homemade treats. She'd made a bed for Wicca in the Cottage close to the warmth of the woodstove on the days when Callie needed to work at the farm. Lucy and Gloria were wonderful about working extra days when Wicca first came home. And Lucy had stayed with the lab at the house on Sunday while Callie taught the herbal Christmas workshop.

Luckily, the weather changed and turned mild again although it was rainy for the first weekend class. Callie was able to hold it in one end of the greenhouse where the attendees could craft, paint, and work without fear of mess. It had been especially convenient when talking about the herb plants that related to the holiday to be in the greenhouse surrounded by fragrant plants. Gloria had helped since the number of attendees was so large. She was also able to set up an elaborate Christmas tea buffet in the Cottage while Callie taught. Afterwards, sales had been so good that Gloria and Callie were able to incorporate three shop displays into one, which created space for the second workshop to be held in the Cottage the following weekend.

With typical Indiana contrariness, the weather turned frigid again, and working in the cool, damp greenhouse was not an option. The classes had managed to work in the limited space in the Cottage, but only barely. After the final class, Callie put prices on all the finished projects that she'd used for demonstration during the classes and made a new display incorporating many of the herbs of the Nativity.

That evening, Callie penned an article for this week's column on "The Manger Herbs" which included information on growing them and the symbolism of the herbs traditionally believed to have been in the manger when Christ was born. She wrote about thyme, pennyroyal, sweet marjoram, and horehound. The legend of rosemary was included. Then, as an afterthought, she added a recipe for a Christmas potpourri that included frankincense, myrrh, rosemary, lavender, Silver King Artemisia, rose hips, sage for the wise men, red rose petals, golden calendula, and two cups of needles from this year's Christmas tree. She explained that making the potpourri this year and letting it ripen during the coming months would make it even more long-lasting and fragrant for the holiday next year. Maybe she could stimulate a few last minute sales.

The holidays were a mixed blessing for Callie. The holiday workshops had gone well, and sales were good after each one. However, sales during the week were very, very low. By the third week, they had dropped to nothing. Everyone was too busy to drive out into the country. Callie thought they were probably hitting the malls where they could shop in a variety of stores. She made a note to close in mid-December next year. It was very disappointing, but unless she had a huge sale, marking things down until there was little profit and spending a chunk of cash on advertising, it wasn't going to work. Next year, she'd have a holiday open house, sell off the Christmas merchandise, and then close. Unless, she had a barn. The thought just kept floating into her mind and into her plans. With a barn, she'd have room for a much broader range of inventory, and maybe people would come. Maybe....

Dr. Tyler had come for dinner twice this month to check on his patient, he said. Callie loved his company, and Wicca did as well. With the changing weather and then frigid temperatures, his practice was busy with minor injuries and the usual animal viruses and illnesses that accompany poor weather. Callie was able to test some recipes on the willing veterinarian since she did not plan to have her girlfriends come to fold newsletters in December. There would be no newsletter mailed for January since the farm would be closed.

However, Callie's girlfriends decided that they should get together for a Christmas party. This time, Sandy was going to be the hostess. Everyone was meeting at her apartment and bringing their favorite holiday dish. Callie didn't want Wicca to be alone, so Lucy came to the farmhouse to keep her company for the evening.

Sandy's apartment was as cheerful and overflowing with stuff as Callie had suspected it would be. Books were piled in front of overflowing bookshelves, and pillows in every color of the rainbow spilled off the sofa and onto the floor for casual seating. Houseplants, many of which Callie recognized as coming from Joyful Heart, filled the windowsills, and a tray of culinary herbs sat on a corner of the kitchen counter. The apartment's artwork was a crazy mixture of travel posters and excellent paintings. Callie recognized the landscape over the fireplace as LouAnn's work. An assortment of Christmas music wafted through the apartment over the evening. The Mormon Tabernacle Choir singing "O Holy Night" was followed by "Grandma Got Run Over by a Reindeer". Callie gave her hostess a big hug. She just loved the woman's creative style and cheerful attitude.

"When you see as much bad as I do, you have to come home to something a little crazy and fun," was Sandy's response. "Being a reporter is not generally a happy task."

Dinner was served on a mismatched set of dishes, which the women carried into the living room. They sat on the floor or the mismatched chairs, exchanging gossip and recipes. They sipped eggnog and nibbled an array of Christmas goodies. White elephant gifts were exchanged. The group had drawn names at their last get-together. LouAnn gave Callie a bag of rocks, which Callie exclaimed were perfect. She'd use them to top fairy gardens and maybe paint the rounded ones into "pet" animals. Sandy gave Cecilia an old briefcase that she'd covered in decoupage flowers and filled with tea bags. Cecilia nearly always had a mug of tea at her side at work. Callie gave Sandy a car trash bin with matching portable file that she'd made out of old leather handbags so they could hang on the door knobs or be carried easily. Cecilia gave LouAnn a canvas stool for which her husband had made an attachment to hold a lightweight umbrella. It would be perfect for painting outdoors. Everyone groaned that they had eaten too much, but that it had been a joyous way to celebrate the holidays.

When Callie returned home, she was surprised to see her house nearly dark. Only one small lamp burned in the living room she noted as she walked up to her back door. She unlocked the door and called Lucy's name as she entered the kitchen.

"I'm here," an unusually subdued and quiet voice answered.

Callie walked into the living room pulling her coat and scarf off as she moved through the room. Wicca thumped her tail against the floor in greeting but didn't attempt to rise. Callie sat on the floor by her dog's side stroking her ears. Then she looked at Lucy, noticing her tear-stained face.

"Why, Lucy, whatever is wrong?" Callie rose to go sit beside the teenager.

"I've been on the phone with Time," she said quietly, as large tears again began rolling down her cheeks. "He's decided he's not going to college."

"And you think he should go," Callie stated solemnly.

"Of course. Time is bright, and we were going to go to the same college. Now he says he's not going at all. What kind of future will he have if he doesn't go to college?" she began, crying harder.

"Well, maybe he'll go to a school that specializes in photography," Callie suggested. "That is what he likes to do best, isn't it?"

"Well, yes, he likes photography, but he says he's not going to go to school of any kind," she sobbed. "How can we keep seeing each other if I'm off at college, and he stays here in Heartland?"

"Things more difficult than that have been overcome," Callie assured her. "Here, dry your eyes, and let's make some hot chocolate. Do you need to call your parents and tell them you're running late or would you rather go on home? You know you're welcome to stay here, if you'd like."

"Hot chocolate sounds good. I'd really like to stay if that's okay. My parents will just ask me a bunch of questions, and I don't feel like talking," Lucy said dramatically.

Callie smiled to herself as she went into the kitchen to start the hot chocolate. "Would you pull the bag of marshmallows out of the pantry, Lucy? Then you need to call your folks."

Lucy rummaged in the pantry for the marshmallows, pulled a box of graham crackers off the shelf, and put them on the counter.

"I've got a chocolate bar in my bag," she giggled. "We might as well make Smores since the fire has burned down to such nice coals."

"Sounds great. Call your mother," Callie ordered.

While Lucy told her mother she was staying at Callie's for the night, Callie put their mugs and Smore ingredients on a tray. By the time Lucy had returned, she had located her fondue forks and was threading marshmallows onto the ends.

"Mom says the roads are starting to get a little icy, so it's a good thing I'm staying. My little car just skids right over the surface. I probably need to put some extra weight in the back," Lucy stated.

"The spare room is all made up, and there are new toothbrushes in the top drawer in the bathroom. Just make your self at home," Callie told the young girl.

Lucy was arranging the chocolate onto crackers and sipping her chocolate.

"I like mine to catch fire," she said nodding to the marshmallows Callie was holding over the coals.

"That's gross," Callie laughed. "Here, cook your own!" she teased.

The two women licked their fingers savoring the last of the Smores. Lucy had been quiet, but broke the silence as she placed her empty mug on the tray.

"I just don't understand what's come over Time," she said. "He's so moody and grumpy all the time."

"Lots of athletes go through an emotional slump when their season ends. Maybe Time just feels restless and out of sorts now that football is over," Callie reasoned. "Or, maybe he's suddenly apprehensive about leaving the small town he's always known and going off to a big university. Lots of kids get cold feet when the time comes to start making commitments."

"I know he was really disappointed that he didn't get any offers to go on a football scholarship. I told him if he got one to a smaller college, I'd switch and go there, too," Lucy confided.

"But I thought you were all set to go to Indiana to your dad's alma mater," Callie said. "It's a great school. Beautiful campus, great variety of majors, fantastic library. I loved it there."

"I know," Lucy sighed, "but being with Time is more important to me than all those things."

"You're awfully young to make that decision," Callie commented. "And you haven't dated Time for very long."

"Since May!" Lucy countered. "That's practically forever. And I know he's the man for me. I just know it. I thought you'd understand."

"Oh, I do, Lucy. I really, really do," Callie said emphatically, putting her arm around the girl's shoulders. A few moments passed in silence. Tears began flowing down Lucy's cheeks again.

"Well, maybe Time doesn't think he can afford to go to college without a football scholarship," Callie offered. "I don't think being a conservation officer is a real high-paying job, and maybe his father can't afford to pay for him to go."

"That's true," Lucy said softly. "I hadn't thought of that. I know his dad had a lot of medical bills when Time's mother died. Maybe Time just didn't want to tell me he doesn't have the money to go."

"There are lots of college loans available, though. If Time really wants to go, he and his father should look into it," Callie advised. "There are work-study jobs, and Time might be able to handle one of those if he is a good student."

"You're right, Callie, I shouldn't let him give up, if money is the problem. We might still be able to go to college together after all," she said brightly. "Thanks, Callie. I feel a lot better now."

"I'm glad, Lucy. Now, it's pretty late. Why don't you go on up? I'll help Wicca go outside, and then I'll be right up, too."

Lucy gave Callie a big hug and bounded up the stairs. Callie could see that she was texting a message as she went. Outside, tiny icy balls were falling from the sky forming a coating on the sidewalk. Wicca went gingerly into the darkness while Callie stood under the motion light, moving occasionally so it would continue to burn. When Wicca returned to the door, Callie helped her inside and rubbed her coat with a towel to dry it. She filled the dog's water bowl and banked the fire in the fireplace. Then she refilled her hot chocolate mug and sat in her old rocking chair thinking of her first love, Daniel, and how sure she had been that he was the man of her future.

"Oh, yes, Lucy, I understand. I truly understand," Callie thought.

The sun came out the following morning, and the temperature rose to melt the thin coating of ice. After a hearty breakfast, in which Callie introduced Lucy to grits covered in maple syrup, the girl returned home. She had been bubbly and chatty, so Callie assumed that Time had responded to Lucy's text message in a positive manner.

Callie took advantage of the sunshine to work in the greenhouse. Several of the violas and pansies she'd seeded in November needed to be potted into four-packs, and it was a good day to do it. She loaded her favorite CD of famous arias into the player and spent the entire morning transplanting. No customers came that day, so she spent the afternoon in the greenhouse with her laptop working on her book. It was warm, sunny, and entirely pleasant being surrounded by green plants while the outdoors was muddy and brown. She had just closed down the computer and was preparing to fill the bird feeders at the farm before she locked up when Morgan's patrol car pulled into the parking lot.

She finished filling the first feeder, placed the large bag of seed on one of her green wagons, and replaced the feeder's lid while Morgan approached.

"Here, let me help you with that," he said, lifting the heavy seed bag without effort as Callie pulled off the second lid.

"Thanks, the birds really emptied the feeders fast this week," Callie observed. Once it was filled, Morgan rolled the sack closed and placed it on the wagon. "I'll pull it. Where do you want it to go?" he asked.

"I keep it in that garbage can in the garage," she indicated, pointing to the open door. Together, they walked to the garage where the sack was placed inside the can. Callie put the lid on tightly, and Morgan pulled the heavy doors closed and locked the padlock, handing her the key.

"It's nice to see you again, Morgan. I've been going to call to see if you've made any progress on Wicca's case," Callie ventured.

"Still working on it. Can't really talk about it yet, Ma'am," he said.

"You know, when you call me 'Ma'am,' I feel so old," Callie scolded. "You don't have to be so polite, Deputy."

"Way I was raised, Ma'am," he smiled. "But, you're not old."

"Thanks," she said dryly.

"How's Wicca doing? I didn't see her outside when I drove up," he stated.

"I left her sleeping in the greenhouse where it was warmer," Callie told him. "I'm sure she's ready to come out. Probably heard your car and is dying to see you."

They walked over to the greenhouse where, indeed, the lab was scratching at the door with her good foot and whining pitifully.

"Come on out and say 'hello'," Callie told her dog. Wicca hobbled up to the deputy, who knelt to pet her.

"She's moving pretty well. When does the cast come off?"

"I'm not sure. Dr. Tyler wants to see her next week to make sure everything is healing okay," Callie told him. "She cries if she tries to climb a step, so I know it still hurts, but she's very brave."

"She's a lucky dog," Morgan said, rubbing her ears.

"Let's go to the Cottage," Callie suggested. She noticed that Morgan walked slowly, so Wicca could keep up.

"Nice ramp," Morgan said, motioning to the ramp Callie had built to one side of the step for Wicca's use.

"I'm trying to make it as easy on her as I can. She's been through so much. I don't want her to tear a muscle or pull one of those pins loose," Callie explained, entering the Cottage. The phone began ringing, and Callie pulled it to her ear.

"Joyful Heart Herbs," she said brightly.

"Hey, Callie. It's Mike," came the familiar voice. "I just finished my last drop, so I'm headed toward Muncie. Thought I'd call and see if I could pick up some Chinese in town and come by and see you and Wicca on my way home. It's mother's bridge night, so I'm all on my own unless you'll rescue me from solitude."

"Oh, Mike," Callie said, looking at Morgan. "I'm still at the farm." If she'd hoped for some clue of Morgan's intent before she answered, his blank expression told her nothing.

"It'll be another hour before I can get there, so you don't have to hurry," Mike offered. "How does sweet and sour pork sound? Or maybe you'd prefer chicken cashew? Shrimp spring rolls? You name it, Sweetheart, and it's yours," he laughed, doing his best Humphrey Bogart impression.

Morgan had turned his attention to the lab, so Callie could not see his face. She sighed in frustration. If he'd had any plans for the evening, he hadn't mentioned anything. She'd paused, assuming he'd shake his head or offer an alternative, but he was ignoring her. She hated to ask him outright, but she hated to risk hurting his feelings.

"Just a second Mike, someone's here. Can I call you back?" she said.

"Sure. I have my cell on, but make it quick as you can. I'll head to the restaurant as soon as I get my car," he told her.

"I'll be quick as I can," she promised, hanging up the phone. She stood in silence until Morgan finally stood up.

"Sounds like I should be going," he stated flatly.

"Not necessarily. Did you have any special reason for stopping tonight?" she asked.

"Just checking on you. I'm still on patrol," he said. "Thought maybe we could go out to dinner sometime. It's the holidays."

"I'd love to go out with you. Or, we could cook. We're pretty good at that," she laughed.

"Actually, I was thinking of the law enforcement Christmas dinner," he said bluntly. "It's this Thursday evening. Out at the Country Club. You'd have to wear a dress."

Callie laughed, "I have a dress. Is there anything else I need to know?"

"I'll pick you up at six-thirty, Ma'am," he said, as he walked out the door, closing it behind him.

"Yes, sir," Callie said quietly, as she saluted his retreating back. She paused for a moment glowering at his retreating tail lights, and then dialed the phone to request chicken cashew. "Men!" she sputtered as she waited for Mike to answer.

Callie lit the logs in the fireplace, put on a kettle, and filled a teapot with green tea leaves. She put on a pale apricot sweater and a spritz of her newest perfume creation and brushed out her hair. Wicca was fed and soundly asleep in front of the fire by the time Mike arrived.

"It smells heavenly," Callie sniffed appreciatively. "This was a great idea, Mike."

He leaned over and gave her cheek a quick kiss. "Glad you could rescue me from a night of loneliness. I got fried rice and extra egg rolls. Thought you sounded weak from hunger on the phone," he laughed.

"I'm about to perish," she laughed in return. He pulled her close and kissed her fully.

"MMMmmm, you smell better than the food," he said, nuzzling her neck.

"My newest creation. I'm thinking of offering a workshop on making perfumes next season, so I've been experimenting," she giggled.

"Well, this one is a keeper," he said, sniffing her ear. "A little sweet, mysterious, definitely sexy. What's in it? What are you going to call it?"

"Oh, I haven't even thought about a name. It's a blend of jasmine, a bit of patchouli, and a little musk with a tiny bit of tangerine to brighten it. A little this and a little that thrown in for balance," she said.

"Well, you should give it a great name and sell it," he challenged her.

"Yes, in my spare time," she laughed. "I'm starving, remember? Let's eat while it's still hot." They took the food into the living room and ate in front of the fireplace.

When the meal was finished, they sipped cups of green tea and opened their fortune cookies. Callie crumpled hers into her hand and tossed it into the fireplace as soon as she'd read it.

"Hey, no fair," Mike said. "We're supposed to share what it says."

"Mine said my luck was about to change," Callie lied smoothly. "And, since my luck has actually been pretty good lately," she said knocking her knuckles on the wood of the coffee table, "that wasn't exactly what I wanted to hear."

"Well, mine says 'make new friends, but neglect not the old'" Mike said disappointment tingeing his voice. "Pretty tame stuff."

"But, good advice," Callie said. "One can never have too many friends."

"That's true, but I was hoping it'd say I would win the lottery, or at least win the heart of a fair maiden," he said in mock-sadness.

"So, winning the lottery is more important than winning the maiden," she teased.

"Well, probably if I won the lottery big-time, winning the maiden would be a cinch," he laughed.

"Not unless your maiden was pretty shallow. Money isn't everything, you know," she said seriously.

"This from someone pining away because she can't afford to build a barn," he challenged lightly.

"I'm not pining," she countered.

"Oh, so why does the word 'barn' keep coming up in every other sentence?" he asked.

"It does not."

"Does, too!"

"Does not!"

"Does, too!" They both burst into laughter.

"I'm sorry. I didn't realize my conversation was becoming so one-dimensional," she apologized.

"That's okay. I understand that it's an important decision. If I won the lottery, you know I'd build a barn for you in a New York minute," he said solemnly.

"Well, then I'll just have to hope you get that winning ticket. How many do you buy a week?" she asked.

He stared at her a moment and then hung his head. "Actually, I don't buy any. Always think I will, but then I think of the odds and decide I'd be better off keeping those dollars in my pocket."

Callie began to laugh again. "Well, then I guess I won't need to call my contractor right away, will I?"

"Personally, I hope you never call that contractor again," Mike said sullenly. Callie sat up stiffly and began clearing the cups and saucers. Her hand trembled a bit, and she could feel annoyance rising.

"Now, Callie. Don't get your hackles up," he began.

"My hackles?" Callie said, using her 'teacher discipline' voice.

"Whoa, let's just drop it, shall we?" he said, raising both hands. "We were having such a good time. Let's talk about something else entirely." He rose to place another log on the fire.

"Callie, do you have plans for Christmas?" he asked. "I'd like for you to come have dinner with mother and the rest of my family."

Callie paused as she was putting items on the tray and folded her hands in her lap. "I'm sure I'll be spending the holiday with my mother. This will be the first Christmas without my father. Thanksgiving was very difficult for her, and I doubt Christmas will be any easier."

"Of course. I assumed you'd be there part of the time. How about Christmas Eve? There's always a nice concert and a live Nativity at one of the churches in town," he suggested.

"I'll probably go over to mother's a few days in advance to help her with the preparations. So many of the cousins and their families are coming in from out of town, several from out of state. Many of them will be stopping in to visit and exchange gifts. Of course the big dinner will be at Aunt Louise's since mother had Thanksgiving. Our family rotates the big dinners among all the local relatives," Callie explained. "I may stay a few days afterwards, too. Depends on how Mom is doing and the weather."

"So, that sounds like a 'No'," he said sadly. "I was hoping we could spend some time together over the holiday. I get an extra day off. We could go ice skating."

"Ice skating? I haven't been ice skating in years," Callie told him with a smile. "I'd probably fall down, trip you, and we'd both end up with broken legs. Then wouldn't Wicca and I be a pair, both in casts?"

"Won't she get her cast off soon?" he asked, walking over to pet Wicca's head. The dog was sleeping right next to Callie's feet but woke when Mike's hand touched her.

She yawned and laid her head on the top of Mike's shoe.

"Not until Dr. Tyler thinks she's well-healed. There was a lot of bone damage, you know, and he doesn't want anything to break again," Callie said, looking at her watch. "I should take her outside. It's getting late, and tomorrow is a work day for both of us. Besides, your mother should be finished playing bridge by now. Does she know where you are?"

"Not exactly. I just told her I was having dinner with friends. You and Wicca qualify," he said without looking at her face.

"Mike, is your mother comfortable with your spending time with me?" Callie asked directly.

"Oh, you know mothers. They are cautious about any girl their boy dates," he said, picking up the tray. "My mother is typical. She's never really cared for any girl I showed interest in. Of course, I haven't pushed the issue. Never found anyone I wanted enough to worry about it. And, besides, if I'm happy, my mother will be happy, too," he ended confidently.

"Yes, I think all mothers want their children to be happy," Callie agreed slowly, "but I also think most mothers think they know best, including what or who will be best for their child as well."

"You're probably right," he conceded. "Shall we wash these now?" he said, placing the dishes into the sink.

"No, it's late. I'll do them with the breakfast dishes in the morning," Callie told him, reaching for his coat. "You'd better go home. The roads could be slippery. It feels and looks like more snow."

"You and your weather lore. What? Is there a ring around the moon or something?" he teased.

"No, a ring around the moon means rain soon," she quoted. "I think it's a little too cold for rain."

After Mike had departed, Callie did wash up the dishes. She was restless and agitated. She felt Mike had sidestepped her questions and felt she knew what Alma Shipley's real feelings were. She put the Chinese food cartons into a bag and carried them outdoors to the garbage can. Somehow, the aroma was now disturbing. She stood in the darkness by the garage, listening to the traffic over on the highway. It was one of those nights when the sounds carried for miles and miles.

She wrapped her arms around her chest and stared at the moon, barely peeking from behind a bank of black clouds. There was definitely a front moving in. Things were changing.

Her mother called the following morning to discuss when Callie would arrive for Christmas. The equipment was sold, the accountant had run the numbers, and her mother had a check waiting. She didn't want to send such a large amount through the mail, and besides, Callie needed to come get her father's new truck. Callie suspected that her mother was also lonely, so she made plans to go north as soon as the farm closed on Saturday night. It was hard to believe that after Saturday the farm would be closed to customers until March. The season had gone so very quickly. Callie didn't have much time to think about it since she had to get Wicca over to see Dr. Tyler yet that morning. Gloria would watch the shop for a few hours until Callie returned, and then she was off to help set up the Christmas party for the Heartland Banner employees. Callie had permission to bring Wicca to the party, along with her big round travel bed so the dog could rest in Mac's office. Callie suspected that the bed would be a waste of time since Wicca would rather be the center of attention.

Callie helped Wicca up the ramp she'd made from an old wooden door into the front seat of the truck. It was only a short drive but Callie could tell that the movement of the truck made Wicca's shoulder uncomfortable. Dr. Tyler came out to help her get out of the truck, moving the door Callie had stuck into the back of the truck into position. He studied the dog's movement as she went down the ramp, and then carefully lifted her and carried her up his stairs. Wicca followed him willingly into the examining room. They chatted as he examined the dog, running his fingers over the parts of the shoulder that were not in the cast. He checked the harness to be sure it fitted properly and was not rubbing into her flesh.

"I'd really like to keep her overnight, Callie. She just doesn't seem as solid as I'd expect. I'd like to take another set of X-rays, but I just don't have time to do it right now. I got a call just before you came in to go out to the stable west of town. Have a mare that's down, so I really need to leave now," he stated.

"Well, I'll miss her, but I want you to do whatever you think is best," Callie answered. "Shall I bring her food?"

"No, I have plenty here. I can bring her home in the morning if that's okay," he said. "My office is closed, but I have some calls to make around town mid-morning."

"That will be fine. Come for coffee, and I'll bake my grandmother's coffeecake," she offered.

"Can't pass that up. We'll see you about nine-thirty?" he said, rubbing the lab's head.

"I'll be watching for you," she promised, giving her dog a good-bye hug. She hurried back to the farm where a pair of ladies were making purchases from the sachet-decorated tree. Gloria passed her a couple of notes, a warning look, and made a hasty departure. Callie puzzled over the look as she hung up her coat. She poured herself a mug of hot spiced cider to help warm her hands before she went to help her customers. She was surprised when Alma Shipley turned around, a basket filled with sachets in her hand.

"Hello, Mrs. Shipley. How nice to see you again," she said sweetly. "Are you finding the colors you prefer? I can get a stool and reach the ones at the top if you need a certain shade."

"Well, I'd prefer the ones in red and purple. I'd like to give them to my Red Hat sisters at our party Friday night," she stated. Callie noted there was not much warmth in her tone.

Callie retreated behind the counter where a small stool was stored. While she was there, she could hear the women whispering.

"Do you want the light purple and the dark purple ones?" she asked, placing the stool next to the tree.

"Just the dark purple ones. Lavender is for members under fifty, and we don't have any in that category," she stated firmly. "Give me ten red and ten purple."

"I'm not sure we have that many left. They have been very popular, and it's the very last of my lavender crop," Callie said, stretching to grasp a red one near the top. "I'm planning to grow more next year."

"Oh, do you still plan to be here running the farm next year?" Alma's as yet-un-introduced friend asked.

"Of course. Bradford County is my home now. I've already started growing most of the plants for next season. We'll have a lovely selection of new perennials, and we're expanding into flowering shrubs," Callie informed her. "I just love the fragrance of lilacs, don't you?"

The two women just stood for a moment blinking. Finally, the friend said, "Oh, well, we'd heard that you are going to the county Law Enforcement Christmas Party at the country club Thursday night with Deputy Wright."

"And?" Callie lingered on the word. She could tell the lady was dying to tell her more.

"And, he was seen coming out of the jewelry store yesterday," the lady continued breathlessly.

"And, everyone knows that he has applied for a position with the state police," Alma broke in, "so he'll be moving from the area." Alma squinted her eyes watching for Callie's reaction.

Callie busied herself gathering more of the required sachets from the tree while she composed her face. Morgan had not said a word about applying for a new position. In fact, she'd thought he was very content in his present job. By the time she stepped off the stool, she had a relaxed smile fixed on her face.

"Well, I think I do have ten of each color after all if we include those in your basket. Shall we count them?" she asked, turning to face the ladies and reaching for the basket. She walked to the counter where she divided the two colors into piles of ten each. "Yes, perfect. Will there be anything else, Mrs. Shipley?" The two women stood woodenly by the tree looking at one another. Finally, Mrs. Shipley moved toward the counter.

"I think that's everything," she said.

"Oh, and I want to thank you for the invitation for Christmas dinner. That was very sweet of you to invite me. Unfortunately, I'll be with my mother for a few days over the holiday, but Mike and I would love to have dinner with you before the New Year," she added with another smile, totaling the purchase.

Mrs. Shipley stood speechless until her friend poked her in the ribs with an elbow. Eventually, she recovered and pulled money from her purse.

Callie pushed another button on the cash register, which rang up a new, lower total.

"I'm giving you the family discount," she said sweetly, stressing the word 'family', and watching as horror flashed through Mrs. Shipley's and her friend's eyes. Callie wrapped the sachets in tissue paper and placed them in a box.

Mrs. Shipley coughed twice before she could manage a reply, "That's very nice of you, Callie, but it's certainly not necessary."

"Oh, it's my pleasure," Callie assured her, placing the box in the woman's hands and moving to open the door. "I hope I'll see you both on opening day next spring or perhaps sooner. Merry Christmas!"

Callie watched the two ladies in animated conversation as they hurried to their car. She wished she could hear what they were saying, and she wondered if Mike would hear any of what happened today. She shouldn't have jerked their chains, but she just hadn't been able to help herself.

She picked up her mug, which was now cold, and moved closer to the woodstove. Was Morgan really moving away? The possibility came as a total surprise, and Callie was equally surprised by how much the thought hurt. It was his kiss that sent shocks of heat through her body, his face that filled her mind whenever she heard the Marine anthem or saw a law enforcement vehicle, and his presence that had helped push Daniel from being foremost in her thoughts. Once again, she felt betrayed.

"Oh stop it, Callie," she told herself. "It's not as if you were engaged or anything. Morgan doesn't have to clear his life plans with you." But, she found herself feeling sad the rest of the day.

And, now that she was disturbed, her mind just wouldn't quit. Who had put "pot" plants in her greenhouse? Who had written threats and obscenities on the truck's windows? Who had slashed that first tire? Who left parcels in her Teepee, and why? And who had shot Wicca? There were just too many questions. But the one that kept floating to the surface was, "Is Morgan really leaving?"

There were a few more customers at the shop over the afternoon to distract Callie from her worries. She'd need to bake tonight as they'd consumed the last of the complimentary refreshments. Or, maybe she could start early in the morning. After all, she'd promised Dr. Tyler her grandmother's coffeecake for breakfast, so the oven would already be going. Suddenly, she remembered the Heartland Banner's

Christmas party was tonight. It appeared she'd be baking very early in the morning.

Lucy was disappointed that Wicca had not been able to come to the party, but she soon recovered when Time came in the door. Tonight her hair was Christmas red, and blinking ornaments hung from her ears. She had on a skin-fitting green sweater that didn't come close to reaching the low-slung green stretch pants she wore, displaying a new tattoo of a tiny clock near her navel. Callie suspected the clock signified Time, and not old Father Time. Knee-high boots completed her outfit. Gloria was a total contrast in a designer suit and perfectly upswept hairdo. Mac was resplendent in a dark suit. Everyone teased him about the lack of his normally ever-present pocket protector. Sandy wore a tent-like creation in rippled silk over black slacks, which looked absolutely stunning. Callie felt very dull standing beside her, dressed in a beige sweater and brown slacks. She hadn't felt very festive when she'd selected her outfit. The buffet was outstanding since it had been catered by Dinah's Diner. Mac made a big production of cutting the Yule Log, complete with meringue mushrooms. Callie made a mental note to ask Dinah if she would make the mushrooms next year for fairy days. They would be perfect to serve at a fairy tea party. Fairies love mushrooms.

Halfway through the evening, several of the newspaper employees brought out musical instruments and started playing a mixture of country and Christmas tunes. Mac and Gloria waltzed out onto the floor when they struck the first notes of "I'll Have a Blue Christmas Without You". They were soon followed by a group of couples, including Lucy and Time. Sandy and Callie sat at a table, sipping punch and watching.

"Looks like it's just you and me, babe," Sandy said to Callie, using the lowest pitch she could manage.

"Hey, girlfriend, we could do worse," Callie smiled in response. "Sometimes a girl friend is a heck of a lot easier than a boy friend."

"I wouldn't know," Sandy grumbled, pulling a sad face. "Tell me all about it, just in case I ever meet a willing guy."

Callie laughed and looked at Sandy seriously. "Have you heard any rumors about Morgan Wright leaving the force?"

Sandy turned her punch cup in her fingers, "A few words here and there. Nothing conclusive." She paused and looked at Callie. "Has he said anything to you?"

"Not yet. Mike Shipley's mother told me today," Callie reported.

"Now that's a reliable source," Sandy said sarcastically.

"I know. I'm ashamed to say I was a little catty with her today," Callie admitted.

"I'm stunned, Callie. How could you?" Sandy replied in mock horror.

"It's true. I was," Callie said. "I guess the Devil made me do it." They both burst into laughter, causing several people on the dance floor to turn their way.

By the time the evening had ended, Callie had made arrangements with Gloria to open the farm the following morning, so she could wait for Dr. Tyler. She'd bake for the farm first, so the refreshments would be ready before Gloria arrived.

Dawn had not even thought about making an appearance before Callie was up baking an herb-laden stollen, which she decorated with fresh mint leaves, candied cherries and white frosting as soon as it was cool. While the coffeecake baked, she made a batch of raspberry tea and took the food to the Cottage a little before nine o'clock. Then she hurried back to the house to tidy the kitchen and her hair before Dr. Tyler brought Wicca home.

She heard Gilda pull into her driveway and hurried to greet them. Dr. Tyler lifted Wicca from the van, and she wobbled over to Callie as quickly as she could manage. Callie knelt to greet her with lots of crooning and hugs.

"You're right on time," she said brightly. "So, Doc, what's the verdict? Is she healing properly? Is she going to be okay?"

"The X-rays show she's healing, but more slowly than I expected. The bone hasn't grown solid around the pins yet. She still needs to take it easy. I want to make some changes in her diet and add an antibiotic. There's a little infection beginning that worries me a bit, but the drug should take care of it. Try to keep her quiet and encourage her to drink lots of water," he said, watching the dog maneuver up the ramp into the house.

Wicca slowly went over to her favorite rug in front of the fireplace and circled stiffly before she finally lay down. Callie went to the sink to wash her hands and began pouring hot chocolate into mugs.

"So, where's this famous coffeecake?" Glenn said, looking around the room.

"Still in the oven, but it should be out in three minutes," she replied, checking the timer.

"Do you have lots of plans for the holidays?" he asked.

"Yes, assuming it's okay for Wicca to travel. I'd like to go to my mother's. It will be hard on her this year," Callie said quietly.

"I think she can go as long as she has a ramp. I still don't want her to try any stairs. The incline of a ramp is hard enough on that shoulder. She's doing pretty well on three legs, though. You'll need to keep an eye on her. If you suspect a fever, check her temperature. If it's above normal, call me. Immediately. Don't hesitate," he instructed.

"Are you going away for the holiday?" she asked.

"Just over to the family farm. I'll give you a prescription for a stronger antibiotic, just in case. If her temperature rises at all, go have it filled wherever you are but still call me," he told her.

The timer rang, so Callie pulled the steaming coffeecake from the oven. "We'll need to let this cool a little. We can start with juice and a quiche," she said, cutting the golden circle of cheese-topped eggs into triangles and placing them onto plates.

They spent the next hour talking about Christmas memories of their childhood and their all-time favorite gifts. The ringing of the phone interrupted their conversation. Callie hurried to the studio to answer. It was Gloria with a question from a customer that she couldn't answer.

"I'm sorry. I have to go to the farm," Callie apologized.

"If you won't be long, I'll stay here with Wicca," he said," then she won't try to come along. I'd like her to rest a while longer."

"That's fine. Have more coffeecake, or make coffee, whatever you'd like. You know where the television is if you get bored," she told him as she donned her coat and gloves.   Over at the Cottage, she met two ladies who were interested in having their group come for a presentation and tour. They wanted to discuss topics, what the farm could offer, if they could have a discount on plants, and dates. It took much longer than Callie had hoped, but she couldn't hurry them. A group tour could result in good sales at the farm.

She returned to the house nearly an hour later and found Dr. Tyler sound asleep on her lumpy sofa. His legs extended beyond the end, just as Morgan's did. She stood and watched him sleep for a moment. Wicca had moved over to sleep on the floor beside him, and his hand was lying on her neck. When the dog raised her head to acknowledge Callie's presence, Glenn's eyes opened.

"Wow, I must have been more tired than I thought," he apologized.

"And I was gone much longer than I expected. I'm sorry, but maybe you needed a nice, long nap. Dr. Tyler, I think you've been working way too hard," she said in mock severity.

"And I think that's the pot calling the kettle black," he chuckled as he sat up, rubbing his back. "And you're still sleeping on this thing every night?"

"Yes, until Wicca can do the stairs," she laughed.

"I think Santa should bring you a new sofa," he proclaimed. "This one's too short."

Callie started to reply that she'd had that complaint before but thought better of it. "I don't think it would fit on his sleigh," she laughed instead.

They talked and watched the birds feeding outside her windows.

"What do you have planned the rest of the day?" he said, pulling her hand so she moved into his arms.

"Well, I have to go back to work. Gloria needs to leave at noon. They are heading out to visit her family in Virginia tomorrow, and she still has packing to do," she explained.

"How about this evening? We could watch old Christmas movies," he suggested.

"Oh, I'm sorry, I have plans for this evening," she said sadly. "We could do it tomorrow night. Why don't you come here, so I don't have to leave Wicca alone? You'll have to bring the movies though. I don't have any."

"So, I have to spend my day off by myself?" he pouted teasingly.

"Only half a day because the morning is almost over," she pointed out, leading him toward the door.

"What's your favorite Christmas movie?" he asked.

"Oh, that's a tough one. 'White Christmas?' Maybe 'The Grinch,'" she pondered. "'It's a Wonderful Life' is a classic, but 'Christmas Story' is funnier."

"I'll bring them all," he laughed, "and the wine. Anything else?"

"A Christmas goose?" she teased.

"I don't think so," he said. "How about Christmas pizza?"

"I don't think so," she laughed. "Just come. I'll fix something." He gave her a quick kiss, as she walked him to the door. She stood waving as Gilda complainingly backed onto the road.

Gloria left, carrying gifts for both her and Lucy that Callie had made for them. The rest of the afternoon was slow. Wicca napped by the woodstove, and Callie mentally tried to figure how much of the Christmas inventory could be converted into other displays next year. She also started diagramming a new floor plan for the shop next spring. It was hard to believe she'd be going back to Atlanta in less than three weeks. She glanced at her watch, noting it was only twenty minutes until closing time. She wanted to leave right on the dot, so she could be ready for Morgan to pick her up at six-thirty.

Of course, since that was the case, a customer came in a moment later. It was a lady from the garden club, looking for last minute gifts for some relatives she hadn't known were coming for the weekend. She debated and debated over her purchases, insisting on comparing every item in the shop, or so it appeared to an impatient Callie as the minutes ticked by. Finally, at nearly five thirty, the customer shook her head. "I just can't decide. I guess I'll come back another day."

Callie smiled and assured the woman that would be fine, reminding her that the farm would be closing for the season on Saturday. She hurriedly turned off the coffeemaker and the lights and stored the leftover stollen. As she put on her coat, she wished Wicca could run, but that was not the case. It was a slow, steady pace that they took back to the farmhouse. Wicca was exhausted and ready for another nap by the time they arrived. Callie moved her water bowl next to her favorite rug and ran upstairs to shower. It was already dark by the time she dried her hair and pulled on her favorite dressy dress. The days in December were short ones. She heard a car pull into the driveway before she was half-finished with her minimal make-up and was searching for her shoes in the bottom of her closet when she heard the back door open.

"I'll be right down," she called over her shoulder, wishing her closet were more organized. It didn't help that she hadn't worn strap heels since she'd moved here. "They've got to be somewhere in here!" she grumbled as she dropped to her knees and shoved her head deeper into the closet rummaging through boots and shoes on the floor.

"Now, that's how I like my women! On their knees," growled a ragged voice just behind her.

Callie froze, her head buried between the hanging clothes. That didn't sound like Morgan's voice. Her nose detected the smell of stale tobacco and beer.

"You just stay right there, Missy. I like the view. Nice ass," he chuckled. "See you fixed those windows."

Callie slowly moved her head, inching backward until she could see the stocky form of Joe Suggs. His orange cap sat askew, and he was waving a pistol slowly in his left hand while his right hand worked at the buttons on his bulky coat.

"Mr. Suggs, I wasn't expecting you," Callie stammered, trying to regain her composure.

"Mr. Suggs, is it? Miss Uppity. Well, you can call me Joe. By the time I'm finished, we'll be acquainted real good and proper," he said, swaying slightly, still struggling as he unbuttoned his coat.

"Mr. Suggs, err, Joe, it's nice to see you again. Can I fix you a drink? Or something?" she said, inching her way backwards. She was trying to locate anything in the closet that she could use as a weapon, but there were only shoes. She gripped a heavy hiking boot in each hand.

"I'll take the 'or something'," he chuckled, a drizzle of tobacco juice running down his chin. "Oh, I'll take something, all right. Think I'll have a share of what all the other men around here are getting."

Callie could see the gun dropping slightly lower as he struggled with his belt. She tried to calculate if she could hit him hard enough with a boot and run to the door. He blocked her path, and she'd have to run past him. If she were wearing jeans, she might have a chance, but it was doubtful in this dress. She might not even be able to get up off the floor quickly. It would be very risky.

"Did you break my windows?" she asked, stalling for time. "Who was that with you? I didn't recognize your friend."

Suggs seemed to be puzzled for a moment by her question. He paused to briefly glance at the window and then returned to his belt. Thankfully, it seemed to be giving him trouble.

"Yes, who was your friend? Why didn't you bring him along tonight?" she asked sweetly.

"He's just a kid. This is man's work. Besides, he's turned chicken. Doesn't want to hang around with me anymore," Suggs said, slurring his words more thickly.

"That's too bad. Don't you have any other friends?" she asked slowly. "Maybe friends you go hunting with? I bet you are a good hunter. Did you get a deer this season, Joe?"

He paused again as if trying to remember. He shook his head slightly, and his orange cap fell off onto the bed beside him. "Yeah, I got a big buck. Big buck. Almost too big for me to carry this time," he bragged. Then, his face changed to a scowl. "Bet you know where I got him, too, Miss Uppity No-Hunting-in-My Woods."

"So, it was you. You killed all those deer," she whispered. As soon as she spoke the words, she realized her mistake. She should not have mentioned killing.

"Someone needs to teach you to quit meddling. I'll teach you something all right. You women. You're all too nosey. Ruining my drop off spot. Just can't keep your nose out of someone's business. And, I have a good business, Missy, yes sir," he slurred.

"I imagine the tire business is good during the winter. People need snow tires. You probably work long hard hours, Joe. I bet you're tired. And the boss probably doesn't appreciate how hard you work," Callie babbled, grasping at anything that might keep him off course.

"Tires not good business," he spat. A brown stain ran down her bedspread. "But I use their truck. I can go anywhere in that tire store truck. Stop anywhere. Meet anyone. No one questions me. Meet a semi on the interstate, stop by the road anywhere." He looked down at the stubborn buckle and seemed to make a decision.

"Joe, do you like my new dress?" she said quickly. "It's a new party dress. Why don't we go someplace fun? Do you dance? I bet you are a good dancer. We could go dancing."

"I don't like to dance, Missy," he spat on the bedspread again. "We'll just have our fun right here."

Callie felt like she'd been kneeling for hours, her hands frozen on the boots. She forced herself to concentrate, waiting for an opening. He'd finally managed to free the belt and was making progress with his pants zipper. She watched as he laid the gun on the bed and began moving towards her.

She threw one boot at his head with as much strength as she could manage. It glanced off his shoulder. He roared as he stepped back to grab the gun. Callie had not managed to get to her feet. Between numb legs and a tangled dress, it was impossible. She said a prayer as she threw the second boot and tried to pull her feet free of fabric.

"You bitch," he yelled, "I'll teach you some manners!" He gave a vicious kick to her ribs, which knocked her breathless. He threw his body onto hers. She screamed and grabbed his arm. The gun went off, the sound echoing around the room. She heard Wicca barking and yelled, "Wicca, stay! Stay!" She didn't want the dog tearing open her shoulder by trying to come up the stairs.

Tears streamed down her cheeks, as Suggs pressed his body against hers. His foul mouth covered her lips as she struggled to get free.

"Hold still. You're gonna like this," he grunted. Callie saw him lay the gun down as he pulled the fabric up on her dress and held her with his left arm. He was strong, really strong. She didn't see how she could get free, and there was nothing within reach to use as a weapon.

He pressed his lips against hers again and forced his tongue into her mouth as he ripped her clothing. She nearly retched in disgust, but instead, bit his tongue as hard as she could. He yelled and crashed his fist against the side of her face twice. Callie's eyes closed as the room started circling above her head. She heard the sound as more of her clothing was ripped. His weight on her chest sent piercing pains through her ribcage. She vaguely wondered if his kick had broken her ribs. Suggs grunted in satisfaction as she quit struggling. She couldn't breathe. His hands groped her body as his wet mouth moved down her chest.

Suddenly, his weight was lifted. She felt droplets cover her face, as Suggs's blood and saliva splattered over her. She heard scuffling and attempted to open her eyes. She saw Morgan forcing Suggs' arm behind his back, as he kicked the gun under the bed. He pushed the man onto the floor, bending his arm at a sharp angle.

"Let me go, pig!" Suggs yelled. "Me and her was just havin' a little fun."

"Are you okay Callie?" Morgan called over his shoulder. "Callie, answer me? Were you shot?"

"No, no, I think I'm okay," she mumbled, trying to get to her feet.

"Stay there," he ordered. "Come on, Suggs. Let's go for a walk." He dragged the unwilling man down the stairs and out into the driveway. Callie struggled to her feet, holding onto the bed for support. She moved slowly down the stairs, holding her throbbing head. Wicca stood at the bottom, whining with troubled eyes.

"Good girl," Callie praised her, sitting on the bottom step. "Good girl to stay." Callie buried her face in the dog's coat.

Morgan reappeared in the doorway. "Are you sure you're okay?" he said, drawing a glass of water and grabbing a towel from the counter.

"Where is he?" Callie asked, her voice shaking.

"I've got him handcuffed outside. Had a spare pair under the seat of my car," he told her. "He's not going anywhere. Back-up's on the way." He dipped the towel in the water and began wiping her face.

"Are you sure you're all right," he said, peering into her eyes. "You're getting a lot of purple bruise on the side of your face already."

"He's strong. I didn't know anyone could pack such a whallop," she attempted to laugh. "Feel like I was kicked by a mule."

"He's the one who was killing the deer. He shot my windows. He told me. I bet he shot my dog, too," she stammered. "You got here just in time. I couldn't push him off. He was so strong. I couldn't push him off!" Tears began welling in her eyes.

"You're safe now, Callie. I won't let anything happen to you," he told her, pulling her close. "Take some deep breaths and try to relax. I have to go check on the prisoner." Callie could hear a siren in the distance. Morgan pulled off his suit coat and put it around her shoulders. Her dress was in shreds.

Morgan left the house, pulling the door closed behind him. Callie stumbled into the hallway and looked into the mirror. Morgan was right. A deep purple bruise was already covering the side of her face.

There were still drops of tobacco stain and blood on her face and neck. The front of her torn dress was spattered as well. It was too bad. She'd never wear that dress again, and it had always been her favorite. Daniel had helped her pick it out to wear to her parent's anniversary party last winter.

She felt weak and violated even though the worst had not happened. She had been almost helpless against the man's strength, and that frustrated her. She wanted her father, to be safe in his arms. She wanted to be back at their anniversary party when her parents had been so happy. When Daniel had loved her. The flash of the patrol car's headlights reflected in the mirror. Callie pulled herself together and assured Wicca that everything was all right. She forced herself back up the stairs and washed her face. She went into her closet and pulled a fleece and a pair of jeans from the interior, and went into the spare bedroom to change. She'd have to remove that bedspread and clean the entire room before she could stand to be in there again.

Morgan returned, entering her bedroom. He retrieved the gun from under the bed and placed it in a plastic bag. "Callie, are you up here?" he called.

"I'm coming," she answered. When she entered the room, she found Morgan searching for the spent bullet.

"I heard a shot as I got out of my car," he stated. "There's got to be a cartridge here someplace."

"Can we look for it later?" she said.

"You go on down. Wicca is waiting at the bottom of the stairs. Send the crime scene officer up when he arrives, if I haven't come down already. You know him," he smiled.

Callie retreated to the kitchen and gave Wicca a handful of treats. She put a kettle on and started pulling ingredients from the panty. In times of stress, she baked. It kept her from thinking about reality, and the aromas soothed her soul. She made a pot of tea and began rolling out a crust. When the crime scene officer arrived, she led him to the stairs. She could hear the two men's voices as she opened cans of apple slices that her mother had preserved and sent home with Callie at Thanksgiving. After thickening the fruit, she poured it into the crust and sprinkled it with rosewater. She turned on the oven and began rolling the top crust.

Both officers returned. "Found it," Morgan told her. "Pudge is leaving but he'll be back tomorrow to get your formal statement. Is there anything you can tell us now?"

"He said he killed the deer. He said he shot my windows. He said the man with him was just a kid. Someone who had turned chicken and didn't want to be around him anymore," she said slowly, trying to recall exactly what Suggs had told her. She put the pie in the oven, and Morgan pulled out a chair for her to sit down.

"He said the tire job wasn't good business. But he used their truck, so he could go anywhere, be around anyone, and the police wouldn't be suspicious. Well, he didn't say police, but that's what he meant," she told them. "He said I was too nosey. I interfered with his drop off or something." She paused. "I can't remember anything else."

"That's fine for now," Pudge said. "I'll be back tomorrow. About ten be okay with you, Ma'am?"

"I'll be at the Cottage, so come there," she replied.

"Callie, you've had a rough night. Can't Gloria handle the store tomorrow?" Morgan asked.

"She's leaving with her family for the holidays. I can manage," she said. Pudge nodded and then left. Morgan poured tea into a cup and brought the honey bear from her pantry.

"Here, you need this," he stated, squeezing a generous amount of honey into the tea. Then, he poured a generous splash of brandy into the cup as well.

"I guess we're missing your party," she realized, looking at the clock. "You should go anyway, Morgan."

"I should stay right here," he countered, pulling a chair up beside hers. They sat quietly, his arm around her shoulders, until the pie was done. Morgan placed it on a cooling rack and led her into the living room, bringing the bottle of brandy along.

"Rest," he said, leading her to the sofa. "You've had a shock." He poured another shot of brandy into her cup and handed it to her. "Would you like some music?" he said, walking over to the CD player and flipping through the stack of discs beside it. He didn't wait for her reply, but put on her favorite "Mannheim Steamroller Christmas" disc. They sat quietly. When the lovely strains of "Silent Night" came on, tears rolled down her cheek.

"There is beauty all around you, Callie," he said softly. "Don't let tonight color your world ugly. Think about all your blessings."

"All I can think about is his foul breath and what might have happened if you hadn't come," she stammered. "All the bad things he said, all the terrible things that have happened since I moved here. Maybe I made a mistake coming here."

"But, I did come," he said, gripping her hand. "And you are safe. And Wicca is safe, and people care about you here. Now that he's in jail, you shouldn't have any of those problems again. He'll be in jail for a long, long time." He stroked her hair and pulled her head onto his shoulder.

They sat that way, in silence, through two more discs. By the time the music stopped, Callie was feeling better.

"I'm hungry," Morgan said. "Can we eat that pie, or is it just for decoration?"

"Oh, I'm sorry," Callie exclaimed. "Of course, you didn't have supper. Let's see what's in the refrigerator."

While she looked through the refrigerator blankly, Morgan rummaged through the freezer in the garage. "Are these shrimp for anything special?" he called.

"No, help yourself," she called automatically. Her mind was sluggish, and she didn't feel hungry enough that anything in the shelves of the refrigerator was appealing.

Morgan came in carrying a bag of shrimp and a container of frozen basil pesto. "Any pasta in the pantry?"

"I think so," she said.

"Put a kettle of water on. Come on, cooking will take your mind off your troubles," he taunted. Within moments, he poured olive oil into a saucepan, adding a bit of garlic and onion. Then he ran water over the shrimp to partially thaw it and passed a hunk of Parmesan and the grater to Callie. "Earn your supper," he teased as he set the table.

He put candles on the table and a new batch of CD's in the player. He opened a bottle of white wine and poured a cupful into the sauce, adding the pesto. When the pasta tested al dente, he drained it and poured the basil sauce on top. He dumped the cheese Callie had grated into the top and stirred the entire mixture with a flourish.

"Ma'am," he said, pulling out her chair at the table and pouring her a glass of wine.

He served the pasta and took the chair next to her. Callie hadn't thought she could eat anything, but she nibbled at the delicious dish and sipped her wine. Morgan ate enough for both of them, soaking up the last of the sauce with a piece of bread.

"Hit the shower, Callie," he ordered. "I'll clean up."

"But you cooked, so I should clean up," she argued.

"New rules," he said bluntly, pushing her toward the stairs.

When she came out of the shower, she saw that the stained bedspread had been removed, and the blood splatters had been mopped from her floor. She pulled on a fleece jogging suit and went slowly downstairs. Only the candles on the table and her Christmas tree lights were on.

Morgan had made hot chocolate and was standing by the window watching snow begin to fall.

"It's a beautiful night, Callie," he said, passing her a cup laden with marshmallows.

Callie stared at her face in the mirror the next morning, trying to decide what to do with it. The purple bruise had turned even uglier and bigger in the night. Make-up wouldn't cover it. She was staring at her reflection when she heard the noise of a loud truck. She looked out to see a wrecker pulling into her driveway.

"Now what?" she grumbled, as she pulled her hair into a ponytail and headed gingerly down the stairs. She had slept in the spare bedroom since she couldn't face a night in her own. Morgan had once again slept on the offending sofa, but he was nowhere to be seen as she passed through the room. She grabbed her coat from the peg and went outdoors. Morgan was talking to the driver of the wrecker, who had backed up to the tire store's pick-up. Callie hadn't realized it was in her driveway. Suggs must have driven it here.

"Good morning, Sunshine," the deputy called.

"We'll have this gone in a minute," the wrecker driver shouted, returning to his cab. Callie watched as a winch pulled the front of the truck onto the wrecker's ramp. Morgan waved farewell to the driver and walked to her side.

436

"Pudge is getting a warrant, so we can search the pick-up. We have probable cause anyway, but we'll play it cautious. We want to nail Suggs and make it stick," he said.

Callie watched the wrecker disappear down the road and turned toward the house.

"Want some breakfast?" he asked, falling into step beside her.

"No, just tea," she answered dully. She glanced at her watch and realized she had less than twenty minutes before the farm was supposed to open. She pulled some frozen lavender shortbread from the freezer and filled two jugs with water, while Morgan made the tea.

"Are you going to be okay at the farm alone today? Maybe Sandy could come out. I'm sure she'll want to hear the whole story anyway," he suggested. "She'll read the police record for last night first thing this morning."

"You're probably right. I'll be fine, and Officer Pudge will be here this morning," she reminded him. "Is that his real name, Pudge?"

"No, his name is Walter Pidgeon," Morgan told her, "but he hated it. So, we started calling him Pudge when we were kids. He was kinda chubby."

"He still is," Callie said, smiling. "But I'm not sure Pudge Pidgeon is any better than Walter."

"Don't tell him I told you," he said. "I think he's kind of sweet on you."

"Oh great, just what I need," she grumbled.

"Hey, he's a nice guy. Good officer," Morgan countered.

"Thanks, but after last night, I'm not in the mood for more visitors, especially male ones," she blushed. "I've got to get to the Cottage. It's time to open," she said, reaching for the jugs.

"I'll take those," Morgan said, "You get the cookies and go ahead. Wicca and I can take it a little slower."

"Thanks, Morgan. Thanks for everything," she said, as she hurried out of the house. Tears filled her eyes as she rushed across the road and over to unlock the Cottage. Her ribs hurt and the cold made her face ache. Once inside, she slowly took a breath, inhaling the scent of lavender. It felt good to be surrounded by her little building. She placed the cookies on a platter and put a glass cake cover over the top.

Turning on the music and the lights, she couldn't help noticing how pretty the Cottage looked.

"A lot better than I look," she said, pausing in front of the mirror. The answering machine showed eleven messages, so Callie pushed the button and reached for a pen to jot notes and phone numbers. By the time she'd finished, Wicca and Morgan were at the door. She fluffed Wicca's pillow and poured part of one jug of water into her bowl. She dumped the rest into the coffeemaker and plugged it in.

"If you want me to stay, I can call in," Morgan said, searching her eyes.

"No, go on. I'll be fine. Pudge will be here in an hour, and I have some things to do in the greenhouse before any customers arrive," she assured him. He gave her a quick kiss, looked straight into her eyes, then seeming satisfied, he nodded.

"All right, but you have your cell, right?"

"Right, Deputy Wright. I'll be fine. Now go," she smiled, pushing him out the door.

"And thanks again, Morgan. For everything."

She watched him lope back across the parking lot and into his convertible. When his car left, she felt very alone. She sat on the floor beside Wicca and let the tears she'd been holding in since last night run down her cheeks. Several minutes passed, and she pulled herself together when she heard a car pull into the lot.

"Great," she said looking into the mirror, "now I'm red and purple." She patted her face dry with a tissue and glanced out to see Sandy striding toward the Cottage.

"Oh, Callie, you look terrible. I came right out just as soon as I saw your name on the record. Thank God they caught that man. I never liked that fellow. Gave me the creeps," she babbled as she entered the Cottage. "Now, if you need to rest, I can watch the shop for a while. Mac is gone, but the gal watching the counter will call me if she needs me."

"Thanks, Sandy. As a matter of fact, there is an officer coming to take my formal statement in about an hour. It might be better to do it at the house rather than in front of customers. Besides, with this face, I might just scare them away," Callie said, looking into the mirror. Her face was more swollen and the bruises looked worse than an hour ago.

"You do look like you ran into a train. What happened?" Sandy asked, removing her coat and gloves.

"Suggs punched me. He's strong," Callie said, trying not to remember.

"Probably from all those tires he loads and unloads," Sandy stated. "Talk about lifting weights."

"I'm sure that's it. He was strong enough to pack that big buck out of my woods. He admitted killing it," Callie told her. "He's the one who killed all the deer and tore down my signs."

"Did he give you a reason?" Sandy asked, pulling out her notebook.

"Hey, I'm not giving an interview," Callie said, backing up to lean against the counter. "All this is off the record, friend."

"Okay, if you say so," Sandy pouted, returning her notebook to her purse," but wouldn't it be better to tell your side and give the facts, rather than have people speculate?"

"People are going to speculate and think what they want despite whatever you write, Sandy. I'd rather not go public. It's embarrassing enough as it is," Callie stated flatly.

"You shouldn't be embarrassed. You're the victim here. You didn't do anything wrong," Sandy argued.

"I know that, and you know that, but some people already think I'm questionable. They'll slant this story to make it as juicy as possible," Callie said sadly, recalling Suggs' comments about other men.

"Well, you'll soon know how people feel; the first car is pulling in," Sandy said, pulling back the curtain. "Do you want to go to the house now?"

"Call me a coward, but I really don't think I'm up to public inquiry. Can Wicca stay here? It's a long walk back to the house for her and Dr. Tyler says she's supposed to take it easy. I'll be back to check on her, but if she acts feverish, call me. She's fighting an infection, and I'm supposed to watch her carefully," Callie explained.

"Okay, I'll keep an eye on her," Sandy promised. "Why don't you slip into the greenhouse and then go to the house once those customers come into the shop?" Callie grabbed her coat and walked behind the decorated trees into the greenhouse. She waited until the women had entered the Cottage and scurried as fast as her ribs would allow to the house.

While Officer Pudge Pidgeon took her official statement, Callie watched several cars go into the parking lot. It didn't take long, but Callie was surprised at some of the questions the officer asked that actually led her to recall more details. When he finished, she thanked him. He gave her his card and said to call him if she remembered anything else. "Anything at all," he stressed.

She should return to the farm. Sandy wasn't used to handling the shop by herself. She'd only helped out at special events before, and Callie needed to check Wicca herself. While she debated, the phone rang.

"Callie, this is Sandy. Everything's fine here at the shop, but maybe you should come get Wicca. She's acting pretty mopey. Maybe she just misses you, but maybe she doesn't feel well," she reported.

"I'll be right over," Callie said, reaching for her coat and keys. She drove the truck over, parking as close to the Cottage as she could. There were several cars in the parking lot. With effort, she pulled the old door out and placed it against the step, so Wicca would be able to walk up into the truck. She pulled a loosely knit cap down over her face as far as possible and hurried to the Cottage. Wicca took two tries to rise when she saw Callie come in. Callie removed her coat and placed it under the dog's stomach.

"Help me carry her to the truck," Callie asked Sandy.

"I'll help," said a young man Callie didn't recognize. He carefully helped Callie lift the dog, using the coat as a stretcher.

"I'm Doug Parker, from across the way. I go to school with Lucy and Time," he said. "I heard about your dog getting shot. I'm sorry she's sick."

"Thanks for helping, Doug. I appreciate it," Callie said as they placed the dog in the cab. Doug pulled the ramp from the side of the truck and tossed it easily into the bed.

"Good luck," he called as Callie started the engine. She was already punching in Dr. Tyler's number as she turned onto the road.

"Her fever's definitely up," the vet said flatly, giving the dog an injection. "I want to keep her here."

"Is she going to be okay?" Callie worried.

"You brought her right away. Has she had all her antibiotics on schedule?" he asked.

"Yes, she's had every dose," Callie assured him.

"I thought maybe with all the excitement, you might have forgotten. Understandable, of course," he added.

"No, Wicca is my best friend. Nothing would keep me from taking good care of her," Callie stated.

"And how are you, Callie? It must have been a terrible experience," he said, eyeing her bruised face.

"Not something I'd like to remember," she said, brushing the topic aside. "Are you positive she'll be okay?"

"You know I'll do my best. Go home and get some rest. You look like you need it. Is there anything I can do to help?" he smiled, putting his arm around her shoulder.

"Just take good care of my Wicca," she said.

"You know I will," he said, giving her a light kiss on the forehead. Callie returned to her house, noticing that the parking lot still had several cars. She called Sandy while she sat in her truck thinking that if she needed help, she'd drive on over. Sandy answered in a perky voice, inquired about Wicca, and told Callie to relax. LouAnn had arrived and was giving her a hand, so everything was under control.

Callie went into the house, breathing a prayer of thanks for good friends and a good veterinarian. "And for Morgan Wright," she added before the final "Amen".

She fired up the computer to check her e-mails and stared at the calendar. Tomorrow was her final day to be open. Christmas Eve day. Now she wasn't sure she would go to her mother's. Which would be worse? Disappointing her mother, or leaving Wicca? She finally decided that Wicca was in good hands and that she should go to her mother's. But, how would she explain the big bruise on her face? She'd have to come up with a dandy story and rehearse it all the way to Urbana.

None of the e-mails needed an immediate reply, so she turned off the computer and went to the kitchen. She pulled out her slow cooker and started filling it with the ingredients for Irish Stew. Not exactly traditional holiday fare here in the Midwest, but probably lots of households were fixing just that on the Emerald Isle. She'd like to escape to Ireland or anywhere no one knew her. At least until her face was normal. She finished the stew, put on the lid, and mixed a batch of bread dough. She'd take loaves of homemade bread to her mother's and their traditional cinnamon rolls, placed in the shape of a Christmas tree and decorated with pecan halves, candied cherries, and white frosting sprinkled with green colored sugar. They'd had that for breakfast every Christmas morning since Callie could remember. She'd make one for Sandy and one for LouAnn as a "thank you" for helping out today. She put soothing music on the stereo, a comfrey poultice on her face and ribs, then wrapped her ribs with a cloth to keep the herb mixture in place. Comfrey was reputed to knit bones back together and help bruises to heal. This should be a real test of its abilities.

She moved slowly to the living room. Her farm photo album lay on the coffee table. She flipped it open. She hadn't added any pictures in a long time, so she hooked the camera to the computer and printed off photos of the Christmas décor at the Cottage and snow piled high in the gardens. There was a lovely photo of the hoarfrost one morning and one of the red fox Callie had taken out the window. By the time she'd caught up the album with two dozen or more photos, the bread dough was ready to roll into rolls. During the second rising, Callie dozed on the sofa. The kitchen timer rang to wake her, so she put the coffeecake 'trees' and loaves of bread into the oven.

When LouAnn and Sandy came to the farmhouse, they sniffed appreciatively as the smell of cinnamon and fresh-baked bread reached them.

"If you have time, come in and sit. There's fresh bread and gooseberry jam, and I made hot chocolate," Callie told them.

"Let's celebrate," Sandy said, pulling off her coat.

"What do we have to celebrate?" Callie asked, perplexed, touching the side of her throbbing face.

"You, my good friend and proud business owner, had an outstanding day," Sandy crowed. "Maybe I should consider a career change and go into sales!"

"She was amazing," LouAnn chimed in, pulling her scarf from her neck. "The woman had people begging to take things home! You hardly have a single Christmas item left."

"You're kidding. I was just trying to figure out what I was going to do with all of it, where all the boxes would go," Callie said haltingly.

"Well, that's not a problem now. I think most people came out of curiosity. Oh, there are lots of stories out there, and some of them even have a grain of truth," Sandy expanded, as she scooped more marshmallows onto her hot chocolate, "but once they were in the shop, I plied them with cookies and expounded on the glories of the merchandise, and voila!"

"She's not kidding," LouAnn said admiringly. "You'll need to go over and fill in the bare spots before we open tomorrow."

"We?" Callie said, slicing the bread and placing it on plates.

"Sure, we're on a roll. And besides, you're right. Your face might scare them away," Sandy teased, looking at Callie's face.

"We just had too much fun," LouAnn said, placing a huge stack of cash on the counter.

"Wow," Callie said, weighing the stack of bills in her hands. "Wow!"

The two friends left soon afterwards, carrying their Christmas tree coffeecakes wrapped in clear plastic wrap and ribbons. They promised to return when the shop opened for its final day. Callie felt odd, missing the final day of the season. She somehow felt she was letting her customers down, but obviously Sandy and LouAnn could handle it. Besides, tomorrow might be a slow day. Surely everyone had lots to do on Christmas Eve day. She had just locked the door behind her friends when the UPS van pulled in.

Mike was at the door almost before she had unlocked it.

"Callie, I've been wanting to get here all day. You can imagine what this day has been like. I had a flat tire on the truck, and the local store couldn't send a man out to help for hours. I tried to call, but you didn't answer your cell. Didn't you get my messages?" he said, pulling her into his embrace. "I've been worried sick."

"I'm fine. Really," she said, pulling back a bit as she thought. "I guess I left my cell when I took Wicca to Dr. Tyler. I forgot to look at it for messages," she said, pulling it from the counter. "Yes, here you are," she said staring at the phone. "I'm sorry, Mike."

"Look at your face! So he did beat you! If I could get my hands on that guy, he'd never walk again," he blustered, pulling her close and planting a kiss on her bruised face.

"Ouch!" she cried, pulling away.

"Oh, Callie, I'm sorry," he apologized. "Here, sit down. Can I get you an aspirin or something. Did you see a doctor?"

"No, I don't need a doctor," she replied although the pain in her ribs debated that reply.

"Well, there must be something I can do," he said, looking around the room. "Hey, where is Wicca?"

"She's running a fever. Fighting an infection, Dr. Tyler says. He wants to keep her overnight at least and maybe until after the holidays," she explained.

"Poor girls. You're both having a rough time right now," he said, taking her hand. "Are you still planning to go to your mother's for Christmas?"

"Yes, I think so. Wicca is in good hands, and she'll probably heal faster resting with Glenn than she would riding over to my mother's. And all the grandkids would want to play with her. That could be too much for her," Callie said thoughtfully.

"Maybe too much for you, too?" Mike asked.

"Maybe. But, then again, maybe it's just what I need to take my mind off everything that has been happening here," she sighed.

"Do you want to talk about it?" he asked.

"No, not now. I just need to rest a bit," she hinted, standing and walking toward the door. "You don't mind, do you? I still have a lot to do before our final day tomorrow."

"I can take a hint," he smiled. "I'll try to stop in tomorrow, but I'm sure I'll be overloaded with deliveries. Everything has to get there before Christmas, you know."

"That's okay. I know you'll have a very full day. And your mother would probably like to have you home as early as possible on Christmas Eve. I may be leaving right after we close, so I'll have packing to do, and I'll want to go visit Wicca before I leave. We'll both have very full days, so why don't I just wish you a 'Merry Christmas' right now, and we'll talk after the holidays," she said, rising on tiptoes to give his cheek a peck.

"It won't be as merry as it could be since you'll be out of town," he replied glumly, taking her hand.

"We both need to be with our families. It's a special holiday," she reminded him, easing him toward the door. "Merry Christmas, Mike, and give holiday wishes to your mother for me," she smiled.

Once the truck rumbled away, Callie leaned against the door staring overhead. She could see her favorite constellation, Orion, clearly in the dark sky. It seemed so peaceful outside with the bright pinpoints of light against the ink-black canvas above. A lonely coyote called in the distance, sending prickles along the hairs on her neck. She moved back inside and locked the door.

Callie moved slowly as she carried the refreshments for the final day to the Cottage. Her ribs were painful. Her face was stiff, and the bruises were even darker than the day before. She placed wood in the stove and began filling in displays so the shelves looked presentable again. LouAnn and Sandy were right, sales had been good. She couldn't find any product to put over the offending metal patches on the walls, so in the end, she taped some paper doilies over them, cut into snowflake shapes. It looked festive, and after all, they only had to last for one day. She cut a few more and taped them to the window nearby to co-ordinate the look and hung a few more on a nearby tree. Most of the ornaments had been purchased, so the tree looked a little under decorated. She swept the floor, which was a slow process with her battered ribs. She made a few sale signs to put on some items that would not store well over the winter or that she didn't want for next year's displays on special sale. By the time she had the Cottage ready for customers, Sandy and LouAnn had arrived.

They exchanged greetings, and Callie pointed out the sale items. Her friends assured her they were ready for business and were looking forward to the day, so Callie returned to the house. She wanted to call Glenn to see if Wicca's fever had broken.

"She's doing better," Dr. Tyler told her, "but I want to keep her for a few more days. Her shoulder seems more tender, and I really want her to take it easy."

"I think she tried to come up the stairs. Maybe she injured it again," Callie said sadly. "She was really upset during the attack. She barked and barked. She knew I was in trouble."

"Well, you both need a good rest," he said quietly. "I'm sorry we missed our old movie night last night. Can we reschedule it when you

445

get back? I assume you're still going to your mother's for Christmas tomorrow."

"I'm supposed to leave tonight after the farm closes. I can't think of any way to get out of it even though I hate trying to explain everything that happened," she said flatly.

"It will all work out," he assured her. "Leave your cell phone on. I'll call you if there's any change in Wicca's condition, but I think she'll pull through okay. I'm giving her some strong antibiotics for the infection, and that will also help her sleep. Call me if you need to talk and be sure to call me as soon as you get back."

"I will, Glenn, and thanks," she said.

"Merry Christmas, Callie," he said before hanging up.

Callie packed for a couple of days at her mother's, boxed up the gifts she was taking, and put the food she had promised to fix in travel containers. She tied ribbons and tags on jars of honey, which were "love gifts" for each family, and made extra ones for LouAnn and Sandy. Occasionally, she looked out the window, but the parking lot only had a few cars coming and going. LouAnn came over after noon to tell Callie she was leaving. Sandy could handle the small customer flow by herself.

By three o'clock, there were no customers' cars, so Callie went to the Cottage to send Sandy home. Callie was sure Sandy had preparations to make for the holiday, and she could handle the shop if anyone did show up.

Snowflakes began to fall soon after Sandy left. Callie made a fresh pot of tea and sat by the window overlooking the parking lot. It was nice having the Cottage to herself, all filled with holiday fragrance. She gazed around at the nearly empty displays and sipped her tea thoughtfully until the clock struck five. Her final day of the season. She cleared the cash register, unplugged the tree lights, and emptied the coffeemaker. The last of the refreshments were arranged in a box to take along to her mother's. With a final sigh, Callie locked the door and flipped the "Closed for the Season" sign over. She pulled the gate shut and looked at the falling snowflakes that landed on the Cottage roof. She took one last photo for her album, loaded her truck, and left.

Callie stood in her living room, packing the Christmas lights into a box. It was hard to believe that Christmas was over and New Year's was only five days away. She'd only stayed at her mother's for two nights, pleading that she needed to get back so Wicca could come home. All the family had exclaimed over her bruised face, which she had told them was a result of a fall while she was ice skating. She'd taken lots of teasing over being such a klutz, but it was better than trying to explain the truth.

She'd deposited the check from her mother into her savings account but hadn't even begun to think how it should be used. Her mind just seemed to be numb. The evening of Sugg's attack kept swimming around in her head and filled her dreams when she could sleep.

Dr. Tyler was bringing Wicca home after lunch, and Callie couldn't wait to see her lab again. She baked a batch of Wicca's favorite dog biscuits, flavored with peppermint flakes and beef bouillon, and set them on a rack to cool.

She'd just gone into the studio to get a clipboard when the UPS truck drove in.

"You're back. I saw your dad's truck in the driveway. Why didn't you call?" Mike said as she opened the door.

"I just got home a few minutes ago," she began.

"Did you have a good visit with your family?" he asked.

"Yes, very good. And you?"

"Terrific. Didn't know I had so many relatives," he said, biting into a biscuit. "Hey, these are different, but tasty."

Callie burst into laughter. "I'm glad you like them. They're Wicca's favorite dog biscuit!"

"Dog biscuit!" he sputtered, tossing the remainder into the sink.

"They're a welcome home present. Dr. Tyler is bringing Wicca home in a few minutes," she chuckled.

"I'm sure she'll love them. They weren't half bad," he chuckled in reply. "So, what are your plans for the rest of the week? What are you doing New Year's?"

"Something quiet. I've had all the travel and excitement I need for a while. And, Wicca needs to take it easy, too," she said evasively.

"A bunch of the drivers are throwing a party. Guess you don't want to go with me then," he said sadly.

"Not this year," she smiled.

"Well, I've got to keep moving," he said. "I'll call you this evening, and we can make plans for later this week. Give Wicca a hug for me," he called, waving as he crossed to his truck.

It wasn't long before Gilda rumbled into the driveway. Callie ran outside to meet them. She could see Wicca's eager eyes and wagging tail through the window.

"Welcome home, girl," she called as Glenn opened the van's door and pulled a ramp to the ground. "She looks wonderful, Glenn!"

"She's doing a lot better," he smiled. "I think the infection is clearing up nicely, and her shoulder seems better. She's got more energy, and her vitals are real good." He put a steadying hand on Wicca's good shoulder as she made her way slowly down the ramp and into Callie's waiting arms.

"You look better, too, young lady," he smiled.

"I'm feeling better. Come inside. It's cold out here," she told him.

They moved into the welcoming kitchen where Callie gave Wicca a biscuit and more hugs. Once the dog was settled in her favorite spot, Callie poured hot chocolate into mugs and sliced a cranberry nut bread.

"So, how were your holidays?" Dr. Tyler asked.

"Pretty peaceful, thank goodness. I missed my dog, but I was glad she was with you. I'm sure she got more rest than she would have with my family," Callie smiled.

"She's coming along well now. I think we can remove the cast in another week or so. Encourage her to walk and lots of fluid intake," he advised.

"I can't thank you enough. And, I want to pay her bill right away," Callie told him.

"Hallelujah! I can pay off all my Christmas credit cards," he teased her.

"Seriously, Glenn, let me pay for all your services. I would have lost her if you hadn't been so skillful. And, I know you put a lot of effort into her care. She's given you some sleepless nights, I'm sure," Callie stated.

Glenn put his mug on the table and walked over to her side. "Wicca's not the only girl in the house that's given me some sleepless nights, Callie. I find myself thinking of you at odd hours. I've missed being with you."

He pulled her to her feet and wrapped his arms around her. Just as he lowered his head to hers, a knock sounded at the door.

Callie moved to the door, looking out the window to see two young men. When she recognized Timothy Pease, she opened the door with a smile.

"Well, good afternoon, Time," she greeted him.

"Afternoon, Ma'am. You remember my friend, Doug Parker?" he introduced the well-muscled teen at his side.

"Of course, Doug," Callie said, extending her hand. "I want to thank you again for helping me get Wicca into my truck that day. I really appreciated your willingness to help."

"You're welcome," he said shyly.

"Err..can we come in for a minute?" Time asked hesitantly, looking at Dr. Tyler.

"Do you need me to stay, Callie?" Glenn asked quietly.

"No, I'm sure you need to get back to the clinic. I'll call you later. Thanks again for bringing Wicca home and be sure to get that invoice ready," she told him, as she walked him to the door. Once he was gone, Callie offered the boys hot chocolate, but they declined.

"Doug brought me over, so I could apologize," Time began slowly. "I've lost my driving privileges."

"Oh?" Callie said as she sat down at the table between them.

"I'm really, really sorry about what I did," Time said, staring at the floor.

"Exactly what did you do to be so sorry about, Time," she asked gently.

"I was with Joe Suggs when he shot out your windows. I put the pot plants in your greenhouse," he admitted without looking at her.

"Time! I can't believe that. You are such a nice young man. Lucy thinks the world of you, and you are such a talented photographer," she exclaimed. "Why would you do such a thing?"

"I'm sorry, Miss Callie," he said, his voice quivering. "I needed money for college. My dad said he's still paying medical bills, but he makes just enough that I don't qualify for much financial aid. I met Joe Suggs one day when I had a flat tire, and he said he'd pay me if I would put a package in that old hollow tree back on your place. Doug and I are always running four-wheelers on his farm next door, so it was easy to run over there. Every time I left one, I got paid."

He took a deep breath, and then continued. "Well, at first I didn't know what was in them. Then I got suspicious. Suggs told me I'd been delivering pot and other drugs, and if I didn't help him, he'd see that I got arrested. Said he'd tell the coach and my dad and the sheriff that he saw me get the packages from the semis at the truck stop. It would be my word against his, and he was a law-abiding adult in this community. I was just a kid that everyone knew needed money."

"So, I kept meeting him along the road somewhere, and he'd pass me a package. I'd go to Doug's and then put it in the tree. Doug didn't know anything about it, honest. He's innocent," Time said, pleading with his eyes.

"I believe you," Callie said quietly. "Go on."

"Sometimes Suggs would go get the package, and sometimes the dealers would pick them up. Either way, having you around was a problem. He wanted you to leave. He always used the empty Cottage to hide stuff, and he liked hunting in your woods. And then he got this idea that he'd make more money if he could grow the stuff himself. Cut out the middlemen, he said. So, he got some expensive seeds and planted them. I was supposed to put the plants in your greenhouse and take care of them whenever I came to see Lucy. That worked for a while, but I started getting more nervous."

He swallowed, and looked at Doug, who nodded in encouragement.

"Then one day, the plants were gone. Suggs was really mad. He thought I'd taken them. Or maybe Lucy. He threatened to hurt her. Said he'd mess up her pretty face if I didn't co-operate. So, I kept delivering packages and meeting people at the truck stop on I69. I just didn't know what else to do."

"Why didn't you tell your father? He could have helped," Callie asked.

"You don't know my dad. He's not easy to talk to and especially if you tell him something he doesn't like," Time said. "Oh, he's a good man. It's just that he expects so much from me, but he doesn't have any time for me. We don't talk much. It's been real hard since my mother died."

"I'm sorry," Callie said softly.

"Well, I just kept getting in deeper, and Suggs kept getting meaner. When he shot your dog, I knew I couldn't keep helping him, but I didn't know how to get out of it," Time sighed. "I finally told him I wasn't going to pick up any more packages."

"And you told Lucy you weren't going to college," she said slowly.

"Yeah. I figured either I couldn't afford it, or I'd be in jail. And, I thought if she wasn't my girlfriend, maybe Suggs would leave her alone."

"Well, he's in jail now, and he's going to be there for a long time," Callie assured him.

"Good thing, too," Doug inserted.

"I finally got the courage to tell my dad. He blew the roof and took away my car. Then he made me go talk to the sheriff. I'm on probation until they decide if they are going to press charges. Dad says maybe if I testify against Suggs, I'll get a light sentence, maybe even just community service," Time said slowly. "But, he insisted that I come and tell you I'm sorry, so I'm here. And, truly, Miss Callie, I am really, really sorry."

"Your father will help you get through this, Time," Callie said softly. "Have you told Lucy?"

"No, but I'll tell her when she gets back. She'll hate me," he said miserably.

"Well, I'm sure she'll be surprised and probably disappointed at first. But, Lucy is a strong young woman," Callie offered.

"She's the best. She sure deserves someone better than me," Time said sadly.

"You can turn your life around, Time. Work hard. Be truthful. Make good choices. You can still go to college and have a good future. It may just take a little longer now, but you can do it." Callie said supportively.

"Thanks, Ma'am," he said. "We'd better get going. Dad will be worrying about me."

Callie walked the two boys to the door, their shoulders slouching and heads hunched over. The world was not an easy place.

It was mid-week. The weather was blustery, and Callie was feeling blue. She had come to the Cottage to pack away the holiday items and take down the Christmas trees. It seemed strange to be closed, but she still had an extensive job list. She could hear the furnaces chugging away in the greenhouse and didn't want to think about the heating bills. At least with the money from her mother, she could pay them. She needed to have a long discussion with her accountant soon.

She was loading boxes into her truck when Morgan's patrol car pulled in. She hadn't seen or heard from him since the attack. She paused by the tailgate and watched him walk towards her.

"Morning, Ma'am," he said. "I come on official business."

"If it's about Timothy Pease, he has already come by to explain his part in all my troubles," she said guardedly.

"Well, I'm glad to hear that," he said, "but that's not my mission. Would you like to place an ad on our county law enforcement calendar?" He unrolled a large calendar with a photo of the sheriff in one corner and another of all the deputies in the opposite corner. A tear-off calendar was affixed beneath a square foot of business card sized ads, with the sheriff's office phone number prominently across the bottom.

Callie looked at the calendar numbly. "Deputy Wright! I haven't heard from you in days. Not since Joe Suggs.....not since....not since that night." She still had trouble talking about the attack and tried not to think about the incident at all. "And now, you waltz in here expecting me to talk about buying an advertisement?" Her voice was rising with each word and her hands began to shake.

"What would you like to talk about instead, Ma'am?" he said with amusement.

"Well, how about 'did you have a good holiday'?" she spat.

"Yes, Ma'am. I did," he said blandly.

"How about the rumor that you are leaving Bradford County for another job," she managed. "Were you going to tell me? Or, just let me eventually notice that you were gone?"

"I don't usually pay much attention to rumors myself, Ma'am," he said without emotion.

"How about the fact that you were seen leaving the jewelry store?" she countered.

"Well, Ma'am. I've been visiting all the businesses in the county to see if they want to buy an ad for our calendar. Jewelry store was just one of them," he replied. "It's a nice calendar. Good cause. Always good to support your local sheriff."

Callie stood stiffly, turned, and walked into the Cottage. She wasn't sure what she had expected by repeating the rumors, but she certainly didn't feel happy at the moment. She wasn't happy with either Morgan Wright or herself.

She poured a cup of tea and turned as he entered the door. He saw glistening tears escape the corners of her eyes.

"Why the tears?" he said softly.

"After the holiday blues, I expect," she sniffed. "Always a letdown when it's over. And closing the shop for the season. It's depressing."

"I expect so," he said quietly. "Can we talk a bit?" He led her to the table and pulled out a chair.

"Your face looks like its healing. How are the ribs?" he asked.

"Still sore," she admitted.

"How's Wicca?" he inquired, nodding at the sleeping dog.

"She's been through a rough time. Developed an infection, and I nearly lost her, but Glenn pulled her through. She's exhausted from the walk over, and she's still on medications that help her sleep."

"So, Time told you the whole story?" he asked gently.

"His part. He really got in over his head, didn't he? Will he have to go to jail?" she asked.

"Depends. He's working with the prosecutor. I doubt he'll escape some form of punishment, and he may have to do some jail time. Depends on how many counts they end up with, and how serious they are. He's a minor, so that helps. And he's never been in trouble before," he explained. "He never really sold drugs, so that helps. But, technically, he did have possession of large quantities."

"Are you really leaving?" Callie asked without preamble.

"I'm leaving the sheriff's department, yes," he paused. "I'm training to become a state policeman."

"When do you start?"

"Right after the first of the year," he stated.

"And then what happens?" she asked.

"Then I get assigned to a patrol, probably a section of state highway. I'd like to work my way up to a special task force assignment eventually," he added.

"Not enough danger for you here in Bradford County?" she sighed.

"Guess I'm ambitious," he chuckled.

She stood and walked to the window. "So, I guess I won't be seeing you very often. You'll be busy with a new assignment and maybe working another part of the state?"

"No way of knowing that yet," he said softly.

Callie wanted to move into his arms, to ask if he would miss her, if he would make an attempt to be part of her life, but she remained silent.

Wicca stirred, became aware that Morgan was present and rose stiffly to walk to his side. The officer rubbed her head and talked to her quietly.

"She's seems to be moving better," he observed.

"Yes, she's going to be fine," Callie said, staring out the window. She wished she felt fine, but she already felt that Morgan was far away.

"Well, I'm on duty, so I really have to go, Callie. Think about the ad. I'll stop again before the end of the week," he said, replacing his hat and rolling up the calendar. "Here's the form, if you want to fill it out." He laid a paper on the table and reached for the door knob.

"Ma'am," he said as always, tipping his head and touching the brim of his hat.

Callie watched as the patrol car rolled away, tears streaming down her cheeks.

"Well, Wicca. I'm as dumb as always. I thought Morgan and I were moving towards something really special. I thought maybe he was the one. You know, when you read the romance novels, and you and your body both suddenly recognize that he is 'the one'? Well, no, I guess you don't read, do you?"

Wicca laid her head on Callie's lap and sighed.

"You probably could if you tried," she smiled. "You are a wonder dog."

Wicca nodded in agreement.

"I really thought he might be the one, Wicca. But, you heard him. He's leaving, and there wasn't a bit of regret in his voice. Not one trace of longing, not one hint that he'd like to have me be part of his future. I just can't read men. I can't trust my own instincts. I was totally off again. What's wrong with me?" she asked the dog.

Wicca licked her hand gently, pushed against her thigh.

"Well, at least I have you, Sweetie girl," she sighed, rubbing the dog's thick coat. "Just you and me against the world. We don't need any men in our lives, do we?"

Wicca gave a soft whine that sounded a little skeptical to Callie's ears. They sat in silence as the afternoon sun slide slowly toward the horizon.   Callie moped around for most of the evening and then decided to bake. While the mini-cheesecakes were in the oven, she made a new job list that was headed by "Call the accountant for an appointment." "Start making a shopping list for Atlanta" came next. "Seed more perennials" and "Make replacement plant signs" followed quickly.

Mike had called briefly, but he seemed to sense her mood, and the conversation lagged. She'd checked her e-mails and other than messages from her cousin Eve and Beth, there was little of interest.

She flipped through mail that had been accumulating in a basket, noticing a flyer from the local lawn mower dealership for a winter sale event. She'd need to run some numbers. Maybe it would be cheaper to buy her own mower than hiring the lawn care service she'd used this summer. After all, she could depreciate it on her taxes. She made a note to ask her accountant.

In the studio, she pulled last year's journal from the shelf. She flipped to the page of resolutions and the list of books she'd planned to read.

"You were definitely overly optimistic last year," she told herself, noting that only a dozen of the titles had check marks beside them. "Just too busy to read," she sighed. "Well, at least it won't take long to make this year's list. I can just use this one again."

It was hard to believe that tomorrow was New Year's Eve. An entire year had passed. She'd accomplished a lot, but there had been disappointments, too. She missed her father. She needed to spend more time with her mother. She needed to work harder at being a good friend.

The timer rang, so Callie moved back to the kitchen to pull the cheesecakes from the oven. She opened a can of her mother's peaches, thickened them with cornstarch and cinnamon, added a dash of nutmeg, and set the pan on the stove to heat.

Engrossed in her stirring, Callie started when she heard a knock on the back door. A big smile filled her face when she recognized Sandy's face peering through the window.

"Come in, Sandy! You don't know how welcome you are!" she cried.

"Happy New Year, almost," Sandy laughed, pulling a wildly striped wool scarf from around her neck. "It's getting bitter out there. Where's the brandy?"

"Sorry, no brandy left, but I can offer you some homemade herbal liqueur," Callie smiled. "And give me a couple of minutes and we'll have peach cheesecakes. You've just saved me from eating the entire batch by myself."

"So, what's the occasion? Must be a real downer if you were going to binge," Sandy teased.

"Morgan's leaving," Callie admitted, "and once again, I totally misjudged a man. Am I ever going to learn?"

"Doubtful. It's the failing of women. We see what we want to see, even imagine good qualities that aren't even there," she stated dramatically as she sniffed the peach topping. "How much longer? I'm starving."

"Two minutes. Have patience," Callie chuckled. "So what brought you all the way out here? Couldn't have been the aroma of peach topping."

"Mac's back. He wants a story on Joe Suggs, and he's hoping you'll co-operate," Sandy stated, sipping the warming beverage. "By the way, Lucy is heartbroken again. Mac fired Time and has told Lucy she can't see him."

"So, she knows about his involvement," Callie stated quietly.

"She knows. Time was waiting on their doorstep when they got back from visiting the east coast," Sandy confirmed. "Mac was fit to be tied. Of course, since Time is a juvenile, his name can't be in the article.

Warren Pease is heartbroken, too. It's too bad. He seems like a really nice man. Let work be the main thing in his life, though."

"Is that the pot calling the kettle black, Miss?" Callie teased.

"I have other things in my life besides work," Sandy argued.

"Name something," Callie challenged.

"I have my hobbies," she replied slowly, "and my cat."

"I thought you were ditching the cat," Callie said, recalling the Christmas party.

"Well, maybe I'll keep it a while longer," she said pouting, "although with Morgan gone, I suppose you'll spend more time with Dr. Tyler than before, so I might as well put it out for adoption."

"Maybe it should come live with me," Callie offered. "We could use a mouser at the farm."

"I don't think Bitsy is much of a mouser," Sandy warned. "Anyway, we were talking about my story. Can I have an interview, officially?"

"I still don't want to comment. What's been in the paper is enough, and I'm hoping by the time I open in the spring everyone will have forgotten about it," Callie stated emphatically.

"Okay. No story. But I still get cheesecake, right?" Sandy smiled.

"Of course," Callie assured her, placing three peach covered mounds on a plate.

It was New Year's Eve, and Callie had no plans. She popped popcorn, mixed a blend of herbs with grated cheese and sunflower seeds into the hot kernels, and poured it into a bowl. She planned to watch old movies until the famous ball dropped in Times Square. Earlier in the evening, she'd called Beth and Bob to wish them a "Happy New Year." She'd had a funny e-mail greeting card from her cousin Eve that she forwarded to Sandy and Cecilia. Too bad LouAnn and Suz didn't use their computers more for socializing.

Mike was at his fellow drivers' big party, and Glenn had been called out on an emergency. If she wanted a midnight kiss this New Year's Eve, it would have to come from Wicca.

She pulled her hair into a long ponytail and wrapped it around her head. A pile of rented movies lay on the coffee table next to the popcorn. The remainder of the peach-topped cheesecakes were on a plate next to a glass of wine.

"Quite a celebration, huh girl?" she told the lab. "At least it's better than last year. We were still living amid the boxes and trying to figure out how to start over. All I could think about was Daniel."

The lab sniffed in dismissal, surveyed the offerings on the table, and walked to the pantry.

"Oh, I guess you want something special for the party, too," Callie laughed. She pulled the container with the peppermint biscuits from the pantry and gave the dog a handful. Her thoughts returned to Daniel. She wondered what he was doing this New Year's Eve and if his life had changed as much as hers had.

After the third sappy movie, Callie looked at the clock and wandered to the window. It was a cold, cold night. Snow was falling, and the wind was blustery. She watched the branches clicking against one another forming patterns and pictures as they moved. It was nearly midnight, and she felt much lonelier than she'd expected to feel.

A flash of headlights caught her eye and she hurried to the studio window to peer outside. An unfamiliar car was pulling into her driveway. She pulled a sweater from the chair and shoved her arms through the sleeves as she went to the door.

"Courageous, but cautious," she repeated as she peered through the snowflakes. The man came to her back door, dimly lit by the motion-detecting light that was blanketed by snow. His face was wrapped in a scarf, his collar turned up against the wind.

She opened the door and stood in stunned silence.

"Happy New Year's, Callie," he said quietly and bending his head, he gave her a soul wrenching New Year's kiss. "It's midnight."

All the past New Year's flashed through her mind, as she spiraled downward. Daniels' strong arms supported her as they moved through the doorway.

"Callie Gardener, I love you," he said. "Will you marry me?"

Rosemary

Legend tells that on the night of Christ's birth, Mary laid her blue cloak over the branches of a rosemary bush. Rosemary commonly grew in the region, a shrubby plant with evergreen needles and white blooms. Because of its wonderful fragrance and insect repelling qualities, women often hung their laundry on rosemary shrubs to dry. But on this special night, the rosemary was blessed. Since then, rosemary has a blue flower that matches Mary's cloak.

This is only one of the many stories linked with rosemary. Throughout the ages, this herb has earned a reputation for special powers. Its clean, potent fragrance was thought to cleanse the air of diseases, so sprigs were often strewn or burnt in the sickroom, or carried at funerals. Many also believed rosemary could ward off evil spirits and that placing sprigs under pillows could prevent nightmares.

Because the flavor and fragrance of rosemary is so lasting, even when dried, it was said to have the power to bring back energy, memories, and even to help raise the dead. It was a symbol of lasting friendship. Rosemary is included in bridal bouquets to symbolize enduring remembrances.

Rosemary is a must for any herb garden, or for anyone who wants to cook. Its flavor goes well with fruits, wines, roasted vegetables, meats, and breads. It is especially good with lamb, and stems are often used as skewers for grilling meats or vegetables. It is also used in teas or lemonades.

Because of its lasting fragrance, it is often included in moth repellant mixtures, hair rinses, and soaps.

The cultural requirements for rosemary include a sunny location, well-drained soil, plenty of lime, and frequent watering. It cannot survive a temperature below twenty degrees for extended periods. Where winters are colder, it should be grown in pots and moved indoors. Inside, it requires a sunny window and frequent misting.

Recipes

January's Recipes

New Year's Day Salsa

Traditionally, black eye-peas are served on New Year's Day to bring good luck to the coming year. Drain 1 can black eye-peas. Place in mixing bowl with ½ c. chopped red onion; ½ large green pepper, diced; ¼-1/2 c. finely chopped fresh cilantro; 4 Roma tomatoes, diced; 1 fresh jalapeno pepper, finely chopped; juice of 1 lime, salt and pepper to taste. Stir and chill or serve immediately. Additional hot pepper may be added if more heat is desired. This will be fairly mild, just as Callie prefers it!

Mini Pork Meatballs in Apple Butter Sauce

Mix together: 1 lb. ground pork; 1 tart apple, finely chopped (Granny Smith or Jonathon work well); 1 stalk celery, finely chopped; 2 T. finely chopped onion; ¼ tsp. freshly ground pepper, 10 sesame crackers (like "Toasteds"), rolled into crumbs, and ½ tsp. dried sage. Form into 1" meatballs and broil, turning until browned nicely on all sides.

While the balls are browning, mix in a large saucepan over medium-low heat: 1/2 c. catsup, 1/2 c. apple butter, and ¼ c. apple cider or apple juice. Place browned meatballs into sauce and simmer on low heat for

twenty minutes. Can be refrigerated and reheated just before serving.
Makes 40.

Callie's Beef Balls

Soak 1 slice whole wheat bread torn into very small pieces in 3 T. milk.

Mix together: 1 lb. ground beef, ½ c. finely chopped onion, 1 egg, and ¼ tsp. thyme. Add bread and milk mixture, mixing well. Form into small balls.

Mix together: 1 c. ketchup, 1 c. grape jelly, and ½ c. raisins in a medium saucepan over medium heat. Add meatballs. Simmer for forty-five minutes, or until meatballs are fully cooked. Reduce heat to low until serving time, or refrigerate and reheat just before serving. Makes 36.

Mini Pesto Balls

Mix together: 1 lb. ground lamb, 6 saltine crackers rolled into crumbs, 1 1/2 c. basil pesto, ½ c. grated parmesan cheese, 1 T. sugar, and freshly ground pepper. Roll into small balls, slightly larger than a quarter in diameter. Place balls on baking dish that has been sprayed with cooking oil. Broil, turning balls every four minutes to brown evenly on all sides. This takes about 12 min. If meatballs are not thoroughly cooked through center, turn oven to bake until fully cooked. Serve warm or at room temperature with toothpicks. Recipe can also be made with ground turkey or beef, but lamb is best.

Tabouli

In large bowl, pour enough boiling water over 1 c. bulgur wheat (medium ground, not fine) to cover well. Add a bit more later, if needed. Allow to sit and absorb until wheat is light and fluffy—it should still have a tiny bit of crunch though.

Meanwhile, finely chop a large bunch of parsley (about 30 stems). Thinly slice 4-5 green onions. Peel and dice 1 large cucumber. Remove leaves of a good spearmint until you have a heaping ¼ c., then mince them.

Drain bulgur, if needed. Add herbs and veggies. Sprinkle with 1 tsp. salt. Stir. Add ¼ c. olive oil and ½ c. freshly squeezed lemon juice, freshly ground pepper, and a dash or two of cumin. Taste, and add salt or pepper if desired. Refrigerate for 30 min., to allow flavors to blend. This is a basic recipe, a traditional form. However, depending upon the region of the Middle East, other ingredients, such as tomatoes, black olives, garbanzo beans, celery, or radishes may be added. Think of it as Middle Eastern salsa!

Traditionally this is served with pita bread or on lettuce leaves as a type of sandwich. However, it can also be used as a salad, or served on crackers or pita triangles as an appetizer.

Cinna-Cream Cocktail
Make simple syrup by bringing 1 c. water and 1 c. sugar to a boil to a small saucepan, stirring to dissolve sugar. Remove from heat. Add a handful of cinnamon basil leaves. Cover tightly and allow to steep until cool. Strain and discard leaves. Store in a tightly sealed jar in the refrigerator.

For cocktail, use one part cinnamon basil syrup and 2 parts Bailey's Irish Cream.

February's Recipes

Simple Appetizer Sandwiches
Cut tiny shapes of white or whole wheat bread, or use small crackers. Spread with softened cream cheese mixed with a small amount of snipped chives and freshly ground pepper. Spread a generous layer of rose geranium jelly over the top. Lemon verbena, lavender, mint, or garlic jelly are also delicious! Serve immediately.

Balsamic Pretzel Ball or Log
Combine 2T. Balsamic vinegar, 2 T. olive oil, 1/4 tsp. chopped oregano, ¼ tsp. garlic minced, 1/2 tsp. chopped fresh basil, freshly ground pepper. Mix well.

Add to 8 oz. cream cheese with ¼ c. crushed pretzels, mixing well. Roll into a ball or a log, and then roll into additional crushed pretzels to cover. Chill, or serve immediately with crackers or spread into celery sticks.

Chick Pea Spread

Combine in food processor: 2 c. chick peas, drained; 2 T. mustard; 1 c. mayonnaise; 2 T. chopped herbs, and a dash of freshly ground pepper. Vary with different herbs and mustard choices! Serve with crackers, pita triangles, or raw veggies. Suggestions: fresh dill with honey mustard; garlic chives with horseradish mustard; summer savory with Dijon mustard.

Hot Dilly Clam Dip

Combine 1 6.5 oz. can minced clams, drained with 8 oz. cream cheese, softened. Add ¾ c. finely shredded carrots, 3 T. finely chopped fresh dill (or 2 tsp. dried dillweed), and a dash of ground red cayenne pepper. Place in small shallow baking dish. Mix ½ c. finely ground sesame cracker crumbs (or oyster crackers) with 1 T. melted butter to form crumb topping. Sprinkle over dip to form a topping. Sprinkle with paprika. Bake at 350 degrees just until mixture begins to bubble. Serve warm with crackers, Melba toast, or veggies.

Parsley-Pecan Cheese Ball

Mix together: 1-8 oz. pkg. cream cheese, room temperature; 3 T. finely chopped parsley; ¼ c. finely chopped pecans; 1 tsp. Worcestershire sauce; 2 T. bacon bits, or finely chopped cooked bacon. Roll into ball. Roll ball onto finely chopped pecans to cover. Wrap in plastic wrap. Chill to allow flavors to blend. Serve with crackers.

Rose-Berry Cocktail Punch

Make simple syrup by bringing 1 c. water and 1 c. sugar to a boil in a small saucepan. Stir to dissolve sugar completely. Remove from heat. Push 8 rose-scented geranium leaves into syrup to cover. Place a tight-fitting lid on top and allow to steep until cool. Remove and discard leaves.

To make punch, use equal parts rose geranium syrup, club soda, and blackberry brandy. Garnish with orange rind twist, or rose geranium leaf, or rose geranium flower and serve over ice.

March's Recipes

Chive and Cheese Dip

Melt 1 stick butter in large saucepan. Whisk in 3 T. flour and ½ tsp. dry mustard. Cook, stirring, until flour is absorbed and mixture bubbles. Slowly add 1 c. half and half, stirring constantly. Stir in 2 c. cubed Velveeta cheese, cooking over low heat until cheese is melted. Add 3 T. finely chopped chives and 3 T. finely chopped parsley. Serve warm with veggie sticks, chilled asparagus spears, or pretzel sticks. Also good poured over steamed veggies.

Viola Cheese Spread

In small mixing bowl, combine room-temperature 8-oz. pkg. cream cheese with ½ c. drained crushed pineapple and 2 tsp. curry powder. Mix well. Fold in ½ c. snipped viola petals. Place in bowl and decorate with perfect viola blooms. Chill until ready to serve with crackers or veggies.

Orange Mint Tapenade

In food processor, combine 1 anchovy filet; 1 tsp. drained capers; 1 c. Kalamata olives, pitted & slightly chopped; 1 large clove garlic, sliced; 3 T. olive oil, 2 T. orange mint leaves, finely chopped, and 3 T. orange juice. Process just until well blended. Add freshly ground black pepper to taste. You can also add a bit of orange zest, if desired

Minty Cheese Pitas

Carefully slice a 7" whole wheat pita into two circles. Place on baking sheet. Spread each circle with mint jelly. Cover each with thinly sliced apple or pear. Sprinkle each circle with 2 T. bleu cheese crumbles, and then 1 tsp. chopped parsley. Bake at 375 degrees until cheese begins to melt. Cut each circle into 16 pieces. Serve immediately. Makes 32.

Apple Mint Cocktail

Steep 1 c. mint (spearmint, peppermint, or a mixture of spearmint and peppermint works best) in 1 qt. vodka. Store in a dark place, shaking daily for at least five days. Mix 3 parts apple cider or apple juice with 1 part mint vodka. Serve over ice. Garnish with a slice of bright green Granny Smith apple and a sprig of mint.

April's Recipes

Viola Quiche

Preheat oven to 350 degrees. You will need a 9" pie crust. If frozen, allow to thaw completely. In small pan, sauté ½ c. onion in a bit of olive oil till soft, do not brown. Meanwhile, drain 1 can mixed vegetables and snip in ½ c. viola petals.   Add onion, ½ c. grated cheddar, and ½ c. grated mozzarella cheese. Sprinkle an additional handful of grated cheddar in the bottom of the pie crust. Whisk 3 eggs well and add ½ c. fat free Half and Half. Stir into veggie/viola mixture, pour into crust. Sprinkle 1/3 c. feta cheese over top, and a bit more grated cheddar. If needed, add a bit more Half and Half until pie is full. Grate fresh nutmeg over top. Bake just until center is set, about 35 min.

Shrimp-Stuffed Eggs

Hard boil 10 eggs. Cool, peel. Chop 2 of the eggs into a mixing bowl. Slice the remaining 8 in half. Remove yolks from each half and place with the 2 eggs already in bowl, using a pastry blender to chop them fine. Drain a can of baby shrimp, reserving juice. Set aside 16 nice shrimp for garnish. Add 1 T. Dijon mustard, 1 c. drained canned baby shrimp, ¼ c. mayonnaise; 2 tsp. chopped summer or winter savory, and freshly ground pepper to egg yolks. Mix until well blended, adding a bit of the shrimp liquid if needed to make a nice consistency. Place filling in egg halves. Garnish each egg half with a tiny shrimp and tiny bits of savory. Garnish the serving plate with sprigs of savory.

Pesto-Stuffed Eggs

Hard boil eggs. Cool, peel and cut in half. Remove yolks, placing them in a small bowl. Add 1 tsp. basil pesto per egg, freshly ground pepper and just enough cream or mayonnaise to make a proper consistency. Fill whites with mixture. Sprinkle with finely chopped fresh basil. Serve immediately, or chill.

Salmagundi Spread

A medieval salad is the inspiration for this recipe. It uses many of the herbs of spring, plants that can be harvested in April in central Indiana (Zone 5a).

Hard boil 3 eggs, cool, and peel. Meanwhile, in an approximately 3"x 5" plastic container, place a ½" layer of chopped spinach, using scissors to cut stacks of leaves into small pieces. Put the meat from three cooked chicken legs into a food processor and mince to produce approximately ½ c. (Or use canned chicken.) Spread over spinach evenly. Snip a ½" layer of fresh sorrel, snipped finely over chicken. Drain a 2 oz. tin of anchovies. Using scissors snip them into tiny pieces to form an even layer over the sorrel. Finely chop the 3 eggs, and spread over sorrel. Sprinkle with freshly ground pepper. Snip a thin layer of chives over the top. Add the final layer, a ½" layer of finely snipped spinach.

Mix together in a small bowl: ¾ c. mayonnaise and ¾ tsp. prepared horseradish, stirring well. Spread over spinach. Cover with plastic wrap. Chill until serving time, at least 1 hour. Stir mixture together gently. Serve as a spread over sesame or whole wheat crackers. Garnish each cracker with a snip of chives, if desired.

A Peach of a Cocktail

If time, infuse a 1" piece of fresh, peeled ginger root, sliced thinly in 2 c. rum for 4-5 days, shaking occasionally. Use this ginger-infused rum for the drink. If not enough time, place 4 peach halves (canned and drained, or fresh peeled) in a sturdy blender with ¾ tsp. finely chopped, peeled fresh ginger root. Blend till smooth. Add 1 c. ice, slightly crushed and 3 oz. rum. Process until mixture is smoothie consistency. Pour into a tumbler. Garnish with a slice of fresh peach

May's Recipes

Nasturtium Appetizers

Rinse 12-15 nasturtium blossoms and lay on paper toweling to dry. Mix together:

8 oz. cream cheese, 3 T. chopped chives, and 4 T. chopped green olives. Roll into small balls. Place one ball inside each blossom. Serve immediately.

Flower Stuffed Mushrooms

1 ½ lbs large fresh button mushrooms

Remove stems, wipe caps with damp towel to remove any dirt. Chop stems finely.

Mix together: chopped mushroom stems, ¼ c. snipped chives, 2-8 oz. pkg. cream cheese, softened, ¼ c. finely chopped radishes, ¼ c. finely chopped nasturtium petals, and ¼ c. finely chopped walnuts. Press mixture into mushroom caps. Sprinkle additional nasturtium "confetti" on top. Refrigerate, covered, until serving time. May be made a day ahead. Makes 18-30, depending upon size of mushrooms.

Mini Arugula Sandwiches

Chop 1 1/2 c. fresh arugula. Mix in 1/3 c. mayonnaise, ½ c. finely chopped celery, ¼ c. sweet pickle relish, and ¼ c. finely chopped green onion. Spread thinly on whole grain bread. Cut into small squares, triangles or rectangles, making a tiny open face sandwich.

Flower & Herb Canapé

Cut bread into small shapes, or purchase "party" sized loaf. Place a very thin slice of sweet onion on each piece. In small mixing bowl combine: 1 c. plain yogurt, 2 T. finely chopped cilantro, ¼ c. finely chopped parsley, 1 T. finely chopped spearmint, 2 T. finely chopped nasturtium leaves and 10 nasturtium blossoms, torn or cut into small pieces. Spread mixture over onion slice. Decorate each canapé with a nasturtium petal.

The Best Mint Julep

The traditional drink of the Kentucky Derby and the Old South has many variations. This one is a farm favorite. Make mint-flavored syrup by bringing 1 c. water just to a boil. Remove from heat. Stir in 1 c. sugar and ¼ c. mint sprigs (Cook's Choice, Kentucky Colonel, or Mint the Best have the best flavor). Cover and allow to cool. Strain. Store in a tightly sealed jar in the refrigerator up to two weeks. To make the cocktail, place 3 T. mint simple syrup in bottom of a tall glass. Add 3 sprigs mint, and muddle with the handle of a wooden spoon until mint is fully bruised. Add 3 oz. bourbon. Fill glass with ice. Garnish with a sprig of fresh mint.

June's Recipes

Lavender Glazed Meatballs

Mix together: 1-lb. pkg. sausage (mild or medium) or 1 lb. ground lamb, 2 T. chopped parsley, ¼ c. chopped shallots, ½ c. small curd cottage cheese, 1 egg, 1 ½ t. ground dried lavender flowers, 2 c. whole grain bread crumbs. Mix by hand. Form into 1" balls. Broil until brown, turning to brown all sides. Remove from oven and place in shallow baking dish. Heat 1 jar lavender jelly in microwave until softened. Pour over meatballs. Turn until coated. Serve immediately. Delicious!

Herbs de Provence

Every village and every grandmother has their own version of this traditional seasoning mixture. It is used in and on everything. Simply mix it with cream cheese and spread on crackers for a simple appetizer.

Mix together, 3 T. each dried lavender flowers, marjoram, thyme, and savory;

1 t. each dried rosemary and basil; and ½ t. dried sage.

Black Olives with Herbs de Provence

Drain 1 can large black olives. Place into container with tight fitting lid. Gently stir 2 tsp. Herbs de Provence and 1/2 c. olive oil. Refrigerate, shaking gently once or twice a day for two days. Serve with toothpicks.

Callie's Favorite Tapenade

In food processor, combine 1-7 oz. can well-drained tuna (packed in water), 1- 6 oz. can black olives, pitted and drained; 1 large clove garlic, sliced; and 1 tsp. Herbs de Provence. Process with quick on/off just until chopped into small pieces. Stir in 4 T. olive oil, 3 T. freshly squeezed lemon juice, 1/3 c. medium salsa, and a grind of black pepper. Serve at room temperature.

Fruit Kabobs with Spicy Sauce

Thread pieces of fresh pineapple, peaches, strawberries, blackberries, melon, grapes or kiwi onto small skewers. In small saucepan, mix together 1T. cornstarch and 1T. sugar. Add 1 c. fruit juice (any flavor), 1 tsp. finely chopped fresh ginger, and 1 T. balsamic vinegar, stirring well. Cook and stir until thickened. Add 1 finely minced Thai pepper, stirring well. Pour mixture into small serving bowl. Spoon sauce over fruit as each skewer is served. This is especially good if the fruit skewers are popped onto a hot grill just until they show browned grill marks, then drizzle with sauce.

Stuffed Apricots

Prepare a cup of hot green tea. Cool until slightly warm and pour over 8 oz. pkg. dried apricots. Cover and allow to sit until apricots are plump and softened. Combine: 8 oz. cream cheese at room temperature, ¼ c. finely chopped celery, ¼ c. dried elderberries (or substitute finely chopped raisins) and ½ tsp. cumin. Mix well. Slice the side of each apricot open and stuff with cheese mixture. Chill until serving time. For another flavor, substitute ground dried cinnamon basil or anise hyssop for the cumin.

Lavender-Chocolate Cocktail

Place 3 T. lavender flowers, 1 T. black tea in teapot. Pour 2 c. boiling water over, cover, allow to steep 15 min. Strain and cool in refrigerator. Mix 1 part crème de cacao; 3 parts lavender tea; 1 part brandy. Serve over ice. Garnish with sprig of fresh lavender and a few lavender flowers floating on top.

July's Recipes

Monarda Drop Biscuits

Cream together until light and fluffy: ½ c. sugar and ½ c. butter. Add 2 eggs and beat well. Stir in gently: ¼ c. beebalm petals and leaves, chopped lightly; 1 tsp. rosewater, and ½ tsp. vanilla extract. Mix together 2 c. flour, ¼ tsp. salt, and 2 ½ tsp. baking powder. Gently mix into butter mixture. Do not over mix. Drop by small tablespoon onto lightly buttered cookie sheet. Bake at 350 degrees for 8-9 minutes, just until lightly brown, but still soft. Drizzle with thinned white frosting or honey, sprinkle with additional Monarda blooms. Makes 36.

Callie's Quick Garlic Dip

In food processor, place 8 oz. cream cheese, 3 T. fresh parsley leaves, 3 cloves garlic peeled, 1-6" zucchini, cut into 1" chunks. Process until about the consistency of chunky peanut butter. Season with a bit of freshly ground pepper. Refrigerate until ready to serve with veggies, crackers, or chips. Or, serve over a baked potato!

Daylily Appetizer

Fold ½ c. thinly sliced daylilies into 8 oz softened cream cheese. Add ½ c. sliced salad olives, freshly ground pepper. Roll into balls. Roll balls into additional chopped daylily "confetti". Chill before serving. For a special effect, select small whole daylilies. Rinse and remove stamen and pistol from center, leaving flower intact. Place cheese balls inside daylily, pressing petals slightly to secure. Be sure to use only unsprayed, chemical-free flowers.

Daylily Confetti Sandwiches

Cut bread into small rounds. Spread cut edges with mayonnaise, or cream cheese thinned with orange juice, orange liqueur, etc.

Chop daylilies into confetti. Roll bread lightly to decorate.

You may serve as is, or add a thin slice of cucumber, radish, or top with a bit of confetti.

Stuffed Tomatoes

Halve and remove seeds from 25 small tomatoes. Place on serving plate, cover with plastic wrap, and chill until just before serving. (The variety "Balcony," which is about the size of a small pullet egg works perfectly. It is rosy-pink when ripe and has a wonderful sweet flavor!) In food processor, zap 2/3c. fresh basil leaves and 1 clove garlic with 1 tsp. olive oil. Add 4 oz. cream cheese and 1 stick unsalted butter, processing until smooth. Place a teaspoonful of filling in each tomato half. Sprinkle with grated parmesan cheese. Serve immediately, or refrigerate up to 4 hours. Makes 50 halves.

Callie's Pesto Loaf

In small mixing bowl, combine 8 oz. package cream cheese and 1 stick unsalted butter, both at room temperature. Beat until fluffy. Line a small container with plastic wrap. Spread a 1" thick layer of cheese in the bottom. Spread a ½" layer of basil pesto on top. Repeat until all the cheese mixture is used, ending with the cheese mixture on top. Wrap with plastic wrap and chill until ready to serve with thin slices of Italian bread cut into small pieces, or crackers.

Orange Mint "Mojitos".

Place ¼ c. sugar and 2 oz. orange brandy in a pitcher. Add ½ c. orange mint leaves. Muddle until the leaves are bruised. Add 2 c. club soda and 2 c. light rum. Fill glasses with ice. Pour cocktail over and garnish with sprig of orange mint. (Orange mint does not taste like oranges. It is named for the fragrance of the bergamot fruit which is orange and provides the flavor and scent for Earl Gray tea.)

August's Recipes

Provencal Salsa

Mix all ingredients together and stir gently: ¾ c. finely chopped Roma tomatoes; 3 T. finely chopped black olives; 1 T. drained, minced capers; 2 tsp. red wine vinegar (or lavender vinegar); 2 T. fresh basil, chopped; 1 T. minced shallot; ½ tsp. grated orange zest; ½ tsp. crushed dried lavender blooms, or 1 ½ tsp. fresh blooms, chopped; 1 T. olive oil; 1 small hot pepper, chopped; salt and pepper to taste.

Black Olive Salsa

Combine the following: 3 lb. Tomatoes, chopped; 1 ½ c. sliced black olives; ¼ c. onion, chopped; ½ c. cilantro, chopped; 1 T. basil or basil/hot pepper vinegar; 1 T. finely chopped hot pepper (your choice of variety).

This salsa improves if flavors are allowed to blend for a few hours before serving. Makes 3 ½ c.

Fresh Vegetable Salsa

This salsa is especially pretty and colorful. Feel free to improvise, adding bell peppers, substituting cucumber for the zucchini, etc.

Combine: 4 tomatoes, chopped; 1 young zucchini, diced; 1 small yellow summer squash, diced; 2 T. olive oil; 1/3 c. cilantro, chopped; 1 jar pimentos, drained; 2 small jalapeno or serrano peppers, seeds removed and finely diced; 2 T. fresh lime juice. Makes 2 c.

White Bean Salsa

Combine the following ingredients in a large bowl: 1 15.5 oz. Can white beans, drained; 1 serrano pepper, minced; 1 sweet red pepper, finely chopped; 1 T. red wine vinegar; ½ red onion, finely chopped; 1 tsp. olive oil; 4 tomatoes, chopped; 2 T. fresh cilantro, chopped. Best when chilled 2 hrs. before serving.

Cool Summer Salsa

Combine in large bowl: 2 c. honeydew melon, diced; 2 T. chopped fresh parsley; 2 yellow tomatoes, seeded and diced; 2 tsp. chopped fresh chives; ½ c. peeled, seeded, diced cucumber; 3 tsp. chopped fresh spearmint; 2 T. balsamic vinegar; 2 tsp. sugar; 1 T. light vegetable oil; 1/2 tsp. salt; ½ tsp. pepper. Cover and chill. Makes 4 c. Great with grilled fish!

Callie's Garden Salsa

Combine in large bowl: 4 tomatoes, diced; dash of salt; dashes of cumin; 1- 8" zucchini, diced; 2 sm. Jalapeno or serrano chiles, seeded and finely chopped; 1-8" yellow squash, diced; 2 T. olive oil; 2 T. lime juice; 1/3 c. fresh cilantro, chopped; 1 bell pepper, diced; 1/4 c. finely chopped onion; 1 clove garlic, minced. Cover and chill.

Rosalitas

Add 8-10 rose geranium leaves to a bottle of tequila. Steep for 4-5 days. Make a simple syrup by bringing 1 c. water and 1 c. sugar just to a boil, stirring to dissolve sugar. Add 6-8 rose geranium leaves, cover tightly and allow to cool. Strain. To make rosalita, use 1 part rose-geranium syrup, 4 parts ginger ale, and 2 parts rose-geranium infused tequila. Use rose-geranium flavored sugar to garnish rim of glass (see Herbal Sugar recipe). Garnish drink with floating rose petals.

Herbal Sugars

Sugar has been used to store the wonderful flavors of herbs for centuries. Select the desired herb, rinse, and gently pat dry with a paper towel. Place a ½" to 1" layer of sugar (brown or white as desired, although white sugar is more commonly used) in bottom of a container with a tight-fitting lid. Add a layer of herb, then another layer of sugar. Repeat until desired quantity is reached. Seal tightly. Shake daily. The sharp edges of the sugar crystals will rupture the microscopic oil sacks in the herb leaves. The oil will be absorbed into the crystals, producing a delicious flavor. After four or five days, taste the sugar. If the flavor is good, remove the leaves and store the sugar until needed. Some herbs have less oil content. If a stronger sugar is desired, remove the leaves and repeat the layering process with another batch of herb. Favorite plants for making herb sugars are: scented geraniums, lemon verbena, vanilla bean, calendula, mints, anise hyssop, cinnamon basil, lemon basil, clove basil, violets, clove pinks, jasmine.

September's Recipes

Pesto

Traditional pesto is made with fresh basil leaves. However, since the word pesto means paste in general, it can actually be made with any herb. Callie's favorite pesto for use on baked potatoes and in her torta loaf or lamb meatballs is this one.

In a food processor combine: 2 c. fresh basil leaves; 1 c. fresh parsley leaves; ½ c. olive oil; and 4 cloves garlic, peeled. Process until fairly smooth. Add ½ c. slivered almonds (or you can use walnuts or pine nuts) and ¾ c. grated parmesan cheese. Process briefly to desired consistency. Add more oil, if required. Serve on thinly sliced bread or crackers, steamed vegetables, put dollops into soups or stews. It's a traditional sauce for pasta, too!

Callie's Italian Eggplant Spread

In large skillet, heat 2 t. olive oil over medium heat. Add 1 large onion, finely chopped (about 1 c.). Cook, stirring often, just until onion is golden. Peel and dice 1 large eggplant. Add to skillet with 1 T. finely chopped garlic; ½ tsp. salt; and 1- 6" zucchini, finely chopped. Cook, stirring often, but do not brown. When eggplant is softening, add 6 oz. can tomato paste and 1 c. water. Turn heat to low. Allow to simmer until mixture is soft. Add a bit more water as mixture cooks if needed. Remove from heat. Add 3 T. finely chopped oregano, and pepper and salt to taste. Serve at room temperature over thinly sliced French bread or crackers.

Creamy Basil Dip

In food processor chop 1 peeled medium carrot and 1 medium cucumber until very fine.

Add: 8 oz. cream cheese (room temperature); ½ c. basil leaves; 1/4 c. sour cream and ¼ c. chopped sweet onion. Process until it is a nice consistency for dipping. Add freshly ground pepper to taste. Cover and chill to allow flavors to blend. Serve with crackers, fresh mushrooms, or raw veggies.

Basil Canapés

Use the recipe above. Spread on small squares, triangles, or rounds of crustless bread. Top each with a fresh viola bloom, a bit of basil flower, or a tiny basil leaf. Variation: add black olives to replace cucumber. Use a slice of black olive to decorate each canapé.

Easy Garlic Dip

In food processor, combine 8 oz. cream cheese; 4 cloves garlic; 3 T. fresh parsley leaves; freshly ground pepper; 1-6" zucchini, cubed. Process to dip consistency. Chill. Garnish with parsley and a generous sprinkle of paprika. Serve with crackers or veggies.

Lavender Pizza

Thaw 1 loaf frozen white bread dough according to package directions. Roll dough to a 10" x 12" rectangle. Place dough on baking sheet that has been sprinkled with olive oil. Preheat oven to 475 degrees. Sprinkle dough with 1 T. Herbs d'Provence (see recipe index). Slice 1 Roma tomato very thinly and place on dough. Sprinkle with ½ c. drained, sliced black olives. Sprinkle with 1 c. Italian blend shredded cheese (or a mixture of mozzarella and parmesan). Lightly sprinkle with ½ c. Feta cheese crumbles. Sprinkle an additional 2 tsp. Herbs d'Provence over top. Bake 15 min, until center is done and browned lightly.

Thai Basil Cocktails

Make a simple syrup of 1 c. sugar and 1 c. boiling water, stirring to dissolve. Add a handful of Thai basil, stir, then cover. Shake the next day, and store in refrigerator for a day or two. Strain. Label, refrigerate or freeze. To make cocktail, use 1 part Thai basil syrup, 1 part gin and

1 part tonic water. Serve over ice and garnish with a sprig of Thai basil, if possible.

An alternative is 1 part Thai basil syrup and 1 part bourbon. Serve over ice. Garnish with a slice of lemon or orange.

October's Recipes

Mini Reuben Appetizers

Place slices of party rye bread on a baking sheet. Spread each with a thin layer of Thousand Island dressing. Cover each slice with a thin piece of sliced cooked corned beef. Place a teaspoonful of well-drained sauerkraut on each canapé. Sprinkle the kraut lightly with a mixture of caraway seeds and dillweed. Put a slice of Swiss cheese over each. Place in oven at 350 degrees and bake until cheese is melted and beginning to brown. Serve immediately.

Balsamic Brussel Sprouts

Rinse 1 lb. fresh brussel sprouts and pat to dry. Spray an 8"x8" baking pan with cooking spray. Pour just enough balsamic vinegar to cover the bottom of the pan over sprouts. Sprinkle with 1 tsp. dried rosemary (or 2 tsp. fresh). Cover with foil and bake about 20 min. Remove dish from oven, remove foil, and turn sprouts gently with a fork. Turn oven to broil. Add more balsamic vinegar if all has been absorbed, and broil just until sprouts are fork tender and lightly browned. Remove from oven and allow to cool. Mix ¼ c. balsamic vinegar with ¼ c. sugar-free hazelnut syrup (the type used for flavoring coffee). Place cooked sprouts (and any remaining liquid and rosemary from baking pan) in a container that can be tightly covered. Pour vinegar-syrup over. Cover tightly. Refrigerate overnight, shaking once or twice. Or, refrigerate up to two weeks. Serve chilled or at room temperature, cutting any large sprouts in half to serve.

Hyssop Tuna Pate

In a small mixing bowl, place 1-6 oz. can tuna (packed in oil). Add 1 finely chopped hard-boiled egg, 2 heaping T. plain yoghurt, and 1 tsp.

finely chopped hyssop leaves. Stir well with fork to break tuna up well. Add salt and freshly ground pepper to taste. Serve with Melba toast.

Tarrasette

Make a French tarragon infused vodka, by putting 1/2 c. tarragon leaves in a pint of vodka. Cap and put in a dark place for a week, shaking occasionally. Use 1 part tarragon vodka, 1 part orange juice, and ½ part Anisette. Pour over ice in a tumbler. Garnish with a sprig of tarragon and a half slice of fresh orange.

November's Recipes

Tasty Toast Cups

With biscuit cutter, cut 24 circles of whole wheat bread, avoiding crusts. Flatten with palm of hand or rolling pin. Press each circle into a miniature muffin tin cup that has been sprayed or brushed lightly with olive oil. Bake at 375 degrees for about 10 min., or until lightly browned.

Meanwhile, open 1-3 oz. can smoked oysters, draining oil into a skillet. Set oysters aside. Add and sauté ¾ c. onion, chopped; 1 clove garlic, minced; and 1/3 c. chopped green pepper; just until tender. Add ½ c. chopped tomato, freshly ground pepper, dash of salt, the smoked oysters, lightly chopped; 3 T. chopped parsley, and ½ tsp. dried thyme (or 1 tsp. fresh). Cook just until moisture is absorbed. Remove from heat. Spoon mixture into toast cups. Sprinkle with grated Swiss cheese. Return to oven and bake just until cheese melts. Makes 24.

Mushroom-Thyme Cream with Toast Points

Soak .5 oz. dried porcini mushrooms in 2 c. boiling water for 15 minutes. Meanwhile, in large skillet, melt 5 T. butter and 2 T. olive oil. Add 8 oz. sliced baby Portobello mushrooms, sautéing until just golden, about 3-5 minutes. Remove mushrooms. Over medium heat, add ¼ c. flour, stirring 3-4 minutes until it begins to lightly brown. Reduce heat to medium-low. Add 1 T. butter, ¾ tsp. dried thyme, pinch of salt, freshly ground pepper and liquid from porcini mushrooms. Whisk briskly as it cooks to keep it smooth. Add 2 c. Half & Half, ½ c. red wine (merlot works well), porcini and portobello mushrooms. Reduce heat to low, stirring as it cooks an additional 2-3 min. Serve over toast points. Makes 36.

Asparagus Rounds

Cook 12 asparagus spears just until tender. Drain and chill. Meanwhile, cut crusts from 6 slices whole wheat bread. Roll slices with rolling pin to flatten. Spread each slice with mayonnaise. Sprinkle each slice with 1 heaping T. grated cheddar cheese. Lightly sprinkle each slice with chopped pimento, drained, or capers, using about 1 tsp. per slice. Sprinkle with freshly ground pepper. Place a cooled asparagus slice across one end of slice. Trim asparagus to fit the slice with no overhang. Roll evenly to just encircle the asparagus. Add second asparagus spear, trimming to fit. Finish rolling bread to encircle second spear. Press end to seal. Slice each roll into 4 equal pieces (about 1"). Makes 24.

Herbal Hot Buttered Rum

The traditional recipe for hot buttered rum called for water, sugar, and rum which was heated by plunging a red-hot poker heated in the fireplace coals into the mug. Here's an herbal version, which can have as many variations as one has flavorful plants in the herb garden to make herbal sugars and butters.

In a mug, dissolve 1 heaping teaspoon herbal sugar in ¾ c. hot water, stirring well. Stir in 2 oz. rum and 1 tsp. herbal butter, stirring until butter melts. Enjoy different combinations. Favorites are tarragon, anise hyssop, ginger scented geranium, lemon verbena, rose geranium, orange spice thyme, cinnamon basil, lime scented geranium, and pineapple sage. Use them to make flavored sugars or herbal butters to flavor this drink.

December's Recipes

Cranberry-Rosemary Chutney

Combine in medium heavy saucepan with lid: 1 apple, diced; 1 c. fresh or frozen cranberries; 1 c. dried fruit (apricots, dates, raisins, pears, etc.) ½ c. apple cider or apple juice or cranberry juice; ¼ c. red wine; 3 T. sweet pickle relish; ½ tsp. dried rosemary. Cover. Simmer gently on medium-low heat for about 1 hr, stirring occasionally, until all moisture is absorbed and fruit is soft. Serve on Melba toast, toasted mini-bagels, or make the pretty spirals below. It's also good as an accompaniment to meat or poultry.

Cranberry Chutney Spirals

Purchase 8 oz. thinly sliced ham. Try to get rectangles about 4" x 6".Open 1 8-oz. package crescent rolls. Press two triangles together to form a rectangle. Spread with cranberry chutney. Place a slice of ham on each. Roll to form a 6" log. Cut each log into 6 pieces. Place on baking sheet that has been lightly sprayed with oil. Bake at 375 degrees just until rolls are beginning to brown. Serve warm.

Olive-Rosemary Butter

Melt 2 T. butter in a small skillet. Add 1 ½ tsp. chopped rosemary. Sauté gently for 2 min. Remove from heat. In small bowl, mix ½ c. unsalted butter with 2 T. finely chopped black olives, 1 tsp. finely chopped garlic, and 1 tsp. freshly ground black pepper. Stir in sautéed rosemary. Spoon into bowl and chill, or serve immediately on crackers or thinly sliced French bread.

Horseradish-Apple Pita

Carefully slice 7" whole wheat pita bread in half to form two circles. Spread each circle with a thin layer of Boar's Head horseradish sauce. Cover with thinly sliced apples, Granny Smith or Jonagold work well (1 large apple should do both circles). Sprinkle with finely grated Cheddar cheese. Sprinkle with chopped parsley. Bake at 350 degrees just until cheese begins to brown and apples are almost tender, about

fifteen to twenty min. Cut each circle into 16 triangles. Serve warm.
Makes 32.

Holiday Mint Crackers

Choose a rich, buttery crackers (like Ritz). Spread each with a generous layer of softened cream cheese, forming a shallow "well" in the center. Spoon bright green mint jelly into center. Serve immediately.

Callie's Lemon Liqueur

Carefully peel the yellow skin from two lemons, avoiding the white bitter part. Place peel in 1 pt. vodka with a handful of lemon herbs. Shake daily for three days. Meanwhile, make a simple syrup of 1 c. sugar and 1 c. boiling water, stirring until sugar is dissolved. Place in a large jar with a handful of lemon herbs (lemon verbena, lemon balm, lemon scented geraniums are best). Seal and shake daily. Strain. For cocktail, mix 1 part lemon vodka and 1 part lemon herb syrup. Serve at room temperature, or over ice.

For further reading:

Ellis, Hattie. <u>Sweetness & Light, the Mysterious History of the Honeybee</u>. New York: Harmony Books, 2004.

Louv, Richard. <u>Last Child in the Woods, Saving our Children from Nature-Deficit Disorder</u>. Chapel Hill, NC: Algonquin Books, 2005.

Sorin, Fran. <u>Digging Deep, Unearthing Your Creative Roots Through Gardening</u>. New York: Warner Books, 2004.

Index of Recipes

Cool Summer Salsa	August
Cranberry-Rosemary Chutney	December
Cranberry-Rosemary Chutney Spirals	December
Creamy Basil Dip	September
Daylily Appetizer	July
Daylily Confetti Sandwich	July
Dilly Clam Dip	February
Easy Garlic Dip	September
Eggplant Spread	September
Flower & Herb Canapé	May
Flower Stuffed Mushrooms	May
Fresh Vegetable Salsa	August
Fruit Kabobs with Spicy Sauce	June
Herbal Sugars	August
Herbs de Provence	June
Holiday Mint Crackers	December
Horseradish-Apple Pita	December
Hot Herbal Buttered Rum	November
Hot Mushroom-Thyme Cream on Toast Points	November
Hyssop Tuna Pate	October
Lavender-Chocolate Cocktail	June
Lavender Glazed Meatballs	June
Lavender Pizza	September
Lemon Liqueur	December
Mini Arugula Sandwiches	May
Mini Reuben Appetizers	October
Mint Julep	May
Minty Cheese Pitas	March
Monarda Drop Biscuits	July
Mushroom Thyme Cream with Toast Points	November
Nasturtium Appetizers	May
New Year's Day Salsa	January
Olive-Rosemary Butter	December
Orange-Mint Mojitos	July

Orange-Mint Tapenade	March
Parsley-Pecan Cheese Ball	February
Peach of A Cocktail	April
Pesto	September
Pesto Meatballs	January
Pesto Stuffed Eggs	April
Pork Meatballs in Apple Sauce	January
Provencal Salsa	August
Rose-Berry Cocktail	February
Rosalitas	August
Salmagundi Spread	April
Salsa, Black Olive	August
Salsa, Callie's Summer Garden	August
Salsa, Cool Summer Salsa	August
Salsa, Fresh Vegetable	August
Salsa, New Year's Day	January
Salsa, Provencal	August
Salsa, White Bean	August
Sandwich, Daylily Confetti	July
Sandwich, Mini Arugula	May
Sandwich, Simple Appetizer	February
Shrimp Stuffed Eggs	April
Stuffed Apricots	June
Stuffed Tomatoes	July
Tabouli	January
Tarrasette	October
Tasty Toast Cups	November
Thai Basil Cocktails	September
Viola Cheese Spread	March
Viola Quiche	April
White Bean Salsa	August

Printed in the United States
126779LV00007B/4/P